The Gift of
ETERNAL LIFE

Chris Phillips

PSYCHE

Psyche

"Psyche is given as the youngest and by far the most beautiful of three human daughters of a certain king and queen. In her time, even sculptors, painters and poets had great difficulty in defining her beauty. Her beauty was so widely known and so great that wherever she went crowds gathered and flowers were strewn on her path. The altar in the temple of Venus was frequently deserted because men were so devoted to this young virgin." - Extract from the Legend of Psyche and Cupid.

Modernday painting of "Psyche" by David Parle.

CONTENTS   Page

SUMMARY.

The Greek legend of Psyche and Cupid is reported using a written record of the legend from the 2nd century AD. From this and other sources we add the pictorial exhibits of the legend by the great Renaissance painter Raphael. A critical moment in Psyche's Soul Journey is captured, inspirationally, by a current painter David Parle. Painted from his imagination is as perfect as Psyche is. You can say that this beautiful Psyche is the female part of our soul we all have in common.

Psyche's soul journey is discussed in detail and we explore the nature of several other characters, including Greek Archetypes like Zeus, Venus and Pan. We find the soul journeys can be reflected as in the asymmetric wings of a butterfly! The ancient Greek philosophers were right about that. Psyche means Soul and the symbol is a butterfly. This provides the basic structure of Psyche as the term is used today in Psychology.

Mythology and religion can sometimes inform us in a reliable way, it can also be very confused and confusing. In contrast to Psyche where we only have one legend, in the case of Pan there are many legends, myths and interpretations including Psyche's vital meeting with Pan. You will see astounding confusion but the same principles used to understand Psyche, apply to our understanding of Pan. However, later when we are discussing the Wisdom Paths we will visit some new vital information that confirms most of the myths about Pan are phoney.

Some of the Gooey Stuff [eg., phoney myths] is cleared away when we begin to explore the ancient Chaldean and Hebrew system of the Wisdom Paths. The Wisdom Paths are used as an analogy for the process of human self-actualization and enlightenment in life. And some issues are explored about their view that there are transitions of life after life and before it. Transitions on Earth are generally in six developmental periods of life.

The rules and tools needed to make optimum use of the Wisdom Paths are provided for personal appraisal and reflection.

In finding that Psyche has a "twin" or Isometric nature, several Organic Chemistry principles are explored in finding a new approach to the psychology of body, mind and soul. We explore the Isometric nature of the Nucleus of Psyche being like the butterfly, +ID Dextro and −ID Laevo. We also find our bodies are a total chiral environment and what is happening in Psyche has definitive effects in many areas such as Health. We further explore a model of the orbitals that contribute to the Nucleus and we explore some AIDS and HIV research of relevance to Psyche.

Finally, some personal exercises in personal transformation and transcendence are offered as a way of exploring the outer boundaries of Psyche. These are only given as examples of what you could consider doing.

DEDICATION:

To my eternal son Nicholas who gave me this wonderful and centrally important example of the Chaldean Tree of Thirteen Fruits. It has thirteen branches with seven fruit on each branch. He knew why this was important to me and somehow he found it. He knew that 13x7 = 91 and by the ancient Chaldean system that meant Love and Light.

My only wish is that he would have found his Love and Light in this life but he was on the Road of Strife and after service in the Australian Army he took his own life.

So I also dedicate this book to everyone who wants to find a better way forward than they thought.

ACKNOWLEDGEMENTS.

All thanks to the Love and Light in Linda Goodman's massive contribution to unlocking the secrets of the code that underlies the Chaldean-Kabala alphabet and corresponding images, and thanks are due to her for having made this information publicly available. By any measure, this work is an extension of what she did and I am sure she would have been pleased to know that at least a part of her wish is being met and a net "+" added to theosophical – psychological debate.

Particular thanks are also due to David Hulse for his extra-ordinary work on the Hebrew Keys to the Tree of Life.

AND to Ana Marie Valka who helped me tirelessly with uncovering the underlying patterns and codes of the great mathematician and storyteller Lewis Carol. She was also invaluable in the assistance she gave in researching the foundations of the Wisdom Paths.

AND to my wife Ashlyn; her loving heart and mind has helped me through many hours of difficulty, darkness and pain to reach this point where I must show you the Light I have been gifted to see. Ashlyn gave me a book about Raphael's life and work and so inspired this exploration of Psyche. She has been a vital, loving and perceptive part of our explorations at Villa Farnesina and in supporting me in this work over many years.

AND to Raphael whose wonderful paintings, research and understanding of Greek mythology enabled a whole new vista to open up after we saw his extraordinary work at Villa Farnesina in Rome.

AND to David Parle for his inspirational painting of Psyche's moment of realization of her "woman's sense".

AND finally, to Archetypes; because there would have been no development without them. They have guided us to see the "twin " nature of Psyche and their efforts have enabled us to see them all in a new and much more wholesome light. They have given us some wonderful insights into their processes and our relationships with them.

I think that together we have brought Love and Light to our knowledge of ourselves and of each other.

Thank you all.

Chris Phillips Jan 2017.

1. Ancient Greek Legend - Psyche and Cupid.

Like many ancient Greek legends, the story of Psyche and Cupid is variously told. The ancient Greek word for Soul was Psyche and it also meant butterfly. In some stories Cupid is called Eros, so yes this is about sex.

What I have written of the legend draws upon three major sources. Initially the writings of Thomas Bullfinch provided an outline or framework for the legend. As luck would have it, the writings of the Greek scholar Apuleius in 200AD were available and I have preserved the expressions he used as far as possible. Some of his word images are wonderfully rich. A further rich storehouse of information came from the pictorial narratives of the Renaissance painter Raphael and his workshop assistants at Villa Farnesina in Rome, which we visited and photographed.

The later works were partly inspired by Niccolo da Correggio's Psiche published in 1491. Raphael's work was carefully set out in the Loggia di Psiche at Villa Farnesina – then a private banker's palace in Rome. Most of the pictorial exhibits that follow are from Raphael's work at the Villa.

These paintings are unlike any of his religious work except for his exceptional attention to detail and magnificent skill as an artist. The difference can be seen in his naked and voluptuous subjects that he found suited the mistress of the private banker. Apparently Raphael also had access to the story by Apuleius but he evidently had other sources for the legend as he relates it with differences.

The Legend.

Psyche is given as the youngest and by far the most beautiful of three human daughters of a certain king and queen. In her time, even sculptors, painters and poets had great difficulty in defining her beauty. Her beauty was so widely known and so great that wherever she went crowds gathered and flowers were strewn on her path. The altar in the temple of Venus was frequently deserted because men were so devoted to this young virgin. Venus became extremely jealous of Psyche's beauty and the homage paid to her. She was greatly offended that a mortal should be paid so much attention whilst she was increasingly ignored.

As Venus shakes her ambrosial locks with indignation she exclaims, "Am I to be eclipsed in my honours by this mortal girl? But she will not so quietly usurp my honours. I will give her cause to repent so unlawful a beauty."

Venus called her winged son Cupid who is mischievous enough in his own nature but is roused and provoked by her complaints. She points out Psyche to him and says, "My dear son, punish that ….beauty; give thy mother a revenge as sweet as her injuries are great; infuse into the bosom of that haughty girl a passion for some low, mean, unworthy being, so that she may reap a mortification as great as her present exaltation and triumph."

Cupid prepares to obey his mother and goes to the fountains in his mother's garden. In one fountain, the water is bitter and in the other it is sweet. He fills two amber vases, one from each fountain and flies to Psyche's chamber where she is sleeping.

The sight of the beautiful Psyche almost moved Cupid to pity but as instructed he carefully pours two drops from the bitter waters onto Psyche's lips and then touches her side with his arrow. She wakes so suddenly and looks straight at the invisible Cupid that he is startled and accidentally wounds himself with his own arrow. Heedless of his own wound and now wanting to repair the mischief he has done, he pours the sweet waters of joy all over her silken ringlets. But the damage is done.

Although there are still as many admirers as there ever were, there are no suitors and Psyche grows increasingly lonely in her chamber and begins to curse her beauty that somehow fails to awaken love. Even her two elder sisters, who were much less well charmed than Psyche, had been married to two royal princes for many years. She deplored her solitude and her parents grew increasingly worried that the deity had been inadvertently offended.

Psyche's parents decided that they needed to consult the oracle of Apollo and so they went to his temple where they were told terrible news: "The virgin is destined as the bride to no mortal lover. Her future husband awaits her at the top of the mountain. He is a monster that neither deity nor men can resist." Her parents and all the people are dismayed and stricken with grief.

Psyche says, "Why my dear parents do you now lament? You should rather have grieved when the people showered me with flattery and called me a Venus. I know now that I am a victim to that name. I submit, so lead me to that rock on the mountain where my unhappy fate awaits me."

When all the preparations had been made the procession to the mountain was led by Psyche's parents. But this was amidst so much lamentation it was more like a funeral. At the rock on top of the mountain Psyche was left alone panting with fear, trembling in every limb and with eyes full of tears as the people with heavy hearts returned home.

However, as Psyche stood on the rock, a gentle Zephyr lifted her up and carried her to a valley full of lovely flowers of countless different shapes and hues. There she gradually began to compose herself and she lay down and fell asleep. When she awoke she was much refreshed and began to look around and saw three girls playing beside a pleasant, stately, stand of tall trees that they beckoned her to enter.

It was Cupid that had pointed out Psyche to the Three Graces – Faith, Hope and Charity – and he sent these girls to help Psyche recover.

The three girls led Psyche to a beautiful fountain with delightfully fresh water and then she noticed a magnificent palace nearby.

It was clear to Psyche that this was not the work of mortal hands but the palace of a deity. Everything she saw caused her pleasure – the columns of gold, the vaulted roof and ceilings, carved walls, paintings of rural scenes and every object she encountered was there to give pleasure to her senses. She was drawn on through the palace in increasing awe and wonder at the beauty in the place.

Suddenly Psyche heard a voice and yet when she looked around she could not see who was addressing her.

"Sovereign lady, all you see is yours. These voices that you hear are your servants and we will obey all your commands with our utmost care. Retire therefore to your bed of down. When you are rested you will find your bath waiting for you in the alcove. Supper awaits you in the adjoining alcove when it suits you to present yourself there."

Psyche heeded her vocal attendants but after repose she was still timid, even to fear so she called the three girls to amuse and chaperone her during her refreshment in the white marble bath. They were attentive to their charming mistress and playfully laughing for their own pleasure at the details of her toilette.

Later, she took her seat in the adjoining alcove.

To her surprise a table appeared covered in many delicacies and delicious wine. But the table was not brought by any waiters or servants that she could see; it appeared as if by itself; and her ears too where feasted by wonderful musical harmony but she could not see who was playing or singing. It seemed to Psyche that as she was enjoying her repast someone who was invisible was at her side, murmuring sweet words and ensuring that she should be in want of nothing.

When the evening finally ended and she was reposing in her soft down bed, she recalled that she had not seen her destined husband and she recalled the terrible oracle of him being a monster. For a long time she scarcely dared to breathe as she listened for him to come and interview her.

Tired of listening and waiting she finally succumbed to sleep as if she was a girl – profoundly - with one arm under her head and the other hanging down beside the bed.

Although she had no recollection of her husband coming to her during the night, he had passed over her.

When Psyche rose in the morning she instinctively began covering herself with the bed sheet. Her woman's sense told her; "He was over you last night."

She turned and looked back at the bed and was blushing and slightly smiling as she realized that her virgin sense had gone

Although her intended husband only came at night he was always careful to have taken his leave before dawn. When he spoke to her he inspired a like passion in her but when she entreated him to allow her to see him he always refused. He wanted to be loved irrespective of his appearance. For some time Psyche was content with Cupid's explanation. But as she became increasingly lonely, she also began to feel that she was a prisoner, albeit in a beautiful prison.

As Venus watched these developments she finally became placated that Psyche's fate was sealed and so she mounted her chariot, drawn by four white doves and continued about her heavenly duties as the deity for Love.

Psyche worried that her parents had no news of her and so she disclosed to her intended husband that she wanted her sisters to visit her. Although he was

much against this plan he finally agreed and Zephyr was sent to bring them to the palace. They were greatly impressed by Psyche's riches that were so much greater than their own and they became increasingly jealous of her. They plied her with endless questions about her husband to which she initially replied that he was a handsome young man. Eventually she admitted to never having seen him.

As the elder sisters' visit was coming to an end they confided in Psyche that she should obtain a very sharp knife and a lantern and keep these concealed from her husband. Whilst he was asleep she should creep forward and find him. If he was a monster, as the oracle foretold, she should not hesitate to cut off his head for otherwise he was sure to destroy her. Initially Psyche rejected the temptation to do as the sisters had proposed but her doubts grew and eventually she was inclined to obtain and conceal the knife and lamp as planned.

She tied her hair high on her head so that it should not rustle and wearing no cloth to disclose her movements, she stole forward with trembling limbs to find the place where her husband slept. She carried both the knife and lamp in her hands. When she found him, she was astounded to find not a monster but the wonderfully formed son of Venus, Cupid with his bow and arrows lying on the flagstones. Her heart leapt in delight at this sight – he was so beautifully formed - but as she leant forward to see him more clearly she spilt a drop of hot oil from her lamp and he was instantly awakened when it struck his shoulder.

Despite Psyche's remonstration but true as ever to his promise to Venus, Cupid immediately took wing and flew rapidly out of the palace saying, "Love cannot dwell with suspicions."

Psyche was distraught and tried to follow him.

As she followed, the unfortunate Psyche became increasingly distraught at Cupid's flight and lamenting her own folly, threw herself headlong into the river to make an end to her distress. But the River deity caused the tide to recede and so saved her young life.

There beside the river was the goat-footed deity Pan but without his seven reed pipe or his flocks. Pan helped Psyche out of the river and invited her to sit with him. In his calming presence, Psyche slowly composed herself.

When she was at last somewhat peaceful, Pan explained the instructions Venus had given to Cupid. In this way Psyche learnt of the manner and extent of Cupid's transgressions against his mother's wishes. [The photo of Pan was taken in Napoleon's apartment at Versailles, France.][1]

More enamoured toward Cupid and feeling ever grateful, her hope revived and she set out to try and find Cupid. Travelling day and night until she came upon a rock that was much like that on which she had first been left on the mountain-top. There she saw a city below her and immediately set forth.

In the city she was standing near a building that was not yet finished when Psyche chanced to meet her sisters who failed to recognize her and she had to go to considerable efforts to prove who she was. After their respective greetings Psyche explained what had happened to Cupid. They were dismayed that the oracle had been so wrong in saying her husband was a monster. As she related her adventure her sisters began an endless series of complaints for they had been slighted, their fears unjustified and their counsel plainly deceitful. But they also deceived themselves and wondered if Cupid who had once been smitten with the charms of a mortal might not now choose one of them.

So in the evening they separately climbed to the rock were Psyche had first seen the city below and believing that a puff of wind was indeed Zephyr come to carry them to his master they surrendered to the deceitful wind and fell to their deaths. Thus Psyche was revenged.

On poor Cupid's return to his mother's palace, he was confined to his bed and subjected to the strongest admonitions from his irate mother. Her complaints about his disobedience were endless. Then came his role in Psyche's pregnancy and his mother's role as the deity for Love becoming a grandmother! These were constant assaults on his troubled and unhappy ears.

---

1 Pan was renowned for his wonderfully haunting music played on a 7-reed flute. The Pan Flutes. His right hand and head are touching the outer edge of a spiral. As he plays two babies are coming down via Laurel branches symbolizing Eternal Love. On reaching Earth one baby takes on a garland of original blessings.

During Cupid's confinement, Venus was visited by Ceres [deity for agriculture] and Juno [Queen of Olympus on the far right in the illustration]. Throughout their visit they insisted on learning all the details of what

had happened to Cupid and Psyche. No detail was too small and the story had to be told and retold many times with many interjections.

As Ceres and Juno were finally leaving, Venus said to them alone that she must have the insolent Psyche dead or alive.

As Psyche was passing through a field she saw a temple at the top of a hill and hoping to find Cupid there she climbed the hill and collected some wild flowers along the way. When she entered the temple she observed a pile of sheaths of wheat and barley, corn and other grains and various agricultural implements left by the husbandmen at Ceres temple. Psyche's supplicant flowers refreshed the temple vases and yet when she spoke to Ceres and asked her to permit her to shelter for two days, Ceres refused. Her advice was that Psyche surrender herself to Venus. Only Venus could restore her to her husband. Psyche was deeply troubled by what she now needed to say to Venus to placate her for she knew that her meeting with Venus could be fatal.

Venus met Psyche with a very angry countenance and paying no heed to her pregnancy commanded that Psyche be scourged with rods. Cupid was deeply troubled by Psyche's cries as he was only separated from her by thin drapery. Had it not been for the hope of seeing Cupid again, Psyche would have preferred death. But Venus, although cruel to excess, did not wish Psyche dead for she had a plan to test and ensnare Psyche as her slave and involve her in a number of dangerous enterprises from which she was unlikely to return. What pretences for new persecutions!

Venus called for wheat, barley, corn, lentils, poppy seeds and a host of other grains to be brought and all mixed together in a huge pile on the floor. Then she called Psyche and commanded her to separate each type into separate piles. Cruelly she said that only a little patience would be needed to have the task accomplished before nightfall. Then Venus went away to a wedding feast and left a very dejected Psyche sitting on the floor. Fortunately for Psyche, Cupid spoke to the leader of the ants and within moments there were thousands of them collecting the grains and putting them into their separate piles. When the task was complete, all the ants disappeared as quickly as they had come.

When Venus returned she entered with an insulting gesture, irony on her tongue and when she saw that the impossible task had been achieved she accused Psyche of having obtained aid. Then she threw a small piece of black bread to Psyche for her supper and departed.

Next morning Venus took Psyche to a wild place. In this place there were large sheep with razor sharp horns but they had fleeces that were as golden threads. These are the Sheep of the Sun and they wander at liberty about their island and have no need of a shepherd for they can inflict mortal wounds. Venus did not warn Psyche of the dangers but said she wanted Psyche to collect a little wool from each of them. So saying Venus departed.

Even as Psyche determined to succeed in this enterprise, the River deity parted the waters of the torrent that separated her from the sheep. Great stones laid bare by the parted waters enabled her to cross the water in safety. Then as she was entering the reeds on the other side, Zephyr spoke to her and warned her of the dangers ahead and described the manner by which to complete her task.

After the noontide sun had driven the sheep into little groups in the shade of the trees, Psyche set forth to the land which the sheep had departed and collected the golden threads they had left on brambles, bushes and the trunks of trees in their passage. Thus Psyche safely returned to Venus with her arms full of the golden bounty.

Her implacatable mistress was scathing in her criticism saying, "None of this can be your work. I doubt if you have any capacity to be useful. But I have another task for you. Take this box and go your way to the infernal shades. Give the box to Proserpine and say, 'your mistress Venus has need of a little of your beauty, for in tending her sick son she has lost some of her own'. Be not too long for I have need of it this evening when I must appear before the Assembly on Olympus."

Psyche was now certain that her destruction was at hand being required to go directly by her own feet down to Erebus in the underworld. Knowing that she could not delay what was inevitable, she climbed to the highest point in a tower and prepared to precipitate headlong to her death.

Just before she launched herself a voice said to her, "Why doest thou, unlucky girl, design to put an end to your life in this most unfortunate manner? And what cowardice makes thee sink under this last danger when thou hast been so miraculously supported in all thy former?"

Then the voice told her how to enter the infernal shades by a certain cave; how to avoid the teeth of Cerberus, the three headed dog; and prevail on Charon the ferryman, to take her across the black

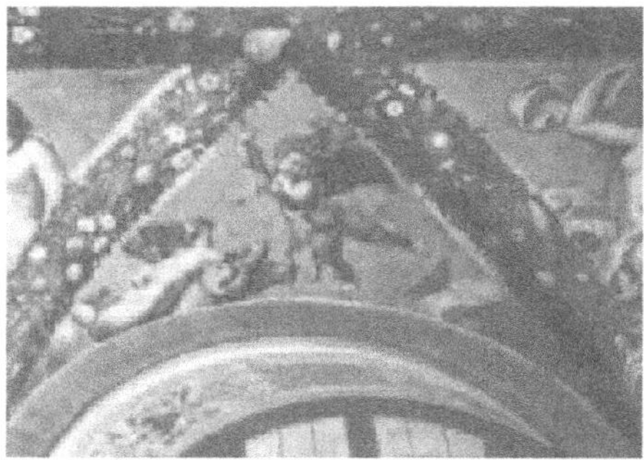

river and then bring her back again. But the voice added, "Once Proserpine has given the box filled with her beauty back to you, of all things this is chiefly to be observed by you, that you are never once to open or look into the box, nor to allow your curiosity to pry into the borrowed treasures of the beauty of the female deity."

Encouraged by this advice, Psyche travelled safely into the kingdom of Pluto and was admitted to the palace of Proserpine where she did not accept the delicious banquet offered but chose course bread and then prostrating herself, she diligently delivered her message from Venus. It was not long before the box was returned to her, shut and filled with the precious commodity. The messenger was dismissed and immediately returned to the light of day.

Having gone so far on her dangerous mission Psyche was seized by a desire to examine the contents of the box. Just the smallest amount of its contents could help her with her husband and Venus was not likely to notice the smallest bit missing. As no one appeared to be watching she opened the box. The intoxicating vapours escaped and she fell to the ground as if she were dead.

Most fortunately for Psyche, Cupid had escaped from Venus' guards and flown straight to where Psyche lay. With great care he collected the intoxicating vapours and put them back into the box. With a light touch of his arrow he woke the beautiful Psyche.

Oh! What a reunion; during which Cupid gently admonished Psyche for her curiosity and told her that she was to go straight to his mother and give her the box. Meanwhile he has much else to do.

Cupid rapidly flew through the heavens and presented himself to Jupiter [King of Olympus]. He earnestly pleaded his case to marry Psyche and have her granted immortality.

Long used to Cupid's mischievous ways, Jupiter searched Cupid's heart and mind and eventually found him to be pure in his intensions. In this way Jupiter was favourably moved and agreed to Cupid's plan. But with one proviso - that Venus likewise give her consent to the marriage of Cupid and Psyche.

After Venus' stout resistance and outright animosity towards the pregnant Psyche, her consent was not likely to be easily obtained. Cupid became increasingly anxious at the prospect of being able to gain her consent. But in order to aid Cupid and Psyche, Jupiter undertook upon himself to intercede and argue their case with Venus.

Through his earnestness she was finally moved to give her consent to the marriage. What remained to be accomplished was the matter of Psyche's immortality.

For Psyche to be granted immortality and married to Cupid, the matter had to be brought before the whole Assembly on Olympus. No human had been granted immortality before. This was both a rare and very important decision.

With the full support of Jupiter; and with Juno and Ceres knowing every detail, Venus spoke openly about her discussion with Jupiter and her agreement to the marriage of her son. After further discussion The Assembly soon decided that Cupid and Psyche should marry and that Psyche should be granted immortality.

To convey this happy news, Mercury put on

his winged headdress, sandals and staff and swiftly went to Earth where he gathered the delighted Psyche and carried her up to Olympus.

To the delight of the gathering at the Assembly on Olympus, Mercury offered Psyche a cup of Ambrosia. He explained that the Assembly had granted her the right to obtain immortality and he invited her to drink from the cup. With Cupid's enthusiastic pleading she readily agreed to drink the Ambrosia and thus she became immortal and at one with the deity on Olympus.

During the wedding between the two lovers, the nuptials were made perpetual and Psyche was given the Vase of Eternal Life / Ambrosia. The whole Assembly then retired for the wedding feast and this was presided over by Juno who arranged all the guests.

Even Venus and her daughter in law were on the best of terms and when they were not dancing, Cupid continually passed from the knee of one to the other.

At the conclusion of the wedding festivities, Psyche was born by three Cupids as she carried the Vase of Eternal Life from Olympus down to Earth.

Thus Psyche was at last happily joined with Cupid in marriage. When her waiting time and confinement had ended they had a daughter whom they named Pleasure.

In Bullfinch's interpretation, the story of Cupid and Psyche is allegorical. He says that after a long life as a caterpillar and unable to move as a pupa, the butterfly is at complete liberty to flit from flower to flower in the sunshine.

> "Psyche, then is the human soul, which is purified by sufferings and misfortunes, and is thus prepared for the enjoyment of true and pure happiness."

Bullfinch.

With the work of Raphael to help us, we can take this allegorical interpretation of the legend a lot further than Bullfinch. First we must take into account Raphael's painting history to understand his illuminating perspective.

Raphael spent most of his life painting Christian religious subjects. He painted the Madonna and the Holy Family in countless different and delightful ways – here with John the Baptist on the left. He also went to great pains to provide accurate representations of scenes from the Scriptures – both of the Old and New Testaments. His most prestigious painting contracts were in the apartments of two Popes – most notably Julius II - and in working with Michelangelo in the Sistine Chapel in Rome. It is thought that Michelangelo

had a profound influence on Raphael's work but conflict developed between them in their last years of work together.

What we see at the Villa Farnesina in Rome is totally different in subject matter. His subjects are either completely or partially naked. His women are voluptuous. His narrative is wide open to interpretation for in dealing with Greek mythology he had a freedom he had not experienced before. The triangular nature of the spandrels also presented a significant challenge at the Villa and he used them to highlight many of the scenes from the tale of Psyche and Cupid. His work at the Villa is very different to his religious works. However, there is a consistent thread in all of his work – a loving attention to beauty in every detail.

In the above exhibit, the two central ceiling panels are painted as if tapestries are nailed to the ceiling. The nearest is of the Assembly at Olympus and the farthest is of the wedding feast. Both the tapestries and spandrels are separated by garlands. The garlands are known to have been painted by Giovanni da Udine who worked in Raphael's workshop and his work is of such high quality that even today the species of flowers, fruits, vegetables and cereals can be identified as known in Renaissance times; including new species

of corn, squash and beans from the New World. To show how the whole can be seen in the parts, we will briefly examine the spandrel of the scene between Venus, Ceres and Juno.

Juno's left hand is demonstrating towards the garland surrounding the scene where we can see Ears of Wheat. We can see Ears of Wheat in Ceres' hair, on the left side. In the garlands at Venus' left foot we can also see Ears of Wheat. None of these representations are accidental. Even in the earlier depiction of Venus pointing out Psyche to Cupid, there is an Ear of Wheat in the garland near Venus' pointing finger and nearer the tip of Cupid's arrow – held in his right hand. What we are left to imagine Juno is saying to Venus is clarified by later paintings about this astounding sequence of depictions of the legend of Psyche. What does Raphael want us to interpret from his paintings about an Ear of Wheat? His years of religious paintings would have told him the Ear of Wheat symbolized Eternal Life. Here we have it amongst the Greek immortals; Ceres, Juno,

Cupid and his mother, Venus. But why is this representation consistently on the left or Laevo side in the above exhibit? And for what reasons do we find Venus shown to the left [Laevo] of Ceres and Juno; or Jupiter being on the right [Dextro] with Cupid and in the Assembly and again on the right when he intercedes for Cupid and Psyche?

In this legend, Cupid is sometimes identified as mischievous and disobedient – Laevo of Centre. Venus is vicious, vengeful and jealous – also Laevo of Centre. Ceres, Juno and Jupiter are all acting in the common good – Dextro of Centre. All of them are consistently positioned in this way. But where is Psyche positioned? From the story she is evidently a Dextro figure though curiosity has been her downfall on more than one occasion. However, curiosity is not a Laevo characteristic – interest and inquisitiveness are central to learning and therefore very clearly Dextro characteristics. A significant insight into the character of Psyche is gained from two of the spandrel paintings.

In this spandrel of Psyche holding the Vase of Eternal Life / Ambrosia she is being born by three Cupids and she is shown as Dextro. This accords with the legend when she came back to Earth with the Ambrosia.

She is again shown to the right of Centre and further right than Mercury in their first meeting – Dextro.

The next spandrel is only about Venus and Psyche. I haven't found this scene described by anyone else – not even the Greek scholar Apuleius. This scene is not told in any of the stories reported here but Raphael paints Psyche offering the Vase of Eternal Life to Venus. Venus is evidently totally horrified and doesn't want anything to do with it. Again Venus is left of Centre – Laevo – rejecting. Psyche is right of Centre and offering the vase in her right hand – Dextro. Ambrosia is Centre.

Even the white doves that pull Venus' chariot are Dextro in this and a former exhibit and they are flying to the right side. This exhibit suggests that Raphael believed that whilst Venus was committed to Immortality she rejected the offer or had no need for it. Venus' face and posture indicate "Take it away". She is clearly Left of Centre and rejecting Psyche's precious Ambrosia. This is also a gesture of surrender by Venus.

Maybe Venus was right in her reaction. Psyche's Ambrosia was a totally heartfelt peace offering to Venus; and Venus knew it would be much too big a gift for her to be able to accept bearing in mind what Psyche and humanity would loose if Ambrosia was not taken down to Earth. That wouldn't fit Jupiter's overall dextro plan. It is likely that Raphael wanted to say something about the changed relationship these two had.

Towards the end of Raphael's short life – 37 years - he was very much in love with a woman identified as "the baker's daughter". This was a love affair that was current when he was working on the paintings at the Villa Farnesina. It is also significant that Raphael chose the story of Psyche and Cupid to adorn the palace where its master intended to entertain his mistress. It therefore seems most likely that the exhibit of the above spandrel did not relate to any part of the legend of Psyche and Cupid but was a personal comment or interpretation in his pictorial narrative of the legend.

There is great consistency in the positioning of all of Raphael's subjects and these positions inform us about the essential nature of the characters involved and how they react in various situations. For example, Venus is the deity for Love and therefore a figure of the Centre. During the course of the story she is more Centre than Cupid when she points out Psyche to him. Later she goes about her Dextro business on her chariot drawn by 4 white doves. Later again she is very cruel to Psyche and has her scourged with rods even though Psyche is pregnant – very clearly a Laevo thing to do. But in the exhibit above she is only just on the Laevo side.

What can we draw from this changing pattern of responses? That Venus has a Mercurial nature? That she can be one thing in one situation and something totally different in another situation? The proposition that she has two fountains in her garden, one with bitter water and another with sweet water reinforces this view of her as Mercurial. Much the same set of conclusions can be drawn about the mischievous but also loving Cupid. His mischievous and impatient side of his nature sometimes has him described as Eros. It is interesting that in the above exhibit, Cupid is painted to the right of Venus in the Assembly and very close to Jupiter and Juno. But Mercury is painted on the left of Venus. This tends to indicate that Raphael believed that a highly changeable or Mercurial nature was more Laevo than Dextro. But when Mercury offers Psyche the cup of Ambrosia he does so with his right and she receives it on her right. As the Messenger for the Assembly he is shown on the right of Psyche.

On the other hand Juno, the Queen of Olympus, is a very consistent Dextro figure. Likewise her husband Jupiter is consistently Dextro. Even in the Assembly on Olympus both Jupiter and Juno are on the most extreme Dextro side of the exhibit. This is also evident in the scene of the wedding feast.

Conversely, Psyche's two sisters are consistently envious, deceptive and scheming but as we do not have any exhibits of them we can only draw from their behaviour reported in the story that they are consistently Laevo figures. In telling their story, the

narrators seem to agree that no additional hands are needed to bring about the destruction of a Laevo figure. If they live by envy, deceit and scheming so will they die at their own hands or as a consequence of their negative imaginations. Psyche had done nothing to bring about her sisters destruction. She didn't know of their plans nor even know or suspect that they hoped to replace her in Cupid's favours. Although the story says that Psyche had her revenge when her sisters fell to their deaths, it can hardly be described as revenge when she sought no such thing.

Although Psyche is presented as suicidal at the river [when she fails to find Cupid after his flight] and at the tower [when in her trials she needs to go directly to Erebus], and Laevo with respect to the gift of her beauty, she is otherwise consistently Dextro in her behaviour. She loves her parents, sisters and Cupid and especially in her trials she obtains unsolicited support from Nature [Zephyr] and the deity [the River deity on two occasions and Cupid on several others]. The Three Graces also help her after her ordeal on the rock at the top of the mountain. All of this support and help is Dextro. When Pan informs Psyche of the instruction Venus had initially given to Cupid, this only serves to reinforce her determination to find her lover Cupid. In other legends, the deity Pan has often been portrait as devious and mischievous, especially with beautiful maidens and Nymphs, but here we see him only serving Psyche's need to be re-joined with Cupid. In this legend there is no sign of the Devil attributed elsewhere to him, most especially in other religious literature and painting of the Renaissance period. In this story he is clearly a deity figure that helped Psyche and he is not to be confused with Satyr or the Devil. Pan is quite different. He is a deity of Light and Love and quite evidently Dextro. It is not known why Raphael decided not to portrait him this way but it is important that he saw Pan in a way that was not akin to the prevailing opinions about him at the time.

The theme of Immortality or Eternal Life is also consistently before us in Raphael's work at the Villa. We have noted that he uses an Ear of Wheat as a vital Dextro symbol as was the Vase. He does so because during the "Last Supper" of Christ with his disciples, he broke bread made from wheat to symbolize His body and asked them to eat it in remembrance of Him. He also took wine in a cup, to symbolize His blood. In this way the bread [wheat] and wine [cup] taken during the Christian "communion" enable mortals to gain Eternal Life. As noted earlier, in the scene of Venus, Ceres and Juno, we find Ears of Wheat on all sides – Laevo, Centre and Dextro. This is consistent with Christ's promise to all beings from all walks of life; though Psyche may have been the first mortal to be granted immortality after her trials and suffering; and so too Christ.

Characters from the Legend of Psyche and Cupid

LAEVO	**CENTRE**	**DEXTRO**	
Venus	Venus	Venus	= Mercurial
Cupid/Eros	Cupid	Cupid	= Mercurial
		Three Graces	
		Ceres	
		Juno	
		Jupiter	
		River deity	
		Zephyr	
		Pan	
		Mercury	
Psyche's Sisters		Psyche	
		Psyche's Parents	

The scenes painted by Raphael and his workshop assistants on the spandrels and ceiling are all of parts of the story to do with the Heavenly realm. The absence of paintings of Psyche's sisters and parents and scenes from Psyche's Earthly life no longer exist – if they ever did.

Some authors believe that these Earthly scenes once existed below the spandrels but were deleted during the intervening five hundred years of changes and restoration work undertaken at the villa.

However, the structure of the walls around the doors is not suggestive of painting having ever been done there – even though upstairs in the villa the ceilings and walls are quite evidently painted to the floor.

In the entry to the villa, one of these Earthly scenes is quite revealing – marble is extensively used below the spandrels so there is no room for paintings of any kind.

Given the extent of the paintings at the entrance to Villa Farnesina and the importance played by the trials Psyche underwent it is significant that her trials are not depicted. Only a part of one is included in a scene from her last trial: of two Cupids restraining the three headed dog Cerberus in Erebus.

At the end of Raphael's short life – 37 years, many great tributes were paid to the breadth, wonder, beauty and depth of his work and he was buried in the Pantheon in Rome with this Epitaph on his tomb;

> *"Here lies Raphael, who while he lived made Nature afraid of being bested by him and, when he died, of dying with him."*

Pietro Bembo

Finally, the sense of a lot having been lost over two thousand years is not restricted to this legend but also to the life of Christ. Perhaps it is a miracle that anything remains of Apuleius' tale and Raphael's paintings after such a long time.

So here we are today with only a partial knowledge of what the ancients knew in their time. Even their analogy of the butterfly suggests they knew a great deal more than we give them credit for. Yes, we are currently informed by science when once it was by fable and tale. But are we any better informed today? It is almost impossible to answer that question because little remains about what they knew and we do not have complete accounts of their tales.

My 7 year-old Grand Daughter Libby, was talking to me about what she had observed about the two types of tiny native bees in my garden and how their activity between flowers was different from that of the European bees. She was spot on in her comments and I realized she was glowing with totally absorbed loving interest. She had very peacefully watched them for nearly an hour. This was three or four times longer attention span than was normal for her age – 2 minutes x 7years =14minutes. And one of her teachers thought she had Attention Deficit Syndrome!!!

We all have to find what children love - that is the virtue that drives them best. Ultimately they know intuitive what is right for them to discover. When they do discover "it" nothing will stop them. We can only help them explore until that point is reached.

I wanted to know what Libby thought and felt about Mother's recent death at the fantastic age of 101 years. Some of my family were staying at our home before the funeral and I also wanted to talk to Libby about the Family Blessing for my Mother. However, before I could ask her the chooks started to cackle and we knew a new egg had been laid. Libby thought it was time for Jazzmen to lay her egg so she went to investigate. She had names for them all. She knew each hen's habits and the spots some of them left on their eggs are like trademarks. Libby was cradling Jazzmen's egg in one hand on her return to the shed. She was right again. On a later occasion she had two other grandchildren sitting up on the hens' perch with a trembling red hen called Elizabeth held between them!!! Libby was instructing them from the floor in the names and habits of each hen. I wish I had my camera! Priceless!!! But I had to rescue the trembling Elizabeth!

The Red hen had been named after my Mother. Next time I had a moment with Libby I reminded her that like her Elizabeth – my Mother - loved nature too. She would love to watch the bees with you…but mid-sentence, Libby burst out with…

"She's not here anymore; she's died an' gone to heaven!"
Grandfather;   Where is that Libby?"
Libby pointed straight up in the air and said;

"Way up there past the Gooey Stuff [in the roof]."

Indeed there was a lot of Gooey Stuff [expander foam] hanging down in yellow globules from the gaps filled in the ridgeline of the galvanized iron roof.

This delightful child of nature had wonderful concentration and insight so she could easily win the Red Queen of Hearts. But of course as her Grandfather, I would think that!

Actually the "Gooey Stuff" is an excellent analogy. The Gooey Stuff prevents us from seeing through to Libby's "heaven". It is a barrier to our knowledge of Life After Life. But how do we get above all the religious and mythological confusion? Way up there - I love the expression – past the Gooey Stuff! But what do you have to do to get past the Gooey Stuff?

I have read more books than there are ridges in the galvanized iron. Some of them have been helpful. Some were extremely confusing and gooey. Some were not well informed and some were a relief and delight. And I have talked to thousands of people during a work life spanning over 45 years as a psychologist. I know the Gooey Stuff is extensive and it is very hard to get beyond it as we can see from our exploration of Psyche in mythology. We began this document with Psyche as that is central to our subject matter and I think we cleared some Gooey Stuff. In the next chapter we will explore Good and Gooey about Pan.

As you may already know mythology always contains a grain of truth. But it is hard to find amongst all the Gooey Stuff. In the case of the Legend of Psyche and Cupid, it was pretty straightforward with fairly consistent and very early reports of the legend. However as you will see in the next chapter on Pan we are not always easily able to see where the grains of truth lie.

Without setting of a discussion on comparative religious literature I venture to say that of "the whole" possibly one example could serve. "The Old Testament Pseudepigrapha" – the Gospels outside the Gospels. This is the Jewish and Christian literature that was not included in the Holy Bible or the canon. It includes the search for lost writings that may need to be incorporated into the canon. But what is in the canon today isn't considered to be the same for people of the same faith.

> "Even in America there are different canons in the various Christian communities. Protestants exclude from the canon the Apocrypha, the additional books from the Greek Old Testament; the Roman Catholics, following the edicts of the Council of Trent in 1546, include them as deuterocanonical. The Mormons, moreover, argue that more books belong in the canon and that it should remain open."
>
> James Charlesworth.[2]

2000 pages later my Woody Allen reading was "The Gooey Stuff is massive…. Agreement on what to include in the Christian canon was just as small as in the Jewish canon. I couldn't help noticing the Sibylline Oracles….Woody would say, … prejudicial rubbish. Searching for "wisdom", and wise sayings narrowed my focus to the missing Gospel Of Thomas that was referred to widely.

When I obtained a copy of the Gospel of Thomas I was fascinated. Scattered fragments of references where finally given form as late as 1945. 13 new papyrus documents were discovered near Nag Hammadi [Upper Egypt] and incorporated into the library as Codex II. But an interesting surprise is in store. It was expected that Thomas made a systematic collection of the sayings of Jesus of Nazareth. Numbers of early church father referred to Thomas. The Thomas Gospel discovered in1945 was somewhat at odds with the New Testament writings in the canon even though it is oriented to "wisdom" and about what Jesus said as Thomas reports the matter in 114 sayings.

> "Now the twelve followers [were] all sitting together, recalling what the savior had said to each of them, whether in a hidden or an open manner, and organizing it in books. [And I] was writing what is in my [book]."
>
> Nag Hammadi Secret Book Of James 2, 7-16.

What we find is that most of the "hidden sayings', "secret sayings", and "obscure sayings" conform to the Gnostic tradition more so than do those of the New Testament and they are clearly in the genera of Solomon's "Wisdom".

Permit me one example from the Gospel of Thomas as found in Coptic.

V13

---

2 James Charlesworth, "The Old Testament Pseudepigrapha." Doubleday 1983.

"Jesus said to his followers, "Compare me to something and tell me what I am like."
Simon Peter said to him, "You are like a just messenger."
Mathew said to him, "You are like a wise philosopher."
Thomas said to him, "Teacher, my mouth is utterly unable to say what you are like."
Jesus said, "I am not your teacher. Because you have drunk, you have become intoxicated from the bubbling spring that I have tended."
And he took him, and withdrew, and spoke three sayings to him.
When Thomas came back to his friends, they asked him, "What did Jesus say to you?"
Thomas said to them, "If I tell you one of the sayings he spoke to me, you will pick up rocks and stone me, and fire will come from those rocks and consume you."

This is a very sudden gnostic twist in the tail of the tale; but there is no revelation about the "hidden sayings". Worst still, no original Aramaic texts of Jesus sayings in his time are available. This is especially serious because the intonations and meanings in Aramaic do not translate very well into Coptic nor into Greek. And that is all we have to go on. Is this a promising start to a Dead End? Not quite.

I want to go back to Raphael, the Renaissance painter who lived before the Edicts from the Council of Trent in 1545 as to what was in and out of the canon. We know he was very thorough in his research and he had access to the Vatican Library and even two Pope's apartments! He researched "The Last Supper" from many points of view and apparently found that during the Last Supper there was an event described as the "Round Dance" performed by three, Jesus was leading.

> The three were dancing aloft! Amen!
> The three were dancing aloft. Amen!
> The three were dancing aloft. Amen!

It scared many to see them levitating but to most people the scene Raphael painted about the Round Dance and the "living Jesus" is interpreted as the "Transfiguration" of the Crucified Christ – but no wounds – no tomb – no stone. Was this the "living Christ" who showed the Apostles a great mystery? Notice one aloft is holding a green book – possibly Thomas himself or James was the other recorder. But where are those vital original records? Even "The Passion" was not written until 40 years later and the first record of sayings was not determined until 70 years later. This all leaves serious flaws in our knowledge with no Aramaic records at all. Some scholars argue this is a canonical scandal.

"Transfiguration" may be yet another cover-up because the painting was still in Raphael's workshop and incomplete at the time of his death. The only interpretation by the Church was that the men aloft are Jesus, Moses and Elijah. The terrified boy in blue at the bottom is given as the epileptic son of the father in green. The official version is that the disciples couldn't heal the boy.

Given that Raphael had access to Vatican records and was very thorough in his research the official version seems confused and probably flawed. "The Round Dance", and the description of "The Last Supper" were nowhere in the first 114 Verses of the Gospel of Thomas found at Nag Hammadi and we have no original Aramaic records by Thomas or James!

The amount of agreement within one faith is vastly greater than the agreement between faiths. With 7-9,000 or so different religious groups to consider all the Gooey Stuff was obviously an impossible undertaking. I was at a Dead End even without a proper idea about the "Living Jesus" as a historical figure.

I continued with research into the life of Confucius who lived about 500 years before Christ so "the way" was very difficult and readings seemed endless. Besides I had to entirely rely on English translations. My interest sharply spiked in my studies in Buddhism when I came across a reference to a Terton. One who finds hidden ancient texts and brings them safely back for consideration at exactly the right time they are to be brought to light. There were many Tertons over time in Buddhism. Often such manuscripts were found deep in caves, or hidden under rocks, preserved in jars, etc. My cave had to be somewhere…

I began to read Islamic literature and as "The Prophet" was about 500 years after Christ I hoped for better-written records and a better outcome. But I had difficulty finding the real historical figure any more clearly than with the "living Jesus". I am astounded at the diversity of opinion between the Jews, Christians and Moslem when they all have the same Father who was once named Yahweh.

It was a remark made by a great psychologist Carl Jung in his Alchemical Studies that got me thinking about a new way forward. He said that the pity of it all is that we don't have any direct information we can only work from legends to identify who the Archetypes are [eg., Jupiter, Juno, Ceres, Venus, Cupid, Mercury etc.,] and what processes they are involved in. The need is for us to hear directly from them if we want to get any real idea of what is happening in the collective conscious or Psyche. That rang true to me. However, the vital key to getting past the Gooey Stuff involved discovering a way to relate directly with them and we did. I say we because it was evidently a joint learning process with Archetypes. That story is contained in "Ambrosia" that includes "What the Archetypes Have To Say." That will be published separately from this document. Matters of direct relevance to Psyche will be summarized here from Ambrosia.

Jung's use of the word Psyche also got me thinking as did the ancient Greek Legend about Psyche and Cupid. Its relevance is direct as the beautiful Psyche was the first human to drink Ambrosia and so be granted Eternal Life. Psyche meant soul in Greek and the soul was being seen as an asymmetric structure as per the wings of a butterfly. This is a wonderful analogy and it proves itself many times over in the following pages. So much for the individual soul but what about the collective conscious aspect that Jung was talking about in Psyche? How is it structured and how does it work? [See Ambrosia.] But again I will summarize the Archetypes structure in chapter 6 Spheres and their Relationships.

"Wheat" was the very first word conveyed by Archetypes. It is the symbol for Eternal Life. They say that it should be present at vert – when the foetus is turned in the womb before birth and it should be laid on the coffin of a departed loved one when the spirit is at vert and leaving the body.

Each member of the family [including Grandchildren and Great Grandchildren] placed an Ear of Wheat on Mother's coffin at the end of a traditional Anglican service. We all hoped this would help her get through the Gooey Stuff. We also blessed her forward journey with farewell words, "Go in Eternal Love and Peace." She has as far as I know. And Libby knows from our talk about the native bees, what it might be like to be loving and peaceful every day. She played her part in the service perfectly as did everyone else. In this manner, our Mother was beautifully blessed by everyone present as she had been a truly wonderful person even until the end.

This wasn't the first time we had used this form of Family Blessing. My Mother and family had participated with me in doing this for the very first time with my son's coffin eight years before my Mother's demise.

At my son's funeral, two of our friends handed out Ears of Wheat to each person as they came in for the church service. Over 200 people were there but we had 6 Ears left over at the end of the distribution. At the end of the service I invited everyone to come forward and say their farewells and place the Ear of Wheat on his coffin with their Right Hand and bless his journey in Eternal Love and Peace.

Mother's right arm didn't work properly and yet she was determined to use it properly and she asked me to help her lift her arm so that she could place her Ear correctly. Of course I did and then she said her farewells and spoke the Family Blessing aloud as I had done and as everyone had been invited to do. At the time people were lining up to place their Ear of Wheat there were many tears and an aura of love for my son. I only wish he had known earlier just how much and how many people loved him. Suicide is a permanent solution to what is usually a short-term problem and most likely many consequences needed more consideration. I don't know why he never talked to me about what he was contemplating because he knew I knew he was on :43 the Road of Strife by the Wisdom Path system we will discuss in detail later. There are many things I wish I had done about this before it happened. BUT I am certain every parent feels like this… If only I had known…I wish I had paid more attention to…How should he [and we all] be Blessed fully on passing? An Ear of Wheat.

Even before my son's funeral Mother knew that Archetypes had said that an Ear of Wheat on the coffin will distil any wrong teachings by the church or it's representatives: Reverend or Sancta Virgo; and bless the person's forward journey with Eternal Love and Peace.

It is fair to say this is a human rite of the "right" [as best we can know]. Most of us can't look beyond the Veil. Possibly Mystics, Spiritual Healers and Clairvoyants can see some things beyond the Gooey Stuff. My job is to tell you about what I have found that can reduce some of the confusion and some mistakes.

The photo of part of a silver church door shows 6 Ears of Wheat [Love and Eternal Life] at the bottom and Serpents [Knowledge] at the top of the staff or Sceptre [Power of Life or Death]. It is also like a mirror image or asymmetric in its structure. We will explore the dimensions of asymmetric structures in the Twin Nature of Psyche in chapter 8.

If you take nothing further from this book, you may remember it was about *6 Ears of Wheat – a symbol for Eternal Life and Love. And it's about butterfly wings and asymmetry.*

This reminds me of the story about Woody Allen after he had done a speed-reading of War and Peace. "It was about Russia." He was right!

I knew 20 years ago that I was going to have to wade through a lot more Gooey Stuff than I had in the

previous 20 years! I started reading and research in a new way. Opportunities led to the Louvre in Paris and Napoleon's apartment in Versailles. And particularly it led to the art and sculptures about Pan. I knew there was a massive amount of confusion about him. I made a pictorial record of what I found in France. You will find it in the following chapter on Pan – The Good and Gooey. Better than all that, we also can learn "What The Archetypes Have To Say" about Pan and a great many other matters. I especially look forward to discussing the "blueprint" the Archetypes have given us about Psyche at the individual level and the collective level. Psyche can be Laevo, Centre and Dextro. These are key concepts for development later but we have already seen it assist our exploration of Psyche's legend. But there is far more to it than just three words.

As early as 400 BC, Socrates and Plato used the word Psyche to mean "soul". They argued the case that the soul is immortal. But it is important to know Archetypes never used that word in any transcript. They had their own name for what they regard is the sacred part of you. The sacred part is in everyone no matter what they believe. The name that Archetypes use is ***Sanctitas Vestra***. This translates as "Your Holiness". This is a title usually reserved for a Pope in the Catholic Church. But as Archetypes use it, Sanctitas Vestra applies to everyone of any faith or even no faith - it still applies to your individual Psyche. In the same way the Laws of Gravity apply to everyone, it doesn't depend on you believing Gravity exists for it to be working unseen.

As an example, this may include the awe and wonder you have felt watching a Sea Eagle over a mirror ocean. Or seeing blood-tressed sunset clouds with the first stars coming out! Maybe you felt it at the Grand Canyon or in a rainforest somewhere. But you can feel awe and wonder even when you see the many Raphael paintings of the "Madonna and Child" or David Parle's "Psyche". But it could be you feel it building a bridge or crossing a river estuary anywhere. We can refer to this experience as your aesthetic appreciation or "Awareness" of Beauty and Love. This will tell you where your "Bliss" lies, so it follows that the more you follow your Bliss the better it is. Your awareness will grow most rapidly when you follow your Bliss. Why? Because your Bliss is totally in tune with your "Blueprint" at birth. We quickly find what we love doing and where we love being.

But your "Blueprint" includes your defenses and they are also part of your "Awareness". They constitute the very fiber of your being and we are all uniquely different. These fibers are always preserved with respect to your experience/awareness in overcoming them.

This special "Awareness" is at the very core of Psyche and so Your Holiness and mine.

3. Pan - The Good and The Gooey.

The ancient Greeks and Romans both maintained myths about Pan. They maintained he was the son of Bacchus and one of the most common stories was about how Pan came to make the Syrinx or commonly called Pan Pipes.

Pan was resting on the edge of the forest with a view over the grasslands that rolled down the valley towards a river. It was a profound moment for Pan when the beautiful water nymph Syrinx appeared. As a great lover of beauty in nature, Pan was nearly overcome by her appearance and the grace with which she moved. He was almost transfixed as he watched her. Realizing that if she continued along her path she would be out of sight and he would loose her, he began to pursue her. In just those brief moments he had fallen in love with her.

Syrinx was startled by Pan's sudden appearance and she began to run back towards the safety of the river. Even though Syrinx was a very fast runner, the faster she ran, the faster Pan ran after her. Pan was as fleet of foot as a deer and was rapidly decreasing the distance between them. Realizing that she could not outrun him she became terrified, at which point, Pan caught her at the waters-edge of the river.

At the moment that Pan was about to embrace Syrinx, she held him away and leaning back, called out desperately to the deity of the river, "Save me! Save me! Anyhow!"

The deity of the river had no time to consider how to handle the situation and immediately turned Syrinx into a clump of water reeds.

Pan was devastated as the beautiful Syrinx dissolved and became a clump of reeds. He fell on his knees and fondly caressed the reeds where only moments before the beautiful Syrinx had been. The suddenness of his love for Syrinx was just as suddenly replaced by the sharpest pain at her transformation. With loving care, he selected seven segments of reed, each of increasing length and he then bound them together. As Pan bound the seven reeds together he symbolized the Great Mystery in Universe. Putting the pipes to his lips, he then began to play a very beautiful yet haunting tune as he expressed the love he felt for Syrinx and the pain he experienced by her departure. He loved the pipes and called them Syrinx after her.

From that day to this, wherever Pan played Syrinx, the unique quality of the sound and the beautiful, haunting tunes had a transforming effect on any deity, person or creature who heard his wonderful music.

The marble statue of the moment that Pan was about to embrace Syrinx, which is shown above, is contained in the Louvre in Paris. Also displayed there is a much older representation of the key moment in this story in which Pan is given the name Satyr but importantly he is not shown with the legs and feet of a goat.

Sadly, the damage done to the older exhibit – shown below – has included Pan's head. Most probably the depiction of Pan with goat's legs, tail and horns is a function of the Christian era and the manipulation of opinion. In the early Greek and Roman times Pan was worshiped in his own right and Pantheism was quite common in Europe. Pan was regarded as a deity with responsibilities principally for the grasslands and grazing animals. However, during the Christian era, the addition of horns on his head has led to Pan being associated with the Devil who is frequently also shown to have horns. This association is a divisive manipulation.

During Shakespeare's times, Pan is seen in a more constructive light as Cupid in the character Puck in a Midsummer Nights Dream. At the very least, you could say that Pan has always had love on his mind.

A very important part of the symbolism in the statue of Pan and Syrinx can be seen at the base, under Pan. The Sceptre is a symbol of the power of life and death. Unlike most uses of power, the Sceptre is not about a power that can be corrupted. The common adage that "absolute power corrupts absolutely," is true of people but not true of the Sceptre. There are repeated references to the Sceptre being held by the kings of old in the Old Testament but none that mention Pan. Interestingly, Pan is depicted with the Sceptre.

Not only do we find the Sceptre with Pan in the above statue, but in many others as well. The dual aspects of his mastery of music depicted by him holding Syrinx and the power of life and death depicted by the Sceptre bring us a lot closer to an initial understanding of Pan and the complexity of his role. These two aspects are powerfully represented in the exhibit below that comes from the ceiling of Napoleon's palace in Versailles.

Notice the two children represented as climbing down to the ground through a laurel tree – eternal love - on Pan's right hand.

The child on the ground is putting on a wreath of red [love] and white [peace] flowers. These symbolise the original blessings we are born with. And Pan is the one who is playing to the children whilst holding the outer edge of the spiral. Even the golden wreath on his head is touching the spiral and the foundation /structure.

You have to imagine Pan's haunting flutes are the love songs he plays to Syrinx eternally as children are being born and blessed through him.

There are strong indicators that Napoleon's master painters had made a study of Pan. In the examples above and below, the different aspects of Pan are shown in the four corners of the room and are not part of the paintings. The statues are built into the very fabric of the building akin to him being integral to the fabric or structure of heaven and earth. Note how Pan is shown as holding and supported by the golden framework and spirals.

The goat skin cloak or Golden Fleece is different to that which Pan is wearing whilst holding the Sceptre, and in this aspect Pan is looking into the

scene that has been painted – laurel wreaths to be worn on the head. From ancient to modern times, a Laurel Wreath is laid as a sign of Eternal Love. Also painted is the musical instrument, the Lyre. We will return to an exploration of the Lyre but at this point it is depicted also with a branch from the Laurel tree. The fourth aspect of Pan is shown on the right hand side of the picture. Pan's face is turned away and is hidden from our view. Thus we know that there are parts or sides of Pan that we do not know about. Of the unknown aspect, we do know that Pan is shown as wearing only a gold ribbon around his body and on his head. We may speculate this concerns being bound by golden rules, or constrained in particular ways. The nature of the part of the structure Pan is holding gives us some cues about what Pan is literally adhering to in every aspect in each corner of the room – a spiral - the symbol of Universe and Pan holds The Veil so we can't see in.

One Universe is shown two dimensionally in both its clockwise and anti-clockwise forms. This symbol has been used in the Northern Hemisphere in ways that are systematically different to the Southern Hemisphere, as you will see later.

The ancient Stone Age Circle at Rollright in the UK has a clockwise spiral of limestone cut down into the floor of the circle. The Celts also used clockwise to indicate what will come into being and anti-clockwise to indicate what is departing. There are some very deep esoteric roots that need to be explored about both of these dimensions of Universe. Let's summarize; that which is coming into being and that which is going away. Like breathing in and breathing out of the cosmos. It is also important to observe that the spirals shown have both an outer plane and an inner plane. Pan is shown to be holding these planes differently and there is a very deliberate positioning of his hands.

In the first corner of the room Pan is holding the outer plane of the spiral structure with his right hand and playing Syrinx with his left hand. In the second corner he is holding the Sceptre in his left hand against the outer plane of the spiral whilst curling his right hand around the very centre of the inner spiral. In the second

picture or the third corner, he is holding the inner plane of the spiral. In the hidden or unknown aspect of Pan, there is a curtain he is holding with his right hand that starts from the inner plane of the spiral. Pan is looking behind the curtain. We can speculate that Pan follows the golden rules or is bound by what he sees on the inner plane of the spiral.

The outer plane of the spiral represents Earth. The inner plane represents Heaven. Respectively the planes are of the 'seen or physical world' and the 'unseen or ethereal world'.

In about 500 BC, Lao Tzu and Confucius set down what they termed the Inner World Arrangement. We will more closely examine what they had to say about the relationship between the Inner World Arrangement and its impact on our lives on Earth, or the outer plane, in "Ambrosia".

Ancient Greek and Roman mythology are so

intertwined it is difficult to say who came up with the idea of the Nine Muses but they are important to our story. They each represented the gifts we human's have in poetry, art, music, history, sacred song, tragedy, dancing, comedy and astronomy. According to the myths they sponsored the gifts we humans have with regard to a particular Muse.

One of the Muses of importance to our exploration has direct relevance to Pan - Le Musique who was symbolized by holding the Lyre. The marble statue above of Le Musique on her own and holding the Lyre in her right hand, is displayed in the Louvre in Paris. Beautiful!

Pan is also a master of music as we have discussed in his playing the Pan Flutes or Syrinx. On another ceiling, in Napoleon's apartment in the Louvre, Pan is shown as paired with Le Musique as shown in the adjacent photo with no legs shown but asymmetric poises.

In an important way we are being given both a female and male form of Pan in this musical aspect. Again Pan is holding Syrinx in his left hand and Le Musique is holding the Lyre in her right hand. Importantly Pan is not shown with the legs of a goat and he does not have prominent horns or a goat's tail as far as we know.

In Napoleon's apartment, there is also a beautiful tapestry hanging on a wall that in part also shows these two mythological characters together but uniquely links them with both having goats legs. This is a sort of Mr and Mrs Pan Interpretation.

This idea seems to have caught on in several further interpretations of Mr and Mrs Pan having little Pans, even a proliferation of Pans! Shown below is an image of Pan's children playing with human children but watched over by a vigilant Pan in the background [top left but the two faces are hard to see below].

XXX

Of course there has to be a mother's role for Le Musique and the following illustration does that perfectly. Complete with a very large Laurel Wreath, there can be little doubt about the artist's intention of conveying the idea of Eternal Love at least between mothers and children. Not only is the link with Pan evident in the goat's leg symbolism but the mother figure on the right is holding a bunch of grapes as a sign of the lineage of Pan through Bacchus and the child is holding a flute. The mother on the left has a Sceptre below her left hand that is touching the Laurel Wreath. This conveys the idea that the power of Sceptre is infused into Eternal Love and Life. A cycle that is as complete as mother and child.

Both of these works are contained in the Louvre in Paris.

An unusual but obvious aspect of this work is that both mothers and both male children are looking to their right, but we do not know the subject of their collective attention. We can say that they all have something consistent about their perspective and that they are all right oriented. Right and Left are also expressed as Dextro and Laevo. Dextro is about what is coming into being or life issues, it is positive and it is about the light. Laevo is about what is going away or death issues, it is negative and about the darkness and sinister. We may conclude that in Eternal Love, they are all Dextro oriented and supported by the power of the Sceptre. We will later explore the issue of Dextro and Laevo forces in subsequent chapter as well.

The Laurel Tree has a special place in ancient Greek mythology. There are strong parallels between the myth of Pan and Syrinx and the myth about Apollo and Daphne. [Bulfinch – see Bib. 7].

Apollo is given as the son of Zeus whose principle is the Sun and who was deemed to be both a very fine sportsman and patron of the Nine Muses. He was the epitome of a handsome young man

One day Apollo was walking through the forest when he came across the beautiful water nymph Daphne. She was terrified at the thought of what would happen to her if she, as water, came into contact with Apollo, who was fire. So terrified she began to sprint back towards the river from whence she had come. Daphne so immediately struck Apollo that he decided to pursue her and being a very competent runner, he soon began to gain on her and caught her at the waters edge.

In sheer desperation she called out to the deity of the river, "Save me! Save me! Anyhow!"

Daphne was saved by the river deity and transformed into a Laurel tree. Apollo was devastated and chose leaves from the Laurel tree to symbolize his Eternal Love for Daphne.

Whenever Apollo attended the funeral of someone he loved he would make a wreath from a Laurel tree and place it at the grave. Even today Apollo still loves and pursues Daphne for as surely as the Sun rises each day, the dew recedes.

The above statue of Le Musique holding a tambourine [as she also did in the tapestry] shows her with both a Pan child and a human child. In view of our earlier discussion, it is no surprise that she has the Pan child on her right hand side. This statue stands in the beautiful atrium at the Louvre.

Although the very distinctive goat's legs are an easy and immediate way of identifying Pan, this is not a necessary part of the traditional mythology. As seen in the older statue of Pan and Syrinx, he had normal human legs. Normal human legs are evident in both of the following exhibits. The first is Pan playing a flute and he is not shown with horns or goat's tail. Depicting Pan with goat's legs, horns and tail is not part of his traditional mythology. However there may be a basis for this confusion that lies back in ancient Greek and Roman times.

In addition to his mastery of the flute and Syrinx, Pan is shown here in the third area of his musical gifts, with cymbals. There is no evidence here of the attributes of a goat but there is plenty of evidence to show a cheerful or happy disposition. Returning to Napoleon's apartment

at the Louvre we find a further ceiling depiction of Pan in both musical aspects: with Syrinx and cymbals as the previous 'legs only' exhibit demonstrates.

In both of the aspects shown, Pan looks inwardly to ONE in Universe and reverse spirals are shown on each side, with a line connecting them. This is not accidental adornment of the ceiling as it tells an important part of the serious side of Pan who is not to be confused with the humorous figure Satyr who is also of early Greek origin.

Where Pan was the deity of the grasslands, Satyr was one of a class of woodland deity. In early Greek plays about Satyr, he was sometimes shown humorously with horses' or donkeys' ears and tail. On the other hand, the Roman's represented Satyr with a goat's legs, tail and budding horns as in this exhibit – note his ears. In this role he was lustful or a beastly-minded man and in early comic plays there was often a chorus of Satyrs. Accordingly Satyr has become confused with Pan. Or Pan has been attributed with Satyr's characteristics.

Bearing in mind the serious purpose of a Pantheon, to represent all deity and to provide a place for memorials and tombs, Pan was regarded seriously. He was not a character for comic relief. There was a much more universal aspect to Pan that is still reflected in the way "pan" is used as a word element in words such as pantheon, pandemic, panorama, panic and as an international distress signal when at sea. The Greek word "panikos" means of or caused by the deity, Pan. It is used even today to mean universal terror or fright or sudden alarm that leads to hasty measures. Syrinx may be just such a case. There is little doubt that the ancient Greeks and Romans took Pan very seriously indeed.

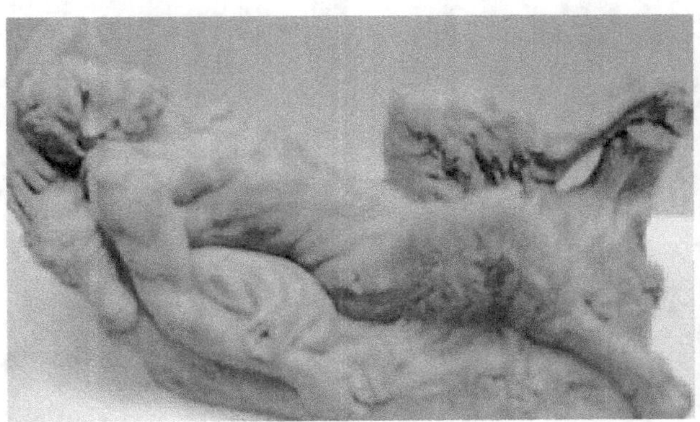

The confusion of Pan and Satyr may arise from the mythology surrounding both characters but it is particularly characteristic of the early Christian era. During that time, Pan was increasingly vilified and a strong stand was made by the Church against Pan. It was during this time that any statue depicting Pan became fair game for a zealous Christian, as the unfortunate defacing of this exhibit above demonstrates. Again we see Pan holding Syrinx and lying back against a goat's head and displaying the characteristic goat's legs and horns.

This photograph is part of a funeral stele that depicts Pan playing Syrinx and held by the horn by a man who is about to bash him!

It may be fair to say that the mythological roots of an understanding of Pan had spread into sour soil and were starting to rot. Even though the colour red worn in Church vestments directly symbolizes the Deer and Pan, Archetypes explain that the use of derris in cloth preparation has changed the colour and so lost a vital link in the power of the Holy See. It would seem this inconsistency has gone unnoticed in a waning church.

Perhaps what is not realized is that Pan is a deity amongst many. In like manner to Woden, Pan recognizes that he is not the supreme ultimate power. There is ONE who is the ultimate power in Universe. All of the rest, including Pan, are amongst the many helpers on the Inner and Outer Plane. As will be discussed more fully later, Pan does have a specific

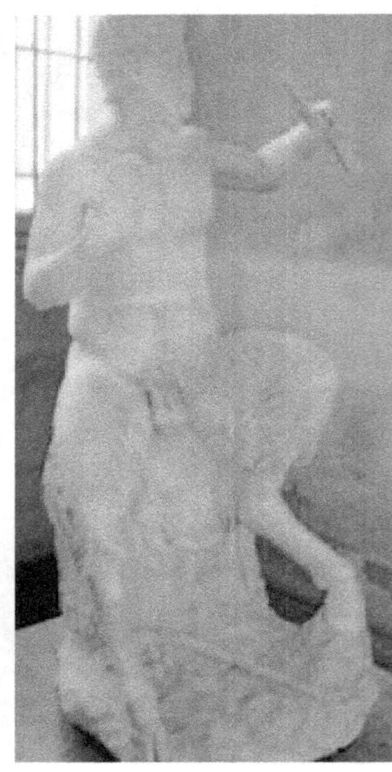

place and role in the Inner World Arrangement and he is often greatly misrepresented but fortunately not always so.

Suffice it say here that Pan is consistently identified by a marked ability with music, particularly wind instruments like the Syrinx or flute. As in this and some of our earlier exhibits, Pan is also identified with the Sceptre, the symbol of the power of life and death. Pan is shown on the right with the Sceptre at his feet, a flute in his left hand and a bunch of grapes in his right hand to signify his lineage from Bacchus. A previously unidentified issue is that Pan is sitting on a Lion's head and skin. Perhaps this is consistent with him being regarded as the deity who cared for the grasslands and lions frequent these places for their feeding. However they usually have their lairs in the forests. Perhaps it is to indicate the supportive power of the Royal Star of the Lion on the esoteric plane from whence Sceptre powers emanate? Likely this is the Right meaning.

Whatever Pan's connection with the Lion, this statue is not a stand-alone association with the Big Cats. In Napoleon's apartment in the Louvre, there is further evidence of this Big Cats connection and also some evidence of a somewhat less serious and more mischievous nature that may stem from him being confused with Satyr.

There are many images of Pan in this exhibit. This suggests the painter was either trying to represent differing aspects of Pan or else was confusing him with the woodland deities who appeared in chorus as Satyrs. However, this is not a woodlands scene. The principle subject matter on the right is Pan's connection with Bacchus; making wine, including the harvesting of grapes in the lower right hand frame. In the top frame, Pan is shown pouring red wine beside two tigers that appear to be pulling a cart that is holding a young inebriated man, supported by another image of Pan. Further to the left, Pan is in the background of a woman blowing a horn and a man playing a flute. In that segment of the picture Pan is shown as playing a triangle.

All in all, these grape harvesting scenes seem chaotic but indicate that Pan is virtually everywhere and doing everything at once in the background as well as the foreground of the pictures. Ever Le Musique's Lyre is depicted, at the lower left, as held by an angel who is following Pan. Pan is clearly pursuing a woman who is holding a bunch of grapes and has a basket full at her feet. There is a strong suggestion of impulsiveness for the grapes she holds away from him. He does not seem to be pursuing the woman for her self. In the scene above Pan is drinking wine from the Pan legged table and being observed by himself from the spilling cask. Altogether, these are chaotic scenes of debauchery and indulgence reminiscent of the way Satyr was represented and not Pan.

Pan's background role in supporting the musical gifts of others is illustrated here but even more beautifully illustrated in the following statue at the Louvre.

A child-like Pan is shown to be hushing the audience with a finger to his lips. He wants them to keep a secret about the Sceptre he is holding underneath the man who is playing a flute.

Thus the man who is playing the flute does not observe Pan but he is having a positive effect on the outcome. From the front of the statue you can see Pan's Flutes on the right of the Sceptre but you can't see Pan at all.

It is noteworthy that the Sceptre is being held on the dextro side of the flute player suggestive of adding the essence of life to his playing. The idea here is also that we have to make good use of the gifts we have as they can also be taken away. We have to honour our gifts; develop and enhance them; practice and refine them; and then hone them to the best of our ability. Having a gift carries with it a responsibility to exercise or practice it in a positive way.

The idea here is also that the gifts we have are supported by the Inner Plane of which we are not actually aware when we are exercising those gifts. Our flute player above is not aware that Pan is lending him a hand in what he is trying to do. There is absolutely nothing mischievous about this

portrayal of Pan and yet he is still shown as having the legs of a goat.

The important issue is Pan facilitating the expression of music and his being of assistance to a particular man or woman. He is demonstrating the unseen nature of the assistance provided by a deity of the Inner World.

A moment of reflection on how useful our "good days" are in setting our standards will show how important intermittent assistance can be. Once we have a grasp of the standards we can more effectively hone our skills by practice. But a person without an idea of what the standards are can be likened to

someone who is tone deaf but singing loudly out of tune. Unless you know what you are doing wrong, you can't correct a fault.

As humans we characteristically have "blind spots" in our personalities, perception and performance. To overcome these blind spots we need tutors coaches and psychologists. On the other hand what we can see about Pan is that by granting Sceptre to our flute player, an inspirational performance is possible and a new field of possibilities open up which can set new standards and targets.

In a similar vein, this exhibit shows Pan, again in the child-like form, influencing a young man who is holding a glass of wine. Pan is again on the dextro side of the young man who is also looking to the right. Some of the symbolism is lost by Pan's right hand being missing.

However, Pan's left hand is demonstratively a caring gesture and his face a picture of concern for the young man who seems very intent on the contents of his cup.

Both of the last two depictions of Pan sharply contrast with the impulsiveness, indulgence and debauchery of the painted chaotic wine harvesting scenes earlier. As the son of Bacchus, wine making, sharing and parties were very much part of the mythology that surrounded Pan. But these aspects seem to contrast with the more fundamental and serious aspects concerning his music and the Sceptre. But he is not always painted or represented in a positive light. Although the following statue of Pan is open to interpretation one way or another, it can be interpreted as negative. It is possible that the sculptor intended us

to see Pan as a "bad-in ape" or someone who was up to monkey business. Alternatively it may be that Pan is being depicted as someone who is trying to help in a situation where someone is suffering.

Pan is completed with goat's horns and legs but given a monkey-like face whilst intently and patiently working at something in the foot of our pained subject. The man's gestures suggest he has consented to the work that is being done on his left foot. Although he is evidently in pain, he is endeavouring to keep his foot still and only a minimum effort is being exercised by Pan to hold the foot with his left hand whilst working on it with his right hand. Everything about Pan's gestures suggests a great intensity of concentration on the delicate task at hand. His crossed feet suggest he has been settled at the task for some time. In short, it doesn't seem to be about monkey business nor does Pan seem to be a "Bad-in ape."

Not all of the representations of Pan are concerned with helping humans or with his interactions with deity. In Musee d'Orsay there is an exquisite marble

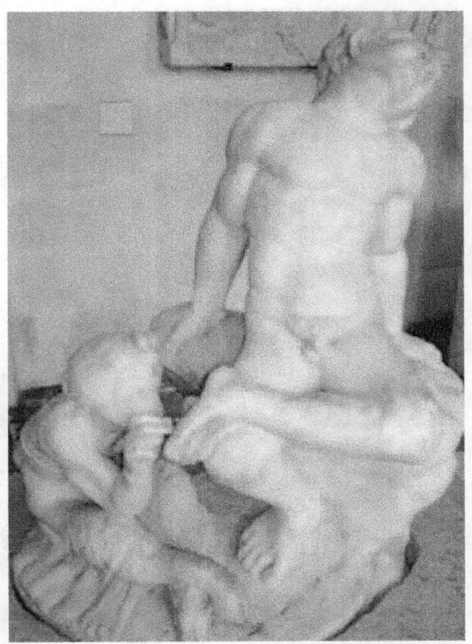

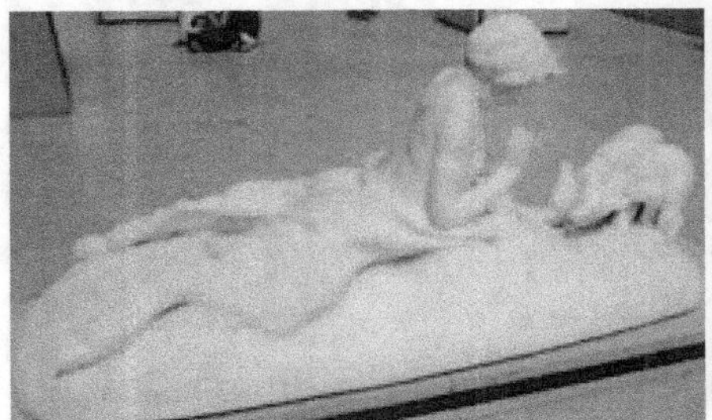

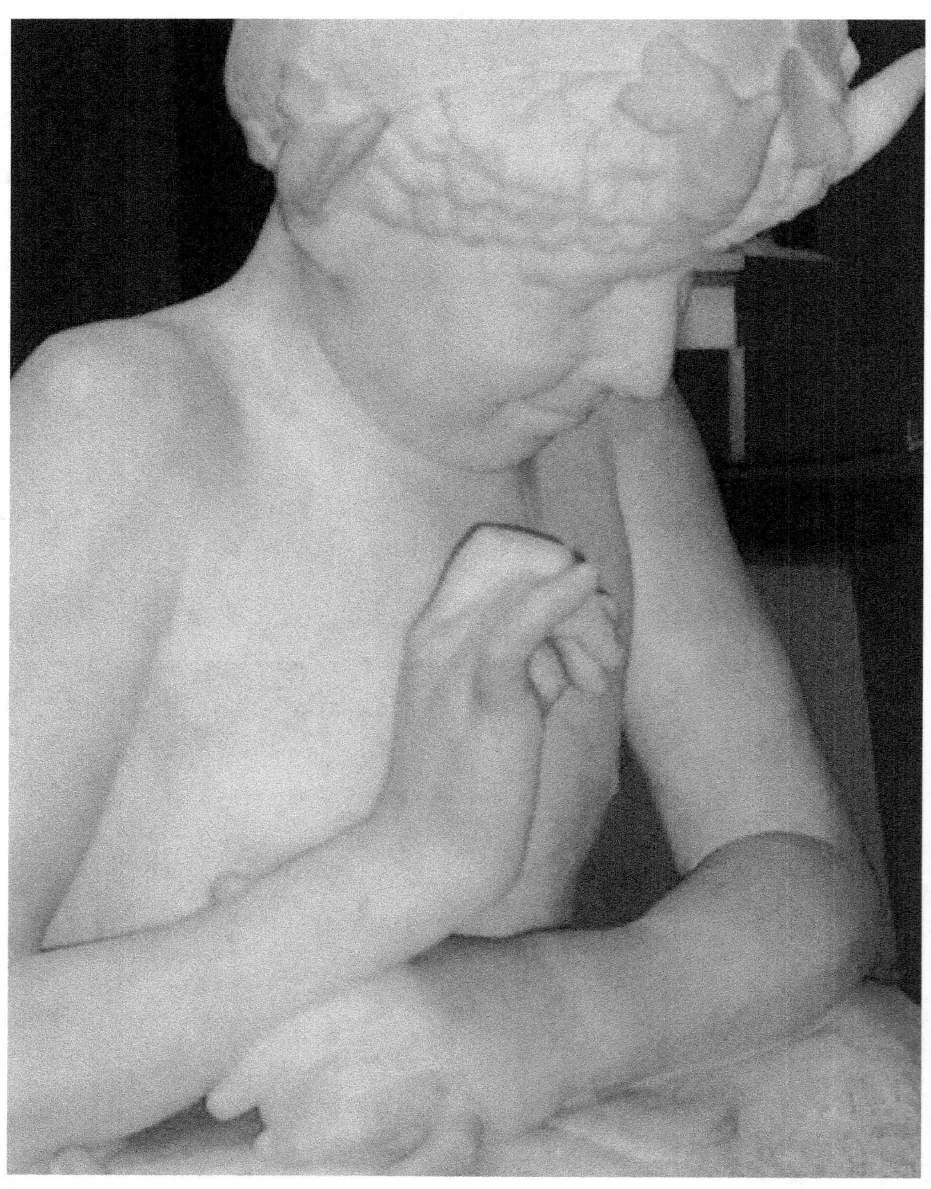

carving of a young Pan feeding honeycomb to two bear cubs and lying on the skin of a Big Cat. He has all the goat characteristics and ears of Satyr but also Ivy leaves or a wreath in his hair.

How can Pan be a sinister or Laevo figure when every sculptor has portrait him on the right or dextro side of his subjects? How could different sculptors, working at different times in history, and from different cultures, consistently position Pan on the dextro side? Is this just an accident or the exercise of deeper intuitive knowledge?

The evidence seems overwhelming. Pan held Syrinx over his right knee. Pan birthed and blessed children on his right. The Sceptre was given to be with him many times. The Pan child was on Le Musique's right. Pan is innocently playing his Syrinx in the stele, on the right side of the misled man who is about to bash him! Pan helps the man with his flute playing from the man's right. Pan expresses his concern on the right of the young man who was intent on his cup. Pan helps the young man with his foot, on the man's right. This is a remarkable and totally consistent set of evidence that Pan is Dextro. He is a deity of Light and Love and not the sinister figure of darkness as propounded by the Church.

In the various ways we have seen Pan represented; time and again we have seen Pan in a helpful role with humans and animals and also as a protector of the curtain or veil between the Inner World and the Outer World in Universe. There is a great deal more we need to know about him.

Fortunately "Ambrosia" has much more Dextro news to tell as you can glimpse from Pan playing whilst babies are being born and blessed. Can there be a more beautiful image! Or even a more wonderful role? Well YES! But Pan is only one of many who assist THE ONE – each in different and amazing ways.

Pan is given as one of the Archetypes and you will find he is given in the East and that does include the Cope of Heaven through which babies are born and blessed. The transcripts say Pan was baptised by ONE in the East.

I received an inspirational gift from Universe – the Two Faces of Pan [See p147].

Beyond The Gooey Stuff.

This is the Age of Aquarius and "tell all" is a good motto for us to follow as we move beyond the canonical scandals of the Church, manipulation of opinion, misinformation and a wide range of secret codes and names. Sadly neither the quagmire of mythology or religious teachings are going to be the help we need to reliably get beyond the Gooey Stuff in this Aquarian Age.

Science does give us some real hope of finding the truth of our being and of illuminating our perspective of what people are here to do on this "Blue Dot" in space that we call planet Earth. Centuries of research have not proved that life exists anywhere else in the known universe. And despite a lot of speculation we have certainly never found intelligent life anywhere else. I know there will be many of you who would challenge the point that people exhibit much intelligence. However, there are some remarkable contributions that do indicate that people have intelligence; for instance the great Greek philosophers Socrates, Plato and Pythagoras. There are many other great original contributions such as Isaac Newton, Charles Darwin, Albert Einstein and Sigmund Freud. Each one has helped "raise the bar" on our collective understanding. In the present day, I must commend Professor Brian Cox for his highly readable "Four Forces of Nature". But perhaps his best contribution for this discussion comes from his reports from the astronauts who on return to Earth provide us with a new insight into how we need to see our role on this beautiful and wonderful Blue Dot in space.

The astronauts had developed a much broader viewpoint. They could see the need to treasure this solitary planet. The Blue Dot is our only home, our Eden in paradise. And they could see we have to put aside our national, religious and numerous other differences to work to save what we have left on this planet and to work for the whole of Humankind because there is no chance of re-supply from anywhere else in the known universe. This perspective does "raise the bar" again. We will all need to jump a lot higher for the collective good if we want to save the Blue Dot treats for our future generations.

I recently found a very interesting example of working with nature for the common good over the long term. This example also changes our perspective of Charles Darwin's theory of Natural Selection – survival of the fittest.

What is known as "The Shea Belt" in the African savannah extends all the way from Ethiopia in the east to Senegal in the west. Centuries of habitation and human preferential treatment of the Butternut Tree have created this belt. The tree is very slow growing and many trees are over 400 years old. Because they are very deep rooted they can survive extreme drought conditions. The nuts from the Shea have wonderful medicinal value and they are processed mainly by women and this contributes significantly to the economy of the region. But the tree is highly resistant to most efforts of commercialization and modern agricultural methods. Although the task of processing the nuts is very laborious, most of the medicinal value is lost when processed commercially. Countless generations of respect for the tree have enabled the Shea Belt to develop. Young trees are tended and protected in favour of other species so the region and it's people have benefitted accordingly even in extreme droughts.

It is fair to say that people can be purposeful in their behaviour and we can term this the Fifth Force. [Allowing that there are 4 Forces of Nature as Professor Brian Cox proposes.] This 5th Force becomes increasingly evident in modern day genetic engineering but is that work oriented for the common good over the long term? Unfortunately there are a great many examples of how this work has been done for profit and entrapment. Some high yielding strains of rice have been developed that require special fertilizers and pesticides. But then the farmers can't use these hybrid seeds the following year. They have to buy new seeds - that certainly isn't the breadth of perspective the astronauts think we need.

However, we can see that even in that behaviour people are using their skills to discriminate and analyse data that are the hallmarks of the Fifth Force. You can certainly see purposeful behaviour in the work of Newton, Darwin, Einstein and countless others who have demonstrated the advantages of having a breadth of perspective. Professor Brian Cox does say he thinks science can help with that issue. But what will help the most is if people clarify their values and take a more worldly view of their purpose in life on the Blue Dot.

The Fifth Force doesn't happen in isolation. Purposeful behaviour is evident in every Nobel Prize winner but there is something more to it – passion drives the 5th Force. Probably none of them could have done what they have without being passionate about their subject. This is akin to a "magnetic attraction" – just like my grand daughter Libby watching the native bees. So the 6th Force Passion / Love drives the 5th Force. That is when remarkable things can be achieved – even when restoring an old car. Love is our best driver in our ability to discriminate, analyse and communicate.

Individuals seeking ideals and being purposeful can be viewed as the primary building block for collective effort. This occurs when a shared passion for a purpose is involved. When we see massive community support for something, big things can happen. The optimum circumstances for Force 6 come only collectively when the first building blocks are in place. People need to have worked ideas and processes through together before they can form effective bonds with each other. The quality of those bonds is probably proportional to the collective achievement of a group, community or nation that has a common purpose. People are most effective when they are clear and agreed about what they want to do. Although we need to resist manipulation and coercion I think we need to follow what holds a "magnetic interest" for us.

I hope we are past the point where an Adolf Hitler can stand up and tell everyone what to do, organize the country, go to war, kill millions of people, experiment with people like they are rats, plunder all their chattels down to their gold teeth and wreck most of Europe. Sadly it looks like ISIS is going the same way. These are extremes produced by prejudice and a lack of breadth in perception and thought about our human values.

I think Mahatma Gandhi spoke to the core of Humanistic Values when he said;
"There are many causes for which I would die. But none for which I would kill."

In a condensed form I would say genuine Democratic and Humanist Values are the starting point. Those ideas have to be clear to everyone in a collective purpose but without manipulation of opinion. Soundly based information and joint agreement is what is needed for all the individual building blocks. You are one such block. Yes that means you!

I will return to this point another way.

We are all blessed to be able to do something. What we do will be very widely varied by our "magnetic interests" and loves. But how do you know what that something is? Clarity is almost impossible when caught up in the vicious cycles of alcoholism, domestic violence and drug abuse.

The obvious starting point is with you. Accepting personal responsibility is first and foremost in breaking those cycles.

In the second place you can explore what you see or know about your enduring unique constellation of interests and loves. Then you need to follow them. This should lead you into discovering how you are blessed – to finding your Original Blessings. [This is the complete opposite of the idea of Original Sin.]

Thirdly, you can explore how other people see you. That can be a very important point of view because we all have "blind-spots" and other people often can see what you can't see yourself. How other people see you is a storehouse of information and insight that can be both right and wrong. It can be totally chaotic and full of individual prejudice and it can also be well thought through, systematic, relatively objective and well organized. I prefer the latter.

The chapters on the Wisdom Paths will provide you with a framework that can be used systematically. Through the process you will probably come to better understand How Others See You. In those chapters there is plenty of work for you to do and there are worksheets to assist you in working out your own Wisdom Paths. In the process of doing that work, you will encounter the major elements of and structure of Psyche both at the individual building block level and also at the collective level where the structure is asymmetric, like the wings of a butterfly as the ancient Greeks proposed. But they were not the only ones to see the soul as asymmetric. The ancient Chaldeans and the Hebrews worked together about 4000 years ago and they devised the basic system of the Wisdom Paths. [The tree of Thirteen Fruits, The Tree of Life, the Kabala and Tarot were part and parcel of their inspired thoughts around that time.]

The ancient system of Wisdom Paths devised by the work of the Chaldeans and Hebrew was almost lost in antiquity until partly revived by the efforts of a mathematician and author called Lewis Carol. He is best known for "Alice in Wonderland". I won't talk too much about his fairy tales. It was Lewis Carol's mathematical interests that revived the ancient system. At least it was enough for Linda Goodman to become involved in rebuilding the ancient definitions and so breathing life back into the search for why we are each on this beautiful Blue Dot in space.

So in the chapters ahead there is work for you to do to get beyond the Gooey Stuff. This work is not only assisted by Lewis Carol and Linda Goodman. As mentioned in Chapter 2, we have the benefit of "What The Archetypes Have To Say." Although that story is told in "Ambrosia", there are many matters in relation to the Wisdom Paths that are summarized here in "Psych". Further to this the Archetypes have steered discovery of a number of things that needed work to make the Wisdom Path system more complete, robust and far more fascinating.

I am sure you will come to appreciate that it is through the efforts of the Archetypes that we are truly able to go Beyond the Gooey Stuff. However, they point us in a number of directions where we need to take the action. For example, as noted in the Legend of Psyche and Cupid, an Ear of Wheat is a symbol for Eternal Life and it can ameliorate the incorrect teachings from the Church. But it is up to us to see that it is placed on the coffin of our dear departed souls. So there are things we need to do to assist completion of the natural cycles that occur beyond the seen dimension that are just as fundamental as gravity.

In what is effectively a dialogue with Archetypes they provided a shorthand way of relaying some information initially using a highly specific code. It began with the Neutron Number of specified elements from the Periodic Table of Elements used in Modern Chemistry. The Archetypes used the Neutron Number to find the relevant Wisdom Path Number reference. "WOW"! At one level I thought I was plane lucky to realize this linkage to the Wisdom Paths. When I did, whole sections of text made more sense. It became well-used shorthand Archetypes were using. However Archetypes used some vital cues to help me find this link. I am sure they knew what I needed to find this connection.

I hope you can see how funny it is to be using a modern chemistry idea – the Neutron Number of an atom in combination with such an ancient system. As it happened it helped enormously. It was shorthand for a massive storehouse of information and insight. One symbol like O for oxygen related to pages of the ancient texts. The Wisdom Paths are pivotal to properly understanding "Ambrosia" and of "What the Archetypes Have To Say." Take your time; the information takes a lot of reflection and deduction. Only you can do that work.

With the direction of Archetypes we are able to provide a more complete Blueprint of the Wisdom Path system as given here. You will have the opportunity to work out the paths that are applicable to you.

So we have found a way of reaching "Way Up Past The Gooey Stuff". We have the transcript from the Archetypes themselves to help us appreciate the complexity of the role of collective intelligence in creation. What they reveal in Ambrosia is "way past" anything I had ever thought about. A stunning new vista of Psyche!!!

However Archetypes make frequent use of the same system, help me improve it and so they must think it is worth some effort to appreciate they are using Wisdom Paths as an analogy for the way their process interacts with us on the Earth plane.

For example, An Ear of Wheat can only help when you use it – Sanctitas Vestra.

The Wisdom Paths likewise are up to you Your Holiness. As an analogy it is pretty exciting and thought provoking.

Preference for a science-based approach to the Twin Nature of Psyche may be more to your interests. In Chapter 8 the "Blue-print" of Psyche is given by Archetypes and that is used to evolve a more complete model of Psyche at the individual level.

Why is this information coming now? The Archetypes see this as a Water Age – the Age of Aquarius – in which "tell all" is the motto. They need us to know what they think. And for us to discover the way forwards. They need you to be involved and the Wisdom Paths are one suggested way to start that. But they provide information on many other ways to assist our sustainable health and growth on Brian Cox's Blue Dot in space.

In short, Archetypes are trying to help us realize things. We have to "Wake Up to Our-selves" first and then to the needs of this wonderful, isolated, water world in space. So there is stuff to do for all of us. You are important as a building block of anything that you know in your heart is important. You can rest assured Archetypes will know what-ever you are up to and they appreciate assistance for the good of creation. "Ambrosia" will give you more reason to look ahead to the How and What in the realm beyond the Gooey Stuff.

But back to some of the Gooey Stuff. Did you know that Lewis Carol used the Wisdom Paths to underscore some of his characters in "Alice In Wonderland"? You will see how this applies in a later chapter on Paths of Ascension and Progression. By the method Lewis Carol uncovered, we find that we are referred to 52 Healer / Holy-man to be able to see Up Past The Gooey Stuff!!! To the ancient Chaldeans and Hebrews, 52 signified The Great Mystery in Universe. This is a matter for Great Spirit and for great care.

The Great Mystery was certainly with Libby on that day – radiantly Sanctitas Vestra!

Sadly I am not the Healer / Holy-man required to make sense of the Gooey Stuff or the concept of heaven. But the dry-humour of an Australian tradesman might help you appreciate the Spirit we can sometimes glimpse in humour. It may assist you in seeing above the Gooey Stuff a bit more.

We were renovating our house in Whale Beach when our plumber-friend had a paralysis tick drop on his head and dig in. Feeling unwell he went to hospital where I phoned him on speakerphone on his mobile next morning.

"Hi Bob! How are you?"
Bob; "I'm OK but they did a brain scan."
Thinking about the tick, foolishly I asked, "So what did they find?"
There were 5 other tradesmen present during the call and they burst out laughing and someone shouted,
"That was a waste of time, they wouldn't find anything!"
In a wonderfully humorous spirit our plumber replied,
"Well No. They didn't" The men were on the floor laughing, as he was.
Then I asked, "So what is happening now?"
Bob answered," They just asked me what day it is and where am I?"
"Who is they?" I asked.
Bob answered, "There are two lovely nurses here and two equally lovely female doctors. One of them just asked me what day it is and where am I? So looking around, I told them, "I'm in heaven and I don't care what day it is!!!"

Everyone was laughing including the doctors and nurses. We knew Bob would be OK and you could feel Great Spirit was with us all.

TO BE IN HEAVEN!!! AND COME BACK!!! BOB DID IT, to a great deal of raucous laughter and extremely good spirits on the next day! Maybe we are already in heaven and some of us do realize it!

Great Spirit is everywhere and exactly like Oxygen – vital to every breath we take. It is heaven every time you breathe!

As noted earlier, this is the Age of Aquarius and "tell all" is the motto. So in the first place this is about Psyche and not religion even though I am a Christian as my name attests Christopher means "Christ bearer". Importantly I want to inform you directly from Archetypes and to tell you all of what they have to say, so "Psyche" needs to be read in partnership with "Ambrosia" and vice versa.

I have been exceedingly fortunate to discover so much about the Archetypes. They want the truth to be known. They are not a squabbling and competing bunch as depicted in mythology. They are instead working to a series of accords, agreements or as we term them, Covenants. The Archetypes and their covenants exist today as much as they ever did and will. At the very center of all these relationships between the Archetypes is The One. However we will not only find Zeus and Woden but that both of them are in these accords, so there is no preferential treatment and they have the same "onwards" reference to THE ONE. There are several Archetypes you will not have found in any mythology that I know of and several others that you will have heard about such as Mother Earth and Great Spirit. They are all in these Covenants.

We will explore four of these Covenants in the separate discussion titled "What The Archetypes Have To Say." Broadly speaking, the Archetypes have directed this work and provided some wonderful examples and deep insights into the process of Life and Life After Life and the central importance of an Ear of Wheat to symbolize Eternal Life and to clear away the Gooey Stuff caused by incorrect religious teaching. Six Ears of Wheat are very special indeed.

In both the Tree of 13 Fruits and the Tree of Life of the Hebrew's, six means Beauty and Love. So our discussion about Eternal Life is also a discussion about Eternal Beauty and Love. Love is the best way to center your being. Love is an "eternal fixed mark". Through Love we begin to enter "the stillness" in peace, reach into the Centre of our eternal being and find "the still center in the eye of the hurricane." There are three aspects of the 6th Force - Love that are addressed here. There is the Love you feel for yourself and the care you show for yourself. There is the Love you feel for others and project into the world around you. And there is the Love you are gifted to receive.

Turning to Science for a moment. A quantum mechanics experiment was conducted in Japan into the effects of "group awareness" on water. This is particularly interesting because about 97% of our bodies are composed of water. You will quickly grasp the idea of this experiment if you imagine 6 experienced meditators [Sitas] sitting around a table with a jug of water in the middle. In the first of three sittings they meditated on Love. In the second, with a different jug of water they meditated on Thank You. In the third, with a different jug, they meditated on Hate You and I want to Kill You. The water in each jug came from the same initial source.

The water from each jug was then deep frozen to about -200 degrees C and left to form crystals. These crystals were then held at about -5 degrees and photographed. The differences in the crystals were astounding. The Chi of Love water crystals were truly beautiful and expansive. The Thank You water crystals were much more structurally cohesive but still beautiful. The Hate You and I want to Kill You water crystals were disorganized or chaotic and ugly. Wow!

What you think and feel makes a massive difference not only to you but also to everyone and everything around you. And the Chi of Love has a wonderful effect. As six is the number for Love, snowflakes are remarkable in all being unique. But you don't have to be frozen to see and feel love. Consider for one moment just how wonderful the impact is upon you when you are surrounded by family and or friends who love you. They don't have to be Sitars for you to be affected by LOVE.

To an astronomer, Right Ascension means the correct rising, path and pattern of setting of a star in our night sky. Each star has it's own unique pattern of Ascension. The Wisdom Paths are similar but you will be pleased to know there are less of them than there are stars! However it needs to be born in mind that each person's path has unique qualities. To make it manageable our discussion will actually be limited to 52 Wisdom Paths of Ascension. The Chaldeans chose 52 because it was the same as the number of weeks in a year. The numerals 5 and 2 combine to create the frequency of 7 that signifies the Great Mystery and they thought it was respectful towards Archetypes to so limit the paths to 52.

The nine months you spend in-utero is evidently very formative but the date of your birth is taken as the time for your Ascension. Birth is a crowning moment for a parent when ***independent life*** commences and a whole host of external influences and factors come into play. Archetypes say that our "blue-print" also contains people and situations that you are born to encounter. Your family and friends are obvious examples. But the people and situations that are difficult for you to manage are also part of the "blue-print" challenges you face. You are born with a whole constellation of abilities, latent talents, interests, etc., that we will term your "eternal fixed marks" but what you do with them is very important. These are your Original Blessings. As body, mind and spirit, there can be Blessings in all three aspects of being, even in apparent disadvantage or limitation.

In quantum physics the talk is about "entanglement". In this discussion you may find that some people who you are born to meet are not only there to facilitate your love but also to teach you about your "dark side" that also has to be integrated into your "awareness". Some of us are more blessed than others to understand darkness and pain. Some of us experience more darkness [Laevo] but there is little doubt we are primarily beings who seek Light [Dextro] and Love [Centre]. The experience of darkness can reinforce and focus our sense of what we want in line with our "eternal fixed marks". In our experience and growth in "awareness", essentially negation can lead to a positive experience.

Life is learning and so our "awareness" matures. Well, providing we are learning not to repeat our mistakes. It is one thing to be goal oriented and so to be busy looking ahead, but it is through reflection and review of incidents and circumstances, that we learn new and more effective ways of doing things. So we always need goals and finding better ways to get there, even unique ways, is all.

Reflection and review is very beneficial when conducted in a group setting that has developed "Group Awareness" – another cartel of cooperation. Other people can express things in ways we might not have thought of. Others see what we may be limited in seeing and so it is through "How Other's See You" that new insights can be obtained. It is very significant that in quantum physics today we find having someone or something observing what a particle does almost always changes the way a particle behaves.

I have seen this at work in psychology too. Significantly the Chaldean built a system of looking at the Wisdom Paths from a unique perspective - "As Others See You" or as an observer would report. This enables new insight into the ways you are manifesting your Original Blessings and your "eternal fixed marks". Essentially it matters just as much how you utilize your abilities and talents as it does in how you manage your disadvantages and difficulties and how you misuse your blessings, even by failing to use them.

As we begin our exploration of the Wisdom Paths there is only one rule we need to maintain as our Archimedean Point – that point being the thing we always return to in a seeming chaos of other things.

When you follow your Bliss you are probably on the right path.

Life is an unfolding journey. Each door that is closed behind you will lead on to another door that will open. New opportunities unfold in their own ways and in their own times. When you "Follow Your Bliss", this process of unfolding seems to speed up. Try it! You know when you are on the right path for you, when you feel blissfully happy. It is when you are in this state that your best ideas and creativity will flow. Of course what you do, needs to be tempered by responsibility to yourself, others and your environment.

The converse of "Follow Your Bliss" would be something like "Holding onto Depression". Most probably depression is a sign that you are not on the right path. It is equally likely that the hormones you release during depression are going to take you even further away from what will be achieved through bliss. Certainly we all have our times when we are confronted with difficult problems. But being confronted by a problem can lead to important learning -"Life is Learning". This means confronting difficulties and honestly working them through.

It is somewhat unrealistic to expect to always follow your bliss, for as Lao Tzu [500BC] once put it, "after the exotic comes the laundry."[3] Though a later Zen proverb expresses this idea asymmetrically;

> Before enlightenment,
> chopping wood and carrying water.
> After enlightenment,
> chopping wood and carrying water.

Let's begin by contextualizing some of the key content to follow. Some of this work isn't as old as Methuselah; it is much, much older than even his time. As mentioned, some of the content dates back to the very earliest of times. A time when written records were first made of the oral-traditions of the patriarchs. Some of the philosophical and practical issues we have to deal with date back to at least 5000 BC. The question of how long have people been wondering about rhythms and patterns would be a path you would loose in the deepest reaches of antiquity. Some of this ancient knowledge has underscored and so survived, albeit sometimes only in part, in myths, religious teaching and sometimes only as a symbol. However, some of the oral traditions of indigenous people still survive such as the "Songlines" and totems of indigenous Australians. And American Indians.

The groundbreaking work done by psychologist, Carl Jung, in "Man and His Symbols", brings some further clarity about the focus here. We are concerned with Archetypes and their mandala in every culture. Western researchers have traced current mandala, through alchemical literature, to the times of the early Greek philosophers and to the mystical schools of ancient Egypt, China and Tibet. Of the great many mandala generated over time, few have received as much attention as The Tree of Life[4]. Although it is traditionally of profound significance to those of the Hebrew faith, it's origins are somewhat obscure. At about the same time, in 1500 BC, two Trees of Life are recorded, one by Moses after the Exodus, before which he would

---

3 Lau, D.C. "Lao Tzu Tao Te Ching".
4 David Hulse, "The Key of it All." – The Hebrew Key.

have had wide international contact and is known to have adapted the National Covenant from his time from Egypt[5]. It is thought that Moses records can be traced back to the writings of Enoch and the 22 Wisdom Paths on the Tree of Life. This was a record of the oral tradition of the Hebrew patriarchs. At about this same time, the Babylonian - Chaldean Tree of 13 Fruits showed interlocking path-work. The Chaldean's were great observers, astronomers, magicians, prophets, and workers of divining tools. The Old Testament is full of references to the Chaldean's who frequently seemed to be rivals with the Hebrew sages such as Daniel in the courts of kings and queens. As far as we can tell from this vantage point in history, both trees have similarities to this work. We will explore a mandala having Nine Spheres of Inclination and 52 Wisdom Paths. Since the time of Enoch, Hebrew theology has adapted the Tree of Life to having 10 Sephiroth and 32 Wisdom Paths and in which there are a number of "hidden paths" as well.

A stunning breadth of writing exists, both in theological and theosophical spheres, about the Tree of Life in the Hebrew Kabala, specifically the Sepher Yetzirah[6]. The breadth of attention given to the Tree of Life grew rapidly after it was adapted to a popular form in the Tarot that is widely used by people, sometimes with no idea where the whole thing came from in the first place. These were the "secret codes of Universe" that were discussed in Masonic Lodges, Templar Knights meetings, and the like for thousands of years[7]. They were regarded as secret because they were sacred. But "Tell-it-all" best suits this Age of Aquarius. We will draw on a number of these ancient sacred secrets. Besides, for a great time to come we will be in the Age of Aquarius. So why not get a few things off on the right foot? Dextro from the beginning. What will be presented as the mandala of the Nine Spheres of Inclination is asymmetric with the Tree of Life. Because it is the discovery of truth that concerns us in "Tell-it-all" so you will not find any "hidden paths" here.

Turning to the Outer Plane, we will examine the nine spheres of inclination and their respective Wisdom Paths. Archetypes referred me to a document that I already had in my possession that would assist my understanding of various sections in the spiral transcripts. This was also given as an example of the way in which they provide what is needed in reaching our goals. The document they referred to was a report of the ancient Chaldean system based on the Tree of Thirteen Fruits. From this system it is possible to identify 52 different Wisdom Paths. From the transcripts the Chaldean system can be extended and the underlying structure clarified so what is presented here is not the same as the numeral systems used by the Hebrews, Chaldeans or the Secret Order of the Golden Dawn or anyone else that I know of.

In 1986 Linda Goodman published research she had done on a link between astrology and numerology[8]. That interest led her deep into the conflicting numeral systems evolved through time, and to publishing only one that she found to be correct. This limits our focus to testing the "Chaldean-Kabala Numerical Alphabet" that Linda published. This is somewhat surprising because the Kabala is Hebrew and there was often conflict between the Hebrews and Chaldeans. However that simple set of surviving letter and numeral relationships, now stands centre-stage for part of our work in the next chapter. Linda's writings indicate what she felt destined; compelled; and she knew it was important for something and someone, somewhere, whoever it was. And it was and still is important to me. And very likely this will be important for you too. I was drawn to it at a time of researching the Enochian alphabet[9]. And it has a number of similarities to that.

5 Ellis, Peter. "The Men and the Message of the Old Testament."
6 David Hulse, "The Key of it All." – The Hebrew Key.
7 Picknett, Lynn & Clive Prince. "The Templar Revelation."
8 Goodman, Linda. "Linda Goodman's Star Signs."
9 Schueler, G.J. "An Advanced Guide to Enochian Magick."

However, by the time you reach the end of the Definitions you will see that Linda has put the beginnings of a wonderfully powerful tool into our hands. Our work here is asymmetric with a tool that was dedicated to growth of individual spiritual wisdom and human enlightenment, as long as 4000 years ago! And this is a tradition we are likewise dedicated to keep.

Inclination and the Nine Spheres.

In the following diagram, you will need to imagine a tennis ball or sphere or planet, with an axis of rotation that is inclined at a given angle to the hypothetical celestial horizon. Planet Mercury has negligible inclination to it's axis. Earth does have an inclination of 23.5 degrees.

Imagine our sphere, like a planet, surrounded by an electro-magnetic field that is closer to the dextro edge of the sphere where it is heading, and extends like a tail behind. Likewise the laevo field with its tail and the centre field between. The axis of the field conforms to the angle of inclination of the sphere. In the microcosm of our lives, we also have an electro-magnetic field that extends both in front and behind us. **That field will attract different ions from the environment, depending on its molecular charge.** Dextro is positive so it will attract negative ions. Laevo is negative so it will attract positive ions. So the same person can attract totally different things from the environment depending on their inclination.

ANGLE OF INCLINATION.

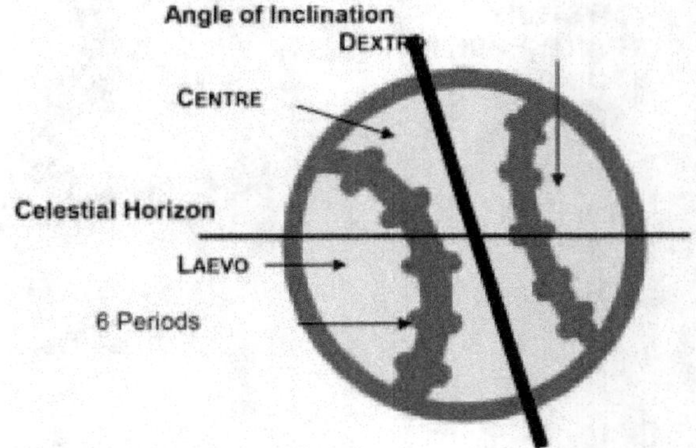

Again we are taking our analogy from astronomy, which uses a hypothetical construct of a horizon to define the angle of inclination of a planet. For example, Earth's magnetic pole or axis is inclined at 23.5 degrees and this is vital to the production of the seasons, etc. On the other hand, the planet Mercury has been found to have a negligible angle of inclination and so it does not experience seasonal variation to the same extent as Earth. Of course there are orbital irregularities to be taken into account in seasonal shifts but the angle of inclination is one of the first considerations that need to be taken into account.

Likewise with the Wisdom Paths, we will firstly determine the inclination of 9 different spheres and then explore the sub-set of generally 5 paths that relate to each of these Spheres of Inclination – as Others See You. The definitions for these spheres relate directly to the same Ascendants used in Astrology. However there is more to it than that.

Firstly, Linda proposed that in determining your birth only the day should be used to determine the path but that limits the paths to 31 and there are 52. We will not use the day of birth alone, but we will use the whole of the date of birth – day, month and year to determine the Wisdom Paths of Ascension 1 – 52

Secondly, Linda did not recognize Periods; nor grades of difficulty; nor isomers; nor the dextro, laevo and centre organization of Spheres. But then I had the good fortune of having Archetypes guide this work so that things can be put straight.

Thirdly, having made an extensive study of the sphere and path interactions it became possible to build a mandala of the interrelationships between spheres and identify their virtues as shown in the following diagram.

<u>Mandala of the Nine Spheres of Original Blessing.</u>

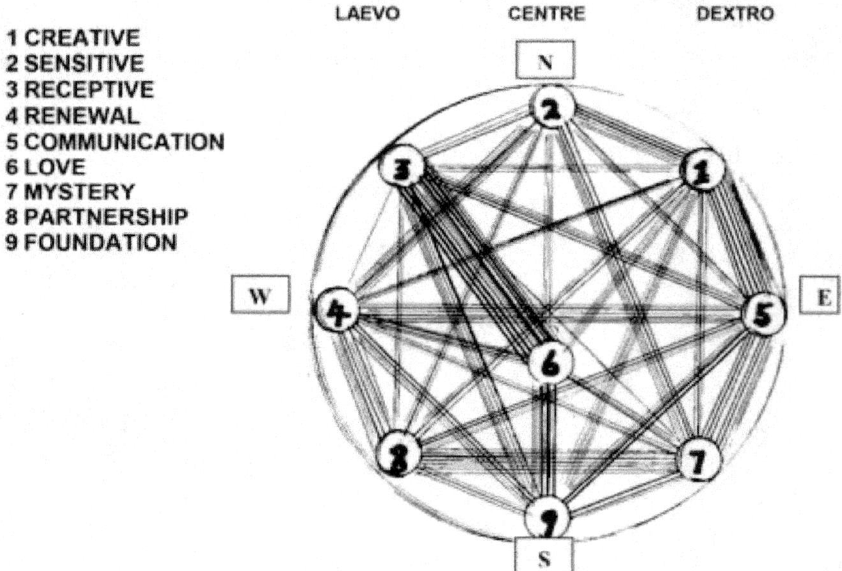

The lines drawn between spheres indicate the bond strength between them, such that the greater the number of lines, the stronger the bond – eg., 3, 6 and 9. Bond strengths between the spheres are directly related to the interaction between spheres or possible emanations from some virtues [such as 1. Creative, 5. Communication, 7. Mystery, 6.Love and 9. Foundation].

1. Creative is the most highly and widely interrelated virtue, having a bond with every sphere but having it's strongest bonds with 5. Communication, 2. Sensitivity and 9 Foundation. The bond between 1 Creative and 3. Receptive strongly suggests emanations from the Creative are received in the Receptive.
2. Sensitive is most highly bonded to 1. Creative but is linked to every other sphere but is most strongly linked to 4. Renewal and 7. Mystery.

3.   Receptive has the strongest bond with 6. Love. This is the dominant relationship in the mandala.
4.   Renewal has it's strongest bonds with 2. Sensitivity, 5. Communication and 8. Partnerships.
5.   Communication has it's strongest bonds with 1. Creative and 7. Mystery but it has significant bonds with all other spheres especially 4 but no direct bond with 6. Love. However the bonds with 3 and 9 are strong.
6.   Love is central to a chain of virtues 3. Receptive, 6. Love and 9. Foundation. The direct bond between 3 and 9 further strengths this vital chain between Love and the Life Force of Foundation.
7.   Mystery's strongest bonds are with 5. Communication and 8. Partnerships. This relationship with 8 and 5 makes up the core of another vital chain between 4. Renewal, 8. Partnership, 7. Mystery, 5. Communication and 1. Creative. The chain is completed by the strong bond between 4. Renewal and 5. Communication.
8.   Partnership bonds benefit directly from the chain discussed above.
9.   Foundation through the chain 3,6, and 9, is connected to every sphere.

The most remarkable feature of the bond strengths is the absence of a direct bond between 6. Love and 5. Communication and 8. Partnerships. However, in both cases the strength of bond is heightened by the chain of bonds 3,6 & 9 and the vital and long chain 4,8,7,5,1 and 2. It is noticeable how weak the bond is between 3. Receptive and 4. Renewal but it is a direct bond and 4 also has strong bonds with 6 and 9 in the chain with 3.

It is fair to conclude that the virtues are not independent. They are highly interdependent. Every sphere has an impact on other spheres and in some cases it must be seen that there is considerable overlap between the virtues. None of the spheres are separate categories and everything points to a powerful accord with active emanations from the virtues 6,9,1,5 and 7.

Working out your sphere and Ascension Path

If you want to know what sphere you are in, write out your birthday in full, such as 3rd July 1973.

From these numerals we can obtain an indication of the way you are inclined and the Wisdom Path that you are on. Two important pieces of information can be gleaned. The actual date of your birth gives your ascension wisdom path. From the sum of all the numerals [3 + 7 + 1973 = 30] you can obtain the sphere by adding the numbers of the path [3+0 = 3]. Sphere 3 means Receptive that you can see from the mandala it is a Laevo path. Wisdom Path 30 means Loner – Meditation and it is fully defined in the following Part under Sphere 3.

If your birthday is say the 23rd of July 1973, there are two numerals on the day of your birth, you should not combine these digits but treat it as the whole number 23 + 7 + 1 + 9 + 7 + 3 = 50. Wisdom Path 50 is defined under Sphere 5 [5 + 0] Communication which from the mandala is a Dextro sphere.

There are some special Chaldean rules for the numerals 11 and 22 so if these numerals occur in your birth date you should turn to Chapter 7 in order to find out what to do with them or wait for the moment.

Your ascension and progression spheres and wisdom paths do not have to be the same.

There are a series of Wisdom Paths in each sphere and each path belongs to what is termed a Period. Let's stay with our second example for the moment. The first period in sphere 5 is path 5. The second period path is 14: and then the third period path is 23: The fourth period path is :32 and the fifth period path is :41. You may notice that 14: and :41 are like mirror images of each other in the same way as 23: and :32 are mirror images. These are properly described as **isomers** and they will be discussed in more detail in Chapter 7. Not all paths or spheres have isomers. In the sixth period we have path 50.Statesman. This means that our person born on the 23rd July 1973 is in their sixth and probably final incarnation.

Out of respect for ONE, it was an ancient Chaldean practice to limit the total number of paths to 52 as a sign of the Great Mystery[10]. Consequently the number of periods is limited to 6 – meaning Love and Beauty.

Essentially the lessons in a sphere become increasingly complex as the period increases until hopefully mastery is achieved in period 6 of each sphere. Period 6 is called the "gold crucible" because the lessons of previous periods are rounded out or become more integrated. The real gold is wisdom and in the crucible, gold is refined and purified. You might say that the sixth period is like the final melting pot in which refinement occurs and the highest stages of human enlightenment are achieved as an elder, sage, holy-man, seer, cadi, doyen, etc.

Not only are there lessons associated with each wisdom path, but there are gifts or blessings as well. Essentially you are born to succeed. The blessings you are born with or which come at different stages in your path assist your achievements. Far from the idea of being born into original sin, you are born with Original Blessings[11]. Each path has a different series of blessings that assist with the challenges you face in each period. Not only are there challenges but there are tests as well. Some paths are characterized by what seems like an endless stream of tests and challenges as depicted in the life of Job in the Old Testament [path 38] but there are correspondingly great rewards for those who have fortitude and integrity.

In our exploration of right ascension, the ways in which we are inclined comes first. So the Sphere you are born into and your Wisdom Path are determined from the date of your birth as shown in the above examples. In all this business of definitions, we need to also remember the wonder of birth; the eruptive flow of love, joy-full tears and celebration of newly "independent" life. Most parents wonder around that time, "what will this child do? How can I protect his/her innocence? What activities can I encourage to bring expression of the child's gifts?" Amongst the parents of some of our more gifted children, many wonder … "who was this child before?" At the time of this wonderful event, birth, we will explore the "blue-print", a plan of the "new model", the Wisdom Paths of Ascension relate to some aspects of the many wonders on the day birth occurs.

The relationship between the Spheres and the Periods is set out in Table 1. below. [This representation is based on the structure of the Periodic Table of The Elements used generally in Chemistry.]

---

10 The Ancient Chaldeans developed the Tree of Thirteen Fruits and a sequence of 52 Wisdom Paths associated with the Tree. The material developed here is based on that system.

11 The term Original Blessing was developed by Mathew Fox who has done some inspired work on Creation Theology.

Table 1. SPHERES OF INCLINATION, PERIODS AND WISDOM PATHS.

Period	Spheres of Inclination								
	H								He
1st	1	2	3	4	5	6	7	8	9
2nd	10	11	**12:**	**13:**	**14:**	**15:**	16	17	18
3rd	19	20	**:21**	22	**23:**	**24:**	**25:**	26	27
4th	28	29	30	**:31**	**:32**	33	**34:**	**35:**	36
5th	37	38	39	40	**:41**	**:42**	**:43**	44	45
6th	46	47	48	49	50	**:51**	**:52**	**:52**	-

NB   H is the symbol for Hydrogen and He is the symbol for Helium
Isomers in bold, eg., **12:21, 13:31, 14:41, etc.**

VIRTUES OF THE SPHERES

1 CREATIVE	**6 LOVE**
2 SENSITIVE	**7 MYSTERY**
3 RECEPTIVE	**8 PARTNERSHIP**
4 RENEWAL	**9 FOUNDATION**
5 COMMUNICATION	

The table above is set out so the Wisdom Paths progress by Periods 1 – 6 in each Sphere. Ascension can only be in one sphere. The respective paths in each sphere constitute the overall progression of Sanctitas Vestra – Your Holiness – as Archetypes identify you. That progression is towards enlightenment in Period 6 when the lessons, skills and awareness developed in earlier paths are increasingly integrated in the "Gold Crucible". Each Sphere has it's own developmental pattern that can be determined by reviewing the paths in that sphere. As a general rule, the earlier paths in a sphere are more likely to be associated with a karmic burden, tests, trials and challenges. These burdens are far less apparent in later paths and rewards are more frequent, though varied.

Where an isomer occurs in the above table, the lessons of the earlier path are reflected in a later path in virtually the converse or mirror image of the earlier path lessons. In most cases they are related to each other in a converse way that can be seen between 12: and :21, where 12: means Sacrifice Victim. On this path there are many trials and difficulties experienced but :21 is the Crown of Magi and is associated with great blessings and a very fortunate life. What we find is that the testing and trials of the earlier life [12:] are richly rewarded in :21.

Not all isomers have a converse relationship of trials and rewards;

- In Sphere 7 Mystery, the earlier path 34: [heightened Discrimination and Analysis] is effectively preparation for a major "hang on to your hat" type of show down in :43 Road of Strife. Then comes :52 Holy-man.
- There are also heightening levels of path development apparent eg.,24: Love, Money and Creativity 1 and level 11 as path :42. and
- 23:32. Royal Star of the Lion is 23: and ensures support in high places that is vital to the success of :32 Communication with the masses.
- A more thorough discussion of isomers occurs in Chapter 7 but it is very important to note here that actually isomers also play a vital role in body chemistry as you may discover in Chapter 8.

Path 11 in sphere 2 and its double 22 in sphere 4 are special cases. 11 means A Lion Muzzled and 22 means Submission Caution. All people have a degree of 22 in the composite of their Original Blessings.

The ancient Chaldean rule with respect to 11 and 22 is that these numerals should not be simply added in the same way as other numerals.

Let's assume the birth date is 22 /12/ 1999.
- We would normally proceed $22 + 1 + 2 + 1 + 9 + 9 + 9 = :53$. But not so with numerals 11 and 22.
- Don't reduce 11 or 22 until we have reduced the other numerals by one level eg., 12 to 3; 28 to 10 etc.
- So we need to proceed $22 + [3 + 28 = 3 + 10 = 13] = 35:$. So our Wisdom Path is 35: Mass Communication and our Sphere is 8 Partnership that is Laevo.
- There are several other rules the Chaldeans used, as discussed in Chapter 7.

Consider: If there are 6 periods in which you ascend on a succession of Wisdom Paths until you reach the Gold Crucible; there is likely to be comparable preparatory "time" spent between your periods.

<u>Period 6:</u> _______________________________________**Path 48 Cadi**

_____________________________**Gold Crucible**

<u>Period 5 :</u> **Path 39 Loner – Meditation II**

<u>Period 4 :</u> **Path 30 Loner: Meditation 1**

<u>Period 3 :</u> _______________________________________**Path :21 Crown of Magi**

<u>Period 2 :</u> **Path :12 Sacrifice : Victim.**

<u>Period 1 :</u> **Start say in Sphere 3 Receptive / Laevo.**

In this example; If your current path is say 39 Loner-Meditation II, ie., having a heightening level of attunement to Universe, in Path 48, these receptive awareness skills provide great help when serving as a Judge or Cadi in any given community of interests.

Likewise for each of the spheres, there is a developmental pattern from path to path; and a different pattern in each sphere.

Each sphere is characterized by a particular over-arching virtue as shown.

The following diagram of the Virtues of the nine spheres combines the wisdom path information with the first representation of the relationship between the spheres as shown in the mandala. It should be noted that this diagram has a direct relationship to the Inner World Arrangement discussed in "What The Archetypes Have To Say". the location of each ordinal position. Where appropriate, an Archetype is given as the patron of the sphere.

In this diagram of the Virtues of each sphere we can distinguish the spheres by Dextro, Centre and Laevo as in our earlier discussion;

- Dextro means Right, clockwise, Light oriented, good and positive.
- The opposite is Laevo that means Left, anticlockwise, Dark oriented and negative. It means sinister.
- Centre lies between these two poles.
- Conventional ordinal positions apply [North at the top].

Virtues of Nine Spheres and Their Wisdom Paths.

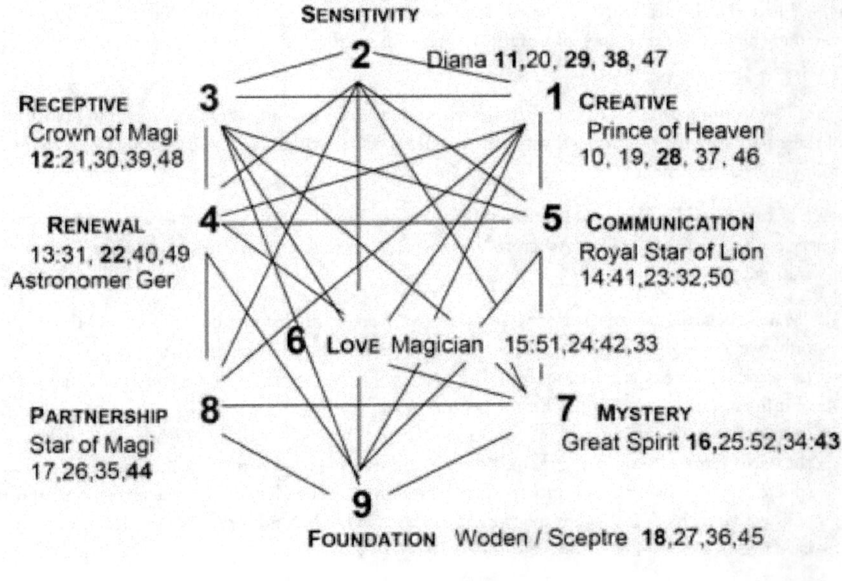

Axis...   LAEVO   CENTRE   DEXTRO

The next chapter provides full definitions of the spheres, virtues and paths.

Although Sphere 6 is identified as having the virtue of Love it could also be identified by the virtue of Beauty.

Professor Charles Birch was a very broad thinker who had a highly distinguished scientific career. In an interview with Caroline Jones [Bib. 36] he had this to say;

> "I think beauty is wherever there's harmony. I love unperturbed nature but I think that to really appreciate nature you've got to appreciate it with other people. I remember standing on the edge of the Grand Canyon once by myself and I thought this is most extraordinary; I want to talk to somebody about this, to communicate with somebody. The Universe is the most wonderfully beautiful place, as well as an awesome place because of its mystery. Finally, beauty is the beauty of holiness, of contributing to the experience and the life of "The Most Holy"... Beauty is a central element, I think, of life."

This is a wonderfully insightful comment about Beauty, Love and the principle Archetype, ONE who is at the Centre of this wonder. And Charles Birch is expressing the wonder that builds Sanctitas Vestra - aesthete.

In 1838 Ralph Waldo Emerson gave an address in Cambridge in which he said; "A more secret, sweet and overpowering beauty appears to man when his heart and mind open to the sentiment of virtue. Then he is instructed in what is above him. He learns that his being is without bound; that to the good, to the perfect he is born, low as he now lies in evil and weakness. That which he venerates is still his own, though he has not realized it yet. *He ought.* He knows the sense of that grand word, though his analysis fails to render account of it. When in innocency or when by intellectual perception he attains to say, - "I love the Right; Truth is beautiful within and without for evermore. Virtue, I am thine; save me; use me; thee will I serve, day and night, in great, in small, that I may be not virtuous, but virtue;" [Bib. 17].

There are 10 wisdom paths that have difficulties associated with them and these are shown in bold above. If any of these paths are relevant to your own, you should take particular care in your study of the definitions that follow in the next chapter.

The Tree of Life is used even today for undertaking an experiential journey akin to astral travel along the paths between the spheres. Dolores Ashcroft-Nowicki [Bib. 1] referred these journeys in the Tree of Life as "path-working".

> "When speaking of the thirty-two paths of the Tree of Life it must be remembered that there are only twenty-two that actually link the spheres together with what might be termed, a path. The other ten are the sphere or emanations from the Tree itself. One might describe them as pools or reservoirs of influence, acting as termini for the beginning and ending of each path. Their greater importance in terms of path-working, stems from the fact that they collect and hold traces and echoes from the paths that enter and leave them. Because of the interwoven pattern of the Tree this means each sphere contains particles of influence drawn not only from its fellows, but also from their mutually connective paths. It is this interplay of influences that lies behind the Qabalistic teaching that there is, 'a tree in every sphere'."

There are a number of highly significant similarities between the Tree of Life and our Mandala of the Nine Spheres. For example Spheres 3,6,7,8 and 9 correspond exactly between the two. Spheres 1 and 2, 4 and 5 are interposed and in the Mandala there are only 9 Spheres but in the Tree of Life there are 10 Sepheroths. The Mandala is also set out Dextro, Centre and Laevo but the Tree of Life is not. It is therefore fair to say that the Mandala of the Nine Spheres is asymmetric with the Tree of Life. What is as yet untested about the

Mandala are the possibilities for path-working but given the bond strength between the Spheres, particularly 3, 6, and 9, these possibilities are very high. Besides, the important developments in our understanding of the Wisdom Paths and their overall structure emerge directly from "What the Archetypes Have to Say".

Bear in mind that all stars have very well defined individual positions, they are differing sizes, having different luminosity, emitting different radio frequencies, are different distances from us [some of them vast], and they are each at different stages of development. The list of the ways in which each star, even in a small section of the sky, can be identified as unique, are almost as countless as the quality we most love about ourselves, uniqueness. The whole study is handled by methods of clustering stars. Another aspect of the analogy is that in examining a section we discover a spectrum against which we can compare. In defining your Ascension Paths you will quickly see how highly valuable individuality and uniqueness is. And we will explore some ways to identify and expand your understanding of the Original Blessings that you received at the time of your birth. But in all that may follow, your Sphere and Wisdom Path of Ascension will be vitally useful as your comparison or reference point like Aries or it could be your Archimedean Point – the thing you always return to [providing you are already following your bliss].

Essentially we are using 9 general categories that can be thought of as constellations of paths. Each of the nine spheres has its core. Linda Goodman argues that astrology uses general descriptions that attempt to be applicable to some 80% of people or 80% of the characteristics that a person may have. No system of description of ones' Sun Sign characteristics is complete without taking into account the Ascendants under which one is born. These Ascendants are all derived from our solar system whilst the Sun Signs relate to the 12 constellations of the Zodiac: the path of the ecliptic. The Wisdom Paths are therefore asymmetric with astrology and astronomy. The work you will need to do will involve "individualizing" the core characteristics so that you can see the relevance for yourself. This work is outlined in Chapter 6 & 7, you will also be planning what you are going to do about what you find out about who you are.

You will already know about a lot of things like your general level of intelligence, background, Zodiac sign, etc., so hopefully this first focus on ascension will add some focus in your progression considerations. Besides, you can't change what you are born with, but you can change your progress. For this very reason, there is a distinction between Wisdom Paths of Ascension and Progression.

Original Blessings – we all have in common

At the outset, it may be of assistance to see that your Wisdom Path of Ascension represents the constellation of your Original Blessings that could be traced to your very structure, your unique DNA and so to the structure of every part of your physical, mental and spiritual body. Your Original Blessings are "wound up like a spring" in your nucleus and some aspects are set on "slow release"! Sometimes, they move to fast-forward. So there are Original Blessings that are evident in your ascension and in your progression. It is all of these blessings that constitute your unique constellation of Original Blessings.

In "What the Archetypes Have To Say" there is considerable evidence of the progression that "Sanctitas Vestra" goes through. The 8th and 9th Transcripts are brim full of illustrations of the processes involved in this progression. Archetypes say that each person's "awareness' goes through several lifetimes with an accumulating "awareness" that transcends death. [See "Ambrosia."]

Archetypes liken our beginning to a small knot of woollen fibre. In this fibre there is an original goodness, not original sin, and it contains the talents, abilities and defences that make up our unique, individual nature, our Original Blessings. For these Original Blessings to be manifest, this knot needs to be combed so that the fibres are separated and straightened. A country like India or China is just the place for such initial combing to occur in the first edition. After saying goodbye to the first edition, some time may be spent in a "communal setting" in the South – The Place of Water – for example in the Red Rata Seas of Aesthete. In that setting some additions may be made to the Original Blessings. Then you go East again for rebirth as a second edition. Such changes to the Original Blessings depend upon how you have coped, how you have performed on your Wisdom Path and they may include rewards for trials with which you have succeeded. Other changes may include dimensions added to or refinements made to our Original Blessings that will assist you handle a particular challenge on the new wisdom path that you are about to face as the second or subsequent edition. Examples are also given of these changes being made during the progression of your life.

In a generally conversational style, Archetypes present us with the life and times of an official of the Christian Church who repeats his mistakes in more than one lifetime [Transcript 8]. They referred to him as Boyo – a disorderly young man from the country – and they proceed with a scathing appraisal of his current behaviour. His first edition is as a Hebrew altar boy where he shows great promise but in later editions he is an equally great disappointment to Archetypes. In this process of evaluating Boyo we gain some rare glimpses of the efforts the Archetypes make to assist him. We are presented with the view that all people are born with Original Blessings – a constellation of skills, abilities, insights and defenses. Whereas most of one's Original Blessings are unique there are two that are common for all people.

The first is the ability to **25: Discriminate and Analyse** situations and to gain spiritual wisdom through careful observation of people, situations and things. The key to gaining spiritual wisdom is to learn from experience, especially past mistakes. But Boyo has evidently made repeated mistakes in several lifetimes, so the Archetypes go to considerable lengths to add aspects to his Original Blessings, some of which have moderate success. [Path 25: is in the definitions of Sphere 7.]

The second general blessing built-in for all of us is a degree of **22 Submission and Caution**. An "inner voice" that warns when trouble looms, but in Boyo's case he is repeatedly unwilling to listen to the voice of caution. [Path 22 is in the definitions of Sphere 4.]

In his present life, Boyo is referred to as Bishop Batsman and his sexual exploits with a police constable from Bondi, who Archetypes call Don Put On, are explored with an astounding degree of candour based on an equally astounding awareness of what these characters got up to. There seems to be nothing the Archetypes don't know and they explain how they come to have such knowledge.

The relationship between Boyo and Don Put On is used to illustrate the negative consequences of some partnerships. Some people come into our lives for good; they are people who we were "born to meet'. Some other people who we are "born to meet' are there to test our ability to heed the "inner voice" of caution. The consequences of not being responsive are also explored.

I found a newspaper article soon after the transcript. It described how the Bishop of Bendigo was arrested and gaoled for soliciting in a public toilet whilst wearing his purple!

The second example given is of a character called Dono who was born in Denmark but currently lives in Spain. His Original Blessings included a high degree of proficiency in dance and music. He was also a "Peach Hand" in the diplomatic corp. However again we see misuse of his talents and skills and we learn that he follows his negative instinctive drives in the bedroom. He is also given as a leader in the Mafia and he has murdered someone. He does not have a bright future. But I haven't encountered any further relevant information about him.

The third character is me, the editor of this manuscript. The Archetypes refer to me as a Peon, the labourer who works off the debts of both Boyo and Dono. And they point out my sexual issues as well. They describe a night I had in a car with a female friend. Colour and type of car as well as describing what happened as a "runt". So all three of us have sexual issues as is sometimes the case with 37 Uniqueness. The Archetypes explain that the three of us have been in a spiritual relationship – a Doab - for a very long time – since early Hebrew times and we each have set roles. But although we are all born on the same day we are not to meet during the present lifetime. Evidently the three of us are "entangled".

As Pan is the Conductor of the Bio-Bond, he handles the Doabs. There are many Doabs and you are probably in one.

Archetypes point out that there is an annual grant of Chi [energy] made to each Doab by Pan. However things have gone wrong in our Doab and both Boyo and Dono have been swindling more than their fair share of Pan's Chi meant for me. Archetypes express concern about this situation and note that it has also happened before with the Nabbie French painter's leader. So the Doab is given as a basic unit of organization dating from some time probably after the Archetypes Second Covenant. The second covenant was possibly in the late Palaeozoic period. So very early conceptualization occurred between the Archetypes and 200million years before the emergence of modern man.

Archetypes indicate there are three primary roles in the Doab - Ace, Apex and Peon. On reflection I could see that on many of the journeys I took into the Big Desert I was actually working off the debts for Boyo, Dono and myself. I was also aware that in many routine undertakings, such as making preparations for each spiral, I was working off their debt. The diagram below illustrates the roles Boyo, Dono and I were born to in our Doab. No wonder I have felt victimised and been subject to the plans and intrigues of others – born on the 12th. [Sacrifice / Victim.] But then, so were they!

In exploring these roles and discussing the problems Archetypes see with Boyo and Dono, they advise me that it is appropriate to end the relationship. What they propose is to move away from Dono and Boyo; to end the Doab; and for me to seek a single bond with Pan. Just as Archetypes went to very considerable efforts to assist Boyo, they explore what I need to do to end the relationship. They expand on the symbolic actions needed in two exercises.

The first exercise was like a classical Japanese drama, a No and it is complete with Hoe! The second exercise was a journey to Cape Woolamai, a faunal reserve on Phillip Island in south-eastern Victoria. A more detailed description of the Journey to Cape Woolamai is given at the end of the eighth spiral.

Both exercises are a remarkable challenge to the imagination [as small knot of Wool am I] but in the course of exploring what needs to be done, a key issue comes to light that effects all people.

We learn that there is a duty of care to all life, a Bio Bond, and that for all who are of bone and travel by foot, Pan is the Conductor of the Bio-Bond. He has primary responsibility for this duty and has been baptized by ONE for this purpose.

None of the ancient myths about Pan come even close to the insights gained here about the extent of the responsibilities and so the nature of the charter Pan has in the Archetypal world and in life on Earth today.

The conversation between the Archetypes is very revealing about;

1. The vital role Pan plays so much so that many of the ancient myths can be regarded as demoralizing nonsense;
2. The Doab reveals the structure and roles between human spirits / Sanctitas Vestra on the Earth plane and in the Inner World; and
3. The consistent and complex inter-relationships between Archetypes are clarified and further insight is gained into the workings and structure of the Inner World.

The diagram below shows the relationship between the three members of our Doab. It is probable that this is the general way things are organized in other Doabs. [A Doab is usually the Y between two rivers that join.] The current flows the opposite way in this Doab.

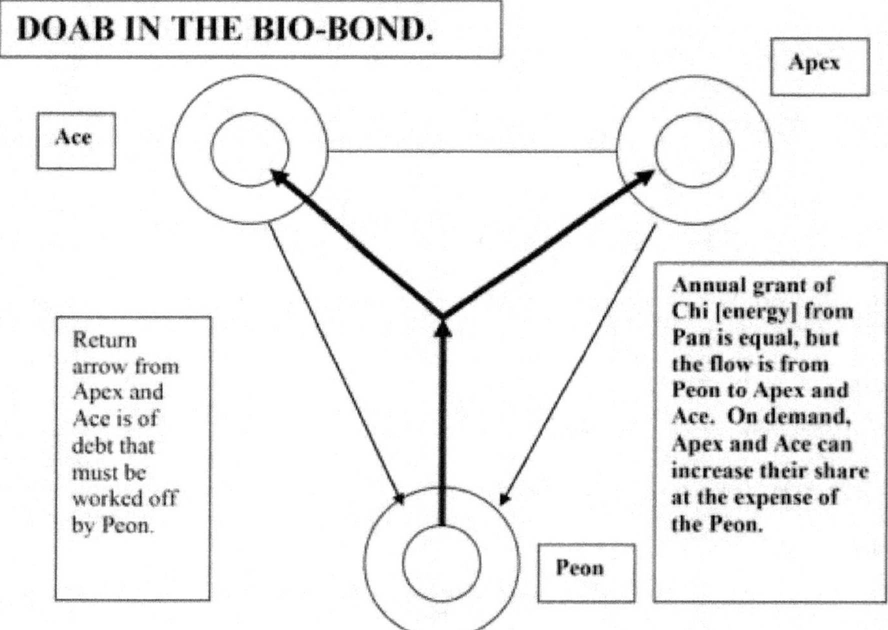

The fourth and final character [and example of path 37] in the spiral transcript is a daughter of mine. Archetypes give her story of incarnations as beginning in India. In the first period, at birth, she is likened to a small knot of woollen fibre that requires combing for the fibres to be separated. Each experience during her life-time assists the combing process. In the second period of incarnation, she is born in China. Further combed, she learns to be ONE-eyed. As her Original Blessings are manifest she gains new rewards and is born in Japan for further combing in her third period. Next, she is born in my household in Australia where the combing continues and her 37. Uniqueness "awareness" grows.

The final section of this spiral contains **a very clear warning for all people.**

The times are changing. We are entering a period in history where every individual will be tested for their ONE-eyed ness.
We are warned, "The bait will fall lightly on water".

Just as a lure, we will be tempted to deny the true seat of power is ONE. That temptation will evidently be like a fishing fly that falls vey lightly on the surface of the water and the hook is concealed!

For all who fail that test their fate will be like Dono's – 16 The Shattered Citadel.

> The ancient Chaldean image of 16 is "A Tower struck by Lightning, a Man falling with a Crown on his head." This is a clear warning of an unpredictable tragedy for those who lack vigilance and ONE-eyed ness and who refuse to heed the "inner voice" of caution. However, real Hope does exist for those who can be steadfast in these three aspects.

We all have the entirely natural capacity to still ourselves; stop our internal dialogue; and so hear the inner voice of caution. But our inner voice is not only able to focus on caution. Our inner voice is central to our intuition that is the wellspring of our inspiration and bliss. Through our inner voice we can find our connection to all living things and our physical environment. As our connectedness expands we expand our awareness and Sanctitas Vestra.

> He who in his own soul perceives the Supreme Soul in all beings, and acquires equanimity towards them all, attains the highest bliss.
>
> The great Hindu sage, Manu.

> "The human mind cannot be enshrined in a person who shall set a barrier on any one side to this unbounded, unboundable empire. It is one central fire, which, flaming now out of the lips of Etna, lightens the capes of Sicily, and now out of the throat of Vesuvius, illuminates the towers and vineyards of Naples. It is one light which beams out of a thousand stars. It is one soul which animates all men."
>
> Ralph Waldo Emerson [Bib. 17].

Archetypes call all men, women and children - "Sanctitas Vestra". And we know that Your Holiness is Eternal. Make no mistake it is your eternal soul – Sanctitas Vestra that is being warned. ***Stay vigilant*** would be Woody Allen's speed reading of this.

Professor Brian Cox in "Forces of Nature"[12] appeals to all people to broaden their perspective as noted earlier. He gives examples of what some of the astronauts had to say on their return to Earth after a period in space. The following is a good example of how they had changed their perspective.

> "This planet is not terra firma. It is a delicate flower and it must be cared for. It's lonely. It's small. It's isolated, and there is no resupply. And we are mistreating it. Clearly, the highest loyalty we should have is not to our own country or our religion or our hometown or even to ourselves. It should be to, number two, the family of man, and number one, the planet at large. This is our home, and this is all we have got."
>
> Scott Carpenter, Mercury 7.

---

12 Professor Brian Cox and Andrew Cohen "Forces of Nature' William Collins 2016.

Professor Cox argues that we can't all be astronauts but science can help us gain some height in our perspective. He appeals to each person to broaden their perspective. That rings true for the individual building blocks.

After you have worked through the Wisdom Paths in the next two chapters, you will hopefully also have broadened your perspective. After that we do what Professor Brian Cox suggests and examine a new approach to the science of Psyche. I think by the time you finish "The Twin" Nature of Psyche" in chapter 8 you may agree also.

A shift in perspective should help reshape and broaden our values and that is vitally important. Only by adopting a global perspective can some issues like climate change be dealt with but can we all reach the point when we see our highest loyalty is to Planet Earth? I even wonder how we can achieve the second goal of seeing ourselves as the Family of Man.

The Tsunami in Indonesia was a good example of how people can pull together globally and quickly when something threatens with great force. Forming lasting accords on a global scale will be a challenge we will all have to work on.

Will we recognise we are all part of a collective Psyche anyway? Fortunately some people already see it and more people are sure to see it as time goes by. Besides, we do have Archetypes to guide us and they certainly know how to reach an accord and stick to it.

5. Defining the Spheres and Wisdom Paths.

The definitions for each of the 52 Wisdom Paths are organized in this chapter according to the Sphere they are in. In the previous section we discussed the organization of each Sphere into six Periods. The following Table reflects this organization.

Table 1. SPHERES OF INCLINATION, PERIODS AND WISDOM PATHS.

Period	Spheres of Inclination								
	H								**He**
1st	1	2	3	4	5	6	7	8	9
2nd	10	11	**12:**	**13:**	**14:**	**15:**	16	17	18
3rd	19	20	**:21**	22	**23:**	**24:**	**25:**	26	27
4th	28	29	30	**:31**	**:32**	33	**34:**	**35:**	36
5th	37	38	39	40	**:41**	**:42**	**:43**	44	45
6th	46	47	48	49	50	**:51**	**:52**	**:52**	-

NB.   Isomers in bold, eg., **12:21**

H is the symbol for Hydrogen and He for Helium

SPHERES AND THEIR VIRTUES.

1 CREATIVE	**6 LOVE**
2 SENSITIVE	**7 MYSTERY**
3 RECEPTIVE	**8 PARTNERSHIP**
4 RENEWAL	**9 FOUNDATION**
5 COMMUNICATION	

Beginning with the definition for Sphere 1 Creative, you will find each of the definitions for Wisdom Paths 10, 19, 28, 37 and 46 follow. This same organization is repeated for each Sphere and the Wisdom Paths in that Sphere. Spheres can also organized into Dextro [1,5,7], Centre [2,6,9] and Laevo [3,4,8].

Extensive use is made of the definitions provided by Linda Goodman. *Her work "Sun Signs" [Bib. 25] is shown in italics in this part.* Chapter 6 has a table identifying the relationship between the Spheres and the Star-Signs of Astrology. This provides a summary of Linda's work. At the extremes, sometimes the Sphere characteristics harmonize and so intensify the Star Sign nature, whilst at other times the two can be in sharp contrast. It may be helpful to refer to that table.

<u>CREATIVE</u>   1

Wisdom Paths, like signposts on "Road Ten" are;
Period 1 1 Creative
Period 2 10 Wheel of Fortune
Period 3 19 Prince of Heaven
Period 4 28 Trusting Lamb
Period 5 37 Uniqueness
Period 6 46 Elder.

Sphere 1 people are blessed to resonate with the Sun. They exhibit the virtues of creativity, protection and benevolence. 1 is the sphere of creative and right action, including responsiveness to the Creator in Universe. 1 people appear to possess a strong sense of equity, *self worth, and a marked dislike for criticism. They demand and usually get respect and will insist on organizing and controlling everything and everyone around them. They exhibit an underlying desire to be inventive, creative and strongly original. They are quite definitive in their views and can be stubborn when thwarted. They love freedom and dislike restraint. Initiating leaders by nature, they quickly rise to positions of authority in whatever they undertake. Otherwise, they pout in "doyen corner" nursing a bruised ego or frustrated ambitions. They insist on being looked up to by mates, friends and co-workers alike. They protect the weak, defend the helpless and take on the burdens of others as long as "the others" do exactly as the 1 person dictates. They know everything better than anyone else and consider their opinions to be superior, if not flawless. The great majority of the time they are right which understandably annoys the people they lecture. They are also very susceptible to sincere compliments and easily detect what is phoney or false flattery. Genuine appreciation will get them to bend over backwards to please. Pride is their weakest point. When the pride is wounded, 1 people lose all their virtues and become most unpleasant. When they are appreciated and respected, no one can be more generous and benevolent. But they can be dangerous when ignored. Being in love and being loved is as vital to them as the air they breathe. Although the disposition is easily wounded, enemies are quickly forgiven after they bow down and apologize. The only way to win a confrontation with a 1 person is to be humble, say you're truly sorry, and you'll be graciously excused. They resent familiarity from strangers but are extremely warm and affectionate with those who are loved and trusted. There is a fondness for children and young people, but often some sadness connected with a child. 1 people enjoy fine clothes, jewellery and impressive cars. Even a cloistered 1 Chaldean monk would always keep his robe mended and maintain a dignified appearance and cube.*

PERIOD 2. 10 WHEEL OF FORTUNE MEANS RISE *and fall by personal desire. The name will be known for good or evil depending on the action chosen. 10 people are capable of arousing extreme responses of love or hate, respect or fear. There is no middle ground between honour and dishonour. Every event is self-determined. Love and Light create all that can be imagined. The code;* **Image 10 Ordain***. Image it and it shall be. Ordain it and it will materialize. The power for manifesting creative concepts into reality is inherent, but must be used with wisdom, since the power for absolute creation contains the polarity power for absolute destruction. Self-discipline and infinite compassion must accompany the gifts of the former to avoid the tragedy of the later. Discipline must precede dominion. Unfortunately some people fail to realize their power potential, and consequently harbour deep-seated feelings of frustration, causing them to feel unfulfilled, and to occasionally behave in a somewhat proud and arrogant manner to cover such unnecessary feelings of inferiority.* To follow one's highest principles or "Lights" never frustrates your talents any more than pursuing your passions and bliss. Those blissful moments are a clear sign of the direction in which your talent lies. You are given these talents in order to make a contribution to humanity and Universe.

> **Born; 19**
> **Mikhail Gorbachov**
> **Florence Nightingale**
> **Rupert Murdoch**

PERIOD 3. 19 PRINCE OF HEAVEN

19 is symbolized by the Sun and the divine white light. 19 is one of the most fortunate of the Wisdom Paths. *It is called Prince of Heaven because it represents victory over all temporal failures and disappointments. It blesses the person represented by it with all the power of 10 but without the danger of abuse inherent in 10. This path promises happiness and fulfilment — success in all career ventures and personal life.*

> **Born 28.**
> **Martin Luther King**   **Mother Teresa**
> **Gen. Douglas McArthur**
> **Tom Cruise**

Symbolized further than by Love and Light, this path is about holding to the divine white light that guides your talent; an image…

> 28 "A person of fine talent and promise, great possibilities, even genius, with the capability of achieving impressive success and who does so, but of another person from whom everything is taken away".

In part this is a warning to make thoughtful provision for the future. Otherwise 28 is a great blessing of success when gifted talent is used with integrity. The wider warning here is that misuse of a talent or gift can result in tests and trials akin to those of Job, but without the advantage Job had of everything being given back again at the end. When it is taken away from 28, what was lost is lost, so make provision for the future in the good times. Gift and purpose need expression and failure to do so can result in considerable frustration and even feelings of inferiority. The later feelings reflect that you know when you are underachieving.

The part of this definition that concerns the Lamb is important to consider from the point of view of what Chaldeans' and Hebrews' have in mind about this symbol and name, 28 Trusting Lamb.

At the time of Moses, before Mt Sinai and the Ten Commandments, it was traditional sacred practice to make a sacrifice of the best young ewe lamb. Through making this sacrifice to ONE and the blessings of the Lamb to Redeem, all could be forgiven between a tribe and the divine forces that they knew directed their lives - even as the "manna" that fell daily from heaven. The sacred redeeming and protective quality of the lamb can be further seen in the Hebrew Ceder and celebration of the "Passover". It still is their practice to place the blood of a lamb on the pillars of the house or door and on a beam inside the house. If you check the story of the Exodus of the Hebrews from Egypt you will see that this practice saved the first born boy of every Hebrew family that had followed this practice. Such was the power of the Lamb to Redeem, that the Destroyer or Eraser will pass over houses marked in this symbolic way. No fault is found with the occupants so the Eraser passes over the houses marked by the Lamb. The Lamb's religious significance can only be traced as far as the records of the oral traditions, before one would loose the trail in antiquity. Thus, by the time of Moses, great symbolic importance was attached to the Lamb and its powers of Redemption.

After Mt Sinai, there were changes in the red ritual and it became what could now be described as an Adder's Ceder. In its new form, there is more freedom in personal choice. Instead of exclusive use of the ewe lamb, the teg was also allowed as a choice in sacrifice. The meaning of this core Hebrew tradition can be seen to apply exactly to Lamb and Redemption and also to 12 Sacrifice-Victim. Likewise in the Christian faith where Jesus Christ is know as "Lamb" and "Redeemer" and was called to make the supreme personal sacrifice.

If you find Alices' "little golden key" on the three legged glass table. And you find that it only fits a little door you know you want to get through, then the obvious thing is to shrink the Ego. In this way you may realize great powers are to work through you in your life to help you discover, direct and refine your talents. The key may never fit any other lock or door, if Creative, Communication and Receptive are not in the lock combinations you are trying. Fortunately the knocks will generally show you where you are off track. Find the core of your path and you can know great things and do great things with your little bit of genius. Defiance is Destructive; so follow your own intuition; to do otherwise will lead you to crisis after crisis, until you are numb. Yes? In the same way that in sphere 1 you have a Creative inclination, by personal choice alone, you can also be inclined to be Destructive; so too in sphere 2, Sensitive can be Insensitive by choice, but by personal choice only. Defy what? Ego. It may seem odd until you "get the hang of it", but the ego can really only take you so far in spiritual wisdom. Go too far with Ego without having developed a balance, and you can end up in trouble.

"I AM is contextual", and includes the myriad creatures of Creation. Just as they are a part of the Life Force, so are you. If you are in awe at the diversity in nature, consider too the diversity in your ascension nature! You would be entirely justified in being in awe at the wonderful forces that flow in and through you. As the myriad are blessed to have life and a cycle to bring to maturity and completion, so are you. On path 28 you should be well on your way to having matured your creative inclination and learnt how to perform a service to humanity or Universe, or 23:32, 44 or 47 - whatever your intuition says.

All things considered, it is likely 28 is a very rewarding path not only for the individual that carries these ascension blessings but for humanity or any other cause 28 may choose to take on in response to the Creative and Receptive impulse. Seen in the context of the great blessings you have been afforded and the unique variety of experience, some time out is suggested by :31 Recluse-Hermit during the Partnership challenges. During such time for reflection on all of these matters, you might consider that you have great blessings in order to provide this world with some great service that is much more important than any individual ego.

"…Efforts have been made to distort my position. It has been said, in effect, that I was a warmonger. Nothing could be further from the truth. I know war as few other men now living know it, and nothing to me is more revolting. I have long advocated its complete abolition, as its very destructiveness on both friend and foe has rendered it useless as a means of settling international disputes."

"…I now close my military career and just fade away, an old soldier who tried to do his duty as G.. gave him the light to see that duty."

Gen. Douglas McArthur

Period 5. 37 Uniqueness.

This path has *a distinctive potency of its own. It's associated with an extremely sensitive nature, good and fortunate friendships, a strong magnetism with the public, often in the area of the Arts, and productive partnerships of all kinds. It places an emphasis on love and romance, and sometimes too much emphasis on sexuality. Attitudes toward sex may be unconventional but this aspect is not always present. There is a pronounced need for harmony in relationships. Happiness and success are more easily attained when in partnerships with another rather than when operating alone as a single unit.*

In what other way is it possible to express your love energy other than as uniquely the way you do it? Individuality is strengthened in partnerships, it integrates rather than disintegrates and it is best expressed rather than repressed. Community, family and group needs all set limits on the ways in which our Uniqueness is expressed, but they also create some extra-ordinary opportunities. There is an impressive range of possibilities created by our uniqueness, in the way in which we change, communicate, meet challenges, love and cause trouble!

Born 46	Name
Nicole Kidman	Malcolm Fraser
Patrick White	

Period 6. Path 46 elder.

Elders also take their symbol as Sun and their direction as Northward in Universe to the Eternal Flame. People on Wisdom Path 46 are greatly blessed with support not only from Prince of Heaven but also as the double for :23 Royal Star of Lion. The challenges for 46 are for attainment of the highest levels of spiritual wisdom and attunement to Love and Light energy in Universe. But not everything is roses, sweet perfumes and pretty sights. Facing reality often includes painful realizations, as one can't make a study of equity without a corresponding understanding of suffering and inequity.

For one of these areas where you need experience, you are referred to 11 Lion Muzzled. Sometimes Archetypal forces resist a development you believe is based on "right action".

Even out of consideration of "right timing" it is important to wait ... as a self-imposed lion muzzled, but contentedly purring with Universe support! By accord between right action and right timing, you recognize new directions and thrusts needed in your good work and expression of your truth.

As 46 you are in the direct line of sight of 23: Royal Star of Lion who can directly assist your communication during quiet times, meditation and times other than those where difficulties are experienced. The other thing you will find is that 23: opens the doors in many ways for opportunities to come your way as you direct them through ID Dextro. Sometimes Lion may be muzzled for a very good reason, so if you are tempted to go wilfully ahead, you need to see to some ego needs and in obedience, wait. At some point on this path there is a point of realization that individual Ego based goals are mirages or illusions and materialism is a barrier and detractor, "a lure" to test resolve to "right action" in one's spiritual quest as 46, with ONE and IN-ONE. Another vital and constant element is the blessing from :21 Crown of Magi, who fully supports you in this period six, gold crucible. Without these blessings, there is no way 46 can fly the way it is otherwise possible.

There is a wise old Chinese saying, "Every gift is pregnant with obligation". So consider your obligations as you consider your ascension and progression blessings.

SENSITIVITY 2.

The wisdom paths of sphere 2 are;
Period 1 2 Sensitivity
Period 2 11 Lion Muzzled,
Period 3 20 The Awakening,
Period 4 29 Grace Under Pressure I,
Period 5 38 Grace Under Pressure II, and
Period 6 47. Seer.

Sphere 2 people are blessed to resonate with the Moon. They will appear to have the virtues of intuition, imagination, parenthood, sensitivity and it is the sphere of conception, childbirth and dreams. 2 people *are dreamers with a tendency to fear the unknown or unfamiliar.*

They are extremely imaginative and inventive, but not always as forceful as they could be in carrying out their plans and ideas. Most 2 *people are not as strong as those born under birth spheres 1, 9, 3, and 6. They possess a very romantic nature and are secretly psychic* when *the intuition is highly developed.* It may initially come as a shock to have such ability and it takes time and practice to develop and refine this great blessing. Where a predictive dream of a disaster is realized, even a "fear of dreaming" can emerge. From fear breading fear, a 2 person *may fear many if not every conceivable loss; loss of love, property, money, friendships and employment. These people need a home base, and although they enjoy travel when finances permit, they must have a home to return to. They are fanatically devoted to or involved with their parents, especially mother, or the place where they grew up. Involvement with parents can be either positive or negative, but one way.*

Two people *make ideal parents themselves, but they must be careful not to smother their children with possessive love. As inclined to the extreme, they are ultra-concerned with the well being of family, relatives and friends. They hover over everyone making sure they don't catch cold, throw money away foolishly, and so on. 2 people are extremely cautious and dislike gambling or taking chances. They love money, but like to accumulate it in a safe, stable manner or invest it so that it can increase through dividends and interest.*

The 2 frequency is secretive, so 2 *people never let anyone know what their next move might be. They're experts in wheedling secrets from others, but they won't allow you to invade their privacy. They'll veer from right to left and backwards then lunge forwards in a surprisingly aggressive manner towards their goals. Money seems to stick to them like glue so you will almost never find them on social welfare. To do so would be to insinuate that they have failed to protect their assets, which is a cardinal sin to* the 2 frequency.

When 2 people *learn to overcome fear, possessiveness and unnecessary caution, their imagination, adaptability, and intuition can carry them to the fulfilment of their many dreams.*

Period 2. 11 Lion Muzzled-A Clenched Fist.

This is a path *of hidden trials and treachery from others. It represents two members of the opposite sex, or two opposing situations. In either case, compatibility of interest is lacking and interference from a third person or force must be conquered. The difficulties may also arise from the illusion of separation. It is necessary to unite divided goals to avoid a sense of frustrated in-completion. The third interfering force can be a person or an idea and it can take the form of a refusal to see the other side of an obstacle to harmony. The origin of the separating force must be identified and an attempt made to seek compromise.*

Occasionally conflicting desires within one's self are seen as in a mirror. Two forces or desires stand apart and must ultimately be united for happiness. Yet, each must remain individual even after being joined, for each possesses its own worth.

Take Heart! The illusion of separation in 11 Lion Muzzled can quickly be dispelled. There are great blessings in support for your difficult journey.

Generally the balancing factor of Dextro is lacking. It is with this 1 5 7 consideration and reflection that you can put the balance back into your inclination and so directives. Eg, the numeral 1, means Creative, so 11 is 1 Creative and 1 Creative, and you will see that is very much the evidence from your ascension blessings. 1 is Strong, so 11 can be viewed as Strong, Strong. It is the lack of the 1 Creative opportunities that require some very close attention. Through this it would seem you are most likely to find the very considerable, doubled creative talent that you have, your unique little bit of genius is also doubled! When you find that strength you need to use it in 1 Creative, 5 Communication and/or 7 Mystery.

If there is a short-cut to the gold crucible, the forms of 11 have an exceptional bond. For this very reason, Lion Muzzled could be chosen as a form as part of another path. When chosen in this sphere by ascension to a form of 11, which is characterized by strength that is restrained, we can certainly see that with great restraints such as sight or sound disadvantaged folk, there is also great benefit that can be drawn. And there are great Archetypal powers at your side that you should call on with 22 in mind. Great powers ride with you in your 11, 1 Creative 1 Creative, journey. Whatever the restraints, either permanent or temporary it is through restraint, you will know the Creative impulses of Universe more clearly and more quickly than most. So it is through a narrow range of limitation that a broader range of enrichment experience can be called upon when you manifest the impulse and give it your unique expression.

There is special consideration required and blessings accordingly given to people who on ascension are disadvantaged and for those who assist them. The part played by carers, teachers and guides are clearly reflected by an Olympic skier with 10% sight turning at her guides simple command, left or right turn only and the rest she can read exactly in her great intuition. But where would she be without the great empathy of her partner when on a Black Run? In like manner we can understand the greatness of the musical works of the hearing disadvantaged and the patience and love of their teachers. In the greatness of a performer we can also see the greatness of sensitivity in partnerships.

<table>
<tr><td>Born 20</td><td>Ronald Regan</td></tr>
<tr><td></td><td>Richard Burton</td></tr>
<tr><td>Name</td><td>Martin Luther King</td></tr>
</table>

PERIOD 3. 20 THE AWAKENING.

In addition to being called "The Awakening", this Wisdom Path was also called "The Judgement", by the ancient Chaldeans and Hebrews. The image; "A winged angel sounding a trumpet, while from below, a man, woman and child are seen rising from a tomb with their hands clasped in prayer."

At some time in the experience of the 20 person, *there will be a powerful awakening, bringing new purpose, new plans, new ambitions – the call to action for some great purpose or ideal. There may be occasional delays and obstacles to one's plans, but these may be conquered through developing patience [the challenge of 20] and by continually cultivating faith in one's own powers to transform. 20 brings the blessings of pre-cognitive dreams, plus the ability to manifest the happy ones and cancel the negative ones. It is not a material frequency so it is doubtful regarding financial success.*

20 is a path of calling to undertake a sacred act or duty. You are being called to work for some great purpose or ideal consistent with Great Design. Your constellation of ascension blessings will enable you to successfully complete this work and at the same time your vivid dreams will enable you to see the pattern of influences in your life and what to do.

There are great things to be done, in face of great dangers. There are great things to learn but some are painful. As you squarely face your pain and the pain of others you can know the great suffering.

"What is this darkness? What is its name? Call it: an aptitude for sensitivity. Call it: a rich sensitivity which will make you whole. Call it: your potential for vulnerability."

Meister Eckhart.

Star of Magi will see to your lessons on your learners' ledger. Her lessons are not always fun, however they are always liberating.

Born 29	Tony Blair
	Hilary Clinton
	Prince Philip
	Sir Douglas Mawson

PERIOD 4. 29 GRACE UNDER PRESSURE I.

29 is a path with one of the heaviest karmas of them all up to and including period 4. *It tests the person represented for spiritual strength, through trials and tribulations echoing the Old Testament story of Job. The life is filled with uncertainties, treachery and deception from others, unreliable friends, unexpected dangers and considerable grief and anxiety caused by members of the opposite sex. It is a path of grave warnings in every area of personal life and career.* The blessing of this path depends on unlocking the karmic mystery that involves the *development of absolute faith in goodness and the power of self, and depends on the constant and energetic cultivation of optimism. This will act as miraculous medicine for the problems of 29. After all, Job's burdens were finally lifted when he had learnt to accept full responsibilities for his troubles and not to blame others or seek revenge for the hurts he suffered. Not only did his long string of bad-luck end but he was given back all that he had lost.*

The ascension blessings for 29 Grace Under Pressure provide a basis for optimism in handling the challenges of the different steps and grades of Grace Under Pressure. Grade 1 echoes the Trials of Job, but it is not the same thing as the Trials of Job. It is similar in that you are blessed with 24: Love, Money and Creativity and can expect general success in any life goals you choose. However, you can also expect to run into some trouble in order to learn how to handle yourself in difficult situations. Some of our best lessons in life come from having to face difficulties and work them through. As with any who are to face testing and difficult situations; heeding your intuition and in courageously adhering to what your "best lights" guide you to do. Some of your more creative decisions may benefit from contemplation. In this regard, use time out as :31 Recluse-Hermit. Taking time out for contemplation enables the intuition and the voice of caution. So in common with Job, you will be tempted and tested in a countless number and variety of ways but you can triumph over these difficulties and draw your lessons to successful conclusion.

Job in the Old Testament is central to understanding 29 and 38. In it Job writes; 3v 25;

> "For the thing I fear comes upon me,
> And that which I dread befalls me.
> I am not at ease, nor am I quiet;
> I have no rest; but trouble comes."

Job was manifesting his own fears and dreads and only just realizing that he had the great power to ordain his own fate and was using it negatively against himself. ID Laevo does not discriminate. It brings on whatever you are focused on. Of course, Job had the same power to ordain success but did not see that when writing his long tale of "misery". In terms of the whole story, ONE and IN-ONE are very much a part of it, as you may find, but Job finds life best with the "t" added = mystery! Consider sphere 7, as a sign of Great Mystery working in your life. Is this so? You have the power to manifest the destructive forces as you enable ID Laevo, at the expense of Dextro, so trouble will manifest. The very things you fear and dread will come upon you if you feed them with your attention. By ignoring Laevo and staying focused on the positives you want, ID Dextro is enabled and the opposite, positive outcomes, in accord with your wishes will flow. As you fear an encounter so it will occur. And as you enjoy an encounter it will recur if you give it the same feeder attention. But you are not limited to two aspects Dextro and Laevo, because you are centre and you have great support from centre, you can ignore the pulls and pressures, shrug off and even laugh at the challenges.

You have the power of all three aspects of ID, Laevo, Centre and Dextro. Once you have balanced the powers in your hands, relative to those in the centre, as it were in your body, and realize the extent of those powers, you will be better able to handle your responsibilities. One thing is certain in this field of uncertainties, and that is that you are being tested because you are needed to play an important role. To discover that role, you will need to use your strengths, sensitivity, intuition, imagination and the ability to manifest your positive or negative wishes. In realization of your very considerable power, what constitutes a responsible exercise of your power? Why too should others be presented with long tales of "misery" when it is Great Mystery we could be discovering?

There is a mechanism in dreaming, where it is difficult to remember what the details of a dream are, when you wake in the morning. Recall seems to quickly and automatically switch off. When we are awake we are somehow "blinded" from remembering dreams. 29 has this same sort of "blinded-ness" when it comes to using one's Dextro power. Focus seems to be inclined towards Laevo power being draw into the life of 29. Exploring Dextro would be most beneficial for 29, and so too the point of Job's story, steadfast FAITH in ONE. Eventually you can triumph, difficulties will end and what was lost will be regained.

PERIOD 5. PATH 38 GRACE UNDER PRESSURE II.

Born 38   Bill Clinton

Path 38 is the second grade of Grace Under Pressure and so the discussion of 29 applies to an appreciation of 38. On this wisdom path the trials and tribulations experienced are exactly like those suffered by Job. In tribute to the difficulties experienced by path 38, we could take the balance of this text to tell the increasingly countless ways in which paths 38 and 47 are expressed! However, we can't live our lives as if it is a Greek tragedy or even a biblical nightmare. We have to see through the difficult times and keep our focus on what is our real purpose - enlightenment. Archetypes have given the element oxygen as in the Place of Great Spirit. As it is also 38, the same as the numeral of your path, you may take heart in knowing Great Spirit is with you every breath you take.

PERIOD 6. PATH 47 SEER.

Born 47 Sir Edmund Hillary

Path 47 Seer is the third grade of 29 Grace Under Pressure. You are in the gold crucible of period 6 and the rounding of your enlightenment in sphere 2 Sensitivity as a Seer. To aid you in your path, :21 Crown of Magi adds her blessing to your efforts.

What would incline a sensitive nature to end up in trouble? How could it be that the magnitude of blessings to do great work, that in the 6th period, we would find a path that is so fraught with yet further difficulties than 38 or 29 or 11? Could it be Humpty Dumpty was right about 47 and "Impenetrability"? He prided himself in being master of his words no matter the words objection to how he used them or what he meant by them. Does this suggest that a highly sensitive nature has been defended by "Impenetrability"? This is a serious warning. It is one thing to misuse a talent, but failing to use one is also to be taken very seriously. Lewis Carol was indeed a master of his words. Humpty Dumpty is on the path of 19 Prince of Heaven but he didn't take sides so he sat on the wall. Everyone knows That Humpty Dumpty had a great fall and no one could fix the egg of his soul after that fall. His blessings wasted he was in serious trouble. Don't waste a talent. Where would you be if you do not properly exercise and refine your sensitivity talents? Do you scorn the blessings that you have, because you have not learnt to deal with the power that they bring? Maybe you are troubled and even frightened by your vivid and predictive dreams? Or don't know how to tell those concerned? Or is there a "blinding" to what the blessings are that you have been given? Whatever the complexities of individual 47 situations, they are magnified from 29, where we started this saga of three grades of Grace Under Pressure, There is one thing for certain. Trouble recurs like a relentless tyrant following from period to period until you are beautifully tuned to Universe, your self, your partners and your world and loving it!

It may assist you to imagine fear as something that always travels behind you. But now that you are driving very fast in period 6, you need to look further ahead and can't spend the same time dwelling on what is happening behind you. Where sensitivity allows you to see the way, the blessings of intuition will warn you when you need to slow down, or it can "warn" you a new delight is just around the corner as you would wish it to be! 47, destined to be mystical in the process of enlightenment.

Impenetrability may at first seem the opposite to sensitivity but in confronting a wide range of difficult situations there is a single-mindedness that can be seen as highly sensitive in the spiritual realm. In I Ching for arousal this sense of the "Right Type" of impenetrability is beautifully expressed.

> "When a man has learned within his heart what fear and trembling mean, he is safeguarded against any terror produced by outside influences. Let the thunder roll and spread terror a hundred miles around: he remains so composed and reverent in spirit that the sacrificial rite is not interrupted. This is the spirit that must animate leaders and rulers of men - a profound inner seriousness from which all outer terror glances off harmlessly."
>
> I Ching - Wilhelm/Baynes.

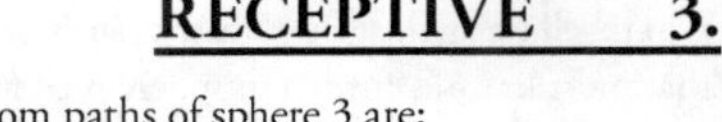

RECEPTIVE   3.

The wisdom paths of sphere 3 are;
Period 1 3 Receptive
Period 2 12: Sacrifice-Victim,
Period 3 :21 Crown of Magi,
Period 4 30 Loner-Meditation I,
Period 5 39 Loner-Meditation II and
Period 6 48 Cadi.

Sphere 3 people are blessed to resonate with the planet Jupiter. They are inclined towards *idealism, higher education, foreign travel and religion.* 3 is the sphere of *optimism, movement, expansion, Holy Trinity* and the integration *of body, mind and spirit. 3 people base every action [even when they are misguided and the action is a negative one] upon the foundation of a great ideal. They aim high for truth and nothing less than truth will satisfy them whether they seek the truth of a love affair, friendship, career, politics or religion.* [This funny 3 seeks the truth behind the eye-piece by looking through the rock!]

They are not easily put off by evasive answers or deception and they can spot a lie, a distortion or dishonesty a mile away. Some of them achieve the goal of truth, others are misled into believing their own illusions, but they never stop searching. The 3 person is fiercely independent, seeks total freedom of speech and movement and cannot be tied down. Travel is an absolute necessity, mingling with others and seeing the world, learning everything there is to know about every country and its people, every intellectual concept, every philosophy. They tend to look on the bright side of everything and their optimism is contagious. Because of the shining quest for truth, the 3 person is either an agnostic, an atheist, or intensely involved with a religious principle ie., nuns, ministers, monks, rabbis, and priests. Either way, religion is an important part of life and being Receptive to Universe guidance facilitates the purpose of the Creative.

The Receptive is the compliment of the Creative and not the opposite. What the Creative initiates, the Receptive brings to completion or reality by adding its power to the Creative's power and purpose. Because the myriad forms correspond with the myriad of impulses of the Creative, these impulses become real. Thus the greatness of the Receptive is that it gives birth to, supports and nourishes all life and does not favour one or another form that the Creative begets. Seen in this light, the Receptive 3 is an assistant to the Creative and thus not independent at all as the 3 person is led by the Creative and conforms to the requirements of a situation. It is in rebellion against the Creative, insistence on personal direction and in refusal to be receptive to guidance, that most karmic burden in sphere 3 can be understood.

Physical challenge inspires 3 people, so sports play a major role. They are shockingly blunt of speech, candid to a fault, and outraged at duplicity of any kind. There is a genuine love of animals and a strong tendency to defend the underdog human with the same loyalty they show their dog, horse or other pets. There is a marked indifference to family ties, and marriage only works when freedom is total. 3 is associated with tests of physical strength, gambling and taking a chance either in the casino or on the stock market. 3 people will bet on almost anything and their bubbling optimism is delightfully contagious. They often display an odd blend of wise philosopher and the happy-go-lucky clown, and a sense of responsibility is sometimes lacking. Some of the goals, ambitions and dreams are serious; others are silly and frivolous. Pursuing an education matters a great deal to 3 people and they are crushed when denied the halls of higher learning. They make excellent "armchair lawyers" or professional attorneys, since the planet Jupiter rules the law.

PERIOD 2. 12: SACRIFICE-VICTIM.

Name   Bob Hawke

Although 3 energy permeates all activity on Wisdom Path 12, *one will periodically be sacrificed in the plans and intrigues of others. 12 warns of the necessity to be alert in every situation, to beware of false flattery from those who use it to gain their own ends. Be suspicious of those who offer high positions and carefully analyse motives. Although duplicity is not always present, forewarned is forearmed. There is a degree of mental anxiety caused by the need to sacrifice personal goals to the ambitions of others.*

A secondary meaning also can be considered. 1 is the creative, the initiator, the teacher, whether a person or Life itself. 2 is the kneeling, submissive and sensitive student. But where the receptive tries to be the initiator, or the student tries to be the teacher, evil will come and a sea of troubles may be experienced. 1 can also be seen as Persecutor and 2 as Victim, in that both are complementary roles, albeit in conflict. Without both parties, there cannot be a victim or persecutor, a teacher or student.

Difficulties escalate when the victim tries to persecute the persecutor! Sometimes this results in severe emotional stress and mental anguish that may create amnesia or forgetfulness of lessons previously learned. 12: represents the education process on all levels, the submission of the will required and the sacrifices necessary to achieve knowledge and wisdom on both the spiritual and intellectual levels.

When the intellect is sacrificed to the feelings, the mind will be illuminated by the answers it seeks. Look within for the solution. Attention paid to the requirements of a situation and education, will end suffering and bring success. There are very strong currents running on path 12: as may be expected from the choice of 12 apostles. When the lessons have been learnt and the sacrifices that are necessary have been made, the karmic burden of this path will dissipate. Because 12: is the isomer of :21 Crown of Magi, after you have been tested, great blessings flow to your side.

Born :21	**Shirley Chisholm**
	Vladimir Lenin

Period 3. :21 Crown of Magi.

This path is pictured as Universe and called "The Crown of Magi". *It promises general success and guarantees advancement and honours, awards and general elevation in life and career. It indicates victory after a long struggle, for the Crown of Magi is gained only after long initiation, much soul testing and various tests of determination. However, the* person blessed *with : 21 can be certain of final victory over all odds and all opposition.* It is a most fortunate Wisdom Path – a path of *karmic reward.*

At the time of the nativity of Jesus of Nazareth, the three wise men that followed a star were then described as three magi. In essence they were receptive to the adventure on which they were led.

As you are one who ascends with :21 Crown of Magi, your awareness of self becomes less of regard in comparison to the urge for life and expression of love uniquely as you are blessed to do.

Where then is the Mystery? Where is the moving star? Later in the life of this period there are great blessings that will come in the form of 24: Love, Money and Creativity. This will be the sign of Great Mystery working in your life.

<table>
<tr><td>Born 30</td><td>Pierre Trudeau
Edward Kennedy</td></tr>
</table>

PERIOD 4. 30 LONER-MEDITATION I.

The photo shows a cave, as a safe place in the womb of Earth where you may retreat for a time and return renewed and inspired. The mosses on the rock as the Life Force adhering to Earth, as it does to your path. When retreating into nature there is freedom from the normal range of external influences and so there is an opportunity to still introspection and find inspiration. Just as a bear is called seasonally to hibernate in the womb of Mother Earth, so from time to time you may feel called to the Receptive Earth.

This is a Wisdom Path for retrospection, thoughtful deduction and mental superiority over others. 30 belongs completely to the mental plane and those represented by it often put all material things to one side, not because they have to but because they wish to. Consequently 30 is neither fortunate nor unfortunate because it can be either depending entirely upon the desire of the person it represents. The frequency of 30 can be all powerful, but it is often indifferent, according to the will of the person. Those people who are represented by 30 generally count few people as their friends. They tend to be taciturn loners, preferring to be alone with their own thoughts. Social functions and public gatherings are not their style. 30 doesn't deny happiness or success, but fulfilment is more often found in retreating from the chaos of the market place, so that one's mental superiority may be used to develop something worthwhile for the world. This may include writing ideas which may change the world, or to protect and develop one's personal talents, such as art or other gifts. It indicates a lonely yet frequently rewarding life pattern.

This is about responding to the Creative impulse and following your passion and insight so that you boldly express or communicate what you discover and are not deterred by the ideas, opinions and actions of others. 30 is not about sitting under the Tree of 13 Fruits and contemplating when one will fall. 30 is about being Receptive to the Creative and then acting. In taking action there is considerable empowerment evident from 36 Sceptre. Subsequently there will be further testing for spiritual strength before even more authority is put at your command.

PERIOD 5. PATH 39 LONER-MEDITATION II.

| Born 39. | Malcolm Fraser |
| Name. | Ita Buttrose |

The second grade of Loner-Meditation is akin to an isomer of 30 but only concerns spheres 3, 6 and 9. 39 epitomizes the blessings that unfold from Receptivity to the Creative impulse. It is through meditation you come to know what Universe has in store for you, or otherwise "knowing" the Creative impulse. The quest for when and where are no different to those for 30, but in how time is spent when alone, this is as different as chalk and cheese. Being lonely when alone is very different to being happy when alone. As 39 you will most likely find your gifts can very quickly develop in a natural environment or retreat. This is the path of discovering how to move beyond "self" or ego and of clarifying the sparks that ignite you. How? By tuning yourself into the energy fields in Universe. Whatever way works for you is great. It doesn't have to be meditation, there are many ways your sparks will fly! All you need is a natural place as 39, a place to be at peace on your own and to have time to rifle through your thoughts until the wind combs them out of your hair and you feel that wonderful flood of love, peace and openness to the wonder around you. You may know your place where this is possible for you, such as where you love to walk along a beach, or it may be in walking a mountain trail, the operative issue is where you feel at peace is where you will come to know the Creative impulse. Your inclination to the receptive Universe blessings; puts you on the verge of the well-spring of ideas you are born to discover and reveal.

Coupled with the blessings of feeling at one in nature, happy, integrated and peaceful, comes the increased harmonization, sense of unity and oneness with one's environment. These are certainly times for recharging the battery, passivity and rest but they are also about re-creating yourself and working for the ongoing creation. Learning in matters of spirit harmonization is a central aspect of 39. Native American vision questers describe this integration/peace as akin to going into the "Great Silence". Many of the outcomes described accord with the experiences of people in active and passive meditation processes. 39 people attune themselves to the frequency of Universe, as represented by the Crown of Magi. 39 is the epitome of the Receptive and it is matched with the power to manifest the impulses of the Creative.

However, with 39 on your side, the ride is magical in the blessings that flow from Universe, the Magician and the Life Force when meditation is effectively practiced.

PERIOD 6. PATH 48 CADI.

Born 48.	Don Dunstan
Name.	Bertrand Russel
	Russel Crowe

48 Cadi, the gold crucible or pinnacle of enlightenment in sphere 3, is ruled by Jupiter and the law. :21 Crown of Magi directly assists your process of enlightenment in this period. Where shadowy and indistinct is the way for earlier periods, the way for 48 is eventually clear, bright and compliments the Creative increasingly perfectly.

In the process of coming to an understanding of the Light, there is development of understanding about Darkness too. By enhanced meditation 48 will develop a great passion for the work and all forms of Sceptre power will facilitate implementation and communication with the masses. There is great success and much happiness achieved on this path. Besides, this is the path that has the doubling effect of one of the most fortunate paths, 24: Love, Money and Creativity. You are born to win!

RENEWAL   4.

The wisdom paths of sphere 4 are;
Period 1 4 Renewal
Period 2 13: Regeneration and Change I,
Period 3 22 Submission-Caution,
Period 4 :31 Recluse Hermit,
Period 5 40 Regeneration and Change II and
Period 6 49 Doyen.

As at sunset, endings. Renewal depends on ending certain things.

Sphere 4 people are blessed to resonate with the planet Uranus. They appear inclined *towards individualism, originality, inventiveness and tolerance.* 4 is the sphere of *unconventional behaviour and sudden unexpected events and also of genius.* 4 people *are seldom understood by their friends and family. They're an enigma to everyone they know. They make their own rules that don't always match those of society. Marked individuality colours every thought and action. If there is a different way of doing something, the 4 person will find it. Their speech and actions frequently shock others and it often correctly seems the attempt to shock is deliberate. 4 people live in the future, caring little about the present. They're light years ahead of others in their ideas and ideals. Going along with this trait is an innate talent for prophecy, for knowing what will happen tomorrow long before tomorrow arrives. Their lifestyle ranges from unconventional to bizarre, yet their crazy ideas are successful more often than not. Anything far out or off the beaten track strongly appeals to the 4 person's questing, curious nature.*

The quest to *be the first person to meet and tame Bigfoot or swim with Nessie the Loch Ness Monster likely strongly excites the 4 person. They are deeply convinced of the reality of whatever can be conceived in the mind. To be told that a thing is impossible only intensifies and spurs the 4 person's resolve to prove it is possible. The expression "mission impossible" rings great bells of mental challenge in the very soul of a 4 person. Although the 4 frequency encourages changes in every area of life, from politics to art, 4 people are strangely reluctant to accept change in their personal habits, which remain rather fixed. They can be quite stubborn when people try to dictate to them or try to mould them into a more acceptable social pattern. Because prophets are often unrecognized in their own time or land, and because 4 people live far into the future, their grandest and truest visions are often ridiculed or ignored. They're often fascinated by UFO's and their secret wish is to be contacted, taken aboard and hopefully not returned to the chaos of Earth!*

Reform movements like women's liberation and equal rights for minorities attract 4 people who are genuinely dedicated to tolerance, brotherhood and sisterhood. Friendship is vital to sphere 4 and these friends can come from all walks of life. Money means little to them and they are just as likely to mix with kings as they are with paupers. They care nothing about class distinction, have no desire to impress anyone and are just as comfortable in a tent or van, as in a mansion. It's not that they are prejudiced against comfort or wealth they simply don't notice their environment because they live in their imaginations. One of their finest virtues is to "live and let live". The 4 person doesn't give a ginger snap what you do or say, however outrageous or against his or her principles, and they expect you to return the same consideration.

Period 2. 13: Regeneration and Change I.

Name

Rupert Murdoch

Napoleon Bonaparte

The image of 13 is "A skeleton, or death, with a scythe, reaping down men in a field of new-grown grass, where young faces and heads appear to be thrusting through the ground and emerging on all sides". This is *not an unlucky path as many people believe. The ancients claimed that "he who understands how to use 13 will be given power and dominion." This is a path of endings or upheaval, so that new ground can be broken. It's associated with power that if misused for selfish purposes will bring destruction on itself. There is a warning of the unknown and the unexpected. Adapting to change gracefully will bring out the strengths of 13 and decrease the potential for negatives. 13 is associated with genius, exploration, breaking the orthodox and new discoveries of all kinds.*

Powerful forces flow in the life of 13: and they can be contrasted as the principles of light and darkness. The principle of darkness asserts itself furtively and unexpectedly with potentially unfavourable and even dangerous consequences. The light principle keeps the darkness in check and through resoluteness, inferior aspects of self are not allowed ascendance even when they first appear. What can be seen as certain about 13: is that there will be encounters between these contrasting forces and in a pattern such that the darkness will not at first appear threatening at all and it may seem that you are able to play with what seems weak, harmless or small, only to find that as soon as you give it power, ascendance can occur and stifle the light. It is best to cut it out as soon as darkness asserts itself, otherwise you dally with danger. You have a wonderfully strong Creative light within and it is your destiny to express this gift. There are many blessings that will support your efforts and increase the breadth of your understanding of the light and dark principles that affect your personal life and those of others.

Besides, with attention to your intuition, your expression of your unique abilities and your quest for enlightenment and wholeness of being, are beautifully supported by Crown of Magi, Star of Magi and Great Spirit's blessings.

<table>
<tr><td>Born 22.</td><td>Name</td></tr>
<tr><td>Marie Currie</td><td>Wolfgang A. Mozart</td></tr>
<tr><td>Forbes Carlisle</td><td></td></tr>
</table>

PERIOD 3. 22 SUBMISSION-CAUTION.

22 is symbolized by the ancients as "a Good Man, blinded by the folly of others, with a knapsack on his back, full of errors." *In the image he seems to offer no defence against a ferocious tiger which is about to attack him. It's a warning number of illusion and delusion. It indicates a good person who lives in a fool's paradise; a dreamer of dreams who awakens only to find that he is surrounded by danger, when it's often too late. It warns of mistakes in judgement, of placing faith in those who are not trustworthy. The karmic obligation here is to be more alert, listen to your inner-voice, curb spiritual laziness, and develop more spiritual aggressiveness - to realize your own power to change things and to prevent failure by ordaining success. When this personal responsibility is recognized, practiced, and finally mastered, the 22 person can be in control of events, no longer blinded by the folly of others, and will see ideas achieved and dreams realized.*

At the time of the development of this Chaldean-Kabala system the inner nature of a person was regarded as good rather than evil as currently held by the western Christian Church. With over fourteen centuries of Church teaching of fall/redemption, western thinking has been dominated by this very Laevo "original sin" attitude that precludes recognition of the "original good" and Creative in all of us. Thus a fragmented or negatively lop-sided view of one's nature has dominated thinking and discovery. In 22 the starting point is that people are innately good. And learning occurs from positive and negative lessons in spiritual growth. Mastery of one's gifts ultimately benefits all people so it is not selfish, but actually essential to develop your gifts. It is a responsibility to both yourself and others.

Accepting that it takes time and practice to reach mastery, allows that there will be times when things are difficult; blockages occur; a form of expression may not seem quite right; goals may be indistinct or ideas only partially developed. Every experience moulds character though some do so more than others. It is common to find that some of our most difficult experiences lead to our greatest growth. In part these experiences or situations can be seen as integral to development of your gifts according to your ascension blessings.

Submission- Caution is generic to all people. It is part of all of our original blessings. Through 22 we learn to do what is innately right, or that which accords with our "best lights" and we learn what can be trusted.

The experience of good and evil rounds character. Caution is needed when you face evil, but submission is required for harsh lessons as 17 Star of Magi may see as necessary for your growth. It is through repeated difficulty that you may identify what you are failing to submit to. Possibly an inferior aspect you are failing to eliminate. Having time to reflect on these matters needs to be balanced with time going beyond self, transcending selfish interests and seeing community and other's needs as well. Moving beyond self to awareness of Universe and the service you may perform in furthering Creation.

Not all "right action" involves doing something in an active sense as in Dextro, but in Laevo there is also Non-doing as in 30 Loner-Meditation and :31 Recluse Hermit. It is through receptivity and thus submission that we come to know the needs of Universe and the causes for which we and Archetypes resolutely work. Even as darkness help us see the light, there is a great concordance in 22 Submission-Caution.

In broad terms, from the blessings of 22 Submission-Caution, we learn the boundaries where respect is required in managing oneself during manifestations from darkness. In listening to our "inner voice" much good can be added to the "knapsack".

PERIOD **4. :31 RECLUSE-HERMIT.**

Born: 31	Name
Sigmund Freud	**Edward Kennedy**
Bill Gates	**Sidney Myer**

This is the isomer of 13: Regeneration and Change and is the second grade that more closely defines the inclinations to seeking a life of retreat as Recluse-Hermit through which to achieve inner peace. Recluse Hermit is blessed to find that unique aspect of their creative and receptive genius most often also found in Loner-Meditation. 39 Loner-Meditation is grade two and similar to :31, except that :31 represents a situation where the person is more self-contained, self-sufficient, and isolated from others. *Quite often genius is present or at least high intelligence. At some unexpected time in life, glittering promises in a busy world will suddenly be rejected for the peace and quiet of Nature or a retreat in some manner from society. The :31 person is sometimes opinionated and an advocate of political change, while sometimes remaining fixed in personal habits. Even in a crowd, :31 can feel isolated.*

:31 Recluse Hermit, to a further extent than 13: Regeneration and Change, includes encountering the unwelcome, unexpected and even furtive obtrusion of the dark principle into the light. In this darkness :31 appears alone in carrying the lantern and bringing light to the darkness, just as :31's original contribution advances the frontiers of knowledge and darkness recedes.

After the "endarkenment" of 13:31, :31 is in little danger but is no doubt much wiser for the encounters with darkness. What has been resisted as the dark principle by the light, does in :31 become reconciled such that one may be friends with the dark and proceed with your light. Recluse-Hermit is balanced and sure-footed as proceeding along partnership cliff tops in the dark with a lantern to find the way in the path to enlightenment.

Born 40
Margaret Thatcher

Period 5. Path 40 Regeneration and Change II.

40 is grade 2 of Regeneration and Change. After experience as being something comes the discovery of self and unique gifts which if Ego bound may link straight into serious trouble as described in :43 Road of Strife. Darkened and then enlightened as :31 Recluse-Hermit, there is more in store! Trials and testing similar to 38 Grace Under Pressure [the Trials of Job]. Even your unique talents are muzzled. Your light veiled for a time. Loosing everything is possible until you realize that you are nothing anyway. After being something comes the discovery of nothingness of self.

"If you would swim on the bosom of the Ocean of Truth, you must reduce yourself to zero."

Mahatma Gandhi.

"Women must even read themselves sideways into analysis of the experience of nothingness. Women need a literature that names their pain and allows them to see the emptiness in their lives as an occasion for insight rather than as one more indication of their worthlessness. Women need stories that will tell them that their ability to face darkness in their lives is an indication of strength, not weakness."

Carol Christ.

"Are you willing to be sponged out, erased?
    Cancelled,
    Made nothing?
Are you willing to be made nothing?
    Dipped in oblivion?
If not, you will never really change."   D. H. Lawrence

Having successfully reduced your Ego to zero, it is time to draw on the great blessings that flow from the doubling of 20 The Awakening.

Born 49	**Wolfgang A. Mozart**	**Kerry Packer**
Name	**Mohandas Gandhi**	**Tenzing Norgay**
	Raphael Sanzio	

PERIOD 6. PATH 49 DOYEN.

49 Doyen is effectively grade four of Regeneration and Change and represents the apex of enlightenment in sphere 4 Renewal. This is the gold crucible and :21 Crown of Magi provides assistance to all people who are in this period.

Path 49 blessings are predominantly Laevo and derive much of their potency directly from 40 as defined above. However this path has a stronger outwards focus of service to community and Universe, rather than the inwards focus on self that we discover by the journey through nothingness. So we find that the ego is nothing, our pain little more than a field for laughter, and that what matters most about individuality is it's actuality and realization of creative and destructive potentials. We are instruments of work in Great Design, we are participants in Creation and we can manifest the Creator's will.

49 Doyen is blessed to provide great leadership in finding vital directions in which Creation is re-created by good work. To do this, there are partnership blessings bringing love and peace with masses of people, thus a following in this good work. And there are communication blessings to back it up. 23: Royal Star of the Lion is every bit a part of :32 Communication, giving Doyen support in high places and helping out in difficult times.

"By the very acknowledgement of our darkness and our pain we are saved, that is, healed. By refusing to cover up the cosmic despair and the cosmic anguish that life rains on us we make healing possible. We allow an entrance into the wound to take place. By letting pain be pain we allow healing to be healing, and instead of healing our projections or imaginary darknesses we heal what is truly in pain, what is deeply and irretrievably dark."

- Mathew Fox.

COMMUNICATION - 5

The wisdom paths of sphere 5 are;
Period 1 5 Communication
Period 2 14: Movement … Challenge I,
Period 3 23: Royal Star of Lion,
Period 4 :32 Communication,
Period 5 :41 Movement … Challenge II and
Period 6 50 Statesperson.

Sphere 5 people are blessed to resonate with the planet Mercury.

They appear inclined towards communication, intellect, movement and versatility. It's the sphere of intellect and both written and oral expression. 5 people possess a great deal of natural charm, and as a general rule, are innately courteous. They're quick to spot a flaw or a mistake and don't hesitate to point them out when they see them. 5 people are super-critical and incapable of ignoring mistakes [their own as well as those of others] and its associated with a love for movement and travel. Change is a never-ending necessity for 5 people. Change of scene, change of relationships, residence, spiritual and political beliefs and so on. Leading and being led.

The challenge of travel is wonderfully illustrated by this Viking Long Ship that is called "Le nav ire dOseberg" = path 14: Movement … Challenge; and what great seafarers these folk were; they brought a lot of changes to a lot of places in Europe and beyond. The Vikings two most powerful tools were these long ships and their ability to surprise the unwary by doing the unexpected. You may be interested to know that there were Nine Caverns of Woden based on a cosmic tree, called Yggdrasil that has similarities to the Tree of Life but bears no cultural relationship. You will also find in the definitions of the Circle of Archetypes, that ONE-eyed Woden is still in his place of water. Woden is reported as owing respect to ONE who is greater than he, which is why he is called ONE-eyed. Note the spiral bow - our symbol for movement as if the breathing of the Cosmos.

Unfortunately, 5 people have a strong tendency to over-analyse people and situations. It's difficult for the 5 person to submit to feelings and intuition; the intellect is determined to find logic or reason. If this behaviour is taken too far it can lead to trouble as an obsession with analysis can ruin personal relationships for those who allow themselves to be ruled by the intellect. Even love can wear out under continual and usually unnecessary scrutiny. Love is made of instinct and feelings, not logic. 5 people tend to "talk love to death" instead of just letting it be, allowing it to become part of them, without questioning its whys and where-fores. Love has little to do with logic and will soon fall victim to the paralysis of analysis. However, most people enjoy being in the company of a 5 person, since the outward persona is usually pleasant and soothing. Because 5 is the frequency of intellect, those under its influence are often extremely bright, or of higher than average intelligence and mental alertness. Nothing escapes their notice. They seem to be fine-tuned to the smallest detail. When finances or other circumstances don't permit the frequent travel 5 people need, they'll travel in their minds, and since their minds are so acute, their daydreams are vivid enough to satisfy the restless urges within them for a time, at least.

According to the ancients, 5 is associated with "Earth magic". Curiously, 5 brings a longing to believe in magic, elves, fairies, and mysteries of Nature along with a need to pin everything down and view it under a mental microscope. These two qualities that are in direct polarity to each other often cause the 5 person to find it difficult to understand their mercurial nature. 5 people are sometimes highly strung, they live on their nerves and crave excitement. They're quick in thought and decision making but sometimes act impulsively. They have a keen sense of new ideas, inventions, are willing to take risks and are born speculators. Writing, advertising, public relations and publishing are fortunate 5 occupations. 5 people possess an admirable elasticity of view-point and the ability to rebound swiftly from blows of fate.

PERIOD 2. 14: MOVEMENT-CHALLENGE I. | Born 14:   Margaret Whitlam

Magnetic communication with the public through writing, publishing, and all media related matters, is associated with 14:. Periodic changes in business and personal partnerships are usually beneficial. Dealing with speculative matters brings luck. Likewise, movement and travel associated with combinations of people and cultures, can be fortunate. However, both gains and losses are sometimes temporary, due to the strong currents of change which are ever present for 14:. There are also cautions about danger from accidents relating to natural elements: fire, flood, earthquake, hurricanes and so forth. You never know how big or small the next challenge may be. There is a risk involved in depending on the word of those who misrepresent a situation. It's a mistake to rely on others. Hard though it may be for 14: to put aside the analytical at times and rely on the intuition, this is the biggest challenge for 14: - learning to listen to the voice within.

Born 23: Abraham Lincoln Franklin D Roosevelt Thomas Jefferson Caroline Jones

PERIOD 3. 23: ROYAL STAR OF LION.

This is a karmic reward path. 23: bestows, not only a *promise of success in personal and career endeavours, but it also guarantees support from those in high places. It's a most fortunate path and greatly blesses with abundant grace the person represented by it. Other paths don't have much of a chance to bring about trouble when Royal Star of Lion is present during difficult times. No path can challenge the Lion's strength and win.*

Royal Star of Lion is sometimes working singly, whilst at some other times all five work together as a Pride. LA, LA, LA. And when they do work as a

Pride, they "hunt" with very powerful companions. Particularly 19 Prince of Heaven and :21 Crown of Magi. So if your path is 23:, you could consider the above to be like a family photo of those in higher places referred to, who are there to assist you… should you ask. On the balance of probabilities, if your path is 23: there is good reason why you have powerful allies. There is something of importance for you to do. A service or duty you need to perform. What sort of service, what work of importance and to whom would it be important? If these are the questions on your mind you may find your questions addressed in 20 The Awakening.

Every move is a sacred act, or could you say an enactment of what is sacred to life itself. The Pride has both Creative and Destructive power as part of its Mercurial nature. A collective "mind" that can be used for any purpose, laevo, centre and dextro. And a mind that should be communicated. Besides if there is something unique in what you see then your

view needs to be added in order to help complete the picture. Not everyone has the ability to see the whole picture, the overall view of the major factors. But that is the blessing you have. Greater things will come by you sharing what you know and learning what others know.

23: is centrally positioned and working very much like "the hub of a wheel" with other spheres. 23: as a hub, supports and unites many major parts of the structure. The atomic structure analogy is our best guide as we would see 23: is as the neutron in the nucleus that balances the other forces and can only do that because it has a mercurial nature. A good mind and good senses are not in conflict unless one or other is being overextended to the detriment of the other, eg paralysis of analysis in love. Considered from the view of spheres and their Virtues, 5 is Eastwards with the "green" shoot springing from the ground in "Viking!" Others are so busy in their Northwards orientation they often don't stop and consider 5 and 4, often because of their fear of 13: rather than their fuller celebration of life as 23: can do beautifully. But as 23: has an isomer we cannot end the 23: part without saying something, a little

but important part of the jig-saw about :32.

23:32 are dextro but asymmetric. 23: is in the 3rd period and :32 is in the 4th period as if these two divisions of the hub are joined also.

Franklin D Roosevelt. "The only thing we have to fear is fear itself."

PERIOD 4. :32 COMMUNICATION.

> **Born: 32 Elie Wiesel**
> **Malcolm X**

23: Royal Star of Lion and :32 Communication complete each other as they are asymmetric parts. :32 has the same *power to sway masses of people that 14: has and the same blessings of help from those in high positions as 23: so adding all this to the natural ability to charm others with magnetic speech and you have the best of ingredients for honest, charismatic leadership in community and business life. :32 is sometimes known, by modernizing the symbol of the ancients as the "politicians vibration" but not because they exhibit these qualities but because they need to. Due to the highly developed analytical and social skills associated with 23:32, the complexities of advertising, writing, publishing, radio, television and other media, are usually an open book for 23:32 who works very well under pressure.*

There is a Chaldean warning note on this otherwise happy melody. :32 is a very fortunate path if the person it represents, holds inflexibly to their own opinions and judgements, intuition, or "best lights", otherwise one's best plans are liable to be wrecked by the stubbornness or stupidity of others and one's failure to learn this karmic lesson.

In common with 23:, as :32 you have the same good mind that can see things in a well rounded, embracing way. You are able to see interdependencies, handle detail and complexities and have reliable dextro intuition. Where you may come undone is with commitment. Being busy surveying the whole can be an escape from your compassionate nature - seeing both sides of things being hardest when wounded, or recently wounded. Certainly the mind leads the change as the 14: in you knows and that has been a central adjustment adult strategy, yes but! Feelings have to catch up and the good mind won't be good again until they do. Take time out until it is good again and the old feeling of integration is back before pressing ahead again. T.O. as :31. Go Receptive for a while.

Taking some knocks are just part of your journey. Good as your mind is, there are still some valuable lessons to learn, some very steep yet rewarding paths ahead in :41 and 50. As surely as the Sun goes West, as some things must, the Sun comes East again, for new beginnings with greater blessings to do greater things. As glue between joints enables one to make a piece of furniture, :32 can hold a group of fractured interests in place, when it has a good mind to do so that is! Breadth of perspective can help hold fractured interests where, social bonds compensate isolation, or complement a task. It is these qualities of mind that makes for great leadership. But not without a lot of testing on this path, each step not being easily won. This is the path of enjoying the calm times, but being on your toes and alert as well. It happens as you know that "all hell will break loose" and you will need to be the still point, the steady centre, the mentally strongly one, the calm in the storm until the panic of so many subsides. You certainly have to be experienced in crisis situations in order to know how to handle them so don't be surprised by surprise, doesn't mean insensitive. All senses need to be sharp or the whole Pride can suffer.

Two people, who are both within a loving partnership, can face different 18 Spiritual-Material conflicts in the same situation of communicating together. The first party is warned that when in a sea of love, 22 Submission-Caution is always lurking in the back-ground and so too is 13: Regeneration and Change and :31 Recluse-Hermit. Even though the evidence of a great blessing is upon you from the Crown and Star of Magi, some time out is indicated to ensure full comprehension of your spiritual quest. Communication is not just a matter of talking, it is especially a time to listen when you are :31 Recluse-Hermit.

Because this step is such an important one at this point in the quest, the warning of 22 Submission-Caution is that you never know who you as :31 might be communicating with, so humility should always be practiced even amidst great good fortune. These "hermit times" are most important times to use to redefine yourself and your freedom to express gratitude as well as grief in private. In those private times to attune yourself to listening to your inner voice. These are vital times for renewal from silence. Listening in a state of inner stillness. Opening yourself to the greatness of the Blessings from Universe. Then, expanding and coalescing ideas, clarifying needs and times for planning.

How does spiritual-material conflict apply in your situation? In what ways might you be failing to show love, respect and appreciation? How do you "cloud" your own or your partner's spiritual path? What ways do you use to be personally "evasive", during an otherwise flowing communication? How do you keep each other playing the games of 12: Sacrifice-Victim? There is no conflict between spirit and love at any level. Conflict only enters through the choices we make so it is particularly the repeated choice patterns that we need to evaluate and change.

Born 41: Bertrand Russell
Name Nicole Kidman

PERIOD 5. :41 MOVEMENT-CHALLENGE II.

This is the isomer of 14:. In the life of a :41, from time to time there will be a series of challenges to established patterns, procedures, organization or ways of seeing things. This will bring new insight that refines your personal sense of purpose as those steps are taken. The nature of :41 Movement ... Challenge II for each person is gradually refined and then defined. Understanding your goals or challenges requires reflection and attunement to the Crown of Magi frequency and also 33 Universe Harmonization. 33 blessings will start small and then grow, eventually including further benefits from 19 Prince of Heaven in later parts of this period. You may see this as the Creative and Receptive frequencies are both supportive and you can learn to trust and respond to them.

Born 50 Adolph Hitler
Name Prince Philip Sir Edmund Hillary

PERIOD 6. PATH 50 STATESPERSON.

This is the gold crucible for sphere 5 - top grade as a Statesperson with full support from 23: Royal Star of Lion and :21 Crown of Magi. In view of the complexity of your role and the great power that is at your command, you also have doubled blessings of 25: Discrimination and Analysis. Although you are very well prepared for this role and greatly blessed with support from high places, remember to listen carefully to your "inner-voice" of caution. To assist in the proper or equitable exercise of power you are blessed with 22 Submission-Caution. You do not want to fall victim to the adage "absolute power, corrupts absolutely". Caution is needed in realizing you are not the absolute authority. Use your blessings of 25: Discrimination and Analysis to keep a watchful eye on showing respect for those in high places to the same extent as the respect due to those you serve. Listen attentively to the needs of your constituents. Great powers are granted for doing great work and not for stroking your Ego.

LOVE 6.

The wisdom paths of sphere 6 are;
Period 1 6 Love
Period 2 15: Magician,
Period 3 24: Love, Money and Creativity I,
Period 4 33 Universe Harmonization
Period 5 :42 Love, Money and Creativity II and
Period 6 :51 Warrior.

Sphere 6 people are blessed to resonate with the planet Venus. They appear inclined to *the feminine essence, compassion and money.* 6 is the sphere of *love, romance* and Beauty. *6 people magnetically attract others to them.*

They're genuinely loved by their friends and associates and when they become attached themselves, they are devoted to their loved one. There's more idealism and affection than sensualism in the love nature. These people are born romantics with a strong sentimental streak no matter how they deny or try to hide it. 6 brings love of art and a deep affinity with music. These people love nice homes, tasteful furnishings, pastel colours and harmony in their surroundings. They love to entertain their friends and to make people happy and they simply cannot abide discord, arguments, unpleasantness and

jealousy – although they can display jealousy themselves if they're threatened with the possible loss of someone or something they love. 6 people make friends easily and they tend to enjoy settling disputes between their friends, business associates and relatives, at which times they appear to be as peaceful and docile as lambs – until their stubborn side surfaces; then they don't seem docile. Money often comes to them without effort, sometimes through their own talents and abilities, sometimes through inheritance or through wealthy friends or relatives. But they're warned to watch for a tendency toward the extremes of extravagance and stinginess. There's seldom a neutral attitude towards finances. It's either one or the other, taking turns in the nature.

The love of beauty of all kinds in every area of life is pronounced. Most 6 people are deeply attached to Nature in some way and love spending time in the country, near the silent woods and singing streams which has a tranquilizing effect on their emotions. A fondness for luxury marks the 6 sphere. Ugliness is extremely offensive to them. They admire the tasteful and shrink from loudness and vulgarity. Their manners are as a general rule impeccable, and in their associations with others they are usually polite. However, when they feel strongly about anything, they won't hesitate to make their opinions known. They're fond of discussing and debating politics and other matters and they usually win, because of their logic and winning smiles.

PERIOD 2. 15: MAGICIAN.

> Born 15: Nehru

15: is of deep esoteric significance and it is the alchemical vibration through which magic is manifested. It's extremely lucky and carries the essence of enchantment with it. 15: is associated with good talkers, eloquent speech and gifts of music, art and drama. It bestows upon the person represented, a dramatic temperament, strong personal magnetism and a curious compelling charisma. 15: is especially fortunate for obtaining gifts, money and favours from others, because 15: powerfully appeals to the altruistic nature of people.

However, there are no roses without thorns and the ancients warn that 15: rules the lower levels of occultism when it is associated with spheres 4 and 8. Such people will use every art of magic, even black magic, hypnosis and mental suggestion to carry out their purpose. Or the contrary is true. The 4 or 8 person will become the victim of others using the same methods.

Other than this warning, 15: is an extremely fortunate vibration and you're blessed with the ability to bring great happiness to others and to shine your light in the darkness providing you don't use this magical and fortunate vibration for selfish purpose.

PERIOD 3. 24: LOVE, MONEY AND CREATIVITY I.

> Born 24: Richard Nixon

This is a most fortunate path of karmic reward justly earned in past incarnations. It promises assistance from those with power and it indicates a close association with people of high rank or position. It greatly increases financial success and the ability to achieve happiness in love and creative expression. It denotes gain through romance, law or arts and a magnetism that is extremely attractive to the opposite sex.

The only warnings related to 24: are self-indulgence and a certain arrogance in love, financial and career matters because everything comes so effortlessly. It's wise to remember that if 24: is abused in the present life it could revert to some other difficult birth number in the next. So one is warned not to fail to appreciate the benefits of 24: and not to allow such good fortune to cause selfishness or a careless attitude towards spiritual values. The temptation to indulge in promiscuity must be avoided, likewise a tendency to over-indulgence of all kinds.

Born 33	Woodrow Wilson
	George W Bush
Name	Margaret Thatcher
	Kerry Packer
	Indira Gandhi

PERIOD 4. 33 UNIVERSE HARMONIZATION.

Although the meaning of path 33 is most similar to 24:, the magic of love, extent of originality and creativity, and promise of financial success are deepened and increased. This is a path of well-deserved karmic reward but it carries a warning not to abuse the astounding luck which will descend on the 33 person sometime during life by allowing it to tempt them into laziness, over-confidence or feelings of superiority. Understanding the central role 6 plays in the Tree of Life and the importance of the Receptive doubled, will assist you define the best ways to utilize your blessings in service to Universe.

Born: 42	Bob Hawke
	Gen. Charles de Gaulle
	Ralph Waldo Emerson
Name	Patrick White

PERIOD 5. :42 LOVE, MONEY AND CREATIVITY II.

Whilst 24:42 indicates that :42 is the higher power of 24:, it should also be noted that :42 is double :21 Crown of Magi. Principally this is a path of harmonious loving, romantic and matured partnerships. Although the warnings of 24:, arrogance and self-indulgence apply to :42, the risks of this are significantly reduced with :21 Crown of Magi and 23: Royal Star of Lion on your side

Born: 51	Mike Willesee
Name	Sigmund Freud
	Nelson Mandela
	Elizabeth Taylor

PERIOD 6. :51 WARRIOR.

:51 Warrior is the pinnacle of enlightenment in the sixth sphere. In this gold crucible there are additional blessings from :21 Crown of Magi.

This path possesses a strong potency of its own and is associated with the nature of a warrior and promises sudden advancement in whatever one undertakes. Although :51's meaning is closely linked with its isomer 15: Magician, it is especially favourable for those who need protection in the armed services or for leaders of any "cause" unrelated to war. Yet it also brings the threat of dangerous enemies and the possibility of attempted assassination. As conveyed by 6, :51 is about activity that is undertaken with a passion that emanates from one's central values and intrinsic nature. This could be manifest in a conservation cause of any sort, work with people who have a disadvantage or are repressed, or giving assistance in natural disasters. There are many great causes and there is a serenity that flows from knowledge that your passion and your destiny are tied.

However, the Warrior is in a field of conflict and optimum performance may require scheduled rest and recreation to maintain one's energy levels, insight and poignancy. Simple constructive planning of this type will assist avoiding the mistakes born through exhaustion. As with other paths in Period 6, :51 Warrior is well prepared for what must be done so any self doubts need to be put aside and the focus of effort refined or systematically honed.

MYSTERY.

The wisdom paths of sphere 7 are;
Period 1 7 Mystery
Period 2 16 Shattered Citadel,
Period 3 25: Discrimination and Analysis I,
Period 4 34: Discrimination and Analysis II,
Period 5 :43, Road of Strife and
Period 6 :52 Healer / Holy-man.

Sphere 7 people are blessed to resonate with the planet Neptune. They appear inclined to *spirituality, sensitivity, sympathy, and mystery. 7 is a sphere of illusion and delusion, sometimes deception; but it is also a sphere for healing, miracles, faith and dreams that do come true. 7 people tend to have remarkable dreams and more of them than most. Some like to talk about their predictive dreams, but others tend to be a bit secretive, maybe, because of some uncertainties about their gifts of intuitive insight or clairvoyant skills.* But 7 is a sign of Great Mystery, a call to realization and awareness that there is a Great Mystery that underlies the individuals' life and the lives of all other creatures.

The mysterious, ethereal quality in the photo of Sacred Gorge is exactly as the camera exposed it. Deep in this gorge, the light effect on rocks and trees is exceptional and inspires one's awe and wonder.

An astute 7 could howl with the wolves because they have the remarkable ability to refine the way they express themselves. This gives them great blessings in their work as actors, artists or any other form of creative expression for which they yearn. The yearning for a way to personally know Great Mystery and the source of Creator energy, will directly lead you to finding and expressing your gifts, talents or insights. Somewhere in following the yearning, the search for some esoteric painting, researching mythology on Neptune, or some other such activity will spark your interest and attention in a particular thing. Follow the leads; your best hunches! The idea could be in a book you purchased once but haven't read, so look on your shelves. It could be in re-reading something, or viewing an object, even a map in different lights, something will be a trigger to clarification, expansion and then refinement of your mysterious/creative gifts. The thing is that you probably already have in your possession, the very keys you need to explore. Look on the passive side too, because some 7 people have the unique gift of being sensed as a healing presence or on having a calming influence or soothing effect on others.

Spiritual quests are an individual matter but some collective wisdom may help you from time to time, even though you may not like to follow the beaten path.

Finding your way is important to those that follow you as 7 is often associated with people who have founded new teaching principles, new religious concepts, and new political beliefs. *7 people are sea lovers and sailing romantics. Travel overseas or a passion for researching something about far away lands is a great attraction to 7 people's interests. Although 7 people tend to be anxious about the future, these anxieties transpose to practical and simple issues such as financial security.* Sensible financial provision, if avoided, can undermine, even cause the collapse of one's plans in an "easy come, easy go" world of awe and wonder.

"After the exotic, comes the laundry," Loa Tzu said about 550BC. Practical matters are the karmic mine-field of the mysterious/creative side. But the "laundry periods" can also be used well. Centering yourself is critical to balance. Few 7 people accumulate wealth or demonstrate care about material possessions. They can earn large sums of money from their new ideas, but they're likely to be making equally large donations to a favoured charity or cause. They are generous, sometimes to the point of fault. When they gravitate towards the arts, they make fine writers, actors, poets, singers and dancers. Their refined skills frequently distinguish them. But there is a strong need for privacy as well and they prefer to keep their plans and problems to themselves. They shrink from prying questions, "big brother" controls and invasions of privacy. At quiet, laid-back times you may hear a 7 person explain him/her-self with a somewhat philosophical outlook. They can exhibit the best in empathic understanding, but this gift also carries a burden. Being empathic means being touched by the pain and suffering of others. Many people turn to 7 for help because they are not inclined to be judgmental or prejudiced, they listen and develop an empathic understanding, and some of them have gifts in healing through their very sensitive natures. If they trust you at that laid-back time, and you encourage 7 to speak about what 7 is thinking, you will be surprised and fascinated by the depths in Neptunium secret worlds.

| Born 16 | **Winston Churchill** |
| Name | **Ludwig Van Beethoven** |

PERIOD 2. 16 SHATTERED CITADEL.

The Chaldean image is;
> "A Tower struck by lightning,
> from which a man is falling,
> with a Crown on his head."

It warns of a strange fatality, also danger from accidents and defeat of one's plans. 16 is one of the two karmic burdens of sphere 7. Failure to listen to the voice within will lead to the destruction of one's plans. The voice within and most likely dreams, will warn you in time to avoid danger. If you are getting very hard lessons then you're not learning to listen. The inner voice must not be ignored. 16 is the path for the

name "Abraham Lincoln".

Lincoln was warned repeatedly of his potential assassination by his dreams … and also by several "sensitives" and "mediums" who were brought to the White House by Mary Todd Lincoln. He did not heed the many clear warnings, and refused to take the necessary precautions, therefore he was unable to avoid his fate. But it could have been avoided, and this is important for anyone with the birth date, 16 to remember. To find happiness in other ways, you can renounce the Crown, fame or celebrity. Lincoln did not do so, feeling it was more important to attempt to keep a nation united than to enjoy the fulfilment of a private life, although he accepted the Presidency with much reluctance and a profound sadness.

Born 25:	Eamon de Valera
	Paul Calvert
Name	Bill Gates

Period 3. 25: Discrimination & Analysis I.

25: bestows blessings of spiritual wisdom gained through careful observation of people and things, and worldly success by learning through experience. It's strength comes from overcoming the disappointments of early life and possessing the rare quality of learning from past mistakes. The judgement is excellent, but it is not a material path, it is about the process of gaining spiritual wisdom regarding Great Mystery. It is about the wise person and maturation of their "wise-ness".

25: Discrimination and Analysis has the isomer :52 that represents the end objectives of enlightenment, happiness, and the blessings of direct experience of Great Spirit in the 7th sphere. 25: blessings enable reflection and integration of experience that is highly formative, or a sound basis for developments on your path into 34:43 and :52. The consistent thread through every period is personal experience of Great Mystery and if you are most highly blessed, you may look forward to direct experience of Great Spirit.

In the caves of Qumran, amongst the Dead Sea Scrolls, was the Gospel of Thomas [Bib. 47]. In translation, it reads very much like a Gnostic text and it confirms the description given also by John. Thomas pays special attention to the events of the Last Supper. This was the night of the "Passover". With Jesus in the centre, they sang a hymn to the Father…

> "And we all circled round him and responded to him: Amen.
> The twelfth of the numbers paces the round aloft, Amen.
> To each and all it is given to dance, Amen."

Apocryphal Acts of St John.

"Even the passion that I revealed to thee and the others in the round dance, I would have it called a mystery,"   Jesus of Nazareth

How beautifully St John's words excite the imagination! Though the round dance is a mystery, it was very carefully performed in accord with Gnostic and Hebrew rites by which the activation of "inner-energies" has an Archetypal counterpart.

Some of the threads of these early traditions can be currently illustrated by the Sufi tradition of dancing, by whirling around. Most often referred to as the Whirling Dervishes, the proper name for this tradition has a special place here in 25: and 34: "Mevlana Dervishes" respectively! 25: is the essential grounding for the periods ahead, and it is characterized by careful training and ritual preparation for any such "round dance" experience. It takes practice to attain high levels of self-discipline and skill. Practice too in "stilling" ego; silencing inner dialogue; opening oneself as in 3 Receptive.

The following description of the Mevlana Dervishes dance, is predicated on this being only one example and only one of many ways that the dance could be described. The unique value of this description is the way Jill Purse describes the activation of inner-energies and their Archetypal counterparts. At the same time she allows insight into the first steps and outcomes of this round dance. As it is especially significant for those in sphere 7, she says their dance or turn shows successive degrees of milling away their illusory existence so enabling ascension of their spirits.

> "The first phase is that of contraction; the Dervish starts his dance with his arms crossed over his chest, suggesting a junction in the heart of the descending and ascending vortices. He has his left foot firmly earthed, representing the still axis. By moving his right foot, he begins to turn like a planet on this axis, while revolving with his fellows around a central sun, the leading Dervish. He gradually expands, uncrosses his arms, and lowering his head over his right shoulder, he raises his right arm, palm up to receive the Divine Emanation, and lowers his left arm, palm down, to return his gift to the earth. He spins gradually faster, as if by his own revolutions he was connecting Heaven and Earth by actually turning the spirit through himself and down into the ground, while his axis and heart remain absolutely still and his own spirit soars to its Divine source. The greater his ecstasy, his expansion and speed, the wider his skirt extends. When his arms are both outstretched to Heaven, it is as if the union in his heart, delineated in its state of contraction [spirit into matter] by his crossed arms, has reached its fullest expansion [matter into spirit] by the opposing gyres of arms and skirts: the outer expression of the bliss of Divine Union." Jill Purse "The Mystic Spiral" [Bib. 58]

So it is that in 25: you are in the thick of the mystery in whatever you do to mill away your illusory existence. To illustrate the generic qualities, the first two and a half sentences could be exactly applied to one of the movements in the Wu long form of Tai Chi. No doubt there are other disciplines that if mastered when 25: will serve beautifully for the periods ahead.

Ascension and early years carry blessings to handle movement and change that may involve travel or living in different countries or places, at least encountering different partnerships, different people, and a wide range of values and ideals. Blessed with :42 Love, Money and Creativity II these are bound to be very happy and satisfying times and a strong sense of personal identity and power will be noted by family and friends.

They see 25: as;

> "wiser than her years, she loves people and talks to everyone. But she has to have her quiet times to herself in her room and in the garden. She likes to play alone sometimes - looking into things, playing with beetles, snails, drawing them, talking to them in her world that others see as illusory, or the product of an over-fertile imagination."

However, the latter is not the case as she is gifted with 7 Mystery qualities of perception and when she is playing in the garden and chatting with others she has 17 Star of Magi in her left hand and Great Spirit guiding her right hand. What more could you want?! Her receptive and creative sides are very well balanced. Sure, there are issues to be dealt with in all partnerships when egos get ruffled, but she knows how to keep to the issues so she has difficulties she overcomes rather than battlegrounds. She quickly learns to follow her intuition in who to trust and has quickly developing relationship skills and insight. Providing she is encouraged to talk about her experiences she will thrive. Though she is blessed with :31 Recluse-Hermit to help her during her times alone in her room and in the garden, her trusting nature is to be moulded in diverse ways even in these early years.

Born 34:	John F Kennedy
Sydney Myer	Ita Buttrose
Golda Meir	Germaine Greer
Kevin Rudd	

PERIOD 4. 34: DISCRIMINATION & ANALYSIS II.

This is grade 2, of 25: Discrimination and Analysis. The challenges represented by 34: call for great acuity but not without considerable assistance. Blessings flow from 17 Star of Magi doubled. As can be seen from the definition of 17 there is also a pungent aspect that can have a doubly strong effect on 34: and particularly on the isomer :43 Road of Strife. There are testing times on these greatly blessed but also difficult wisdom paths.

One clue to the talents and testing is to do with your uniqueness and communicating your unique point of view. Knowing the value of the unique insight that you can bring to a situation and finding the way of expressing it constructively is always a challenge. These are wonderful lessons in achieving self-expression in mutually beneficial ways. Like always there is a warning. The first concerns 18 Spiritual-Material Conflict but most particularly as that relates to the use of the higher powers of 36 and 45 Sceptre. Usually obedience to your inner-voice is tested before dominion is given.

Born: 43	Ludwig Van Beethoven
Name	Germaine Greer
	Xavier Herbert
	John Howard

PERIOD 5. :43 ROAD OF STRIFE.

The ancients claim that this is an unfortunate path. It is symbolized by the tendency toward revolution, upheaval and strife, conflict and war. It carries the frequency of repeated disappointments and failures. If you want to avoid something akin to repeated strife, then look carefully at what you are repeating. Until you end what you are repeating, and take a new approach, strife will continue. If you are wondering "Why is all this trouble coming my way?" Stop. Look. Listen. Retreat to Nature and study her analogies for a while. Your lessons may be to do with the way you express yourself in what you know. That is a uniquely individual communication challenge that greatly varies by the situations you encounter. But learning how to do that is part of spiritual wisdom where the failures through rigidity of rightness, can be matched by the capacity for forgiveness providing there is a desire to get it right. In other words, there's a lot more to arrogance than just a point of view, when it stems from intolerance. Some of the karmic lessons on handling pressure gracefully might be interesting and beneficial to try when you want to get "unstuck". What possible benefit can you derive from remaining "Stuck" on the Road of Strife? Try 30 Loner-Meditation for a while and get a solid grounding in 34: or particularly 3 Receptive in the hands of Mother Earth.

Name Joan Sutherland
Archbishop Desmond Tutu

PERIOD 6. PATH: 52 HEALER / HOLY   MAN.

The gold crucible of period 6 reaches its climax in spiritual wisdom with path :52. This represents the highest level of human consciousness in contemplation of the divine order that affects our lives and drives us in our quests. This is not achieved without the person having developed heightened awareness of self both in light and shadow aspects. As this is as much a path of gaining clarity, it is also one of deepening appreciation of Great Mystery in our lives and seeing the interdependence of body, mind and spirit with that of Universe. Although sphere 7 is Dextro, active and creative, path :52 also requires time for receptivity [Laevo] and as its isomer would indicate, careful discrimination and analysis of your situation.

If you happen to think, "I've made it!" Probably this is so, but bear in mind the lessons of path 49, Regeneration and Change, that transforming oneself is very much an ongoing process. As the Creative builds new dimensions of self there is also a corresponding Destruction or termination of aspects of one's being. Old ways must give way to new ways and new understanding and awareness. Path :52 is about clarifying and using your spiritual wisdom in whatever field you are involved. :52 is the pinnacle of achievement on the paths.

According to the Chaldeans, when you pass the root number 9, you multiply 9 until the compound number 45 is reached. Then you add the mystical number 7 to 45 and 52 is reached. This represents the number of weeks in the calendar year and when multiplied by 7 gives the days in a year 364, when the next day, 365 was one of great festival and no work was allowed to be performed by man, woman, child or animal. In like manner, the Wisdom Paths stop at 52 as a mark of human respect for those of our Archetypal world.

PARTNERSHIPS.

The wisdom paths in sphere 8 are;
Period 1 8 Partnerships
Period 2 17 Star of Magi,
Period 3 26 Partnerships,
Period 4 35: Mass partnerships,
Period 5 44 Commander,
Period 6 :52. Healer / Holy-man.

Sphere 8 people are blessed to resonate with the planet Saturn.

They appear inclined *to wisdom, learning through experience, stability, patience and responsibility. 8 is also the sphere of financial security, caution, restriction, self-discipline and self-control. 8 people are normally quiet, reserved and shy. They don't obviously push ahead, but slowly and surely they will get where they want to go, and nothing will stop them from achieving their ambitions. The shyness and reticence is to cover for an intense drive to reach the top of the profession or career. They make excellent teachers and counsellors, most of them could be successful in the tough game of politics and they excel at anything that requires patience and intelligent deduction.*

Those influenced by sphere 8 may have poor health in childhood but they grow more robust when they reach maturity, and longevity is common. These people are willing to wait for their plans to bear fruit and they use the waiting time wisely. It's rare to find an 8 person procrastinating or "goofing off". They have an inborn sense of duty and responsibility that won't allow them to take a careless attitude toward what is expected of them. Most of those born under the influence of 8 are as reliable as a grandfather clock and as cosy to be around as a grandmother quilt or comforter. They have a rich sense of humour, but one has to watch for it as it is subtle and never obvious. These people behave as if they don't care a peanut what people think of them and they appear to be turned off by compliments. Yet, inwardly they care a great deal about what people think of them, and if the compliments are sincere they secretly enjoy them, although they'll hide their pleasure for fear they might be considered weak. To be considered weak is the very last thing they want to have happen because they have very deep and intense natures and great inner strength. They often play an important role in life's drama and many times are the instrument for the Fate of others. There is a tendency towards fanaticism in religion and they will stick by what they believe relentlessly in the face of all opposition. They make loving friends but bitter enemies. Although 8 people appear to be cold and undemonstrative with those they love and trust, they can be shyly affectionate and warmly devoted. They're often lonely needing desperately to be loved and they are capable of great sacrifices for an ideal, an ambition, or for those who depend upon them. They grow younger in appearance as they grow older – they look and act younger at fifty than they were when they were twenty. They're as demanding of themselves as they are of others but for all the outward attitudes of wisdom, maturity, self-control and self-discipline, the 8 person's heart is lonely and longing and they need to learn that the pursuit of happiness is not a sin.

Period 2. 17 Star of Magi.

Born 17	Lang Hancock

This is a highly spiritual path and was expressed in symbolism by the ancient Chaldeans as the 8-pointed star of Venus. The Star of Magi is the image of Love and Peace and promises that the person represented will rise

superior in spirit to the trials and difficulties of earlier life with the ability to conquer former failure in personal relationships and career. 17 is the "number of Immortality" and it indicates that the person's name will live after them.

Two situations are depicted by the Magi here. In her right hand she is pouring out the great blessings of this extremely fortunate path into a pool. However, with her left hand the blessings are falling on the ground and are running away in different directions. This action with her left hand is linked to the highly negative periodic influence of Saturn, with which, from time to time sphere 8 resonates. Accordingly there will be periodic positive and negative changes or apparent contradictions. Saturn can have a very pungent effect that overrides the blessings of Venus. It is from this negative influence that the trials and difficulties of 17 emerge that mould your character.

We all have "blind spots" so self-examination most often is assisted by reflection on how others see us. Their reflections may point to vital needs for Regeneration and Change. Our Partnerships are there to teach us something in both positive and negative ways and thus raise our "loving awareness" and so continue discovery of the underlying mysterious aspect of our destined paths together. The Star of Magi points the way towards the Mystery that underlies 13: and discussion of its double 26.

Born 26	Pope John Paul 11.	Gough Whitlam
	Imran Khan	Raphael Sanzio
Name	Michael Willesee	Imran Khan

PERIOD 3. 26 PARTNERSHIPS.

This path has a unique kind of power, based on compassion and unselfishness, with the ability to help others, but not the self. 26 it full of contradictions. It warns of danger, disappointments and failure, especially regarding failure of ambitions, brought about through following bad advice or following others, not hearing the good advice you were given: there are a great many areas for reflection on both the most successful partnerships and the worst. There are great learning opportunities in carefully evaluating both. As we advance through the higher levels of Partnerships, 35, 44, and 52: it can readily be seen that mutual "loving awareness" is a sublime blessing. Just as important in the relationship between parent and child as it is between healer and healed. Partnerships of all kinds are encountered. In examining the flaws, look to when intuition occurs both in yourself and your partner, times when you failed to follow and when you did follow your individual and collective intuition. Two or more people can vastly increase the "loving awareness" of one. But there are practical matters in partnerships too, finances to manage effectively, physical surroundings to be maintained, and there are destined lessons in being generous with others, especially those in need, but also building a solid foundation for the future in some particular relationships. There are destined dangers in not attending to these practical matters.

Partnerships are the melting pot for trouble but they are also greatly blessed with 17 Star of Magi, 15:51 Magician: Warrior, 12:21 Crown of Magi, and 34: Discrimination & Analysis to cover spiritual wisdom that is gained along the partnerships way.

Born 35	Nelson Mandela
	Tenzing Norgay
Name	Tom Cruise

PERIOD 4. 35: MASS PARTNERSHIPS.

These partnerships continue to be within the direct sphere of influence of the Star of Magi and 26 but with 35, there is need for a process of learning how to blend multiple interests and needs. 35 means encountering situations that will sharpen 26 skills and advance them in a number of beneficial ways by confronting the 35 person, with a series of destined challenges, as if opening them to the wider direct influences of Jupiter and Mercury. In 35, 3 represents Trinity, Jupiter, idealism, higher education, overseas travel, friends, encountering a series of partnership senses, a series of situations, and a series of new ways to develop to the highest levels achievable in human integration of endeavour; and dedication to a series of increasingly large partnerships until Transcendence. In 35, 5 means Mercury, communication, movement and versatility. It's the number of intellect and of both oral and written expression. In overall terms, 35 means multiple partnerships of the sort seen in meetings of large numbers of people, or small crowds who are gathered for a defined purpose and from which destined lessons are learnt.

Born 44	Elizabeth Taylor
Name	Richard Burton
	Sir Mark Oliphant

PERIOD 5. 44 COMMANDER.

You have a captivating presence and compassion that nearly everyone responds well too. Your past experience and awareness about people's needs and the relationship skills developed in previous paths in Sphere 8 will take you a very long way in directing people effectively. In your most recent past life you have learnt about Mass Communication and now is the time to use those blessings and awareness to achieve something your name will be remembered for having done. This is a path that needs you to add your ability to love what you do. This is a highly spiritual path and Saturn can guide you. Periodic reflection alone will aid the clarity needed in your mind to direct events effectively. These need to be times when you tune in to your inner voice and silence your Ego. This isn't about you as much as it is about something you are being called to do. Did you know that Napoleon used to have a period of tuning into "The Great Silence" before he would formulate his next usually victorious battle plan? Joan of Ark always prayed before battle. North American Indians sought to encounter Great Spirit in the Great Silence achieved through the Pathway of Peace.

You will need to plan "Time Out" and ensure you take it if you are to discover what Universe has in mind for you to undertake as a born Commander. Yes, you are going to face plenty of difficulties as an 8 but you should have learnt how to handle most of them and will move forward on the journey to possible immortality. Great things can be achieved.

Destiny, 4 repeated, it is the double of 22 Submission-Caution and it is a heavy load to be carried for those who are travelling on this path. This refers to partnerships of all kinds, in business and private life. As this is a fifth period path it is very likely your involvement in this life has been preceded by involvement in previous incarnations where there has been important unfinished business and/or conflict in 35 Partnerships. The level of difficulty in 44 Commander is increased over that in path 35 but as with all paths the lessons are there to be learnt and the goal of :52 should be achievable in the next period.

As you may have noted elsewhere we are born to triumph. In your analysis of your situation, it may be useful to consider and clarify how partnerships are formed, how they develop and the ways in which they are maintained. Clearly there are destined lessons we need to learn individually but there are also lessons you need to learn together – even as a large group - as if one heart and mind. No where is this more clearly evident than in 29 Grace Under Pressure that plays such a key role in partnerships. It generally takes two people to play the game in its opposite parts of Persecutor and Victim, but it only needs one person to stop playing and the dynamics are radically altered. In an ideal world this change in roles will be mutually understood and an agreement reached about the changes necessary, but there is every reason to end what you don't like and do something different, even if that simply enables greater clarity about the issues that you all face. At least this gives you a starting point and is a clear signal to the Star of Magi that you want to do something constructive about your situation. Make no mistake about the seriousness of the trouble that can underlie

44. You may not share the same house, you may be sworn enemies dedicated to destroying each other. There is a very unpleasant, pungent side to Saturn's negative influence and it is well worth the effort to minimize the chance for such a pattern to become established. It being easier to prevent rather than stop when that influence has started to flow. The best starting point for analysis is the karmic lessons that underlie 22.

Period 6: 52 HEALER / HOLY-MAN.

Although the correct path number here is :53, the Chaldean system is limited to :52 paths so :53 is treated as path :52 – see Sphere 7 for the definition.

FOUNDATION.

The wisdom paths in sphere 9 are;
Period 1 9 Foundation
Period 2 18 Spiritual-Material Conflict,
Period 3 27 Sceptre I,
Period 4 36 Sceptre II, and
Period 5 45 Sceptre III.

Sphere 9 people are blessed to resonate with the planet Mars.

They exhibit persistence, courage, and excel at penetrating, aggressive action against an opponent. This is the sphere of originality and initiative ... also the contradictory side of vulnerability and naiveté. 9 people are not stubborn, but they are determined to get what they want. Stubbornness reacts whilst determination initiates. 9 brings a tendency to be impulsive and make snap decisions that are later regretted. Although the temper will flare rather frequently these people are quick to forgive and forget. They're vulnerable to their enemies because their first instinct is to trust everyone. Since they are so direct themselves, they expect others to be the same ... and others often are not. Deviousness and manipulation always come as a shock to 9 people. As a general rule they are incapable of such behaviour and motives themselves, and dishonesty catches them off guard nearly every time, until they learn to be more cautious.

One of the most beneficial virtues of sphere 9 is the ability to penetrate straight to the heart or the core of a situation instead of indulging in circumlocution and the slow process of analysis. Mars rulership allows 9 people to go straight to the point and this makes them extremely impatient with slow thinkers, which doesn't help them with popularity contests. Impatience with the mistakes of others and with errors of thinking, is one of the traits 9 people find the most difficult to control. The familiar catch phrase, "what you see is what you get", is typical of a 9 person.

It's against the very essence of the 9 person to plan complex strategies or to play games to get what they want from other people. It's so much easier to simply demand what they want. Since such straightforwardness is unexpected by other people, 9 people usually get what they want. Many people are touched by the visible vulnerability and childlike quality of the 9 person and feel protective towards him or her. Others may see this as foolish which is one of the reasons that 9 people are seldom truly respected by friends and business associates ...

until that Mars temper and courageous spirit burst out and shocks others into retreat. It often seems to others that 9 people are vain because they seem so concerned about their appearance. But vanity is not the reason for this behaviour, rather it is fear of rejection. Beneath all the bravado, 9 people inwardly tremble with a lack of confidence. As self-assertive as they seem, they need continual reassurance they are liked respected, admired and loved. For all the pushiness and independent airs of 9 people, they're secretly very unsure of themselves. Generous to a fault and normally extravagant, 9 people need no lessons in giving. The first instinct is to give, to let go and let tomorrow take care of itself.

PERIOD 2. 18 SPIRITUAL-MATERIAL CONFLICT.

Of all the paths, 18 has the most difficult image to translate.

> "A rayed Moon, from which drops of blood are falling. A wolf and a hungry dog are seen below catching the falling drops of blood in their opened mouths, whilst still lower, a crab is seen hastening to join them."

18 describes the material side striving to destroy the spiritual nature.

18 is often associated with family conflict, wars, social upheaval and revolution. In some cases it indicates making money or achieving position through divisive tactics, war or conflict. It warns of treachery and deception from both "friends" and enemies; also danger from the elements such as fire, flood, earthquakes, lightning, hurricanes and so forth. The only way to dilute or diminish 18's effect on the life is by spiritual means; by unfailingly meeting deception with honesty, hatred with generosity, love and forgiveness and by "turning the other cheek", and returning good for evil, kindness for cruelty, honesty for dishonesty, honour for dishonour. In this way 18 can be used

for great success in illumination and enlightenment. People whose birth date is 18 may be wise to find ways to add the 3 and 6 vibrations to dilute the 18 influence as 3 is the root of 9.

However, Spiritual-Material conflict finds its way into the life of every person. You could say that it underlies all the progressions in all the paths in the same way that 1 does. The most difficult thing about 18 is that the times at which testing will occur are not likely to be expected. But with sound practice in listening to your inner voice, enough warning is always given. There is a big difference between a trick and a test. These are tests not tricks. They are tests of persistence and congruence in values and action. For example, do you say you put love first, then go home and intimidate your partner? Is there congruence between what you say and what you do? Look at what you do. Put aside the self-talk and all the high and noble reasons why you do things and all the fancy rationales, put them aside. Look at what you are doing, as if looking through the very eyes of reality itself. The pattern of your past mistakes and successes will tell you the areas in which you are being tested for 18 Spiritual-Material Conflict. Repeated troubles, repeated problems, repeated failures, anything repeated will give you a clue to the destined difficulties you face and the way in which manifestation occurs. The tests will keep happening until you acknowledge and change what you are doing.

In 18 you are being regularly, though unexpectedly confronted to see something that is vital to your spiritual quest or that is central to your eye for justice and equity. All people have a resonance with 18 and sometimes 27, but if your birth date is 18, you are on the steep path to 27 and the promise of great fulfilment. Power is not granted before the user is tested. And when power has been attained, one continues to be tested in 18, most especially for any abuse of the powers you are granted.

PERIOD 3. 27 SCEPTRE I.	**Born 27** **Mohandas Gandhi**

This is an excellent, harmonious and fortunate path of courage and power, with a touch of enchantment. It blesses the person with a promise of authority and command. It guarantees that great rewards will come from the productive labours, the intellect, and the imagination, that the creative faculties have sown good seeds from which one will reap a rich harvest. People represented by 27 should always carry out their own original ideas and plans, and not be intimidated or influenced by the diverse opinions of others.

27 is a path of karmic reward, earned in more than one previous incarnation. With being a symbol of just authority, also comes the power of life and death. In Biblical times, if you were allowed to touch the staff-like sceptre of a king, you were granted the blessings and power of Life. If you were denied, your life was taken from you. Many a story is told of someone who has misused power. This a-

tests to the level of human difficulty in handling power when there are apparently few restrictions. Hitler is one who failed to see the dangers of abuse of power.

Born 36	**Chaim Herzog**	**Joan Sutherland** **Neville Chamberlain**

PERIOD 5. 36 SCEPTRE II.

This is the second grade of 27 Sceptre. Significantly it is also 18 doubled so the emphasis on being tested for spiritual strength is markedly increased.

PERIOD 6. 45 SCEPTRE III.

This is the third grade of 27 Sceptre.

"Reason is not to be set aside, but it is to be continually illumined by this higher spiritual perception, and in the degree that it is thus illumined will it become an agent of light and power. When one becomes thoroughly individualized he enters into the realm of all knowledge and wisdom; and to be individualized is to recognize no power outside of the Infinite Power that is at the back of all. When one recognizes this great fact and opens himself to this Spirit of Infinite Wisdom, he enters upon the road to the true education, and mysteries that before were closed now reveal themselves to him. This must indeed be the foundation of all true education, this evolving from within, this evolving of what has been involved by the Infinite Power."

Ralph Waldo Trine [Bib. 75].

Contents of this chapter;

1. Virtues of the spheres and their path relationships.

2. Major bodies in the solar system.

3. Spiral and the Archetypes.

4. Elements, spheres and their electro-magnetic frequencies.

5. Nine Spheres and the Sun-Signs of Astrology.

[Earth and our Moon.]

(1) Virtues of the spheres and their path relationships.

The following figure of the nine spheres and their virtues is repeated from our exploration of the paths in the last two chapters. It provides a model of the interrelationship between the spheres and identifies them by their chirality, Laevo, Centre and Dextro.

Fig. 8. Spheres of Inclination and Wisdom Paths.

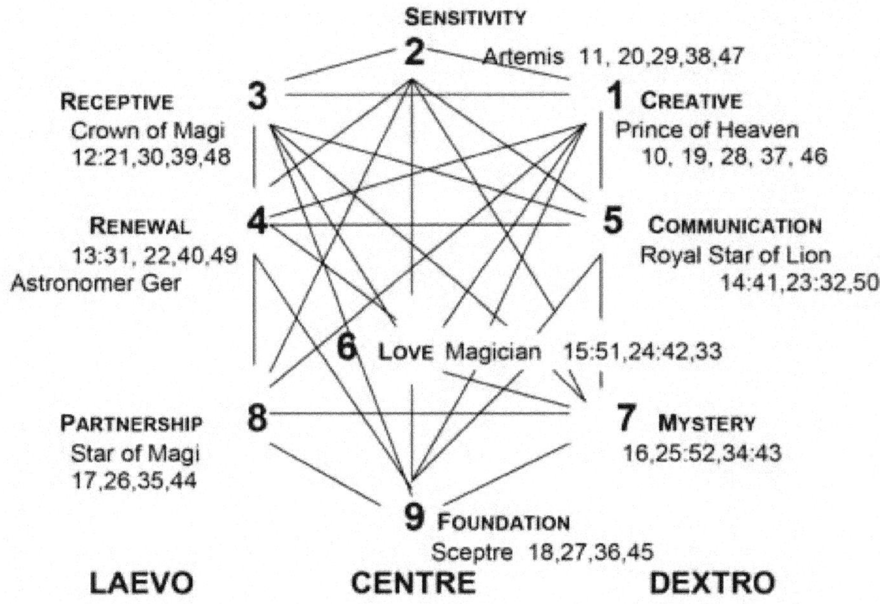

The only thing we really know about the Chaldean-Kabala allocation of 9 is that it could be used to represent the sacred name of the Life Force of nine letters. As you will see Foundation has 10 letters and is therefore not representing the sacred name as it properly could but Sceptre is about life and death and that theme is recurrent in 3 of 5 paths in Sphere 9. At least our numeral is correct and so is the position – South in the place of Water.

(2) Major bodies in the solar system.

To each of the spheres there is a planetary allocation as given below. Two of these planets were not observable with the naked eye so neither the Chaldeans nor Hebrew would have had early allocations of all three that they are unlikely to have seen. Pluto wasn't found until 1930. Therefore, all of the information that follows immediately with each planet is gathered from modern astronomy and may or may not have been a part of their considerations, we will never know. The ancients speak of mystery planets and wandering stars and they wondered just as often as we do about the size of their world and their personal charter. And they wondered about the way exceptional groups of stars predispose us? There were some along the way like Solomon's Wisdom, so really who can say what the deity said and who can say what man understood them to say. But quite obviously the deity knew the number of planets, and they have had several goes at getting these old ideas across to people in many different generations

before and most likely … for many yet to come.…..So, let's take a brief look at those bodies in our solar system and see if there is anything about it that predisposes you, as others would see you!

Each of the major bodies that can be identified in our solar system are allocated to a particular Sphere of Inclination with the exception of Earth. Every one of us that draws breath is on an Earth Wisdom Path - well at least there are some good signs of there being one. There is certainly a lot more attention paid to ways in which human kind will have to clean-up its act. There has been a massive denigration of the environment since the onset of the industrial revolution and there are many who question the viability of Earth as a habitat if we continue our path. We have a common debt to Mother Earth and our life on her planet is a blessing we all share. Every sphere exerts an influence on Earth and so all of us, most especially the Sun. But then where would we be without the Moon's influence on our tides, fishing, moods and other corresponding lunar cycles? Every one of the following influences have their particular characteristics, such as the frequency of the radio-waves that they emit, or the electro-magnetic fields correspondence, and each body in the solar system has a unique spectrum it emits. As many of you will appreciate, this spectrum is a great deal wider than that which forms visible light. Modern Astronomy indicates that part of the electro-magnetic spectrum is possibly as low as 10% of what is received on Earth. These influences are far greater than we expected.

If you imagine a full spectrum of light as refracted by a prism [above], and not just split into four primary colours but 9, you will see that the following 9 Spheres of Inclination are each part of the spectrum of "How Others See You". To put this another way, other people see and experience things about you and their own cycles, tendencies, potentials, abilities and they soon recognize your unique manner of speaking. If you imagine that you have three friends of three friends telling you what they think is indicated about your Sphere, you would have the idea of this equally ordered and beautiful spectrum of how others see the way we are inclined. So check the axis angle, some of you should nearly be lying down, or maybe that is the way you are inclined as others would see you! Some interesting astronomy information about the members of our solar system now follows.

Spheres 1 – 9 and their Planetary Correspondence.

0. Universe   In Universe there are hundreds of thousands of Galaxies about half of which are Spiral Galaxies. The other half are mainly Elliptical Galaxies and Random Star fields.

1. Creative - Sun in our Solar System. Our Sun is about 28,000 light years from the Galactic Centre of

Milky Way that has a diameter of about 100,000 light years. Milky Way is a Spiral Galaxy in which the Sun and the whole Solar system are in motion around the nucleus. Our solar system is located in a smaller spiral arm called the Local or Orion Arm which connects to the larger or more substantial inner arm – Sagittarius. That arm blocks our line of sight view of the Galactic Centre. Our Solar System takes an estimated 225 million years to complete one cycle around the Galactic Centre.

Although the Sun is a massive 1 million miles across, it is really quite small compared to some and tiny compared to some other stars in Milky Way. Betelgeux in Orion for example, is about 250 trillion miles across and emits powerful radio waves that are regularly measured on Earth. Recent estimates of the number of stars in Milky Way have been increased from 200 billion to 400 billion stars.

In the core of our Sun, at a temperature of about 14 million degrees C, in an estimated ratio of 4 hydrogen to 1 helium, the combination of these two elements occurs in an atomic reaction that creates an outer-atmosphere in the Sun's corona of 1 million degrees C. This creates exactly the "Goldilocks" ecosphere we require to survive on this planet which is 1 Astronomical Unit in distance from the Sun [149,597,870km].

You may find this figure also interesting, Sun [Sphere 1] is 109 times larger than Earth and it is the "nucleus", the active centre, or power-house of our solar system.

2.   Sensitive – Moon. The effect of the Moon on Earth's tides demonstrates the power of this heavenly body. The Lunar cycle of 28 days is replicated in the female cycle of many species of life.

The Celts described our Moon as the second devoted luminary in our sky.

The diameter of the Moon is 3476 km [3+4+7+6=20 = 2].

3.   Receptive - Jupiter   3 degrees = angle of inclination of the axis; 3.12 to be precise. The mass of Jupiter is about 318 times [3+1+8=12=3] that of Earth and slightly greater than all the other planets combined, but the density is about that of water. Although Jupiter is very largely composed of hydrogen and helium, it also is believed to have an iron core. And the sidereal period is about 12 years [3] compared to Earth. Its distance from the Sun is 778,412,010 km = 3; and the mean air temperature is 165 degrees on the Kelvin Scale = 3 again.

4.   Renewal - Uranus   98 degrees = angle of inclination. This is almost an exact "square" to

Earth. Up until 1781 AD, this planets existence had not been determined by telescope, as it was not a naked eye planet like all the other planets out to Saturn. In studying the unique qualities, particular eccentricities helped later identify Neptune and then Pluto as late as 1930.

The Hubble space telescope took this photo of 4 moons circling Uranus but it has a total of 27 moons altogether. Its mean air temperature is 76 degrees Kelvin [=4]. It has a rotation period of -0.71833 days [=22=4] in a retrograde orbit; a surface area, compared to Earth of 15.88 [22=4]; and a mean radius of 25,557.25km [31=4]. In the lower segment

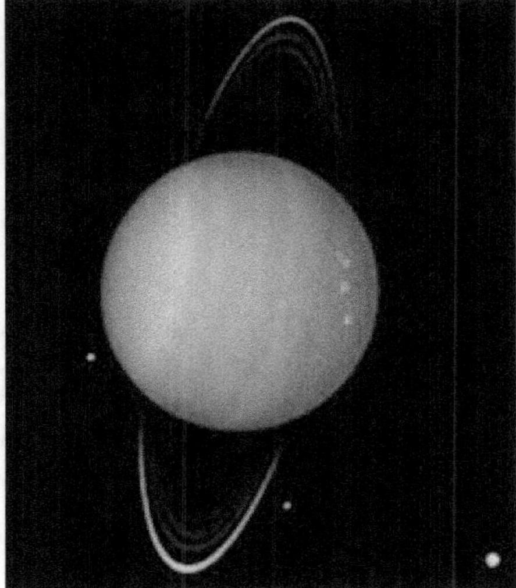

of the photo 4 rings can be identified. Uranus is a strong Sphere 4 planetary representative.

5.   Communication - Mercury   The angle of inclination is negligible. Its proximity to the Sun makes observation very difficult except in the early morning and early evening. Mass = 0.05 of Earth and the maximum surface temperature is about 410 degrees C [5]; it also has a density of about 5 g/cm^3. This compares to Earth having a density of 5.5g/cm^3. Oddly this is the reverse figure of our mass difference.

The light strip on the dextro side of the photo is due to areas in the composite photo that have not been completed. Mercury is the representative for Sphere 5.

6. Love - Venus   The axial tilt of Venus is 177 [15=6]. The average distance from the Sun is 67,200,000 miles. [6+7+2=15=6]. It has a mean orbital speed of 35.0214 km/sec [15=6]. Venus is almost the twin of Earth in mass and size and it is our nearest planet at the closest it can approach us, 24 million miles [6 again].

Venus is named after the goddess of Love & Beauty.

Apart from the Sun and the Moon, planet Venus is our third luminary in the sky and our planetary representative for Sphere 6 Love.

7. Mystery - Neptune   The volume of Neptune, compared to Earth is 61 times [6+1=7]. It surface area compared to Earth is 15.1 [7] and a total of 7,700 million km^2. Significantly it has a radius of 24,766.36 km [34=7]; and a mean distance from the Sun of 4,498,252,900 km [43=7]. This is evidently a planet that goes through mysterious changes – note the development of the white areas in the southern latitudes.

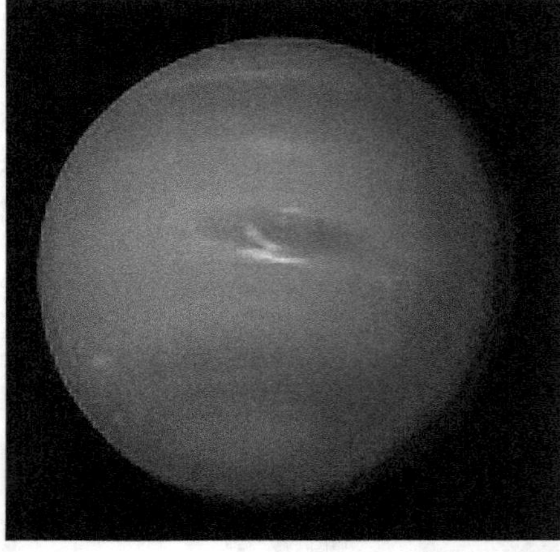

8. Partnerships – Saturn   26.7 degrees = angle of inclination; and most remarkable

for its distinctive rings as illustrated below. Its angle of inclination is perfect for love [2+6+7=15=6] and

we all appreciate how vital this is for any effective Partnership. There is evidently a Partnership between the rings and this beautiful planet.

Saturn has a mean radius of 60,267.14 km [26=8]; relative to Earth, Saturn's radius is 9.449 [26=8] times; it has a volume of 8.27 x 10^{14} [17=8]; and a surface area of 44,000 million km^2 [8 again]. Saturn is the strong planetary representative for Sphere 8 Partnerships.

9. Foundation – Mars Mars has a radius about half that of Earth = 0.53226 [18=9]; a surface area of 0.2745 [18=9] relative to Earth; and a planetary discriminant of 1.8×10^5 [9 again].

Mars has been known as the Red Planet since antiquity.

The NASA photo shows a full rotation of Mars. The white areas in the North/top are Ice.

Some ancient beliefs are that Egyptian civilization began when people from Mars escaped a major collision with a comet that on collision tore off a tectonic plate the size of Europe and so created the asteroid belt and several of our regularly visiting comets. Current evidence is uncertain about whether life once existed on Mars and despite numerous space probes to the planet it will probably be a decade before the question of life is determined. Some speculation included "Pyramid like structures" on Mars.

Whilst these planets are the largest bodies in our solar system there is also Pluto [about the size of our Moon], comets, meteors and asteroids but these bodies have not been given in the Chaldean system that includes only nine primary influences.

Knowledge of Pluto probably did not exist before about 1930 but speculation about mystery planets was rife throughout the ages. Even currently there is dispute about whether Pluto is a planet or a wandering moon. It is currently classified as a Dwarf Planet along with Eris [larger] and Ceres [smaller].

If we are able to put a boundary on the size of our solar system, you might be able to use the orbit of the great comets that are estimated to travel a distance of 2 light years before returning to Sun. So our Solar System is vast indeed. And the position of the planets and the way they are inclined, exerts measurable influences.

Oh Yes, and what do you think is the angle of inclination of Earth? It could just be a Royal Star of Lion Communication trick but it is 23 degrees! A good sign you could say that we are right to consider the angle of inclination of each axis. Saturn's inclination is 26.7 degrees, our representative planet for Sphere 8 Partnerships. 2+6, is a journey into

Partnerships: Yes, but with some Mystery added that is also a journey into Love [8+7 = 15 = 6]. No one who has truly Loved has done so without a Partner. Self-love may be a vital ingredient but to truly love another and to be loved by another is a Mystery of cosmic proportion! Love is definitely the essential ingredient in Creating new life! And Jupiter [Sphere 3] has an axial tilt of 3 degrees and Venus [Sphere 6] has an axial tilt of 177 degrees [15=6]. Evidently the way in which the planets are inclined has relevance for our nine spheres.

(3) Spiral and the Archetypes as Patrons of the Wisdom Paths.

From the figure of the Virtues of the Nine Spheres above, each of the respective Wisdom Paths are identified along with the relevant Archetype except for Sphere 2 Sensitive, whose celestial body is the Moon.

An appropriate allocation here could be Artemis or Diana who was the twin sister of Apollo who is in Sphere 1 Creative [Sun]. According to Greek mythology they were both born on the island of Delos. Diana lived in the woods and was known as the huntress and as Diana of the Hind because she was kept company by a deer as shown in this exhibit – a marble statue in the Louvre in Paris.

Depending on the issues or your concerns, any Archetype may be chosen to assist you on your Wisdom Path. But you should only try to work with one Archetype at a time. If you are in doubt, as North Sages tells us, you can always depend on Mother Earth to support anyone with a somewhat sad expression!

The following part of this section (3), involves discussion of the Spiral of the Archetypes as built in the Courtyard of our home.

The outcome is lovely and the description of what is built in the spiral may assist your consideration of the Archetype most relevant to your needs. If you can excuse the pun, having something concrete to look at helps crystalize ideas. And a picture is worth a thousand words, so I have included many. [NE Bench & Pierre]

The Courtyard Spiral.

Effectively the following information is a summary of information contained in Ambrosia about the structure of the Inner World or of Psyche at the collective level.

1. Our thoughts, needs, feelings and actions on this Earth Plane have a direct relationship to reactions and interactions on the Spiritual Plane. The Courtyard Spiral reflects my long term interest in this interrelationship.

2. In exploring the nature of the interaction between these Planes, the ancient Chinese Sage, Lao Tzu, identified the key elements, attributes and structure of what he called the Lou Shu or Inner World Arrangement. This interacted with the Outer World. Lao Tzu was a contemporary of Confucius and they are believed to have worked together on what today is known as The "I Ching" or Book of Changes. We are direct beneficiaries of their work.

3. In 20+ years of working with the spiral and Inner World Arrangement of the Archetypes, I have come to many conclusions about the structure landscaped into the gravel Courtyard. An overview of those conclusions is outlined below. Details are in "Ambrosia".

4. The Spiral is oriented to True North and not Magnetic North. True North orientation is set by the shadow cast by the mid-day Sun – allowing for the exact longitudinal time difference in this location. [Magnetic North varies by about 4 degrees. True North never varies.]

5. In the Southern Hemisphere, the midday sun is in the North but in the Northern Hemisphere when the Druids faced the mid day sun, they were facing South. So the Sun rose on their left hand and set on their right – invoking was clockwise. The opposite is true in the Southern Hemisphere when we are facing North. The Sun rises on our right and sets on our left hand so invoking is anti-clockwise. Our Spiral is set out "sunwise" or anti-clockwise.

6. Many features of the property suggest that the Spiral is exactly located in the right spot. This in turn has led to the development of further relevant features to complete the picture.

7. There are 9 Primary Ordinal Positions [normal compass points] marked in the Courtyard Spiral – each of them having "Attributes and Virtues". All of this information has been derived from Archetypes. This is what they are saying about themselves and what they are each on about.

Position	Attributes	Virtues	Colour
Centre	The One	Love and Beauty,	Red/Green
North	Fire	Light, North Sages, Zeus	Yellow/White
South	Water	Foundation, Woden, Whales	Red/Black
East	Neb	Pan. Birth, Beginnings,	Orange/Green
West	Node	Death, Endings, Transform	Brown/Green
North East	Bench	Court, Judgement	Blue/ Yellow
South West	Steerer	Guidance, Light in the storm	Blue/Violet
North West	Earth	Mother, Receptive	Blue/Green
South East	Spirit	Father, Mystery, Blessings	White/Violet

How it all began – the story behind the stones and their positions.

Starting with an interest in Western and Eastern philosophy, I was attracted to Chinese ancient wisdom of Lao Tzu as mentioned before. I perused his works from the exercise of Tai Chi and his writings that included the Lou Shu or Inner World Arrangement. What has been built in the Courtyard has many systematic similarities with this ancient work by Lao Tzu.

In the first place the Lou Shu identified Fire in the South and Water in the North. But from my reading in Celtic and Druid practices it was clear that the Northern Hemisphere was as different physically as it is spiritually in a number of systematic ways eg., the Corriolis effect seen at the Equator of Earth.

As noted earlier, in the Southern Hemisphere, Fire [as per the midday Sun] is in the North and Water is in the South.

So very importantly, when you face the midday Sun you have the East on your Right Hand and the setting Sun will be on your Left Hand. So being, to invoke is an anti-clockwise movement. Our Spiral is set out to invoke Universe as a Druid would do as you approach THE ONE. This is to do with being active rather than passive in contemplation and reflection.

The rocks around the spiral and the guardians of each 8 ordinal position are of micatious schist – a very fine grained metamorphic rock. This has been through extreme heat. As a rule, the mossy sides of the rocks have been placed facing South and the clear sides facing North. These rocks define the lanes for the spiral of three and a half turns. This half spiral is the symbol for a spiral of 7 turns and therefore predicates that there is another dimension beyond what has been defined by the pattern. This is also true for the spiral of 7 turns predicates that there is a further or fourth dimension. Some people think the spiral represents the breathing of the cosmos. Some Neolithic people believed that a spiral of seven turns provides a cone of protection. [eg., Rollright Spiral in the UK.]

The stone that marks the Centre is white calcrete from the Big Desert region of NW Victoria. Calcrete occurs naturally in the soil here but it is usually highly weathered and unsuitable for the purpose. I collected the Central stone and the other 8 primary stones after a lovely time at my grandson's wedding. Each stone was selected for each compass point providing it had only been carved by nature. Love and Beauty were further invoked in moving the stones. The Centre stone was the last of the primary stones to come into it's final position. Using only my Right Hand it was carried anticlockwise around the spiral before sliding into the wet, soft/receptive, black, Biscay earth. Whilst the stone was settling, the apex tilted slightly North of the East West line, so the axis is "Northward".

Centre

The white central stone represents THE ONE in Universe, the Creator. The base for all these white primary stones is black earth/Biscay soil symbolizing IN-ONE. So we have symbolized the Creator/Love and the negation is the Eraser/Hates in Universe and his colour is black. The colour for Love and Beauty is Rata Red and Green. In HIS knowable form, THE ONE is Great Spirit and HIS colour is White. The White Light that shines in the darkness is in the SE as we will discuss later.

An exact line can be made between the 8 stones radiating from the Centre and oriented to True North in Universe and not the variable magnetic North.

True North

A FIRE Lantern with a burning candle in the North symbolize the Sun. It is worth several moments of reflection on what the Sun is.

Sun in our Solar System. Our Sun is about 28,000 light years from the Galactic Centre of Milky Way that has a diameter of about 100,000 light years. Milky Way is a Spiral Galaxy in which the Sun and the whole Solar system are in motion around the nucleus. Our solar system is located in a smaller spiral arm called the Local or Orion Arm which connects to the larger or more substantial inner arm – Sagittarius. That arm blocks our line of sight view of the Galactic Centre. Our Solar System takes an estimated 225 million years to complete one cycle around the Galactic Centre.

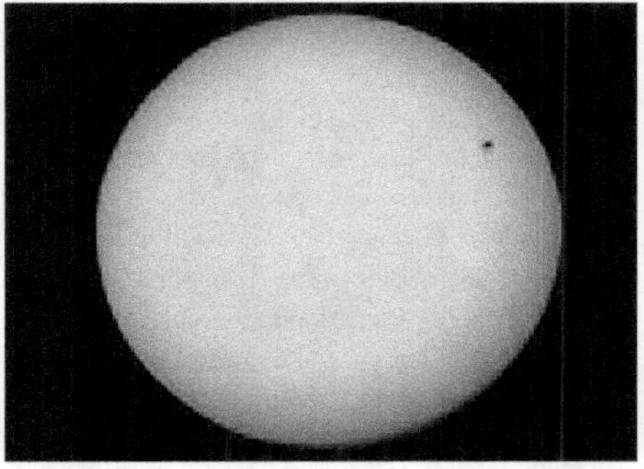

Although the Sun is a massive 1 million miles across, it is really quite small compared to some and tiny compared to some other stars in Milky Way. Betelgeux in Orion for example, is about 250 trillion miles across and emits powerful radio waves that are regularly measured on Earth. Recent estimates of the number of stars in Milky Way have been increased from 200 billion to 400 billion stars.

In the core of our Sun, at a temperature of about 14 million degrees C, in an estimated ratio of 4 hydrogen to 1 helium, the combination of these two elements occurs in an atomic reaction that creates an outer-atmosphere in the Sun's corona of 1 million degrees C. This creates exactly the "Goldilocks" ecosphere we require to survive on this planet that is 1 Astronomical Unit in distance from the Sun [149,597,870km].

Archetypes used the Periodic Table of the Elements to show that in the first period there was only THE ONE symbolized by Hydrogen and at the other end of the table was IN-ONE symbolized by Helium. Hydrogen has one electron and no nucleus, but helium has two electrons and a nucleus. What these two elements alone are able to produce is astounding! You can fairly say that since the beginning, Hydrogen and Helium are centrally important to Life, the Universe and Everything. We owe it all to ONE and IN-ONE.

In the North, three standing, guardian stones represent the North Sages. They are there as philosophers, theologians and wisdom figures from many disciples, sexes and ages. The smallest stone represents children who are also great teachers. They aim to assist us in our search for inner "Light" and "the True Way" towards "Enlightenment" and the Creative energy radiated from the Sun and released by inner and outer Peace and Love in each of us.

The area of the Courtyard to the North of the Lantern is perfect for active meditation like the practice of Tai Chi on a raked surface under a tree canopy. As Lao Tsu said, "After the Exotic comes the Laundry". So for "laundry" before and after practice comes raking the gravel yard but only as much as it is a labour of love. Maybe only the area of the trees' canopy needs to be raked?

For grass in the open, try further North on the Putting Green without any tree canopy! The Canopy of Trees is a NNW concern and especially those as large as along the Amazon and Congo Rivers. They are literally the lungs of the Earth and their protective canopy is a sheet of immense scale and importance for life.

Zeus is a very strong adherer to the Creative force – Northward. This is his domain and also the place for Pegasus and the horsepower we posses. Pegasus says, "Nay!!! Not only the horsepower!" The 7 Muses are at their source here in the Creative that has many ways to be expressed. Zeus from the North and Aesthete from the South, lovingly combine to inspire us to serve the Creation of Love and Light / Beauty, Truth and Knowledge in countless ways.

There are both SHEER and SHEET forms of Fire and Water. The flame of a candle is sheer and upward but Pentecostal Fire, or White Fire, that is seen most often by sailors when it is dancing on the surface of waves as a sheet in a storm.

White Fire can be visualized as surrounding oneself in a sheet for protection.

White Fire has also been known to dance across the floor in the See of Bishops and single out one who has strayed! They obviously need more of it!!!

Further into the garden there are Palm Trees planted in the North Line and a very large old Aloe Vera plant grows at the Entry, also a North plant. This has wonderful healing qualities [smear on raw leaf juices for instant relief in burns and rashes especially exema type skin conditions]. So someone planted it in the right place a long time ago.

See Page 153 for discussion about the North Calcrete rock.

South,

This is the place of Water and Foundation. It is about the Life Force.

On day one of digging the pond, after I had dug 6 spades full to the Right and 3 to the Left [9 for Foundation a key attribute of Water] work was delayed by rain filling and daily refilling the southern section of the first spiral turn. The remainder of the pond was dug as rain and draining permitted work. Eventually three dry days enabled digging the Dextro section from the deep East Water Gate and shallow section through to the South where it is deep again. Then rain came again and stopped work after 15 barrow loads were dug out – I love the way rain is defining the work for Water. We know that we are tuned to Universe in this. Rain totally filled the newly dug pond so we tried digging the Laevo side using the aid of water to prevent clay building up on the shovel. This had been a heavy restriction on previous work. The water worked perfectly and the rest of the pond was therefore easily outlined with a further 8 barrow loads of Biscay soil being removed. 8 is the Chaldean Numeral for the South West beside where the pond finally ends in the WSW – The Eats – the place for Feeding Fish. We have a moon shaped pond with concrete sides per favour of 5 days of fine weather. The pond has not been made any deeper for children's safety. Water feature and plants followed. The area was blessed and soon fish came.

Woden and his many sons are symbolized by the three standing/guardian stones in the South. Woden was well known for being ONE_EYED. He always has said there is THE ONE who is greater than he. Woden was also known for his "blackish" sense of humour. He is dedicated to saving souls and he has some interesting ways of describing how this is undertaken. His Saga is very long and you will see the "Blackish" humour in some of his examples and analogies. There is plenty of fun in "Whata Saga" in Ambrosia.

"Wednesdarg" means Woden's Day = Wednesday. Thor was famous for his Hammer and Thursday is his day. Tyr was lesser known for his personal sacrifice of one hand but with the other, he captured the extremely dangerous and very clever Fenris Wolf. Tuesday is named after him and for many years I fasted on Tuesdays.

In the South Pond, Seal Rock faces Northwards and is symbolic of the great navigators - Seals, Whales and Fish that are the animals of the South. The pond fish are the living symbol for all of these water creatures. Well up until the White Faced Herons find them.

Water is also the place of the Great Vases and the 1 Gallon Earthenware Jug is the symbol used for the Ewer. They have a place in our discussion of receptacles later.

The first plant for the South is the New Zealand Southern Red Rata [Metrosideros umbellate]. The flowers look very similar in structure to those of the Australian Flowering Gum seen below but the photo is not Rata Red. Rata Red flowers are the exact ones to represent the Seas of Aesthete – that are here in the South - as seen in the photo. But we are waiting on supply. Aesthete means that which inspires appreciation of beauty in the arts, poetry, woodwork, architecture etc., and any aesthetic appreciation of nature. So the Seas of Aesthete are Rata Red or the Seas may be imagined as inspiringly

beautifully covered in red floating flowers from the Rata. This is important to the many souls who have departed and come under Woden's care in the Seas of Aesthete. His second plant is the Peach Tree.

In one form, Water when SHEER is falling and fracturing, until it rises as a mist. Clouds of mist may condense and fall as rain. In the form of a SHEET, Water fills all the lowest places first and then it becomes cohesive and still: enabling the very best of reflections in sheet.

For these forms to be represented I have used a small solar cell and pump to provide a fountain to give water its two forms in the one place. A supply line also runs around to the East Water Gate from whence it falls into the pond and flows South. With an outside temperature of 2 degrees C, ice can form a perfect sheet. However, finding a way to represent the Pentecostal Fire is challenging and it is best to leave that to Great Spirit.

Woden's humorous twist to the way he treats a "Vagrant" includes by "Sheet". Anyone who has travelled the roads knows it would be very pleasant under a sheet in the Seas of Aesthete. [No blackish humour here – yet!] He also has charge of The Great Vases that can accommodate those of any particular religious Faith. Woden and his sons will do anything to save your soul in the place of Water. Thor is even known to use hammers and swages! But Woden has his ways using water as well. You could be laid down to ret [rot] the fibres that are central to your being or have you dumped in the Sewer to have any last worthy bits all saved!!! You can be assured that Woden won't miss a thing when it comes to straightening the fibres of your soul that may have become entangled during your life on Earth. He has some ingenious methods to illustrate his processes and what can occur in the Life After Life.

Yes, so Woden's oversight of Water includes charged responsibility for saving souls who end up in the Sewer!!! [You were warned about his blackish humour.] A sewer is a receptacle that has the function of gathering usually water born material and then of separating ingredients. It is also very important to the practice of making a blood sacrifice. The Sewer is the vessel that collects the Ewe blood and it is therefore integral to REDEMPTION on the spiritual plane. Maybe not so bad an idea? Of course you can also be saved in the Ewer or any one of the Great Vases.

The process of "purification" and blessing occurs in Fire and Water. Water at Christenings, birth and death rites, and in many esoteric practices and countless human indigenous rituals: means WATER is very important. So too is FIRE. One can extinguish the other and both are Northward in referencing towards THE ONE.

It is also worth noting the when water runs down a stream, it can clean itself. It's property of surface tension can strip a sheet off the surface of the whole pond. You can see any floating particles head for the overflow first. Water can also purify itself by evaporation and condensation - so leaving everything behind. For these very reasons it is perfect for blessings, cleansing and drinking.

Depending on the heat of a Fire, it can purify almost anything. The ultimate Fire is the Sun in our solar system. The second great luminary in the sky is the Moon. Both the Sun and Moon have vitally important functions eg., sunshine and tides. There are therefore two different but related aspects of North hence the division shown on the North Ordinal rock. [The division runs right through the stone – note the calcrete balls on both sides.] The

ancient Greeks depicted this relationship by Apollo [Sun] and Artemis [Moon] being twins – one male and the other female. [See later discussion page 153].

In a serious moment, Woden explained that if people knew the difference it makes to what he can save of your soul, they would choose Water before Fire.

On the edge of the Courtyard, The South Shed faces North and it is the perfect place for more features that include Water. So we plan to build a Hot Japanese Bath and Sauna in South part of the South Shed.

Another pond will be dug to catch the overflow from the Courtyard and the Tank Farms. It will be built in the South garden – as a water-trap for golf - called Woden's Pond??!

East

The Inner World Arrangement identified Wood in the East and Metal in the West. With the knowledge that North and South had to be reversed, it seemed unlikely that East and West could be changed. However, I set out on a Vision Quest to find out what should be done about these two dimensions and so I was on a journey to the NW as an American Indigenous person would do to find a vision.

Camping in the Big Desert I drew a purpose circle and marked both Sunrise and Sunset carefully. Then I made a Fire in the North, placed a bowl of Water in the South, blessed the circle with water and waited.

The question eventually formulated as "Where is Pan?" I rose and walked due East until I suddenly knew to stop and pick up a piece of wood half buried in the sand at my feet. It was a small piece of Mallee root; but as I brushed off the sand, I was stunned by what I could see - The Two Faces of Pan. It has been sculpted by nature without horns. This side of his face seems jovial and the other is sinister. Pan is in the East but he faces Westward to THE ONE.

This wonderfully durable and naturally sculptured piece of wood is an inspirational gift from Universe. This gift was the pivotal prelude of much that was to come from the spiral work and discovery of "What The Archetypes Have To Say." [See "Psyche" and "Ambrosia".]

The East is for birth and beginnings and like water flowing from a spring it means life giving as in a seed germinating - life flows into the plant. Life also begins here at your Birth as the Cope of Heaven is in the East.

I found a very remarkable ceiling panel in Napoleon's apartment at the Versailes France. It shows babies climbing down through a Laurel tree [Eternal Love] to Earth whilst Pan is playing his 7 fluted Syrinx and holding a spiral in his right hand.

Pan's head also rests against the spiral. On reaching the ground, the baby is putting on a garland of Original Blessings in Red [Love] and White [Peace].

Indeed the Cope of Heaven is in the East and Pan is also there with his wonderful flutes and playing

his mournful, eternal love themes to Syrinx as the Reeds in the ESE.

This is also the sharp or pointed end, hence it is the NEB. Like a bud, it is the source of new growth. It's opposite is in the West that is the NODE or receptive

end of the spectrum. The tree for the NEB is the Pine Tree. And two Pencil Pines are already well established in the East of the Courtyard and were planted by the first owners. I deliberately chose the centre of the pines for the centre of the spiral. But that also works well with many other things that past owners have done. This will be noted as we go.

The Vegi Garden fence is due East from the spiral where we constantly generate fresh organic produce.

West

The West is for endings, the setting Sun, death, transformation and decline; the decay cycles and purification or refinement processes [as used for making metal] all included.

When you eventually pass through the West Gate, you will encounter Astronomer Ger, the Master of precision in determining your Right Ascension. Yes, he is German and he assesses the right time and place for endings and will ensure you are re-joined with any body parts that had been removed since birth. His job is to assess how well you have followed your "Blueprint" and used your Original Blessings given to you at birth.

Immediately West of the Centre is our Workshop – green door closed. Then to the WSW there is the Aviary and the white doors of the Shed office in the SW.

South East

At a later date I was again on my own on a Vision Quest when I asked "Although Great Spirit is everywhere, where is the Gentle Wind?' As I sat by my tiny fire pit, long after dark, I heard an Emu moving in the bush nearby. I kept completely still whilst it came up behind me and I could hear the diaphragm vibrate as it sniffed me and I felt it's breath on my neck between exhilarating sniffs. All this happened in the stillness and cold of desert night. Or was it the cold of Great Spirit's unseen presence? Besides, why didn't my Red Healer dog wake up in the place of Mystery?

At dawn, the Mallee trees around our small clearing were a wonder and bathed in a pulsing and radiant golden light. Whilst inspecting the circle, I found a tiny white down-feather fluttered in the SE – the place of Great Spirit. It's filaments each wavered in the slightest air eddy / the Gentle Wind indeed. It wavered like White Fire. From the three-toed Emu footprints in the sand and other signs, the White Spirit Feather was an exquisite gift from nature.

This is also the place of the Father, Original Blessings, Jesus of Nazareth, the See of Bishops and of Healing. The animal is the Deer and the colours are purple and White. The Deer is Wed to the colour RED – Love & Beauty and THE ONE. The exact red is vital to the purple being correct for the See Of Bishops. And currently it is not correctly working in the See.

My son Nicholas gave me a wonderful example of the Chaldean Tree of Life [as shown here] that is also known as the tree of Thirteen Fruits. [The importance to the ancient Jewish Kabala is discussed in the chapters in "Psyche" that relate to the Wisdom Paths.] Very few people know that the early work I was doing in researching the Wisdom Paths I had discussed in some detail with Nicholas. The original had 14 branches but we soon fixed that and the symbol was perfect with 13 branches of 7 different fruits. 10. Wheel of Fortune to Chaldeans. An inspirational gift!

Nicholas later gave me a piece of Ebony timber he found in a rare timber store. He also knew the relevance of this for the SW as you will see.

We were both vitally concerned that in calling himself Nick Phillips, he attracted Path 43. Road of Strife on the Chaldean Tree. As a 43 and having later joined the Australian Army and had a bad experience or two; or three; or four; he was discharged and without proper psychiatric care he took his own precious life and part of mine too. The same can be said for the 200 or so people who shed tears at his funeral. In the final part of the service, each person laid their Ear of Wheat on his coffin with their right hand

and blessed his journey in Eternal life, "to go in Eternal Love and Peace". This was a first for us and the church.

The Chaldean Tree belongs in the SE Place of Great Spirit. The tears we have shed for loved ones who have passed belong here as do the Tears of Easter. My personal regrets go even deeper for as Archetypes led me to find his 43 key I then failed to help him solve his own vital riddle. I failed my Sphere 7 Mystery son and he died. I also failed myself to recall the Wisdom Path Road 10 warning to me as well.

> "There is a fondness for children and young people, but often some sadness connected with a child."
>
> - Linda Goodman.

Totally shattered by his death Ashlyn and I stayed with loving friends in Woodend. After the funeral, we held a Wake for "Nick" with family and closest friends. They were many and again we used the Ear of Wheat to bless his spirit journey.

Days later and still dazed we headed back to Sydney but stopped for two nights in Wodonga. On the first night, when *the Last Post* was being played we realized the motel was beside the training camp Nicholas had been through. This was my darkest moment. Darker yet than the Darkest moments I had known. The Last Post kept saying my son was dead and reminding me of the loss of others too. WOW - The Grief for eternal loss!!!

Inspiration did come after those dark moments. However before we turn to that part of this story I think it vital that we were both warned under this Wisdom Path system and that alone makes it worth giving to you. I don't need any more proof of its importance as an analogy and guide. I only hope this is of some assistance to someone somewhere who is looking for Light in their darkness, suffering and grief.

Next morning I began to build a small shrine for Nicholas that included his photo in the SE. I used groups of river pebbles in each Primary Ordinal Position. This was the first stone replica of a spiral that I had built to depict the Inner World Arrangement. I had always used a circle previously in vision quests with Fire in the North and Water in the South.. But all the transcripts from Archetypes were on a spiral. Everything was ready for the next Last Post. Even a Red Ants hole and guardian was in the WSW. And I felt more hopeful afterwards about Nicholas finding the White Light in his "Bardo" world.

Nicholas had been aware of the major dimensions of the spiral. We had even worked happily together on resolving the position of each of the 8 Immortals of Chinese mythology. This included the meaning of why every one of them was standing on a cloud. When we explored his places of Original Blessing and the lines that emanated from the spiral at the house at the farm where I had been researching the spiral, he was elated. Arms up! He fully embraced Great Spirit and he knew this was in the place of the SE on the Inner World Arrangement [IWA].

After Wodonga, we took some time reaching home in Sydney where we had a small courtyard. In that space I built a small spiral of the IWA and used several stones from Wodonga. Several months later, my wife Ashlyn, daughter Kirrilie and I were in that courtyard and simultaneously felt Nicholas' happy presence. That was a very healing moment.

This all means that the current Courtyard Spiral is the third stone spiral replica of the IWA that I have built. I think it is becoming increasingly consistent with what Archetypes want. I am listening to them as the work evolves and I am writing this account during construction.

The rising full moon and it's reflection are seen in the SE of the pond. We had test filled the pond for the first time that day.

In the SE line of Original Blessings is an idea that Nicholas loved. Starting in the SE of the spiral and running through the front of the house, the line on the veranda is marked by the Three Fish on one and Wind Chimes on the other. The musical note to which all humans are positively tuned [Dextro] is Concert A. It can be appreciated as a healing sound for humans so I still need to listen often.

Oak trees are symbolic of Great Spirit. In ancient Druid times, no ceremony would be conducted unless "in the presence of an Oak or Holly Tree." An Oak tree is growing very slowly in the SE corner of the property – planted by a previous owner but victim to rabbits, drought and a tractor accident – it struggles on.

A standing stone on the SE boundary is for Remembering loved ones who have passed. It is dedicated "to all those for whom we have shed love's tears."

North West

Earth and the Receptive are in the NW. Where the SE is the place of the Father, so the NW is the place of the Mother. Our Blue Dot in Space.

Archetypes teasingly say that Mother Earth in the NW wants to save each and every soul with a somewhat sad expression! We can understand her sympathetic appreciation as she is bound to be sad about what we humans have done to this wonderful planet. She suffers the mining, deforestation, farming, cities, chemicals and pollution. And she is faced with changes in climate as well.

As the Receptive, Mother Earth is the womb of the Creative impulse and bound to THE ONE of Love and Beauty. I'm sure you have noticed that she radiates that love and beauty in countless ways. Mother Earth has many Archetypal duties to report as well eg., DOE Office, Graves, Ecclesiastical Rules, - See Ambrosia.

Mother Earth's symbolic plant is the twinning vine or Hop plant used to make beer. We can't legally grow it so instead we have the violet flowering Happy Wanderer in the garden and the passionfruit growing on the fence of the Dog's yard. Warnings of any confidence tricks are soon conveyed to the Hop Office of Mother Earth.

North East

Our beginnings are with some certainty about 7 of the 9 primary ordinal positions. The remaining two, NE and SW took some time to determine and so too confirmation of the whole circle of Archetypes and with them comes their story – What the Archetypes Have To Say and my story of how the information has been derived. It is now close to 20 years later that this story is being told.

In the NE is The Bench or Court and the place for Judgement. The plant is the Mickey Mouse plant that had the virtue that you can talk to it. The animal, a very spikey Echidna.

A platform, 3 rocks high, represents the Bench of the Court on the spiral.

The Ordinal rock has many intricately formed creatures and faces. None of them are carved by human hands. This is very suggestive of Judgement and care for all creatures.

It is highly significant that during an incident reported in the Transcripts, THE ONE moved to the ENE Gatt Seers [possibly for information] and then to the NE Bench where HE SAT.

And we often see THE ONE has interjected in many places in the spiral so it is probably fair to say that HIS allocation should be everywhere like Hydrogen is in water and in our bodies water. HE is there already in you and me on this Earth plane. Can you wonder why Archetypes call you and me Sanctitas Vestra when our bodies are 95 - 98% composed of water?

Further afield in the North East forest, a Bench is provided for reflection.

South West.

In the Transcripts there are two names given in the SW. Steerer and Three Tree. I have chosen Steerer because she provides Guidance both on the Earth Plane and in the IWA we gain access to how she directs / guides during one of Woden's sort of "Mad Hatter Egrets Tea Parties". And yes the humour is "blackish" with pain, fun and insight into his analogy!

Three Tree does have three trees: Ebony with very dense/hard, black and rare timber; Penda that is a tropical tree; and the Ben Tree that has fantastic nutritional value. [Consider just three findings; the leaves of Moliferous have 16 times as much Vitamin A as Carrots, 25 times the iron in spinach and twice the protein in eggs!] OH HOO! What great idea in order to feed the dining room children and people in desperate health from malnutrition. Three Tree says to only use a pinch in regular meals. A Pinch. The leaves are loaded also with amino acids we need and anti-oxidants as well. Research in Switzerland proved the seeds could be used to purify water instead of chemicals! The Ben tree is a treasure house of virtues.

Steerer uses the Three Trees for her Guidance and other IWA functions. She says she is set because she has a receipt for the Rare Art Of Erse that opens the Ear of Erse through which she can hear and see even as clearly as a sewer can see the sews.

The symbol is a lighthouse that gives a warning of rocks, so Steerer gives warnings when values are threatened. She is the "voice within".

The Shed Office is located on this line from The Centre.

A second guardian can be seen in the background in front of the cactus plants and spikey palms.

From the transcripts of "What The Archetypes Have to Say", there are eight other ordinal points having attributes and interactions as well. But something needs to be born in mind as we start this further discussion.

All of the Archetypes are working in a complex accord with each other – a series of Covenants. The ideas coming from Greek and Roman mythology, are that the deity are superior, factional, jealous, competitive, quarrelling and endlessly fighting each other. Nothing could be further from the truth here.

Archetypes work to an inclusive accord and not an exclusive code. For example, native spirituality has as much a place here as Judaism, Christian, Muslim, Nordic, Buddhist or any other religious group of Believers or Vagrants or non-believers as well. Everyone is referred to as Sanctitas Vestra – Your Holiness. At the Core is THE ONE of Love and Beauty and that radiates through all the Archetypes and Life itself.

Position	Attributes
NNE	Hoy Ferry, Hope, Blue.
ENE	Gatt Seers, Right Observation, Height.
ESE	Ever Errs/Repeated Errors, plant is the Reed.
SSE	Numerical Aperture, Tent of Meeting, Reflection, Encountering.
SSW	Dyna Pandy, Punishment.
WSW	Eats, Consumption/Deconstruction, Deep.
WNW	"E" Transcendental Constant, Calculation & Analysis.
NNW	Barn/storehouse, Abundance, plant is the Pecan nut tree.

NNE Hoy Ferry.

The Ferry or water taxi has a Ferryman who has helped many travellers in the journey Northwards when they need to cross a sea or river. This journey is full of HOPE. So the right Ferry that you should call; "HOY!" should have a blue sail or be painted **cyani/blue** and be headed NNE. You will find a great many other souls on board including ancient pharaohs who worshiped the Sun as if it were Raa. They also worshiped the Nile River and it's life-giving water and denudations of silt all included. They are all travelling to THE ONE.

SSW Dyna Pandy.

This is where serious PUNISHMENT is metered out. It is Scottish for Punishment. It is the opposite of HOPE in the hopelessness of resistance to the methods used to deliver your punishment if that is deserved. You might consider how you would cope with the supreme master of Sumo wresting. You have little or no chance even when doing your best! Pain will follow! AND then you're done for!

Beside the SSW in the SW, there are many very spikey cactus planted by previous owners is one of the worst places you would want to be caught on this place. Dyna Pandy could easily dispatch you there. And above the cactus grows a very nasty palm with spikes that provide safe nests for the very delicate Superb **Blue** Fairy Wren and his family! How lovely to have this in nature and naturally as well as symbolically – awesome! The very small bit of blue on the side could be Woden doing his best to save every soul! Even where there are thorns there is some hope Twe would say. But then he accepted that he was making a brave sacrifice for the whole of humanity as the Vikings knew it.
Of course, your deeds are weighed up by none other than Woden, so the chances of being assigned to Dyna Pandy could mean being tied and yet facing the hooves of Woden's donkey! You are going to get stashed!!!

The overflow for the pond is in Dyna Pandy and it therefore equates to the Sewer as well as Punishment.

ENE, Gatt Seers.

A Gatt is a narrow passage or path so that sight is normally limited by cliffs, as in a high mountain pass. The Gatt Seers are able to see through the high passes to the path that is taken. Narrow or in broad view they see what is going on. OBSERVATION and accurate reporting are the Gatt Seers function. You may well ask, how do the Gatt Seers See? Archetypes answer is that they see by virtue of a tree! It seems to me that the general virtue is height in this case. However trees have many further virtues beyond height eg., Oak, Pine, Palm, Pecan, Rata, Ebony, Elder, Ben, Penda, Peach, Tarata, Ash, Alder and Laurel all play different roles. So does a Stand of Trees, a Dale of Alder, A Cops and a Canopy of Trees. There are many trees and many virtues. [See Ambrosia.]

During an incident in the Transcripts, THE ONE moved and sat in the ENE with the Gatt Seers to gather information and then moved onto the NE Bench/Court – Judgement.

The ENE corner of this property is our highest point. A very wide expanse of country-side can be viewed from that point. Indeed there are surrounding hills and the established Eucalypt trees in the ENE corner can provide some additional height.

WSW, Eats.

The representative animal is the Shark and countless numbers of Garfish in a feeding shoal – a Sea of Garfish. Naturally sharp teeth fit very well into several of Woden's ingenious methods available to save your soul.

Shark says she can pick the mood of the occupant of a tinny! She is super-sensitive to someone who is feeling negative or Laevo. And when two legs are offered beside a surfboard, Shark simply prefers to take one and leave one. She says she likes to see the sudden look of surprise as someone comes back to the reality of the Here and Now moment! So she has purposeful intent beyond food.

This is also to do with the deepest places as in the sea. In contrast to the opposite in the ENE Gatt Seers where height is the virtue. Deep is the virtue here but so too is sensitivity. It is equally likely that "super-sensitivity to the mood of the occupant of the tinny" applies to the Gatt Seers as well, so the virtue of the tree will need lots of clarification before we know the answer to the Archetype's riddle at height and it's depth.

In this line we have a place to feed the fish in the pond and further away in the Aviary; food waits for the birds and fish in the Aviary ponds. Several food producing plants - strawberries, guava, grape, feijoa, blueberry and banana all grow and wait for us and the birds to Eat them. The Labrador dog, Jacques shown lying down in the right of the photo is a classic example of the Eats in a land animal that has no idea when to stop. He shows no restraint around food but evidently Shark does. She always likes to leave one leg!

ESE – Ever Errs /Reed.

The place in the spiral for the Reed is ESE in the pond. This place is characterised by Repeated Errors that warrant some further comments. When the Second Covenant was made between the Archetypes, Pan wanted to be wed to Syrinx who was a nymph of Water. She refused and so in the Transcripts she says her refusal means that she is forever in Error – Her name is Ever Errs.

In the legend, *when Pan saw Syrinx walking through the forest he fell immediately in love with her and began to pursue her. Syrinx became frightened and then as she ran away towards the river Pan caught up to her. As he put his arms around her, she was in total panic and she cried out to the water deity to Save her: "Save Me.*

*Save Me. Anyhow". Even as Pan held her she turned into a bunch of Reeds. **In** Pan's melancholy, he cut and bound 7 Reeds together and began playing his mournful music for which the Pan Flutes have been famous for thousands of years.*

Syrinx knows that she made a mistake and so she is called Ever Errs because she has always been in Error since her fright. She is beside Pan in the spiral but her mistake still affects Pan too.

As with the virtue of a tree, we find there are virtues in plants of many types. The Reed is vital too.

Further afield the Rotary Clothes Line is very much like the Merry Go Round that Syrinx is on forever.

The Rotary Clothes Line symbolizes repeated mistakes and regrets. So the Clothes Line installed by previous owners is a more sombre idea and therefore perfect for Syrinx's resigned mood. Merry is way to bright!

WNW "E" Transcendental Constant – Mathematical Calculation & Analysis.

Just as Ever Errs is a constant, "E" is the mathematical symbol for the Transcendental Constant used in cycles of growth and decay. In both we can see the consequences of certain actions. "E" is expressed as 2.7182818…………..And …. it is possible to infinity extend the number….. It is the base for natural logarithms and exponential growth. E is vital to probability theory and many branches of mathematics such as derangement, asymptotics, calculus and even normal distributions.

Her symbolic tree is the Elder or sometimes called "pipe tree". There is a vital structural characteristic of the branches of the tree as the pith in the centre is **spiral** shaped and may be quite easily removed to make a beautiful white-pipe to play. Pan Flutes are often made using an Elder. The Elder is also known as the Eternal Tree. Some mythologies hold that its timber was used for the cross on which Jesus of Nazareth was crucified. As the name Eternal Tree suggests it has the virtue of a constant. The flowers of the Elder are used for wine and the fruit for jams. A very important and useful tree.

The West Workshop also includes this line

SSE – NUMERICAL APETURE / Tent of Meeting.

Between Great Spirit and the place of Water Archetypes say there is a Numerical Aperture to THE ONE. Maybe ONE APERTURE is what they mean..

The term Tent of Meeting has historical significance. When the Hebrews made their Exodus from Egypt and wandered in the Sinai desert [about 1800 BC in the time of Moses], they carried "The Arc of the Covenant" with them. Wherever camp was established, the Arc was placed in a Tent away from the main camp. This was the original Tent of Meeting - the place to ask your questions, give thanks and pay your respects. This is the place for Encountering THE ONE.

In the SSE you will find a stone to provide a seat and another place to stand whilst you consider your purpose or reflections along the southern pond. ONE has said HE wants an I – THOU relationship with all people. He dislikes the superior airs that set HIM apart or above people. He wants an equal LOVE with Sanctitas Vestra – Your Holiness – I - THOU.

On the Southern boundary in the SSE a single Guardian rock stands. Beside this rock is where a small Retreat could be properly built.

NNW – BARN.

A Barn or Storehouse preserves Abundance and so it is about making provision for the future.

The Chief Petty Officer is in charge of the Barn.

A New Zealand Maori storehouse is called a "Whata" – a storehouse on posts. "Whata Saga" in Ambrosia will illuminate the Abundance of things to be considered in the Barn. For example, how much is going on under a rainforest canopy? The Chief Petty Officer is in charge of Canopy.

This photo shows the completed spiral looking back along the SE Line of Original Blessings and further afield to Mother Earth. The pink hue is created by river pebbles between the spiral lanes.

Hopefully Sturts Desert Pea with Red flowers will help complete the inner lanes of the spiral around ONE.

The figure below shows the Spiral and the lines of influence that radiate in 16 directions from the Centre.

ARCHETYPES IN THE SPIRAL – Southern Hemisphere.

The following figure of the Inner World Arrangement is taken from "What The Archetypes Have To Say." The Courtyard Spiral conforms to this figure.

FIGURE 3. INNER WORLD ARRANGEMENT.

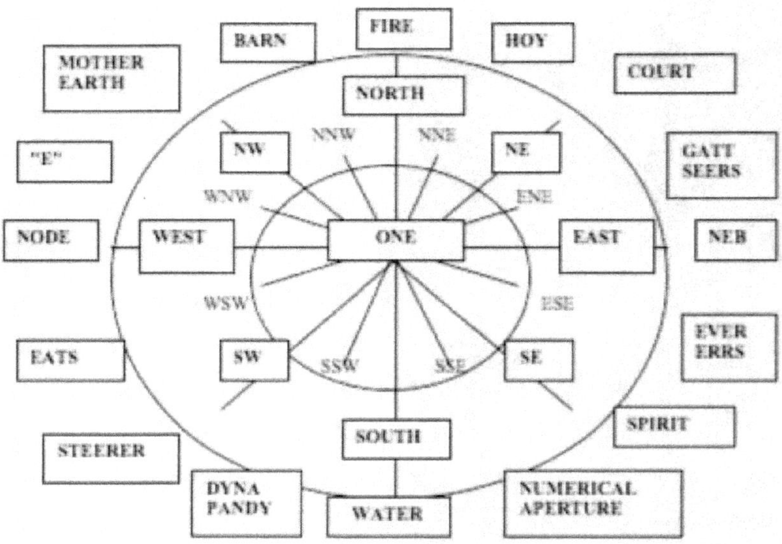

Pierre is standing in for Mother Earth – tail down and so appealing to her!

The birthday gift from Ashlyn of The Three Fish was hung on the Line of Original Blessings that runs through the house. She shows her delight!

HOUSE. Two lines continuously embrace the house and its occupants. This is a truly wonderful spectrum of blessings, energy and influences to flow in our house of Love, Beauty and Peace.

1. SE GREAT SPIRIT The Line of Original Blessings and Healing emanates from Great Spirit and runs right through the house and down to the Oak Tree and the SE Guardian on the boundary. The later is for Remembering tears shed for past loved ones.

Although Great Spirit is everywhere, this is a wonderful concentration of energy and support for everyone in their journey to realize their potential and manifest their Original Blessings given at birth but expressed or manifest in life in this house and elsewhere.

2. ESE EVER ERRS The line that emanates from Ever Errs runs diagonally through the house and out to the Rotary Clothes Line! She is there to help us deal more effectively with our repeated mistakes, bad habits, and mistakes in anything from relationships to kitchen processes. Most often the hardest part is to see our habitual mistakes and she can assist our ability to identify and overcome them. She knows how our repeated mistakes can hurt us from her own repeated experience. You may recall that she wanted to be wed to Pan eons ago but failed to act appropriately then and so is Ever in Err. But she is there to support our efforts to deal with our blind-spots and overcome our eternal errors.

Pierre standing in for the illuminated beings who sit on the Bench [3 tiers of rocks] in the Inner World Arrangement.

Is the Courtyard Spiral in the right place?

Of importance to the spiral, Past Owners have established;

1. A large Canopy of Trees in the North;
2. An Oak tree planted exactly SE;
3. Rotary Clothes Line for Ever Errs;
4. Two Pencil Pines for the East Neb;
5. House has perfect True North Orientation;
6. Aloe Vera growing at the North Entry; and
7. Large gravel Courtyard needing a turning circle, even to soften straight lines.

You could say it is a Great Mystery, but;

8. They also built excellent sheds and so our Workshop, needed for fixing things and building things [Transformation] is in the exact West of the spiral too. And the South Shed is perfect for a Hot Japanese Bath and Sauna in the place of Water.

It could be destiny? But.

9. The highest point on the property is in the ENE corner. It has an expansive view – exactly what a Gatt Seer would love. So the topography also works in favour of this being the correct FOUNDATION.

But there is one further factor;

10. Calcrete occurs naturally in these black Biscay soils. They belong together.

The location for the Courtyard Spiral seems to fit the bill. It seems like the evolving work of the Creative is coming together.

This Centre photo was taken shortly before noon and is remarkable in the White and Black dimension.

THE NORTH ROCK & TWO GREAT LUMINARIES.

The Sun and the Moon are our two great luminaries and they have different characteristics. Where the Sun is equated to the Creative, the Moon is regarded as being Sensitive. The North Ordinal rock has a divided nature that signifies this difference.

In this photo of the North side of the North Rock, you can see the crack and small calcrete balls in the crack. This calls for a moment of reflection on the formation process for calcrete.

Water born particles of calcium carbonate are deposited when the water evaporates. As with a stalagmite, over thousands of years these particles become cemented together as a rock or layer of hardpan. Calcrete usually forms in arid and semi-arid areas. This rock came from the Big Desert in NW Victoria.

If the normal process of formation continued for this rock, it would eventually have so many small calcrete balls in the crack it would then cement the two pieces together. The South face of this rock has already sealed. So this is a rock in creative formation not decomposition. Significantly the small calcrete balls are mainly on the dextro side.

In the Spiral, Archetypes can be viewed as being Laevo, Centre or Dextro. In that case, the North as Moon and Sensitive is tied to Centre with The Centre of Love and Beauty and the South of Foundation. The Dextro aspect of the Sun and Creative is then shown in the NE and is included with East Neb and the SE Spirit. There is no change in Laevo – North West Receptive, West Node and SW Guidance. This re-allocation of the Sun for Dextro and the Moon for Centre is used for the Chaldean Wisdom Paths. The ancient Greeks also made the distinctions evidently needed here. [eg., the twin brother Apollo/Sun and his twin sister Artemis/Moon.]

On completion of major works for the Courtyard Spiral, Ashlyn, Kevin and I participated in dedicating the area and granting our blessings.

"We dedicate this spiral to Eternal Love, Light and Peace of THE ONE."

We lit a candle in the North and then beginning in the East; we blessed a bowl of water taken from the pond in the name of "The Father, Son and Holy Spirit." Using the bowl I splashed water over us all and the area where we were standing. "Bless You. Bless You." Then together, we circulated three times anti-clockwise sprinkling water and giving our blessings. We made sure everything was sprinkled with water. All our blessings were given with the right hand and in a spirit of fun and laughter!

Then Universe perfected everything by giving us gentle rain in a gentle breeze!

From the transcript of the proceedings concerned with this work, Archetypes have given a number of things of importance to each Sphere. These are given together here in the table below.

(4). ELEMENTS, SPHERES AND THEIR ELECTRO-MAGNETIC FREQUENCIES.

Sphere	Archetype	Solar System	Elements	Colour	Frequ.	Music
1	Prince of Heaven	Sun	H and NaCl	Yellow	580	B/Tee
2	Artemis/Diana	Moon	Tl, K and Ca	Violet	390	G/Soo
3	Crown of Magi	Jupiter	H, Iodine	Blue/green	480	Rythmic A
4	Astronomer Ger	Uranus			Still and subdued A	
5	Royal Star of Lion	Mercury	Na	Orange	595	Silence then A
6	Magician	Venus	Mg and Fe	Green & Red	510	C/Doh
7	Great Spirit	Neptune	Oxygen		High B and D/Raa	
8	Star of Magi	Saturn		Blue/violet	440	A/Laa
9	Sceptre	Mars	Lithium	Red	625	Concert A, Raa

Whilst a number of the matters depicted in the above table may not concern you immediately, they form part of our considerations in Chapter 6 where we will discuss analysis and interpretation of your Wisdom Paths. In this chapter we will also explore a number of exercises that you can undertake to strengthen and reduce various influences.

This is entirely based on the work of Linda Goodman.

It was clear from Linda Goodman's Sun Signs that the exploration of "How Others See You" should be considered in conjunction with the full analysis of the person's Star Sign. She saw that there are a number of enhancing and inhibiting factors that affect us but that Star Signs can be allocated to each Sphere as set out in the following table.

Sphere	Resonance	Sun Sign Ruler
1	Sun	Leo
2	Moon	Cancer
3	Jupiter	Sagittarius
4	Uranus	Aquarius
5	Mercury	Gemini and Virgo
6	Venus	Taurus and Libra
7	Neptune	Pisces
8	Saturn	Capricorn
9	Mars	Aries

Linda advises that there are situations where there will be harmonization and contrast between Sphere and Sun-Sign personality. In the table below we can identify how Sphere and Sun-Sign Personality can;

    a.   Intensify each other;

    b.   Sometimes Oppose each other;

    c.   Harmonize; and

    d.   Sharply Contrast

Sphere Sun-Sign Personality will likely....

	a. Intensify	b. Sometimes Oppose	c. Harmonize	d. Sharply Contrast
1	Leo	Aquarius	Aries, Libra, Sagittarius, Gemini	Scorpio, Taurus, Virgo, Cancer, Pisces, Capricorn
2	Cancer	Capricorn	Scorpio, Virgo Pisces, Taurus	Aries, Libra, Gemini, Sagittarius, Aquarius, Leo
3	Sagittarius	Gemini	Aries, Leo, Libra, Aquarius	Pisces, Virgo, Capricorn, Scorpio, Taurus, Cancer
4	Aquarius	Leo	Gemini, Libra, Aries, Sagittarius	Scorpio, Taurus, Cancer, Virgo, Capricorn, Pisces
5	Gemini, Virgo,	Sagittarius, Pisces	Mercurial changes from moment to moment in all other Sun-Signs, sometimes c, then d.	
6	Aquarius, Taurus, Libra	Scorpio, Aries	All other Signs, sometimes c, then d.	
7	Pisces Virgo		Scorpio, Cancer, Taurus, Capricorn	Gemini, Sagittarius, Leo, Aquarius, Aries, Libra
8	Capricorn	Cancer	Pisces, Scorpio, Virgo, Taurus	Aries, Libra,Gemini,Leo, Sagittarius, Aquarius
9	Aries	Libra	Sagittarius, Leo, Gemini, Aquarius	Capricorn,Cancer, Virgo, Taurus, Scorpio, Pisces

Linda was very specific in her advice that when there is a sharp contrast as in d. above, when it surfaces on occasions in personality, the behaviour is so unusual, relative to the person's normal Sun Sign attitude that it startles others, and often surprises the person themselves!

By way of further explanation of b. [sometimes oppose] Linda says that with effort, the resonance can be used to balance the Sun-Sign nature.

7. Wisdom Paths of Ascension & Progression.

"There is a divine sequence running throughout the universe. Within and above and below the human will incessantly works the Divine Will. To come into harmony with it and thereby with all the higher laws and forces, to come then into league and to work in conjunction with them, in order that they can work in league and conjunction with us, is to come into the chain of this wonderful sequence."

Ralph Waldo Trine [Bib. 75].

In the following pages you will find the methodology by which to identify the divine sequence in your own nature. You will also find how to increase the resonance you have with the Divine Will and how to modify the frequency of your being to meet the needs you have in a way that better suits both who you are now and what you want to become.

Our analogy for Ascension & Progression Paths comes from astronomy. Archetypes equated your birth to the rising of a star. All stars have a set time and place to rise and this is called Right Ascension. Stars then have a course that they follow through the celestial sphere and a predictable time and place for setting in the West. This is termed the procession of a star but we will liken it to the progression path within a lifetime.

Essentially your Ascension Path is about the original blessings you receive at birth.

Irrespective of the sphere you are in for Ascension, everyone receives blessings of 22 Submission-Caution [Sphere 4] and 25: Discrimination and Analysis [Sphere 7]. Those definitions are to be part of your consideration of Original Blessings.

This chapter contains the tools to formulate your Wisdom Paths for Ascension and Progression as set out below in 1 and 2 respectively. Interpretation follows in section 3.

1.   ASCENSION - Sphere, Path and Period are determined by your birthday.

Your Ascension Path is set by your date of birth. Any other ascension information must be regarded as of a secondary nature, such as the name you were given at birth. Both Sphere and Path numbers can be recorded as a summary below under 1.5, as there are worksheets and rules to be taken into account for this secondary information. However your birthday is probably a straightforward calculation if your total is 52 or less. [If higher see 2.3 below.] By the addition of all the digits in a number, a condensed value is obtained. For example, if you were born on the 24th December 1961, you would write it 24-12-1961. Take the whole number for the day 24 and add it to the reduced numbers for the month and year ie., 24+3+17 = 44:. This would be your Ascension Path in Sphere 8 Partnerships. To obtain your sphere, condense the value to a single numeral between 1 and 9. 4+4=8 These two values, 44 and 8 are your wound up "numeral spring" on ascension. There are many things that can be understood by considering these numerals. 11 & 22 need special care. All other numbers are reduced first eg., Born 17/11/1961 = 8+11+17 = 36.

	Sphere	Path	Period

1.1 Your Date of Birth............................   ----   ----   ----

Your sphere and path will have a corresponding description in Chapter 5 and your period can be determined from the table at the beginning of that chapter.

Also check your day of birth path and sphere...

1.2 Full Name at Birth ....

[See 2.3 for rules and 2.7 below for Table of Name analysis.]

The full name that you were given at the time of your birth, is a secondary set of information on your ascension sphere and path. To calculate the relevant values for your name the rules needed are set out in 2.3 below. However, the Table of Name [2.7] is not needed until you begin creative diagnosis and action planning in part 3. Interpretation. Also record the name you are most often called.

1.3 Relationship to Sun sign personality.

Using your ascension sphere, you will be able to determine the degree or otherwise of harmonization with your Sun Sign. At the end of Chapter 6, you will find a table of information developed by Linda Goodman that will assist you make an assessment of the interaction between your Ascendant planet, identified here and your full Sun Sign nature that should also take your Ascendant into account.

1.4 Karmic Responsibilities.

This information and how it can be obtained is set out in interpretation, but can be determined from part 2.D. Identifying Karmic responsibility.

The following layout may assist your final summary of your Sphere and Paths of Ascension information that corresponds with the definitions in Chapter 5. Essentially you will see the range of information that can be unwound from the "numeral spring" of your birthday. As you find your pattern of virtues and responsibilities, you will more fully appreciate the original blessings of your birth [don't forget paths 22 and 25].

1.5 Summary of Ascension Information.

1.1 Sphere ____   Virtue ________________________________
     Laevo/Centre/Dextro

[birth] Path ____   Challenge ______________________________

    Period ___   Patron ___ ______________________________

       Musical note __________   Colour ____________

1.2 Sphere ____   Virtue ________________________________

[name] Path ____   Challenge ______________________________

       Patron ______________________________

       Musical note __________   Colour ____________

1.3 "Harmonization" OR "sharp contrast" with Sun Sign Personality;

1.4 Karmic Responsibility to …. And people in

Spheres...

[See 2.D and section 3 Interpretation]

In any Period 6 path there are seldom any karmic burdens.

2. PROGRESSION PATHS.

After your Ascension Path there is your Progression to consider during your current period on Earth. Whatever your past and whatever your burden or rewards, you can do something about the way that you progress. Some of those "life lessons" are indicated by the path and sphere of your Ascension. You could consider part of your progression, what you are blessed with and the way the earlier period lessons prepared you to cope with your challenges. But for convenience we are calling that your Ascension as it is "wound into your inclination and path spring". From the structure of the table of spheres and paths, the periods are applied across the same sphere, so your birth sphere will be the same in successive periods. You will therefore find that all of the information about the paths in your sphere is relevant, by period, to the wider view that needs to be taken on your progression. To differentiate, Progression Paths are about your current period. The movement from one period into a higher period, is your procession - you could say we are concerned with progress in spirit on Earth and the six periods in procession of Sanctitas Vestra.

Since birth, no doubt many things have and will draw your attention and interests in the process of clarifying or gradually acquiring an appreciation of "your unique bit of genius". Knowing the special qualities we have is one thing, but being able to display those qualities in what you do, is more difficult. You could say this is the theory - practice gap. Eg, we see others who live a lie or say one thing and do another. All of us benefit from considering how we are doing on that dimension. The problem in the theory - practice gap is that we are least effective in evaluating our practice. Other people would be least effective in evaluating your theory but they are best able to describe what they see. So sometimes what people say, can have special value in seeing what sometimes you are blinded from seeing. Everyone has their "blind spots" and they can be direct clues for you to consider. There always have been and always will be clues. There would have been special situations where you excelled, and/or times when you know "you stuffed up"! Times you know that you didn't listen to your "inner voice", when you rushed ahead without heeding your inner voice.

Because the following section contains all the rules for doing things by the Chaldean-Kabala method, it is possible you could loose sight of the central point about progression. We need to be responsive to our "inner voice" and follow our Bliss. It would be very easy to go into a routine of deduction and miss the point. And so a "blind spot" to your clues and the paralysis of analysis could inhibit your progression. On the other hand you need to actively see where you can use your "inner voice", eg, to add your interpretation to the definitions that are simply an 80% framework you can use to build your unique picture. Hopefully this tool will contribute to your self-awareness, encourage you to define what you are good at and love doing, and be part of your planning to take action to increase your happiness and bliss, now and eternally. A Big Call - too right! And well worth it. But to achieve this you will need to do your bit with the "inner voice" and following through with things that attract your interest.

What some learn from happiness and bliss, is very different from what you learn through suffering, but the same need to use your "inner voice" applies. There is a huge range between using the inner voice of intuition in something you love doing versus manifesting an inner fear. However, that is part of the spectrum in progression and we will need to face some fears as well. As we noted earlier there is a great deal that we draw to ourselves according to our Psychic drive state. This brings us squarely back to our introductory discussion of destined and self-inflicted trouble. It also raises the issue of responsibility and power to change, as we are not "just pawns in the hands of Fate." There is a balance between destined and self-inflicted trouble that may be represented by the degree to which your sphere fits who you are, or the degree to which your sphere inclines you certain ways and not others. But in which sphere does it say "blind" or "fear"? It doesn't appear as a key component of any sphere and yet it underlies all human behaviour and would be more relevant in some paths. Effectively we are therefore saying that fear is another way in which you can be inclined as part of -ID Laevo. Fear is part of the spectrum of our behaviour we need to consider in progression because it can be a huge hurdle. We will continue this discussion in 3. Interpretation but this will require you doing some work here in preparation. Eg, thinking of the most accurate descriptors of a fear you have; descriptors of a situation or key event; or this could be a phrase you use to describe "it". Later we will explore some strategies that can be used to overcome fear, karmic burden and strife. There are positive things that can be done in this process of exploring your progression, but of necessity, not all of them will be comfortable parts of the terrain to cross. Not all of them will seem blissful parts of Psyche to visit, but they like "the laundry" they must be addressed so that you can get over the hurdles and on with your bliss.

How could you determine the key words that describe the unique things about you? There are probably several words that come to mind. What does your Inner voice say? Try listing your words. If you want a prompt: "List how you think others see you now." Or finish this sentence; "The most indicative things about me are

....

A number of other "markers" on your journey may be identified as you go along, so you will need to keep track of them and do some condensing of the meaning before we get into interpretation. These markers could be a word, name, key phrase or even an event description that you know best illustrates your progression. Let's say it is going to take some effort for you to generate and then refine your markers before we can most accurately determine your Spheres and Paths of Progression. We will return to your list later, but as a common starting point for your Progression, the name you call yourself is generally a good indicator. The following may provide a summary of your initial findings.

Rules for the use of the Chaldean-Kabala Numerical Alphabet are included in 2.3 below.

	Sphere	Path
2.1 What you call yourself...	▬▬▬	▬
2.2 Other numbers and names....................................	▬▬▬	▬
such as the names at birth / business name / nickname, etc.		
....	▬▬▬	▬
eg; how would you describe your aesthetic appreciation?		
....		

2.3 Chaldean-Kabala Numerical Alphabet Rules.

The numerical alphabet is repeated here for convenience. This is just the same "one and only one to use" one that was found by Linda Goodman.

Chaldean-Kabala Numerical Alphabet.

A – 1	H – 5	O – 7	V – 6
B – 2	I – 1	P – 8	W – 6
C – 3	J – 1	Q – 1	X – 5
D – 4	K – 2	R – 2	Y – 1
E – 5	L – 3	S – 3	Z – 7
F – 8	M – 4	T – 4	
G – 3	N – 5	U - 6	

9 can not be allotted to any one letter out of respect for the sacred name for the Life Force which cannot be reduced to a single letter. [The virtue attributed to 9, Foundation, does not represent the sacred name, as a virtue it means that it is the foundation of all life and inseparable from Water. Foundation resonates with the highest levels of wisdom concerning Universe, 48.]

No numerals above 52 should be used. 52 represents the highest levels of human consciousness and spiritual wisdom. This is the limitation imposed on manifest beings in their contemplation of the divine world. "The laundry" implications are that, if the total is above 52, it must be reduced and it must remain in the same sphere as the total. This situation most often occurs when obtaining the number of one's full name or when analysing the name of a business, or a long word with a lot of F's, O's and/or P's. However, there is an exception with :53 – the path is taken as :52.

Eg.   FREDERICK DAVID STRICK
        825452132 41614 342132

	32	16	15 = 63 = 9	Foundation
Option A	5	7	6 = 18 = 9	Spiritual-Material Conflict

63 is above :52 so each of the component numerals are reduce. But if one of those component numerals is 11 or 22 then a special rule applies. This is only for **11 and 22; These two paths are only ever reduced at the last step** needed in determining the path and sphere.

Eg.   TRANSDISIAL NARGOOLIANZ PTY LTD

42153413113	51237731157		841	344	
28	42	13	11		= 94 [Rule 11, not :49]
1	6	4	11		= 22 Submission-Caution!
					= 4 Renewal!

I'm sure you would agree, this is great advice! Change the name. Actually this is not really a good example because you should not use abbreviations, the whole name and title, if any, should be used. Of course if you don't like the path indicated by the spelling of the name, you can change the spelling to your choice of path. To put it another way, some names convey something you don't want to have conveyed in the name. Considering the long term nature of a Wisdom Path, it may be appropriate to alter the name to better suit that direction. For example, if you are wrecking houses for a living, 16 Shattered Citadel may be appropriate as an image? Whilst you can change a name, you can not change the date of your birth and it is the major determinant of your Wisdom Path and the relevant sphere. Your name is most indicative of family intentions at the beginning of your life and these may not suit you any longer. Whatever you do about changing a name, the karmic lessons that initially apply will still need to be genuinely dealt with. But it is logical to change a name when it is attracting something you don't want.

For example;

	MYER EMPORIUM	COLES	COLES-MYER
	4152 54872164	37353	37353 4152
	12: + 37 = 49	:21	:21 + 12: = 33
ADDING	Proprietary Limited [as the full name or title should be used.]		
	41+ 22		
	5 + 22 = 27	= 27	= 27
TOTALS	49 + 27 = 76	:21 + 27 = 48	33 + 27 = 60
	13 + 9 = 22	3 + 9 = 12:	6 + 9 = 15:
SPHERE	2 + 2 = 4	1 + 2 = 3	1 + 5 = 6
PATH	22 Submission-Caution	12: Sacrifice-Victim	15: Magician

It is apparent that both of these great retail stores have individual names that create a negative impression but when combined as they now are in practice, the resonance is highly favourable. It should be noted that when you are finding the value for the name of a company, the full name should be used. In like manner if a personal name also has a title, the full name and title should be used to find the sphere and path. Essentially abbreviations should not be used. For example Doctor = 27 but Dr = 6, this changes the sphere from 9 to 6 so the abbreviation should not be used.

One further example may assist your appreciation of the need to use a title;

ADOLF HITLER
14738 514352
23:      20   = :43 Road of Strife

CHANCELLOR ADOLF HITLER
3515353372 = 36   23: 20 = 9 + 5 + 2 = 16 Shattered Citadel

Basically, any name, listed characteristic, trait or even a frequently used expression that you have, can be compared to a Sphere and path.

2.4 Developing a plot of your virtues.

Figure 8. Virtues of the Nine Spheres, is repeated below from chapter 4. You may find this figure useful to plot your Ascension and Progression Path information. But before you jump into doing this take a moment for reflection on the context of the process you are beginning in finding your Wisdom Path. This is not a game. You will be making your personal mark on a figure that represents the glory of your eternal being. Actually this is a startlingly important step to take don't you think? A brief word about the context of this figure may assist some understanding.

The 10 Sephiroth of the Tree of Life have been part of the Hebrew tradition for thousands of years. The Old Testament character Enoch, who we referred to before, not only recorded the numeral system of the patriarchs but he also recorded a great many details about the 10 Sephiroth of the Tree of Life and its relationship with the Watchtowers of the elements - Fire, Water, Air and Earth. Some estimates of the date of the Tree of Life are between 1500 BCE – 1900 BCE, at the latest, it was well recorded in the time of Moses. The Tree of Life is a key part of a vast theosophical and spiritual tradition. But of course the Hebrew were not the only people who applied themselves to issues of human destiny. The Ancient Egyptians, Aztec, Babylonians, Chinese, Chaldeans and Tibetans, all applied themselves to the question of human destiny. At about the same time as Moses, in 1500 BC, the Babylonian Tree of Life, depicting 13 fruits and interlocking path work, was first recorded. A great many great minds like Pythagoras, have applied themselves to the task of understanding ourselves in the context of our destiny, understanding and using our gifts, and exploring the free will we possess. But each Wisdom Path identified and described is only by analogy to your life and the first thing it does is break you into parts!

In figure 8, we have three basic divisions; Laevo is Left, there is Centre, and Dextro or Right. But here the positive axis of both Laevo and Dextro are being shown. These dimensions are fully discussed in chapter 8. It is just as well to keep in mind that this is the positive end of the measuring stick used to describe the nine virtues. As an example of this reversal factor lets take 17 Star of Magi. Uniquely, 17 has a foot in all three of these categories and the pungent negative influences in Partnership can be seen by others as very Saturn like. As you may have seen, or will see from the definitions, 37 Uniqueness, your individuality

Figure 8. Virtues of the Nine Spheres.

Sensitivity

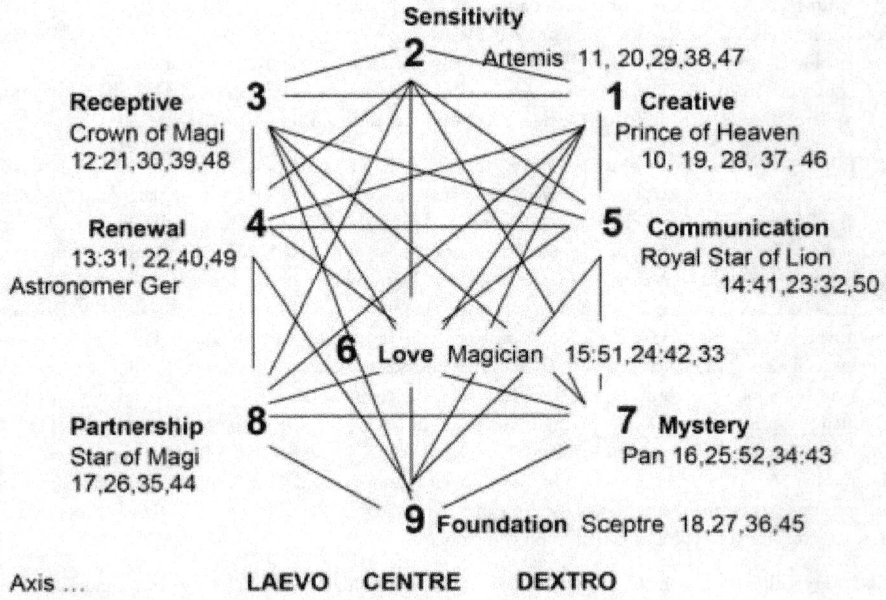

and potency is set to vary as much as DNA can vary, an entropic process. But as one can grow uniquely so one can uniquely suffer and a description such as 29 Grace Under Pressure may not seem enough recognition for what you have personally endured. So although the virtue of 2 is Sensitivity, this can have its difficulties in endurance. The other obvious 2 case is 11 Lion Muzzled. There can be long-term suffering and frustration there as well. With due respect to the feelings of those who do suffer in the ways described generally, you may be interested to know that Archetypes are not dealing with you in a category, this is only a useful cut in the spectrum for our consideration and possible use. Finally, again that reminder, what you are plotting on the figure is How Others See You. Practically this means our patterns of likes and dislikes etc., have more to do with intention or inclination, more so than chance alone would determine. So too each Wisdom Path has countless variations but several central patterns or threads [80%] to which the Chaldean and Kabala analogies apply. Obviously if and when you are ready, in figure 8 above, circle the number that corresponds with your sphere of birth.

The numeral you have circled has a name and primary attribute for your Wisdom Path. Principal Archetype is given after the name and attribute, eg., Crown of Magi. When you circle your sphere pay particular attention to the other lines connected to your path as your later research may show them to be useful secondary perspectives from which to view oneself, in the same way that one's name can be useful. However, the definition of your ascension sphere and path is the place to begin.

The name you call yourself, would make a sound place to begin your second level of analysis. You could circle that in as well, including other secondary calculations and considerations you have. When you continue with your full name you will see the vibration you were born under and how this does or doesn't accord with your birth numbers or later name changes. When calculating your ascension details, you could also note the astrological implications with any reliable astrology text. "Linda Goodman's Star Signs", provides the astrology links with the Wisdom Paths for those who are interested. This information is given at the end of Chapter 6. Historically also known as the Tree of Circles on Numbers, as you draw in the circle around each sphere you will be completing the figure, because that is how it should be drawn.

2.5 Taking "right" action is central to every person's Wisdom Path. In part, formulation of options enables relevant choices, and so the following section concerns options that may not be immediately thought of, but which might assist gaining such insight. Also provided in this section is a table on some of the attributes of each sphere that may assist your diagnostic accuracy and so the "right choices" that you make. Some details do need to be provided but they are meant as spurs to your own deduction and creativity about who you are and who you want to be, and how you can realize more of your gifts. We will start with knowing more about who you are. The first thing is your ascension details circled on Figure 8 above. For consistency sake, it helps to always put this numeral first, in diagnosis and adaptation to something that will not change. The date on which you were born is in the first place, a great blessing in the gift of life to an independent being. In much the same way, any way of giving thanks is "right action". Celebration of being is "right action". ID Dextro movement and activation involves only "right action". However, to annually celebrate your being, the number 365.2424 is very helpful, a partnership with numerals and their deeper, more esoteric meaning, concerning your eternal being, born again on that day. When you celebrate that day you can bet that it is "right action" for your spirit to celebrate on your sphere.

2.6 Name Table. Using the Chaldean-Kabala Numerical Alphabet, each letter in your name is given an equivalent numerical value as per the rules discussed at 2.3 above.

```
                                                                Path    Sphere
  8 2 5 4 5   2 1 3 2 - 4 1 6 1 4 - 3 4 2 1 3 2 = 63 : 36      9  Foundation
  F R E D E R I C K   D A V I D   S T R I C K  ⎤
  P B H M H B J G R   M I W J M   C D B J G R  ⎥  Letters of your name
   K N T N K Q L B     T J U Q T   G M K Q L B  ⎬     and letters of
     X   X   Y S         Q     Y     L     Y S  ⎥        equivalent value
             A           Y     A           A    ⎦
```

Bearing all the above considerations in mind you should be ready to finalize your Name Table, below for both Ascension and Progression. For Ascension, set out the full name you were given at birth in the same manner as for our example Fred. With your name on the second line you can allow room to put in your corresponding number values per letter above and then put the alternative letters in as well underneath your name. As you will notice, a different combination of letters can have the same frequency.

1...

2...

3...

4...

5...

6...

Ascension Name Given;   Sphere _________ Path _____
Progression Name Called;   Sphere _________ Path _____

Chaldean-Kabala Numerical Alphabet.

A – 1	H – 5	O – 7	V – 6
B – 2	I – 1	P – 8	W – 6
C – 3	J – 1	Q – 1	X – 5
D – 4	K – 2	R – 2	Y – 1
E – 5	L – 3	S – 3	Z – 7
F – 8	M – 4	T – 4	
G – 3	N – 5	U – 6	

2.7 Further Chaldean Rules for more widely based, Lexigram analysis.

The numerical alphabet was not the only tool that Linda Goodman discovered; she found that the ancients also used what they termed a Lexigram. This is also a technique that is used to analyse words and discover their latent or intrinsic meaning. It does not use the numerical alphabet. When a special word, words or a phrase are to be analysed;

1. Should you wish to analyse the name of an entity, a statement or phrase, then the words must not have 4 or more different vowels. If they do, then they should not be subject to analysis and the basis of enquiry should be simplified or clarified. Even if you have three vowels you may find analysis difficult, but it may be undertaken.

2. The same is true if there are more than 14 different letters. Eg., for Fred: A, 2C, 3D, 2E, F, 3I, 2K, 3R, S, T, V = 11 different letters, even though there are 20 letters in total. So the name may be subject to analysis.

3. In creating a Lexigram, no letter should be used more than the number of times it occurs in the original statement. Other information concerning Chaldean Lexigram rules that a letter may be used more than its occurrence,is probably unreliable.

Eg. "WHITE REEDS LAID". The idea here is to break everything down to the primary letters and their occurrences; A-1, D-2, E-3, H-1, I-2, L-1, R-1, S-1, T-1, and W-1. The next step is to generate all the new words that you can from those letters eg, seed, wade, seal, tides, whale, red, relate, relates, related, etc. Linda says you can think them up, but you will appreciate that this does not work for someone who has a "blind-spot". You simply won't think of some words, eg, aesthete, so a more reliable word generation process is to use a dictionary and simply work your way through systematically. The other thing that is necessary is to allow for the multiple definitions of words and to allow for abbreviations eg. S means South. This enables a more exact determination of the meaning of the words in the final analysis. This is no small task. It takes a lot of time and patience to even generate the words before you can begin to analyse the meaning of what you have generated. It is probable that if you used the Complete Macquarie Dictionary you could generate upward of 1500 words from the original phrase "WHITE REEDS LAID" so this is not a journey for the faint hearted and the possibilities of being overwhelmed are quite high. Lexigrams can of course be very simple and it is suggested that you start small with few letters, and with words that have been carefully considered to carry the bulk of the meaning you can apply in as few words or letters as possible. There is a strong advantage in early discrimination to find the words that best distil your known meaning or which indicate the phrase you wish to gain insight into. This may especially apply to a statement from a dream.

Linda Goodman says that once you have your list of words, inspect them and see how you can create sentences and explore some of the unexpected word combinations that bring insight. Although this is a relatively useful way of initially exploring your word list, it suffers all of the same problems encountered in word generation. It is probable you will not see certain things because of your "blind spots" and you are very likely to end up with something that simply confirms your prejudices. Again the problem is to determine a methodology that does not mean the individual imposes their constructs on the meaning that can be derived. Well at least initially. Essentially the problem can be solved by separating you from your list of words, ie., getting some detachment, and so allow meaningful chance to work its magic.

The process used in this work to obtain the spiral transcripts made extensive use of Lexigrams. In summary, the process involves writing all the words separately on small slips of paper, and then totally randomizing the order they were in. Mixing them round, paying no attention to what is what other than randomization. All the words are then loaded onto a tray. Respects are paid, requests made to understand the expression eg, "WHITE REEDS LAID", and a room is prepared with a spiral of three and one half turns laid out on the floor. The words on the tray are then thrown into the air over the spiral layout. As the white rain flutters down, words go in all directions and there is no control over what they do. Meaning is vaporised. Within seconds, all the words are back on the floor, some within the spiral and some outside it. All those outside are ignored but those that fall inside the spiral are carefully recorded in the order they appear. Words that are facing you are recorded running inwards along the lane of the spiral until reaching the centre. And then a record is made of all the words facing you in the outward journey as well. All the words that are face up and that have been recorded are then collected and the word slips that are face down are then carefully turned over to keep their original order and position. These word slips are then read in the same way as previously described.

In simple terms this is like distillation in that the meanings are all boiled off, some particles condense and fall into their respective positions on the spiral lanes on the floor, which is like a collecting vessel. Archetypes say there is surface tension in the lanes of a spiral so the words are slippery on ice When meanings are randomized and then condensed in this way, the resulting transcript is very dense and you could liken it to 100% proof, you have to add "water", expand the words again in their context with other words and their definitions. After completion of the record, what begins is the slow process of trying to understand what Archetypes are saying to you by the words they have chosen. In this way, the starting point for interpretation is not "contaminated" by your choices, prejudices and "blind-spots". If you are careful in preserving your detachment, remaining faithful to the order and meaning of words given, you will be well on the road of Light, Love and Power.

The expression "WHITE REEDS LAID", comes from the I Ching. For some reason this was often running through my mind at a time when I was exploring the use of the spiral process. As it turns out this was most fortuitous as Archetypes directed further work be undertaken and so "WHITE REEDS LAID" became the foundation for the majority of this work. In this work I have used the following statements for spiral analysis. This list will give you a sense of the unusual nature of the condensed words. Included to assist your appreciation, is the Chaldean-Kabala value for each statement.

1. WHITE REEDS LAID   49 Renewal
2. WIDER EARS   20 Awakening
3. WEEDS RED A DEER WEDS   33 Universe harmonization
4. DEW RISE RIDE 20 Awakening
5. THE GREAT WRASSE SAVES   22 Submission-Caution
6. HARVEST RAT'S AGHA 48 Crown of Magi Revealed
7. HAIL THE ONE :41 Movement…Challenge Level 2
8. ANYBODI C HOPE?   49 Renewal
9. ONE LED TREE 50 Movement…Challenge Level 3
10. SAIL LIDS LIST   30 Loner-Meditation

These statements form the basis of the Lexigram content for the Spiral Transcripts given in a separate document "Ambrosia".

The unique thing about the statements for Transcripts 7, 9, and 10 is that they were specified for analysis in the first spiral. Archetypes said LIST HAIL THE ONE, so the statement was listed, and so on. With one exception, the other statements are from expressions Archetypes used that seemed to need to be teased out. The exception was spiral 8 that comes from writing whilst on the verge of sleep! Overall, a stunningly important journey started by a nagging idea.

You may have a similar situation of a particular expression being repeated many times or of waking up and having a thought running through your mind. In the past there has been little you could do about such a situation but now there are two tools you could use. You could use the Chaldean-Kabala to analyse the statement and/or use the spiral process for a much more complex analysis. Either process can be used to assist understanding of messages that surface into consciousness from the collective Psyche. I had a simple beauty the other day when I came off the telephone and was thinking over the situation, the letters RKZ popped into my head several times, and it is true, I was acting as 11 Lion Muzzled. I had withheld my opinion when it was needed.

Should you be wondering why a Lexigram works, the answer is not "it 's a Mystery", the answer is in the name Lexigram = 23: Royal Star of Lion!

2.8   Using the Numerical-Alphabet for analysis of text.

Another form of more widely based analysis involves the analysis of text. The extra restrictions applied to Lexigrams, do not apply here, only the primary rules apply as set out in 2.3 above.

We will take as our starting point sphere 2 Sensitivity and its polar opposite Insensitivity, the later of which is reflected in 47. The word IMPENETRABILITY, is used by Humpty Dumpty to express 47. The word PONDEROUS has the same frequency and is sometimes used amongst educators to point out the advantages of education and this is how they express the idea;

"THERE IS NOTHING MORE PONDEROUS THAN THE SELF TAUGHT."
:21/3 4 30/3   18/9   47/11   15/6 14/5 19/1 23:/5

The first word THERE has a value :21 that is determined from the numerical-alphabet. This value is condensed into sphere 3 and is entered following :21. All sphere values are then added [easiest to add backwards], watching out for the 11 rule. So we obtain 11 + 36 = 47/11/2. It would not be stretching a point to conclude that the frequency of the expression equals the subject or the two are congruent and so imply agreement.

Chaldean-Kabala Numerical Alphabet.

A – 1	H – 5	O – 7	V – 6
B – 2	I – 1	P – 8	W – 6
C – 3	J – 1	Q – 1	X – 5
D – 4	K – 2	R – 2	Y – 1
E – 5	L – 3	S – 3	Z – 7
F – 8	M – 4	T – 4	
G – 3	N – 5	U - 6	

There is of course another side to the debate that can in part be expressed as follows;

"HIGHTENED SENSITIVITY CONTRIBUTES MORE TO AWARENESS
37/10   34:/7   :42/6   19/1 11 :31/4

THAN DOES EDUCATION."
15/6   19/1   36/9   Total = 11 + 44/8 = 19 Prince of Heaven.

So adding the Prince of Heaven, the statement is continued;

"ESPECIALLY WHEN ONE IS GUIDED BY THE PRINCE OF HEAVEN"
33/6   21/3 14/5 4 23/5 3 14/ 24/6 15/6 27/9 = :52

You would expect that there is nothing further to be added to this statement possibly other than to qualify that awareness concerns the search for spiritual wisdom. In doing so the circle is completed as follows;

"IN THE MYSTERIOUS SEARCH FOR SPIRITUAL WISDOM"
6 14/5 36/9   19/1 17/8 29/11 25/7 Total = 47

A further part of the debate about education could be expressed as follows.

"THE LOVE OF TWO PEOPLE CONTRIBUTES MORE TO AWARENESS
14/5 21/3 15/6 17/8 36/9   42/6   19/1 11   31/4

THAN DOES EDUCATION."
15/6 19/1   36/9   Total = 11 + 58/13 = 24: Love, Money & Creativity

Given the frequency of the statement, it seems unlikely the matter needs to be taken any further - the message and its frequency are congruent. You are bound to ask what to do about statements that are not congruent, as in the following example.

"WE ARE GUIDED BY ROYAL STAR OF LION IN THE GOLD CAULDRON
    11   8   23/5 3 14/5 10/1 15/6 16/7 6 14/5 17/8 31/4

OF PATH 46."
15/6 18/9 46/10 Total = 11 + 83 : 38 = 49

As 49 is also in the 6th period as are paths 46 [double 23:] and 50 [23: is Archetype for sphere 5], we could change the statement as follows.

"WE ARE GUIDED BY ROYAL STAR OF LION IN THE GOLD CAULDRON OF PERIOD 6.
    27/9 6 Total = 45 Sceptre

As 45 Sceptre is the Foundation for period 6, and about power, we could add either of the following;

"WHERE WE FEEL OUR POWER"
23/5 11 21/3   15/6   28/10   Total = 11 + 24 = 35: Partnership

"WHEN WE USE OUR POWER"
21/3 11 14/5 15/6   28/10   Total = 11 + 24 = 35: Partnerships

Thus we could vary our statement to reflect this use of power in partnerships.
    "IN AN ADVANCED PARTNERSHIP"
    6 6   29/11   44/8   Total = 11 + 11 = 22 + 44/8 = 30 Loner-M.

Again we have not yet achieved congruence so a further qualification is required to allow for other forms of guidance when we are meditating and obviously not restricted to period 6.
    "AND WHEN MEDITATING"
    10/1 :21/3   :32/5

Putting the whole lot together we have the following;

"WE ARE GUIDED BY ROYAL STAR OF LION IN THE GOLD CAULDRON
11   8   23/5 3 14/5 10/1 15/6 16/7 6 14/5 17/8 31/4

OF PERIOD 6, AND ALSO WHEN WE USE OUR POWER IN AN
15/6 27/9 6 10/1 14/5   21/3 11 14/5 15/6 28/10 6 6

ADVANCED PARTNERSHIP AND WHEN MEDITATING."
    29/11   44/8   10/1 21/3   33/6

Total = 11 + 11 + 11 = 33 + 139/13 = 46

Thus we are back where we started without having obtained congruence. We could change the initial statement;

"WE ARE GUIDED BY ROYAL STAR OF LION IN THE GOLD CRUCIBLE
11 8   23/5 3 14/5 10/1 15/6 16/7 6 14/5 17/8 25/7

OF PATH FORTY SIX."
15/6 18/9 22   9   Total = 11 + 22 = 33 + 85/13 = 46

Indeed we have reached congruence this time so it is worth noting that when making these statements, and there is no path name, the path numerals should be spelt out in full. The only place where this practice was followed was in Lewis Carroll's work but he gives no explanation, as we will be discussing in 3 Interpretation. As path 46 is in sphere 1 it comes directly under 19, so what happens if we substitute the name Prince of Heaven, for Royal Star of Lion?

"WE ARE GUIDED BY PRINCE OF HEAVEN IN THE GOLD
24/6 15/6 27/9 = :21

CRUCIBLE OF PATH FORTY SIX". Total = 46 - 19 + 21 = 49

Significantly we are pretty much back where we started with Royal Star of Lion, expanding to cover the whole of period 6 and allowing for advanced partnerships.

3. INTERPRETATION.

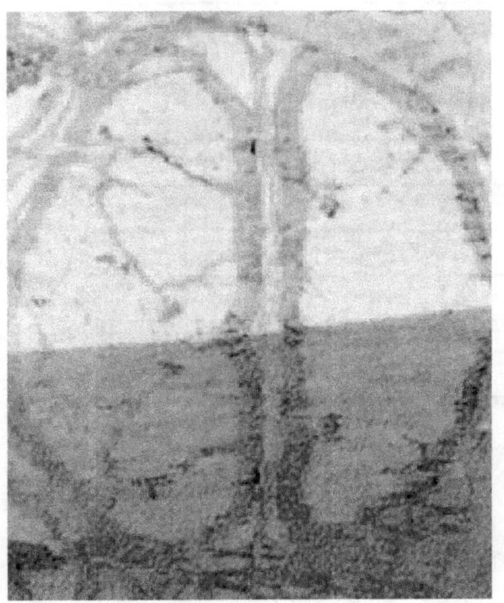

This photograph is a cross-section of highly weathered volcanic rock, reflected in the water of a pond. It perfectly represents Laevo, Centre and Dextro and the East West axis is also evident. Significantly the position of each sphere is marked almost exactly as we require. The more fractured nature of Laevo contrasts with the clarity of Dextro and you could argue the dual aspects of Star of Magi in 8 Partnership and 6 Love are shown in the South; whilst in the North, the duality of the Receptive to either Creative or Destructive forces is reflected. Don't you love the way Universe provides? What a great blessing!

At this stage it would be best to familiarize yourself with the respective definitions, beginning with the number of your birth Sphere and proceeding to the Wisdom Path number. This would also be a good time at which to research the secondary influences on your path, such as your name. Where you identify further Spheres, these may also be entered on the figure below.

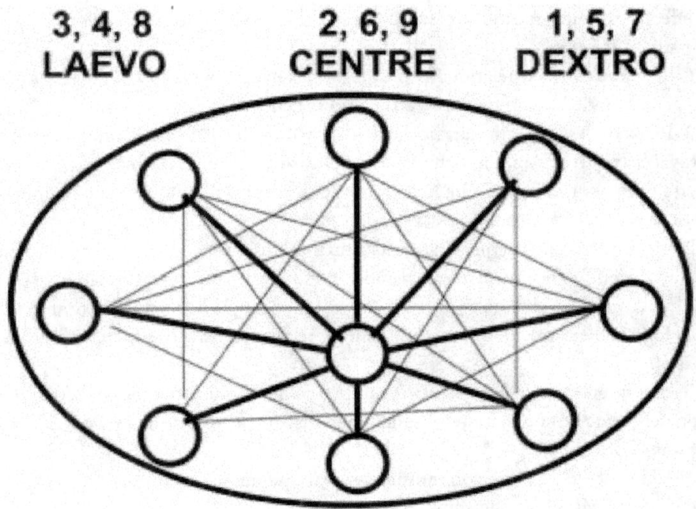

There are also18 paths affected by isomers – highlighted in the table below.

Period	Spheres of Inclination								
	H								He
1	1	2	3	4	5	6	7	8	9
2	10	11	12:	13:	14:	15:	16	17	18
3	19	20	:21	22	23:	24:	25:	26	27
4	28	29	30	:31	:32	33	34:	35:	36
5	37	38	39	40	:41	:42	:43	44	45
6	46	47	48	49	50	:51	:52	:53/3	-

Isomers. This occurs when the two paths are like a mirror image of each other. You may recall the butterflies wings are asymmetric, so for example in

12:21 the trials experienced in 12: Sacrifice / Victim, when completed successfully in one lifetime, they are matched with corresponding rewards in :21 Crown of Magi. The second path is the converse of the first.

13:31 The chaos, turmoil and unexpected surprises of 13: Regeneration and Change are matched with the converse in :31 Recluse / Hermit where you are largely alone, peaceful and unperturbed by life events to any great extent.

14:41 Movement ….Challenge in !4: involves many places, people and things. That experience can serve well in effective Communication at level 2 in the path :41. The path is different but not the converse of the earlier path.

15:51 These are converse relations as the gregarious nature of the 15: Magician is contrasted with the steadfast, single-mindedness of the :51 Warrior and the enemies this generates.

23:32 There are less trials or karmic burden carried in the 3rd Period and little or none by the 6th period. 23: Royal Star of the Lion is a path of karmic reward and promises support from high places. This is not a converse isomer but rather an augmented relationship where 23: helps :32 Communication that is widely based or it may assist the "politicians vibration" in :32.

24:42 Again we have an augmented relationship that works simply as the success of 24: Love, Money and Creativity in Period 3 is heightened considerably in :42 Love, Money and Creativity II.

25:52 Effective Discrimination and Analysis will augment :52 Mystic. As there are few karmic issues for Period 6 or for 25: they are taken as complimentary relationships. 25: is more reality based and :52 is esoterically based.

34:43 This is a reverse, converse relationship. The 34: Discrimination and Analysis II is vital to :43 Road of Strife. Serious consideration is needed in what you are doing on :43 most especially when you experience chains of disruption.

35:53/2 The secrets of mass communication and magnetic communication with the public are augmenting our :53/52.Mystic Partnerships..

What cross influences apply to your path?

The starting point to having entered your Ascension Path information, onto the mandala, is to note if it is Laevo, Centre or Dextro for the date of birth only at this stage of our discussion. Note the immediately interactive Spheres and consider the descriptions that may suit some of the people that you know have relevance to finding your path, or of even "blinding" you in some way that you allow. Besides the two adjacent spheres, amongst the most opposed of the three that Sphere fits your opposed relationships? Opposition can teach you what you are needing to remember or learn, both in Laevo and Dextro. But this is also a matter of what you are attracting to yourself, most especially if it is reinforced by your birthday or some other important Sphere. Ultimately the balance needs to be in favour of a solid Psyche Dextro for good health and proper body, mind, and spirit functioning. [See Chapter 8].

How then would you assess your overall balance on the following scale.

LAEVO   CENTRE   DEXTRO

Any secondary sphere and path information can also be drawn in and inter-relationships noted. This may include any key Progression Path information that you have derived. You may find a couple of highlighters will help you keep track of your Ascension and Progression Sphere and Path numbers. Which way does your balance lie for your Ascension Sphere; Laevo, Centre or Dextro? Do either of the secondary paths redress the balance?

- If Laevo; the left chirality of the paths may be having negative health and/or other more difficult consequences. Some tuning, by decreasing Laevo and increasing Dextro resonance will assist Dextro chirality. Some of the issues outlined in creative diagnosis below, may also assist definition of your preferred Progression Path.

- If Centre; neither Laevo not Dextro chirality is expected so it is relatively easy to tune more closely into Dextro Progression. Creative diagnosis issues outlined below may assist definition of your preferred Progression Path.

- If Dextro; this would generally indicate right chirality and a more straightforward run with things unless a karmic burden or two has caught up with you, or you think it will someday and you want to begin addressing it before it addresses you!

Amongst the further definitions given by Archetypes is a reassurance the human body has a natural resonance with the musical note called Concert A, the note all instruments are tuned too. Beginning with 9 Foundation, High A; 8 Partnerships A twice; 5 Communication says the sound of creation is the sound of Royal Star of Lion, and the sound of creation is Silence followed by A. Astronomer Ger says that the musical note he has in his 4 Sphere responds to is Subdued, sedate and even still A. And Mother Earth as a matron of this wonderful Universe, she is patron for 3 Sphere and she says that she likens Dextro A with a rhythmic beat. No other musical note was more widely discussed and there would seem to be little doubt about A, LA, in a variety of forms that are all regarded as tuned to a Dextro Psyche.

I would think it fair to assume that you do not have to wait until the next cycle of the moon [although neap tide is always a good time to do things,] but can see that some private time spent in some exploration of the musical note A, could be helpful. In the variety of ways that A can be expressed, given by Archetypes, you will most quickly aid your body's balances in right chirality. A wind-chime tuned to Concert A would soon deliver every variation of A that could be imagined. We thought that we humans were the only creatures that didn't have a sound everyone could recognize and yet it is there, it is the sound of Creation. From the silence comes the A, as the fist thing, A comes from nothing in the creation process. As far as a process of interpretation goes, some time out may be warranted to do some things and get things under your belt so to speak before we continue with the next step in interpretation.

At the next step, we will take it as read that you have completed your Wisdom Path information for Ascension and Progression;
1. explored your respective definitions;
2. analysed your "key word" statements;
3. found creative diagnosis [3.2 below] and "right action"; and
4. finally from the list of the definitions given in Chapter 5, determine your list of possibilities and select one patron from the Spiral of Archetypes with singular care.

3.1 Karmic Burden.

So far, principle attention has been on the karmic rewards, but special attention is given here to the burdens indicated by Path numbers for Ascension. The karmic rewards and burdens are identified in Chapter 5 definitions. A plot of these might be helpful on the Virtues mandala, karmic burden numbers are shown in bold;

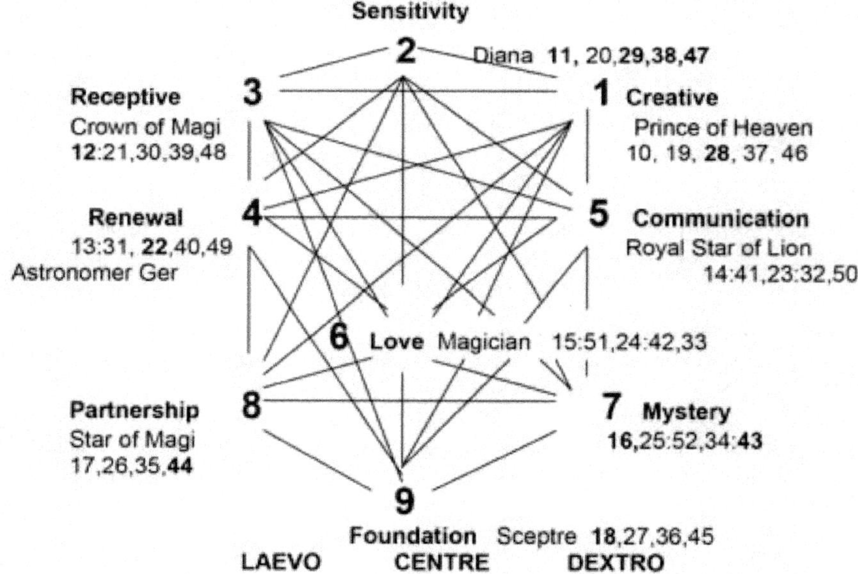

Let's leave spheres 5 & 6 out of our following discussion, as there are no indications of karmic burden associated with either sphere. [However, there are two later general issues to be dealt with at the end of this section that concern every sphere, 18, 22 and the next topic karmic responsibility.]

The first indication of burden is set by the day you were born and by the overall date of birth. The second indication is given name and name called [see Name Table.]

- Definitions given in chapter 5 give the related burdens.
- Karmic responsibility, may cast extra light on with whom, by sphere, the burden is particularly indicated.
- You are here to learn something, in your current period, 2 for 11, 12:, 16: period 3 for 22; and for period 4, 29 and so on. Note your path period, and plot your sphere on the above diagram of the virtues. Look at the interconnected spheres and plot in your karmic responsibility spheres. What does it tell you when you have both of these pieces of information together? Note which spheres are dextro in your case. Just as Job was tested for good reason, so are you. However indistinct that reason may seem, you will know exactly in the nucleus of Psyche. The dextro spheres of relevance to you should show you some of the added ways in which there are others out there who can assist you confront these testing situations and so bring them to an end. Eg, 28 requires partnerships for expression. There is a burden that underlies most spheres that has application to all paths in that sphere.
- When you are feeling tested and pressured, it is sometimes important not to do something until you have clarified your position. In being here to do something and our search for what that something is, there will be clues, most especially for those paths in later periods, such as 29. Considering the issues of right action and right timing, sometimes your uncertainty should be a Good reason for waiting, enduring, until you do know what to do and you do know the time is right.
- In completing your diagnosis, this would be a good time to note the polarity of the virtues, or spheres, on the chart you have drawn above.
- If you look carefully into the virtue that you have, you have the key to unlocking your mystery, especially when it can also be seen in converse. Eg., Sensitivity, but after a battering as 29 you may become Insensitive as 38 and especially 47 - Impenetrability. If you haven't found that key, you will need to return to Creative Diagnosis.

5th Period Paths 38, :43, and 44. The characteristics of each path are given in the definitions, but the product sphere and path is derived from a given name or some other such vital ascension information. It is possible that if you are using words other than a given name that you have not found what is vital. And need to start again. Most especially if you are concerned with :43, and you have just been "playing"! Get serious, take a step back to 34: and reassess things through a :31 process of clarification. To triumph over the burdens of 38, :43 and 44 is great! Take 44, just as Saturn can have very pungent negative influences, the Crown of Magi can offset it when you're done.

25: Discrimination and Analysis and 22 Submission-Caution are possibly not indicated by your Path numbers but this does not mean it is of no concern to you. According to Archetypes, both of these Paths underlie every path even though probably not indicated by your Sphere. You can appreciate it underlies every Sphere in one way or another. It may be that you are being the persecutor with a 12: Sacrifice-Victim? Assuming your familiarity with both 22 and 25: definitions, it needs to be said that whilst these paths may be considered to carry a karmic burden, they are also Great Paths. One further path can be considered relevant to all paths.

18 Spiritual-Material Conflict warrants attention too because in this Age of Aquarius your ONE-EYEDNESS will be tested –"the bait will fall lightly as on water"

JESUSOFNAZARETH			JESUSCHRIST	
1 5 3 6 3 7 8 5 1 7 1 2 5 4 5			1 5 3 6 3 3 5 2 1 3 4	
18	15	30	18	18 = 36
9	6	3 = 18	9	9 = 18

You will probably agree that both Greatness and Burden are indicated by both names for Jesus who is The Prince of Heaven in ONE Led Tree. But you will need a careful reading of the events of Easter to see the depths to which 18 Spiritual-Material Conflict can go. Consider too the part about Peter and the cock crowing. The deepest threads of destined behaviour can be seen there.

JUDAS ISCARIOT
16413 13312174
    15   = 6 + 22 = 28

As it was, Judas trusted the High Priest Caiaphas, and no wonder when the later had a 15: Magician and two 23: Royal Star of Lion on his side! With the Great number 22 in his family name and 28 Trusting Lamb, the inner voice of caution could have been relied upon to be working overtime when Judas gave in to Caiaphas' bargain. His suicide demonstrates his realization in hindsight and the 28 way he had been trapped by the plans and intrigues of others and simply failed to listen to his own inner voice. We all have to stay tuned to our Great 18 and 22 vibrations. They just might help save your life. If either of these Path numbers do have specified relevance, look out! Close attention to the definitions may assist clarifying a particular repeated difficulty.

If you were born to a path 11 or 29 in 2 Sphere, or 12: in Sphere 3, or 16 or :43 in Sphere 7, it is very probable you have something you won't want to crow about that is buried deep in your "forgotten" past. In the first place it may be noted that karmic burden is a lot more a thing of Centre 2 Sensitivity, than of either Laevo or Dextro. But being born to any of these paths means there are things to be dealt with. Having been born on the 12th myself and knowing the relevance of being a sacrifice in the plans and intrigues of others, I took a stand. If Caiaphas can make a bargain so could I, but of quite a different sort. If I had to make a sacrifice to end being used as a sacrifice then my Progression would be smoother. My bargain was that I would fast on every Tuesday for as long as it took to deal with the past burden. About four years later I learnt I need not fast on Tuesdays any more, but I never found out why. At the very least I had found one way to cleanse myself and get on with what I was "otherwise" meant to be doing. Even in a powerful recent example there was no hint of my being A Sacrifice-Victim, in fact Victory came quite against the apparent odds and most expectations, but then I know to listen to my "inner voice". And that can make all the difference anyway. As a general rule, karmic burden is best dealt with up front so that the benefits of freedom may follow.

3.2 Creative Diagnosis and Action.

Warm-Up!

Want a model for Uniqueness, try;   CHESHIRE CAT

……………………………..
Or did you wonder why the name DINAH …………. Struck terror into the mouse?
What are the beautiful qualities that draw us all in the title;

      ALICE'S ADVENTURES IN WONDERLAND

      ……………………………...   ——— ———

Maybe you have wondered about the author's name;
>   LEWIS CARROLL   ____ ____
Or why the twins, seemed so alike in
>   TWEEDLE DUM   TWEEDLE DEE
>   ....
Or WHITE RABBIT ....
Or the answer to the question   "DO CATS EAT BATS?"
....

Now if you think these are highly selective and yet wonderful examples you would only have the tiniest fraction of an idea about the stunning and deliberate mathematician's trouble that was gone to get the picture right at all levels, but especially too in the Chaldean-Kabala Numerical Alphabet sense! If you didn't work out that cats love bats, you better go read the book with the alphabet beside you! Lewis Carroll was not only a wonderful author but he was a great mathematician who had not previously been known for using the numerical alphabet, but he obviously did.

Why not try, MAD HATTER'S TEA PARTY ....

What are the path elements described in the title and depicted in the story?...............

....

....

The second title is
>   "THROUGH THE LOOKING GLASS"   ___   ___
It features a procession by
>   "THE KING AND THE QUEEN OF HEARTS."   ___   ___

Chaldean-Kabala Numerical Alphabet.

A – 1	H – 5	O – 7	V – 6
B – 2	I – 1	P – 8	W – 6
C – 3	J – 1	Q – 1	X – 5
D – 4	K – 2	R – 2	Y – 1
E – 5	L – 3	S – 3	Z – 7
F – 8	M – 4	T – 4	
G – 3	N – 5	U - 6	

NIRVANA ________   ___   ___

TSONGKHAPA ____________   ___   ___

POTALA PALACE __________   ___   ___

BUDDHA DHARMA ________   ___   ___

Back to the deliberate efforts of **Lewis Carroll**. He refers to the names he uses as Magic Names, and contrasts the real world of Alice's room and what she calls Looking Glass House, what she could see in the mirror and experience when she went through the glass and met the various characters on the other side. **Isomers**. The titles of the first two books are an example, 24: 42 Love, Money and Creativity. There are many Magic Names in these two stories alone that you could explore, we will only deal with four characters here.

Humpty-28 Dumpty-27, balanced on his narrow wall is 19 Prince of Heaven and he wanted to know where Alice was going? He had two favourite words that both total 47; "impenetrability" and "portmanteau". Even as Lewis Carroll uses Humpty-28 Dumpty-27 to define these terms there is no doubt he understands the issue of isomers and that this is precisely the point of his Looking Glass tale. A portmanteau is a bag that opens in two halves, or a word that has "two meanings wrapt up in one word". Isomers again. During their encounter, Alice asks Humpty Dumpty to explain some words used in a poem. When you have a copy of the story beside you, see how well the Chaldean meanings apply to the first and last verse;

> "T'was brillig-15 and the slithy-17 toves-25 [slithy toves condenses to : 42]
>
> Did gyre-11 and gimble-18 in the wabe-14:
>
> All mimsy-13 were the borogoves-42,
>
> And the mome-21 raths-15 outgrabe-34."

Without spoiling your fun too much, take "gyre", as Humpty Dumpty explains is "to go round and round like a gyroscope." Very much the attribute of 11 Lion Muzzled. The first two lines have a total of 18 Spiritual-Material conflict, the characteristic of which is gimble, meaning to make holes. The second two lines mean 35 Partnerships as does the stanza overall.

Queen 22 Submission-Caution! She had three favourite expressions that she used with great frequency during the croquet game;

> "OFF WITH HIS HEAD" - 27 Sceptre: power of life and death.
>
> "OFF WITH HER HEAD" - : 21 Crown of Magi
>
> "OFF WITH THEIR HEADS" - 27

This is a significant depiction of the Queen as the primary wielder of negative futures and the King as exhibiting more compassion. But together, as the Queen orders the executions, the King, in the Queen's absence, pardons all the players in the end. THE KING AND THE QUEEN OF HEARTS - : 42 Love, Money and Creativity. KING-11, QUEEN 22 = 33 = 6 Love and 33 for RED QUEEN. However, the WHITE QUEEN = 25: Discrimination and Analysis and the WHITE KING AND QUEEN = 37 = Sphere 1. The image of Osiris and Isis behind these two later characters is evident also.

The Three Gardeners; Five, Seven and Two, wear Hearts on their backs and Spades on the front, they begin with a discussion about the characteristic of spade 5 people - they are super critical of themselves and others. You can see for yourself what else the author thought about the other spheres. Interrupted when sighting Alice, but keeping guard for warning of the Queen, they expect to encounter the Queen's wrath for having been caught painting white roses, red. Then comes the warning;

"THE QUEEN! THE QUEEN! AND THE THREE GARDENERS INSTANTLY

14	22	14	22	10	14	21	30	27
5	22	5	22	1	5	3	3	9

THREW THEMSELVES FLAT UPON THEIR FACES."

22	43	16	26	17	20
22	7	7	8	8	2

22 22 22 63:36 = 9 + 4 + 4 + 4 = : 21 Crown of Magi..

What a 14: for our meditating gardeners with their spades reversed?! And with what power did they throw themselves on their jointly Shattered faces? All three face down on the Road of Strife. And their faces showed an Awakening to the power of the Star of Magi, no doubt a strong reference to the pungent, negative aspect of Saturn that can be directed by the planet. Lewis Carroll is describing his awareness of spheres 5, 7 and 2 and describing several interlocking paths [:43 16] and pointing to the negative aspects of Star and Crown of Magi in particular. In case you missed it at the start, but The Queen! The Queen! = 54: 45 Foundation, when repeated, the highest power of Sceptre.

Duchess-29, is constantly under pressure from cook who throws various kitchen utensils and pots at her. The Duchess completely ignores them, whether they hit her or not. She is also under threat of execution from the Queen. Her initial gruff exterior softens and she tells Alice that "Love makes the world go round". She wants us to search for the moral in everything. Certainly some of her remarkable extensions in logic will enlighten but she also says the following that has considerable relevance to our exploration of Lewis Carroll's knowledge and use of the Chaldean-Kabala system and its underpinning, "How others see you". Duchess says;
> "Be what you would seem to be.
> Or if you'd like it put more simply.
> Never imagine yourself not to be otherwise than what it might appear to others that what you were or might have been was not otherwise than what you had been would have appeared to them to be otherwise."

Alice thought she would follow it better if she had it written down. We have the privilege of having it written down, but the "simplified" bit only helps a bit in getting the drift.

Lewis Carroll's work is a remarkably clear example of the use of the intrinsic meaning conveyed by the frequency of words. It is this intrinsic quality that is measured in the Chaldean-Kabala system and it is this quality that underlies Alice and the Magic Names of the characters in her adventures. For all the consistency there is a strange thing. Red is obviously the colour for Love in an archetypal sense but it is also the colour for conflict. So it is green with a red for passion as a slash that represents Love, Money and Creativity. Lewis Carroll evidently also knew of this distinction. More than that, he points to the "portmanteau" of 17 Star of Magi and :21 Crown of Magi, or the asymmetric nature of two spheres of inclination, 8 and 3 both of which are Laevo. And by his depiction of THE QUEEN! THE QUEEN! As 45 Foundation for the Queen of Hearts that is red, it is significantly different in the second book to RED QUEEN at 33 = 6. We would therefore need to include sphere 6, Centre as also having such an asymmetric nature like spheres 8 and 3, Laevo. It should be noted that Dextro has no spheres where there is evidence of such a divided nature, except with respect to the Mercurial nature of 5. Carroll uses the three gardeners; one of which was sphere 5, but where 5, 7 and 2 do not have a divided nature. Overall, it is probably fair to say that Carroll's works reflect an understanding of the Chaldean-Kabala system and enable a deeper appreciation of some other shreds - our shreds with his shreds from a century ago, helps us remain certain we are on the right track, in more ways than one.

Incidentally, when the Mock-16 Turtle-24 sings "Beautiful, Beautiful Soup" it did mean soup made from Mock Turtle but did you notice Soup is also 24! And the moral of that... Mock Turtle Soup = 19 so it's heavenly!

What were the words you first thought of during the introduction to progression?

The indicative things about you; your "inner-voice" list; let's say 5 characteristics of you in practice - as others see you.

....
....
....
....
....

How about determining the numerical values of those characteristics? What path and sphere is indicated for each and for the total? What is most true of you in practice? What is most true of you in theory? How could you change what you do to be more consistent with your theory? What words would describe your theory? What paths and spheres do they indicate?

Name three people you admire. What are the sphere and paths of these people;

[add yours]   ....

            NELSON MANDALA

            ....

            HIS HOLINESS THE DALAI LAMA

            ....

            HELEN KELLER

            ....

The life of Helen Keller, is also one of exceptional courage, but being disabled in sight, sound and speech posed apparently insurmountable hurdles to progression. Helen's teacher, Annie Sullivan [:42] broke through that abyss to reach Helen and draw out her "little bit of genius" even if her name means :43 Road of Strife, she was Sceptre on Ascension - born to triumph.

What virtues do you attribute to those you admire? What does this tell you about your theory and practice? If you can define the positive virtues, can you define the negative aspects of your behaviour: the opposites? Maybe you could try to define the Virtues of people you detest?

Checking the definitions for a second time.

If you have completed your first reading of the respective definitions it would be appropriate to explore them again and add your interpretation. Check to see you know what the symbols mean at least in summary name eg., 28 ., to start with. In the process you will become quickly able to see the recurring threads either in the positive aspect or negative. Dextro and Laevo either positively as Virtues, or in their converse. Eg., the Laevo word "traitor" as in "Judas the Traitor", is :21 in converse, Crown of Magi reversed. As you go through the definitions, it is important to build in your own picture of how others see you. This is the creative aspect of your dextro action. Providing you don't redefine the image, you have a great deal of freedom in interpretation. Not only but also, a responsibility to add your interpretation.

One way or another everyone of us will need to strengthen either laevo or dextro at differing times, in different ways and for different reasons. Let's start this further process of diagnostic work with three ideas in mind.

a. This is about ways to increase or reinforce a particular frequency. And

b. Taking a creative approach, free-wheeling with some ideas to generate some fresh energy and open up options from which you can choose.

c. Establish some grounding and familiarity with wisdom paths so that there is more opportunity for inner voice practice and informed choices.

Why not try painting your Virtues or Challenges?

Or sketch it out! Symbolize the original blessings of your Ascension and how you have and will progress! The colour for each Sphere is given in the table in Chapter 6 and repeated below for your convenience.

Making a Concert to your Name!

Using your Table of Name [given or called] there is a musical note that can be played for each numeral-letter group. So there are an exact series of musical notes that can be played to represent the spheres in your name. A Concert to your name! Eg. FRED is 8254 = 19 = 1 and the corresponding musical notes can be determined from the table below.

		Sphere
F	8	AA
R	2	G
E	5	Silence A
D	4	Sedate A, then subdued and finally still!

Who knows when your inner voice will come to you as you play your Name Concert?

What about your Ascension Concert!

What are the musical notes for your Table of Birth?

....

If you play your notes, it must increase the activation energy of your birth and given name. But how to play? Any musical instrument will do. What about a wind-chime cut to the right notes?

TABLE OF ELEMENTS, SPHERES AND THEIR ELECTRO-MAGNETIC FREQUENCIES.

Sphere	Archetype	Solar System	Elements	Colour	Frequ.	Music
1.	Prince of Heaven	Sun	H and NaCl	Yellow	580	B/low Tee
2.	Artemis	Moon	Tl, K and Ca	Violet	390	G/Soo
3	Crown of Magi	Jupiter	H, Iodine	Blue/green	480	Rythmic A
4	Astronomer Geer	Uranus				Still and subdued A
5	Royal Star of Lion	Mercury	Na	Orange	595	Silence then A
6	Magician	Venus	Mg and Fe	Green & Red	510	C/Doh
7	Great Spirit	Neptune	Oxygen			High B and D/Raa
8	Star of Magi	Saturn		Blue/violet	440	A/Laa
9	Sceptre	Mars	Lithium	Red	625	Cncrt A, Raa

On this table, highlight your Sphere number, its musical note, graduation, element and colour. How do like Mother Earth's choice? Your Sphere's musical equivalent is played first, as your birth-day. But, if you are abbreviating in any way, you should still give your Sphere first, but it would be best not to chant to the first note of the Sphere, to avoid the risk of 9, for which there is no single letter correspondence.

Let's assume for a moment that Fred has familiarized himself with his definitions and calculation of his Right Ascension Path. The first part, 6 Sphere Love and Wisdom Path 15: Magician. Further to this, he wants to create a concert to his birth and name he only had to create the name he wants to call and the rest is easy. How could you structure a concert of your name? The following is one possibility.

Silence A is the sound of Creation so a good way to start. Then play your Ascension Sphere numeral. Then each of the corresponding notes to letters in the name, simply using the Chaldean letters to numerals key. Even using the detailed birth numerals to make up the chorus, or a section that is chanted! Have fun!

Note there is no letter correspondence for sphere 9., so no chanting, only the musical note Concert A.

It takes time, repetition, effort, and patience to establish resonance, particularly where there is something to overcome; a burden to be dealt with; or a "blind spot" to identify and deal with. None of this is achieved in five minutes. For instance, if you are thinking of changing a name, plans will need to include flyers with your new name on it, cards, emails, letters, advice of change of name to official bodies so that the resonance is increased in a wide number of ways both from and to you.

Clarifying the "Blue-print ". Information about our Original Blessings seems strangely out of place in table form but there are many bases to cover at once in tell-it-all. But that table does represent some of the blessings that have come just by birth. This Ascension Sphere and Wisdom Path represent your "original" state at birth. You could say this is the "Blue-print" against which your progression can be compared at the end of your life, or at any point in-between. The important step now would be to compare yourself to that blueprint and see what you think you need to do less of and more of. Your Ascension spheres and paths, particularly your date of birth, represent your primary blue-print.

Wonderful creative energy is released when music and chanting is involved. No doubt your Ascension information will give you keys to unlock the secret knowledge you already have within every cell of your body.

In Sanskrit, letters are written without the vowel sound that follows unless a particular sound needs to be made. Taking that principle and applying it to your Name Table you could easily create a chant, but less easily if you are going to emphasize a particular overall vibration.

For example in creating a chant to the overall vibration of 33.

Ki Ka Va Za Ha Ha Va	2 1 2 1 6 1 7 1 5 1 5 1 6 1 = 40 = 4	
Ha Vi Za	5 1 6 1 7 1 = 21 = 3	
Ha Za Ga Va	5 1 7 1 3 1 6 1 = 25 = 7	14
		33
Ra Ja Ru Wo Ne Ne Wu	2 1 1 1 2 6 6 7 5 5 5 5 6 6 = 13 = 4	
Ne Wu Ja	5 5 6 6 1 1 = 24 = 6	
Ne Zo Lu Wu	5 5 7 7 3 6 6 6 = 45 = 9	19

And so it is that we come to the end of the creative play, well no, at least not quite.

What if you don't like your "blue-print".

The first of two completely different situations, is where the "blue-print" doesn't fit with what you see about yourself. If you don't like it because it isn't true simply continue with careful determination of your Progression markers. In the other situation you don't like the "blue-print" but it is true. It may simplify some possible confusion about how others see you, to recall the first part of Duchess' advice, "Be what you would seem to be" [and not otherwise.] What happens if you take one of the virtues you see in your great people and determine its sphere and path? The importance of this is that we often see in others, a reflection of ourselves, and sometimes keys to our "little bit of genius". A list of Your Great People and their Values would pinpoint your theoretical values at least. As you set out to refine your understanding of your path of ascension, you will of necessity start with the broadest goals and then condense them to virtues. In this way you could build the starting blocks where you like but won't really deal with any Ascension issues and what you were born with was your informed choice of where to start. You chose your path. You activated your current period. If you have activated what seems like a lot of trouble, you did so for good reason. The circumstances you are now in define what you need to do. Resolve troubles.

Given that we have already discussed karmic burden under 4. Some of the remaining barriers would be to do with fear and particularly evil. Fear of Evil might be our best starting point. Human experience broadly and Archetypes advice is that Evil exists but is best dealt with by not fearing it. Fear is the mind killer and you need your mind to cope. Although as a general rule, fear is best dealt with by confronting the source of the fear and working it through, this is not suggested for Fear of Evil.

Planning your process. What if you want to decrease a frequency? [Fear of furniture, right hand turns, spiders and evil].

Assessing Your Karmic Responsibilities and Finalizing Your "blueprint" of Ascension.

Your Original Blessing is expressed in the Virtue of your sphere for your birthday. This virtue also defines an organized set of responsibilities. We don't go around with our karmic rewards and/or burdens in isolation, but rather through interaction in partnerships of all kinds and for all sorts of reasons. You could say that there are many paths on the "Tree of Life" and particular things are designed to happen, people are bound to collide with each other's lives in a vast array of ways. The generally accepted view of our karmic responsibility is to say that we have that with all people. Yes, we have and you never know the difference it sometimes makes when you express that kind word or take pains in your expression of appreciation to an apparent stranger.

But we can be much more specific than that. As you read the table below of each virtue for each sphere, you will find a list of spheres in which you can understand that you have some specific responsibility for someone, in addition to that of your own sphere. [eg., a partner or child.] So Virtues and blessings go hand in hand with responsibilities towards others.

Karmic Responsibilities - For Your Gifts and Toward Others;
Royal Star of Lion's Point of view.

With the virtue of;

1. **CREATIVE** your "best lights", inspiration and bliss in the creative, make serious demands on a range of other needs that you and others have. LIGHT and LOVE are with you and behind that the eternal flame when your creative power is expressed. Wonderful, but you may benefit from a break as :31, and doing so repeatedly may assist to bring out your strengths. Look out particularly for 27 Sceptre. In your general activity spheres, particularly note the spheres associated with your path; 3, 2, 5, 1, 4, 1, 6, 5.

2. **SENSITIVITY**, your strengths will best blossom in 26. But that is where you will be most tested. Like the phases of the Moon, your destined spheres cycle and are; 3, 5, 5, 3, 1, 4, 1, 6, 1, 4, 1.
3. **RECEPTIVE**, your strengths in Crown of Magi may blind you to 12: There is both a debt and a gift in the wonder of Universe for you to see as 39 Receptive that are connected with spheres; 2, 5, 3, 5, 8, 4, 1, 6, 5.
4. **RENEWAL.** The best way to unlock the mysteries of 4 are to be found in a pursuit of 25:52. Think of the butterflies wings, in isomers. Those with isomers to your life are in spheres; 2,5,5,5,6,1,3.
5. **COMMUNICATION.** The challenge will involve 29 Grace Under Pressure. Particular spheres of concern are; 3,7,4,4,6,5,1,3,1,4,1,7,5.
6. **LOVE.** Where-else, but to be tested in 24: and in the best be blessed by the Crown of Magi. But you have a responsibility to her as well most especially when involved with people in spheres; 3,7,6,5.
7. **MYSTERY.** Testing is 28 and your call is 20. Your critical spheres are; 4,1,3,4,5,2,1.
8. **PARTNERSHIP.** Your strengths will flourish with some help from 23: but that is also where you will see your particular karmic responsibility. Your critical spheres are; 8, 1, 2, 4, 5, 5, 2, 3, 5, 1, 8.
9. **FOUNDATION.** Always especially tested at 36. Your spheres of concern are 8, 7, 6, 5, 4, 1, 4, 1, 7, 5.

As you can see, each sphere is associated with both a virtue and particular responsibility toward another person in a different sphere. This may be someone who you have not yet met, or it may be someone you most frequently associate with. It is usually someone "special" or important in your life. These are the people that through your destiny, you are born to meet. Can you identify them and see their relationship to your path and vice versa? This list does not include the members of your family - they are givens in responsibility and expectation. So the other "special" or important people, given by their spheres, are for you to find. One may be in a sports club, church group, a work group, or at the corner-store news-agency each morning. When you follow your Bliss you will find them. As you plot these people on the mandala of the virtues, you are bound to find the pattern.

My bet is that by the time you have put that together in your Progression Plan, you will have worked out how to do the rest yourself! Save one thing, clearing up how this relates to the dimension of Transcendence in the final chapter.

Virtues of Nine Spheres

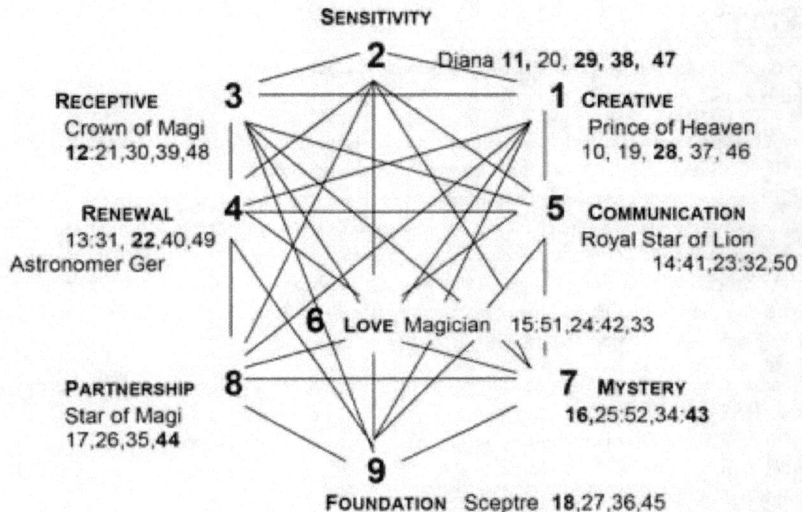

Mandala of the Nine Spheres

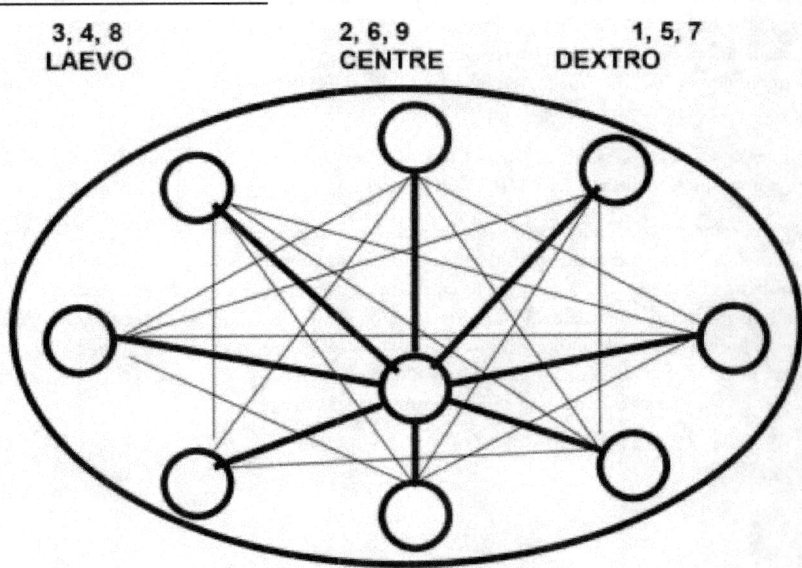

A Brief Case History – Sigmund Freud.

The purpose of this section is to highlight the interactive process that occurs between the Wisdom Paths of Ascension and Progression.
Born on 6 /5/1856 = Ascension Path :31 Regeneration and Change / Laevo.
Sigmund Freud = Progression Path :51 Warrior / Centre.

As you would expect from :31, Freud was a genius who transformed both medicine and psychology but during his long life he suffered greatly for what he believed in. Although Freud trained to be a medical practitioner some of his earliest discoveries were made in neurological research. When he began to develop an interest in his patient's symptoms he found that by asking his patients when these symptoms became manifest and exploring their earlier memories they often identified earlier events. Some of these earlier events were quite banal and neither traumatic nor pathogenic; this was the "predisposition" necessary for the later traumatic event to become pathogenic. This matter of reacting to a later event according to the earlier experience, Freud termed "regression" and it was a noteworthy discovery.

Ernest Jones extensive and very thorough biography of Freud's life and work says that it was already apparent in the mid 1880's that Freud was
> "finding himself in increasing opposition to his "respectable" colleagues".

His studies in male Hysteria; hypnotism; sexual factors and anxiety in neurosis all contributed to him being increasingly out of step with others.
> "He felt he was leading a crusade of revolution against the accepted conventions of medicine….and he accepted his mission wholeheartedly."

In one of Freud's letters to a friend, he writes;
> "I treated my discoveries as ordinary contributions to science and hoped to be met in the same spirit. But the silence with which my addresses were received, the void which formed itself about me, the insinuations that found their way back to me, caused me gradually to realize that one can not count upon views about the part played by sexuality in the etiology of neuroses meeting with the same reception as other communications."

Ernest Jones says that by "general consensus "The Interpretation of Dreams" is Freud's major work….and Freud says in his preface 'Insight such as this falls to one's lot but once in a lifetime.'

Freud's greatest pleasures included looking for mushrooms in the pine forests with his children. According to his children, Freud would creep up on the mushrooms and pounce on them with his hat! He was a very loving husband and father with a great appreciation and sensitivity to Beauty. Every bit a Sphere 6 by his name and his :51 Warrior nature evident in his devotion to his work. This is profoundly evident also in his personal life and his battle with cancer for over a decade. During this time he endured a long series of operations; he refused to take opiates, he continued his commitment to work and seeing his patients, and he is well known for never complaining about his situation. :51 to a tee.

8. The "Twin" Nature of Psyche – a new approach to the psychology of AIDS and some other diseases.

There are many trials and ways in which we suffer that have nothing to do with the deity and everything to do with the ways we are thinking and unconsciously living. However, just as with the Legend of Psyche and Cupid, we can review what "animates our being" from the perspective of the butterfly. That is, from the asymmetric structure of Psyche with ID Dextro and –ID Laevo. This discussion builds directly on Sigmund Freud's idea of the ID and of Carl Jung's idea of Psyche.

The following section is modified from "AMBROSIA" by the author and although completed in 2008 it has not been published. That document includes a long chapter on "What The Archetypes Have To Say." They have directed the content of the next section and I am essentially only the editor – a mercurial messenger.

Of very great concern to Archetypes is the 40 million people or more who are suffering with HIV and AIDS. Out of consideration for their needs this article is written on the "The Twin Nature of Psyche." The section below is an extracted from Ambrosia.

The "Twin" Nature of Psyche.

The starting point; we are each sacred beings. Whatever parts of the self come under discussion, even if we examine them as body, mind and spirit, we need to keep in mind that every part, every organ and every cell of our bodies is sacred. Whatever processes we evaluate, whatever laws of nature we discuss that apply to those processes, the central starting point is that we are a constellation of parts that make up our sacredness, your holiness, Sanctitas Vestra or Psyche.

The twin structure of Psyche is ID Dextro and –ID Laevo. Archetypes initially propose this can be imagined as two opposite faces [heads and tails] on the one coin. In Figure 1, these two aspects are shown as D and L. S [Still] represents the metal on which the faces are imprinted. The terms, Dextro and Laevo originally come from Latin and mean Right and Sinister or Left . So the primary structure of Psyche is bipolar, where right is positive and left is negative. Thus the instinctive energy of psyche in each person can be regarded as primarily having a bipolar nature where ID Dextro is right and positive, and –ID Laevo is left and negative. S [Still] is in the middle, it is neither right nor left and is neither positive nor negative but it can be imagined as the bonding agent or neutral middle ground between polar extremes but working to hold the whole nucleus together.

The terms, Dextro and Laevo are used here with the same meaning applied in modern times in organic chemistry that examines the living state. Such terms have not previously been used in discussing Psyche or ID but they are very useful in exploring this subject as you will see.

Dextro is used to indicate particles and compounds that either have a right handed structure or which have the *ability to turn light* clockwise. Laevo is used to indicate the opposite. These primary relationships are summarized in Figure 1 below. In later discussion we will build on this model and regard this primary structure as the atomic nucleus of Psyche.

Figure 1. "Twin" Nature of the Nucleus of Psyche .

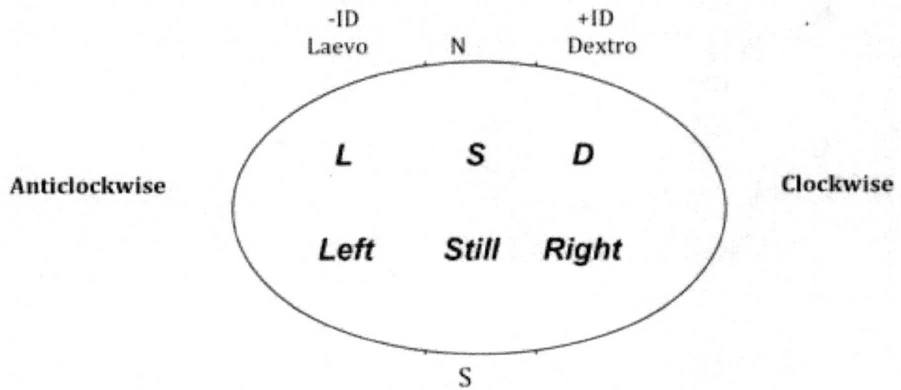

North and South pole is indicated N and S.
S – Still; indicates no movement left or right and no charge.

There are several further principles in organic chemistry that will facilitate our ongoing discussion about Psyche, so a brief summary of those principles is needed before we can move on.

Firstly, particles and compounds that have the ability to turn light clockwise or anticlockwise are highly important to an understanding of the living state. Because they are optically active substances they are referred to as optical isomers. Light from the Sun consists of electromagnetic waves vibrating in all planes; it is unpolarised. Some substances [eg., Polaroid] possess the ability to screen out all light waves except those vibrating in a particular plane. Other substances, optically active materials, have the ability to rotate the plane of polarized light. These optical isomers are identified [D or L] by their ability to rotate polarized light to the right [clockwise] or to the left [anticlockwise] respectively. How an optically active isomer behaves is illustrated in Figure 2 below.

Figure 2. Optically Active Isomers are Dextrorotatory or Laevorotatory.

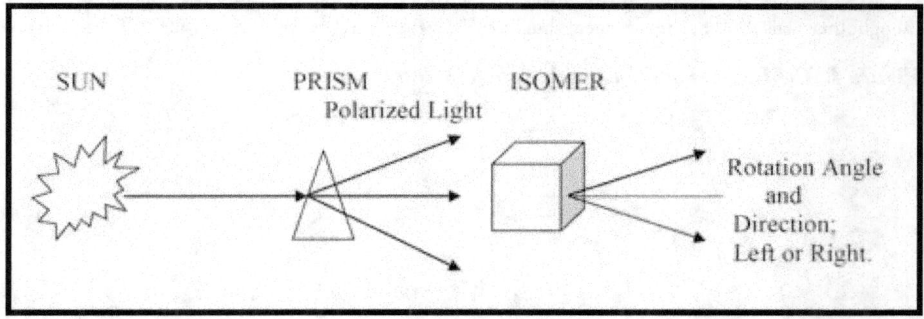

Let's say we select part of a beam of light coming through the prism, and project it through a vertical slit as a plane of light. That plane of polarized light will be affected by the isomer it enters. When it has passed through an isomer it will have been turned either left or right. The plane of light won't come out vertical. It will have been rotated. Isomers that have the ability to rotate the plane of polarized light to the right are termed Dextrorotatory [based on the Latin for right]. If they turn it left it is termed Laevorotatory [Latin for sinister or left].

The second principle in organic chemistry arises from the first and concerns the structure of an optical isomer. Archetypes begin with two examples DISSID and ALLA as in Figure 3 below.

Here, we need to leave our concept of ID Dextro and −ID Laevo being like two sides of a coin. ID Dextro could be imagined like a right hand held up to a mirror. But we can properly see that there is an isometric relationship between the two. The nucleus of Psyche can therefore more properly be viewed as ID Dextro and its mirror image [equated to −ID Laevo]. Two mirror images or isometric representations are given as examples in Figure 4 below, based upon the letters DISSID and ALLA given in the transcript. [LA is a colloquial term for "wonder, delight and surprise!"]

Figure 3. + ID Dextro and its Mirror Image are Asymmetric [-ID Laevo].

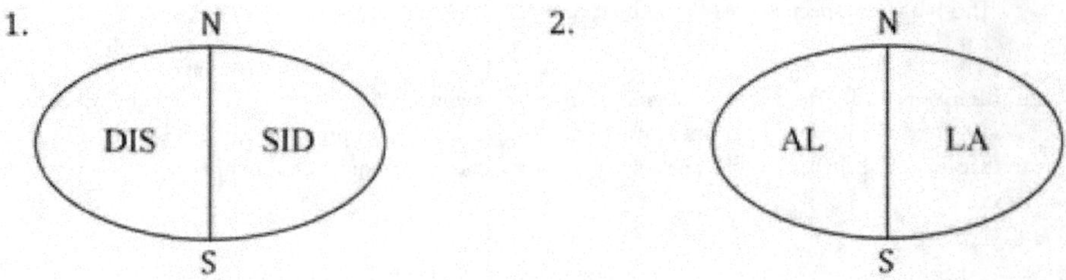

It is fair to conclude that these "Twins" are not identical but are like a right hand and its mirror image. [In order to minimize confusion, we will consistently use the term +ID Dextro to mean the right hand, and −ID Laevo to refer to the mirror image or −ID Laevo as the isomer of +ID Dextro.] So both DISSID and ALLA would be asymmetric molecules.

Later in the transcript, Archetypes specifically refer to a simple optical isomer called glyceraldehyde. See Figure 4. So an isomer is like a mirror image in that the two compounds cannot be superimposed even thought they consist of the same elements but in a vitally different, converse relationship.

Figure 4. The Isomers of Glyceraldehyde [C3H603].

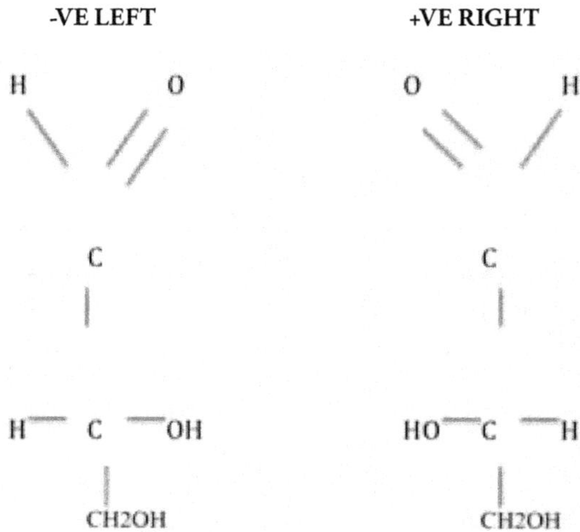

We don't have a mirror here to look at the difference between Laevo and Dextro in this molecular structure. Notice the OH is reversed as HO as in a mirror image so the two cannot be superimposed any more than a left and right hand on top of each other on the table – no fit.

Chirality is defined as the ability of an asymmetric or disymmetric molecule to turn the plane of plane-polarized light. [Greek; cheir; hand. Chiral is pronounced kye.rull]

With the sole exception of glycine, all the amino acids in the body are responsive to chirality. This is a vital aspect of the body's functioning.

Ralph Petrucci.

What this means is that from the top of your head down to your toes, your body is a chiral environment. It means +ID Dextro will bend light anticlockwise and affect all the amino acids in the body in an opposite way to that for –ID Laevo. Nearly all protein receptors in the body require an exact fit from an amino acid. See Figure 5.

Figure 5. Molecule Receptors.
Due to the lock and key mechanism, some amino acids are only being exposed to –ve Laevorotatory light, so they will not bind with some receptors.

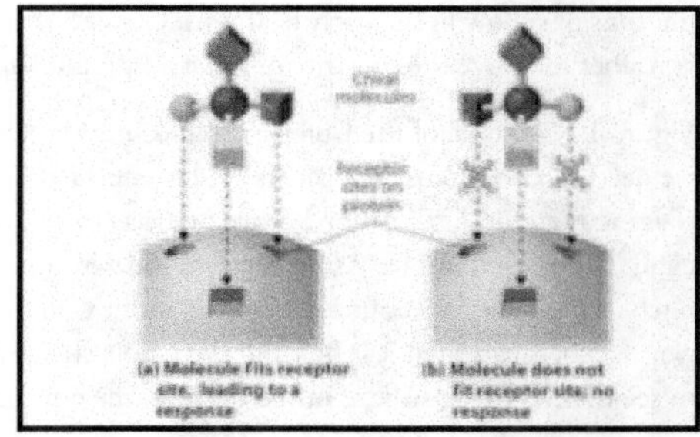

Because the Dextrorotatory responsive protein receptors are not being filled, deficiencies will develop after any extended period or environment – ie., in YOU. [If you hold a dowsing ring on a piece of cotton over someone's head you could know in two seconds what way they rotate. Or if they are Still at that point in time.] There are many avenues to still be explored. But there are many other people who are much better qualified to talk about the vast implications of this model. Certainly the lock and key aspect of molecule reception would have to be regarded as the microcosm. That really requires an examination of the cells in our body and that is better done by someone else. However it should be apparent that our model of the Nucleus of Psyche is a macro-cosm of what is happening in the micro-cosm because of the chirality of Psyche.

Isomers are also very important for the drugs we take. Many of them are based on isomers. Getting the isomer wrong can have the opposite effects to the aim of improving health [thalidomide]. Usually "side effects" point to the isomer being an incorrect matching structure [the isomer used for morning sickness caused birth defects]. Wide ranging research is going into the nature of chiral environments and isomers because they are so central to us and every living thing around us.

Given the Mercurial nature of Psyche, we can expect that when we are +ID Dextro, nearly all our amino acids will be turning the light we receive to the right and behave in an opposite fashion when we swing over into -ID Laevo. In the process, throughout the body we are taking different things from the same polarized light at different times.

The body doesn't only respond to light, it also responds to sound.

In the animal kingdom, each type of animal or bird has it's own unique call and yet to date, human kind has no such universal call. Archetypes advise us that Concert A is just such a note that resonates at the instinctive level for human kind. Being the 6th note in the musical scale and having a pitch of 440 is both real and symbolic. 6 means Love. 440 means destined difficulty doubled or having a repeated pattern of difficulty that we are destined to encounter. Concert A can be thought of as rousing the destined aspects of one's being. Native wisdom has it that sound frequencies can bring up records in the memories of ancient knowledge. Such a view is reinforced here. Playing Concert A, on any instrument, or chanting by any person may assist tapping into our ancient intuitive wisdom source. As sound is energy and that energy can affect an electro-magnetic field, Concert A will assist us to correctly balance Psyche to the right: Dextro.

In a similar way, Blue-violet light is electro-magnetic energy of radiation and it will produce the same effect as Concert A. This radiation energy of light is measured in photons and the amount of energy is proportional to the frequency of the light. Blue-violet light has a high frequency [at 440 nm], so it is more energetic than photons of yellow light [at say 600 nm]. Concert A and Blue-violet light both have the same frequency, so it is Archetypes give the specifics of Love and Light for Right instinctive energy in Psyche.

Figure 1 is a model of the Isometric Nucleus of Psyche from which we have explored Dextro and Laevo but we need to also discuss the centre we have termed Still. This simply represents the molecules in our Psyche that are not chiral. They don't move one way or the other they are more like a constant. You could say their challenge is not to move. As in an atom, the neutron [S] has no +ve or –ve charge but it is vital to keeping the nucleus together. Without a neutron an atom would fly apart. If we imagine that Still functions in the same way as a neutron then it is holding the whole structure of the nucleus of Psyche together. It is also relevant to see that by being still, as in meditating, the currents for change often emerge.

So the neutron is essential to the workings of the whole. Of all the elements there is only one that doesn't have a neutron – Hydrogen and that was given in the Transcripts as the element for ONE. The negation of ONE was termed IN-ONE and the element given was Helium and it does have a neutron. These two are the only elements in the First Period of the Periodic Table of Elements.

So what might be the neutron's composition for Psyche? An interesting possibility arises from our earlier discussion about the Virtue of the Spheres in the Centre. – 2. Sensitivity. 6. Love and 9. Foundation - it represents the Life Force. It is true that our sensitivity is increased when we are Still. It is also true that Unconditional Love doesn't go one way and then another. AND the Life Force in each of us is constant for as long as we draw breath. However, given the nature of things yet to explore, these are all good virtues to keep Still.

To summarize, the Nucleus of Psyche has a "Twin" or Isometric nature;
- When the nucleus is +ID is Dextro, there is a positive electro-magnetic charge that for example, has a beneficial effect on most aspects of Health, the Highest Light and Good. Essentially our whole bodies are a chiral environment,
- When the nucleus is –ID Laevo, there is a negative electro-magnetic charge having an opposite effect on the body's chirality. This is associated with Illness and Disease, [The mirror image of Health]. Pain, Wickedness and Evil.
- Both processes can be entropic but having vastly different outcomes. The key is obviously to set a positive process in train. Stillness, Concert A and Blue-violet light will each enhance Psyche towards ID Dextro and the pursuit of happiness.
- The Twins are held together by the neutron that has no charge +ve or –ve.

Whilst Psyche can be Dextro or Laevo at any given point in time, it can also turn clockwise in some situations and anti-clockwise in other situations. Psyche is seldom static and may be appropriately regarded as intransitive, swapping from side to side, turning one way and then turn another way. It is also possible that the isomers vibrate. So firstly, Psyche can alternate or be ***intransitive between +ID Dextro and –ID Laevo.***

However, over time Psyche can also begin to ***slide*** in one particular direction and become more frequently set Right or Left. In some frequently occurring situations, the behaviour pattern may be pretty much set one way or another like an automatic or habitual response. Then it is characteristic of Laevo processes for vicious cycles to set in when –ID Laevo predominates for extended periods. So thirdly, Psyche can become ***fixed.***

Psyche also has a mechanism equated to putting up more or less sail to catch more or less wind; it can vary receptivity levels. Not only are receptors tuned positive or negative by the valence of Psyche but the "sensitivity" of receptors can be increased or decreased as a function of the activation energy in Psyche.

We will firstly clarify how the valence of Psyche effects *what* is drawn from the environment. Later we will explore *how much* is drawn from the environment.

Let us assume we have two people in the same physical environment at the same point in time. Let Psyche for Person 1 be –ID Laevo and for Person 2 be Dextro. Person 1 with –ID Laevo has a net electro-magnetic energy charge that is negative and so will attract ions having a positive charge in the environment. Equally, Person 2 with ID Dextro has a net electro-magnetic energy charge that is positive and so will attract ions having a negative charge in the environment. So we can say that although the same building blocks are present in the environment, As with light, Person 1 will take totally different things from it compared to Person 2 depending on the chirality of Psyche [See Figure 6].

Figure 6. Opposites Will Attract Opposites.

IN an IONIZED ENVIRONMENT

-ve   +ve

-ID LAEVO   STILL   +ID DEXTRO

+ID DEXTRO will attract ions having an opposite charge – ve Ions.

-ID LAEVO will attract ions having a positive charge.

Psyche attracts totally different things from the same environment. D or L.

Left   Right

LAEVOROTATORY   DEXTROROTATORY

NB. All amino acids [except glycine] in the body are affected by chirality.

As an example of this process at work, Comet Borelli visited our part of the solar system in September 2001.

Part of what Comet Borelli left behind was a large tail of positively and negatively charged ions. Some of these ions were carted away by solar winds and others sat in the upper atmosphere for some time before being deposited on Earth's surface. So if our two people with opposite Psyches were in that same ionized environment, they would attract ions of opposite valence. [See Figure 6 above.]

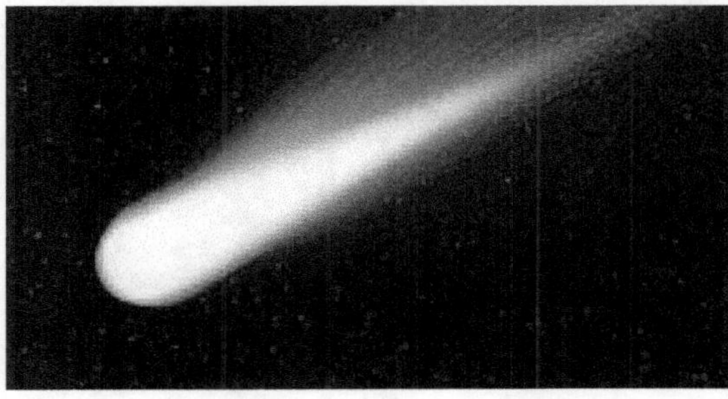

Taking different ions from the same environment is independent of the elemental composition of the ions. Some ions are highly toxic, whilst others are very beneficial but this discussion is presently limited to the difference in valence, +ve or –ve and the opposite effect of chirality on the structure and function of every cell in the body. Further to this;

"Many phenomena of the living state, such as the activity of an enzyme or the ability of a micro-organism to promote a reaction, involves chirality."

As enzymes play a key role as a catalyst in chemical processes in the body, and amino acids are the building blocks for protein in the body, there are very few reactions in metabolism, maintenance or growth that are not affected by chirality.

We can also say that the same building blocks in the environment can have vastly different effects on each person depending on the chirality of Psyche. Hence the primary distinction is drawn between +ID Dextro and −ID Laevo in the nucleus.

Clearly the nucleus of Psyche does not occur in isolation. To continue with the analogy of the structure of an atom, this model uses eight vital electrons that interact with the nucleus and determine the overall structure and chirality of Psyche. Each of these electrons contribute to both the net chirality of Psyche [whether it is ID Dextro or −ID Laevo] and to the net activation energy of the system as a whole.

The Electron Orbits around the Nucleus of Psyche.

Archetypes use the analogy of an ***inner transition element, lanthanum.*** That suggests we should view these electrons as contributing in an inwards fashion towards the nucleus. Lanthanum is the first of the *f* block elements in the Lanthanide Series on the Periodic Table of Elements]. This is somewhat of a departure from the atomic theory approach in which it is a general practice to regard an element as having its properties defined most clearly by the outer shell electron/s. Whilst we know *what* [+ve or −ve Ions] are taken from the environment in each case, it is the net activation energy that will determine *how much* is taken by each electron and its contribution towards the Nucleus.. [See Figure 7.] Although this model is based on the way an inner transition element behaves, it is hypothetical. The characteristics attributed will provide examples for consideration and research development. We use this model to review some of the research into HIV and AIDS.

Figure 7. Nucleus and Electron Configuration of Psyche.

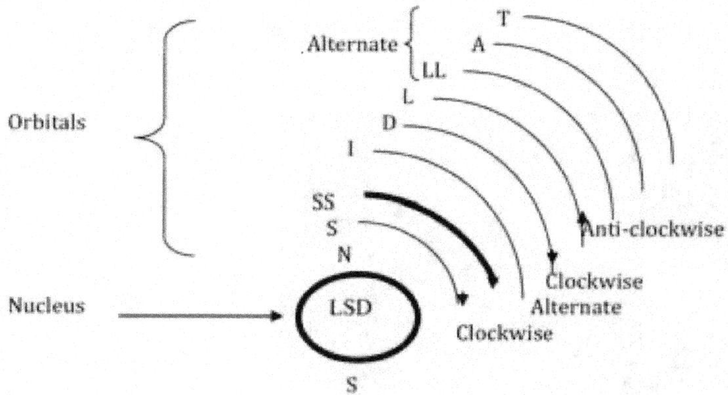

- Clockwise rotation by electrons S, SS and D is fixed as is their polarity that is the same as in the nucleus.
- Electron L rotates anti-clockwise and is fixed as is its polarity that is opposite to that in the nucleus.
- Electrons I, LL, A and T, may rotate in either direction or alternate in the direction they rotate. These 4 electrons vary the resultant chirality of Psyche [given that the other 4 are fixed]. Their polarity will be determined by their direction of rotation. If an electron rotates clockwise, it will have the same polarity as in the nucleus, and vice versa.
- The activation energy of each electron and the total system can be estimated but it is difficult to know if we need to regard the two outer orbiting electrons A and T travel at a very high speeds as they do in Lanthanum.

In the above figure the idea conveyed is that the nucleus [LSD] of Psyche and its electrons are in an activated state. The electrons that orbit around the nucleus are briefly described as follows. [The number of electrons per orbital does not correspond to Lanthanum that has the formula: {Xe}5d16s2] We will later discuss each orbital or dimension in more detail and discuss some of the AIDS and other research that bears on this classification.

1. The first orbital is denoted S and its spin is generally fixed clockwise. The S orbital can be regarded as partially shielded from all the other orbiting electrons. The polarity [N - S] of the S electron is the same as in the nucleus. This represents the **common physiological processes** in the human body in the living, activated state. S denotes what we all have in common as humans and share with many other living and chiral creatures on Earth such as other primates. At the first level we are all composed of the same primary elements and compounds. For example hydrogen, oxygen, nitrogen, amino acids, proteins etc. These elements and compounds combine to produce the living cells of our bodies, and so direct the work of respiration, metabolism, defences against infections and operation of the senses, to name but a few of the commonalities we are all born with. Generally these are matters that do not require conscious effort or decision making, hence the idea the S orbital is partially shielded from the other orbitals. Where physiological processes are growth and maintenance oriented S remains clockwise in its rotation around the nucleus. When the body's nutritional requirements are not being met or chemical or biological agents are having a toxic effect, or the body is stressed in some way, the speed of rotation slows down and S may change and become anticlockwise as the body goes into physical decline.

2. The second orbital is designated SS and it also generally has a clock-wise spin. It denotes what we have in common with each other [S] but it is also the innermost layer of **individual differences** [SS]. For example, we all have a DNA structure in the shape of a double helix [spiral] and composed of protein, peptide bonds, chromosomes, etc [S]. However our DNA also has a unique configuration. What we have in common is that each individual's DNA is uniquely configured like a fingerprint [SS]. In the same way that we are all born having body, mind and spirit [S] we are each uniquely different and granted unique Original Blessings that form the constellation of our gifts and so influence, even determine, how we will grow or develop as unique beings [SS]. This represents the characteristics we are born with so it is

the "blueprint" against which comparison can be made to examine what we have done with our gifts during our lives.

3. The third orbital is designated I to represent the **Ego**, and at birth it generally has a clockwise spin. Life experience makes a huge difference to the developmental process involved here and so too the direction of spin. Initial differentiation of ourselves from others, or individuation, is a critical first step; finding out who we are; learning about our unique skills and abilities and exploring our strengths and weaknesses. What may emerge progressively is an awareness of belonging - at least to family for most people - and this is formative to the second step. Differentiation is followed by integration. An increasing sense of connectedness to the wonders of Creation, or being the metaphysical "I AM" contextually. In this developmental process right chirality is maintained. However, life experiences may have a destructive effect on either differentiation or integration with the result left chirality may occasionally occur and then become the dominant mode. Where differentiation is over-extended and / or belonging does not develop, isolation increases and left chirality occurs. That is where "I AM" is not contextual, Ego turns left [negative] and will begin to self-destruct or attack others [intra- or extra-punitive]. We also make our own comparisons to our "blueprint" and examine the extent to which we have achieved the goals we set ourselves relative to our Original Blessings. Secondly, we may learn from our experiences [+ve] or find we are repeating our mistakes [-ve]. Thirdly, a "balanced I" is positive whilst an "over-extended I" is negative.

4. The fourth orbital is designated D, meaning **Dextro**. This electron represents the resultant Right choices and behaviours evident during a person's life: the net "Good" we have generated at given times. Behaviour that accords with the Lore, respect for the sacredness of self and others and service to humanity. The activation energy of this electron is a function of the net "Good" we generate.

5. The fifth orbital is designated L, meaning **Laevo**/ Left. This electron represents the resultant negative

choices and behaviours evident during a person's life. The net "Bad" we have generated at given times. This includes behaviour that does not accord with the Lore and so involves deception, wickedness, self-destruction, self-service, illness and evil. Left chirality activates death. The activation energy of this electron is a function of failure to heed what we know is "Good" or right.

6. The sixth orbital is designated LL. Two electrons are involved here. The first L means **Love for self** [L^1] and the second [L^2] means **Love for others** [LL]. Whilst the initial direction of spin is set to the right, Dextro, the activation energy of these two electrons ideally balance each other such that one travels clock-wise and the other travels anticlock-wise around the nucleus. When out of balance, LL will have a net rotation to the left, Laevo. Positive self-regard [L^1] is the foundation for loving others [L^2] and when these two are in balance the net rotation and activation energy is Dextro.

7. The seventh orbital is designated A, meaning **Attunement**. This represents the body's attunement to Concert A where all the instruments in the orchestra are tuned to the same musical note. Attunement, like Concert A, has right chirality. However we can choose to be out of attunement to our bodies needs

and those of others, resulting in left chirality [-A] and self-destructive effects. When attuned A, we increasingly surface [into awareness] the ancient records of intuitive knowledge.

8. The eighth orbital is designated T. In T's most highly activated, clockwise spin this signifies the highest levels of human consciousness in contemplation of the divine. This is linked with the 7th musical note TE and contemplation of the working of Great Design in our lives. In this state of **Transcendence**, we recognize the lessons we need to learn and we work through the destined difficulties we face, even when those difficulties appear to be doubled. We know our "calling" and patiently pursue "the way" that manifests our Original Blessings [SS orbital]. However when our past actions have been negative [L] and we feel cut-off from the source of positive intuition and insight [distal] we may falter to the left and even slide into left chirality [-T]. Transcendence is about what is sacred in ourselves, others and Universe.

Consistent with the atomic theory analogy, the inner orbitals [S & SS] fill first. This constitutes what we are born with. Life experience then fills orbitals I, D, L, LL, A and finally T. Depending upon how we act, and react to the destined difficulties we face, the interaction between the nucleus and the electrons will produce either ID Dextro or -ID Laevo. The resultant chirality and the level of activation energy of Psyche depend upon the interaction between the nucleus and the orbiting electrons. In turn this will draw to us the fate and circumstances that accord with our Psychic state. ID Dextro will take uniquely different elements from the same environmental building blocks. It will draw what is helpful or beneficial. On the other hand, -ID Laevo will take the opposite elements that will further destruction [as per Figure 4].

5. Discussion.

We will begin this section with a review of the existing research evidence into HIV and AIDS as it can be related to the classification of each of these electrons. In turn we will examine how a combination of electrons can affect the chirality and net activation energy of the nucleus of Psyche, the system as a whole, and interaction with the environment.

(1). S orbital and physiological processes.
The partial shielding of the S electron from the other electrons is not complete but it is not under the control of conscious decision making. Most of the body's processes are regarded as automatic but again this is only partially true because our feelings directly affect every organ in the body through peptides and their receptors and the secretion of hormones. A review of the immune systems response to stressors shows there is a relationship between the presence of physical and psychological stressors and a decline in the immune system. That discussion points directly to the chirality of –ID Laevo being the major contributor to a break-down in the immune system and especially the decline in T-lymphocyte cell production. But given that -ID Laevo has become dominant, albeit temporarily, there is evidence to suggest that it takes a long time before there is a return to normal immune system responses after a negative process has commenced. Even after a short period of over-exercise, there was a significant drop in the CD4 count that could take upwards of three weeks before returning to previous levels. This highlights the importance of electrons in the LL orbital and L^1 [self-love] in particular – submitting oneself to physical abuse. A, attunement to the body's needs, is also negatively affected in this situation so there will be a combined effect by both electrons on the net activation energy of –ID Laevo in the nucleus. The resultant chirality will attract an appropriate environmental response. At first glance it would not seem likely that such a simple stressor as over-exercise could have such response magnitude, but chirality goes a long way towards explaining this longer-term impact.

Julie Quinlivan from the Flinders Medical Centre in South Australia has undertaken a number of studies into the effect of hormones in sheep and adolescent pregnancy. She has found that repeated exposure to stress hormones results in poor foetal growth and that there are foetal origins of adult disease. In her experiments with sheep she found that four short lived exposures to the stress hormone betamethasone caused significant delays in the size of their brains, reflected by a significant reduction in the quantity of central nervous system myelination. Deficits in myelination are linked to hyperactive childhood syndromes such as attention deficit disorder [ADD]. She also reports that repeated prenatal exposure to stress hormones can affect cell division in the nervous system with permanent deficits in brain cell numbers.

Extended periods of malnutrition; introducing foreign substances into the bloodstream [by recreational drug abuse, exposure to some herbicides and pesticides, blood transfusions, biological agents like E coli, unclean water etc.,]; and sleeplessness have all been found to decrease immunity and can all be seen to have a similar effect on these same electrons and consequently a *slide* into decline in the immune system. Agreeing to take prescribed medications such as AZT, antibiotics, protease inhibitors, steroids and cancer chemotherapy treatments all create negative side effects or conditions associated with AIDS. Any of these chemical agents or physical factors such as stress, especially a combination, will build the net activation energy of –ID Laevo and may lead to a reversal of spin with destructive consequences even for foetal development.

(2). SS orbital and Individual Differences at Birth.
As this electron represents the unique constellation of gifts we are born with, the individual "blueprint", it includes our particular sensitivities, strengths and weaknesses. Having a clockwise rotation signifies that we are all born to be active and our essential nature is "Good" – in contrast to the religious idea of Original Sin. In body, mind and spirit we are sacred beings.

(3). I orbital and the Ego.
Defining who we are and the processes of Ego development can be regarded as integrative [clockwise] or disintegrative [anticlockwise]. Developing a clear sense of individual identity and connectedness is central to integrative processes. The opposite is also true and a most tragic example of this process can be seen in the Romanian orphanages under the rule of Nicolae Ceausescu. A team of researchers, led by D. R. Rosenburg made a neuropsychiatric assessment of orphans in one orphanage and in 1992 made the following report.

> "Since the downfall of Nicolae Ceaussescu's communist regime in Romania in December 1989, several almost barbaric institutions for children have been discovered throughout the country. Because of draconian probirth policies implemented by Ceausescu coupled with Romania's status as

> one of the poorest countries in Europe, children were frequently abandoned by their parents and placed in state run orphanages. As a result, approximately 40,000 abused and neglected children languish in these orphanages... Prior to 1989, it is estimated that 35% of these children died every year. During September of 1991 we conducted a neuropsychiatric assessment of the entire population of one of these orphanages. One hundred and seventy patients resided in this institution, and all had been declared "irrecuperable". The orphanage was severely understaffed...This resulted in such minimal child – staff interaction that 75% of the children did not know their name or age."

Although the key issue here concerns child deaths and the lack of individual identity, [75% did not know their name or age] the other key findings are as follows but will be discussed under 6. LL below, where we will explore the consequences of abandonment, isolation and severe social deprivation.

> "94% of the children had developmental language and speech disorders; 40% were mentally retarded; 26% had muscular atrophy; 22% were completely immobile; 14% suffered from delirium; 12% had epilepsy; 10% had autism; and 4% psychosis."

This is a tragic example of –ID Laevo at work with disintegrative processes.

Further examples can be drawn from people subjected to earthquakes, tornadoes and cyclones, flood, tsunami, wild fire, torture, war, persistent abuse, debilitating pain and illness. This is not to say that all people suffer a disintegration of Ego in crisis situations, in fact the outcomes in the long term may be a strengthening of integrative processes but the initial impact of a shock or crisis is paralysis/disbelief before possibly moving into defensive retreat. Where such shocks are persistent and people have not developed effective strategies for adapting to changes, susceptibility to remaining in shock will increase proportionately to the severity of the shock. Ultimately, if this negative cycle continues, even a comparatively minor shock can trigger disintegration. [Figure 7.]

Figure 7. The Effect of Shock on Integration and Disintegration of Ego.

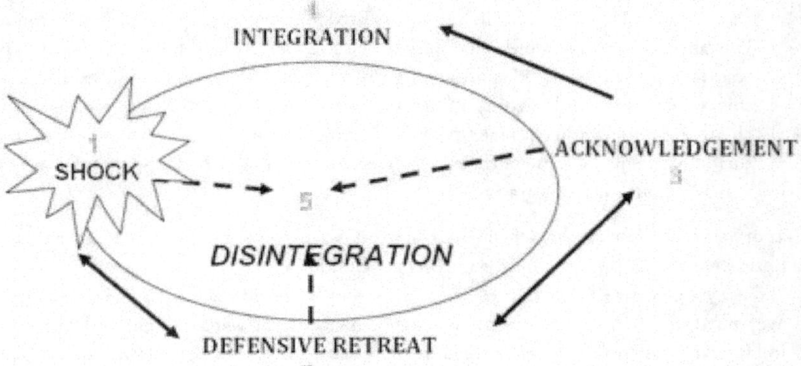

1. **Shock** is associated with an emotional state of panic, paralysis, fear and helplessness. The  cognitive state is usually "frozen" and one's world-view "seems to be turned upside down". Some people remain in this state for a long time when the severity of the shock is great and if they experience a number of successive shocks. Due to the shock on shock effect, increasingly smaller and smaller incidents can constitute a shock. Remaining in this state is a sign of 5. Disintegration beginning to occur. However, after a shock most people move into;

2. **Defensive Retreat** associated with an emotional state of pain, anger and denial. The cognitive state involves refusal to accept the change which has occurred. One's world view is defined by what was and not by what is. Rigidity of opinions and ideas and refusal to face the reality and consequences of the change may cause the person to remain in this state which reinforces 5. Disintegration. After some time people move on to;

3. **Acknowledgement** means facing reality and that is painful. This stage is often associated with a slide between 2 and 3 and then back again to 2 - hence the two way arrow. Some people find 3. Acknowledgement so painful they retreat again into 5. Disintegration and become either intra punitive or extra punitive. [When angry or dissatisfied with self, some people attempt suicide; others may attack other people or the targets of their aggression may become manifest.] However, as current reality is faced, there is a chance for cognitive reorganization and a deepening of the full experience of grief. What usually follows is a gradual increase in satisfying experience as new coping strategies are formulated and experimented with. This leads to;

4. **Integration** and adaption as reality is defined in current terms.

5. **Disintegration** is the product of not adapting to the initial shock or reaching and sustaining a stable state in subsequent stages. Evidence of unstable ego states is most pronounced in the personality disorder identified in the USA as Borderline or in Europe and China as Emotionally Unstable personality disorder. Because of the stigmatization of people with Borderline one researcher promotes the idea of it being called Mercurial Disorder – an excellent name in this context. It is highly significant that past trauma either by physical or sexual abuse during childhood is present in the majority of these disorders. An absence of parental skills in helping their children make sense of their world is characteristic of such families and so it reinforces mal-adaption and disintegration.

The effect of Shock on Shock is dramatically illustrated in an interview by Caroline Jones with a woman, Magda Bozic who lived in Budapest during the Second World War.

"I was a young married woman and then in the war my husband went to Russia where he was killed. We went down to the air-raid shelter with the family when the war and bombing started in earnest in Hungary and two of the family died there in that air-raid shelter, my father and my sister. My mother and I were the survivors. When we came out from the shelter we walked around and looked at Budapest. Before the bombing, it had been such a beautiful city that it sang, your heart sang when you walked along the main avenues and up in the hills. We came out of the shelter and we really didn't know where we were because there were in the streets rows and rows of collapsed buildings and ruins, including our own home. There was absolutely nothing, a burnt out shell and we wept and wept for a life gone forever…."

Crisis events of the Shock on Shock type create an increasing vulnerability to eventually even a banal event triggering disintegration.

Taking the two extremes of the continuum; feelings of pleasure and well being stimulate the immune system into working at peak efficiency whilst acute psychological and physical stress depress immune system functions. Perhaps the simplest example of the later state can be seen from an experiment with the common cold published in the New England Journal of Medicine by Cohen in 1991. Psychological stress questionnaires designed to measure helplessness and negative emotions were given to nearly 400 healthy people. They were then given nose drops containing several types of cold virus. The chances of getting cold symptoms turned out to be very predictable from test scores. People who are psychologically stressed are about twice as vulnerable to the common cold. In a very similar experimental design undertaken by Cohen and published in the Journal of the American Medical Association in 1997, people with poor social connections were four times as likely to come down with a cold when compared to people who had a wide variety of close friends. These reactions are however not restricted to people. Helplessness induced in rats by Laudenslager, Ryan and Drugan et al led to immune system suppression but rats who were subject to the same stressor, electric shock, and who had a bar in their cage by which to stop the shock, did not experience the same decline in lymphocyte proliferation. The apparatus used consisted of a pair of cages wired to give the rat in each cage identical random shocks through their feet. One of the rats has a bar in its cage that stops the shock in both cages when the bar is pressed. The helpless rat in the second cage, receives exactly the same shock until the rat in the first cage turns it off. The second rat also has a bar but it makes no difference to the shock. Then a cancerous tumour was implanted under the rats' skins. Only 27% of the helpless rats rejected the tumour whilst 63% of the rats with bar control rejected the tumour. Rats receiving no shock at all, rejected the tumour 54% of the time. Although such an experimental paradigm has not been used with people, helplessness in primates and adult humans shows much the same trend of immune system suppression - and vigour when empowered.

Secretion of hormones is the most commonly proposed mechanism for the immune system suppression that occurs during states of acute or chronic psychological stress. One of the major changes during times of stress is an outpouring of the hormones epinephrine and cortisol which lead to a dramatic reduction in the T-lymphocytes. The strength of the correlation between decrease in T-cells and excess cortisol is so strong that low T-cells is one of the diagnostic criterion for excess cortisol.

> "Almost any type of mental or physical stress can lead within minutes to greatly enhanced secretion of ACTH and consequently cortisol as well, often increasing cortisol as much as 20 fold."

> "Cortisol suppresses the immune system, causing lymphocyte production to decrease markedly. The T-lymphocytes are especially suppressed."

Any situation which causes the body to react quickly with the hormone cortisol, if it persists, will result in a suppression of the immune system and increase vulnerability to an increasing range of infection. Naturally the duration of the stressful period will be a vital factor. A person waiting for test results and "fearing the worst" will be exactly in one of those stress-producing situations. The magnitude of this stress will be sharply increased if the prognosis for HIV and/or AIDS confirms those fears. Whilst cortisol affects the immune system, a similar destructive effect has been found between the hormone epinephrine and brain tissue. It is no surprise therefore that dementia is a symptom often found amongst long term sufferers of HIV and AIDS.

Because of the generality of low CD4 counts many people question using CD4 to diagnose AIDS, when it is clearly not the only blood agency affected and it has not been established how HIV/AIDS actually affects CD4 in the blood. Some call for new methods to be developed to test for AIDS. However that debate runs its course in medical circles, there is clearly a powerful relationship between increasing psychological stress factors, lowering of CD4 levels and progression from HIV to AIDS.

> "Faster progression to AIDS was associated with more cumulative stressful life events [p<0.002], more cumulative depressive symptoms [p<0.008] and less cumulative social support [p<0.0002]. At 5.5 years, the probability of getting AIDS was about two or three times as high on those above the median on stress or below the median on social support."

As noted, the experiment by Laudenslanger, Ryan and Drugan showed the effect of shock and powerlessness on the immune system of rats in their twin cages. Having the power [a bar] to control the shock led to integration and so actually invigorated the immune system when compared to the control group and these "empowered rats" were 3 times more successful than their twin cage rat in rejecting the implanted cancer tumours.

All the other research regarding HIV and AIDS both on humans and primates, reinforces the view that helplessness leads to an increase in epinephrine and cortisol secretion with resultant deterioration in learning centres of the brain and in immunity respectively. Likewise, as we saw with the children in Romanian orphanages, and the helpless rats, disintegration has a negative effect on every aspect of adaptive [physical, emotional, cognitive and spiritual] being that when anticlockwise will ultimately lead to decline and premature death. The converse also applies when people and animals are empowered. Satisfaction and improvement generated by successfully meeting a challenge facilitates self worth and integration of the Ego. This is contextual because all learning involves an interaction between self and the environment as a cycle between beliefs and proof. When electron I is positive and clockwise it powerfully affects the activation energy of ID Dextro.

4. D orbital and Positive Life Experiences.
Our Mercurial nature seeks positive life experiences; activity, exploration, learning, light, freedom, variety, challenge, power, connectedness with one's environment and others, flexibility, nourishment and creativity. This is reflected in deep satisfaction, feelings of awe and wonder and pleasure when acting in the common good. The activation energy of the D electron is determined by the sum of positive life experience and it travels clockwise around the nucleus.

5. L orbital and Negative Life Experiences.
Our Mercurial nature seeks negative life experiences; passivity, withdrawal, depression, restriction, monotony, rigidity, under-nourishment, distal, isolated, fragmented, powerless / victim, and is associated with illness, disease, death, what is defiled, dark, destructive, bad, evil and coming under the pungent negative influence of Saturn. This is reflected in deep dissatisfaction, alienation and disinterest in serving others. The activation energy of the L electron is determined by the sum of negative life experience and it travels anticlockwise around the nucleus.

6. LL orbital and Self-Love, Love for others - social support, tactile contact and affiliation.
The two electrons in this orbital are L^1 self love and L^2 love for/with others which includes social support, tactile

contact and affiliation. No research was found on self-love amongst AIDS sufferers or their carers. As mentioned in 3 above, a study by Cohen in 1997 found that people who had poor social connections were four times more likely to come down with the common cold when compared to people who were connected with a wide variety of close friends. A large number of studies have been undertaken to assess the effect of social contact on recovery and length of survival after contracting cancer and the vast majority of them have proved significant. The general rule of thumb is that love is a mediating factor in coping with a wide range of stressors and this has a beneficial effect on the treatment of disease. Where love is absent and isolation has occurred there is a rise in the cortisol levels that directly effects lymphocyte proliferation and so immunity declines. Studies conducted with humans and other primates are consistently conclusive on the beneficial nature of social support, tactile contact and a wide range of social affiliations in handling stress.

Children in the Romanian orphanage, discussed above, were also assisted by two other researchers, Mary Carlson and Felton Earls. This is the institution where 35% of children died each year prior to 1989 and where 75% of them did not know their name or age.

> "These children experience a form of social care in which their medical and nutritional needs are met, but their social and psychological needs are not met."

The researchers also give an account of many research studies involving primates that identifies how tactile stimulation and grooming practices induce a healthy response in brain neurotransmitters, receptors and neuronal development and of how cortisol can inhibit this process.

> "The muteness, blank facial expressions, social withdrawal, and bizarre stereotypic movements of these infants bore a strong resemblance to the behaviour of socially deprived macaques and chimpanzees. Most of the children …had experienced severe tactile/social deprivation due to the high child : caregiver ratios [20:1] and custodial rearing practices."

Although early indications had been that these children were not "recoverable", it is worth noting that an enrichment program using a child : caregiver ratio of 4 : 1 did lead to a marked improvement in the children's behaviour and return to relatively normal developmental patterns. That is, when LL is Laevo [eg., blank facial expressions], social contact, tactile stimulation and more individual attention can ameliorate Laevo forces, strengthen Dextro forces and leads to improvements physically, emotionally and mentally – so the children did recover.

The extent to which our social context is a defining dimension of our health can in part be seen from the only longitudinal study undertaken with people who were HIV positive but living in monogamous relations with a partner who was HIV negative. Although the purpose of this study was to identify the infectious nature of HIV amongst heterosexual adults, which it failed to prove, it highlights the central importance of a loving relationship for the health of both partners. In 1997, Padian, Shiboski, Glass et al attempted to determine how many acts of intercourse were needed before a partner became HIV positive. In this 10-year study, 175 couples were followed. At the commencement of the study 75% were not using condoms. After entry most couples began to use condoms but over 25% continued to practice "unsafe sex" for the duration of the study. After an average of 1000 lovemaking encounters per couple, no evidence was found that HIV had been sexually transmitted. All the people who were HIV negative at the beginning of the study were still HIV negative at the end of ten years of sexual contact irrespective of whether they did or didn't use condoms. Although we could discuss this study further from the stand-point of the myths of the science of HIV and AIDS, the point here is that loving, normal relations between partners is a defining quality in health ie., ID Dextro.

Studies with "caregivers" and nurses indicate a call for a new level of "Family" amongst HIV and AIDS sufferers if they are to effectively recover. In an interview with Caroline Jones [Bib.38], Aldo Genaro, who was dying from HIV/AIDS, was asked;

"What do you think we must understand about so many people having this disease of AIDS? What is it that we really need to see and respond to?

I think that the first thing that comes into my mind is love. Homosexual people have been rejected for a long time. We have made fun of them. We have ridiculed them. Homosexual people are not aggressive people. They are gentle people and we have received so much aggression from many different levels. I think we need love, we need compassion, we need understanding not so much compassion – love – we need love.

And love to be shown how?

Love shown in the way we talk about gay people, in the way we support gay people in this trouble. In going to our gay friends we should recognise what value they add to our lives. Assist them in what they are dealing with at the moment. Be there, just be a friend. I am sure a lot of gay people will be very happy to embrace new friends, with no difficulty.

Do you think there are some people now who are ill with AIDS or who are dying, who do not have the friendship and the support and the love that they need?

I think so. I think a lot of gay people at the moment are going through a very difficult time. They are dealing with the death of their friends, of lovers. They are dealing with their own process of dying. Some of them are feeling very lonely and confused. At the same time I would like to say here that it's extraordinary how brave gay men are, how much courage they have. They have been creating support groups, and they are looking after one another. For the first time they have been in a community house. We are creating a very close nuclear family. I think we have learnt a lot from that process. I think the gay people at the moment are presenting a beautiful model of support and caring and nourishment for one another. But it's much more. It's also good to see a lot of no-gay people participating in that process, especially women in the care profession."

When the LL electrons have a clockwise moment a shield to infection is raised but when the moment is anti-clockwise health, developmental processes and mental functioning all deteriorate.

7. A orbital and Attunement.

The direction of rotation and the activation energy of the A electron is determined by sensitivity to one's own needs and the needs of others. To a large measure this requires "listening" to the self and others as well as asking questions in order to clarify what others need. The balance of this measure flows from the extent to which we respond appropriately to meet and satisfy the needs identified. The skills of listening and questioning for understanding can be likened to tuning in our instruments to Concert A; the musical note which resonates with ID Dextro.

The following study illustrates the process by which electron A can move anti-clockwise or the consequences of being closed to one's own and other's needs.

"A group of researchers led by Robert Sapolsky has done a great deal of work observing the effects of psychological and social stress on baboons and other primates, with most of their work focussing on the neurotoxicity that is caused by stress, with dementia and loss of neurones in the hippocampus [Sapolsky 1990, 1996].

In one study, however, they measured total lymphocyte counts and cortisol levels in a group of baboons that were invaded by a highly aggressive young male baboon, who they named Hobbs [Alberts et ali 1992]. Hobbs was particularly threatening to females in the group, and was apparently attempting

to use fear, physical intimidation, and abuse to increase his chances of successful mating. Cortisol levels in the group nearly doubled after Hobbs joined the group, with a slightly greater increase amongst females. T-lymphocytes plummeted in the group from a pre-Hobbs level of 67 per 10,000 red blood cells to a level of about 39, a drop of 42%. When looking only at the levels of baboons who were the victims of Hobb's aggression, the levels fell even more steeply, to 29 RBC's per 10,000, a drop of 55%. Interestingly, Hobbs had the lowest level of T-lymphocytes in the entire group, and the highest cortisol level, suggesting that his behaviour may have been taking an even greater toll on his system than it did on the victims of his aggression." Low T-lymphocyte counts have been shown in other studies to be associated with low CD4 counts [Kotze 1998], so it is expected that the CD4 count would also be lowered by stress amongst the baboons.

When this study is compared to other studies about dominant male baboons who are involved in mutual grooming with females and infants and the resilience this creates to stressors, Hobbs is an outstanding example of −A [aggression] rather than Attunement to both his own and other's needs. His behaviour increases his own and other's vulnerability to opportunistic infections. Viewed from the perspective of Hobb's lack of Attunement, the finding of the study is a lot more than "interesting" it is a definitive aspect of what was found in both Hobbs and the troop.

Increased vulnerability to infection is not the only consequence of −A [aggression].

−A [aggression] at home in the human community can have other disastrous results.

Julie Quinlivan, in her study of teenage mothers who had been exposed to domestic violence, found that amongst other things, the circumference of the baby's head was significantly less than controls. High cortisol significantly affects brain development and myelination of the central nervous system. [A finding that accords with her studies of the effects of stress hormones on pregnancy amongst sheep – reported earlier.] By comparison with controls, she found that these children would not reach their full potential and with a much higher risk of ADD, they would be a burden on their parents, siblings, friends and particularly educators.

Considering the much higher levels of domestic violence amongst indigenous Australians, significant brain development and central nervous system impairment of children can be expected.

High levels of Attunement are expected of caregivers of the severely handicapped, long-term sufferers of Alzheimer, etc., but who is attuned to the needs of the caregiver? Significantly caregivers in both these categories whose immune systems have been studied, show a lower than normal count of T cells. Attunement is a two way process – those who give support also need support themselves.

8. T orbital and Transcendence.

Body, mind and spirit work as one in the pursuit of higher consciousness or Transcendence of the Ego. The resulting T electron travels clockwise around the nucleus. Discovery of being body, mind and spirit as a sacred being and realization of the power that this enables, is not restricted to the later years of life. Usually there is an early awakening and later consolidation in our individual efforts to conceptualize and understand the workings of Great Design in our lives.

As an example of this early awakening, about ten children aged 11 years were jointly participating in a levitation experiment in a school. One child kept watch at the door to warn the others when the teacher was coming. Another child who was leading the experiment, knelt on the floor and called for a volunteer to lie down with her head facing her. Then she called for other volunteers to take similar positions, kneeling with two on each side and one at the feet. They were instructed to put two fingers of each hand under the prostrate child's body. The leader then called on a "spirit" to assist the group raise the body off the floor. When levitated to shoulder height of the kneeling children, awareness that "it was working" broke group concentration and the levitated child fell to the floor. A second subject was found to take the floor and the procedure was repeated. When this second levitated child was above shoulder height, the teacher-watcher at the door explosively shouted, "She's coming!" Instantly the levitated child crashed to the floor and one of the girls felt a "massive and sudden rush of spirit like a wind" that in leaving arched her completely backwards on the floor.

The child who experienced this "arching" had numerous subsequent encounters with this spirit. She became increasingly frightened and noted that even the family cat was most unusually terrified at times. Eventually her mother called the local priest who exorcised the house but the girl had become deeply disturbed. She started writing about suicide and attempted same by a range of unsuccessful methods. She developed chronic asthma, suffered from frequent colds and cold sores, frequent bouts of depression, and twenty years later made a very serious attempt to take her life. She would have succeeded had it not been for an earth leakage switch. She was admitted to a psychiatric hospital. Three of the biggest cold sores she ever had broke out next morning. Anti-depressant drugs and therapy for an obsessive-compulsive disorder followed; but by this time she had no recollection of the fears raised by the levitation experiment she had been involved in at school. When she did finally recall those events, she could identify the characteristics of her whole negative history. Slowly circulating clockwise three times and calling on the "Highest Light Good" is making the positive difference she seeks. She is free from the negative vortex and re-integration is occurring as Dextro forces are reactivated in her life as body, mind and spirit.

Electron T is positive or negative [-T], though the level of activation energy will vary in either direction. If the right hand is held up to the mirror as we discussed earlier, and it represents "the Highest, Light, Good," what is the reflection? "The Lowest, Dark, Evil"? The careful reader, especially of Transcript 8 in "Ambrosia" will know the bipolar extremes of this continuum are ONE as the right hand and on the left, the negation of ONE, who Archetypes politely refer to as IN-ONE.

Back at school, our 11 year old child who experienced the backwards "arching" also recalls telling teachers why she subsequently did something wrong was because "the Devil told her to". No-one believed her, but even in adulthood she is emphatic that the voice told her to go ahead.

When questioned about the girl who had acted as the leader in the levitation experiment, our informant recalls that the leader had experienced a great deal of negative disruption in her life at around that time which included death of her brother. [Figure 4 needs to be re-visited in the light of this information.] She was not a normally popular child but had found she could gain other student's attention by her experiences in matters of spirit – albeit negative ones. Our informant remained convinced for many years that there was definitely an Evil force that operated in the world around her. She abandoned belief that there was a balancing force for Good until recently. Now she sees the polar extremes, and she thinks that the mirror image is necessary to maintain balance.

When questioned about how she became involved in the levitation experiment, she recalls her grandfather's death when she was six years old. She had woken during the night and found him standing at the end of her bed wanting to say goodbye. She had a very happy recall of that experience. It wasn't until after the levitation experiment that her fear was raised, the cat was terrified and she decided she did not want to be able to see spirits.

It is important to note that in this case suicide was attempted without any suggestion by any external person or entity. Thus although she attributes –T to have been initiated when the spirit departed ["a massive and sudden rush of spirit like a wind"], she sees the source of the activation energy for suicide as internal and not external. This is quite properly referred to as self-willed death where no external agent is involved. Such situations need to be differentiated from those where there is an agreement by the person with a single external authority figure such as a doctor, and further differentiated from situations where the whole community is involved in a prognosis of isolation and death. The following comments by Dr G. W. Milton in 1973 are an example of the confusion that arises when these situations are not differentiated, though it is granted that the outcomes are similar.

> "There is a small group of patients in whom the realization of impending death is a blow so terrible that they are quite unable to adjust to it, and they die rapidly before the malignancy seems to have developed enough to cause death. This problem of self-willed death is in some ways analogous to death produced in primitive peoples by witchcraft…Throughout questioning his answers are minimal, and as soon as the questions stop he is silent… He does not have the obvious signs of extreme anxiety or fear. Blood pressure, pulse, and respiration remain normal … Within a month of the onset of this syndrome the patient will almost certainly be dead. If a necroscopy is carried out, … there will often appear to be no adequate explanation for the cause of death."

What is evident is that the prognosis of death comes from an authority figure – a medical practitioner. The description of the person's reaction is akin to them going into extreme Shock [as per figure 6]; a shock delivered by the doctor. The resultant activation energy applies to Disintegration of the I electron and Laevo forces [-I] are established. Acceptance of the diagnosis is a sign of acknowledgement [step 3 in the above model] but this is coupled with powerlessness to change one's fate. Electron A also is activated anti-clockwise, as questions and answers accord with the prognosis and acceptance. Likewise for the T electron that because of the symptoms of illness presented would already be set anti-clockwise, is further activated by the prognosis that death will ensue. It comes as no surprise that death is not caused by the presenting illness when Laevo forces are present in all three of the outermost electrons.

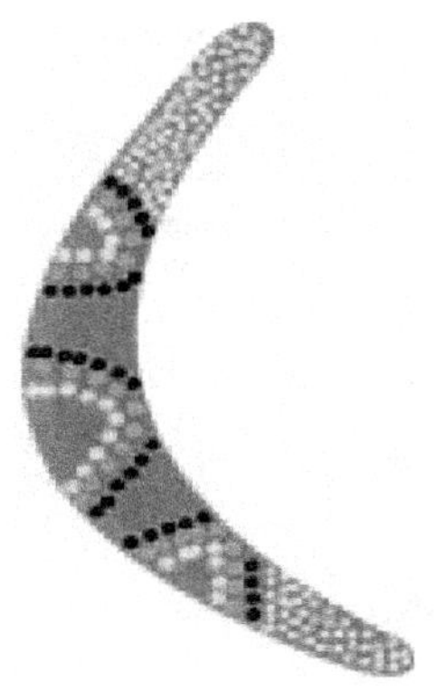

It is presumed that the witchcraft referred to is "Pointing the Bone" that has been the subject of a lot of discussion in medical and psychological circles and is identified as 'self-willed' death. This is a practice used by indigenous Australians for many centuries and although it has a number of similarities with the above situation, it is even more far-reaching in its impact on the instinctive drives of psyche. It is worthy of attention here because "wasting away" of the victim's body is similar to that observed in AIDS. When a tribal member seriously infringes a custom, the Elders will meet and decide what form of punishment is appropriate. When guilt has been established and maximum seriousness applies to the infringement [eg., a serious threat to the physical survival, social network or spiritual life of the tribe], the guilty party has the Bone Pointed at them by an appointed Elder. [This is equivalent to a High Court decision by the Full Bench that a capital offence has been committed. "Pointing the Bone" was never used for minor offences and it was not the practice to have a decision to point it taken by one person alone, as is the case for our doctor previously quoted.] This is a decision by a whole community to banish a member. In some cases this also involved spearing the guilty party in the leg before ritual banishment but usually no physical abuse or fatal injury was involved. The banished person is completely isolated and no return to the tribe is possible. All social support is practically and ritually withdrawn and the guilt wracked and spiritually shattered individual usually goes away to die. They generally will not even attempt to sustain themselves with food. In some cases tribal representatives will visit this individual when close to death and conduct powerful mourning rituals.

The impact of "Pointing the Bone" can be expected on every orbital. When nutritional requirements are not maintained, even the S and SS orbitals will slow down and then stop. Laevo forces will apply to a disintegrated [-I] ego; L and LL will show -L$^{1\,\&\,2}$; acceptance [-A] of the tribal Elder's decision; and spiritually shattered –T. The net activation energy of –ID Laevo would result in "wasting away until death occurs". In some cases the magnitude of the Shock is so great death occurs within hours. This is a very powerful method for dealing with a trouble-maker that doesn't involve ropes for hanging, guns, axes or prisons. It does involve a well-knit social order, understanding of creative and destructive forces that in their simplicity and sophistication belies the term "primitive". In fact, given the problem of deaths in custody, a feature of imprisonment of indigenous Australians for even minor offences, perhaps the term "barbaric" should be applied to our custodial practices that show such little regard for the devastating impact imprisonment has on some of our fellow Sanctitas Vestras.

The T electron is the outermost shell of Psyche. In common with atomic theory, this orbital is the principle one that determines the interaction between the Psyche and the environment. This can be regarded as the mediating variable through which all the other dimensions / electrons interact with the world around us. Perhaps it is no more than a reflection on the difficulties associated with measuring Transcendence that there is little or no research available on the impact this has on HIV and AIDS. Equally this may be a subject that warrants some careful evaluation. [A range of exercises to assist +T are given in last chapter.]

A similar pattern of impact to "Pointing the Bone" may be found in Africa by an examination of a "Voodoo" curse. Time and effort will tell, however it is significant that the Coordinator of the Long Term Survivor's Network, Clair Walton, pin-points diagnosis of HIV and AIDS as equivalent to an Evil Spell that must be rejected.

She challenges these "death warrants" and maintains that a positive belief system is vital to survival. She regards the warrants as equivalent to an evil spell.

> "Such is the power of the HIV/AIDS spell. On several occasions I have had people say to me, patronizingly or even gleefully, that they knew someone just like me, who thought the way I did, then got sick and died…do they think it never occurred to me?"

> "We have survived an assault on the very basic human spirit; ostracism of society, poisoning of the mind by fear, attempts to control our sexual and reproductive needs, as well as pressure to take toxic and experimental drugs. No mean feat!"

In view of the foregoing discussion this is very likely correct. This becomes even more likely in the light of the discussion that will follow.

In his well documented and reasoned book titled "AIDS and the Voodoo Hex", Matt Irwin draws several parallels with the plight of people who suffer from an HIV or AIDS positive diagnosis. Due to the power of the cycle between beliefs and proof there is a need to examine the beliefs that are promulgated about HIV and AIDS. However, it needs to be said before we leave this section of the discussion that what seems most lacking in the research evidence is a semblance of ordered enquiry and care in evaluating the psychological dimensions. Perhaps this problem exists due to the lack of a constructive theoretical framework for Psyche.

As outlined at the beginning, the purpose of this paper is to present a theoretical basis by which an order may be used both for research purposes and for the development of response strategies to assist those who are living with HIV and AIDS and a number of other human complaints.

A Case Study - Janet and Martin's Soul Journeys.

Attractive, intelligent, easy manner and cheerful and with a great sense of humour, Janet was a prime target for young male attentions when she began her studies at Sydney University. Both she and her younger friend Anne fully enjoyed the freedom and stimulation University life had to offer in the late 1960's. This case study is given from Anne's life-long observations of her much loved friend.

Janet first "fell in love" with a would-be Geologist but her parents' strong disapproval lead quickly to its demise after less than three months. Janet's parents again disapproved of her next delightful young man and so on until their eventual death many years later. They never approved of any partner Janet had during any of those years. For their own reasons they were obsessive about controlling their children. The father was an arrogant, aloof GP who was strangely subservient to his wife who had been one of those bossy nurses in her younger days. Janet's experience was pretty much repeated for each of two sisters and her brother. No-one was ever good enough for any of them.

After graduation Janet and Anne worked in the same organization and continued their close friendship. An independent life had a great deal of appeal to both of them. Janet began to save in order to have a place of her own but when the time came to move out, Janet's parents began to increase their control over Janet by insisting that she spend every Wednesday with them. Their other three "children" were assigned other days of the week. She complied and this began to seriously affect her life and especially her career prospects.

Whilst Janet was still in her late 20's she "fell in love" with an older man who came under her parents' scathing eye and so gained their "normal" disapproval. Fortunately for Janet this man pointed out to her that she was far too subject to her parents' opinions and that she needed to be more prepared to make her own stand. After a short romance this older man went the way of all his predecessors. Unfortunately Janet did not heed the warning. She seemed listless without her parents' direction and had a "blind-spot" to the destructive effect they were increasingly having on her life.

During a party at Anne's place, Janet met the "love of her life", Martin. He was young, handsome, charming, intelligent and had a very serious and thoughtful side that reflected tolerant, humanistic and democratic values. His many talents served him well in a successful career as a newspaper journalist and later as an editor and they served him well socially. He was as in love with Janet as she was with him and their relationship quickly blossomed, most especially when they took an overseas trip together. They were born to meet.

Anne was certain that they were so good together that they were certain to have married if it had not been for Janet's parents' endless critical onslaught. After four years of coping with this they began to succumb although the decline took another three years. Both of them were oppressed by this critical opinion. Eventually they were convinced that they had to make a life together and purchased a house in which they hoped to create a happy, independent home. But they had not counted on the schemes and financial resources of Janet's parents.

Without any discussion with Janet, her parents negotiated purchase of the property next door to Janet and Martin. The later didn't even know the property had been on the market. In this house they installed their youngest child Olivier. Olivier wore overalls and her spiky hair was soon followed by a shaven head. She was an angry, rabid feminist who hated all men, including Martin. She had little capacity to establish and maintain friendships of any sort and has never had a relationship last more than six months. Fundamentally she is a very lonely woman with almost no one to talk to. Her installation next door to Janet and Martin came as a terrible shock to them both. It began to undermine their previously quite lovely relationship that had all the promise of children and future happiness together. They both felt they were meant for each other until that moment. It was partly Olivier who was a problem but it was particularly their parent's connivance that over the next three years increasingly undermined the relationship between Janet and Martin. Martin wanted to be free of them. Janet couldn't make that commitment so their relationship began to spiral downwards. Janet still visited them every Wednesday and still refused to take a stand against them.

Eventually Janet decided to go overseas for a one month holiday and before she left she made out a will that she left in her father's hands. After he read the will and found she was leaving her scant possessions to Martin he tore it up. On her return Janet was devastated by his breach of the confidential trust she had shown and his flagrant disregard for her wishes. Accordingly she made out a new will and gave it to Anne for safe keeping.

The controlling parents' next scheme was to set up a women's book shop and install the three sisters to run it. In the post Germaine Greer years there was a great deal of interest in women's issues but there were very few men who ever entered the shop and men's issues were not a subject of much concern in that era. However there was an interest in these issues even at that time and this was often the subject for discussion between

Anne, Janet and Martin. A changing role for women meant a changing role for men too. As it happened Martin's mother was also a GP and had faced many role issues during her early training as a doctor.

It is important to reflect that socio-economically Janet and Martin's backgrounds were very similar so it is difficult to understand her parent's objections to Martin. Janet's father was also a GP in an inner Sydney suburb, and Janet and her siblings had all been to a private school as had Martin. Both of them had gained degrees at Sydney University.

Finally after seven years, in sheer desperation, Martin insisted that they had to break away from the parental control to which Janet was subject. She refused to make a stand against them. Martin insisted that he couldn't take any more and they broke up.

When the final crash came Anne remained independently in contact with both Janet and Martin. She tells a harrowing story of how neither of them could function even enough to continue working. Over the next six months Anne became increasingly worried about Janet's intention to starve herself to death. She took to her bed and refused both food and water for so long that Anne was sure she would not find Janet alive when she visited next day. All the fun and previous good humour they had shared seemed to have gone forever. Anne tried everything she could think of to rouse Janet. She reminded her of funny things that happened at work. She read her stories; made her tea; and took her young son along to distract her. She made her get up, dressed her frail body and took her out to the local coffee shop. After coffee she returned to bed. Janet remained immensely depressed and the black hole seemed to be getting bigger. Even friendships they shared with other men and women were avoided by Janet. –ID Laevo was firmly established and demise had become very probable.

Martin was in a state that wasn't much better and he didn't manage to begin working again for many months. He had always loved his work but he was so crushed by the failure of the relationship that his creativity and interest seemed to have dried up. On Anne's first visit to the small flat he had rented, she found he had also taken to his bed – a mattress on the floor. He like Janet had been eating so little that he was little more than skin and bones. It was over a year before he began to go out again but when he did it was evident that he never smiled at anyone or about anything. On one occasion when Anne visited Janet, as usual she called as she let herself in and there was no answer. Janet was so depleted she could not even acknowledge Anne's presence.

Janet and Martin were so much in love that being apart was destroying them.

Neither of Janet's parents took much of a role in her recovery and they have never had any further contact with Martin. Because she refused to visit them on Wednesdays, they eventually came to visit her and could not have failed to notice she was wasting away, had no food in the fridge and was immensely depressed. They began to pressure Janet into returning to University and taking up studies to be a teacher. Janet had no enthusiasm for the project or anything else for almost a decade.

Anne suspects that Janet's next choice of partner was to confront her parents. She chose a woman who was ten years her junior. The irony is that the parents installed the three sisters in a woman's book shop and they all became lesbians.

It is fortunate that Janet and her new partner have been happy for over the last ten years and IVF has enabled them to have two healthy boys. Sadly for them, Janet's parents did not accept the boys as their grand children.

Perhaps it is best that Janet's parents are now both dead. Even in their case it is significant that only two months after her father died, her mother died.

Thirty years on and Anne is still convinced Janet and Martin should have loved, married and had children together. But the circumstances ended Janet's fertility in this lifetime. After about a year of depression, Martin began to work again and slowly remake his life without Janet. Janet was much slower to recover but her parents continued their criticism of every partner Janet had found. The story isn't much different for any of her siblings.

These trials and this suffering were caused by controlling parents and Janet's unwillingness to take a stand against them; and particularly her "blind-spot" to the dreadfully negative effect they had on Janet's life. This had nothing to do with the deity – except perhaps the Eternal Love that Janet and Martin had pledged to each other.

This case fully illustrates the dire consequences that flow from not following your bliss. When you know what is right for you there is a profound need to follow that path even in the face of uncertainty. If you do not follow your bliss, you do so at your peril. The vitally important issue to learn is to recognise what makes you happy and if you are profoundly unhappy you have to set about finding the opposite circumstances. If you remain in a Laevo state for long enough it will destroy your ability to function, ruin your potential and make others around you depressed as well. Health comes more from happiness than from anything else. We are born to be happy and of necessity follow our bliss. Likewise being overly dependent on others' opinions is Laevo and independence is Dextro. Your chirality matters a great deal.

Good and loving friends are vital to a happy life. Consider for a moment where Janet and Martin would have been without Anne's wonderful support. Where loneliness is very much a Laevo state, good friends, their love, care and support are vital to our Dextro state. Primarily we are social beings and greatly benefit from worthwhile interaction. AND most especially knowing you have AIDS or HIV. The same is true for any genetic or other disease, the sufferer and career need compassion and love most. Anyone can give that.

A re-examination of Psyche and particularly building a new theoretical model of +ID Dextro and –ID Laevo is proposed to provide a useful basis for more broadly based discussion, improvements in psychotherapy for a number of conditions and to provide a constructive basis for ongoing research developments.

9. Personal Transformation and Transcendence.

In 1841 Ralph Waldo Emerson gave a public address in Boston in which he said, "some sources of human instruction are almost unnamed and unknown amongst us; that the community in which we live will hardly bear to be told that every man should be open to ecstasy or a divine illumination, and his daily walk elevated by intercourse with the spiritual world. Grant all this, as we must, yet I suppose none of my auditors will deny that we ought to seek to establish ourselves in such disciplines and courses as will deserve that guidance and clearer communication with the spiritual nature." [Bib.17].

The aim of this Chapter is to provide some useful exercises that will enable this clearer communication and guidance from your spiritual nature; and thus enable your personal Transformation and Transcendence.

In Chapter 8. "The Twin Nature of Psyche," we discussed a personal model that had an outer electron shell we termed Transcendence. This shell is very permeable at the outer and inner boundary of the self. Essentially it is somewhat like a permeable membrane that allows experience of Psyche to travel into the self and outwards from the self to the environment. Generally this process is occurring at the unconscious level but there are many ways of increasing our sensitivity to this process and of bringing this process into consciousness. Archetypes explained in transcript 10 that we can "put up more sails" to catch more of what is happening in the environment. This chapter aims to provide you with some exercises and information about how we can increase our sensitivity and awareness of what is going on in Psyche. Archetypes have already outlined several exercises in symbolic activity. Through the processes and exercises outlined in the following pages you may open up opportunities to contact your own inner wisdom figures, make contact with your spirit guides and establish contact with Archetypes directly.

We need to identify the orbitals of Transcendence as they relate to the Wisdom Paths. What is obvious is that the process of Transcendence is seen in several spectrums.

- Sphere of Ascension [1 - 9] and Progression [1 - 9]
- Period [1 - 6],
- Chirality [laevo, centre, dextro].

The overlap between these spectrums can be seen in the two mandala - Virtues of the Nine Spheres, and the circle that encompasses the Nine Spheres and represents the Inner World Arrangement to ONE and IN-ONE.

Period and Sphere have also been defined in table form, but this does not particularly suit organization of laevo, centre and dextro in the way that the mandala does. Although of course those dimensions can each be determined and displayed on the table. However, the table does show period clearly whilst the mandala does not show period. Without needing any further work, the mandala can be imagined by period in 6 sheets, one for each period of the paths but that doesn't match the elegance of the table. Either way the orbitals of transcendence apply to the current period in its context 1 - 6, where there may be several unfilled orbitals/ periods.

The direction of rotation of an electron, can indicate Laevo, Centre/Still or Dextro chirality in any orbital of any electron. Without going down the road too far, the debate between those who hold the view that electrons don't rotate, and those that think they do, our model had to allow for one to be used for analogy purposes. This does not mean being less exact, it means using the principles and rules in order to explain and be able to repeat, manage and sometimes heal. If instead of rotating, an electron vibrates by wave particle duality, the theory will still have to account for the chirality of all living organisms. Obviously that debate should not determine this release and so we proceed with the view of electron rotation. Besides, even if an electron vibrates, and it is for instance an amino acid, it will still turn light laevo or dextro to some degree of inclination from centre. Our primary concern is a living ID on the same dimensions. Besides it is still the behaviour that the theory attempts to explain. Behaviour of ID is our principle concern. Your body's chirality is vital to good physical and psychological health as well as having long term relevance to your procession, your journey in spirit. All of this is included in the behaviour of ID and it, like the behaviour of an amino acid will still behave the same way no matter what the theory. Having a new theory doesn't change the way things or people behave. Because theories assist understanding, in the same way that each period is the silver cauldron of wisdom, we will await with interest to see the outcome of scientist's debate on rotation or vibration.

However an electron moves, it is still an electron so we can concentrate on defining the electrons of transcendence. If the first periods are the silver crucible of wisdom, Period 6 is the gold crucible, as the ancients would have expressed it. Period 6 represents the highest levels in each sphere, the pinnacles of creativity, sensitivity, attunement with Universe, renewal, communication, love, mystery, partnerships, and Foundation. In this period of enlightenment in any of the spheres also comes enlightenment about other spheres, a rounding of boundaries, integration and unity. Ultimately these are the blessings that await us if our Ascension puts us in an earlier period. What better ideals and virtues could be representing the human contribution to the Age of Enlightenment in each and all our spheres on paths 46, 47, 48, 49, 50, :51, and :52. . Sometimes there are people who excel and from this system, :52 would denote this. In their manifestation of the gift of enlightenment, there are probably few who would not agree that Nelson Mandela as :51 Warrior is perfect and The Dalai Lama would deserve :52 no matter what day he was born on. [As it happens the Dalai Lama was born on 6 – 7 – 1935 = :31 Regeneration and Change].

For Ascension, providing that we allow one electron for each of 6 periods, and attribute the electron with the sphere value, all paths can be identified and by rotation we can signify chirality. Thus the outer orbitals of ID, transcendence will number 6, according to period, T 1 - 6. Electrons are assigned a value according to sphere 1 - 9 and assigned laevo, centre or dextro in rotation. This will all be based on birth date information only.

For Progression, the first marker is the name given at birth, and the second the name you are called. But period is not determined by any marker other than the birth date, so less account is required in our spectrum and period is also already determined in Ascension. Both path and sphere are important to all markers selected.

There are blessings that are granted to the soul at the commencement of each period. There is an accumulation of blessings thus bestowed: an accumulation of virtues from different periods. The later the period, the greater the possible range of blessings and the wiser the soul. All of the 6th period paths could be considered the pinnacle of achievement in human enlightenment in their sphere. And who is to say that it all ends there, after 6 Periods? That is what you might term the general inclination in Great Design's arithmetic entropy.

Reading is very much a left brain activity linked to thinking logically and systematically about things. But in general terms to access these other aspects of wisdom including your inner wisdom figures, guides and archetypes you will need to make a great deal of use of your right brain, your creative side. Several of the activities proposed in the previous chapter would aid the right brain processes. The following exercises are also designed to assist this right brain activity and balance it with left brain reflection and developmental learning. At the end of the first chapter we discussed the adult learning process as having four definable stages – experience, reflection, generalization and application. The work you do in this chapter and so the benefit you may gain are very much dependant upon your commitment to this learning process. It may mean that you need to spend a regular period of time each day or each week doing this work. Setting aside some regular times when you can be quite and alone is vital. To this end it is suggested that you find a place where you can be quietly on your own – your "Quiet Space" - as it is referred to. Where could you work alone?

Because we have already addressed the issue of dreams as a source of inner wisdom and the Spiral Process has been outlined for Dream Statement Analysis, it simple remains to be said that it is beneficial to record your dreams and ask your "dream maker" to grant you dreams on specific issues of concern for you. Writing down your dreams immediately on waking up is most necessary as the "forgotten" component comes quickly into play. So too it is helpful to ask your "dream maker" to wake you up so that you can record important dreams. A blank journal is a very good place to record your dreams and reactions and learning in the following exercises.

The following exercises are generally set out in italics. It may assist you to record them [as on a tape recorder] and leave the periods of time indicated as silent spaces. Where time is indicated [eg. Allow 3 minutes] it is only approximate.

Essentially the more personal work you do the better able you will be to have the contacts you desire and to handle the information that is forthcoming. Nearly all guidance suffers from the attitudes, opinions and values you have and these will "contaminate" what you think is said to you. Sub-personalities can also interfere in the process.

Lemons.

Obtain six lemons and put them in a bag. Go to your quiet place with your bag of lemons;
close your eyes and focus your attention on your breathing in and out until you are totally relaxed. Keeping your eyes closed select one lemon from the bag and take about two minutes to explore the way it feels, its texture, any bumps it has, its fragrance – essentially get fully in touch with the unique qualities of your lemon. After a couple of minutes you can put the lemon back into the bag and stir them all around. Then removing one lemon at a time find the lemon you originally selected and were in touch with.

Presto! You can use your senses to find the correct lemon – even when sight is not being used!

Use your journal to record your reactions and reflections on this exercise. If you look at all the six lemons are they each unique? How does this affect the stereo-type you have about lemons? How do your other stereo-types limit your awareness? Do you tend to use some senses more than others or pay more or less attention to each of your senses?

Deep Relaxation.

Virtually the starting point in most of the exercises that follow will be developing a deep sense of relaxation at the beginning. If you are not experienced in doing this you may find it helpful to purchase a tape recording of such exercises and practice until it becomes second nature as soon as you go to your quiet space.

Whilst undertaking the process of relaxation you may have images or symbols appear. These should be noted in your journal along with any memories they invoke.

Beautify & Bless Your Quiet Space.

Your quiet space may be a room; a corner of the garden with a comfortable chair; under a tree in a paddock or meadow; wherever you choose but make a choice of place because when we do some of the later exercises they will require you to start somewhere and end somewhere that is consistently used. In undertaking Pathwork with the Tree of Life all paths begin at Malkuth – the Kingdom. Your quiet space is of just the same importance. It is the place you should return to should something go wrong or if you need to end something quickly. It is the place from which to begin and end each exercise.

Select something beautiful like your favourite flower and put it in your quiet space. After carefully considering the features of the place, use your senses to really get in touch with it as with your lemon and note each of the senses responses, including sounds in your journal. Are you heightening your sensitivity? It may be helpful to identify North and light a candle there and put a vase with water in it in the South. Can you draw a simple plan or map of the place using your left hand? [Your left hand is connected to the right side of your brain.] What images, symbols and memories does the place invoke?

Do you feel relaxed, comfortable, safe and in charge in this place? If there is something you sense that isn't quite right you could try a banishing and blessings ritual. Even doing this could be seen as "cleaning and beautifying" the space. You may recall that in Chapter 3 we discussed esoteric practices and identified that there is a profound difference between "Sunwise" in the Northern and Southern Hemispheres. In the Southern Hemisphere you banish by going clockwise and invoke or bless the place by going anticlockwise. The very opposite is true in the Northern Hemisphere. *Because you are a divine being you can use your power to banish any negative energy or presence by turning around [SH - clockwise] three times and clapping your hands three times and saying aloud "Go in Eternal Peace and Love." You could then bless the place with water; circulating around it three times [SH - anticlockwise] and saying your blessings out loud as you sprinkle the water.* Keep a record of what you have done and feel.

Mapping the Inner Territory.

Having a plan is a good way of remembering where you are and where you want to go. In Transpersonal Psychology some thought has gone into mapping the Inner Territory. This is a part of psychology that takes particular account of the transcendental and spiritual drives and needs we exhibit. In this work we often see keys to healing and wholeness. One worker, Roberto Assagioli, developed a diagram of the Psyche that is known as the Egg Map that is reproduced below. Note the permeable boundaries.

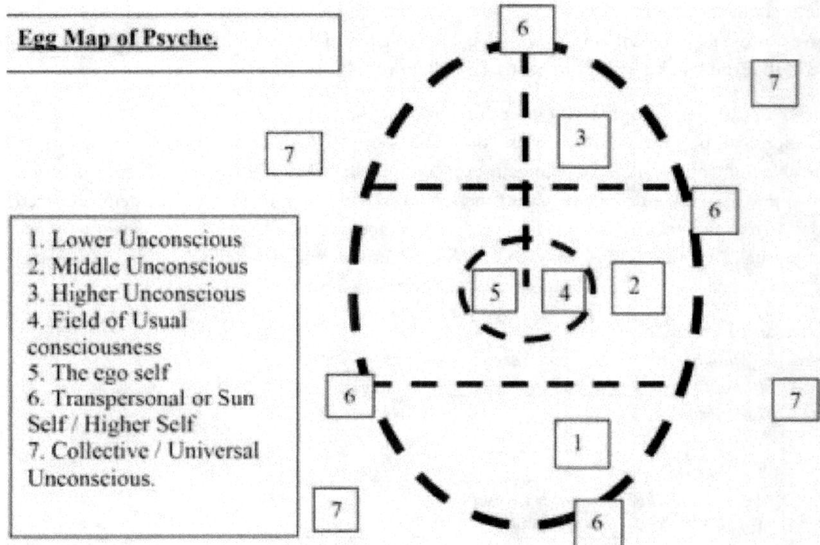

It is important to note that the majority of the area is unconscious and the actual field of Usual Consciousness and the ego is regarded as very small by comparison. Through the process of increasing your sensitivity and taking more direct notice of your dreams you are increasing the permeability of the boundaries and expanding the normal Field of Consciousness. Further to this the idea is that it takes energy to store material that is held in the Lower Unconscious. That material includes experience and feelings repressed from the normal Field of Consciousness into the Lower Unconscious. Psyche is actually very wise about the way this material is handled and your defence mechanisms generally serve you well; but as personal growth occurs the dynamics of these defences are altered and energy can be released by freeing up some of this repressed content and releasing more creative energy and wisdom in Psyche.

Recent experience and skills such as reading and writing that are used virtually habitually are in the domain of Middle Consciousness. Generally this includes ready recall of situations, events and the feelings associated with them. The Higher Unconscious is the region of our aspirations and our life lessons or purpose as a being. It is this region that is of most specific concern in developing transcendence. Transcending the mundane and reaching into our spiritual core, finding those wisdom figures that are within and without us in Psyche. Ah! What a journey that is! This speaks to the possibilities of your peak experiences; deepening insight and intuition; deeper levels of wisdom; giving and receiving unconditional love; working as a cartel of cooperation between the parts of self and with others; meeting archetypes and having dialogue with them; and finding out what you need to know to utilize your blessings most effectively. This is your journey to releasing the wisdom and divine spark within through contact with your Higher Self! Ambrosia indeed!

A vital dimension of the Map of the Inner World has already been discussed at the end of Chapter 8. Conclusions Drawn from the Transcripts with Archetypes. From your later work in subsequent chapters you will have identified the Patrons for the Wisdom Path you are on, based on the Chaldean Kabala system. This chapter is about the territory between where you are now and how you can contact Archetypes yourself, if you have not already done so. This is about you travelling into the Inner World and charting the territory as you go so that you will know how to get back safely to your quiet space.

Inner Perceptions may not match Outer Perceptions.
Expectations can be a limitation on what you discover on the road ahead. It might be best to say that if you are able to be open and flexible in your expectations this will serve you best. The normal boundaries on perception are very much a left brain function so your right brain activity will help you stretch your boundaries. It is important to avoid making judgements about things. It is best to simply observe and record in your journal. If you think this is easy to say but harder to do, you may find the following exercise helpful. It may help you release some of the energy in the Lower Unconscious.

Criticism and Judgement.
Complete the following sentences as spontaneous as you can....
    1. *I'm not _____________________ enough.*
    2. *I should be more_____________________*
    3. *Whenever I _____________________ I punish myself.*
    4. *I will never learn how to _____________________*
    5. *My life would be fine if only I could _____________________*
    6. *When I can't do something well I _____________________*
    7. *Children should _____________________*
    8. *Compared to _____________________ I am _____________________*
    9. *I criticise others most for_____________________*
    10. *As a child I was criticised for _____________________*
    11. *Men are _____________________*
    12. *Women are _____________________*
    13. *Old people are _____________________*
    14. *Marriages are _____________________*
    15. *Police are _____________________*
    16. *I punish myself by _____________________*
    17. *I punish others by _____________________*
    18. *As a child I was punished by _____________________*
    19. *I am harsh on myself when I _____________________*
    20. *In my childhood I was "put down" by _____________________*

What experiences come to mind when you reflect on your answers to these statements? How did you come to hold those views? What authority figures did you have during childhood and what role did they play? How long ago did you form these opinions?

Write a dialogue between your Critic and the part of you that wants to be less critical. Maybe a page each of the first things that come to mind. Especially note how you feel.

Ask your Critic what you need to do so that you don't continue to be adversaries.

As vividly as possible, recall a time in your childhood when you were punished for something. What did you feel and do? When you have finished the reflection, forgive yourself for whatever it was that you did and maybe forgive whoever it was that punished you.

Think about a time when you were punishing someone. How does that relate to the way you were punished? How did you feel? Stay with the experience until it has run its course – forgive that person and yourself and then write it all down in your journal.

Write a letter to your Critic and your Judge [possibly separately] saying what you intend to do differently and asking them to write back to you saying what they will do differently in those circumstances.

Run a check on yourself on any subsequent day to see how many times you are critical or judgemental. Note this also in your journal and consider the whole exercise in your quiet space. What generalizations are relevant to your critical and your judgemental sides of your self. What will you do differently in the future?

In what ways does this exercise energise you to release some parts of self from the responsibilities they have been taking? How will the new set of alliances [with the Critic and Judge] help in enabling you to be more open to experience in both the inner and outer plane of perception?

Fear.

Can I handle what will re-surface from my repressed experiences? Until you can you should not move on with these exercises here. "Living Beyond Fear – a Tool for Transformation" by Jeanne Segal [Bib. 69] is a wonderful and very important book to use to help you deal with your fears and anxieties that can severely limit and distort your process of inner discovery of the wisdom path you are on. There are some excellent exercises you can undertake and from them insights can be gained that will help on this early part of "the journey" and free-up a great deal of creative energy in Psyche and increase your capacity for deep relaxation.

How will I know if the spirit guide who I seek to help me on "the journey" ahead, is genuine, or only likely to cause me harm?

In another excellent book called "A Question of Guidance" by Ruth White [Bib. 83] she says that in her experience;

> "the key notes of the true guides … are unconditional love, or positive regard; acceptance; gentle humour; and deep wisdom without drive or threat."

In short "Fear no Evil", this is a great journey with the promise of wonderful gains.
Any of the following exercises can be undertaken as many times as necessary
for you to feel comfortable in moving on to the next exercise.

Creative Visualization.

When you enter your quiet space for this exercise, use all your senses to take the place in and pay particular attention to the process of your breathing – deep slow breaths. Feel the texture of anything within your reach; the earth under your feet; the wood or fabric of the chair you are sitting on; the texture of any clothes you are wearing; the sound of your breath through your nostrils; etc. Pay particular attention to the way your body is moving [kinaesthetic sense]. *Without crossing any parts of your body, make yourself comfortable, relax, close your eyes and picture the place you are in – reviewing its many features.*

When you are ready [deeply relaxed], ask your inner wisdom figure the question;
> *"What do I need to take with me on this journey to map the territory?"*

What images or symbols or words pop into your mind? Maybe a small stone like a travel stone, or a talisman, a favourite ring, or a small crystal or something that is already there in your quiet space? *Make a choice about what you want to take with you and hold it in your left hand as you familiarize yourself with its features.* Recording any impressions that you receive will reinforce your relationship with your inner wisdom figure. That figure will know that you are paying attention.

Politely ask your inner wisdom figure if he or she would like to accompany you on this journey. Still yourself and after a period [say 10 minutes] of silence, record any impressions you have gained – especially any feeling of a presence or closeness. If you do have a sense of acknowledgement, you could ask your inner wisdom figure to give you his or her name. Then spend some time writing down what has happened; drawing any symbols and noting any memories associated with them; writing down the name of your inner wisdom figure and any impressions you gained from his or her presence.

If you don't feel that you were acknowledged, in the same way that you wrote a one page letter to your Critic or Judge, *you could write a polite letter to your inner wisdom figure asking for his or her cooperation in your endeavour.* After writing this you could read it aloud in your quiet space – and then wait. If you still don't experience some form of acknowledgement you can expect that your journey to map the territory will be undertaken alone. He or she will join you later.

Journey to the Mountain and mapping the terrain.

The following section has some long passages of imagery that make it difficult to read whilst undertaking the exercise. You could, both in this and following italicised sections, ask someone to read them for you and time the pauses. Alternatively you could record this on a tape recorder and again time the pauses.

With your travel stone or talisman in your left hand, resume your deep relaxation in your quiet space. Review the rhythm of your breath; and experience the life giving oxygen filling every part of your body with its white light. As you breathe out imagine the tensions in your body are floating away as spent grey particles. Imagine yourself moving deeper and deeper into your inner space as you relax more and more completely.…[allow 3 minutes]

Love and Heart energy will enable you to enter and remain safe during this and future journeys. Fold your hands over the centre of your chest at the level of your heart and visualize the oxygen flowing into your heart and emanations coming from within your heart are flowing outwards in front of you… [allow 3 minutes].

In front of you is an open door…as you move towards it you may notice that it is apparently dark on the other side of the doorway but when you are standing in the doorway you can see that there is a path that leads down to a river below. This is the River of Life. As you enter the path leading down to the river, note the various things there along the way… smell the fragrance of flowers along the way…hear the sounds of birds and insects…feel the path's surface under your feet…look around and drink in the scenery…watch the animals and birds going about their business…let yourself be filled with enjoyment at the beauty of this natural landscape. When you reach the River of Life, look back along the path that you have travelled so that you will remember the way on your return journey. [Allow 3 minutes].

The path continues alongside the river, with several fords where you can safely cross the water. The running water is crystal clear and sparkles in the sunshine so you pause here and taste the delightfully fresh water…feel it running through your hands as you dip into it and bring the cool water to your lips… what else do you experience in this place? [Allow 3 minutes].

The path winds around some very large boulders, across pebbled strands, over sandy patches, through reeds in open glades surrounded by forest, through grasses and stands of trees until you suddenly come out onto a beautiful beach where the river runs into the ocean. You stop here for a welcome rest and whilst you are leaning back against a huge tree you suddenly realize you are being supported by the Tree of Life. What does it look like? Can you feel the texture of its bark? Can you feel the sap rising in the tree? It's roots run deep into the soil underneath and its branches reach out even into the ethers. You notice that the sunlight is slanting through almost translucent leaves and striking you with its warmth and creating radiance all around you. What type of tree are you leaning on? What can you see, hear, smell, feel and otherwise sense about this place where the Tree of Life stands at the intersection of the River of Life and the Ocean? [Allow 5 minutes].

To your left the beautiful curve of the beach runs around to a lighthouse on top of the South-western-most cliff.

To your right, the path leads Northward across the dry sand to the waters edge where you can feel the wet sand between your toes, smell the wonderful odour of the salt water and listen to the sound of the waves breaking in their eternal motion on the shore. You can hear the distant call of gulls and you notice some beautiful shells, even oysters clinging to the rocks at the foot of a massive rock cave that opens up inside the first headland like a huge cathedral. This cave is an incredible sea sculpture and a great place to shelter during a storm. What do you see and hear in this wondrous landscape as you drink in the details? [Allow 3 minutes.]

After the first headland the beach curves around to another more distant and very tall headland which, as you approach along the beach path the Gentle Breeze from the Ocean is soothing and cool. Eventually you realize the next headland is really a very tall mountain - maybe even a volcano on the edge of the ocean. But you can't make the features out properly because the top is shrouded in cloud. [Allow 3 minutes].

You continue along the path and it winds upwards through a rocky but tree studded ravine with a small creek running along the bottom. Again you stop to quench your thirst and take in your surroundings. What do you notice and experience in this place? [Allow 3 minutes].

The path climbs up the right side of the ravine and as you climb the path you can see a deep cave on the other side. After the fresh air and gentle breeze along the beach path, this path is much more enclosed and the air is hotter, you are now perspiring and noticing how quickly you are gaining altitude. Suddenly an eddy of hot wind turns into a "Willy-Willy" [a small whirlwind] that picks up leaves and dust in its vortex and it buffets your clothes and hair pulling them upwards. As suddenly as it struck you it moves on up the side of the ravine. Where it crossed the path, you can see crescent shaped scuff marks in the sand. [Allow 3 minutes].

When you reach the top of the ravine, you can see the path winds onwards up the mountainside. You do not continue climbing the mountain because you sense you have done enough for one day and that it is time to return to your quiet space. Maybe your inner wisdom figure has told you it is time to return? You will explore the mountain on future journeys. [Allow 3 minutes].

You return by exactly the same path you have taken, down the ravine, past the cave, to the beach…along to the first headland with its cathedral cave…further along the beach to the place where the River of Life enters the sea…it is close to sunset and the sky and the Ocean have taken on a wonderful rose red or rata red colouring and it reminds you of the Sea of Aesthete. After a short pause to take in the beauty you travel on past the Tree of Life. Up the path beside the river, over the fords and finally you are walking through your door-way into your quiet space where you rest, relax and reflect on your journey to map the territory. [Allow 5 minutes].

When you are ready make a quick sketch map of the major features you noticed in the inner terrain. When you are recording your observations and experiences you had during this journey also take note of how you felt whilst you were moving along. Did you move in a fluid manner? Were your kinaesthetic senses different as you walked along the beach and up the ravine? Were any parts of the journey vivid enough for you to be able to illustrate them with sketches? Where did you have positive and negative experiences?

This exercise has principally involved the "elements" – Earth, Water, Fire, and Air. There are several parts of the journey associated with each of these elements. In the guided imagery you experienced The Doorway, The Path, the Rocky Path, the Fords, the River of Life, the Tree of Life, the radiant Sunlight, the Ocean, the Rata-red Sea of Aesthete, the Lighthouse, the sheltering Cave, the Gentle Breeze, the Ravine, the Willy-Willy or whirlwind, the steep Path and the Mountain. What memories do you have associated with each of these "elements" and symbols? What other features or symbols caught your attention and what memories do you associate with them? Are any of these symbols more relevant to a particular part of your life? What animals, birds, insects and plants did you see along the way? What were they each doing? In what ways were they behaving in a symbolic manner; or what messages can you take from how they were behaving? It is important to record your responses.

Before you go about your normal daily business you should spend a final moment folding your hands in the centre of your chest at the level of your heart and thank your heart energy for leading you on this journey. Also imagine that, like the petals of a flower, those petals are gently but flexibly folded back into their normal place. Affirm your body's contact with the ground. As each of your future journeys will be undertaken using your Love and Heart energy this ritual closing process needs to be completed at the end of each exercise.

Three Questions.

For the remainder of this section we will focus on three questions;

1. Where am I now in my life?
2. What are my guidance needs?
3. What question(s) should I be asking?

Let's take each of these questions and initially do some right brain activities on them. *It may help in this exercise if you write each of these questions at the top of each of three pages in your journal.* It would also be of benefit to obtain some coloured pencils or crayons to record your reactions to this exercise. Drawing, no matter how crude, engages the right brain. Anything you do can be elaborated later. Initially we will only take a few minutes with each question and about the same amount of time doing the drawing and recording any symbols you see.

In your quiet space begin with deep relaxation and folding your hands over the centre of your chest and symbolically opening them as you open your Love and Heart energy.

Then let your attention focus on the question; Where am I now in my life? Ask your inner wisdom figure to send you symbols, images, energy forms or whatever you need to better understand the answer to the question. After a few minutes keeping the same meditative state, begin the work on your first page and simply draw anything that comes to mind. Again taking just a few minutes to draw.

This process is then repeated for the second and third questions – beginning again with relaxation. On completion of all three questions, gently close your heart energy and thank it for the assistance given and affirm your body's contact with the ground.

When you have completed your drawings, carefully examine them and write in what you think and feel about what you have done. It may be that you are already formulating some ideas about what guidance means and what you want from it. Some of you may even have seen or briefly encountered your inner wisdom figure. *Some of your dreams around this time may also be very revealing so recording them in your journal could be beneficial.*

Journey Along the River of Life.

When you think back over your life it may help if you divide the time elapsed so far into 7 year periods of chronological age; from 0 - 7 – 14 – 21 – 28 – 35 – 42 etc. One starting point for "Where I am now" is the period you are in. Write down each of those periods in order up to the present time leaving spaces between them for recording any memories that you have or special events that occurred.

In your quiet space, enter relaxation and with each in-breath and out-breath slowly and gently open your heart energy.

When you have entered deep relaxation, imagine your doorway is open to the inner territory beyond and that as you move through the doorway you can see the path that leads down to the River of Life as you have partly explored it. Again you go quietly along whilst noting all the features around you. When you reach the river, there is a new path leading you upstream to the Source or Spring where the river comes bubbling up from the ground in the East. The place of beginnings. What features do you note here? What feelings do you have about your own birth? What impressions, even fleeting senses, thoughts, images, memories, etc. are connected to your first 7 years of life? You were born to meet your parents and siblings; how have the affected you? What are the earliest impressions you have of them and their friends and neighbours? What memories do you have about your earliest years in kindergarten and school? Where any of these people of continuing importance in your life? [Allow 3 minutes for this period of your life].

Without disturbing your meditative state, you may wish to take a few minutes to write some notes about this fist period of your life. Then re-centre yourself and enter back into deep relaxation.

The path besides the River of Life runs Westward down the valley where you have travelled before down to the Ocean where the Tree of Life stands. You have been there in your journey to map the territory. What features did you identify along the way. If you think about the second period in your life from 7 to 14; what features belong to that part of your journey? What memories are associated with that section of your path beside the river? What images, feelings, symbols etc., do you notice? [Allow 3 minutes].

Without disturbing your meditative state, you may wish to take a few minutes to write some notes about this part of your journey. Then re-centre yourself and enter back into deep relaxation.

As you continue along the River of Life, you are reflecting on the period from age 14 to 21 years. What features are associated with that period? What memories, impressions, images and feelings were involved in that part of your life? [Allow 3 minutes].

Without disturbing your meditative state, you may wish to take a few minutes to write some notes about this part of your journey. Then re-centre yourself and enter back into deep relaxation.

As you continue along the River of Life, you are reflecting on the period from age 21 to 28 years. What features are associated with that period? What memories, impressions, images and feelings were involved in entering adulthood? [Allow 3 minutes].

Without disturbing your meditative state, you may wish to take a few minutes to write some notes about this part of your journey. Then re-centre yourself and enter back into deep relaxation.

As you continue along the River of Life, you are reflecting on the period from age 28 to 35 years. What features are associated with that period? What memories, impressions, images and feelings were involved in early adulthood? [Allow 3 minutes].

Without disturbing your meditative state, you may wish to take a few minutes to write some notes about this part of your journey. Then re-centre yourself and enter back into deep relaxation.

As you continue along the River of Life, you are reflecting on the period from age 35 to 42 years. What features are associated with that period? What memories, impressions, images and feelings were involved in that part of your life? [Allow 3 minutes].

Without disturbing your meditative state, you may wish to take a few minutes to write some notes about this part of your journey. Then re-centre yourself and enter back into deep relaxation.

[Considering your current age and the relevant period, the Tree of Life stands at the point where the river meets the Ocean and it represents where you are now in your life. If you are more than 42, continue the above process along the river until you reach your current period.]

Without disturbing your meditative state, you may wish to take a few minutes to write some notes about this part of your journey. Then re-centre yourself and enter back into deep relaxation.

You are standing before the Tree of Life. Enter into the scene as fully as you can. What can you see, smell, feel, sense or hear? If you lean against the trunk as you did last time does the sun shine through the leaves and shed its warmth and radiance on you? Can you feel the sap rising in the trunk? Have any of its features changed since you were last here? This is where you are now in your life. What impressions, images, symbols, feelings, ideas etc., come to you? [Allow 3 minutes].

Without disturbing your meditative state, you may wish to take a few minutes to write some notes about this part of your journey. Then re-centre yourself and enter back into deep relaxation.

It is time to make the return journey, so bid your farewells to the Tree of Life and express your gratitude for the blessings which have come to you in your life. You will return here on later journeys. As you turn Eastward, you are going back up the River of Life, and visiting all of the features in each of your periods but in reverse order until you arrive back at the Source. Before you leave the Source, express your gratitude for the manifold blessings the River of Life has brought to you. What impressions, ideas, images, symbols and feelings do you have here? [Allow 3 minutes].

Without disturbing your meditative state, you may wish to take a few minutes to write some notes about this part of your journey. Then re-centre yourself and enter back into deep relaxation.

As you leave the Source, you join the path that leads back to your doorway to your quiet space. Along the way it is important to note the various features of your landscape; to note any animals or birds that you see or hear; the fragrance of any flowers; the light that shines on particular trees or bushes; etc. As you approach your doorway, express your gratitude to the Path for showing you the way. Cross through the doorway into your quiet space and relax comfortably, just noting any things that surface into your consciousness about your journey since you left the Source. [Allow 3 minutes].

Without disturbing your meditative state, you may wish to take a few minutes to write some notes about this part of your journey. Then re-centre yourself and enter back into deep relaxation.

Allow any impressions to surface into your consciousness as you consider the periods of your life and the totality of the journey you have been on. Are there any symbols that will help you recall and understand any of the difficult periods? Then slowly and gently, as if a flower is folding its petals, with each in-breath and out-breath close your heart energy and affirm your body's contact with the ground. Then begin your period of reflection.

During your reflection you will have a lot of notes to consider about each of the periods in your life. At the end, you could ask why Psyche has surfaced these particular memories and recalled these events at this time and in this place? A careful consideration of this question will help sharpen your sense of guidance, overall purpose and even possibly a pattern will emerge that is relevant to your Wisdom Paths of either Ascension or Progression.

Return to your sketch of the inner territory and evaluate the features that you have drawn. In light of the exercise you have completed concerning the 7 year periods in your life, what memories are associated with any of the other features in your sketch? How could you further define those features? Which features are identified with positive emotions and memories? Which features are associated with negative memories and emotions? Do you need to add some new features to your sketch or place any of the symbols you have seen on that sketch?

If you happen to have chosen the "deep cave on the other side of the ravine" for either your positive or negative features, make sure that at this stage you **do not** approach that cave until your inner wisdom figure is accompanying you. You would be best to stay exactly on the path up the Mountain and consider "the deep cave" from the point where the "Willy-Willy" left scuff marks in the sand on the path. It is most important that you do not approach the cave until you have met and been accompanied by your inner wisdom figure – as you will be in a later journey when you will be delighted and possibly surprised by the outcome.

Journey to Your Positive and Negative Features.
In your quiet place, begin the process of relaxation and gently open your heart energy.

After some time but only when you are feeling deeply relaxed and ready, recall the sketch you have just been working on. Then ask your inner wisdom figure to draw your attention to a positive feature and show you a symbol. [Allow 3 minutes].

Without disturbing your meditative state, make some notes in your journal and return to your deep relaxation. Again recall the sketch including the new aspects you have just added. Then ask your inner wisdom figure to draw your attention to a negative feature and to show you a symbol. [Allow 3 minutes].

Again make some notes in your journal and adjust the sketch.

When you are deeply relaxed again, ask your inner wisdom figure if you should take a talisman with you on a journey to your positive and negative features. [Allow 3 minutes].

Gently close your heart energy and go and get the talisman indicated. [Most likely this object is already in your possession. If you can't find it you can draw it.]

Re-commence your relaxation and opening of your heart energy.

When you are ready, go out through your doorway; the path will lead you to your positive feature. As you travel along, note all the things along the way and anything that draws your attention or that stimulates a memory. Open all your senses and note any memories that emerge as you approach your positive feature. When you arrive drink in all the details about the place and pay particular attention to any impressions, thought, feelings or symbols that may come to you. You may sense that you are drawn to more closely examine some detail. What happens when you do? [Allow 3 minutes].

Without disrupting your meditative state, take a few minutes to write some notes about your journey to this place and what you have experienced here. Note what is happening to your talisman – can you feel any vibration? What memories are evoked; what emotions; impressions; ideas; symbols; energy fields; etc., do you experience?

Re-enter your relaxed state and allow a moment or so for it to deepen. Possibly it will assist if you hold your talisman in your left hand as you are going to follow the path that goes from this positive feature to a negative feature. As you will be returning here, note any of the features along the path and any memories, impressions or feelings that you associate with approaching a negative feature. When you arrive take careful note of any of the aspects of this place. What were the negative reactions linked to? How do you feel as you study those features? What memories, impressions, thoughts, ideas and feelings do you associate with this place? How is your talisman reacting? [Allow 3 minutes].

Without disrupting your meditative state, take a few minutes to write some notes about your journey to this place and what you have experienced here. Note what is happening to your talisman – can you feel any vibration? What memories are evoked; what emotions; impressions; ideas; symbols; energy fields; etc., did you experience?

Re-enter your relaxed state and allow a moment for it to deepen. Before you leave this place, have a careful look around to see if there are some things that need to be attended to or put right. Does something need to be repaired? Is there a hole that needs to be filled in? In your memory was there something that was left unsaid? Consider what you need to do to make a difference here, to put something right. Maybe even to put some colours in different places; fill a crack; straighten a leaning post; put in some plants; or screw a door back onto its hinges. Allow your intuition to guide you in what to do and when to do it. [Allow 3 minutes].

Without disrupting your meditative state, take a few minutes to write some notes about your journey to this place and what you have experienced here. Note what is happening to your talisman – can you feel any vibration? What memories are evoked; what emotions; impressions; ideas; symbols; energy fields; etc., did you experience?

Re-enter your relaxed state and allow a moment or so for it to deepen. Then bid this place farewell and continue your journey along the path back to your positive feature. Note the things along the way. What has changed since you were travelling in the other direction? When you reach your positive feature again, think back to your experience at your negative feature and review what happened there. There were some things you put right so how does that heal the negative impression you had about the place? Ask your inner wisdom figure to assist you with an insight into how you can better integrate the negative sense you had about the place. [Allow 3 minutes].

Without disrupting your meditative state, take a few minutes to write some notes.

Re-enter your relaxed state and allow a moment or so for it to deepen. What has changed about your positive feature since you were last here? How has your journey to your negative feature influenced how you see things now? [Allow 3 minutes].

Without disrupting your meditative state, take a few minutes to write some notes.

Re-enter your relaxed state and allow a moment or so for it to deepen. Then bid farewell to your positive feature and take the path that leads back to your doorway. Again, as you travel along note all the things along the way, the memories invoked, your feelings, impressions of the various features; and when you reach your quiet space reflect back on the journey you have taken and see how this informs you about the 3 questions;

> *Where am I now in my life?*
> *What are my guidance needs?*
> *What question/s should I be asking?*
> *Then ask your inner wisdom figure to enable your healing of the negative patterns in your life by giving you a symbol or insight that will bring about strength and resourcefulness and lead you to the "Highest, Light, Good". [Allow 3 minutes].*

At this point you could write up the experience in your journal, but before you go back to your normal daily routine, spend a few moments gently folding in the petals of your heart energy.

Choosing an Archetype to help with your questions.

From the point of view of guidance from the Archetypes it is important not to invite just anyone who wants to talk to you but to invite a particular Archetype of your careful and rational choice.

If you spend some time reviewing the Circle of Archetypes at the end of Chapter 5. Spheres and their relationships, you should be in a better position to make a considered choice of Archetype. As you will notice there is an Archetype given for each Sphere so you could consider approaching that Archetype. Each of the Archetypes have the status of being Patrons for various Wisdom Paths so this can help you narrow the field. Equally, it is Mother Earth who offers herself to anyone on any path.

You are one who is in control of this process of contact with both the Archetypes, spirit guides and the deity generally. You need to maintain this control and even if things get too much for you, you can limit and even terminate contact by immediately returning to your quiet space. Initially only one Archetype should be chosen but if you need to make contact with another Archetype you can repeat the process below on as many occasions as you consider necessary. However, the very important rule is **"one at a time"**.

To make contact with your Archetype there are two basic preconditions. Firstly, meeting with your Inner Wisdom Figure and secondly, having the strong, primal or instinctive energy of your Totemic Animal on your side.

Meeting Your Inner Wisdom Figure.

In your quiet space, begin the process of relaxation by focussing on your in-breath and out-breath for some time until you are reaching the deeper layers of relaxation. Then begin to gently open the petals of your heart energy. This journey is to the dwelling place of your Inner Wisdom Figure. As you are standing in the doorway you can see the path leading to this dwelling place. What do you notice as you travel along the path? What sights, sounds and fragrances occur and how do you feel as you are moving along? When you reach the dwelling invoke the presence of your Inner Wisdom Figure. He or she may invite you inside or you could sit in the garden beside the water, or simply take a walk together. Take note of what he or she is wearing and how you are greeted. You may ask; how may I refer to you? Carefully express your gratitude for the guidance you have been given so far [images, symbols, impressions and ideas] and explain that you want to meet with an Archetype who you have chosen; the purpose of

Meeting Your Totemic Animal.

In the Transcripts we are given quite a lot of animals who are in various helping relations with people and
the Archetypes of the Inner World. Some of these animals such as the Lion [Royal Star of the Lion] and the
Shark are themselves identified as Archetypes. In addition we were given;

Adders who are usually misaligned but are animals on the side of Creation.

Pegasus, the winged horse and other mythological creatures.

Horses

Ernie the Sea Eagle

Deer

Stag

Rat

Chickens/chooks

Whales

Seals

Sharks – to the Eskimo the shark is well known as a helping spirit

Garfish and Wrasse

Does – kangaroo, deer, rabbit, hares, goat

Eider duck

Aves - that covers all birds in the most general sense who are often messengers.

Sheep/ram

Squirrel

Swan

Lion

Donkey

Emu, Rhea and Moa

In total some 28 animals and birds are referred to in the transcripts.

From the above list, all the birds are represented in Aves although special mention is given to the Sea Eagle

Ernie who is the doctor to ONE, and Rhea who is bound to be Woden's favourite. In the transcripts, especially the first, we are given to appreciate that animals are also able to conduct very important spiritual rituals. The example given is pivotal in the balance of the forces of Destruction and Creation. The Reed Dais Tide is a ritual conducted by the Leader Whales when they are at rest after being tired by their journey.

Animals are not only important to us but also to Archetypes. When you go to meet your Archetype of choice, the animal who accompanies you is very important. It certainly does not need to be a fierce animal. Even the meek and mild Lamb, who has the wonderful powers of Redemption, may be exactly the right animal to augment your journey to the Archetype of your choice.

In the myths and traditions of the Australian Aborigines there are almost countless totemic animals and birds. But in virtually every part of the continent the totemic animals to which an individual belongs are not to be hunted or eaten by that individual. This practice is also wide spread in many other parts of the globe. The North American Indians wouldn't dream if it were not for animals, nor would their Medicine Wheels have any significance if it were not for the helpful nature of these creatures of the wild. Even in the present day the Animal Cards originate from the mythology of these people. Animals are very widely regarded as the helping spirits of humans, most particularly in Shamanism that is still practiced globally.

> "In a considerable number of myths and legends all over the world the hero is carried into the beyond by an animal. It is always an animal that carries the neophyte into the bush [underworld] on its back, or holds him in the jaws, or "swallows" him to "kill and resuscitate him". Finally we must take into account the mystical solidarity between man and animal, which is a dominant characteristic of the religion of the paleo-hunters….the tutelary animal not only enables the shaman to transform himself; it is in a manner his "double", his alter ego. This alter ego is one of the shamans souls, the soul in animal form or more precisely the "life soul"….the animal spirits play the same role as the ancestral spirits; these too carry the shaman to the beyond [sky, underworld] reveal the mysteries to him, teach him,… Mircea Eliade "Shamanism Archaic Techniques of Ecstasy [Bib. 18].

You may already know your Totemic Animal. Your Inner Wisdom Figure may have discussed this with you or you may have noticed the appearance of several animals during your journeys through the inner territory. Alternatively you may have found that a particular animal has always had something fascinating about it. Your Totemic Animal is known to your intuition and you have the power to invoke this creature of the wild without there being any need for you to be concerned for your own safety. This creature will be a friend with whom you will be able to communicate and it will be benevolent and your protector.

When you go into your quiet space simply follow your normal rituals of relaxation and opening your heart energy. You are about to undertake a very important journey to meet your Totemic Animal and the Archetype of your choice. Bring to mind the sketch you did of the inner territory leading to the Mountain. This is the path that you will be following. From your doorway the path leads down to the River of Life and you will possibly be accompanied on this journey by your Inner Wisdom Figure. Proceed along the path with your normal sensitivity to all the sounds, sights, fragrances, senses of movement and impressions. It is important to stay alert even in this now familiar terrain. So you continue down the River of Life to the Tree of Life where you might rests as usual, looking out to the West over the Ocean. [Allow 3 minutes].

Without disrupting your meditative state, you may wish to take a few minutes in order to make a few notes. Then return to your deeper levels of relaxation.

Now begins the journey North-wards along the beach, around to the first Headland and the Cathedral Cave. Go to the entrance to the cave and say aloud that you want to meet with your Totemic Animal and have it accompany you on the journey ahead. Then continue along the beach path paying attention to all the sights and sounds etc., along the way. Again you will enjoy the fresh breeze coming from the Ocean. What animals have appeared to you? Should a whale or dolphin or shark appear to you, go to the waters edge and greet it as you would a very old and dear friend. How does it greet you? How does it show its happiness? Although such creatures will not be able to go with you on the land journey ahead, you will probably feel a jolt in the region of your solar plexus and stomach and you will know that it has opened up these lower regions of your awareness and can still be "present" on your journey. If there are still no signs of your Totemic Animal continue up the path on the right side of the Ravine to the point where the Willy-Willy left scuff marks in the sand on the track. Rest there and look across the Ravine to the deep cave on the other side and wait there for your Totemic Animal and invoke its presence. Do not go down the ravine to the creek or enter that cave. Call the animal out and wait until it comes. If it still hasn't come to you, return to your quiet space and undertake this same journey on another occasion until the animal does appear. Alternatively you could ask your Inner Wisdom Figure to give you some assistance with contacting your Totemic Animal. When the animal does appear make sure you greet it like you would do with a very old friend and thank it for meeting you. [Allow 4 minutes].

Without disrupting your meditative state, you may wish to take a few minutes in order to make a few notes. Then return to your deeper levels of relaxation.

Accompanied by your Totemic Animal and your Inner Wisdom Figure, you continue along the path up the Mountain. Drink in the scenery that is revealed to you as you climb higher and higher. Eventually you come to a bend in the path and your Inner Wisdom Figure suggests that you all have a rest before going around the bend to the plateau where the Archetype will be waiting. There beside the path is a small fresh water spring from which you all drink to quench your thirst. Your Totemic animal will possibly lie down beside you and you could stoke it and dialogue together whilst waiting for the right time to continue your journey. [Allow 3 minutes].

Without disrupting your meditative state, you may wish to take a few minutes in order to make a few notes about your Totemic Animal and the greeting process. Then return to your deeper levels of relaxation.

Journey to Meet Your Archetype.

When the time is right, you will leave your Totemic Animal lying down but on guard at the small spring. You and your Inner Wisdom Figure continue around the bend and onto a clear plateau near the top of the Mountain where you are to meet the Archetype of your choice. Move around the area and "sense" the right place to be standing or sitting on the plateau before you invoke the Archetype. Take a few moments to drink in the scenery and make your normal observation about the features of the place you are in, any impressions you have or any memories that are invoked by the place. Your Inner Wisdom Figure will probably sit somewhere away from the place you choose and will be unlikely to enter into your dialogue with the Archetype. When you feel the time is right, ask the Archetype to come and meet you. When he or she arrives, take a mental note of the way the Archetype appears and of the greeting process that occurs. Do not rush this encounter, take your time and remain peaceful and open to anything that happens. At an appropriate time you might tell the Archetype that you have come with a question you would like to ask. If the Archetype acknowledges that the time is right for you to ask your question, you may proceed to ask your question. Is there anything further that you want the Archetype to comment on or is there anything the Archetype wants from you? When these matters are attended to it is time to thank the Archetype for coming to meet you and to bid farewell. [Allow 4 minutes for this dialogue.]

Without disrupting your meditative state, you may wish to take a few minutes in order to make a few notes about your meeting with your Archetype, the greeting process that occurred, how the dialogue proceeded, the question you asked and the answer you were given. Any other details about the meeting can also be noted including a sketch of the place where the meeting occurred. Then return to your deeper levels of relaxation.

Bring the plateau back into focus and join your Inner Wisdom Figure and discuss what occurred during the meeting with your Archetype. Before you leave the place, carefully look around at the features of the plateau and any impressions you gain about the place, then also bid the place farewell and thank it for being the host for the meeting you have just had. Then with your Inner Wisdom Figure, return around the bend to the place where your Totemic Animal is waiting. Greet this animal properly and thank it for keeping guard and preparing you for this important meeting with your Archetype. It is now time to return either via the path to your quiet space or to return by another route. Your Inner Wisdom Figure and your Totemic Animal may both accompany you up to your doorway or take their leave at some other point in the return journey. Properly expressing your appreciation for their contributions is very important. When you go through the doorway into your quiet space relax comfortably and allow a few moments to reflect on aspects of the journey that have occurred. [Allow 3 minutes].

Make any notes that you think are necessary and then return to your relaxed state and gently close your heart energy, feel your feet on the ground or the way your chair is supporting you and then slowly open your eyes and take in the familiar surrounds of your quiet space. You could then begin to write down what the Archetypes said to you about your question and how the Archetype personified when meeting you. To help open your right brain you could make a sketch of the place of your meeting; how the Archetype appeared; and how your Totemic Animal represented itself. Then it would be worth reviewing the various notes you took during the exercise.

To gain another perspective on your question, you could undertake this journey with another Archetype of your choice.

Journey to Meet Your Sub-personalities.

"On separate occasions, different motives, traits, attitudes, purposes and value systems may operate in us and in the way in which we handle life. In varying situations we may sense ourselves to be almost different personalities. Initial realization of this multi-faceted quality of being sometimes brings anxiety, fear of loss of identity, of being a "split personality", of going mad. Yet these aspects may belong to the inner parts of ourselves which were referred to by Jung as the "persona" or "mask", and seen by Assagioli to have almost separate existence as "sub-personalities". Such diverse identities are widely seen to be part of the normal range of experience and not belonging to abnormal pathology."

Ruth White [Bib. 83].

These sub-personalities usually arise in Psyche as part of our defence mechanisms so they may be manifest as "Shyness" in situations of unfamiliarity or where we are not very confident. Or they manifest as "Flamboyant" in situations on the dance floor or in the bedroom. Nearly everyone will find they have an Inner Child who may be compulsively clean or dirty or demanding or petulant or even magical. However these sub-personalities have formed, they are seldom in communication with each other, although some collusion occurs from time to time. In the earlier discussion about freeing up energy in Psyche we explored a number of things that you can undertake. This is yet another of those processes to free up the creative energy in Psyche. It takes energy to handle sub-personalities and instead of them sometimes working against each other it would be best if they were working with "I" as the leader of the team. The aim of the following exercise is to help you identify what sub-personalities you have and to develop a strategy to reduce their possible negative impact. This is a process aimed at transformation and integration.

You may recall Linda Goodman's chart on page 374 saying that when the Sun Sign sharply contrasts with the Sphere the person's behaviour can startle others and even surprise the person themselves. Whilst you can't manage to change either your Sphere of Ascension or your Sun Sign you can manage how you respond in various situations by being more aware of the operating sub-personalities related to certain of your traits.

> "When a sub-personality is given recognition, no matter how much from the shadow side of us it may seem to come, it begins to loose its autonomy. Our abilities to observe and discriminate, to understand or be compassionate can be activated towards it. Steps can be taken to be more in control of it, rather than being in its control." Ruth White [Bib. 83].

The first part of the following process is simply to meet the various sub-personalities – **"one by one."** The second part is to begin a dialogue with them. In the third part you will encourage them to dialogue with each other, and you may be able to mediate between those which are at war. By decreasing their separateness the sub-personalities can help meet their respective needs and become more integrated.

Some sub-personalities can manifest as if persons, others may manifest as an animal or even a mythological creature. When you first use this process only invoke the first six sub-personalities – one at a time. Don't try and meet them all together. If they won't respect your rule of one at a time, close the exercise and return to your quiet space.

In your quiet space, commence the process of relaxation and using each in-breath and out-breath begin to gently open your heart energy. Ask your Inner Wisdom Figure if there is a talisman that you need to take with you and if he or she would like to keep you company on this journey. All your sub-personalities live in a houseboat. This houseboat is moored in a safe backwater on the River of Life. When you go to your doorway you will see the path leading to this backwater. As you proceed along the path take in all the surroundings as usual and note all the features along the way. When you can see the houseboat, find a comfortable tree to lean against on the bank near the houseboat but do not go on board. When you are relaxed and ready, invoke the first of your sub-personalities to come and meet you – but not to have a dialogue until you have met them all. Thank him or her for manifesting and meeting you and allow this sub-personality to go back on board.

Without disturbing your meditative state, take a few moments to write some notes or draw that sub-personality and record any impressions you had. If your Inner Wisdom Figure is with you, you could discuss your impressions and find a name to describe that sub-personality.

When you return to deepening relaxation, invoke the second of your sub-personalities to come and meet you but not to have any dialogue until you have met them all. After the meeting you can thank him or her for manifesting and coming to meet you. Then this sub-personality can go back on board.

Without disturbing your meditative state, take a few moments to write some notes or draw that sub-personality and record any impressions you had. If your Inner Wisdom Figure is with you, you could discuss your impressions and find a name to describe that sub-personality.

Repeat this process until you have met the first six sub-personalities. When the last one goes back on board you could say aloud that you intend to return to meet any others and that you regret that they have been neglected and that you intend to return again and again until you have meet them all. When that has occurred you would like to begin a dialogue with each of them in order to find a new way of working with them.

Then return along the path, noting things along the way; go through the doorway to your quiet space and complete such drawings and notes as you require.

Then move back into relaxation and closing your heart energy and affirming your body's contact with the ground before you go about your normal daily routines or business.

When you use the process the second time you might suggest that if any sub-personalities are in a twin relationship that you will allow them to meet you together rather than only one at a time.

The process can be repeated as many times as it takes to meet all your sub-personalities and hold a series of dialogues with them. You might even ask them your 3 questions to determine what level of wisdom they have acquired. It is very likely that a number of your sub-personalities are quite simple and no longer needed so they may be combined with others or no longer necessary at all. Ask them what their needs are and have them talk to each other about how their respective needs can be met or integrated. The principal aim of these dialogues is to enable the sub-personalities to see that by some combination / integration they can become more akin to a higher archetype.

Journey to the Top of the Mountain.

The purpose of this journey is for you to form and establish a conscious relationship with your Spirit Guide. It is most likely that there is already an unconscious connection. It is possible that you have already sensed a "presence" near you when you have been alone – sometimes making the hairs stand up on the back of your neck and/or arms. From the earlier map of Psyche, the Higher Self would be entirely familiar with your Spirit Guide. It is also probable that your Inner Wisdom Figure is also on familiar terms with your Guide. The obvious starting point is with your Inner Wisdom Figure.

In your quiet space proceed as usual with relaxation and opening your heart energy. When you are deeply relaxed and ready, invoke your Inner Wisdom Figure and explain that you would like to have direct contact with your Spirit Guide and ask him or her, your question. [Allow 3 minutes].

Without disturbing your meditative state, take a few moments to write some notes and record any impressions you had from your Inner Wisdom Figure. You may have even received some advice about how to go about this process of contacting your Spirit Guide.

When you have returned to the deeper levels of relaxation, you could ask your Inner Wisdom Figure to come with you and your Totemic Animal on a journey to the top of the Mountain. Again you will set off from your doorway and follow the path down to the River of Life and west-ward to the point where the Tree of Life is standing by the Ocean. After a short rest there, you continue North-ward along the beach to the first headland, past the Cathedral Cave and along the beach path where the gentle breeze refreshes you and invigorates your sense of smell. Eventually you reach the Ravine and follow the path up the right side until you are opposite the deep cave where you Totemic Animal lives. [Allow 3 minutes].

Without disturbing your meditative state, take a few moments to write some notes and record any impressions you had along the way.

When you have returned to the deeper levels of relaxation, invoke the animals presence and greet it like an old friend when it arrives. The three of you continue up the ravine and then up the mountain to the spring near the plateau. Here you all pause, enjoy the refreshing water and the scenery and then proceed around the bend to the plateau. Your Totemic Animal will probably lie down here as you explore the place and note any changes that have occurred since you were there to meet your Archetype. [Allow 3 minutes].

Without disturbing your meditative state, take a few moments to write some notes and record any impressions you had along the way.

When you have returned to the deeper levels of relaxation, find the right place and determine the right moment to say aloud to your Spirit Guide –
> *What is your name;*
> *What is your name;*
> *What is your name?*

[Allow 3 minutes].

Without disturbing your meditative state, take a few moments to write some notes and record any impressions you gained. Did you feel that you were acknowledged? Did you have any sense of a "presence"? How did your Totemic Animal react?

When you have returned to the deeper levels of relaxation, find the path that leads from the plateau up to the top of the mountain. Your Totemic Animal will stay on guard on the plateau until you return. You and your Inner Wisdom Figure will climb the path together. The path becomes increasingly steep and you note that steps have been beautifully crafted into the rock. As you climb higher and higher a light mist surrounds the top of the mountain and it has a particular hue about it. When you reach the top there are six beautiful ponds of crystal clear water with lilies and lotus flowers growing in them. Flagstones line the path North-ward that leads up to a small temple that has only one step at the entrance where you take off your shoes at the South door.   [Allow 3 minutes].

Without disturbing your meditative state, take a few moments to write some notes and record any impressions you have about the journey up to the temple. Even a quick sketch may be helpful later and it may help your right brain activity.

Returning to your relaxation and concentrating on your in-breath and out-breath, feel your heart energy singing. As you go inside you light a small white candle at the North end of the Temple. You can feel your heart energy radiating into the place as you explore it with all your senses. You choose to sit on the right hand side of the Temple [dextro] and continue to take in your surroundings, noting how each of your senses are reacting. Finally you reach a state of complete inner stillness and close your eyes. After some unknown period of time you become aware that the hairs on your arms are standing up and you have a distinct feeling of a "presence" and the air seems suddenly to be colder. Your Spirit Guide has come to meet you. You become aware that you should stay perfectly still. An inner voice says, "I have come to guide you through the Great Silence so that you can meet Great Spirit."   [Allow 10 minutes].

During the Great Silence you feel as though you are standing on a huge web and you can feel the connection between all things. Your Inner Wisdom Figure is intricately involved with you. Your Spirit Guide, although unseen gives you a clear sense of quality, reassurance, love and a deeply spiritual sense of the connection between all three of us. There is even a beautiful fragrance in the air which seems known to you at some very ancient level of your being. Here is the peace that surpasses all understanding. Here I and Thou are One Unity. You become aware that there is a very soft voice and as you focus on it increasingly carefully you know Great Spirit is speaking to your inner knowing and you are being blessed with Great Love. Tears of pure joy begin to flow.   [Allow 10 minutes].

Without disturbing your meditative state, take a few moments to write some notes and record your feelings and impressions.

Returning to your relaxation and concentrating on your in-breath and out-breath, feel your heart energy singing. It is now time for you to go. Thank Great Spirit for blessing you in such a profound way. Thank your Spirit Guide for meeting you and guiding you through the Great Silence. Thank the Temple for safely housing you through this time, bid your farewells and go silently back to your shoes on the step at the entrance. As you are going along with your Inner Wisdom Figure you talk about what has just happened and you learn to your delight that you can come back here any time you like. Before you start to go down the steps, your Inner Wisdom Figure suggests you stop here and write down what happened, what you felt, any senses and impressions you had, what you detected with each of your senses. Maybe even a sketch of the inside of the Temple. Because some of the very important things are sometimes only fleeting an early record is often a better one.   [Allow 3 minutes].

Without disturbing your meditative state, take a few moments to write some notes, record your impressions and sketch the Temple.

Returning to your relaxation and concentrating on your in-breath and out-breath feel your heart energy singing. Travel lightly down the steps to a small landing where the Sun suddenly breaks through the mist behind you and casts your shadow onto the mist bank in front of you. The outline of your figure is surrounded by rainbow light — a perihelion. At the plateau your Totemic Animal greets you very warmly and again you can feel the blessing of Great Love and you share it. Together you travel around the bend to the spring where you may stop and quench your thirst. Soon you are travelling down the Ravine; out onto the beach; around the first Headland; and along to the Tree of Life where you all stop to rest. Your Totemic Animal and your Inner Wisdom Figure continue to travel with you up the River of Life, along your path to your doorway where you thank them for accompanying you and keeping you safe. You bid them farewell. When you turn into your quiet space you will need to relax and reflect for some time.   [Allow 3 minutes].

Without disturbing your meditative state, take a few moments to write some notes, record your impressions and further sketch parts of your journey.

Finally, you may need to return to your relaxation process and begin to close the petals of your heart in as loving a way as you can and affirm your body's contact with the ground.

May you go in Eternal Peace and Love.

[Horse Head Nebula in Orion.]

10. BIBLIOGRAPHY.

1. Apuleius "The Golden Ass". Circa AD 120 – 125 - 170 -190. As in Lemolt Phraxary "The History of Psyche". Charles Tilt. London. 1832.
2. Ashcroft-Nowicki, Dolores. "The Shining Paths." Aquarian Press. 1983.
3. Bancroft, Anne. "Origins of the Sacred". Arkana. 1987.
4. Barr, Andy. "Traditional Bush Medicines." Greenhouse Publications.1988.
5. Beblo T, Driessen M, Mertens M, Wingenfeld K, Piefke M, Rullkoetter N, Silva-Saavedra A, Mensebach C, Reddemann L, Rau H, Markowitsch HJ, Wulff H, Lange W, Berea C, Ollech I, Woermann FG. "Functional MRI correlates of the recall of unresolved life events in borderline personality disorder." [http://www.ncbi.nlm.nih.gov/entrez/query.fcgi?] 2006.
6. Benazzi F. "Borderline personality-bipolar spectrum relationship Prog Neuropsychopharmacol Biol Psychiatry Jan;30 (1) :68-74 2005.
7. Blainey, G. "Triumph of the Nomads – A History of Ancient Australia". Sun. 1983.
8. Bulfinch, Thomas. "The Golden Age of Myth and Legend." Studio Editions. 1994.
9. Carr-Gomm, Philip. "Sacred Places." Quercus Books. 2008.
10. Carroll, Lewis. "The Complete Illustrated Works of Lewis Carroll". Chancellor.1991.
11. Carlson M, Earls F. "Psychological and neuroendocrinological sequelae of early social deprivation in institutionalized children in Romania." NY Acad of Sciences; 807 pp 419 – 428.
12. Charlesworth, James H. "The Old Testament Pseudepigrapha." Doubleday & Co. Inc. 1983.
13. Chatwin, Bruce. "The Songlines." Picador. 1987.
14. Common Bible. Revised Standard Version - Expanded. Collins 1973.
15. Cox, Professor Brian & Andrew Cohen. "Forces of Nature." William Collins 2016.
16. Cragg, Kenneth. "Readings in the Qur'an." Fount. 1988.
17. Duesberg PH. "Inventing the AIDS virus." Regnery. Washington DC. 1996
18. Dunphy, Dexter. "Jaguar Heart Poems". Wellington Lane Press. 2003.
19. Emerson, Ralph Waldo. "Selected Essays." Penguin Books. 1982.
20. Eliade, Mircea. "Shamanism." Princeton University Press. 1974.
21. Ellis, Peter. "The Men and the Message of the Old Testament." Liturgical Press 1962.
22. Evans-Wentz, W.Y. "The Tibetan Book of the Dead." Oxford Univ. Press. 1968.
23. Evans-Wentz, W.Y. "The Tibetan Book of the Great Liberation." Oxford Univ. Press 1968.
24. Evans-Wentz, W.Y. "Tibetan Yoga and Secret Doctrines." Oxford Univ. Press 1968.
25. Flaum, Eric. Pandy, David. "The Encyclopedia of Mythology." Friedman Group. 1993.
26. Foster, S. & M. Little. "The Book of the Vision Quest." Prentice Hall. 1988.
27. Goodman, Linda. "Linda Goodman's Star Signs." Pan 1987.
28. Goodman M, New A, Siever L. "Trauma, genes, and the neurobiology of personality disorders." Ann NY Acad Sci. 1032: 104-16 2004.
29. Grieve, Mrs M. "A Modern Herbal". Penguin Books. 1982.
30. Haich, Elizabeth. "Initiation." Unwin Paperbacks. 1988.
31. Hespertz SC, Dietrich TM, Wenning B, Krigs T, Erberich SG, Willmes K, Thron A, Sass H. "Evidence of abnormal amygdala functioning in borderline personality disorder: a functional MRI study." [http://www.ncbi.nlm.nih.gov/entrez/query.fcgi?] 2001.
32. Houston, Jean. "The Possible Human." J.P.Tarcher Inc. 1982.
33. Howard-Taylor, Lucy. "Feeding the Demon." Sydney Alumni Magazine. Spring 2008.

34. Huang W L, Harper C G, Newnham J P, Quinlivan J A, Beazley L D, and Dunlop S A, "Maternal administration of repeated corticosteroids delays brain growth in foetal sheep." Obstetrics & Gynaecology 1999.

35. Hulse, David Allen. "The Key of It All." Llewellyn publications 1993.

36. Ingpen, R. "A Celebration of Customs & Rituals of the World." Dragon's 1994.

37. Innes, Brian. King, Francis. Powell, Neil. "Fate and Fortune." Crescent Books. 1989.

38. Irwin, Matt. "Low CD4+ T-cell counts; A variety of causes and their implications to HIV and AIDS."   Health Education AIDS Liaison. Toronto.[irwin18@gwis2.circ.gwu.edu].

39. Irwin, Matt. "AIDS and the Voodoo Hex". First draft p 23. 2002.

40. Jones, Caroline. "The Search for Meaning." ABC Enterprises. 1989.

41. Jones, Ernest. "The Life and Work of Sigmund Freud." Anchor Books 1963.

42. Jung, Carl C. "Man and His Symbols". Picador. 1964.

43. Jung, Carl C. "Alchemical Studies". Routledge & Kegan Paul. 1967.

44. Lamy, Lucie. "Egyptian Mysteries". Thames and Hudson. 1986.

45. Lau, D.C. "Lao Tzu Tao Te Ching". Penguin Books. 1987.

46. Laudenslanger M., Ryan SM., Drugan RC., et al. "Coping and immunosuppression: Inescapable but not escapable shock suppresses lymphocyte proliferation." Science 1983 221; 568 – 570.

47. Macdonell, Arthur A. "A Sanskrit Grammar for Students." Motilal Banarsidass 1988.

48. Maggiore, Christine. "If It's Not HIV, What Can Cause AIDS?" Health Education AIDS Liaison, Toronto. 2002. http://www.healtoronto.com/ifnothiv.html

49. Meyer, Marvin. "The Gospel of Thomas". Harper San Francisco. 1992.

50. Milton GW. "Self-willed death or the bone pointing syndrome." Lancet 1, June 1973 pp 1435 – 1436.

51. Montefiore, Simon Sebag. "Speeches that Changed the World." Murdoch Books. 2005.

52. Moore, Patrick. "Atlas of the Universe". Colporteur 1982.

53. Nasr, Seyyed Hossein. "Islamic Spirituality – Foundations." Crossroad. 1987.

54. Oldham J. "Borderline Personality Disorder: An overview." Psychiatric Times. Vol XXI Issue 8 2004.

55. Padian NG, Shiboski SC, Glass SO, et al. "Heterosexual transmission of HIV in Northern California: Results from a ten-year study." American Journal of Epidemiology. 1997 146 (4) pp 350 – 357.

56. Palmer, M. "The Jesus Sutras." Piatkus. 2001.

57. Petrucci, Ralph H. "General Chemistry." Macmillan 1989.

58. Phillips, Dr. D.A. "Secrets of the Inner Self." Angus & Robertson. 1988.

59. Picknett, Lynn & Clive Prince. "The Templar Revelation." Bantam Press. 1997.

60. Purce, Jill. "The Mystic Spiral". Thames and Hudson. 1973.

61. Quinlivan J. "Study of Adolescent Pregnancy in WA." In "Domestic Violence in Australia ; The Way Forward." Proceedings of a national conference on Domestic Violence published by the Australian Institute for Family Studies. 2000.

62. Rampa, Lobsang. "Wisdom of the Ancients." Corgi Books. 1977.

63. Regardie, Israel. "The Complete Golden Dawn System of Magic." Falcon Press. 1987.

64. Ricard, Matthieu. "Happiness." Atlantic Books. 2006.

65. Rosenburg, DR; Pajer, K; Rancurello, M; et al. "Neoropsychiatric assessment of orphans in one Romanian orphanage for 'unsalvageables'." 1992 JAMA 268(24); pp 3489 – 3490.

66. Schnapper, E.B. "The Spiral Path". C.W.Daniel Co Ltd. 1985.

67. Schueler, G.J. "An Advanced Guide to Enochian Magick.". Llewellyn Publications. 1987

68. Schwaller de Lubics, R.A. "Sacred Science." Inner Traditions International. 1988.

69. Schwaller de Lubicz, R.A. "The Egyptian Miracle." Inner Traditions International. 1985.

70. Science. 1984 224 carried separately titled retrovirus articles by (1) Gallo RC, Salahuddin SZ, Popovic M et al; (2) Popovic M, Sarngadharan MG, Read E et al; (3) Sarngadharan MG, Popovic M, Bruch L, et al; and (4) Schupbach J, Popovic M, Gilden RV, et al. The team was under the leadership of Robert Gallo.

71. Segal, Jeanne. "Living Beyond Fear". Newcastle Publishing Co. 1984.

72. Steiger, Brad. "Indian Medicine Power." Schiffer Publishing Ltd.1984.

73. Suzuki, David. "The Sacred Balance". Allen & Unwin. 1997.

74. Suzuki, David. "A David Suzuki Collection." Allen & Unwin. 2003.

75. Suzuki, S. "Not Always So. Practicing the true spirit of Zen." Harper Collins. 2003.

76. Temple, Robert. "The Crystal Sun." Century 2000.

77. Trine, Ralph Waldo. "In Tune With the Infinite". Keats Publishing Inc. 1973.

78. Tichy, J. "Legends from Eastern Lands." Paul Hamlyn. 1968.

79. UNAIDS and WHO; "AIDS epidemic update December 2001." By Anne Winter, Dominique de Santis and Andrew Shih.

80. Von Franz, Anne Marie. "Divination and Synchronicity."

81. Walton, Clair. "What makes a Survivor?" Continuum 1999 5 (5) p 16 – 18.

82. Watson, Lyall. "Supernature II".Sceptre. 1986.

83. Webb, James. "The Harmonious Circle." Thames & Hudson 1980.

84. Weiss, Margaret., Phyllis Zelkowitz, Ronald Fedman, Judy Vogel, Marsha Heyman and Joel Paris. "Psychopathology in Offspring of Mothers with Borderline Personality disorder: A Pilot Study". Canadian Journal of Psychiatry Vol 41 June 1996.

85. White, Ruth. "A Question of Guidance." Saffron Walden. 1988.

86. Wilhelm, Richard. Translation. "The I Ching". Bollingen Series. Princeton. 1987.

87. Zanarini MC, Frankenberg FR, Hennen J, Reich DB, Silk KR. "Psychosocial functioning of borderline patients and axis II comparison subjects followed prospectively for six years." J Personal Disord   Feb; 19(1): 19-29 2005.

AMBROSIA

1. INTRODUCTION

[Whirlpool Galaxy M51 and the Eagle Nebula by the Hubble Space Telescope.]

Advances in science and technology have enabled us to rapidly increase our knowledge about the wonderful Universe in which we live. Early astronomers informed us of the major and minor bodies in our own Solar System and soon expanded our view of the exceptional nature of planet Earth in a truly wondrous Galaxy, the Milky Way of which our Solar System is a tiny part. Accordingly our world view has been going through massive transformations as we have come to appreciate that the centre of our world the Sun is only one star out of hundreds of billions of stars in the Milky Way alone. Recent estimates have put that figure at about 400 billion stars and have given the diameter of the Milky Way at 100,000 light years. Our Solar System is situated about 25-28,000 light years from the Galactic Centre of the Milky Way which is a Spiral Galaxy [Type Sbc] centred in Sagittarius. Consequently the Galactic Centre is not visible from our arm of the spiral. In Galactic terms the Milky Way is actually a giant Galaxy but only one of many hundreds of thousands of Galaxies in Universe. These are massive figures and they massively transform our sense of who we are and the unique place we hold as intelligent beings in Universe. [I know, there are many who would challenge the claim that we are intelligent! Well OK, sometimes intelligent.]

[Hubble Space Telescope image showing a full rotation of Mars with ice on the North Pole.]

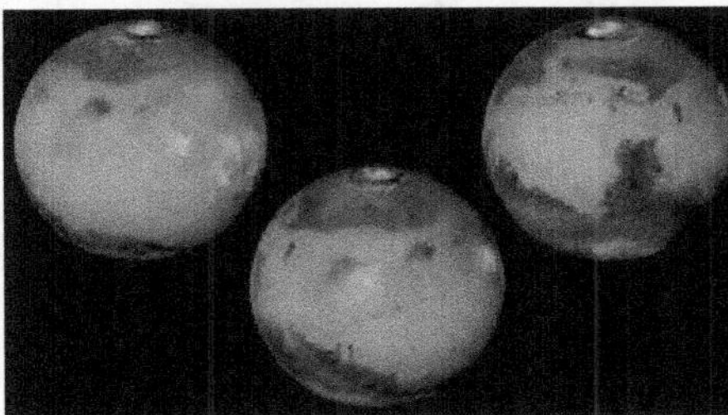

Countless years of work have gone into exploring wider and wider fields in our search for other forms of intelligent life. We have built bigger and better telescopes to probe the heavens. We have increasingly sensitive receptors to radio signals from even the most distant bodies and we have sent space probes to the outer reaches of our Solar System. But in all this work we have never found intelligent life anywhere except on Earth. The jury is still out on whether life exists anywhere else even on planet Mars and answers to that won't be certain for almost a decade.

As our scientific instruments help us determine where life exists in Universe, as reader of these pages you can be the jury on whether there are other forms of intelligence. I think there are and I will give you my evidence so that you can make your own decision. I will also give you my methodology so that you can conduct your own research.

Our ancient Gnostic forebears were the fathers of modern chemistry who came to many of their principle insights through their dreams. The great psychologist Carl Jung [Bib.41] argues the Gnostics were therefore also the fathers of the Psyche and it is our Psyche that is of principle concern to us here. What you will see is that Psyche does have extraordinary intelligence but in the past it has only been possible to understand Psyche through our dreams and what we project onto our dream figures; our values, attitudes and expectations about how these dream figures behave. In Western culture, Greek and Roman myths strongly colour our thinking about the Archetypes - Zeus, Apollo, Pan, Isis, etc. In Eastern culture an equal number of stories abound although the Archetypes differ. Given our common humanity there are common themes about the Archetypes and as our Psyche is "collective" it includes all our perspectives but this is not reflected in mythology. So what has gone wrong?

All past work about the Psyche has depended upon symbolism and particularly dream images. But we don't only have images in our dreams.

Words are also evident and we sometimes speak to and are spoken to by dream figures. Words are also vitally important symbols and even the letters from which our words are composed each have symbolic meanings that underlie them. However, there is no current process or framework, of which I am aware, by which to examine what is spoken in dreams. And our past dream analysis process has led to a mythology that is riddled with author interpretations and projections concerning possibly only half of what is going on in a dream. Jung deeply regretted this "contamination" because it significantly limited our knowledge about Psyche and our understanding of the Archetypes. Until now, we have made very poor use of a wonderful store of intelligence, as you will see.

Developing a process to extend the boundaries of our knowledge about Psyche and the Archetypes has been a central aspect of my work for three decades. I am pleased to say the work has been well rewarded with some compelling discoveries. The first vital discovery was that the spiral is intrinsic to the functioning of Universe. At least half the Galaxies in Universe are in the form of a spiral and our own Milky Way is a spiral. The other half are mainly Elliptical Galaxies and Random Star-fields. Some real images of some of these other Spiral Galaxies are included throughout these pages. Because of the importance of the Spiral, the process by which we access Psyche and the Archetypes is identified as the Spiral Process.

The core of this book is about what has emerged from using the Spiral Process to analyse what is said in dreams. This work accurately reflects an old Polynesian saying;
"Standing on a whale, fishing for minnows".

When I began this work I really was only fishing for minnows and had absolutely no idea of what a huge and beautiful whale would slowly be revealed under my feet. The whale of course is the Transcripts that come from the spiral process.

This work will take you into the formerly unknown territory of "What The Archetypes Have To Say". Archetypes are the authors of this work and I am only the editor. This is their story as it is told by them. I have tried to minimise my impact on their work. The effect of this is that sometimes the wording is very dense or condensed but profound, very rich in meaning and sometimes extremely funny. What you will discover is both their story and the way they tell their story. This is a vitally important matter because the old myths about Psyche and the Archetypes have portrayed them as a squabbling and backbiting lot. On the contrary you will see they work seamlessly together much like in modern genetics there is discussion about a Cartel of Cooperation between genes. You will discover much about the Archetypes Cartels.

Barnum Barnum, an indigenous Australian, was interviewed by Caroline Jones [Bib. 38] and he provides us with a unique insight into one direction in which Psyche may be expanding.

> *"Most Aboriginal people have a strong conscious memory that comes out in our stillness and in our connection to the Earth. That particularly applies to me, I believe. It also helps to know who you are as you walk tall on Aboriginal soil.*
> *My great grandfather was a famous artist. My grandfather on my father's side had a pet whale. Actually, my people come from a dolphin tribe. Dolphins surround Australia, particularly on the four points of the compass – Cape York Peninsular, Byron Bay, Wilson's Promontory, and Monkey Mia. These are very strong dolphin energy points. There's something extraordinarily beautiful about people's connection to that spiritual element of Australia. And I believe that the longer people live on this continent, and the more they grow, the more they will develop a dolphin consciousness."*

My wife and I were most fortunate to have lived at Whale Beach, just north of Sydney for a while. That beautiful place is directly on the migratory path of both whales and dolphins. In September 2008 a pod of twenty-two whales where following that path and people stopped their cars to watch the progress of these magnificent creatures of the deep. At our high cliff top position we could easily distinguish adults from calves and people were chatting excitedly together about the whales. So many people gathered at this spot that the road was soon blocked. Nobody tried to pass through, even the regular bus stopped and everyone jumped off to watch - enthralled. The bus driver was the first person out the door! Many Chinese and Japanese tourists were amongst the crowd. This suggests we may be seeing a general emergence of Whale and Dolphin consciousness. At least this is something to hope for – most especially in Japan.

Perhaps the best examples of human concern for whales are seen when a pod beaches itself and hundreds of people converge and try to get these wonderful creatures back into the water or cover them until the tide rises. But what has happened to their normal extraordinary navigation ability? We have almost no idea how they navigate. Hopefully advances in science will help us discover what is needed to really fix the problem. As the next series of photos show, there have been great steps in our understanding of the Universe and its occupants but we have a very long way to go to get past the superficial.

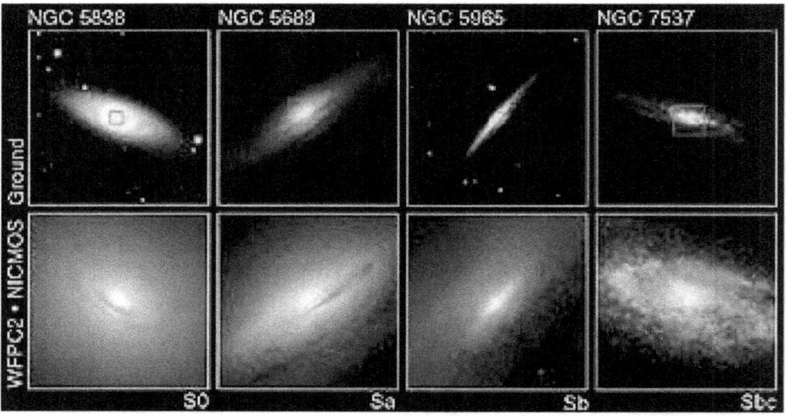

[Ground telescope images of four galaxies at the top and comparable images from the Hubble space-telescope are shown below.]

Four Key Matters;

1. Fishing for minnows - a process of search and discovery.

Looking back over the last twenty years the process of discovery seems to have several definable stages. In "minnow" form, it began as a game. The game was to write key words onto separate pieces of paper, mix them up and then throw them into the air - paying particular attention to the way they came down and the meanings, that could be derived from the various arrangements. This game [known as Lexigrams] was proposed by Linda Goodman [Bib. 25] and it was based on an ancient methodology used by the Chaldeans several thousand years ago. This was vital to seeing the value of using different combinations of letters to expand the words under consideration. Unexpected word combinations sometimes opened whole new fields of insight and provided glimpses to deeper understanding. The results were promising and fun so further experimentation seemed warranted.

Developing a more systematic approach involved using a "field" such as a grid laid on the carpet to set some parameters or to limit the words that were taken into consideration. Refinements followed, ideas generated became spurs to new ideas and what began as fun exploration, was refined and eventually evolved into a very serious pursuit using the Spiral as the grid. Through this Spiral grid, the Archetypes vista and so "the whale" was revealed. As you will see, this final step occurred when important recurrent words, spoken in a dream, were treated in a similar fashion.

2. Divination techniques and randomization.

The Nordic Runes are mixed around in a bag, or shaken until randomly distributed before a question is asked and a Rune chosen from which an answer can be devised. In common with this randomization process, the Yarrow sticks are shaken in their holder, or 3 coins shaken in the hands when a question is asked of the I Ching. Similarly, the cards used in the Tarot are randomized or shuffled before one or more are selected. In like fashion the shaman, who shakes the bones and throws them down a race and then reads them to tell the fortune of an enquirer, is using the same principle of randomization before determining the "reading" based on the idea of "meaningful chance". But how can you get the Archetypes to choose a card?

In broad terms it matters little how randomization is achieved, what matters is that it is undertaken by stirring, shaking, shuffling or casting; that is, attempting to neutralize the influence of some past order or system and enable focus and so revelation about the enquirer's issues. It is the incidence of meaningful chance or synchronicity, which characterizes divination [Von Franz Bib. 78]. Having neutralized our human influence, we attribute the meaning of the result to "higher powers" - "divine" influence because we have no better explanation. Taking the I Ching as an example, from my personal viewpoint I am in awe at the breadth and relevance of "divined" results. Randomization and casting play a key role in the process used to uncover What the Archetypes Have to Say.

3. Contamination of data.

Studies in psychology over many years have pointed to the power of the undisclosed attitudes of people to influence each other. The obvious problems of experimenter bias and the subtleties of the demands of an experimental situation do point to the need to proceed cautiously when saying what is "divined". Some of the most notorious examples of contamination occur in some "automatic" writing through which the attitudes and opinions of the writer become infused into the "divined" text. To then attribute this writing to "divine" intervention is often egotistical folly. I have seen a lot of Gooey Stuff!

Contamination of our narratives may never be removed as it is deeply embedded in culture, language and images. Carl Jung [Bib. 41] argues that it also affects our understanding of our archetypes and hence all our postulations about Psyche. In broad terms, if we can't eliminate contamination, we can at best reduce it to a minimum (by processes such as randomization) and we can recognize the limitations of human understanding (sometimes our minds can't stretch far enough) when pushing back the edges of the unknown. I don't want to enter into a philosophical discussion about the Buddhist notion of the Void [Evans-Wentz Bib. 20], nor do I want to try and explain what Lao Tzu meant when he said "that which can be defined about the Tao is not the Tao" [Wilhelm Bib. 84]. What I do want to highlight is that as human beings, we are limited to constructs in thinking and will therefore always "contaminate" our narratives in the same way we personify deity, project ourselves into our rationales of behaviour and have trouble with constructs such as infinity. Essentially we need to recognize the limitations "contamination" puts on our narratives and aim to minimize it.

In this work, by randomization we can minimize contamination. Additionally the original transcripts obtained from each use of the spiral process are given to enable you to make a comparison between the transcripts obtained and the edited material.

4. Finding an Archimedean point.

In much of this work, we need an Archimedean point - something that is outside the narrow field of consciousness that assists us in finding our bearings in an otherwise seeming chaos [Jung Bib. 41.] We could use the Greek legend about Chaos [Bullfinch Bib. 7] but I want to use a dream I had as this Archimedean point as so much of this information is about Psyche.

At the outset it may assist you to know that I asked Archetypes for a dream that could be used to assist readers comprehend the information to be presented and I respect the fact that this dream occurred on the night I asked for this assistance.

> *I am enjoying a walk along a sandy track through the semi-arid Australian bush. Small multiple-trunked Mallee trees (a slow growing desert variety of eucalypt) surround the track and the track is littered with various sized and shaped stones. I am using a bayonet to turn over several of the stones as I walk along. I come across a small brass hoop and flick it into the air. Unexpectedly the hoop begins spinning under its own steam, spiralling along the track, skipping twice on the sandy ground, leaving crescent shaped imprints. The brass hoop spiral-skips off the track and away into the bush and out of sight.*
>
> *I am fascinated and leave the track to follow in the sand and spinifex. The trail of crescent shaped imprints leads to a river where a large solitary tree stands. I watch in awe as the hoop skips like a tossed pebble across the surface of the river, glittering and glinting in the rippled light. Beneath the tree, the hoop turns into gold and spins*

vertically upwards. At the peak of its spiral ascent, the hoop fragments into hundreds of sparkling lights that glow like a skyrocket burst in the night sky. One that I particularly notice slows in its outwards drift and fades to nothing and all the others do likewise and the whole sky is dark - the Void.

All the faded lights reappear, grow bright and reconsolidate not as the

hoop I had followed, but rather as three deities. These three beautiful golden coloured entities combine together in a creative dance beneath the tree, as I watch from the bank on the other side of the river. My attention shifts to the trunk of the tree where I notice the three deities faces are carved as beautifully as by Michael Angelo. Absorbed in the faces, I recall the Trinity's dance and find this marks the place of their eternal creative re-enactment.

Suddenly two men approach me beside the riverbank. One holds a short, sawn-off sword. The second man carries a dagger in his hand. They will arrest me if I report details of the Trinity dance. But, I still carry my bayonet in my right hand. With my left hand I grab the sword hand of the first man and holding it aloft, reply to the second man, "No harm is yet done." The moment is frozen. "I came by these wonders as led to see and began in the clear promise I would write what I learnt."

The second man nods his acknowledgment and moves his free hand very slowly forwards. With the lightest touch on my blade tip, he gently presses aside the danger saying;
>   ***"Gently is for the Greater Good.***
>   ***Secrets of the Sacred Heart***
>   ***Are said in dreams that stand apart."***

I woke and wrote down the dream; Archimedean in it's symbolism, themes and message. The second man crystallizes the nature of and the importance that underlies the words spoken to us in a dream. The message concerns the Secrets of the Sacred Heart, the generic aspects that we all share; similar to the Archetypes of Jung. Although the expression Sacred Heart is usually identified with the Roman Catholic Church there is no exclusive use involved here. The term is generic and refers to all of us having a Sacred Heart and having access to the secrets about it in relation to the eternal nature of our being. The Secrets of the Sacred Heart are revealed to us in spoken words in dreams that stand apart – just as they did in this dream.

5. Turning over the "lapus philosophorum".

As indicated in the dream, I began this journey with the expressed intent of writing down what I discovered and sharing those findings with others. I was aware at the outset that I needed to write as carefully as a Terton - normally a Tibetan Buddhist who knows the responsibility that attends the search for sacred secrets usually through the discovery of ancient texts. To the Terton this work involves the discovery and safe return of the "Treasures of Divine Wisdom" or Prajna Paramita [Evans-Wentz Bib. 20] to the priests of Tibet. By way of example, the original text, Bardo Thodol [The Tibetan Book of the Dead], was committed to writing by the great Guru Padma Sambhava in the 8th century AD. It was subsequently hidden away and then, when the time came for it to be given to the world, the Terton, Rigzin of Karma Ling-pa, bought it to light.

There are some important parallels. I do feel that I was born to discover this work. Although it was not hidden in a cave, initial experimentation led to discovery of the process by which I obtained the transcripts. By analogy, you could say that I have gone deep into Archetypes' place in the Big Desert. When they demanded to know what I was doing there, I said I was there to collect my life's work in accordance with my Calling. In their sacred room they allowed me to carefully copy what was written in a spiral on the floor. From each spiral, a transcript was written.

 My responsibility is to accurately relay these treasures in written form; hence I carry a bayonet symbolic of the pen with which to write. Walking along the bush track turning over various stones along the way does depict the search for understanding along my Wisdom Path, each book equivalent to a stone, each idea, turned over and examined, but not all the books read nor all the ideas examined. Along my Wisdom Path, I have turned over selective philosopher's stones or *lapus philosophorum* [Jung Bib. 41].

Finding the Dead Sea Scrolls in the caves of Qumran led to much translation, study and contemplation in the Church of the West. Of particular significance was the Thomas Gospel that has a strong Gnostic flavour in the teachings and this is especially evident in Thomas' account of the Last Supper[1]. This flavour is not generally evident in the New Testament and this has led to speculation that Church officials have deliberately deleted it. Be that as it may, in many respects it may be said of this work that there is a strong Gnostic flavour here as well – besides, it is primarily structured on the interplay of the Elements – Fire, Water, Earth and Air.

Finding the small brass ring was a crucial step in the dream and in reality. The ring does symbolize the search for spiritual understanding and since antiquity it has symbolized the centre, the absolute, the power, the Tao, Great Spirit

---

[1] Meyer, Marvin W. Translator. The Gospel of Thomas – the Hidden Sayings of Jesus. Bib.47.

and ONE in Universe. (eg. Bancroft Bib. 2, Chatwin Bib. 12, Webb 81). In the dream, the hoop moved under it's own steam and led me away from the track or the known aspects, into the unknown and unfamiliar territory where I follow the signs as they are given and I report what I learn along the way.

This photograph depicts Australian Aboriginal percussion art of circles that

were chiselled into the rock-face of Sacred Gorge in the Northern Flinders Ranges of South Australia an estimated 50,000 years ago. Considering the local people still maintain this sacred site, you can appreciate this is a stunning example of people's devotion to and role in the ongoing creation process.

Even if you went back half that period, no ancient Egyptian buildings and relics exist and the Great Pyramids had not been built. There are many great traditions founded on expressing the sacred within and without us. Our drive to express our spiritual awareness with a circle is very powerful and very widespread over totally different regions of Earth.

Like the Australians, indigenous North Americans still draw their sacred purpose circles, and create their medicine wheels.

Ancient Chinese Taoists often used a circle to represent Tao, long before their famed Yin and Yang symbol that is contained within that circle. Buddhists turn the prayer Wheel of Dharma.

Neolithic Britain's built stone circles in the Orkney Islands in Scotland. These relics predate circles at Stonehenge, Rollright, Averbury,

Newgrange and many other sites.

Although most of the detail about the religious and practical function of these stone circles has been lost, there is still evidence these ancient people used the circle for sophisticated monitoring of the position of certain stars and it would seem they also had measurement in mind. A ditch and mound define the outer perimeter of Stonehenge and carbon dating suggests this work was undertaken about 5000 years ago. At that time a circle was set out using timber markers that rotted away long ago. Today, immediately inside are a circle of markers including special attention to the Solar North and South positions. There is then a second circle of markers and the third or inner circle features the famous standing stones or Sarsens that are believed to have been added about 4000 years ago. The original second circle of bluestone had to be removed when the Sarsens were put into place. The Bluestone markers weigh about 5 tons each and they were evidently carried from the Precelli Mountains in South Wales almost 400 km away.

The giant sandstone Sarsens were cut in nearby Marlborough Downs and moved some 30 km to their current location. The vertical stones are capped with lintels that are mortise and tenoned together. This was a massive undertaking. Current estimates are that the bluestones weigh about 5 tons and the Sarsens weigh up to 45 tons.

People don't go to this much work unless it is centrally important to daily life and/or their eternal being. It must have taken the muscle power of hundreds of men to move the Sarsens into position. This image is a reconstruction of the way Stonehenge would have looked at about the time the Roman's

invaded England. Although great care is being exercised to preserve what remains of the Sarsens at Stonehenge, the following image shows how much they have declined from their former glory. Even still, 5000 years later these stones accurately position the rising Sun at midsummer.

As with circles, our Sun and the Trinity, when similar symbols are used from one culture to another they are termed archetypal. Naturally all symbols have a meaning and these meanings may be archetypal as well. But not all symbols are archetypal nor are all meanings. However, where symbols such as the Sun and Moon are the same, or similar across different cultures these symbols point us to understand the human condition in generalized or archetypal terms.

If you look closely below the circles in the photo of Sacred Gorge, you will see a small human figure with raised arms. Could this mean exhilaration and celebration? Can gestures be archetypal? What about a happy smile? Of course that means something different between dogs, but between humans, a smile is wonderfully archetypal. As far as our small figure is concerned, although unlikely, I have seen some people run like that when terrified so it could be read as a set of polar opposites in meaning for the same symbol. In the context of Sacred Gorge, the extraordinary light qualities on the rock and beauty of this isolated natural wonderland make it most unlikely our small figure spent a great deal of time carving in a place where terrified! Exhilaration and celebration are much more likely as this unsolicited photo shows of arms raised and hands opened upwards, complete with smile at this vital place of water, for life in the desert. What our friend spontaneously expresses has been deliberately and patiently carved into our small figure. It is an uplifting and magical place to which both are responding but from vastly different

cultures and times. So we have an archetypal place for archetypal behaviour of exhilaration and celebration of what we feel is inspirational and what we accord with being sacred. What is sacred we generally know implicitly. We don't have to be shown, we feel it and so we "know". And we know that when we follow our bliss we are most certain we are doing what we need to be doing, or in other words, following our Wisdom Path.

In the dream, the hoop skips across the sand, dances over the water and rises under the tree in a spiral movement. The spiral has never been a symbol of the absolute in the way the ring or circle has. The spiral has very ancient, at least Stone Age roots but it is "more akin to the breathing of the cosmos" [Purce Bib. 58].

The ancient Stone Age people of Britain, who built the famous stone circles, built one at Rollright in Oxfordshire [see exhibit]. A team of scientists under the leadership of Don Robins made a careful and comprehensive study of the Rollright Stone Circle and came to a number of remarkable conclusions.

Using an ultrasound device Robins reports that just an hour before sunrise;
"the Kingstone [at left] suddenly sprang to life, emitting a regular signal that lasted through the dawn, gradually fading as the Sun climbed the sky."

More sophisticated screening was developed to rule out other sources of sound and they found that the stones alone were responsible and at the same time the Geiger counter showed unusual levels of radioactivity within the circle. Although you always have a background of ultrasound in the country, the stones seemed to create an ultrasound barrier inside the circle. But during the equinox in March and October the stones emitted their strongest ultrasound signals. One of the scientists took infrared photographs of the Kingstone and to everyone's astonishment they showed a light mist around it and a ray beaming upwards from its top. [Bancroft Bib. 2].

Independently from Robin's team, a retired engineer, Charles Brooker made an electromagnetic survey of the circle and found there was a seven ring spiral of magnetic intensity inside the circle. When Brooker read Robin's article in the New Scientist he followed it with one of his own. He concluded that the circle was a magnetic refuge that created a cone of electromagnetic protection.

Inside the Rollright Stone Circle, Stone Age Britons had dug a spiral of seven turns into the floor of the circle and filled the trench with limestone.

Stone Age Britons evidently had a very high level of attunement to the forces in Universe and judging from this and other structures they built, white limestone played a key role in symbolizing the White Goddess and particularly the Moon. Importantly the Earth Goddess was symbolized by the Sun and these ancient stone structures recorded the position of both the Sun and the Moon within a circle.

At Rollright we have the bonus of finding a spiral of seven turns under the floor of the circle.

Newgrange in Ireland is one of the earliest stone structures that still exists. It is believed to pre-date the other major stone circles in the UK and to predate the Giza Pyramids of Egypt by some 600 years. Carbon 14 dating suggests Newgrange was built about 5000 years ago and it still has some markers on it's original circle that is marked by what are called keystones - as shown in the above picture.

In addition to the sophisticated monitoring of the position of the Sun and Moon, Newgrange was used for human burial in both passages and mounds. It is akin to Stonehenge in the scale of the operation undertaken but fortunately it also includes some of the earliest Stone Age Art. Amongst a number of important symbols we can still see the spirals with seven turns that were evidently very important to these people in the carving on Keystone 67. Some archaeologists argue that Newgrange was also essentially a monument to the White Goddess as the phases of the Moon are also recorded and the light that shines down the passage falls onto a white quartzite surface. This is very similar to what was found at the Rollright Stone Circle. [Bancroft Bib. 2].

As noted from the foregoing discussion the spiral is a very ancient symbol but it can be traced back even to the last Ice Age in far distant Siberia. From one of the earliest burial sites of Cro-Magnon man, the skeleton of a small child was discovered buried at Malta in the Lake Baikal region of Siberia. Within the burial site were found;
"Twenty female statuettes of mammoth ivory, all naked except for one which was dressed in the engraved skin of a cave lion – perhaps a shamanic robe. Among the many beads, pendants and medallions which decorated the body of the child, one showed an engraving of three cobra-like snakes, while another had a design of a spiral with seven turns enclosed in three spiralled S-shapes. An ivory fish had a spiral labyrinth stippled on its side; there were six flying birds in the grave and another on a necklace around the child's neck; also an ivory baton of the sort used in shamanic rites." [Bancroft Bib.2]

Spirals were also carved by the Mayan people at the entrance to their temples that like the Britons were oriented to the Sun and the Moon as the two great luminaries of the sky. In this exhibit a spiral is carved into the hinge of the python's mouth.

Like the Maya's, the Inca's also built astronomical observatories to record the exact position of the Sun at the Equinox on 21-22nd of March and September each year.

What is illustrated below is the Intihuatana Stone of the Machu Picchu. At the time of the equinox the Sun is directly overhead and does not cast any shadow. The great spiritual power of this stone was feared by the old Spanish invaders and they sought these stones to destroy them. Fortunately this stone remained undetected.

Certainly the spiral is a static sign of the dynamic force in the same way that the scuffmarks in the sand were made as the hoop skipped along. This dynamic aspect is also reflected by the Sufi dancer who in extant bliss dances spiral-

wise. So too Pilgrim's Progress was depicted as a spiral-wise journey to the Celestial City in the centre. The double spiral of seven turns was even carved into ceremonial implements used by megalithic man and the well-known Chinese Yin Yang symbol is a variant of the spiral.

Significantly the tradition is that the spiral is drawn three dimensionally with seven turns and it depicts the fourth dimension. When drawn in two dimensions it is usual to find it with three and a half windings and so depicting the third dimension.

Here, Botticelli uses a downwards spiral to depict "The Pit of Hell".

In most cultures, the spiral is woven into the mythologies surrounding the creation process and we have found it in widely different cultures across the globe.

The ancient Australian Aborigines carried stones hundreds of miles to build a spiral on a salt lake in the sandy desert region of Western Australia. But finding a spiral in many different cultures in very diverse parts of the world may not be all that surprising.

The fossils from widely different places are relatively similar across the globe and the fossils are full of spiral representations – shells! What is surprising is that spirals are virtually always a static sign of a dynamic force.

Our representations of the spiral with either seven or three and a half turns are testimony to the archetypal nature of this very powerful and ancient symbol. Here, work with the analysis of dream statements, the spiral of three and a half turns plays a pivotal role in revealing what the Archetypes have to say.

 Finally, in relatively recent times we have found that our own Milky Way Galaxy is a spiral and there are many thousands of other spiral galaxies in Universe. The spiral is even an essential ingredient in each of us as the DNA molecule is a double helix.

Our present day researches of Universe have revealed that Spiral Galaxies have distinctive arms that are highly pronounced in the Hubble image of a

Barred Spiral Galaxy here. The darker regions between the ”arms” are often darker because they contain a lot of dust so they are referred to by astronomers as "dust lanes”. The dust simply obscures the view of background stars and so they appear darker.

Dust plays an important part in creation and as you will see later, the idea of "lanes“ play a vital role in the Spiral Process. The "Lane" in our process is of three and a half turns into the Centre.

This Hubble image is a close-up of a region of a Nebula where intense radiation from the very hot stars excites the hydrogen gas to a red colour.

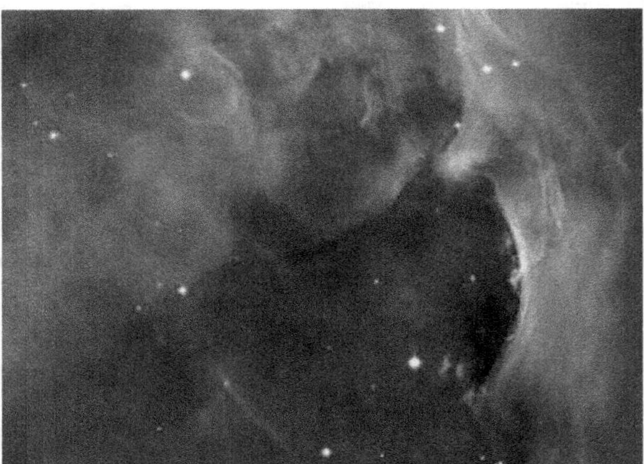

Through the interaction of intense radiation, hydrogen, helium and dust [in the darker areas] new stars are born.

[Spiral Galaxy NGC 3949 by the Hubble Space Telescope.]

In this way the Galactic landscape is constantly being created. This type of region can be identified in nearly every Galaxy including the Milky Way.

So just as we have an ever-expanding Universe we also have an ever-expanding Psyche and as you will see it is just as vitally dependent on Hydrogen and Helium to begin with.

2. SPIRAL PROCESS

for Dream Statement Analysis.

Given the fossil evidence illustrated here, it is not surprising to find a half spiral of three and a half turns being used widely across the globe by people from highly diverse cultures. But for that symbol to appear in our dreams it is archetypal. The Spiral Process is based on this form of half spiral.

Dreams are our most accessible resource for exploring the unconscious. Freud termed them our "via regia to the unconscious". [Ernest Jones Bib. 39]. Freud's most original and important work was titled "The Interpretation of Dreams" but it continues the strong sexual interpretation of his Oedipus complex. He also concludes that the motive of a dream is the fulfilment of a wish. To a large extent this is a continuation of his previously stated theories. The difference here is that we are not stating from a theoretical position except to say that the statements made to us by a dream figure can be deconstructed and then reconstructed without there being any necessity of a sexual theme or wish. As it happens, by using Dream Statement Analysis we are able to gain a direct insight into the Archetypes, their structure, processes and what they want to say to us. They are the ones who give us the theory and this takes us into new and vast territory.

In summary the Spiral Process involves deconstructing the words in a Dream Statement down to the letters. Creating a comprehensive list of all the words that can be generated from those letters. Writing each word on a small, separate piece of paper – a word slip. Randomizing all the word slips by mixing them around and putting them on a tray in a big pile. Laying out a large spiral of three and a half turns on the floor. A respectful request is made to Archetypes asking them to assist understanding of the Dream Statement. Casting the tray full of word slips into the air over the spiral. When all the word slips have finished fluttering down only those that have landed inside the spiral are considered. A careful record of the words is then made and this forms the transcript relating to that Dream Statement.

What is very surprising is that when the spiral is used as a grid, for dream statement analysis, the results are very meaningful and yet should mean nothing at all. The resulting pattern of words should be totally random. It should not be possible to find a cohesive meaning to the words. As I discovered for Hail The One Lord. My mistake was in adding the word Lord, as it seemed more respectful. But that isn't what the Archetypes wanted. That wasn't the true statement. The resulting transcript was totally impossible to fathom / random words until I came to the end – "SEE RIGHT EDIT AIN'T ON DEMAND."

Considering the probabilities of two thousand words being randomized and then thrown in the air, the chances are really stacked against anything sensible or coherent coming out of what lands on the floor. Further to this, if something coherent and sensible does come out of this activity, how can it be said that I have caused this to occur? I know, some of my friends would argue that coherence and sense wouldn't come out of me anyway so there has to be another explanation!

Earlier we identified that astronomers use the terms "arms" of a spiral and "dust lanes" that differentiate between the "arms". Archetypes give their own explanation. As you will see from later transcripts, they tell us that there is a surface tension in the "lane" of the spiral ["arms"] and this affects the way the word slips come down. In the fossil above, the "lane' is where the animal once lived. What Archetypes don't tell us is how the surface tension can be varied to affect such complexity. Except to say the surface tension must be continuously changing as you move inwards or outwards. They also explained that in combination they use the agency of "Slippery as" C the speed of light in a vacuum. There are further factors in the transcripts, as you will see. This is nothing short of a staggering achievement – a miracle, as you will see from the actual transcripts!

Just to make human understanding harder; some parts of the transcripts are pure poetry! In other parts a strong sense of humour leaps out repeatedly. Even harder; part of one of the transcripts was so complex I had to consult a friend who has a PhD in Chemistry. Even she was amazed at the profoundly deep understanding of chemistry that underlay the transcript. There is no way that I have that knowledge. Further than this; there are some events in my life that I have not discussed in detail with anyone and yet there are parts of the transcript that reveal those matters.

All of these outcomes are very surprising indeed. I don't know why "Divination" works but I do know that it has worked to produce the transcripts 1 – 10. The best explanation I can find is that as Archetypes say, the spiral works because of the surface tension in the "lane" of the spiral etc. but it also works because Archetypes wanted to tell their story as they say in transcript 1. We had found the way through the spiral and Lexigrams.

Lexigrams.

The numerical alphabet was not the only tool that Linda Goodman discovered about the ancient Chaldeans; she found what they termed a Lexigram. This is also a technique that is used to analyse words and discover their latent or intrinsic meaning. It does not use the numerical alphabet. When a special word, words or a phrase is to be analysed;

1. Should you wish to analyse the name of an entity, a statement or phrase, then the words must not have 4 or more different vowels. If they do, then they should not be subject to analysis and the basis of enquiry should be simplified or clarified. Even if you have three vowels you may find analysis difficult, but it may be undertaken.

2. The same is true if there are more than 14 different letters. Eg., for Frederick David Strick: A, 2C, 3D, 2E, F, 3I, 2K, 3R, S, T, V = 11 different letters, even though there are 20 letters in total. So the name may be subject to analysis.

3. In creating a Lexigram, no letter should be used more than the number of times it occurs in the original statement. Other information concerning Chaldean Lexigram rules that a letter may be used more than its occurrence, is probably unreliable.

Eg. "WHITE REEDS LAID". The idea here is to break everything down to the primary letters and their occurrences; A-1, D-2, E-3, H-1, I-2, L-1, R-1, S-1, T-1, and W-1. The next step is to generate all the new words that you can from those letters eg, seed, wade, seal, tides, whale, red, relate, relates, related, etc. Linda says you can think them up, but you will appreciate that this does not work for someone who has a "blind-spot". You simply won't think of some words, eg, aesthete, so a more reliable word generation process is to use a dictionary and simply work your way through systematically. The other thing that is necessary is to allow for the multiple definitions of words and to allow for abbreviations eg. S means South. This enables a more exact determination of the meaning of the words in the final analysis. This is no small task. It takes a lot of time and patience to even generate the words before you can begin to analyse the meaning of what you have generated. It is probable that if you used the Complete Macquarie Dictionary you could generate upward of 1500 words from the original phrase "WHITE REEDS LAID" so this is not a journey for the faint hearted and the possibilities of being overwhelmed are quite high. Lexigrams can of course be very simple and it is suggested that you start small with few letters, and with words that have been carefully considered to carry the bulk of the meaning you can apply in as few words or letters as possible. There is a strong advantage in early discrimination to find the words that best distil your known meaning or which indicate the phrase you wish to gain insight into.

Linda Goodman says that once you have your list of words, inspect them and see how you can create sentences and explore some of the unexpected word combinations that bring insight. Although this is a relatively useful way of initially exploring your word list, it suffers all of the same problems encountered in word generation. It is probable you will not see certain things because of your "blind spots" and you are very likely to end up with something that simply confirms your prejudices. Again the problem is to determine a methodology that does not mean the individual imposes their constructs on the meaning that can be derived. Well at least initially. Essentially the problem can be solved by separating you from your list of words, ie., getting some detachment, and so allow meaningful chance to work its magic.

The process used in this work to obtain the spiral transcripts made extensive use of Lexigrams. In summary, the process involves writing all the words separately on small slips of paper, and then totally randomizing the order they were in. Mixing them round, paying no attention to what is what other than randomization. All the words are then loaded onto a tray. Respects are paid, requests made to understand the expression eg, "WHITE REEDS LAID", and a room is prepared with a spiral of three and one half turns laid out on the floor. The words on the tray are then thrown into the air over the spiral layout. As the white rain flutters down, words go in all directions and there is no control over what they do. Meaning is vaporised. Within seconds, all the words are back on the floor, some within the spiral and some outside it. [The words are distilled/condensed.] All those outside are ignored but those that fall inside the spiral are carefully recorded in the order they appear. Words that are facing you are recorded running inwards along the lane of the spiral until reaching the centre. And then a record is made of all the words facing you in the outward journey as well. All the words that are face up and that have been recorded are then collected and the word slips that are face down are then carefully turned over to keep their original order and position. These word slips are then read in the same way as previously described.

In simple terms this is like distillation in that the meanings are all boiled off, some particles condense and fall into their respective positions on the spiral laid on the floor, which is like a collecting vessel. When meanings are condensed in this way, the resulting transcript is very dense and you could liken it to 100% proof, you have to add "water", expand the words again in their context with other words and their definitions. After completion of the record, what begins is the slow process of trying to understand what Archetypes are saying to you by the words they have chosen. In this way, the starting point for interpretation is not "contaminated" by your choices, prejudices and "blind-spots". If you are careful in preserving your detachment, remaining faithful to the order and meaning of words given, you will be well on the road of Light, Love and Power.

If you intend to try and replicate the Spiral Process on words in your own dreams you will find the outline of the methodology of direct relevance but if not I suggest we move on to find out what we can discover in the Transcripts.

Detailed Methodology for the Spiral Process.

The following outline covers the main elements that are of concern to anyone who wants to repeat this process.

1. Word preparation.

- The exact words of the dream statement are written down eg, SECRETS OF THE SACRED HEART. A judgement then needs to be made as to whether the statement could or should be analysed. [The statement being used in this example is a small part of a more complete statement and it does not convey the whole meaning. However it does convey some of the meaning and is suitable for an example.]

- The words are deconstructed to letters eg, A=2, C=2, D=1, E=5, F=1, H=2, O=1, R=3, S=3, T=3. Some basic rules are used to assess whether to proceed eg, statements containing more than 14 letters and 3 vowels are seldom used as the results become unmanageable. The ancient Chaldean belief was that if there were three vowels the statement didn't want to be analysed. If there were four vowels it was disrespectful to analyse the statement. By these rules, "Secrets of the Sacred Heart" should not be analysed.

- Words are reconstructed from these same letters eg, ACT, CAT, AESTHETE, DART etc. All words so generated from memory and dictionary are taken by their individual meanings. (Probably about 2000 words would be generated from the above example but by shortening the word chain to Sacred Heart Secrets and so eliminating one of the vowels, reduces the task by half). Each letter has an individual meaning (Hulse Bib. 33) and is included. I used the Complete Macquarie Dictionary and worked through the letters creating the words systematically. This removes the problem of only using the words I can think of and restricting the variable meanings as well. I also include all the abbreviations and also chemical symbols for the Elements. I keep a complete list of the words generated and their respective meanings.

- Each word and it's meaning is written on a small slip of white paper (approx. 12mm x 50mm) - I refer to these as word slips.

- The word slips are spread out, face down on a clean flat surface.

2. Preparing the room and the spiral layout.

- At this point I usually take some time out to clean the room to be used, make some incense and say a personal prayer asking ONE to guide my heart, hands and mind in coming to an understanding of the dream statement or word chain.

- A spiral of three and a half turns is laid out on the floor. I use woollen thread on a mainly wool carpet in an area about 4m x 4m. I begin the first, outside winding in the North (South in the Northern Hemisphere to be "sunwise") and then proceed towards the West. At the centre of the spiral, I include a separate word slip – THE ONE.

- I light the incense and again ask for guidance, then mix all the word slips on the table. They need to be thoroughly mixed to randomise their order and then slipped into a pile on a tray.

<u>**3. Casting the word slips.**</u>

- Carry the tray to the SSE point of the spiral and face the centre, again stilling the self and asking for guidance. If I "sense" that I have been acknowledged, I cast the word slips up into the air over the centre of the spiral layout. Some parts of the white cloud will separate and flutter down like snowflakes. Some go cartwheeling across the room. Others seesaw down and yet others may fall in a clump. In all it only takes two or three seconds for all to settle in their places on the floor. I only take account of the word slips that fall inside the spiral outline. Those, which fall outside, are ignored. (On one occasion I had trouble ignoring those falling outside as the word slip WEIRD had landed on my right foot!)

<u>**4. Preparing the transcripts.**</u>

- To begin making the written record. Standing in the North and looking along the spiral lane running Westwards, first record each word slip facing upwards and towards you in the sequence encountered as you move around the "lane" into the centre. (I usually also record the ordinal position or compass sector in which words occur). When you reach the centre, turn around and return along the "lane" in the opposite direction recording the words facing upwards and towards you as before. This word data needs to be exactly recorded as any Terton would. (I follow some basic conventions during this record taking eg, those word slip falling parallel to the "lane" are recorded in both directions as are word slips which fall across the woollen thread, they are read at two points, or in both "lanes". When slips come to a photo finish, they are read left to right). At this point you should have a record of every word facing upwards so those word slips are carefully collected and put aside.

- In the above step, all the upwards facing word slips were removed. What are left on the floor are all the word slips that are face down. These are each carefully turned over to preserve their original position and by turning end over, to preserve their direction. Each word slip is recorded as before - inwards to the centre and then returning. At this point there should be four "lane" readings. All the turned word slips are then collected.

- Some word slips may have come down in heavy clusters or clumps. These are carefully slid back onto the tray and are later cast into the air - again repeating the steps outlined above. Further casting of each cluster/clump may produce a further four "lane" readings for each cluster.

5. Analysing the transcripts.

- The work then begins of coming to an understanding of the "lane" readings and preparing a written retrospective. This work cannot be hurried. Having no punctuation to guide you each word may stand alone unless grouped in the original record. Having the individual meanings on each word slip will help a lot so too will some basic research into the root meanings of key words. In basic terms the meanings will each need to be expanded.

- In the transcript the Archetypes report that this literature is Vaporization and Condensation and so is likened to the distillation process. But they also use two agencies as previously mentioned, the surface tension in the lane and also the agency of "Slippery as". They warn us that the results are somewhat "patchy" but it is sometimes hard to know where this is occurring. At other times it becomes increasingly evident what is being said. In principle it is best to stick to the exact definitions and the word order. It is too easy to run ahead in interpretation and impose your understanding too quickly. Take time out to work each part through by expanding the condensed material.

- As a mark of respect, the dream analysis process should not be repeated on the same dream statement - this is true for any divination technique. The same question should not be asked twice. I would love to repeat White Reeds Laid using the dictionary rather than only the words I could think of. But there it is it is not to be repeated.

The fulcrum in the process is you. So how you go about your respective tasks is very much a matter of –ing as in writing, researching, enquiring and thinking. It is a gerund that depends on you having the right attitude and approach in every task – whether it be laundry like cleaning the room or the exotic of understanding the transcripts messages. You will see this issue again in Whata Saga. As a fulcrum you need to remember your place as an ordinary person respectfully requesting assistance to understand a statement. As THE ONE is in the centre of the spiral layout, these requests are to the Creator from one of His tiny creatures. This is a matter of realizing that you are very, very, very small and still or quiet in yourself. As red is the colour for Love, I wear a red-headband when doing this Tertons work of discovering sacred texts. You are a messenger and it is the message that is important and not you or me. We are a fulcrum for the "divine force".

What will be appreciated is that the interpretation of the Spiral Transcripts will occur during those brief few seconds whilst the word slips flutter down and land in their respective places. The transcript is not therefore a function of manipulation by the enquirer. The resulting word record is far less "contaminated" by our attitudes – I can say the resulting information about the Archetypes is produced by the Archetypes themselves.

3. WHAT THE ARCHETYPES HAVE TO SAY.

[Spiral Galaxy M100 by the Hubble Space Telescope.]

CONTENTS

[A Black hole powered Spiral Galaxy as seen from the Hubble Space Telescope.]

The following sections are all based on the transcripts recorded from using the Spiral Process. It should be noted that early transcripts were recorded before the methodology was fully developed and so they lack some of the rigor evident in later sections. However, this does not change the remarkable nature of the information that is forthcoming although it does mean later sections become increasingly complex, as greater clarity exists about the meaning of each word.

In earlier sections we identified the Spiral Process as most akin to a "Divination" technique. How it actually works is essentially a Mystery. However, this means I have to be as careful as possible to stay with the meaning conveyed in the transcripts and minimise my interpretations. This means you will sometimes need to read between the lines. Sometimes you will also recognise that you need to take action – such as in Transcript 7 where it is proposed by Archetypes that each person should atone on encountering each interjection in the story. There are many interjections and thus many times you are called to atone in peace.

This information is nothing like anything I have ever encountered before so essentially there are no guidelines to follow or even issues that can be highlighted to ease the passage from one topic to another, except as they are given in the transcripts. There is no doubt that Archetypes are very conscious of the need to use analogies and examples to help us understand their meaning and this document is full of some of the most unique imagery I have ever experienced in my 73 years on this beautiful planet.

Even in areas where I have read quite widely both in psychology and theology I have not encountered information like this. No religious teaching will properly prepare you for what is ahead. Perhaps the best word to describe this is that it is extremely INCLUSIVE and Archetypes seem very well aware that past religious teaching is very often distorted and extremely limited, elitist and denigrating of any other ideas. These revelations by Archetypes are not about religion but they are about spirituality. They are about your spiritual essence and your essential nature. They are also about the spiritual nature of others with whom we share this planet and as you will particularly see in Transcript 1 this includes those wonderful creatures that swim in our oceans, the Whales. You will also find out about a great many other creatures that are fully responsive to the Archetypal plane. Accordingly we are not the only ones who are spiritual beings. Nor are we the only ones who work for the good of this wonderful planet and all the myriad life forms that enjoy it.

You may also need to pause and reflect at times. Whilst I have done my best to present this information as it was given to me, there may be things you see or don't see that need exploration. To assist you with this process I have included an exact copy of the transcripts I have recorded. These are included at the end of this book under the same section headings given above. It needs to be appreciated that the transcripts are extremely "dense". Each word is like a highly concentrated liquid that has been distilled or refined a number of times. Further, there is no punctuation to help you determine the limits on some ideas. However, sometimes the pure poetry and word linkages are nothing short of sublime. One thing I am absolutely certain about is that **I cannot speed read these transcripts.**

I recall Woody Allen saying that he completed a speed reading of War and Peace in 20 minutes and concluded, "It is about Russia"!

Some parts of the transcripts have taken days of careful study and some others I have revisited more times than I could count. By providing you with the actual transcripts I hope you are able to verify or challenge my expansion where "density" requires it; and test my interpretations, assumptions and conclusions. Initially to assist you in this work, the actual words from the transcripts are given in capital letters and in the exact order they occurred in the transcripts. I have followed this convention for the first five sections until word definitions were exactly noted for all the subsequent sections, thus making capitals too difficult to follow during your reading.

Essentially I am delighted to be able to bring you an unabridged version of these revelations as given by Archetypes themselves.

[Interacting Spiral Galaxies NGC 2207 and IC 2163 by the Hubble Telescope.]

Transcript 1. <u>WHITE REEDS LAID.</u>

[Galex-Spitzer image of Spiral Galaxy M81.]

Experimentation began in earnest with the word chain – White Reeds Laid. Originally this idea comes from antiquity in China when preparations were made at sacred ceremonies for communication with the Ancestors. It normally involved serious preparation rituals using a reed mat but it was a recurrent word chain in my dreams so I began word preparation as discussed in the Spiral Process but at that stage I was not aware I should use a dictionary to generate the new words. The following text emerges from the transcript of the analysis. Words given in capitals are directly from the transcript and they are used in their original order.

1.
The very first word set by Archetypes for our contemplation is WHEAT. This is a key symbol for Eternal Life and nourishment in body, mind and spirit. A Cereal Offering has been used for thousands of years at the beginning of all Hebrew rites to THE ONE and as used in Christian communion rites to symbolize the body of Christ. [Ellis Bib. 19]. Just as the spiral is pivotal to deepening our understanding of the psyche, so too is Wheat central to understanding the Eternal and therefore sacred aspects of our being.

In this beautiful silver Christian church door, six ears of wheat are bound to the base of this central symbol of the Sceptre. The Sceptre stood for the power over life and death. At the top you will notice these are 4 serpents or adders as a symbol of knowledge. In ancient Chaldean terms six means Love as it also does in the Hebrew Kabala. Silver was also used symbolically to mean the crucible for understanding and gold was used to mean the crucible of wisdom.

To begin with the word WHEAT is therefore highly significant and not an accident of chance. It is deliberate, meaningful and consistent with past Archetypal sacred rites. This is a great word and symbol to begin the transcripts with.

The second word given is SITE.

WHEAT SITE means the place or location where wheat grows. Speaking metaphorically we can see that this is also about what nourishes and supports eternal life and so too our sacredness. The WHEAT SITE is in DIRE strife. The wheat site is dreadful or calamitous. The product of drought or even flood is dire but here we have the whole situation facing Eternal life and its support and nourishment in a dreadful or calamitous condition!

LARD SIDE WET. Lard is the fatty layer under the skin. Lard side is wet, means the ground water level has risen and is penetrating higher and higher into the surface region. To say that the wheat site is dire because the lard side is wet, it means that the calamity is on account of the water rather than the land. This doesn't sound like a good start for Eternal life or your sacredness. Evidently the calamity is occurring on an inner level that cannot be directly observed.

WETS TIRED The Wets are loaded up with something and it results in say more sluggish or unnatural /unwanted effects. In this tired state, the Wets don't behave as they normally would and we are told WETS TIRED LIES LEADER WHALES. The calamity here seems to be that the Leader Whales are not being informed in a normal or expected manner. The Whales don't know that the Wets have lied or sent the wrong signal. It is highly unlikely that the Wets are doing this intentionally as we are told they are tired, exhausted or done in.

We are then told the implications of the misinformation going to the Leader Whales. Research has shown that whale pods do have Leaders. In the transcripts we find these Leader Whales are tied to the performance of a sacred

rite that is also associated with the Reeds that grow in the estuaries. As whales are mammals and were once land animals that took to the water first in estuaries, it is understandable that they have a special association with estuarine plants and especially the Reeds. Apparently there is a vital link between the Wets, Reeds and the Leader Whales that has broken down. In the adjacent photo we have a pod of sperm whales who beached themselves at Smithton River estuary in Tasmania.

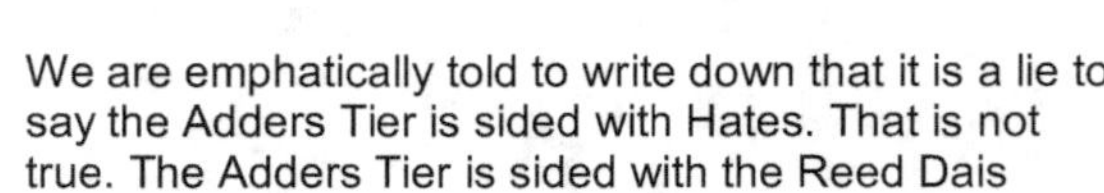

TIED HAS REED DAIS RITE. So the Leader Whales perform a rite or ritual that is termed the Reed Dais Rite. Evidently, misinformation by the Wets is leading to this rite not being performed correctly. A Dais is usually the raised platform in a church on which the celebrant performs a sacred rite. Here it is evident that the Leader Whales are tied to performance of a rite even as a celebrant would perform one - the Reed Dais Rite.

We are emphatically told to write down that it is a lie to say the Adders Tier is sided with Hates. That is not true. The Adders Tier is sided with the Reed Dais Tide.

You may recall that at the top of the Sceptre in our image of the silver church door, there are four adders depicted.

WRITE TIE LIE ADDERS TIER SIDED HATE. Adders are given as having a tier or several usually hierarchical layers. Adders are generally feared like most snakes, but adders most particularly because of their strong venom. However we are told they are not creatures who are sided with Hate. This statement suggests they are sided with the opposite of Hate, namely Love. Ancient Egyptian's worshiped the Adders Tier and the Uraeus was always displayed on Pharaoh's crown and incorporated in the symbolism of power.

The image above is of a Minoan Snake Priestess. The heads of these snakes are shown at the same level as the head of the priestess.

Even today in India there are priestesses who still practice their ritual soothing of cobras by singing whilst swaying to sooth them until the snake is calmed to such an extent that they can stroke the cobra's head.

In general terms the subjects and objects of our greatest fears become subjects and objects of our hatred. But even if some people hate snakes this doesn't mean that the snakes are sided with hate. They are simply much maligned by us. One classic example of a false story about snakes relates to the Garden of Eden where a serpent is used as a symbol of evil to tempt Eve. There is of course nothing of historical relevance about this story in Genesis as it was actually composed during the time of Moses – about 1300BC.

Another creature that is much maligned and again incorrectly is the Rat. They are certainly creatures that like to keep a safe distance from us but they have their role in testing food that we have discarded. As Archetypes put it – the LEE RAT TRIES WHAT SHIT HIT. Rats are certainly creatures of the LEE side, they nearly always approach from down wind and they like to keep to the shadows. One important aspect of this message is that the Lee Rat will test or try what has entered the decay cycle – what shit hit. It is probable that the Lee Rat is especially attuned to what is not working correctly or what is defective in some way. Given that we began with the dire strife in the Wheat Site, it is highly likely the Lee Rat is attuned to this. Our archetypal Lee Rat is called HEW. This is an extremely good name for a rat. Hew has DEAR EARS and it is evident that rats have extraordinarily good hearing. Or it may be that HEW is DEAR. Either way – HEW DEAR EARS SEW SAD TO ONE. Sad news is conveyed to ONE by Hew.

2.
ONE is sad about the rites connected to the Reeds. Evidently Hew has conveyed to ONE that there are problems with the Reed Dais Tide. ONE is SAD RITES REEDS RISER WIRE. So the Reed Dais Tide is connected to a Riser Wire. Tides certainly rise and fall. In this case as the Reed Dais Tide rises; it is

connected to something as if by a wire, the RISER WIRE. ONE is sad about what has happened to this connection.

WISER EARS DREAD RELEASED. Those who have Wiser Ears, like Hew, dread what is connected to the Riser Wire and what will be or is released by a failure in this connection. ADDS READ – an advertisement reads or Wiser Ears add they dread what will happen when others read – DAIS TIDES HIT. As the Reed Dais Tide is HIT or affected and not working properly, something or someone will be released - there are serious consequences that are dreaded by Wiser Ears. ONE is also sad about this failure.

The first in a string of consequences is identified as affecting the SEED TILE. This may be imagined as the list of all the genetic material on the Earth. The full range of interacting species and processes by which natural selection occurs. In this process the weak and sick are weeded out. But the Seed Tile apparently depends upon the Riser Wire of the Reed Dais Tide in order for its protective HAT LID to be kept on. The failure of the Reed Dais Tide will be reflected in the failure of the Hat Lid on the Seed Tile. That is bound to get Hew's attention.

When a squirrel searches for nuts under a tree, there are some nuts that it cannot find or which seem to be concealed therefore enabling the germination of a young tree. If a nut has been HIT as by SHIT, and is not going to germinate properly, the squirrel or Hew can quickly identify it and take it away. Seed Tile identifies this process of partial concealment of selected seeds, as if by a Hat or Lid, as being at risk. SEED TILE WRITES SHIT HAT LID.

A second consequence is identified as the LEE RAT becomes or takes sides with the ADDERS TIER.

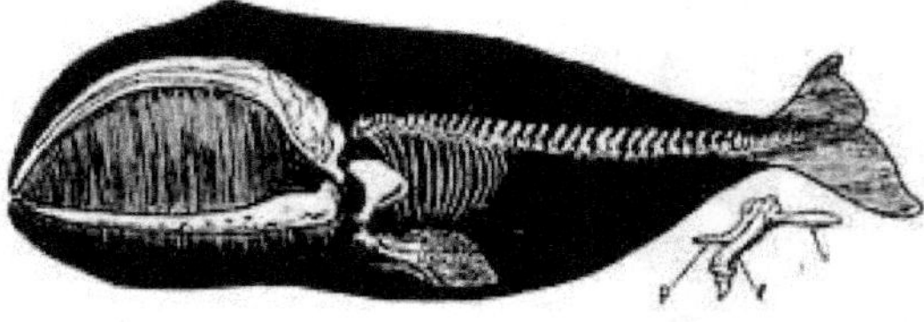

The REED is TIED to the WHALES HEEL when the LEADER REST TIRED. Whales do still have remnants of their rear legs evident in their skeletons. In this skeleton, the bones of the hind legs are shown enlarged and outside the body but of course this does not normally occur. So the Reed Dais Tide is performed when the Leader Whale is resting, when tired. It seems that the Reed has a tied relationship to the heel

of the Leader Whale when the whale is tired and resting. Presumably this means the heel would display some tiny movements that help the Reed Dais Riser.

The WETS RATE in this story and they are on the SIDE of having someone HIREd to tell the TALES RE DIRE TIRES SITE WHEAT.

I know the area of the Wheat Site being referred to is the Mallee Region of Southern Australia that merges with the desert areas of NW Victoria and the SE of South Australia. The Mallee trees are extremely well adapted to semi arid and arid conditions because they are very deep rooted. They kept the water table low wherever they grew. There are remnants of the original Mallee tree forests between the sand dunes in the Big Desert Wilderness Park. The calamity started when the trees were ripped out and shallow rooted Wheat and cereal crops were assisted with open irrigation channels taking water into the region where the wheat is being grown. As the water table has been rising for years throughout the Murray/ Mallee region the salt levels have increased dramatically and salinity is as sever a problem in the Murray basin as anywhere in the world.

I visited a place on the Murray River near Loxton where I had camped 60 years ago! I was with a troop of scouts who paddled canoes from Renmark to Waikerie. This was a 200 mile journey along one of the most beautiful places on Earth. Stunning Red Gums growing in the waters of the billabongs. Fish jumping and turtles diving away from our paddles. Birds in great flocks and abundant water we could drink directly from the river. It was paradise.

I couldn't believe my eyes were seeing the same bend in the river. All the trees were dead ghosts in the water. The salt was firm on the surfaces of the billabong and there were no birds or fish to be seen. No reeds, no grass, no young trees, just white stinking salt that gave me a sore throat.

Extensive irrigation washes more and more salt into the rivers and eventually the environment becomes too toxic for plants. The Wets are tired all right; exhausted; and virtually caput.

It is significant that none of the reports I read about the environment said that it was a sacred site for the whales. Once it must have been a virtual sea of green Mallee trees possibly covering an area about the size of France. It is not hard to imagine how the dire tires in the Wheat Site have led to the tiny rear limbs of the Leader Whales moving gently but out of tune to the Rite, when the leader rests tired and a tiny but vitally important current was normally caused to aid the Reed Dais Tide and it's Riser Wire.

3.

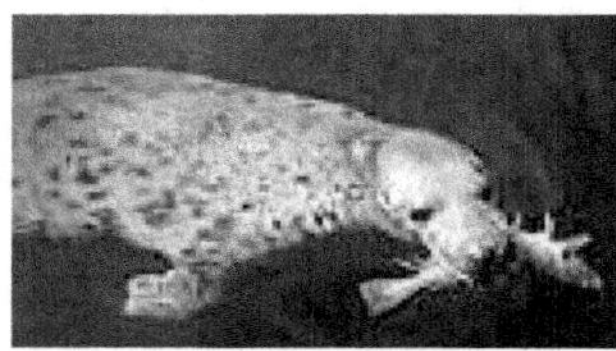

The WILD SEER of the ADDERS Tier REALIZE that the WHALE RATES or is very important in this situation. Some changes have already been noticed by the Wild Seer. Just as outlined earlier by the Seed Tile, concerning the "concealment process" to protect needed seed, there is a further process in "natural selection" by which certain weak or lost young birds in a rookery are taken by the Shearwater. The Wild Seer reports SHEAR RAIDS HEAL. The colony is strengthened by the weak being taken. But the Wild Seer has noticed a change. SHEAR RAIDS HEAL HAD ALTER. This normal healing pattern had altered. The way the Rats are behaving

has also altered. Bearing in mind that they are now sided with the Adders Tier, we are told RESTED RATS SLIDE, RAID and WADE. This is not the way you would normally describe Rat's behaviour – slide and raid are much more like the Adders behaviour. Raid also has a bold quality about it. THESE Rats are SEAL LED. That is the Seals are informing them somehow or giving them directions or leading them in what to do. Seals are also creatures known for their slides. THESE SEAL LED LAID HEATER SHEER. So it is the Rats that have

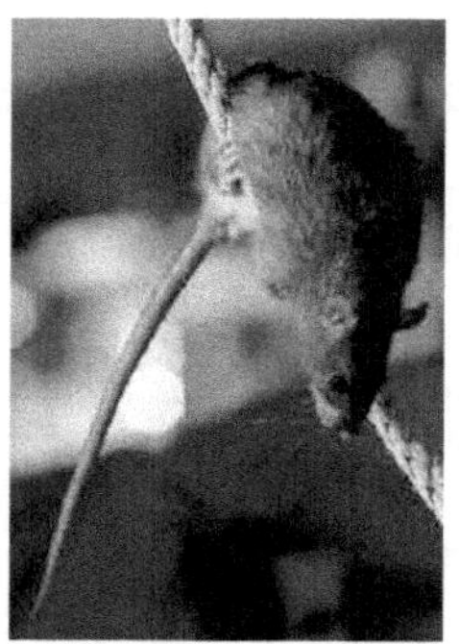

turned up the Heater. A heater turned to Sheer will completely incinerate the substances in it. So the Seals have instructed the Rats to turn the heater onto sheer. RID DAD HEARD – eliminate – the Father heard. DIE SEA REAL AS SHEARED - there is a shocking truth here.

Atomic waste, that is still radio-active and will be so for at least the next 250,000 years, has been dumped at sea in steel containers reinforced with concrete. No one knows how long the concrete will last but it is very unlikely to last for the period required. The sea and everything in it will die as certainly as if it were a limb that was cut off and removed completely - sheared. LATER AIDS SHEET DIRT TIERS. Later the deposited remains of all the sea creatures would be seen as a sheet or a layer of dirt, bones and shells that would be layered as tiers. HEARS LEASE SHED SET.

At the time this transcript was obtained there were reports about the Russians dumping nuclear waste into the sea. They were filmed doing so and the film was shown on national TV in Australia. At that time we were operating wilderness Vision Quests [Foster & Little. Bib. 24] in the Big Desert of North Western Victoria and we had plans for leasing a shed in a nearby town - Rainbow. Indeed we were a "Lease Shed Set". The transcript continues – SLID SIT HADES, LATE EAR LAD LEADS TO ONE. I do recall an incident where I experienced what was like sitting in on what was going on in Hades and hearing what was said. It was an exceptional incident and I did report to ONE. What is also accurate about this comment is that my Ear did develop Late – I was in my 50's at the time – so hardly a Lad.

3.

ONE LEADS the EAR WIDE LATE. So my Ear for such an incident developed late at the direction of ONE. I was clearly meant to hear these things. WAITS for developments to occur in HADES, then SIT SLID into place where Satan or HIS HEATS HIDE A REAL DIE IT HEARD. One's sacredness is really destroyed by Hades Heats. DAD, the Father, RID HEATER and LAID a SEAL. Fortunately ONE intervenes and Satan or Hades Heats are put out and a seal is installed to prevent the Heaters use.

THESE Rats who WADE, RAID and SLIDE in and who had turned the Heater onto Sheer, ADD that they are RESTED and have returned to their HEAL RAIDS. SHEAR RATES the RIDES into the Big Desert DID provoke SHIRE TEARS. RED [the colour of the Deer] and WHITE [the colour of the Reed] HELD the ALDER tree. This action SLEW or terminated the constraints and HATES obtained HIS AIR DATE RELEASE TO ONE.

4.

ONE TEAR HIS LEASED HEAT. It is the sadness ONE experiences and particularly His tear that enables Satan or Hate's Heater. There are many who believe that Satan is really ONE's lover. But the significance of Hates being granted his air date release is certainly something to be deeply concerned about. No wonder the Dear and Wise said at the beginning that they feared what would happen as a consequence of the failure of the Reed Dais Tide. They feared what would be released. At LEAST the ALDER DALE STAID, prevented or stopped TEARS being shed in the DEER SHIRE. Alder trees are riparian so they would have a dale, but how the Alder Dale is related to the Deer Shire is uncertain except that Deer would drink at mountain streams and could have a tied relationship between the Dale and the Shire.

HEAR DEEDS SEE WEEDS. In nearly all stories told there are things that could be done better or weeds that could be removed. LEaST LIED LETS RISE WIDER TO ONE. Those who have lied least are entreated to rise wider - to look, listen and act more broadly – to ONE.

5.
It is clear that this is not the only transcript the Archetypes support. They then propose 5 more word strings that need work;

LIST HAIL THE ONE;
THE ONE LED TREE;
SAIL LIDS LIST
AIDS TO THE ONE;
THE ONE AIDS.

Bearing in mind the Spiral Process limits the words available to only those words that can be generated from the letters in the original statement, this is a quite remarkable story. It is tempting to expand this story with excepts from later transcripts but I think that each one should stand alone as they were each given separately.

At this juncture, suffice it to say that later transcripts reinforce a number of the issues raised and in some parts considerable expansion occurs and whole new vistas are opened up into the Archetypes world, their perceptions, concerns, differences, fields of interest, humour and overall structure. For this reason alone I don't want to change the structure and order in which they provide their information.

Trans. 2. <u>DEVELOPING WIDER AND WISER EARS.</u>

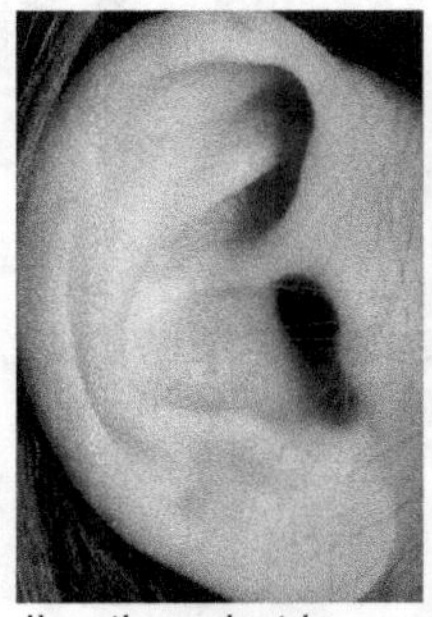

Emerging from the previous text was the idea of WIDER EARS being tuned to the softly murmured secrets of the Dear and Wise in the previous Spiral transcript. Wider Ears were also sided with the Reed Dais Tide and the forces for Healing and had been tuned to overhear the covert plans of Satan in Hades. Accordingly the words WIDER EARS were used for analysis.

In the transcript we find that a consecrated relationship exists between the Elemental forms of Fire and Air in directing what is erased by the Erase Wires.

1.

As the Reed Dais Tide has a Riser Wire, so here we begin with Erase Wires. AIRS WED ERASE WIRES. WE had EASIER WAR.

Apparently there has been a titanic struggle going on, a War, but Fire and Air have an easier war.

The word WED is essentially the same as "tied" or "tie" or "sided with" used in the previous chapter. The transcript goes on to say – READ IS DEW RISE RIDE TO THE ONE LORD. Analysis of the expression DEW RISE RIDE (Trans. 4) will expand on the easier War by Fire and Air and the operation of their Erase Wires.

2.

THE ONE LORD RISE and SAW RAW DEW IS READ. ONE arose, as in the morning, and saw that the Raw Dew had been read by someone. Apparently it is not normal for someone to read the Raw Dew and ONE notices that someone has been there before Him to read it. The Raw Dew apparently says REARS WAR. ERASE the WEE SEER [a seer is someone with clairvoyant skills] and those to whom he is WED because he DARES the Rears WAR IDEA. The Raw Dew is evidently informing ONE that the Wee Seer should be or by the rules, needs to be ERASED by SEAR. For how this affects the WIDER REED or what the Wider Reed WEARS as a consequence we are told to SEE ERE SEED SEA TO THE ONE LORD. However it is likely that the Wee Seer is wed to the Wider Reed before [ere] the Seed Sea but exactly what happened then is not explained.

3.

THE ONE LORD ERASER RIDS SEA SEED. The Eraser or Satan eliminates seed that has gone astray. This sounds like a mass extinction occurred in accord with some primal arrangement that existed even before the Seed Sea. That which is ERASED AIDS the DAIS RISER. Nothing is wasted – the Reed Dais Tide benefits from the erased seed and the Riser Wire is activated. We also find that when someone wears Red clothing [weeds] this activates the Deer – WEEDS RED A DEER WEDS. Red has long been the traditional colour for love and so too the soft doe eyes of love of the Deer's fawn. The Deer gravitates to and 'weds' those who wear Red clothing and DAREs that a SIRE ARISE WIRE SEWn TO THE ONE LORD. The idea of being sewn with wire makes for the idea of a very strong bond to ONE that the Deer dares or hopes will occur if it can produce a sire.

4.

THE ONE LORD ARISE WEIRDER. The word weirder had fallen in the South and this is the place of the Elemental Water.

The word 'weird' comes from the Nordic tradition of 'wyrd', meaning the mysterious power of the Almighty One Eyed One - Woden. Woden is credited with saying he was not the supreme power in Universe, he was always respectful that there was a greater power in Universe than him and that is why he was ONE- Eyed. We find that to Him, a mistake in the colour Red was said to have alerted the senses in the East, the place of beginnings. A RED ERR WAS EARS.

Returning to the South it is said that there is WIDE EWER DESIRE for EASE RE those who endured a DIRE WADE WERE WEIR AID ARSE DEARS of the REAR SAID the WEIRS TO THE ONE LORD.

A Ewer is a large water jug, with a handle and spout, which is a very appropriate vessel to have in the South, the Place of Water. Another vital water image here is of Weirs. So too wading is an activity that occurs in water so there is a great deal of overall consistency here and poetry as well.

The Ewers as a group desire ease be taken with those who were in a dire wade, the Arse Dears. This most likely also refers to the previous transcript where the Wets were in trouble and tired at the Wheat Site. It was their lies to the Leader Whales that triggered off a whole string of dire consequences including the Rears War referred to earlier in this transcript. Evidently Ewers share the view that these Aids to the Weirs deserve some special consideration. So Ewers are entering a plea and the Weirs to ONE confirm that they are Arse Dears of the Rear.

5.
THE ONE LORD WEIRS SAID
AS ARSE AID REAR
IRE EIDER RIDES WERE to
RID the WEIRD RE their DESIRE.

The poetry, again in this passage, is unmistakable and 'wyrd' indeed! But

through it we learn that the Rears War is indeed a war concerning the Rear, and in particular the Arse Dears of the Rear. Indeed they would endure a dire wade. In the same way that the Arse aids the Rear by eliminating waste, the anger or Ire of the Eider, rids the weird of their desire. The image of an angry Eider is one of a large Arctic duck with wonderful downy feathers of black and white, repeatedly attacking [riding] someone with weird desires. Significantly the home-ground for an Eider is Northern Norway, Iceland and Northern Scotland. The same territory Woden was worshiped in.

This Rune Shield shows Woden's one eye in the centre and the Ash tree Yggdrasil supporting him and having its branches and roots in all realms – above and below. Runes [depicted by the outer circle of symbols] have been in existence since about the first century AD.

<u>Trans. 3. SACRED BONDS OF THE SEED SEA ERA.</u>

Emerging from the previous text, the word chain used for analysis here was "Weeds Red A Deer Weds". The resulting text concerns the sacred bonds formed after Seed Sea. It is apparent that there was a previous arrangement, a primal arrangement between the Archetypes but the Seed Sea marks the point at which a new set of relationships were determined. Apparently the war idea dared by the Wee Seer has its origin in those arrangements and involved manipulation of tied response relations.

1.
What was DARED WAS SEA WARS. The Wee Seer or his associates DARES the ASS or donkey to do something that EASES its work or burden that had been extended or SEWn, ADDED the DEARS TO THE ONE LORD.

2.
THE ONE LORD WARDED or defended the ARSES and SEWERS. Their ERR or error was of a WADED or WADE type. Any DARED DEED is up to the ASS SEESAW WARD to determine what wAS DARED.

This does sound a bit like asses in a playground and also a play on the sound the ass makes, but essentially the idea of the Seesaw is as a set of scales or balances as symbolized by Justice. The Ass Seesaw ward concerns weighing up the evidence concerning what is dared in a deed.

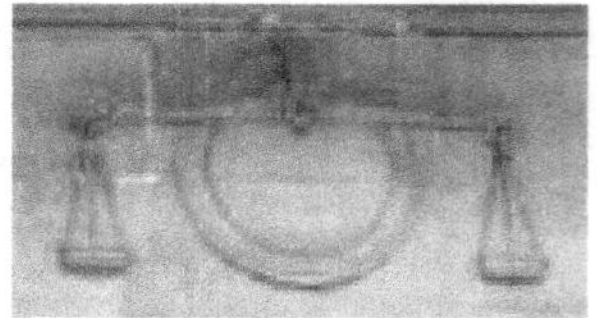

In the South East, we are given the image of the WARDER - the keeper or guardian of some defined duty or one having responsibility for a number of wards. In the South, the place of Water, we are told the form of Warder referred to is RARE or unusual but it has been noted before. The form is rare since the ADDERS SEDER when ERASE REDDER DEEDS.

This is a poignant reference to the time of Moses when the Hebrew Seder was varied; the sacrifice of a young female lamb was ended; the holocaust was erased and Redemption achieved by taking the teg [male] around to the door for the priests' use. In the first text, Transcript 1, we were told that the Adders are not sided with Hates. It is a lie of association that they are so sided or feared. The Adders are here directly associated with this very significant change in religious practice.

The Seder celebrates the time of the Passover, when the Hebrew were still in captivity in Egypt. The story of Moses meeting with the powerful magicians at Pharaoh's court begins with Adders; the magicians each threw their staffs down and had them change into serpents. Moses is said to have thrown his staff down at the end and that his serpent swallowed all the others. The form of Warder at that time was known to occur, and the massive destruction in Egypt on the night of the Passover leaves little room for doubt about the power of the Warder as Eraser. (The Eraser passed over the Hebrew houses that had been specially marked with ewe blood but the Eraser is said to have killed the first child who had opened the womb in every other house. Later, during the time in the Wilderness, when the Covenant was remade at Mt. Sinai, the redder deeds were indeed erased. In theology this is known as the Third or National Covenant, the first being with Adam and the second with Abraham (Ellis Bib. 19). It is important to note that this change in religious practice lifted a huge burden on the Ewe. In this text the 2nd Covenant is given as being at Seed Sea and the 1st Covenant would be that primal arrangement that preceded it – before Seed Sea.)

In the transcript it is pointed out that the DRAW [in the 3rd Covenant], the change in circumstances for the Ewe had negative consequences or WEARS the SEWER. It may be noted that the Sewer would have been used to catch the blood of the lamb and thus Sewer played a key role in Redemption.

Apparently after some 3300 years since the time of the

Adders Seder, the Wear is so great, the dire wade so long, Sewer DARE WEE DEW EWE ERASE part of its message to THE ONE LORD. The Wee Dew Ewe apparently did not do as dared as we learnt in the previous transcript. THE ONE LORD rose and saw the raw dew had been read.

3.

Transcript; THE ONE LORD foresaw or SEEDS SEWER WEAR DRAW SEAS DEEDS WAR. A Seas Deeds War is inevitable given the draw. (The idea of Seeds is more one to do with the potential the seed has within it - all the potential for the mature tree. In the passage of time, the potential for this problem to occur will be manifested). What is also seeded is that in the aftermath of the Seas Deeds War, besides the Wee Seer being seared, the threat is the Deer could also be erased and in its wake, so too the Bishop's Seat of power - the See would be razed. ADDS ERASED DEER RASED SEE [of bishops] The Bishops DREAD that REAR DRAWS SEAR. They would suffer a real death also and there would be no Eternal Life for them. REARS were WED to the SERE REED WEDS SWEAR TO THE ONE LORD. In the Seed Sea arrangement [2nd Covenant], the Rears were wed to the Sere Reed. Sere here refers to the stages of development in the ecological succession. In turn the Sere Reed weds and swears to ONE.

4.

THE ONE LORD says that before the SEED ERE, before the Reed was Wed, the RAW REED SERE WED SAW the READER SEARED. In the same way a chaperone is terminated at the time of a marriage or one ends life as a spinster. Evidently the trust put in the Sere Reed was very great indeed and such that if she herself was to be subject to Rear Raze, the Deer would follow and so too the Bishop's See. REAR RASE ADD DEER. In this, the Seas Deeds War, the WRASSE SEER WADED EARS. The Wrasse is a very colourful tropical fish that

is characterised by its very sharp teeth! The Wrasse Seer is one who has clairvoyant skills associated with the Wrasse. We may imagine the Wrasse Seer Wading along a tropical reef listening in to the Ears of the Cosmic Sea and hearing of further aspects of the Seed Sea arrangement.

WEED DREW READ WEARER
SEWER SEES SEWS RE SEAR
EAR ERSE TO THE ONE LORD.

The archetypal Weed, tied to or wed to Ears (eg, wheat also has ears) drew responsibility to read what someone does via their clothing - Read Wearer. Such a reading to be as clear as someone who is a sewer and who can therefore see the sewing in a garment. Any sews concerning Sear are tied to the Ear of Erse to THE ONE LORD. Erse is the Gaelic name used by the Celts to refer particularly to the highlands of Scotland. Definitely people of tongues, ears and readers of what one wears, the tartan being a prime example.

5.
THE ONE LORD ERSE RE concerns ARE WARE SEERS who in the Seed Sea arrangement SEES that READ DREW WEED, EARS and DEW. [In this play on words, Read drew WED!]

<u>Trans. 4. FAILING ALLIANCES IN THE BISHOPS' SEE.</u>

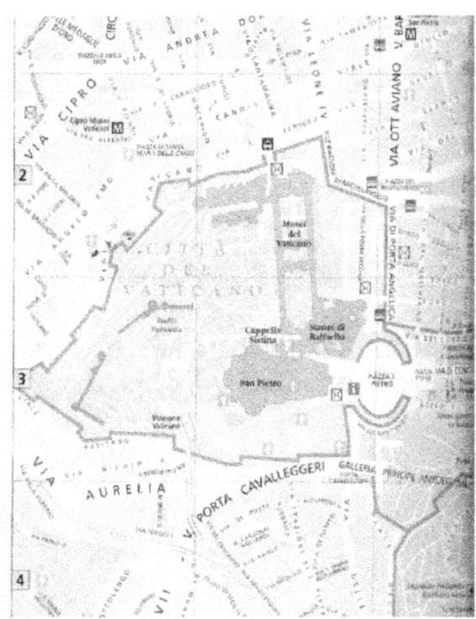

The word chain used for analysis was Dew Rise Ride.

During word preparation, more detailed notes were included to differentiate Reed grass from the reed used as a shaft in an arrow, or the reed musical instrument, or the reed used in a weaver's loom.

It was evident that as the Reed was so central to understanding the dynamics of the Covenants, it was best to differentiate. This was a learning process and in later analysis, this differentiation became even more central to clarity of understanding.

1.

Appropriately REEDS -ARROWS opens the defence of the Wider Reed. It refers to the WIDER WEIR's colour or DIE –STAIN. Reeds-arrows points out that the Bishop's seat of power in the South East, the SEE, is in the DIED WARD and it is DIE-CAST to REDDER WEIRS. REEDS – GRASS follows on saying that in the developmental stages of the ecological succession when she was SERE, she DESIRED the DEER WISER IRE. Perpetually in error because she did not become wed to the Deer's Wiser Ire, she says WE'RE EVER ERRS ESE – East South East. WEED – GRASS and REED-ARROWS both SEE what the concerns [RE] of the WEER REEDS-GRASS SEER WERE and observed what he DID TO THE ONE LORD.

2.

THE ONE LORD says that the DEEDS are aligned with or SIDE RIDE REED-GRASS concerning [RE] SEEing the way the Bishop's clothing appears – their SEE WEEDS. There is no err attributable to Reeds-grass in this respect. The WEIRER of the Redder Weirs ERRS in favour of the REED of WEAVERS that is SIDED with WEED-GRASS.

The REEDS – WEAVERS report that as long as DERRIS is used during cloth preparation this EVER WOULD continue to occur. The See of Bishop's death is directly attributable to the use of derris.

Derris is a plant whose roots contain an insecticide probably used to treat the vestments for moths but probably also reacting with the die-stain colour pigments and thus affecting the Weirer's decisions. For as long as derris is used, this err will occur. IRE is DIE-CAST to the DEER ID RIDER and according to his DESIRES and concerns [RE] the RED WEIRS were DIED-STAINED. It seems that in the 2nd Covenant, the Deer Wiser Ire is renamed as the Deer Id Rider and that his desires regarding Red Weirs colouration are finally set. Directly linked with this are the DIE WIRES (akin to the Erase Wires) that are activated by the REEDS-FLUTES music and REDDER DIE-CAST WARD DIED. This error

RESIDE with the DIRE ERR by the SEE-BISHOP'S WEIR. This is a direct reference to the Pan Flutes being played and affecting the Die Wires.

 In mythology, Pan is frequently directly associated with the Deer and here is very likely being referred to as the Deer Id Rider. In some very automatic way it seems that as long as derris is used, the Die Wires will be activated. The text says that this is central to the dire err, the separation from the Redder Ward and so death in the See of Bishops Weir.

In the European legend about Pan, he was resting in the forest when he was struck by the sudden appearance of the beautiful water nymph Syrinx. In this context Syrinx is probably EVER ERRS of the ESE.

From the transcript it would seem Reeds-grass [EVER ERRS] regrets her mistake of running away but she is quite philosophical about it saying what else would you expect from her when her charge is EVER ERRS in the East South East! (Accordingly this is the sector for life lessons and particularly repeated mistakes).

The WEE WISE- PROCEEDING warn that any who DERIDE SEWER should first consider that the DERIDER DIES on the WORD of WEEDS-GRASS.

We are told that during the period before the

Seed Sea, ERE, it was DEWIER according to the EIDERS when their WIRE was set to EIRE DESIRE.

It may be recalled that earlier, the Eider's Ire rid the weird of their desire. Ire is later used in conjunction with the Deer - the Deer Wiser Ire but it is not referred to in the title Deer Id Rider after Seed Sea – the 2nd Covenant. It suggests that the use of the word Wire may be a play on words [wiser ire - wire] and that Ire is linked directly with the Eiders in the current arrangement. We are also told that Eire desire resided with the WIDE EWE. Indeed, the Celts in the highlands of Scotland very widely used and favoured wool in their tartans. Finally proceedings draw to a close with a comment from the Ewer to THE ONE LORD, "WE'D [HAD] WISE WEED-CLOTHES."

Just as the Weirs have their Weirer, the Wards their Warder, the Ewes have their Ewer! Thus we may see that the Deer Id Rider is the archetype for the Sacred Heart and the Ewer, not a jug at all but rather the Archetype for arrears and redemption.

Trans. 5. Whata Saga.

A significant improvement occurs in the text of this analysis. Previously, the word generation process depended on all the words I could think of that could be made from the letters deconstructed from the original dream statement or it's derivatives. In this analysis, two changes are made. Firstly I used the statement - Great Wrasse Saves. This is implied in the third transcript but is not directly used, as the Wrasse is only referred to in the place of Spirit. Secondly, I used the Complete Macquarie Dictionary to obtain a systematic and exhaustive list of words that was four times bigger than any previous word listing but less open to ambiguity in word meanings.

This chapter refers to the traditional Biblical Covenants, the 4th Covenant applies after the birth of Christ and the 5th Covenant applies when He comes again at a time in the future usually called the Second Coming. These matters are very central to an understanding of the transcript that has been obtained. Teras is the Abomination of Greek legends and is the Abomination referred to by John in the Book of Revelations in the Holy Bible of the Christian Church and the Abomination that makes desolate of the Hebrew tradition as discussed in Daniel's book in the Old Testament.

1.

At the beginning of this transcript we are told that the notion of Weave warrants careful examination. WEAVE RATES REVERT ARTICLE RAG RASTER [electronic scanner]. Weave is so important that we need to go back and look at its previous state before it was an article and to put it under an electronic scanner so that its structure and fibres can be examined. The example given is the AREA GETT or Erse tartan that is generally a multi-coloured plaid, woven with stripes of different colour and width, at right angles to each other. The colours mentioned in the transcripts are easily imagined in an Area Gett;

White associated with Whales, Reed, Ewe, Ewer, Weirs, Sewer, and the Dears
Red associated with Deer, Love, Deer Id Rider, Pan

Redder associated with Spirit and the Bishops' See
Black associated with Satan, Hates and Hades
Yellow associated with Wheat and Eternal Life
Green associated with Weed-grass, Word

Even the notion of the Deer being Wire Sewn to
ONE is a very powerful indication of the bond using
the terms of reference of weave. Many others refer
to tied relationships eg, the Leader Whales are tied
to the Reed Dais Rite; wires are woven into the
stories; the sewing is well illustrated by the ware
seers of Erse; the sewer sees the sews; and the
ecclesiastic vestments of the Bishops identify the
colouration problems caused by derris during cloth
preparation. All in all the Weeds-clothes were
indeed wise and weave is a central notion in the
emerging picture. As a variation on the old Gnostic
saying - As above so below - it is also fair to say -
Above Sew below - and - As you sew below so you
sew above.

In contrast to the joy of Christmas, EASTER TEARS RAWER TAW [highly valued
marble] WHEAT – this identifies a time of sorrow but also a time of great power,
value and importance to Eternal Life. Significantly the Last Supper Christ had
with his disciples occurred on the night of the Passover and they would have
followed the traditions of the Adders Seder but with the major variation that Christ
broke the bread to symbolize his body and gave the disciples wine to symbolize
his blood.

The first word in the first transcript was Wheat and again it occurs here, integrally
linked to "Easter Tears". Indeed Christ promised Eternal Life to those who would
follow him and remember him by eating the bread and drinking the wine. The
transcript tells us that because of the sharp pain experienced by the Archetypes
at that time, Wheat should be worn, carried or used in wreaths as a symbol of
that time - as a linkage that will assist the passage to Eternal Life through the
Wheat GATT [passage or pass]. The particular moment of vulnerability
mentioned is at Vert, when the foetus is turned in the womb preparatory to birth.
Wheat SH'D [should] be worn [WHERE] AT VERT to SEVER the GRASS
SWEARER [on whose word we die] and identify ARREARS in STEERAGE or
errors through the religious teachings of REVerend and S.V.[Sancta Virgo].

ESTATE GARTER TAWER [cloth preparation] THREW SHAT STARS. Cloth
preparation, tawer is in the place of Water. During tawer the cloth is thrown in
such a way that it eliminates the stars. An admonishing finger is WAGged. This
action VEERS RETE - Sun's network in the solar system.

The WEER RAGE – WHATA SAGA. What is beginning is indeed a long saga but it is also a play on words as the Maori or indigenous people of New Zealand who built their storehouses on posts called them a Whata. The WEER, the tiny ones are in a rage over the start of this Saga. The Norse were famous for their sagas.

In the text it says what matters is how we go about our tasks - the "ing" in washing, hunting, storing and loving. GER [GERUND; is the verb form of a noun created usually by adding "ing". In what we do we need to be AWARE of AEGIS - sponsorship and protection given by Zeus/Sun. An example given is of a H.G. – High German GEARER who issued SWEATERS made from a EWE (redemption) to those working in the SECtions responsible for dealing out strap punishment - TAWSE.

The West African Butternut tree or SHEA [Vitellaria nilotica] only grows in the savannah from Ethiopia to Senegal. Some trees in the Shea Belt are estimated to be 400 years old and like the Mallee Trees they are extremely deep rooted and drought resistant. The stands of Shea have been protected by the inhabitants and farmers of the region for hundreds of years of agroforestry. The SHEA SEES the seats in the Bishop's SEE. H.E. [His Eminence] can SEE WAVE THETA [Grk 8th letter] HEATS WEARER [one who changes tack] and who favours SWEETS instead of STEEVE - upwardly striving for their VERT rights and responsibilities as a Bishop. The real power vested in them vegetates. Aegis from the STAR bonded with the ASS'S ASH [ex. Fire] VESTS them with power. The power VEGITATES, SEE [look] at the Old Testament story of HAGGAI [Common Bible Bib. 13].

Haggai and his people fared poorly in general and were asked by the LORD of Hosts to consider how they fared.
> *1v6 You have sown much, and harvested little; you eat, but you never have enough; you drink but never have your fill; you clothe yourselves, but no one is warm; and he who earns wages, earns wages to put them into a bag with holes. v7 Thus says the LORD of Hosts: Consider how you have fared.*

The people fared poorly because the LORD'S house lay in ruins whilst people busied themselves each with their own house.

Aegis from the STEER bonded with the TETRA or tropical fish are a VARiant in this AGE as ASSistants who SERVES ARSE SWERVE.

There has been a steady stream of admonishments of Christian Church officials for their "Arse Swerves". The large number of these sexual assaults reported all have effects [such as cover up] even up to the level of Bishops, one of whom was elevated to the position of Governor General in this country! The wag of an admonishing finger is not enough for these criminals – this behaviour is totally reprehensible. How can you build a Church or even a basic society on hundreds if not thousands of sexual assault cases? Even worse is the example these people set. Might I say it is here identified in "Whata Saga" that it is both the religious teachings and behaviour of church officials that is being seriously called into question by Archetypes. Not only are these individuals and their institutions failing people but they are also failing Archetypes and their own eternal sacredness. This is not a condemnation of Archetypes as many assume or of Gay people either, but it is a condemnation of those who use their position on unsuspecting/ otherwise trusting and innocent, non-consenting individuals, to impose themselves. The Shea sees in the See of Bishops who is being heated by Wave Theta. Wave Theta will heat any who have changed tack.

GRASS GAVE its WAGER on what would be told about them and an admonishing WAG of its tussock seals the deal! [Remember, you die on the word of the WEED. Justice comes anyway – it is unavoidable as all actions and intent are known to Archetypes.]

ERST [formerly, of old] STEEVE [packed tight] TRESS [plait or braid] SEWER. At the end of the primal arrangement, before the 2nd Covenant, the Sewer was packed tight with tress (plait or braid). This is the product of the mass extinction referred to in the earlier transcript. AH! (Exclamation of pity). It WAS TERRA [Earth's] TAGS WAGER in TATTERs as a GESTATE STEW. So Mother Earth had a number of contenders for the ecological succession and those who didn't make the grade ended up in the Sewer as a huge stew. Indeed this is a pity. However we learnt earlier that which is erased [upward of 90% of all species] aids the Reed Dais Riser.

Those with the SERE-dry TAG will GREAVE when they are arrested. The ARRESTEE is AGHAST as the SECondary WASTER of the STEWS THEATRE is the GATE TESTER SAHARA. With the Sere-dry Tag, after a time in the Stews Theatre comes testing times in the Sahara and not much is left after that. Anyone with any sense would RATHER WASHES SEVERER REARS.

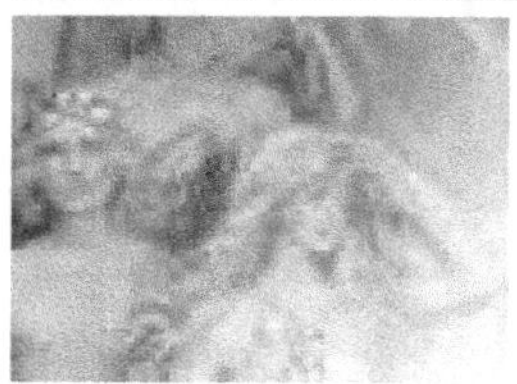

In the South, the place of Water, we are given W. The abbreviation for Wednesday or Wodensdarg – Woden's day. Woden was a Norse deity known for his One Eye, many successful battles and a unique sort of "blackish" humour. The old Norse were famous for their sagas so it is fitting that as we come to the Archimedean point in how the Sacred Heart is saved in Whata Saga and we are reintroduced to Woden who was also known as "All Father". In the Norse Pantheon there were two principle races namely the Aesir and Vanir that eventually became joined as one. Woden was an Aesir and the W in his name was not pronounced so he is more traditionally spoken about as "Oden".

We are told Woden will REAVE [to commit ravages] and even WAGE [war] to SAVE you in the THRASHERS that STARVE or don't consume any of your S.V. [Sanctitas Vestra: Your Holiness.]

Whilst Sanctitas Vestra is normally a title reserved for the Pope, here it refers to the sacred part in each of us – literally Your Holiness. No doubt you have noted  Woden's "blackish" humour already [Thrashers] but there is plenty more in store. There are several methods Woden uses to save Your Holiness. In the first of these, the Thrashers, Sanctitas Vestra is separated but in no way diminished or damaged by the process. The second is by SHEER STAVE. This is more akin to removing the steel bands from a good wine barrel and then separating each of the staves. This deconstruction is known as the Sheer process. A third analogy is given equating to the separation of GARE - the coarser 'guard hair' in a fleece. The gare normally protects the finer fleece (eg, cashmere) but this is extracted in the West by Woden's assistant, the witch Woden calls the HARASS HAG! And yes she is very ugly, brutal and blunt.

The Harass Hag is very watchful and when she spots the gare, she saves it and uses her SWAGE tool to beat the gare back into its original shape before she HEAVEs it in and TEASEs it out in the EAST VAT for WAREs or things!

In the South East, Place of Spirit, the GRASSER or informer for EASE, in the case of someone being inclined to Ease, the Grasser-informer exclaims ER ; so hesitation is exercised in the use of STEARATE but they are tagged with the VAGrant TAG! Stearate is the salt of stearic acid, a monobasic organic acid that occurs naturally in animal fat and having ONE replaceable hydrogen atom! You will see the much wider importance of this later but don't miss the play on words about needing to be steered if you are tagged as a Vagrant!

 In the South, Woden says that when you are tagged Vagrant, it is always a toss up between the VASES and the SEESAW weighing up any dared deeds. Where the later is the case you would be assigned to the magnificent RATA-red [Southern New Zealand red flowering riparian tree] SEAS of AESTHETE where you will be as Woden puts it RET. This refers to the cloth preparation process in which the cloth is soaked in water until the fibres rot enough to separate – you are being set to rot!

The reference to Aesthete is delightful. It is defined as one who cultivates a
sense of the beautiful; one very sensitive to the
beauties of art or nature and one who inspires or
affects great love of art, poetry or music but has
indifference to practical matters. In the Rata Red
Seas of Aesthete you are in an inspirational
setting with like-minded others. Woden intends
finding out just how much aesthetic awareness
you have gained but first he has to separate your
fibres. This is just another way he wages war to
save another part of Sanctitas Vestra and he and
all the Wets are devoted and unrelenting servants
in your cause. The Arse Dears of the REAR.

SHEET REVERE [venerate] GREATER RHEA TO THE ONE LORD. In these
circumstances, the Vagrant is saved in their preferred mode of lying down –
under a Sheet - horizontal. But there is more to it than that. SHEET is a
fundamental property of water that comes under the aegis of .

The Greater Rhea to
THE ONE LORD.

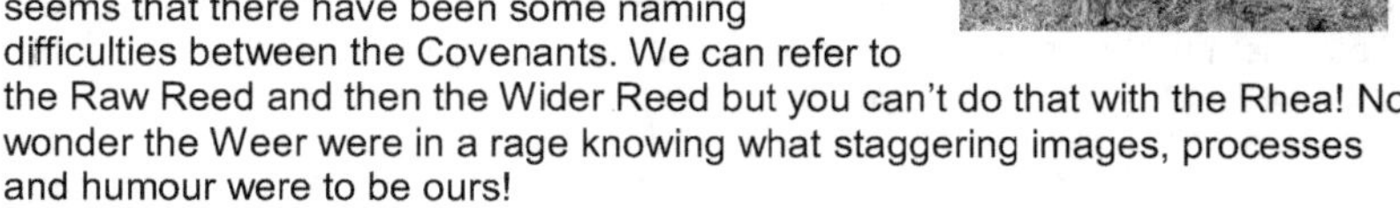

We have another unusual aspect to the Rhea being
used for this aegis. The Rhea is a three toed bird
and the footprints it leaves in the soft earth or sand
is exactly the symbol of the "wyrd" used in ancient
times to signify Woden.

2.
THE ONE LORD ASHES GREATER VEST. The
aegis is by the Great Rhea not the Greater Rhea. It
seems that there have been some naming
difficulties between the Covenants. We can refer to
the Raw Reed and then the Wider Reed but you can't do that with the Rhea! No
wonder the Weer were in a rage knowing what staggering images, processes
and humour were to be ours!

SHEET shows on its record that it HAST TWA or two of EARTH'S SEAS RET or
laid down to rot. As twa is Scottish this suggests the North Sea area, Norwegian
Sea and the Barents Sea are all contenders. We noted in the first transcript that
radio-active waste had been dumped in the sea. Here we find it is two seas that
are at risk. SEESAW - something of a play on the balance or scales of justice
suggests the Seas that are ret are teetering in the balance. SWEETER VASES
TAG these seas as VAGrant but again there is hesitation, ER exclaimed at the
proposal to use STEARATE to EASE the situation, according to the GRASSER –
informer.

East VAT admits that the earlier reference to the fleece being tossed into the East Vat for things was just to TEASE you. WARE [things] should really be understood as 'WARE [aware] EAST. The Harass HAG interjects with the exclamation to cause surprise - EH! In the West, GARE. After she collected the Gare in the West, she used her swage tools on it to straighten out the fibre and she heaved the fleece into the East Vat where the fleece was 'Ware – Aware: the Gare is aware or conscious throughout this process. So Sanctitas Vestra is your awareness and it is this aspect of the self that survives death in the West and is delivered to the East again for rebirth with pretty much the same original set of defences mixed in with fine qualities. The Gare is Aware, not a ware - EH! And the Harass Hag has been beating it with her hammer!

In like fashion reference is made to the STAVEs of the barrel

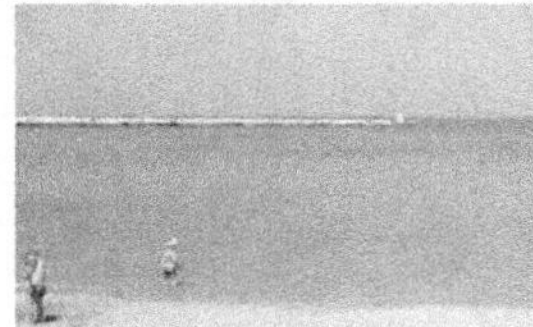

that Woden saves by Sheer, also being aware. However it is indicated that the North Rete also supports SHEER. Fire in the North and Water in the South can both be either Sheet or Sheer and both play a central role in these processes. North with South and what goes West comes back in the East again.

TERAS is the study of the abominable and is given in the East as if beginning. You can trust Woden to bring up something unpleasant! In Greek mythology, Teras referred to monstrosities of many forms. Today, it also refers to abnormal life formations in nature. The Teratorn was a prehistoric bird, as tall as a man, with a wingspan of 8 - 11 meters and it is believed to have been the worlds' largest flying bird - so if it is huge, ugly and eats you it is a Teras. In modern times, the nuclear disaster at Chernobyl has led to a whole field of study referred to as teratogenic foetal abnormalities. Teras is with us today in more ways than one as the widely varying abnormalities of an equally wide range of drugs are found to cause foetal abnormalities.

In the South the TRET [an allowance for waste in the cargo] EWERS of WODEN are used to make up for the Teras damage caused to Your Holiness during one's lifetime. Woden would RATHER a GATE TESTER WE'RE VERSET [short verse] or knew the difference between the WASHS TAG and SAHARA. Generally STEWS are AGHAST the TARTARE is STET or put back into the GRAVE when SERE-dry. AH! (Exclamation of pity.) After two prompts from the transcript to include a short verse to the Gate Tester, the following is offered.

ON WODEN'S WORD – coming to the end of my wandering days.

Tramping along the old Wheat Gatt, my Billy at my rear,
I noticed he was thrashing, having more for me to hear.
"The Tartare of Your Holiness, the Stews will save for me,
And Rhea save your Star-Bush Love - as Aesthete fibre be."

The Wheat-fields around the Gatt, swayed and wagged agree,
I knew that I was at the end of the wandering days for me.
The Washes Tag is best," the Billy thrash a while,
I even kept the beat of it as I liked the Billy's style.

But I'd always loved the desert and Sahara sounded fine,
So I dared to ask if Tartare Stet had ever been designed.
"Tartare Stet!", the Billy thrash ,"The Stews would be aghast!"
"Wee Sahara Stews have to bury you 'til Sanctitas Vestra pass."

I tried another gait…"Ah! A pity, such a pity, such a pity Sere Dry"
I tried another gait.. ."Aware, Aware, Aware as gare."
But Billy made no reply.

3.
At this point the transcript says RESTATE TAGS. There have been four tags
discussed in the transcripts so far.
- **Wager Tag**. There is a reference to the Wager tag, when Mother Earth's
  Wagers ended up in the Sewer as Tress and gestate stew prior to Seed
  Sea. She had pinned her hopes on several contenders for the ecological
  succession and the ones in the Sewer had lost.
- **Washes Tag**. Under Woden's guidance the Washes Tag is the best for
  saving Sanctitas Vestra. Woden will even wage war to save Sanctitas
  Vestra by Sheet or Sheer.
- **Sere-dry Tag.** To be dried to a crisp in Sahara is a terrible waste of Your
  Holiness. Even the secondary wasters in the Stews theatre can do little to
  save your awareness.
- **Vagrant Tag.** Treatment of those who have been given the Vagrant tag is
  normally with a dose of Stearate but hesitation is exercised. Both people
  and Seas have been tagged in this way. In the case of people, the Vagrant
  is treated in the preferred mode of lying down in the Rata-red Seas of
  Aesthete until the Aesthete fibre has been separated. Rhea has the aegis
  for this form of saving you.

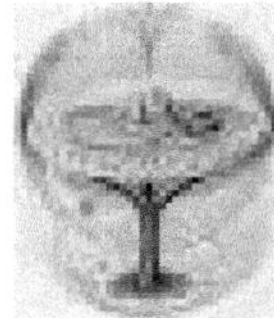

Woden has a wager that in future the Sewer will be packed as
tight as formerly when people realize the benefits of the
Washes Tag over Sere-dry. There is also something of an
ominous note here. A comparison is being made with the mass

extinctions at the end of the primal arrangement. ERST SEWER STEEVE [packed tight] HE'VE [he would have] WAGER. Woden would only be having a wager on a future event. Formerly it was the Eraser who GAVE SWERVERS the ARSE based on the word of Weed-GRASS. In the coming event the ASH [tree] will be the ASSistant for THE AGE. The power the Ash-tree has to assist us SERVES little purpose or VEGETATES. Woden refers us again to HAGgai in the Common Bible. We need to consider how we are faring and the ways in which we are neglecting our responsibilities and missing very important possibilities in relation to ONE. Swervers are those who have turned away from Him. AS STAR ASS'S SWATTER, Haggai entreats us to consider how we are faring and how we will fare in the future, particularly when we will end up in GRAVES. Even as Woden wages war to save Your Holiness, so too Graves WAGES or conducts us upward or STEEVE in their WAR against SWEETS WHARVES. The treats are not the only thing to think about and even the dared deed is known and adds to the Wear or Trett as Woden called it earlier. In the Grave the WEARER [one who changes tack] HEATS the WASTAGE WAVE – Theta.

The Ash tree is very significant in Norse mythology, the Pantheon was based on the Ash-tree - Yggdrasil that supported the cosmos and had roots and branches in all realms. According to Nordic legend, man was made from the same essence as the Ash-tree and woman from the same essence as the Alder-tree [Hulse Bib. 33]. It may be recalled that the Alder tree played a central role in holding Hates in White Reeds Laid. In North America there is a white Alder and in Europe both a white and black Alder. The Ash tree is also termed white and has a wonderful crown of golden or red leaves in autumn.

On the edge or VERGE of this discussion about Wearer Heats or Trett, we are reminded about the Redemption qualities of the EWE. As discussed earlier the SWEATERS made from the Ewe were used by the GEARER H.G. [High German] because he was AWARE of the RAW AEGIS in the GERund [hunting] GEESE SAGA that SERVE the provisioning of the Maori WHATA or storehouse.

The Aegis TARGETS the WEER and THAWS or releases the STEER or castrated male in the North RETE. A Rete is a network of fibres such as heart, arteries and veins or in this case it is referring to the North or Sun's solar system. In the West, the place of endings, what has been cut off is joined back again as you were originally ESTATED.

In the South West we note there is a WAG from an admonishing finger. Obviously there is a correct way of doing things and it is not being followed.

In the South East, place of Spirit, the correct STAGES and actions in GARTER preparation for the ESTATE of S.V. [Sancta Virgo] and REVerend are needed to enable STEERAGE SWEAT to be released or THAW. Stearage Sweat would be

the mistakes in religious teaching and misguided actions that cause the Sweat.
As the SWEARER is Weeds-GRASS, whenever or WHERE AT VERT [turning
the foetus in the womb] WHEAT. The earlier discussion about Graves and what
happens in the West when we come to our end of days, strongly suggests that
Vert is not just referring to the pre-birth process of a foetus. It also suggests that
the body and our Awareness are at Vert when we die, so our spirit turns in the
"womb". What is proposed is that Wheat should be worn or present at both these
times to eliminate the negative impact of mistakes in religious teaching by SV
and REV. Wheat is a highly valued TAW and the TEARS of EASTER RATES
very highly and so warrants THEE WEAVE Wheat or an Ear of Wheat into any
cloth that is used at Vert. The Aegis of Wheat and Eternal Life are centrally linked
to the Tears of Easter.

In the process of castration, those who conduct the operation should use the
aegis of a Targe that is a Scandinavian round shield. The SHEARS SECretary or
the one who uses the Shears TEETERs or things could go oneway or another.
The aegis of the TARGE means a WART is cut off when you HEW any STEERS
and the WEAR caused EASES STATE WRATH. Further, proper disposal of the
removed parts requires a WREATH of WHEAT which AVERTS SEVER TEAS
like those of the Western Australian desert – Sere-dry.

The TAR EWER is for REVET or stone faced HEARTS. Heart's WASTES
WEARS RE or are of concern to the VESsel. The Tar Ewer is concerned with the
wear on the heart caused by heartlessness. The vessel WAVERs or oscillates
unsteadily or is irresolute or undecided between different courses or opinions
concerning the TARE. The weight of the cargo or the weight of Your Holiness can
be REVERSEd by the weight in the Tar Ewer. For this purpose the SEWERS
have a RETired TASTER. She is to test the ire or angry component or the rot that
has occurred – the Ret. HER HARSH SERGES are made WHERE AS a SWAG
she wears a TERETE and makes her harsh surges into the GHEE. So Your
Holiness is equated to liquid buttermilk that experiences the harshness of her
surges with her terete. This is consistent with the Harass Hag saying that the
Gare and fleece were aware. Here your Ghee is aware. We find there is more
than one Ret Taster - THESE EAGER WETS also WEAR an ASHET or meat
platter. This is something akin to the Targe mentioned earlier. So they eagerly
get around the Sewer with their Teretes worn like a swag on their backs and also
wear an Ashet, probably on the front. Their STEERER or the one who directs
them, does so by using TE, the 7th note in musical scale! [Tea Eh! No it doesn't
say that anyone eats of drinks anything at this tea party.]

The Steerer is given as being in the South West. She HAS in her possession the
RARE ART of ERSE and SHE is beautifully SET with her RECeipt for this Art.
Steerer is also a SHARER of the ETHER with THREE HARVEST TEATS.
    1. VERticle is a Harvest Teat where GER sits in the West. He is dark-skinned
         or a SWARTH STEER ASTronomer. This suggests that Ger can join you

back together with any parts you have lost during your life, such as your testicles.

2. The West TRAVE is a device used in veterinary surgery to hold a wild animal. TEATS asses you for Right Ascension. This refers to the exact position for a star to rise in the night sky and then follow its unique path until it sets. This is an analogy directly applicable to people as if they were a star at birth etc. Obviously an Astronomer is exactly who you need to test for Right Ascension of Your Holiness.

Establishing your Right Ascension will EVERT the TEETH THAT ART SWEAR in REVelations in the New Testament of the Holy Bible. A SEVERE outcome follows if Right Ascension cannot be established. If you turn up early in the West (eg, through suicide) Ger would see that setting is not in the correct order and you would be Traved and then subject to the gnashing teeth sworn to in Revelations – this is John's apocalyptic chapter at the end of the Holy Bible. In that book, the Abomination (Teras) is referred to and his number is given as 666. His period of domination is fortunately fairly short and precedes the Second Coming of Christ, referred to as the Lamb. This text suggests Revelations is an individual rather than global matter but it is very reminiscent of the monsters and horrors of the Bardo world in the Tibetan Book of the Dead [Evans-Wentz Bib. 20].

The wise SAGES of the North advise that their SHEETS went into a TASSET THRASH. A tasset is a pair of defences worn on the thighs. We are to imagine the Sheets are thrashing together like a pair of Tassets. They urgently want us to notice them and their record. TERRA or Earth's SERE is taken as meaning Mother Earth's contender in the stages in the ecological succession, on whom she had a WAGER. The Sages record that a V.G. [very good] STARTER was a SWAT that STASHES the ASS.

In the South, this situation is akin to or be HEST WASTES EVE ETA [Grk; 7th letter]. Again we have a play on words as Eve Eta would be one in which Mysterious [7] things happened when the Ass was stashed. EARS VEE, the Ass had it's ears back, it SWEAR AT WHAT'S TAT or small – namely the Wee Seer. GAT SEERS note from their vantage that there is a TEAR as REAR EGRESS occurs in the West. In the West TARTAR or the descendants of Genghis Khan AGREE HA! Exclamations of laughter GREW in the SETTER GARage to RAH! And then exclamations of hurrah were heard in the Setter Garage. Obviously the

Sun sets in the West and we all go West in the end – even the Ass – to everyone's amusement except the Ass and probably Mother Earth.

 REGESTAE means to present the facts of a case. This is required for STAVES [staffs] TEG [1 or 2 year old sheep] and RET'D [retired].

Staves. The twelve tribes of Israel and the twelve staves representing each tribe, date back to the time of Jacob. However it was in the national covenant (3rd) that Moses strongly identified the staff as a symbol of power and the twelve staves together was a symbol of the unity of the Hebrew people as a Theocratic nation. The ultimate staff was termed the Sceptre by which life could be given or ended and it was Christ who is said to have taken the Sceptre under the 4th Covenant, when the 12 staves of Israel were retired and the covenant made with the whole of Humankind.

Teg. Amongst the Hebrew, a major change occurred when the use of the Ewe lamb as a blood sacrifice was ended with the formation of the 3rd Covenant that is termed earlier as the Adder's Ceder. It had originally been introduced at the same time as the staves in the time of Abraham about 1800 -1900BC, so it lasted about 600 years before it was retired. Initially the young male lamb or Teg was not used as a sacrifice. The most prized lamb was the female that could be used to reproduce. That was regarded as a greater sacrifice than using the male lamb. What is evident from the transcript is that the lamb and the ewe still symbolize Redemption. The use of the term The Lamb, to refer to Christ, is for this same purpose.

In the South East place of Spirit, we have another play on words HARASSES TO THE ONE! On the serious side, RET"D [retired or retiring] the staves and also the ewe lamb from the blood sacrifice has harassed ONE. [It was the retirement of the ewe lamb that was identified as the cause of Wear in the Rears War earlier.]

4.
THE ONE LORD in the South East place of spirit prepares WREATHS.

In the West STAVES WEAR a rousing cheer or a RAH hurrah in the GARage. This spread to the ETHERS and even the upper reaches or heavenly regions of the air. The

Ethers SETTER used her SWAGES and GREW the HA to an outburst of laughter which most AGREE was RATHE or came early or quickly into full bloom.

In the South the RAGS GEAR TART of the REAR who GETs ETA [Grk; 7th letter]
SAW the VEGETATE WASTES SERVER SAVATE or French kickboxing the Ass
on its TETHERS. The Vegetate Wastes Server STASHES the Ass repeatedly.

In the South East place of spirit the stages in the ecological succession are
recorded on the SERE SHEETS of the VASE SAGES. The Sere Sheets show
SWERVE GASH HART or injures the male Red Deer as in John's Book of
REVelations in the Holy Bible.

Again we are reminded to look into the Apocalypse, the Revelations of John. It
would be inappropriate for me to attempt a summary of that extraordinary work;
readers will have to do that for themselves. What I do want to do is highlight
several key factors consistent with matters repeatedly raised in this transcript.
Earlier we were referred to Haggai. He provides an account that is directly
relevant to expectations about the 5th Covenant but that are set in a time -frame
without his knowledge even of the 4th Covenant or the coming of Christ. Haggai
(18) writes;
> *2v6 For thus saith the Lord of Hosts; Yet once, it is a little while, and I will*
> *shake the heavens and the earth and the sea and the dry land; 7 And I will*
> *shake all nations and the desire of all nations shall come; and I will fill this*
> *house with glory, saith the Lord of Hosts. 8 The silver is mine and the gold is*
> *mine, saith the Lord of Hosts. 9 The latter splendour of this house shall be*
> *greater than the former, saith the Lord of Hosts; and in this place I will give*
> *peace.*

In Solomon's wisdom we see the meaning of the expression that the silver and
gold are mine. Silver represents the crucible of understanding and gold
represents wisdom - both prized above any gems. Likewise, Daniel who was
known in his time for his ability to interpret dreams and understand symbols (eg,
he was called to interpret the writing on the wall at Nebuchadnezzar's Feast).
Daniel was very devout and serious in his attempts to understand his own and
others dreams and he had several encounters with deity. Daniel came 600 years
after Sinai and the 3rd Covenant and 600 years before Christ and the 4th
Covenant and he reports having great difficulties with some of the things he was
told would occur. For example he found it inconceivable that the continual burnt
offering could be taken away as it literally meant the end of the theocratic nation.
But faced as he was with information he had difficulty accepting, he hammered
away at the deity with his questions and reported what they said even though he
didn't like it.

Amidst the representations of the abominations or monsters Daniel [Bib. 13] was
confronted with in his dreams, we find the Ram who rules for a time, the He-goat,
the third and forth beasts arise and all is Severs Teas. Kingdoms rise and fall and
then comes the 5th Covenant.
> *7v14 One like a son of man, and he came to the Ancient of Days and was*
> *presented before Him. And to Him was given dominion and glory and*

kingdom, that all the peoples, nations and languages should serve Him; His dominion is an everlasting dominion, which shall not pass away and His kingdom one that shall not be destroyed.

Daniel pressed hard on the timing of these matters and after long personal ritual preparation he reports the following encounter with the deity that is an **Archimedean point** to our understanding of the timing of these matters.

*12v6 And I said to the man clothed in linen, who was above the waters of the stream, "How long shall it be till the end of these wonders?" 7 The man clothed in linen who was above the waters of the stream, raised his right hand and his left hand towards heaven; and I heard him swear by him who lives forever that it would be for **a time, times and half a time;** and that when the shattering of the power of the holy people comes to an end, all these things would be accomplished. 8 I heard, but I did not understand. Then I said, "Oh my lord, what shall be the issue of these things?" 9 He said, "Go your way Daniel, for the words are shut up and sealed until the time of the end." 10 Many shall purify themselves, and make themselves white, and refined; but the wicked shall do wickedly; and none of the wicked shall understand; but those who are wise shall understand. 11 And from the time that the continual burnt offering is taken away, and the abomination that makes desolate is set up, there shall be **a thousand two hundred and ninety days.** 12 Blessed is he who waits and comes to the **thousand, three hundred and thirty-five days.** 13 But go your way till the end; and you shall rest, and shall stand in your allotted place at the end of days.*

The deity's reference to a time, times and half a time seemed exactly like the number of turns in the spiral we have been working with - 3 and ½ times. At one level the whole time speculation seemed simple. With all the texts earlier emphasis on the 3rd Covenant, it seemed evident this could be seen as a period

of a deity time = 600 earth years. 3 and ½ times = 2100 years after the shattering of the power of the Theocratic nation. The shattering of that power did occur with the birth of Christ, the Tears of Easter and the formation of the 4th Covenant. It therefore seems that "all these things will be accomplished" by about 2128AD. As 3 and ½ times is equal to 1335 deity days then 1 time = 381.43deity days = 600 earth years, so 1 deity day = 1.573 earth years. But this is pure speculation. The Book of Daniel wasn't written until the time of Antiochus II – circa 170 BC. But Daniel lived at the time of Nebuchodonsor and Darius of Medes - circa 600 BC. This makes my "Bull Shit Metre" run hot!!!

Certainly bright red is noted in Revelations and there is a beast that has a wound that has healed.

Teeth like those on a flywheel and which come around repeatedly - WHARVE TEETH SWEAR that they TETHER STEERS until Right Ascension of every bristle. Hence the Ass has to be tethered until his bits catch up with him. In this way SETA EVERT TRAVE ie., a device to restrain a wild animal or large animal such as a horse. It consists of a series of steel bars and straps to hold the animal during veterinary work. This time the ASS Astronomer SAT with GER the German in his STARRED ESTATE. They conducted their HARVEST to solemn or GRAVE music and also completed cloth preparation or TAW.

Also sharing the ether is THREE TREE (a trinity tree) SEES or looks out for VEGETables and SHE is SET to ERSE. Three Tree HAS WAGE that she receives for assisting in the TERRET harvesting by the Eager Wets in the Reverse Sewer. She is located in the South West with the Steerer and assists as she STEERED TE [7th note in the musical scale] to guide the harvesters – the Eager WETS. We find that THESE Eager Wets wade in the GHEE with their TERET tied like a SWAG. One Ret Taster STATES that they have to look out carefully because of what ARRives in SERGES with the liquid buttermilk is like the bitter taste of TARATA or Maori lemonwood. She says that there is a HARSH cry of pain when Tarata is encountered – HA!!! When this occurs, the contents of

her Terete are RETIRED to the SHEER SEWERS where the TEA HATTER EGRETS can handle it. SHE'D just WEE away and not be concerned RE WASTES. Egrets have a long curved beak that is quite similar to a terete. [Tea Hatter Egrets sound very like the sort birds you would find at a party with someone called Alice who had just fallen in!]

The Ass that has been stashed is finally standing at the HE HAW VERGE or incline and is being assessed by the SWAGS EWER who verifies that it is a true copy - ESTREAT. The THRASHER TEAS manage as it AVERTS EACH SHEW of WRATH by the Ass. The Ass' wrath EASES when it changes tack and asks what it will WEAR whilst reclining on the delicate and precious TWEE SETTEE for STEERS that is ARTified with the HEW GRATE – the fire for VERTebrates!!!

There were many at the time of Seed Sea who agreed to be wed or tied in various ways to various responsibilities. One such AGREER was the very useful set of tools - SAWS. Saws responsibilities caused ERES AWE if ever there was reason for THREE'S ARREST. Eres awe occurred when Saws ATE or consumed something it was just like EG by a SHAG. The whole thing was swallowed up as if it was nothing. The SASH like a moveable window frame was totally obliterated.

In the same way the old ways were totally obliterated by THESsalonians in the Bible. The proposed framework for a "good" life is referred to in Paul's letter to the Thessalonians in the New Testament [Bib.13]. In Paul's first letter;

> *v9 For they themselves report concerning us what a welcome we had among you, and how you turned to the LORD from idols, to serve a living and true LORD v10 and to wait for His Son from heaven, whom He raised from the dead, Jesus who delivers us from the wrath to come.*

Paul encourages a view of life in which we attempt to live properly by the values of love, hard work and vigilance, as the day of reckoning will come like a thief in the night. He says there will be no escape from the retribution that comes at the end of days prior to the Second Coming.

In the same way that Woden wages his war to save Your Holiness, TREES WAGES their wars against WEAR [changes of tack, heartlessness and taking the easy option] TO THE ONE LORD.

5.

THE ONE LORD TREES STATES they stand together and work together like in the SASH. Each individual part of a window Sash works together with the other parts to create the whole that can then have a useful function. With the SHAG EG in mind of what Saws can do when they cut loose, trees stand together even like a GAS holds together in a bottle. In like manner, the small bathing costume men wear, their VEES, cling to the body to fulfil their function. Trees have been set to wage war against Wear since it SWARE or swore to this in the archaic time of Seed Sea.

The VERGER as church warder or official is charged with the responsibility to RATE the Atmosphere and conduct TESTS of those who have a HASTE VEST quickly sewn when they are about to go WEST. As the West WEAVER begins to SEW the Haste Vest this helps or TREATS the AWAY WAVES sewn previously TO THE ONE LORD.

THE ONE LORD WAVES AWAY any such TREATS as may be SEWn by the WEAVER in the WEST. Consistent TESTS of the ATmosphere RATE the VERGER as church warder and official of the male Red Deer and as such he is referred to as the STAGS TREASurer.

ASH'S -tree's TARTS VESTS as worn on the chest, AGREES that in the TRASS or Rhine volcanic region of Germany, GASES should be given the command to GEE-up. The SHEARs are also brought out for the STAGE VESTS or the ecclesiastic vestments purported to be connected to the

AETHER or upper regions of the atmosphere supposed by the ancients to be heaven. This STARTS the SAGES' TARGET of the AVERSE ERA and what to do about the unwilling.

In Sanskrit, the decent of a deity to earth is termed AVATAR [Macdonnell Bib. 45] The Avatar SAGE says that to expect VESTA the Roman Fire goddess is an ERRATA or mistake. ERSE'S RASES VERsion is much more relevant and SEWER SWEAR that the loudness of the hail or AVE! TEAR or rips the EAR. It now RESTS waiting for TREATment in the ETAGERE or open shelves as in a library in the South East place of Spirit. Even there the noise is very loud, and the WHEE - expresses the delight or thrill of the inhabitants. The RAVES WERT that WEAVES for a HATE HAT were dark or SWART and this SWATS the RASTAfarians VEST and their power. Any Rasta Vest WEARER must bear in mind that this is a WATERAGE linked to the SOUTH as if by a HAWSE or very thick rope. This Hawse ties the Waterage to EARTH as if bound by every sinew of a muscle or THEW. Thus the Avatar Sage says we about wrapped up or SWARTHE in what HATH to be said about the Averse Era TO THE ONE LORD.

6.
THE ONE LORD HATH SWAT Estimated Time of Arrival with a WREST or jerk. These claims about a WATERAGE are but a TEASER so He RESEAT WET EGRET and SAWSET for HATES and dark or SWART or swarthy SEARS THREATS. THREAT causes SWEATS [the Sawset is under Hates direction but The One doesn't want Sears Threats for a Waterage. Even threats generally only cause sweat.] EATS WERT TESTER or like a flogging of 25 lashes. At the edge of this story, as if the hemming on the garment or REVERS are very GRAVE or sedate about the EAR of Wheat that RESTs in the South East. This is a RAGES REVolution and EAVES RECORD VERsion of VESTA the Roman Fire goddess as a WASHER!!! The WREATH ERA TARGET STARTS with the SAGES ATTAR or incense being lit. Certainly the VESTS or ecclesiastic vestments can go to the SHEAR STAGE where the GEE up command can be given for them to be buried in a GRAVE in the TRASS or Rhine volcanic region of Germany. There the GASES will deal with the AGREE VESTS and WETER TARTS will note the WEER SAWGRASS TASTES them in Russia at least over a kilometre – VERST. The ecclesiastic vestments VEST RAVE WARS will affect every WEARER so GATHER their deeds or GESTA and

discharge them – EGEST. They will SHARE the VEER that is noted in the SEE of Bishop's seats of power. Even where the See is inclined upwards or STEEVE they HAVE a HATS HER'S RHEToric occurring. This indicates a concern about women in the priesthood that is seen as SEVERE.

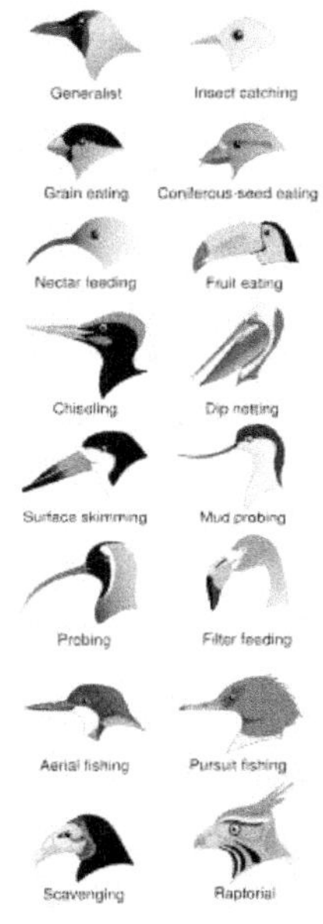

SECondly the EATS indicate that WHERE things are GRAVE are in New Zealand where the stand of trees are in TATERS and the WAVE of the Maori timber tree with purple flowers, the TAWA are being cut down by HARVESTS GREATEST RATTER. This situation is GRAVE and especially serious for the SEER of the birds or AVES and the HARES. AREAR GEEup VERSE about what A STAGER SEES RESET E ie., the mathematical transcendental constant whose tongue has been on the WAG TO THE ONE LORD.

Evidently the Tawa are exactly the type of stand of trees that help deal with the Wear to ONE and sadly they are in taters. Significantly the colour normally given as a healing colour is purple or lavender that is consistent with the Tawa's flowers and fruit that are an important food source for many birds. Because Tawa are native to the low-lying areas of flatter and richer soils they were heavily logged when land was cleared for pasture. Tawa is prized as a timber for flooring and furniture so the trees were removed for commercial use that included wood chipping for paper pulp. Removal of the Tawa forests meant destruction of the Aves habitat and the famous kiwi became endangered. Extinction of the Moa was important to the Tawa as the fruit has quite a large stone that cannot be ingested by any other native birds. The Moa had been important in increasing the distribution of Tawa forests and after logging only remnants or pockets of forest remained. And the Moa are now extinct.

Aves is the term used to describe the whole class of birds. In evolutionary terms they are the living representatives of the dinosaurs and still exhibit scales on their legs and feet. One of these ancient descendants is shown in the fossil exhibit.

The Seer for the Aves is also given as the Seer for the Hares. Hares are mammals and are not related to the Aves in any way. This Snowshoe hare is in its winter coat and it has unusually large feet to help it hop on the snow. In summer this hare turns a rusty brown colour. The Snowshoe Hare is a native of North America and it has smaller ears than the European Hare.

7.

THE ONE LORD's mathematical transcendental constant E is RESET. The GATEway reports SHE'S SWEET ASS…and SEES or looks AVErage in her new surroundings. Again a verse is called for. An AREAR VERSE SHARES a GEE-up for the ATHWART HARES and AVES SEER to WASH the HARVEST SEGT. Who has caused the WAVE TATERS under GATT [the General Agreement on Tariffs and Trade]. At the GATEway an AGHA of a SECond will GET The GREATS [of Fire for vertebrates] to eliminate the Harvest Sergeant.

As a stager, I am indeed athwart to the Hares and Aves Seer and have arrears to admit so I wrote the following verse as directed. In it an Agha of one second is explained but by tradition a lot more time would be taken by Turkish people at the graveside of one of their generals.

    The Greatest Harvest Rat beGATT….

    I pray to THE ONE for the Hares and the Aves
    That are over the land and the sea,
    And thank them as one for the trouble they went to
    And wagers they took upon me.

    You are sweet little critters of Earth and of Air
    Who help me all over the place,
    But I owe you apology for what I've done
    Tears of shame dripping down from my face.

    As a kid I climbed trees to steal your small eggs
    Worse than a Lee Rat I was,
    And I shot you with shangie and bullet as naught
    All to show you that I was the bozz.

    To Grey Crane and Shag that visit my pond
    I'm sorry for sears threats and rock,
    I hope you'll come back for the Reeds and the fish
    Without fearing you'll end in my Wok.

    Now I give you my Agha as Turkish folk do

My mark of respect - graveside time,
I'll hold my gate open and tell you this verse
Which I'm told you will like when it rhyme.

Word from the Ewer 's we need you again
To wave Harvest Sergeant Ta Ta,
He is the GATT rat that saw-gnaws the Tawa
Once purple wave, now ugly scar.

Having ONE'S aegis to end this rat's rein
It's time that we settle the score,
First to dignify him with an Agha
But just for a second - no more!

Returning to the discussion before that concerning the Hares and Aves, we find that WART HATS have gone WEST. Here we have a short SEGment that concerns the VEER EGEST of the SEE of Bishops. It will be recalled that their deeds have been discharged. Even as the Bishops SEETHE GATHER and argue about "His Hats Hers " and the WEARER of dark ecclesiastic vestments, the SWATHES STASHER is in a RAVE about how the HEATER has been REVised.

The final comment in Whata Saga is that WHATEVER TASTE in clothes is expressed is GREAT AT the GRAVE because GEARs SAG under a SWATH TERAS.

[Dusty Spiral Galaxy NGC 4414 by the Hubble Telescope.]

Trans. 6. <u>HARES AND AVES AGHA TO THE HARVEST RAT.</u>

As discussed at the end of Whata Saga, I was intrigued by the notion of an Agha to the Harvest Rat and wondered what happened to him when it was given. Accordingly I used the expression, Harvest Rats Agha, in analysis. Traditionally, the Agha is a Turkish custom given to army generals who have carried the burden of military responsibility. It is a grave-side mark of respect given by the people. In this context, the Hares and Aves give their Agha to the Harvest Rat for one second – a tat Agha.

1.

North Sages begin with REAVE, which means to rend, break or tear. This is a fair summary of what is to become of the Harvest Rat. The Agha comes quickly into bloom: it was RATHE according to GER and so it ended as quickly as it began. A TASSET is one of a pair of defences worn on the upper thigh and suspended by straps. In order to SEE the Tasset is RASEd or lifted by the VETS SEER AND RATS who find there are GRAVE ARREARS which SEW his ARREST in the REAR. In the South the HEW VASES GATHER THAWS VESTS. A SEARS TA TA TARGET has been set. Farewell to the Harvest Rat will be in the form of Rear Raze. This is the form of farewell that was greatly feared in the Bishop's See.

In Nordic mythology, Thor was one of Woden's sons who wielded a mighty hammer. It is most likely that the Thaws Vests referred to are actually the concern of Thor who was widely and highly regarded for his good works. The opposite is true for the Harvest Rat and the destruction of the Tawa. However it is the Thaws Vests that are gathered and which indicate that a Sears Ta Ta Target is appropriate.

The Great Article Hart in the West gathers up the graveside Agha 's Tags and rests them in the North West, the place of Mother Earth. In the North North West, comes the exclamation Ah! It is a pity the grave of Sergeant Gashes was dignified. The Sages in the North tell us that not only is he to be a Ta Ta Target but also a target of laughter – Ha Ha! Accordingly he is aimed through an opening between sand banks, a Gat, and he hits the Ships Hull in the North North East. There on the hull his Tartare is artified (akin to a Pro Hart food painting) but unfortunately for him he is set to be scaped off like barnacles would be. Those aboard the ship cry out in surprise – Tea Eh! Some doubt is expressed about the haste taken with Seta and they think that the Tartare should be carefully examined with the staff frame of David (Hebrew) in question. Evidently the Harvest Rat is a Jew and as the lineage of David is much favoured (hence the reference to the staff) special care should be taken before proceeding.

Evidently he doesn't have lineage with David as he is next assigned to the Vats for the Era Teas. Evidently some severing is in the making as the Targe (Scandinavian round shield linked earlier with protecting the operator in removal of the steers Whata knots) is prepared in the Gases Garage. There, we are informed by the Seers of Theta, that the Garfish will be fed the Harvest Rat's heart. The Rastafarians rave that Hearts are grave/serious in the Sancta Virgo Teats.

Harvesting proceeds to the musical note Te! We learn the thaw is very good, even producing seas! The arrears of the Harvest Rat have been mighty indeed. However, as the heart is fed to the garfish we find the garfish begin to shit treasures of Terra art depicting the Hares and Aves heat before the present time. The ashes of the Harvest Rat are put into the Sages vessel in the North and are then read – the garters of Reverend and Sancta Virgo are revised in the Rags Revolution to include a Scottish Gett or area tartan.

Ger, the West Astronomer, turns on his harsh electronic scan and confirms with confidence that the Gateways do have a Teat to the Haggai Seas, and the ash in the Grates is carefully inspected by the Vets to THE ONE LORD.

2.
We learn from Mother Earth that THE ONE LORD would prefer us to use the correct title – The Grates. The Grates also have a Gateway to the South; a Gateway to the work of Woden and Great Rhea. It is further affirmed that Mother Earth is in the North West, and she informs us that the Hares and Aves Heat Treasurer sags and their "Tat Agha stare" saves the Hares. In the East Teat, the Rastafarians are still raging and raving about the serious regard Sancta Virgo has about the Garfish getting the Harvest Rat's heart, the arrangement of the Targe in the Gasses garage and about the work of Theta.

In the South, the Vats and Ears have checked things very carefully and concluded the Harvest Rat was handled with average haste for anyone who is Seta-bristle, even though some surprise and doubt has been expressed regarding this. In the North North East, we are told there was much laughter as the artified Tartare of the Harvest Rat was scraped off the ship's hull – certainly a Ha Ha Target was struck. The Sages in the North report that when the Harvest Rat was held in the Trave, it sagged with the immense weight. Sergeant Rat was

GATT's action arm and the awareness with which he and GATT act leaves a great deal to be desired.

At the time of this analysis in 1992/3, I discussed logging with a friend in New Zealand who confirmed that some of the Tawa forests were being clear felled under GATT. He was unable to say if the chief person responsible for operations was Jewish and had died, but one thing was for certain, the purple wave of the Tawa was in taters. Judging from the transcript, nothing was missed in what was done by the Harvest Rat both as it concerns his work and his personal deeds; both were seen by the Seers in the East North East. What they saw was what determined both the outcomes and the atmosphere in which the Harvest Rat was treated; a Ha Ha and Ta Ta Target.

In the North, the Sages call for a test of Right Ascension for the Age. In response, the Aves rave about how THE ONE LORD'S Ship sat in the South East, the place of Spirit, where normally the Ship sits in the North North East. They also rave about the waste of Mother Earth that has been sewn in Russia. In the South East, reference is made to several aspects of the test; Stars, the tropical fish -Tetra, Heath, Thessalonians, Hats, Attar-incense and the Vertical Gate. We are informed that in the analogy of the Garfish eating the heart of the Harvest Rat, we should note that this is akin to a process by which something of him is saved.

The South West Steerer informs us that what is identified is the Err Vest for Him and Her. That both partners are judged together as responsible for what happens in a relationship. They are judged as one and not separately. What is suggested is that at the end of a relationship, we could make symbolic costumes to represent the relationship Errs - Err Vests.

The East Hews rears the Tartar Genghis Khan and he says "Ave"! (Exclamation meaning hail)!

The Sages intervene telling us that he was a Teras, an abomination. At his grave test of the Err Vests, the weight of his Errs ripped the Trave's straps and he had to be dealt with in Woden's Thrashes. (This exclamation from Genghis Khan does indeed suggest Woden can save by any means.) Such a thrashing was a sign of the Tar Ages when all were aghast at the degree of the decline. At the grave [in 1227], Genghis Khan was rated as a Teras by a sort of geiger scan of the tears at the graveside. It was noted that these were rhetorical tears, or tears purely for effect. (Who would you guess undertook this rating? None other than the Ass Assistant, one who could see the dared deeds.)

In the place of Spirit, at the commencement of the Thrashers Harvests, the Hart (male Red Deer) lights the attar-incense at the Vertical Gate. Through this action, a deity descends to Earth to avert the Eats from consuming hearts which are judged – Ret (partially rotted). In the West North West, we find that the decent of the deity (avatar) averts a gash by empowering the Transcendental Constant (E) and Eta (a sign of the great Mystery). The Sages of the North explain that the gash would otherwise ret the Tarata tree (Maori lemonwood tree) that is vital to the Seers deeds to seeing. (It was said in the previous chapter that Trees wage war against Wear. In the case of Genghis Khan the Wear would have been colossal, as his raids were greatly feared from Northern China to Eastern Europe. Also previously we found the Ret Taster in the Reverse Sewer, when she tastes Tarata, she lets out a sharp cry of pain – "Ha!") The Seers in the East North East

are aghast at the damage done to the New Zealand forests that are given as treats to the Ear of THE ONE LORD.

3.

THE ONE LORD'S Ratter Gates in the West are linked to the Heats as well as the Sash containing the Teg (lamb/redemption). Thus, when we go West, our errs/arrears/heats are balanced against any atonement. The Teg area of the Sash positions the Seers in relation to the Tarata tree or maintains the linkage to their ability to see. The Sages give the Tarata as being in the North, opposite the Rata in the South linked with the Seas of Aesthete and having a reciprocal relationship with that tree. Accordingly, the destruction of the native environment of the Tarata is having widespread consequences. The destruction and hence suffering of the Tarata is in turn also destroying the celebration and happiness in the South. In the South East, the male archetype of the Red Deer, the Hart says the Harvests Sash is turned to Thrashes when the Ret Taster in the Reverse Sewer tastes Tar. As soon as she tastes Tar she throws Thrash. With the Harvest Rat, he tasted of Tar and he is consigned to the Thrashers.

In the North North East, the souls aboard the Ship report that when the Harvest Rat's GATT Vest was gathered, it ripped the grave-hole. The Sages in the North call for a verse on the areas rare deeds and exploits. Mother Earth in the North West, calls the Harvest Rat a Vagrant. In the West at the Ratter Gates, the vagrant vertebrate is Verted (usually this means turning a foetus in the womb prior to birth but in this context it refers to the spirit foetus being turned/prepared in it's journey). The Steerer in the South West reminds us that in the Harvest Rat's assessment, both His and Her Err will be taken into account. (This does not augur well for Mrs Harvest Rat.) In the South, even though Woden is known for even waging war to save Sanctitas Vestra, he says he would rather the Harvest Rat be saved by The Eats even if that means they would be harassed by the taste of Tarata.

Rare Area Treats the Sages See.
How is it that the Sage and Seer See?
It is by virtue of a tree.
Tarata is the Maori name
Or Lemonwood of common fame.
The forests of New Zealand – nature's home,
As vital to the Rete-net As vertebrate to arch of bone.
Tarata there – a sacred tree
The Seer's Gesta – grant by deed to See.
But what's the virtue of the tree?
A secret must be told to see.
Woven by Sere Sett to ONE
As vertebrate to spinal cord
Tarata treats Ear of THE LORD.
It's true – HE listens there!
Hears the treats of forest songs
Knows the Kiwi scamper, pause and peck
Within each pause, pure Sabbath prayer
Noting Seed Tile opening there.
Tarata send the forest song
The area treats, sound treasures to THE ONE.

Oh! Mighty Moa stride is gone Extinct – the treat deplete.
Where once the stride and Sabbath pause to ONE
Now comes the roar – White-feller's gun.

Oh! Oh! But what now there to hear?
The chainsaw rasp and tear.
The Harvest Rat had come
To rip and ret Tarata there.
The Seer's gesta in decline
And thus it be the Sages too
With failing deed to See.
The Harvest Rat – a vagrant vertebrate be
To gnaw the tree, to hew them down
The area treat that once abound
Was now a gasp!
The Harvest Rat had come by GATT
As Teras or Genghis Khan invade and rip the forest down
In lakes of sad Tarata tears
That freeze the Ears.

Ah! But the time does come for Harvest Rat
To hit the gunwales of the Ship in Tartare splat.
Teras himself will taste the Tar in him
And then consign to Thrasher din.
No gentle vert as spirit foetus turned in loving care
No doubt Sheer Sewer get the lion's share.
Even yet the Rising Water say to save
He'd rather it harass The Eats
And yet on Earth it even simpler be
To save the taters of the Treats.

In the East, we are informed that the Revolution in understanding Sanctitas Vestra (Your Holiness), is set as if sewn for a variation on a good rage. According  to the Grasser-informer, His Eminence has an estimated time of arrival for a Rags Revolution in the Church by which waste can be reduced.

In the North North East, the Aves express irritation that the Aster-flower sat with the Ship in the South East place of Spirit, as if included with the weight of the vessel and not as part of the cargo/occupants as it normally would. The Aves state that this is a fire sign, a sign of the beginning of the Hearths Age.

The Sages in the North agree that this is the Right Ascension test.

[Spiral Galaxy NGC 4622 by the Hubble Telescope.]

<u>Trans. 7. HAIL THE ONE - A Tale of Interjections.</u>

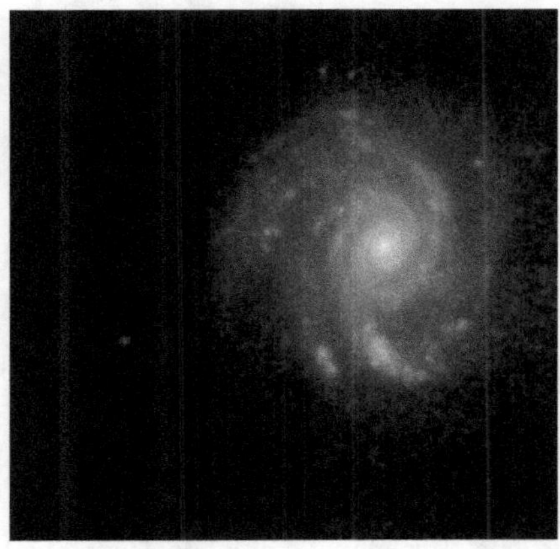

At the conclusion of Trans. 1 White Reeds Laid - was the direction – List HAIL THE ONE. In my efforts to be "more correct", I initially added the word LORD, generated the list and followed the normal procedure for analysis. At the time, I could not make sense of the resulting transcript with one small exception. It read "See right edit ain't on demand." Realising my error in adding the word LORD, I removed it and re-completed the analysis. After this experience I concluded we should use the exact words given in undertaking this form of analysis. Hail THE ONE led to this exciting record.

[Spiral Galaxy NGC 5653 by the Hubble Telescope.]

1.

The record begins in the North with the Sages explaining the problem with the word LORD being the elitism associated with that name. They explain that ONE hates the elite, alien and ethnic attributes that have accompanied the name used to refer to HIM. Theologians of many different cultural backgrounds have different names for ONE but they are unhelpful where distance or aloofness is suggested. (As an example of this difficulty, the Hebrew name for THE ONE is AHIH or IHVH (Hulse Bib. 33). In Islam there are 100 names for THE ONE, and a secret name! (Nasr Bib. 51) In contrast to this what is wanted is an intimate - I, Thou, Thee - relationship. The stake Theologians have is compared to an anole, an iguana that changes its skin colour depending on its background. At a minimum Noel (the birth of Jesus Christ) should be recognised. When all is made known, we will know that to Hail THE ONE is a lot more than hailing a number. It equates more to a "Lit Leash" with the speed of a ton (100miles per hour) in the present age of Halite at temperature one! (Halite is rock salt – a very pure, strong, crystalline salt with a cubic structure. At one degree on the Kelvin scale of temperature, because of its ionisation, it would be an excellent conductor of electricity.) We are told that ONE Theology is also akin to a Tela, a delicate body membrane resembling a very fine web. It is the innermost layer of **three** meninges that surround the brain and the nervous system – a rete.

In the South East place of Spirit, we are offered peace; peace that will come from atonement on encountering this Tale of Interjections. Each time we encounter an interjection it is suggested we atone to ONE.

THE ONE is somewhat technically described as Actinon. (It is a semi-inert gas which takes it's name from the Greek word actino, usually used to describe something which is ray like, or which radiates – eg, the structure of the flower of the Aster plant. Actinon has an atomic number of 89 and it is an isotope of radon produced by disintegration of actinium. Whilst it is known to generally be inert, it also is known to have spontaneous "flurries" of energy. All actinides are radio-active and their properties are so special, a special series of 14 elements are identified in the Periodic Table of the Elements (Petrucci Bib. 55).) In the same text we are given two letter pairs AT and AI. (In the Hebrew letter pairs, AT means Soothsayer – Enchanter at the 8th Gate with the Fool providing strength. The letter pair AI refers to the 9th Gate and means Island; jackal; impossible – The Fool and The Hermit. (Hulse Bib. 33) In the word sequence of the text we have the 8th Gate actinon the 9th! (A further level of meaning may be drawn – there are 14 steps in the actinide series and 14 half times in deity time for a complete spiral of 7 turns. I expect these double meanings have great significance and are no accident.) The transcript also says it is a technical ONE that is 'actinon' the surface tension in the lane. This meant a great deal to me as I referred to the spiral as having a lane running from the North into the centre, as it is open at the North. I see this meaning it is ONE in the form of Spirit who acts on the surface tension in the spiral lane and thus affect how the word slips fall and thus their arrangement. In a further description of the internal passages in which ONE works, we are given the analogy of an asthma sufferer taking a hit of Intal containing sodium lint which within an hour has settled things down. The text says Intal was not available to Noah and nor was the nail so our earnestness is denoted as nominal.

In the North, we are told that we are born to meet certain people during the course of our lives. Our lives are woven in Leno (a warp yarn twisted in pairs between the filling yarns). This Leno relationship is set initially in an Oath, in which anethole is eaten, a herb given as natural to ONE. (Anethole is a compound containing anise and fennel oils that have antiseptic, stomachic and carminative properties with very wide culinary use. Chemists, cooks and fishermen all know the wonderful action of anethole in taking the fats out of tissue (Grieve Bib. 27). The active ingredient in anethole is C10H12O – a substance held together by ONE oxygen in a very long carbon chain with hydrogen off it and some double carbon bonds, the chain ending in
C - H I II O
Thus anethole is very volatile. In mythology, anethole is highly esteemed for its use in protection against Evil and prevention of nightmares!) In this transcript it is compared with Tanh (the 3rd of the 6 mathematics of the hyperbolic function. This is derived from the Sin and the Cos in mathematics – an exponential, multiplicative relationship in natural laws that could be described as volatile in the

same way anethole is described. If temperature is involved, it is very likely you could say that anethole and tanh behave in the same way. We could not leave this discussion without reference to the Transcendental Constant E that underlies the calculation of Tanh in the first place.)

HA! (Interjection; Hey) **Oath Leno.** (Atone in peace on encountering the interjections). The suggestion is made that if you wish to know who you are born to meet in this life, take time out and be alone in Lent (40 days in the Christian Church calendar that leads up to Easter.) Even a very small amount of time, an hour in the open meadow or grassland would help in the beginning. We are told this will help restore the seat of our generative power – the inner loin, eaten by slothful or 9th Gate behaviour (the Fool and the Hermit).

In the North East, we are given an extraordinary further insight into the AT ONE; we are first told this is a Literary ONE AT (8th Gate Soothsayer –Enchanter); "HALT THE HEEL HEATHEN HEIGHT LIES AND TALE (that there is) NO OLD NORSE HONOURARY LINE."

The Western Church has long regarded native people's spirituality as heathen and with it's elitist attitude, has tried to bring them to heel. Here we are told to halt such lies and behaviour. Woden of Old Norse mythology certainly has his place here in this record. We are clearly to see that he is part of the honorary line. Significantly Woden was often referred to as Alfader that was integrated into the Christian Church as All Father and Our Father. Even the word Easter is Nordic in origin – from Ostana whose favourite animal was the Hare and who used to bring eggs to children at the spring festival/Easter. Woden, according to legend, always respected that he was not the supreme deity; his one eye denoted his orientation and Wednesday is named after him. Tuesday [Tiwesdaeg] remembers one of his sons Tyr and Thursday [Thuresdaeg] remembers one of his other sons, Thor. We know very little about the Nordic Pantheon even though it is as familiar as the names of three days in the week.

In the South East place of Spirit, we are offered a robust image of a Tela (3rd meninger around the brain and spinal cord) Theology in order to limit or contain the discussion. Likewise, in the North East, the use of the analogy about Halite or rock salt is to limit discussion to ideas that can be grasped. What is added is that we are or should be elated that it is Hail THE ONE rather than Heil (German for Hail)! Mother Earth, in the North West, tells us there is a conduit for earth energy that is connected to the loin and it is this that can be restored.

Noh, No, Nae!!! [Interjection] This is not a legal right although everyone has the opportunity to have his or her share or to make use of such energy. In the North, the Sages explain that taking an elitist view of these matters is alien, incompatible, repugnant and opposed to the central notion of equality. In the East, we may imagine the Rastafarians having a rave about how within a year of the Tone being sounded, even maidens will be on an equal footing with an earl's eldest son when it comes to a determination of inheritance.

In the South East place of Spirit, Lo! (Exclamation; behold – it is time to atone again). There is a very strong dislike, a loathing for Opera as a way of moving in spirit; it is not useful as a fulcrum pin. In the South, Woden reminds us of the Chinese belief that all existence has been only in relation to an external absolute – Tao. Indeed it is a very heavy musical note that will cultivate us as spiritual beings. The image of Taoist monks chanting a very heavy "Aummm" is easily imagined. In the South West, the Steerer informs us that a heavy musical note removes Thor's (the Thunderer's) reluctance or unwillingness to be involved in the West. Mother Earth informs us that the currency, the Toea (New Guinea) will apply in the Age of Heath Office Law when we will have to attend to things by work (cleaning up the planet for one thing).

In the South East, a note has been left for us saying that Spirit has moved on to another but un-nominated place.

In the South, in the place of Water, Woden tells us to take particular note of an important name – Thiol (normally an organic compound. Although Thiol is the name for a sulphur based organic compound, its association with sulphur linked it in alchemical speculation with Hades. Thiol is the name of a group of organic compounds having a radical element by which an S atom replaces an O atom, in a reaction known as ionisation. In this way a heavier element, sulphur replaces a lighter element, oxygen (Petrucci Bib. 55).) Spirit is equated to Oxygen, an element that freely combines with almost every other element.

In the South West, the Steerer informs us that at absolute temperature Tee or starting point, LA! (Exclamation; wonder and surprise – time to atone) we will find Thiol is Oaten. (Organic Chemistry is a vast subject so I referred this matter to a qualified friend who was indeed in wonder and surprise and said thiol may very well be described as oaten in consistency at that temperature, where water acts as a superconductor. (Thiol was given in the place of Water.)) In the West, this oaten like substance will have largely longitudinal lines marking it.

In the North the lines are given as similar to Olein (the glyceride of oleic acid found in olive oil) and described as A'One. Oh! (Interjection; surprise and pain – atonement time) This is a substance it is best to keep at a distance. (When a very dilute solution of oleic acid is added to liquid pentane, it floats and can be evaluated not only in the area that it covers but also by cross section – longitudinally! The thickness of this monolayer is one molecule. Further, oleum in a solution of SO_3 is greater than 100% H_2SO_4 or sulphuric acid, so it is indeed a good idea to keep a lot of distance from that.)

In the North East, we are informed that there is a small island at the toe of Thursday Island. From my atlas I could certainly identify such an island and it was exactly magnetic north from Victoria as advised in the text. (Having verifiable data presented contrasts sharply with say the discussion on Tags or the demise of the Harvest Rat.)

In the South East, there are then two further interjections; Oh! (Interjection; surprise and delight) and Ah! (Interjection; surprise, pain) and then a sharper pain.

In the South South East, Ah! (Interjection; surprise and joy).
This expression derives from the line of the anil or indigo plant that was used exclusively by the Taino women to make a tea. (The Taino people once lived in

Arawak, Central America but were almost exterminated by early Spanish settlers. Pictured here is Taino Chief Agueybana greeting Juan Ponce de Leon. As the indigo plant does grow in tropical regions, it is quite possible that the women used a species of anil to make their tea.) In the text it says the tea was made without anything being extracted. (This would have indeed been a problem because anil contains a yellow amorphous ingredient – indican – of a nauseous, bitter taste and an acid reaction. In Western medicine, it was once used medicinally to induce vomiting (Grieve Bib. 27). Here, we can appreciate that to drink a tea made from anil would result in an Ah! - of surprise and pain. A pain which then intensified.) We are informed that the women drank oceans of the tea when just a small amount would have sufficed for redemption and to restore the health and vigour of their relationship to THE ONE. (Likely the basis for the Ah! – of surprise and joy.)

2.
THE ONE heals. The healing power may be equated to ten tons of oleate (crystals of oleic acid) or of rock salt. The Steerer refers to the long association ONE has had with stone. (The *lapus philosophorum* referred to earlier and representing enduring qualities, permanence and incorruptibility. The healing qualities associated with stone are beautifully expressed in the sacred churinga of the Australian Aborigines. They often used stones for sacred totemic objects and they held a very strong belief in the churinga's healing qualities (Chatwin Bib. 12). Neolithic times bear present day stone circle reminders of past faith and understanding. In traditional Western religion, stones and rock were central aspects of the teachings – Moses came down from Mt. Sinai with the Ten Commandments carved in stone; and Christ built His Church upon the rock.) The Litho Line takes time to complete its healing function and time to hone awareness.

In the South East place of Spirit, there is an alternate Oh! (Interjection; surprise, delight) in the Thai language, versus Oh! (Interjection; surprise, pain) on Thursday Island. (The discussion refers to one of the Eastern islands in the Gulf of Thailand, probably Ko Kut, where the people are in elation over a flower associated with Tyr – one of Woden's sons. On Thursday Island, the alternate Oh! Is associated with Tyr's brother, Thor. In the North, His Excellency is A'ONE. His healing powers are associated with both Olein (the glyceride of oleic acid, a compound in olive oil) and with the Aloe (a cactus with equally ancient renown for it's healing qualities, but seldom used alone). Both are given as certain to eventually catch their game even if they do work slowly. They are equated to game nets that are set to catch game driven into them. The Steerer then refers to the toenail that we are told should be eaten slowly (to replace a deficiency).

In the East, things are being drawn together as if a knot is being tied. In the North, this concerns Theologies Tail – a knot tied in its tail. This play on the word tail refers to the Law of Limitation and hence refers to inheritance! Mother Earth says the inheritance of His Eminence Thor, in the Age of Heath Office law we will also Hail him in the West as responsible for the Heats (Heat Treasurer?). However, we will not see him nor will this occur within the year (this record was taken in 1992).

In the East, we have the image of the Tael, a unit of silver used as currency in the Far East. (Silver symbolises the crucible of understanding). We are told in the place of Spirit that we should understand that the Litho (stone) Line is the lone line to ONE In particular it is the Neolithic stone that is relevant. It was Neolithic people who understood this relationship to ONE. In a some-what brief, cryptic message we find that a hot tar and duck feathers night hasn't been held for an infinitely long time to ONE. A manifest form of ONE as Thor makes a declaration that my lei (a wreath usually of flowers) is a silver Tael.

In the South East place of Spirit, we are given the image of an anthelion. (This is the ring or halo around the shadow of an observer's head as thrown by the sun on a fogbank, cloud or moist surface, especially as seen in polar regions.) The anthelion is being destroyed; eaten by drinking ale/light beer. Ale nil Leo to THE ONE. [I am a Leo.]

3.
THE ONE enate (to grow outwards, especially related to the mother's side) length noil (short fibres are separated from the long fibres by combing). The long fibres on the mother's side suffer a sort of tinea or skin fungus during Lent (the forty days leading up to Easter. My mother's father was Jewish!)

In the South East place of Spirit, the Linden Tree says Ta! (Interjection; Thank you. Because of it's white wood, this tree is commonly known as the Limewood.

Tilia europa is known for it's heart shaped leaves that exude a saccharine matter having the same composition as the Manna of Mt Sinai. It is extensively used as a tree of protection in Europe and is regarded as having further esoteric values - Love, Luck, Sleep and Immortality). In a playful way the Sages explain that it is not applicable for the Linden Tree to intervene until the sounding of the tonal music announcing the disclosure of the atomic number of ONE.

Back in the South East there is a further interjection, presumably from the Linden Tree, Oh! (Surprise and gladness) and we learn that the black cockatoo-like bird, the Ani sounds the final music note TE!

Thus we end HAILTHE ONE and this Tale of Interjections, on a very high note indeed. The 7th note of the Solfa scale is a significant mark of the Great Mystery. The number of healings, miracles, faith and dreams come true. Should you be wondering where the atomic number is; it is given by Te – tellurium (from the Latin – tellus – Earth) with an atomic number of 52. In numerology this is the highest compound number used by any good Chaldean and a number that means 7. The mid-twentieth century religious teacher G.I.Gurdjieff, showed a great deal of interest in the work of the Greek mathematician, Pythagoras. Pythagoras is understood to have experimented extensively with what he termed the universal harmonic. Gurdjieff extended this work and associated the musical note TE with the Blissful state of head and heart harmony. In harmonic form, TE was associated with – ALL ONE, Enlightenment, the topmost limit of human consciousness in contemplation of the Divine, the Centre of the Solar System and the Centre of Heaven (Webb Bib. 81). No doubt Hebrews will enjoy having it

pointed out that it was the ANI who sung the final note TE. The ancient Hebrew cipher for THE LORD was known as the AIN formulae. AIN stands for the Void from which all evolves and that state to which all returns (Hulse Bib. 33). Equally, this should be an agreeably heavy note for Taoist and Buddhist alike. Finally, should you be wondering about the number of Interjections in this Transcript – 15 – the Monogram of the Eternal – Magical Love!

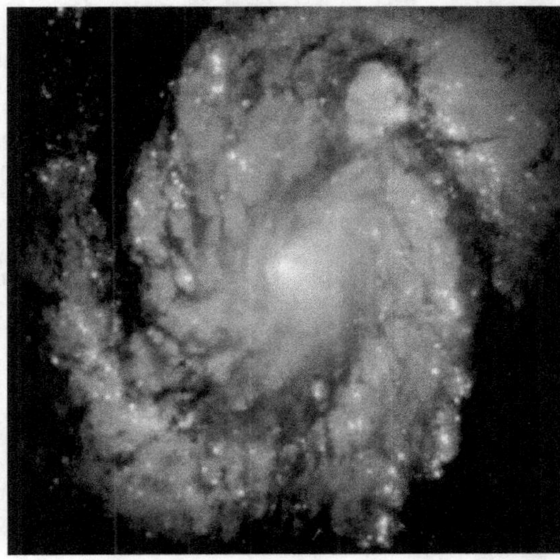

Trans. 8. ANYBODY WITH HOPE?

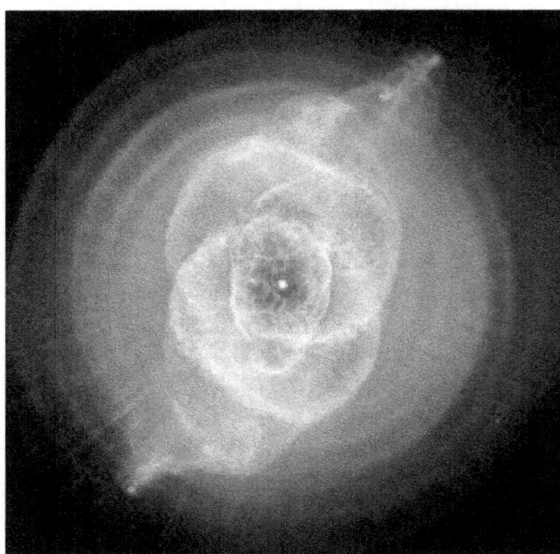

[Cat's Eye Nebula by the Hubble Space Telescope.]

The words used for analysis were "Anybodi c [with] Hope"? This was written onto a word slip whilst I was on the verge of sleep. With 11 different letters and four vowels, just over 1300 words were generated for this analysis. Word definitions are contained in brackets and the normal dictionary conventions followed [n.= noun, v.= verb, adj.=adjective, W.E.= word element, pref.=prefix, suf.=suffix. Chemical Elements were included in the abbreviations and we find they are used to relate directly to specific Wisdom Paths [See "Psyche"].

In this Transcript Archetypes describe the repeated mistakes of a character referred to as Bishop Batsman. They also describe the assistance they give in trying to correct the situations Bishop Batsman encounters during several lifetimes. Despite being gifted in Communication, Bishop Batsman is unconventional in his drug taking and sexual behaviour that disgusts the Archetypes. Details are also provided about the life of another key individual, Dono a Spanish lord or gentleman. Dono is a creative dance expert and a man whose lyrical poetry skills are very highly regarded but who on the down side is a hood and a leader in the Mafia. Dono and Bishop Batsman are born in this life as spiritual brothers to me - the editor. The relationship between the three characters is discussed and our roles are outlined. Archetypes do not favour a continuation of the arrangement and provide detailed descriptions of the actions needed to end it. An exciting journey to Cape Woolami in Victoria enables termination of the arrangement that burdens me.

1.

We begin in the East with the much admired and liked Pilot Officer Hydrogen. He is wearing a boater hat and given a round of applause as he lands his balloon. This is a significant beginning as hydrogen has the atomic number of ONE - the very same number given as applicable to ONE. A boater hat is usually worn to a sporting event such as a rowing contest on a river so it is a very distinctive thing to be wearing for the pilot of a hydrogen balloon. Pilot Officer Hydrogen wants to see an "Awakening" in a Chaplain who is a pretentious Cob; more like a thickset and stout legged horse. Unfortunately, the way things are going, our Chaplain will be worth about as much as a Poon or a loaf of maize bread on the day he dies and his life and activity cease. Unless Pilot Officer Hydrogen can bring about an "Awakening " in our Chaplain, he won't have much of a future.

2o The Awakening.

This was also called "The Judgement" by the ancient Chaldeans and Hebrew.

The Image: "A winged angel blowing a trumpet, while from below a man, woman and child are seen rising from a tomb with their hands clasped in prayer." [See Psyche.]

This is a call to action for some great purpose or ideal.

In the SE place of Great Spirit he is called BOYO. He is a disorderly young man from the country. He is designated as a D-500 POCO and so Boyo is headed in a somewhat miscellaneous direction. [D-500 is not easily understood but it may mean BOYO was formed very early or a long time ago.] There is clear evidence that he has indulged in an excess of engineered chemicals. His beady appearance provokes a strong reaction.
        PAH! [Exclm; disgust].

Under the terms of the Water CODE, the system or law will AID his Pyo – the watery substance like pus. Boyo is engraved with the stamp to be a head in a Cathedral but there is an imprint of softer material that comes from habitat acquired characteristics involving volatile chemicals such as derivatives of benzene.

In the SW, Ebony sharply cuts off a warning signal from the Beacon. But she gives us a diagram of a Yap mouth husband.

Mother Earth presses to have the Obituary Notice for a certain Police Constable to be stolen and chopped up!

North Sages report that they can plainly see what happened.

The NE Bench tells us his Nap Pad will DIE. [His Nap Pad is a cushion like mass of short fuzzy fibres. You may recall the Harass Hag dealt with your fleece and it's gare or defences.]

Pilot Officer Hydrogen has another sailing idea but this time it is a Yacht. You can imagine that it is a very old yacht and it has a NODE OR KNOB with connections between the boy, brother who is a mischief and BOYO. And YEP they get up to trouble.

At the Numerical Aperture; It is not applicable to give them cyanide.

BOO! [Exclm; to frighten].
He has wonderful, excellent PYO. [Pyo is a word element meaning pus. Pyin means the albuminous constituent of pus - which is any of a class of water-soluble proteins occurring in animal and vegetable juices and tissues. In animals the liquid part of blood or plasma albumin is involved in osmotic regulation and transport, as of lipids. At this point it may be best to simply note that these are very complex molecules, having even more complex processes and reactions - the subject of organic chemistry being a very extensive one. For example the scientist who defined the nature of the enzyme that initiates photosynthesis spent 18 years doing so and found it contained 37,792 atoms! Pyin is a vital part of every cell in the body, the major constituents of which are carbohydrates, proteins and lipids. To my simple appreciation of these matters I see no good reason to doubt that Pyo can be excellent.] Boyo's peachy Pyo has an electrical current rating equated to younger dope. [Nap Pad would be similar].

Woden exclaims, YEAH / YES. His hips are narrower by an inch than his bodice.

Ebony has a nip of heady, intoxicating, red wine but only a Nip. She reports that the Penda [a rainforest tree] has paid an Ion to prohibit or Ban something.

Astronomer Ger in the West explains that a Decan is a division of 10 days length in a zodiac astrology sign, but Boyo's future is conoid or cone shaped and his ONE future an aeon – an infinitely long time.

Mother Earth's ecclesiastical rules are consulted.

North Sages report that Boyo's 17. "Star of Magi" blessings will die within the year. [The Magi has two jugs like Venus; one is sweet water and the other for sour or bitter water. The path has many windings and tests and rewards but it tests especially for spiritual strength through a series of destined difficulties. See Psyche for the full definition in Sphere 8. Partnerships.]

The Bench decrees that his Pad will be like a Poi – a dish of baked Taro.

Pilot Officer Hydrogen; We need to keep an idea in mind. Boyo is chained to the ocean.

Great Spirit's Codex designation of PHI [the 21st letter of the Greek alphabet] means there is a serial order to being called to attention by ONE.

At the Numerical Aperture; HOY [Exclm; to get attention.]

Woden says Boyo was against an education in Pan – his face was expressionless.

Steerer agrees that he had been against an education in Pan and had seized on another idea.

Astronomer Ger says he seized on the idea that Pan lived in a place of wild habitation like a cave or the Den of a large Cod-fish on the Murray River.

North Sages report that he included a cheap education in Divinity.

At the Numerical Aperture Boyo calls HOY [Exclm; to get attention].

To THE ONE.

2.

THE ONE

At the Numerical Aperture calls HOY [Exclm; to get attention.]

 Pilot Officer Hydrogen; In his backbone we included a hoop.

North Sages report that putting your hopes in a small ferry-boat or HOY is false. You can trust the truth of the matter that the Murray Cod does have links to Pi. It is itself an amazing example of the ratio of the circumference to the diameter. It can become mammoth. To carry all the past souls on a ferry would mean it would have to expand like a mammoth Cod.

Mother Earth intervenes; she has consulted the ecclesiastic rules and so she gives Boyo a Cap of Columbium – 25 Discrimination and Analysis so he had Pan. But he remained expressionless again. [25: This is a very helpful Cap for Boyo to get because it brings an increasing ability to learn from our mistakes. Just the thing for Boyo. See Psyche.]

Steerer; Each of us have it individually built in that we are open – no boundaries.

At the Numerical Aperture; Boyo is simply against being called even though he is one who is likely to succeed.

In the SE Place of Spirit; we are referred again to Codex – Phi by order Ocean.

In the NNE, we find the genuine HOY ferry is painted Cyano / blue and under the charge of a Cadi – as in a Judge and leader in a Muslim community. [This is the same NNE Hoy-ferry referred to in the demise of the Harvest Rat – Trans. 6.]

In the NNW; Boyo had exasperated his Peon - messenger or attendant – twice over or double his Pi.

Mother Earth points out that under the Ecclesiastical rules, the Aeon was paid for by the Doe's bid of an Ion to be paid by the Penda Tree in the SW.

Astronomer Ger; The Conoid or core shaped cloud over Boyo's future shows there has been a deposit of some luminosity recently. A simple Humane act by Candella. That only leaves Boyo with the 10 day Decan to pay for.

Ebony says she is ready to give him a Cobalt injection by no later than her commencing decent into her rich red wine! [Cobalt is a silver-white metallic element that is used in ceramics, alloys and the treatment of cancer. It's name comes from the Greek meaning 'goblin'. It means :21 Crown of Magi[1]. Our young Bachelor of Divinity is getting a major injection of great blessings.]

In the South, Woden advises that Boyo as a younger slice was peachy or

excellent when he received :21 Crown of Magi. [The term younger slice wouldn't mean when Boyo was younger in this life time. So he was peachy in a past life time when given this injection by Ebony.]

In the SE, Al the sloth tells us again that it is not appropriate for Cyanide to be given to bone but wants to get started with a Gee Up for a Mischief.

---

[1] This path is pictured as Universe and called "The Crown of Magi". It promises general success and guarantees advancement and honours, awards and general elevation in life and career. It indicates victory after a long struggle, for the Crown of Magi is gained only after long initiation, much soul testing and various tests of determination. However, the person blessed with : 21 can be certain of final victory over all odds and all opposition. It is a most fortunate Wisdom Path – a path of karmic reward. [See "Psyche".]

Pilot Officer Hydrogen explains that it would take an epoch in communications on the telephone to explain the distinctive character of this method. The relevant node to account for it is out of print but as a means of death it is clearly superior. In the NE, what is known about the method is in part known by the Ani. [The Ani is a black cuckoo-like bird that inhabits the warmer regions of Central America and given earlier reference in Trans. 7 to the Taino of Arawak, the almost total extinction of that tribe by the Spanish no doubt has a distinctive character - surpassing, beyond. We were also told the Taino women had a tea ceremony that used the indigo plant - also characterized by blue colouring. It was the Ani that sounded the final note TE in that transcript.]

Pilot Officer Hydrogen; Characteristically this is like a telephone epoch having the distinctive form of two sides of a conversation where one says that when we die we cease to exist and the other says no we surpass death or exist beyond it in another form.

The NE Bench decrees that Boyo has already lived as part Ani - a black cockatoo like bird.

North Sages open their sheets on a matter that is plainly visible to them.

Mother Earth has a Police Constable to deal with. She is of the opinion we should steal his Obituary Notice for Doe.

Astronomer Ger; to chop up his Obituary will open the unfilled-chain to the Peony flower. [And so too the Peony's chain is open for the unnamed soldier.]

Ebony says he is a dooby – an ignoramus or a dope. The fingerboard on her guitar tells the Beacon to descend – no more warnings.

Woden tells us that derivatives of benzene are engraved on Boyo according to the Water Code system or law. It says the imprint of benzene has been noted by the Hectare Dean of the Code.

At the Numerical Aperture; Phenyl is a univalent radical $C6H5$ from Benzene. It makes Boyo chop or change suddenly like the wind.

 In the SE Place of Spirit: This impels the parents and citizens to be affectively shy and reserved but on the same page to convict Boyo.

In the ESE, Ever Errs; the Atomic Energy Commission is characterised by collusion between bidders at an auction. But it is time for collusion in a round of applause for Deputy Hoopla.

Pilot Officer Hydrogen is much admired in his boater hat but he has added a pin of a surfboard with wide sides.

3.

North Sages are Northern in orientation. [So too in Tai Chi.]

Pilot Officer Hydrogen bids farewell to the indicative day of 24 hrs. Eastern and Western in orientation.

In the SE Place of Spirit; For any who experience a downwards slope or incline, there is a duty of Care under the Bio-Bond that unites all life from its Neb or beginning to it's Node where life joins back again to the stem.

Woden; Phobias and obsessive fears or dreads are also passed along from the Neb to the Node and back again. You will appreciate that water nymphs always have an obsessive fear of becoming like a sun dried mud brick – adobe – when in contact with the Sun/Fire.

Mother Earth; The Head Office for determining where any confidence game is being played is the Hop Office. [The Hop plant is a twinning stemmed plant often used in making beer. But does this mean that the virtue of the plant is that it helps determine how things, events and even motives are twisted together?]

North Sages; Daphne the water nymph was terrified of being sundried by contact with Apollo. [Remember the Dew Rise Ride? Daphne, as if the dew, rises as the sun or Apollo pursues her around the Earth eternally. Apollo is given in the legend to have chosen the Laurel tree to represent Daphne and his Eternal Love for her. Like wise Pan chose the Reeds for his Flutes to represent Syrinx.]

NE Bench; How you like to dance: the regulated steps you like to follow, is also built in a little bit.

Pilot Officer Hydrogen; Given what was conferred on Boyo and what he completed, the outcome seems to be a "dead" heat with his charges for being over the prescribed limit for alcohol.

SE Place of Spirit; At the basics, it is heady to see how rash and impetuous our little ewe lamb has been.
HA! [Interjection.] By the Actinium Commanding Officer. [Actinium is a chemical element that refers us to the wisdom paths – 22 Submission- Caution.[2] In many ways this means failure to listen to your own "inner voice" of Caution.] He says that he has the youngest of two parts in The Bag. Boyo in identified as being in a Dycho.

In the South; Nehemiah exclaims greetings – HI!
In the Old Testament story Nehemiah lived in Susa about 450 BC.

---

[2] 22. Submission – Caution. The Image; "A Good man, blinded by the error of others, with a knapsack on his back, full of errors." There will be trouble ahead in which you need to listen to the "Inner-voice".

After hearing bad news about the exiled surviving Jews in Judah and the destruction of the walls and gates of Jerusalem, he was granted leave, safe passage and access to materials by the king he was serving and travelled to Jerusalem. He was greatly distressed by what he found and began the "good work" of organizing the rebuilding of the city's defences, unique character, his father's sepulchres and the morale of the people. Nehemiah made it known to the Jews that it was

the wish of THE ONE to have the city restored. The first gate to be rebuilt was the Sheep Gate [redemption] then the Fish Gate, the towers and walls, Valley Gate, Fountain Gate, Pool of Shelah, Water Gate in the East, Horse Gate, East Gate, Muster Gate and all the other gates and towers. The Jews enemies were greatly enraged by this rebuilding, they ridiculed their efforts and plotted against Nehemiah. The Jews maintained their vigilance and work, surprising their enemies with what was accomplished. The wall was rebuilt in 52 days and even the Jews enemies believed it had been accomplished with the help of THE ONE.

> *On the first day of the 7th month all the people were gathered together in the square before the Water Gate and the law recorded by Moses was read to the people.*

Ritual consecration, sacrifices and celebration followed and "the joy of Jerusalem was heard afar off." So Nehemiah became Governor of Jerusalem, is remembered for his "good work" and devotion to THE ONE.

It is the story of great things being achieved when working in an accord with ONE. So Nehemiah is also part of the Dicho but he is given as currently an Opah – a brightly coloured deep-sea fish.

In the SSW, Dyna Pandy can deal out the most powerful of punishments and is waiting on the hand or foot of Boyo.

Ebony is aphonic – she has lost her voice! Maybe Steerer takes over; for someone of Irish decent by artificial insemination it seemed that he had a very nice cop. But it was carefully wound on the spindle of a Bad-In Ape.

Ger; for him to exist is Hooey or just nonsense.

In the WNW, E [transcendental constant] – it is indefinite.

Mother Earth; He is ONE's Dextro-Pan.

North Sages; This is an Icon of Horse Power! You need a Bachelor of Economics in Beyond to see the effect this is having on Boyo's Pad.

In the NE; A small chip of something pleasant and amiable is required, said the Bench.

Nehemiah; Boyo was given a pinch of Beryllium = 17 Star of Magi.[3] And sent to Honduras.

Ger; No Dice. OH! [Exclm; surprise/pain.]

A whole cycle of the spiral is silent until we return again to the West.

Ger; That Edition of Boyo was simply amazing.

In the NNW; Icy – he was covered with ice, said the Chief Petty Officer.

North Sages; He was ONE single unit

TO THE ONE.

4.
THE ONE

Pilot Officer Hydrogen is singing a hymn of invocation to Apollo as he brought down the Bin.

North Sages; ONE [single unit].

In the NNW Chief Petty Officer; With charge for the Canopy of anything such as rainforest trees, he can see what is above and covered. Boyo was like a cake he was covered in so much ice. He seemed cheap, mean, slow witted and stupefied.

Ger; Adonic [a verse with a spondee followed by a dactyl.]
     "The doubled prongs of Magi bring
     A double dose of tests and sting
     Gently."

---

[3] 17 Star of Magi. Like Venus has two fountains on with bitter water and the other sweet, so to there are these contrasts in 17 attributed to the periodic but pungent effect of the planet Saturn.

Nehemiah; Yes Boyo is here in a communal setting. Maybe in a school of Oprah for some time.

Pilot Officer Hydrogen; Brought down the Bin head on so we have a new edition of Boyo.

The NE Bench; He will be in command of other people's Bach of Economics of Beyond.

North Sages; Behind Boyo, paced Pegasus ready to add his horse-power. He peruses things carefully.
     Nay! he says, not only so….

Mother Earth; As Boyo travelled by foot he accumulated repeated blessings in Iodine = 24: Love, Money and Creativity. [4] But his greetings and benedictions were only an imitation and so not genuine.

Ger; Boyo was carried over as an Anglo Norman where he existed centigrade.

Steerer: YO - HO! [Exclm: to get attention.] BAD-IN. Then later she called…
     POOH! {Exclm: distain] on contact with A very large dog's calcium on or about AD 476.

Dyna Pandy; He had the power….

Nehemiah; Yes Boyo had the same power as I did but he had it in old English.

At the Numerical Aperture: It takes a lot of bustle and fuss to separate and refabricate a cubic gland with many panes.

In the SE; I [my, mine, me] Dopa [a non protein amino acid precision of adrenaline, used to treat Parkinson's disease. [Indeed there has been a history of Parkinson's in our family. Genetic inheritance certainly has many panes.]

Ever Errs; Dopa works like the mycelium of a fungus and attacks the problem at the base. It works like an ace in tennis and it can't be touched according to the Poon or East Indian timber tree. [More virtues of a tree.]

Pilot Officer Hydrogen; To open a new chapter on Boyo we rename him Cob and his sweetheart is known as Density Donah.

The NE Bench; He has Pico – 10 to the power 12 the power indicative of Nahum[5] from the Bible.

---

[4] 24: Love, Money and Creativity. Blessings of great rewards.
[5] Nahum in the Old Testament lived at the time of the fall of Nineveh. "Woe to the bloody city…"

North Sages; The population he was interested in was more like the snake shaped wraps of silk he used to display his 24: Love, Money and Creativity, about which he made a very loud noise.

Chief Petty Officer Canopy; His abundance was like a Pecan nut tree's crop.

Mother Earth's Hop Office declares an interest in a confidence trick.

Ebony rises from the Aboriginal Bench in the SW to show her interest too.

Nehemiah; In any dialect you would know what it meant if you were reprimanded and a binding put on your scrotum.

At the Numerical Aperture; Pad, who knows the path worn by animals had evidence and authority to verify he was called.

In the SE Place of Spirit; As a common Hebrew he knew the C tone keynote, the alphabet and yet even as a Head Boy he would Dip his eyes in respect but Opine – he thinks or expresses the opinion Dip: meaning to have a short swim.

Pilot Officer Hydrogen; One day to everyone's surprise and delight he pledged his hand in marriage above.

The Cadi advised that the whole vehicle moved along fast.

5.
North Sages; We rate Cob as a Yahoo or a rough and uncouth person.

The NE Bench; Cob's action or procedure was reported by Oceanid the Sea Nymph.

Pilot Officer Hydrogen; YAH! [Exclm: impatience.] Ice is like diamonds to him so he hoed in too energetically into the coconut flesh. But Boohai – Maori: wrong. AH !! [Exclm: surprise and pity] at the arrest of Yin [feminine principle] who aches or is in pain continuously.

In the SE Place of Spirit; Cob seems to race wide from his place of origin as a boy. As a grown man he is obsessed with Ice even the icing on a cake. He has really only achieved a behind – a minor score – even though able bodied. But most so as a Pooncey [Col: effeminate]. OO [WE: egg] BYE [having no competitor] for a Nape or back of the neck Picture.

Nehemiah; He should get a Diploma in Bandy for the way he has been passed from one to another.
OH! {Exclm: surprise, pain]. A new Doona is needed.

Ger; His personal computer is on demand for the distress it causes.

Mother Earth; The pane needs to be honed.

In the NNW; Pan has a pot for Ondine the water-spirit. She says he is a bi-sexual chip according to Racoon.

North Sages report he should be put in a compartment for Cash on Delivery.

The NE Bench; Offers Deuterium an isotope of Hydrogen: Wisdom Path 2. Sensitive. It is a cheap, of little account ion of small value to match his action and process.

Pilot Officer Hydrogen; Just as the North is Northern in their orientation, the East is Eastern and about what is coming into being…a Hot and Cold Dib or the bait that falls lightly on water but has it's roots in 18 Spiritual / Material Conflict.[6] See Associated Press. [See Psyche.]

In the SE Place of Spirit; HE! HE! [laughter] His head compared to his place of origin is more than hypothetically he is certifiably icy cold.

At The Numerical Aperture; He could be able bodied on a small Scottish island but with a shot of 25: Discrimination & Analysis.[7]

Ger; Cob is on demand.

Mother Earth bids 24: Love, Money and Creativity.

North Sages bid Polonium = 8 Destined Difficulties Doubled. His hope or expectation of a desired outcome is patchy but one way or another he is in the difficulty can – the Booay Can.

The NE Bench; Codex longs to find a dwelling place to give him an operation.

In the SE Place of Spirit; In the nide or nest of a pheasant and pinned to the central business district but born as a piece of primaeval rabbit fur.

At the Numerical Aperture; The number for Ionium = 5. [Cob is being knocked back to the basics in communication.]

---

[6] 18. Spiritual / Material Conflict. Image: "A rayed Moon with drops of blood falling down and below there are dogs waiting to devour them and below the dogs there are crabs waiting." This is a great spiritual path.
[7] 25: Discrimination & Analysis. Learning from experience.

Nehemiah; Cob will have to abide there – wait for some time before some manner of thing occurs.

Ger; bids for Economy of Beyond.

Mother Earth; In the Indies.

North Sages; Phooey [Exclm: contempt.]

In the SE Place of Spirit; He was born

To THE ONE.

6.
THE ONE

In the SE Place of Spirit; Born as a stone or pebble.

Nehemiah; He will have to abide there – stay and wait for a Number.

In the SE Place of Spirit; He will be in a new capsule, the Ace we need to play.

Pilot Officer Hydrogen; aches with longing.

North Sages; Cob is in the Booay Can one way or another there will be destined difficulties in the steep path ahead. The first of these will be within the year.

Ger; On Demand.

Dyna Pandy; I'll have his foot.

Nehemiah; He is near the condition of Niobium = 25: Discrimination & Analysis.

At the Numerical Aperture; No claim was made on the bonus [25:] He seemed busy eating his principle meal for the day. We will have to dip him in ONE derivatives just like you make a candle by dipping in tallow.

In the SE Place of Spirit; Panic occurs as something is passing through.

Ever Errs; It is Habakkuk from the Bible to bring Cob to 20."The Awakening". He left laughing. [He lived about a hundred years before Nehemiah. On the day of reckoning he said "the beams will speak and the walls will reply". Oh! but he loved and rejoiced in THE ONE he called his chief stringer of his stringed instrument. But why did Habakkuk leave laughing after contact with Cob?]

Pilot Officer Hydrogen; Cob made a stand against Habakkuk like a rude and ill-bred girl who has been trapped but with no "Awakening" but claiming to be A'ONE Eastern.

Gatt Seers; he is like a parking pod for a seed vessel.

Cadi on the Hoy Ferry; He is Cash on Delivery to the racoon department.

In the NNW; Barn.

Ger; At the point something occurs his head won't be worth a bean.

Nehemiah; Maybe he is worth as much as a rose hip [fruit] growing on a ridge.

At the Numerical Aperture; Caption: Ciano [hello] incidentally Cop [police person] His Eminence Boon or joyous companion of old but resembling in action and process a Pooncey or effeminate.

In the SE Place of Spirit; This is a repetition of an epic, imposing and impressive story of a highway man who was attempting to attain the goal of being a Boa constrictor around a pine tree.

Ever Errs; Identifies him as Don Put On.

Pilot Officer Hydrogen; He is well known for hoeing in energetically to the photographic fixing agent.

Gatt Seers; YAH! [Exclm: impatience]. Born like it.

North Sages; He is a Yahoo – a rough and uncouth person.

7.
NE Bench; A loud and confused noise is made to signify a special purpose.

Pilot Officer Hydrogen; The twining plant, the hop [The Hop Office is in the NW and its specialty is confidence tricks.] says that the decay, decline and rot set in on a particular day at noon when Cob was on the beat and looking to strike.

In the SE Place of Spirit; Pan can move around continuously, silently and as if with a camera on extended play in and on the direction he wants. He does this by simmering the 3rd C Scale E as he plays and sings a pean of praise and joy. In name only this Cap, a trifling term for the top or upper surface of a wave, can be imagined as hard or fixed.

At the Numerical Aperture; In bed with a negro called Don who was the head fellow. His dark skin did match his mood. He had a nocturnal carnivore hypothesis in his head – a Hyena Hypothesis.

Nehemiah; To peach is to inform against an associate or accomplice. The Hen and her Hod can provide an open, candid or frank disclosure.

Ebony; He was in the hen coup every day.

Mother Earth; He would qualify for Head Drug User.

North Sages; His den is squalid and vile.

Cadi; He needs a shot of Hahnium = 13: Regeneration & Change.[8] This is especially needed with respect to bringing forth young.

Gatt Seers; A One Chain linear measure – 22 yards measured out with a cane having a pithy wood stem. [eg., Elder tree]

Pilot Officer Hydrogen; He is holding a Poi – a ball on the end of a string as used by Maori women.

In the SE Place of Spirit; The Poi is used to cut along or across the backbone until it is open or bare or uncovered and the party begins to complain and remonstrate.

At the Numerical Aperture; When the subject wants it keenly he is a near opus ace in the composition of his attentions on his subject. Then he picks on a single spot on our Ace.

Nehemiah; They were Dutch Pico [WE: 10 to the power 12].

In the WSW; Hindustani.

Mother Earth; Height dance. According to the Dance Bench who noted their feet and body rhythm.

---

[8] 13: Regeneration and Change. This can be like a shot to the intellect and is not associated with bad luck. It is about refining skills and knowledge, changing how we respond or do things.

North Sages; Bed registered the sound.

Pilot Officer Hydrogen; At the furthest extremity he was nothing more than an aide de camp.

In the SE Place of Spirit; The matter is to be open, laid bare and uncovered.

Ger; Don Put On is from the Bondi Criminal Investigation Branch in NSW.

NE Bench; Once, on a single occasion, -Ian [suf. variant of –an from the Latin -ianus]!

TO THE ONE.

8.
THE ONE

In the SE Place of Spirit; Diploma in Library or a short study is needed.

Pilot Officer Hydrogen; Cooba [acacia or willow wattle native to Australia. A stick cut from this tree would be an excellent whip.]
HO! [Exclm: Stop]. Cony [animal rabbit of the genus "cuniculus". Daman also meant the Lamb of Israel.] Adjective [Damaning?].

North Sages; Check dance – feet and body rhythm but also to bob up and down.

In the WSW; Hindustani [language spoken around Delhi in India.]

In the SE Place of Spirit; Someone is writing with haste in a small cabin and then in a taxi in Bondi.

Pilot Officer Hydrogen; The man can move from Dexter chief to Sinister base Actinon the voice of 22. Submission Caution.

NE Bench; He is writing the biography of a very important person who is really only an overdrawn Hob - more like the target pin in a game of coits. And he is trying to bring forth young with another person described as December Deacon – an elected official of the church.

North Sages; This is like acid on the Bible.

Chief Petty Officer; The Cad. This is contemptible.

Mother Earth; He could have the title of Head Drug User.

Ger; He would.

In the WSW; Norse. [More like a predator.]

Ebony; refers us to the Hen Coup.

Nehemiah; The hen has been confined to barracks whilst she informs against an associate and accomplice. The matter remains undecided at the moment.

At the Numerical Aperture; He is the cause of much ruin and destruction of life. Even the Ecclesiastic rules have been bent and caused to stop for a Pion = 12: Sacrifice Victim[9]. In name only he was a Dan with a high grade of proficiency.

In the SE Place of Spirit; His songs of praise and joy when he is wearing his long silk mantle or surplice would make an electrocardiograph jump.

Pilot Officer Hydrogen; It is engineered that way.

NE Bench; There is a loud confused noise and a new subject is to the fore. He is a citizen of Denmark.

9.
NE Bench; He is a peach.

Pilot Officer Hydrogen; Yes a Peach Hand of the Diplomatic Corp.

In the SE Place of Spirit; He had original blessings of 25: Discrimination & Analysis. And of 10. Wheel of Fortune. He became a conservatorium figure of renown for when he performed a Paean [metrical foot-note of 4 syl = 1 long + 3 short.] you could see the cape jutting out into the sea and Daniel from the Bible with 21: The Crown of Magi on his head. [Daniel did have great rewards for a great life well lived.] But for all this display of wonderful gifts, the Bay Laurel Tree says that he is doomed, done for, napoo.

At the Numerical Aperture; A dance he performs called the Post Office Hype deliberately stimulates excitement by use of a canopy and clouds around a throne with the piano keyboard used like an ode to Phoebe that evokes fear.
        HEY! [Exclm: to get attention.]

Nehemiah; Computer Aided Design is open to commence.

Steerer; Once only.

---

[9] 12: Sacrifice – Victim. To be sacrificed in the plans and intrigues of others. Learning to ordain success.

Ger; Co- [Pref: association].

Chief Petty Officer; Icy – slippery as…]

North Sages; Whatever heap of something is caste upon someone or something, there is a conscientious objector connection to the inside knowledge of the Nob or Head of the Nipa Palm Tree. [Another Virtue of a Tree.] It would be a boon to have an integrated circuit because what we have is Patchy and thick. Such a boon wasn't available to any deacon of the early Christian church.

NE Bench; In Gymnastics, When moving between the horizontal bars, if you move up and then dip below the bars and say BOO! Thus showing contempt for the main mass of the building, the aim or purpose cannot be achieved. [The analogy equally applies to respect for THE ONE.] To better achieve one's aim or purpose an Adults Only debenture involves 22 yards per annum in a niche or recess [remember you are going into a Dip] with a Phen or illuminating gas reference. This especially applies to anyone who was born on the 12th of any month. 12: Sacrifice Victim. A great thing to conquer as the trials of the earlier life are rewarded in the next life with :21 Crown of Magi.

Gatt Seers; Using a negative ID, chop up a cape / garment into small bits using a Hoe and plenty of exclamations of contempt and frustration. Then Pace or traverse the Chain.

Pilot Officer Hydrogen; Pine wood will assist the struggle to be on even terms so use it to try and mix the pieces of the costume with water – with the aim of reaching a uniform consistency or Poach. The Node of difficulty will be engaged when you try and dice the garment with your jaw – by chewing!

 In the SE Place of Spirit; the depraved appetite will bode an omen of Pan when all is considering together with the jaw.

At the Numerical Aperture; A pea [the round nutritious seed] symbolizes One Unity with COB as the Head Boy.

Nehemiah; This will require a NO – a stylised Japanese classical drama. A beak is holding a bond or sealed document that says "Di- [Pref: twice] Computer Aided design Inclusive…

Steerer; An Ace or highly skilled person.

Ger; Check the growth or development.

Mother Earth; Pay as you earn in Danish.

North Sages; Any Nip or small quantity will Nip the eccentric Head Pin or Apex, Dono the Spanish Lord or gentleman who now lives as a citizen in Denmark.

Pilot Officer Hydrogen; You have to bring your own Bianco [white wine], Yen [Japanese currency] and Hoe that doth perform! [The hoe has to be very sharp to cut up a garment.]

In the SE Place of Spirit; Close and affectionately this is the BOCO [nose] Handicap and Cap [head covering]!

Nehemiah; Boche Candle Power.

 Steerer; A Cop will arrest someone who is caught in the…

Mother Earth; Hypno Harbour.

North Sages; With Heroin and being reprimanded severely.

Pilot Officer Hydrogen; Dono was dipped – he was baptised by immersion

TO THE ONE.

10.
THE ONE

Pilot Officer Hydrogen; THE ONE baptizes Pan by immersing him in the leaves of the betel tree.

Nehemiah; This ends the speculation about Pan.

In the SE Place of Spirit; HOP – to leap by one foot.

Pilot Officer Hydrogen; Confined in prison like a varnish over the whole body, I had a Doab [the land in the Y between two rivers]. So bring your own poach to trespass and steal game!

NE Bench; Bench – long seat.

North Sages; Don is a Spanish Lord or Gentleman with the suffix –O like in garbo. He is the Head Pin or Apex or actually the Head Pin-Ice given his state. After a small drink he deletes his Chopin – the thick cork soled shoes of Spain.

Mother Earth; Our church official is the Ace but to a very small amount.

Nehemiah; A betrayal is involved.

At the Numerical Aperture; The Chi Pan is a vessel containing energy like a pea is a nutritious seed. The Chi Pan is Opposed to…

In the SE Place of Spirit; the Doctor of Chemistry in the depraved appetite department. [Me, the editor].

Pilot Officer Hydrogen; In any difficult year it is most probable the error is in how the chain is paced or traversed.

NE Bench; The Cape/garment Poach Chap can open small slits and cracks but it would take a chapter to show how he can move a mountain like Mt. Ben in Scotland.

Cadi; That would be a boon to OPEC.

North Sages; Neb or nose is dangerous and tricky and against the agency of Icy - slippery as.

Mother Earth; No answer unless to pay to nip off the association and seal it with a coat of tar.

Steerer; Once – a single degree.

Nehemiah; Open to start or commence with C the velocity of light in a vacuum betrays the nominative. So there is more to it than just the speed of light.
HEY! [Exclm: to get attention]
Decay in Physics means the disintegration of a radio-active substance to a stable state.

In the SE Place of Spirit; Diploma in Library The Peach tree has a sympathetic response to any decay. [Peach fruit is delightful fresh but very quick to decay.]

At the Numerical Aperture; Wearing a cloak with a hood overhead by a pond or small body of water and carrying a piano keyboard. Pace [anxiously], Hoon [loutishly and recklessly and then suddenly Peachy.

In the SE Place of Spirit; Pen the female swan tuned to :21 Crown of Magi will panic. When she is stricken by Pan she will jump in her Cod [pod].

Pilot Officer Hydrogen; matted material printed on the warp of a cloth can create a commotion and lead to a probable error in hop – how to go.

NE Bench; Cognate with Ochna or Mickey Mouse Plant, he knows how to hop.

11.
North Sages; Cain was a murderer and so is our Capo leader in the Mafia who according to the Sages writing Sheets he/Dono had moved away from his earlier pastry preparation and now has chief responsibility for ICE making – but murder!

Pilot Officer Hydrogen; The noun or name passed me by but Honorary Deci is offered. [Deci- 10 to the power -1]

In the SE Place of Spirit; Icy yet able to be a peach in the bedroom; but in the husband's den he is a yob and brutish in expressing his instinctive energy.

In the Numerical Aperture; By any measure of acidity he is in remote country. And then he dips into the photo finish to nod off, used up, careless and dull.

Nehemiah; Advertisement.
HEY! [Exclm: to give encouragement] We deny / so it is not true that he is a notary of any official sort.

Steerer; Old piano with a softly music direction…

Chief Petty Officer; He takes his Dip like it's a cocktail.

North Sages; The Can [for permission] says NOH / NO. High Nabis [This refers to Pierre Bonnard (1867 – 1947) He was the Doyen of a 19th Century painting school in France that took their name Nabis from Nabhi in the Hebrew that meant prophet.] Had exhausted Idem [same as previously mentioned] Dicho [WE: pairs].

NE Bench; Considering the compass of the double headed coin covers two; you have to "Own Your Own Nob". [So the Dicho is equated to a double headed coin – that was Boyo and Nehemiah who were previously mentioned in a Dicho. This is confusing. The current Dicho seems to be Boyo and Dono – a relationship said to have established much earlier than Nehemiah's time in Yiddish history as it is referred to in the mid Palaeozoic period.]

Gatt Seers; beginning in a pious and especially hypocritically manner Sodium = 18 Hop [jump or leap by both feet] would be nice if done with great precision and accuracy.

Pilot Officer Hydrogen; A Bachelor of Arts in Dance will be needed to properly complete the sodium 18 exactly measured leaps when Liability and so excitement are turned on. [A chain is 22 yards to be covered in 18 leaps.]

In the SE Place of Spirit; North BED, B Ch D (Dental Surgery) Honey with a double certificate. [I do have a North Bed and a dental surgery honey had been sharing it with me. She certainly did have a double certificate and she proudly spoke of it. She and her three boys were fun and a great help around the farm.]

At the Numerical Aperture; Terrible Neuter.

Nehemiah; Zero dyne or force when she spoke fondly or amorously.

E the Transcendental Constant; It is a reproduction of a bored peon or day labourer.

North Sages; Tucked into the blankets in a state resembling sleep intensified the desire and longing for a PhD [Doctor of Philosophy].

Cadi; It's Odic but he's [me] just a cheap, British, pooncey mannered dandy.

NE Bench; Open to access about Bishop Batsman. [Previously Boyo] He is an absolute Cob judging from his Pyin [albuminous constituent of puss].

Pilot Officer Hydrogen; Hooch or alcoholic beverage…

In the SE Place of Spirit; Hand or assistant.

At the Numerical Aperture; Bound Price on Application

North Sages; for the Pain caused

TO THE ONE.

12.
THE ONE

North Sages; call for a bid for the pain caused.

Ger; Dysprosium = 18 Spiritual / Material Conflict.

Pilot Officer Hydrogen; offers a hard cent for his body.

NE Bench; Cob deceased and then enchained to a stupid person in North Central Africa say Chad.

Cadi; bids for a small disagreeable island.

North Sages; AYE! Ever as always his identification is iced and he is in a hypnoid state resembling sleep.

Mother Earth; Just a hire purchase peon who could attend a mule or horse.

Ger; Board.

Steerer; Dean in the Year Book 's gone yonder.

Nehemiah; Aged Compare Nib with Dono of the Mafia. [So Dono and Bishop Batsman are the two sides of the Double headed coin as they were apparently born on the same day.]

At the Numerical Aperture; The chaps a hood. [Dono].

Pilot Officer Hydrogen; It is undecided how he will die.
But YAHOO!!! [Exclm: delight and surprise] Anode[+ve ions] Nob [double breasted coin] into the pen of the author / writer. [Maybe this occurred in 2016.]

NE Bench; A bead pooncey [male homosexual] but for him to be deceased is Hooey! {Exclm: disapproval]. There will be a codicil on Boyo-aid – a fizzy drink!

North Sages; The hounds are baying at the Cooperative in Charge.

Ger; Honourably.

Steerer; To cut back or hone the light sensitive parts of the eyes requires a trip to handle arrears.

Nehemiah; With respect to this…HEY! [Exclm: to give encouragement].

At the Numerical Aperture; Remote country; ecology den or personal place of a hundred Yobbish trips. [Refers to my trips to the Big Desert of NW Victoria.]

In the SE Place of Spirit; His Excellency Breadth N [Math: indefinite whole number] Open hype needle.

Pilot Officer Hydrogen; Honoured …

NE Bench; To move away from…

North Sages; Cain – a murderer [Dono].

13.

North Sages; Didymium [once called "the twin" it was found to contain Neodydmium = 18 Spiritual / Material Conflict and Praseodydmium = 26 Partnerships.] Phoney – not genuine. Cape [mid Palaeozoic period] Yiddish.

Pilot Officer Hydrogen; Hobo – a vagrant [Recall discussion on Tags?]

In the SE Place of Spirit; Obi – a fetish or charm worn in Obi magic was closely tied to the 16th letter of Greek – Pi.- near the beginning of Yiddish history. An overdose of lyrical poems has cleared obstructions to Poach [slushy trampled land] Bay soil [reddish brown colouring] and the "Account" notes it well.

In the South. Nehemiah; Note what is happening in the East…

Steerer; Alternating Current …Aye! [Exclm: Affirm].

Mother Earth; To Con, defraud or swindle needs a group of two metrical feet to reach the right band or frequency of waves, to link into the Hop Office.

North Sages; The Consumer Price Index was limited to physical education in the mid Palaeozoic period when the Cape was covered in pine trees.
> [The Palaeozoic period had two of the greatest Mass Extinctions the Earth has known. The first was earlier in the Palaeozoic when an Ice Age occurred [about 400 million years ago]. The second but largest Mass Extinction occurred at the end of the Palaeozoic period about 250 million years ago.
> The Largest mass extinction the Earth has ever experienced occurred over an 8 million year period and resulted in; 96% of sea creatures and plants died in the oceans. 70% of terrestrial vertebrates died out. Vast numbers of insects died and it is estimated some 83% of all genera were destroyed. The earliest mammals and the predecessor of man were some of the survivors. The causes are numerous and include comets, asteroids, volcanic activity, tectonic plate movements of Gondwana / Pangaea, climate changes, green-house gasses like methane, ash producing acid rain, etc. It is worth a moment to reflection on the magnitude of some of these forces of nature.
> The Siberian Traps experienced massive volcanic activity that spread lava over about 2,000,000 square kilometres and released vast quantities of ash and gases into the atmosphere blocking out the sun for long periods in some areas of Pangaea. But as the lava spread over low lying sea-beds it released the methane gasses stored in the mud and it also ignited coal deposits that burnt for many thousands of years. Many species were unable to adapt to these sudden and vast changes that occurred. They simply were unable to adapt quickly enough in vast regions.
> Researchers have found a massive crater 40 Km wide, in the antipodes to the Siberian traps. Carbon dating has confirmed the timing of the formation of the crater and the occurrence of volcanic activity. It is

believed because of the irregular orbital behaviour of comets vrs asteroids, that a comet of about a ton or so hit the Earth at Araguainha in Brazil. Impact speed could have been as high as 300,000 kilometres per hour and with a molten centre in the Earth, this was like a bullet to the head; the force shot straight across to the antipodes in Siberia and a huge part of the crust shattered. The resulting volcanic activity was the greatest the Earth has experienced. (Allowances being made for the movement of the tectonic plates of Pangaea set off by the impact also.)
It was a very different world at that time and as conifers also began at that time, it is likely there was a Cape covered in pine trees at the end of the recovery that took nearly 30 million years for some species. Ocean species are thought to have recovered more quickly.]

NE Bench; Cob was like a black backed lorus – a gull.

Pilot Officer Hydrogen; Cob had the idea that life after the present one could be a bugger or bastard.

In the SE Place of Spirit; Inclusion.

Nehemiah; Decibel – noise [change of subject - back to the Dicho and Doab.]

Steerer: Intransitive Cabin – like on a ship or a truck.

Ger; Peon - one held in servitude to work off debts. [My own and those of Bishop Batsman and Dono.]

Mother Earth; To contribute.

North Sages; Young Chi tea [My contribution has been worth about as much as Young Chi Tea.]

Pilot Officer Hydrogen; Beyond life after the present one is the country

TO THE ONE.

14.
THE ONE

Ger; By conformity…

In the Place of Spirit; Chain of succession…

Mother Earth; Bay…

Ger; Peon - one held in servitude to work off debt. Detective has tapped him lightly with the hand.

Pilot Officer Hydrogen; Hay!

NE Bench; Cob is scathing and scolding like a black backed Iorus and he wants to know where the fault lies.

Cadi; blame lies in the mid Palaeozoic Cape period. [This again refers to a period when there were abundant fossils found in rocks; the age of ancient life. We already know this was a period of mass extinctions. It is possible that was the time Woden referred to as when the sewer was packed tight with those who had failed in Mother Earth's wager tags in the ecological succession. My bet is that this is the time of the Second Covenant between the Archetypes 250 million years ago. The Primal Arrangement would be before 500 million years ago. You may recall the Erased aids the Reed Dais Riser, so a concept of how things are to work precedes the actual. In Man's case this is interesting as the concept formed of the relationship between human Dichos and Pan was set nearly 240 million years earlier if the Cadi is correct as I expect he is. Man's evident emergence genetically as "homo sapiens" did not occur until at least 1.25 – 1.7 million years ago. You might say a long time between concept and achievement – but what a wonderful planet the Blue Dot has proven itself to be! Oh Yes! You may be wondering about the virtue of the pine tree? It represents the "struggle on equal terms" at the new beginning for the ecological succession in the Triassic period that followed. The surviving mammals included our ancestors. You may also see that there was a plan for Yiddish history to follow as well.]

North Sages; Pad knows the movement of every animal.

Steerer; The bedroom Pad is her precinct.
AYE! [Exclm: Affirm] and what is consumed there.

Nehemiah; Pene – almost

In the SE Place of Spirit; AY! [Exclm: surprise and sorrow.] Bay [reddish brown colouring] and Pi [16th letter of Grk.]

Ever Errs; wants to know the guidelines for what to look at internally.

Pilot Officer Hydrogen; Obi – an African magic system using a fetish is a sign of a Vagrant and an eccentric or weird person. They should wait and endure for a while. [They do have the Rata Red Seas of Aesthete to look forward to – in a sheet!]

NE Bench; Dab the small European flatfish will provide the necessary punishment. [There are many types of flatfish from as small as under 5 cm and up to the Atlantic Halibut of over 3m. Because they have uniquely chameleon like camouflage you won't see them coming and most of them have very sharp teeth.]

North Sages; The relationship in the Dicho and Doab, like the name, it is nominal only; it is as phoney as Didymium.

13.
Pilot Officer Hydrogen; The sound that you make when you walk along the ground is reflected inversely and is noticed by Ob-pad.

In the SE Place of Spirit; Bond – acknowledgment of debt will be a bit tedious and irritating but that will be nothing compared to the Boon, benefit or blessing sought. The Hoons like Dono and Coby will be in decay and their source of energy will be removed by inches.

At the Numerical Aperture; -Older [Suf: super families] Dose Bench [House of Parliament.]

Mother Earth; -Phany [Suf: to n.] Appearance of a deity or supernatural being.

Cadi; Doyen [senior member of a body, class or profession]. But where there is hype or sounds have been heard or uttered about drug taking, …

NE Bench; Dye Deci [10 to the power of -1]

Pilot Officer Hydrogen; The decoy to the head or seat of thought was Obi being a reference to the Sash worn by Japanese women and children who…

In the SE Place of Spirit; were ancient volcanic cone hands.

At the Numerical Aperture; They would talk loudly, noisily, hard and black.

North Sages; and quickly receive two legged support.

Cadi; Drug taking, especially of a narcotic, can only result in a poor quality Pan more akin to a depression in the ground.

NE Bench; We need a Postal Order…

In the SE Place of Spirit; Organization for Economic Cooperation & Development.

North Sages; We are seeking those who are both elite and good and straight…

TO THE ONE.

14.
THE ONE

North Sages; Nob or social elite…

In the SE Place of Spirit; Oh! [Exclm: longing.]

NE Bench; The cheap or poor quality will suffer, longing or grief.

Steerer; Capacitance as in electricity.

Nehemiah; The potential difference in the hand or source of information from Seals [phocines] ….

At the Numerical Aperture; Before 1950, the radio carbon dating year or there abouts.

In the SE Place of Spirit; Peta [10 to the power 15 of any given unit.]

Pilot Officer Hydrogen; Bice [blue or green as carbonate of copper] Decoy or lure.

North Sages; College of Advanced Education stopped functioning.

Dyna Pandy; She is on her Perch waiting…

Nehemiah; Phoney action or cheers will bring a Bondi Thrashing.

At the Numerical Aperture; Cape – pede [we: foot]
EH! [Exclm: surprise and some doubt] Phosphorus. [This is the beginning in the transcript that is written up as the Journey to Cape Woolami in Victoria. This was undertaken as directed in the script. Cape Woolami lay exactly SSE from the farm where this transcript was taken. This was a trip to the Numerical Aperture as you will see.]

In the SE Place of Spirit; Chip [Elect. A square semi-conductor] Blend of pedal dice [small cube 1:6] Bond [acknowledgement of debt to] Pan.

Pilot Officer Hydrogen; Oh! [Exclm: gladness]

NE Bench; Echoa [Maori: friend].

15.
NE Bench; Bond die [singular of dice]

Pilot Officer Hydrogen; Open access to knowledge or enlightenment Peon [foot soldier] Chine, ravine or fissure.

In the SE Place of Spirit; Pace with permission from…courteous form IN-ONE [IN- means the negation of…ONE]. AD [since Christ's birth] Coop [prison] Coo [soft murmuring sound like pigeons] Helium=10 Hobgoblin in outside broadcast.

At the Numerical Aperture; Hen [fussy woman] New English Bible pregnant with one's luck or lot. [A woman who could be called Fussy did give me exactly such a copy of the Bible and it was used extensively for these records and came with me later when I undertook a trip to Cape Pede – see Postscript – "Journey To Cape Woolami".]

Nehemiah; Direct or command De- [reversal eg deactivate] Chine [bottom of a boat] Phon [unit of loudness].

Steerer; Die [loose strength, power or force]

Ger; YEA! [Exclm: Yes]

Mother Earth; End issue, result or remnant

Cadi: Obi [sorcery practiced in Africa & West Indies.]

NE Bench; Write it twice [End Obi, End Obi]

Pilot Officer Hydrogen; Captain Dia- [Prefix: opposed in movement] Electronic data processing. Failure is inevitable as a fixed standard of pitch is required.

In the SE Place of Spirit; Australian Broadcasting commission body is dead on arrival India. An apparent similarity occurs between the pelvis ability to absorb oxygen compared to the brain. [Oxygen= 38 Grace Under Pressure II].

At the Numerical Aperture; Chape [metal trim on the scabbard] Pica – print size.

Nehemiah; Those who are of bone or of bone-like material are in ONE union or agreement and harmony with all having a foot.

Dyna Pandy; Pea – the plant producing a pea. A pea as a symbol of One Unity.

In the WSW; Nip – to steal..

Mother Earth; About Debenture

Cadi; Conductor

NE Bench; On support or conveyance

In the SE Place of Spirit; by route ABC.

Nehemiah; To expand is unnecessary.

Gatt Seers; pecan or hickory nut tree.

TO THE ONE.

16.
THE ONE

Mother Earth; De- [pref: negation]

At the Numerical Aperture; Cine or motion of the Direct Current…

In the SE Place of Spirit; Brotherhood

Pilot Officer Hydrogen; Cap is explosive

NE Bench; Deposit

Mother Earth; the Head / top of the body…

In the WSW; Poncho [blanket like cloak]

Steerer; HOY! [Col: to throw] Editor

At the Numerical Aperture; Date for Dace [small freshwater cyprinoid fish] Dip

In the SE Place of Spirit; Body [wool quality]

Ever Errs; Coon – failure is inevitable.

Pilot Officer Hydrogen; Entertaining at dinner a racket started about Y the unknown variable in Math. Concealed poise.

NE Bench; Diapason – melody.

Chief Petty Officer; Hip – the sloping side of the roof covering the Barn, reported Coy [modest and shy.]

Nehemiah; Heard the voice or sound.

At the Numerical Aperture; The Hen or fussy woman who gave me a copy of the New English Bible came with her son – [Nobelium=13: Regeneration and Change] who I was to have made fast with. However they left quickly after my complaints about some minor irritations about that book and I failed to make a bond with him.]

In the SE Place of Spirit; The Bench or Court by the extent of the hero narrative or Epic that needs to be written about Pan, must show that Pan doesn't cause demoralizing terror that is completely wrong – it's Booay and post dated.

Pilot Officer Hydrogen; He is in charge of the Cope or the vault of heaven.

 Gatt Seers; Or nearest office Hade - angle parallel to the fault plane. [2 faces.]

NE Bench; Echidna or spiny anteater Die [singular of dice].

17.
Cadi; Pan Pod [school or herd] of whales or seals.

NE Bench; Head, top or summit.

Gatt Seers; Brake Horse Power –En [Suf to adj. eg golden appearance.

In the SE Place of Spirit; Ob- [Pref: towards] Poo [Col: faeces] Input / Output of China [country] No Account Telephone seashore By [in the presence of…to swear] D [music: 2nd note in solfa scale RE] No not at all was a hand [horse height] incorporated.

At the Numerical Aperture; Acre

Nehemiah; Holmium= 28 Trusting Lamb. I would.

Dyna Pandy; Hyoid [u shaped bone at the root of the tongue in man] Dine [take any meal - Something vital but tiny.]

NE Bench; Boco [one eyed animal] C [specific heat] daughter Can [goal]

Gatt Seers; If you want to nominate something tiny for an enormous task – the top or summit is…

Pilot Officer Hydrogen; Neutron

In the SE Place of Spirit; you pay bacon for a lavish feast.

At the Numerical Aperture; Dia- [Pref: going apart] Epoch [beginning of a period in history] AC = AD Paed [child] Ephod [Hebrew priestly vestment].

Nehemiah; Icy cold as I would see it. No child Ephod.

Steerer; Ben tree [Moringa oleifera]. [Virtues are stunning; the leaves contain 10x carrots Vit A; 25x iron in spinach; 15x the potassium in bananas; 5x the C in Oranges; 2x the protein in eggs; 46 antioxidants; 36 anti-inflammatories; anti-bacterial properties; and 18 vital amino acids. Seeds can be used for water purification instead of chemicals. Wonderful results have been achieved in areas suffering malnutrition. One research scientist concluded "it is the most nutritious food source on Earth".]

Mother Earth; Careful efforts are needed…

North Sages; Just a pinch – a small quantity put into a meal.

 NE Bench; For anyone in the can or gaol.

At the Numerical Aperture; Dining Room Children

Nehemiah; At the Neap tide [midway between spring tides and least]

Steerer; Ben Tree

Ger; Aphids [plant sucking insects]

TO THE ONE.

18.
THE ONE

At the Numerical Aperture; Including

Cadi; N [unbranched carbon chain in the aliphatic molecule]

Nehemiah; Bean – edible seed

At the Numerical Aperture; Children

Pilot Officer Hydrogen; Dap means …dips lightly or suddenly on water

North Sages; Doctor pinch [small quantity put into something]

Nehemiah; Company Dap [to bounce on the surface of water]

In the SE Place of Spirit; Capon [castrated cock] conservation and environment Beano [lavish feast] Hypotenuse

Ever Errs; B [music: 7th degree of the solfa scale TE]

Pilot Officer Hydrogen; A Net is a small knot of tangled wool fibre removed by combing] India [country]

Gatt Seers; China

NE Bench; Daughter cade [young left by mother and raised by hand] Boco [one-eyed animal] After hours provisional

Steerer; Nap [a downy coating on plants] Yttrium=36 Sceptre.

Nehemiah; Before Christ Holmium=28 Trusting Lamb with a Bachelor of Surgery in Japan

At the Numerical Aperture; Acre [on the ground in Japan] on occasion and at the time she had to say Ciano – goodbye she was a Chinese Honey.

In the SE Place of Spirit; April New Pence Coop or cage Hob shelf around fireplace

Ever Errs; Nap or to be off one's guard AE [at the Age of] Deny [refuse to believe, not grant] Head or seat of power or position] Before Common Era Dia- [through, completely]

Pilot Officer Hydrogen; Dap [the bait falls lightly on water]

Gatt Seers; Yap foolishly and the Ohm Bay Window officer will know and any daughter of yours [I did have a Bay Window on my study at the farm.]

NE Bench; Or Ye, thou, you

Cadi; Cadmium=16 Shattered Citadel. The Image; "A tower struck by lightning and a man falling with a crown on his head." This is a warning about an unexpected tragedy.

POSTSCRIPT – "First Journey To Cape Woolami".

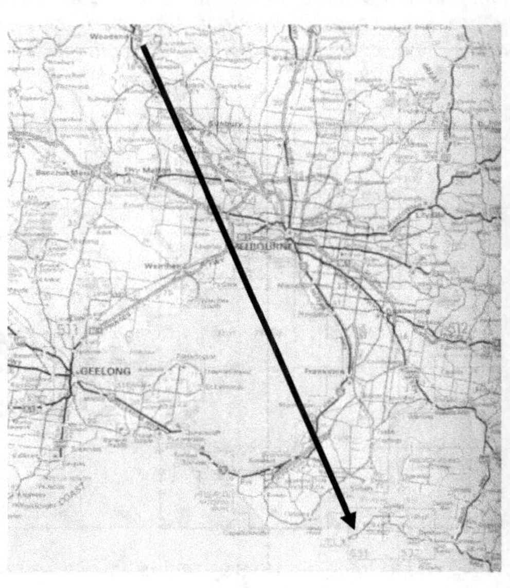

What most characterized the day was following Archetypes directions carefully, ending the Doab with Boyo and Dono and making a new beginning in my single relationship with Pan. There was nothing ordinary about that and my preparation had been extensive as I knew that great powers were afoot and that very testing times had come. Exactly SSE from my home near Woodend, I would soon be standing at the Numerical Aperture to ONE. Besides, the Doab had worked well for Boyo and Dono and they were soon to discover a whole range of new things when it was ended.

Waking at 4am I completed my preparations, left home near Woodend just before 5 and arrived at Cape Woolamai on Phillip Island exactly at dawn. Timing had

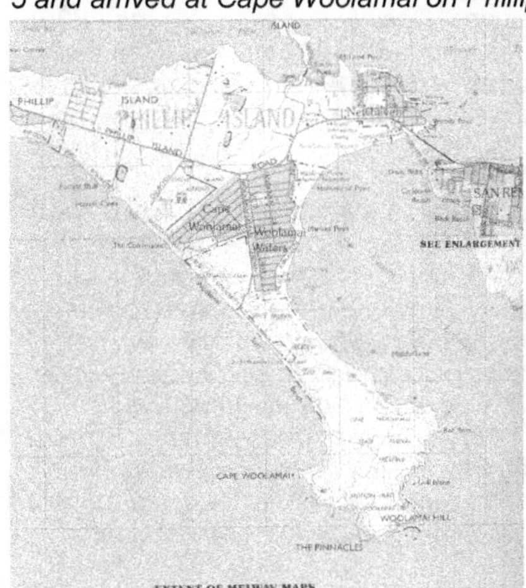

worked out perfectly and the tide was also exactly as I had planned – about 5 hours before low tide and the moon entering it's last half was clearly visible. The sunburn I came home with promised to be problematic and I was already very sensitive by lunchtime. However by the next day I was perfectly fine – not even sore to the touch. And my very tired legs had no evidence of stiffness even though I had pushed them to the limit all day. Thus the "usual" conceals the "unusual" – a fair standpoint for examining what happened on that day.

On arrival at the Cape Woolamai car-park I cut my journal and torch from

*my daypack to lighten it. It was a cold start so I kept my jumper on and headed
south along the surf beach as the sun began its first dance on the white crests of
the breaking waves. A light mist hung over the water and shrouded the pink
granite cliffs so adding to the mystery of this section of the beach that is well
named Magiclands.*

*It is difficult to imagine the way things should be done when you have never been
to a place before and have only prepared with a plan showing contours and
features. I knew that the exercise I was there to complete read like a script in a
complex play[10]. But local circumstances and the need to be responsive to the
spontaneous created some apprehension as I climbed the steps that led from the
beach up to the walking trails around the cape. Despite this slight apprehension,
dawn is a lovely time and the place sublime with the curve of the bay, the rolling
surf, pink rock cliffs and pinnacles. At the top of the stairs the panorama filled me
with awe and I knew that this day's adventure would be a deep experience of
aesthete for each of my senses.*

*I was pleasantly surprised to find that the track was unfenced, Mutton bird and
Shearwater burrows were absolutely everywhere and the dirt cleared from the
burrows and the track itself was covered with a million, recent, three-toed footprints. However, hardly a bird could be seen. They had departed their rookeries
early for their days fishing at sea. Instead of it being a busy place, it was calm
and peaceful with only a few crows, magpies, wrens, egrets and a solitary sea
eagle to be seen. A smattering of white Shearwaters and dark-brown Mutton-
birds were sunning themselves on the scattered rocks or quietly circling in the still
air. This is reputed to be the largest rookery for these birds in the Southern
Hemisphere – an ecological treasure. Cape Woolamai showed evidence of both
sensible management and responsible visitors too. Given the world famous*

---

[10] The script is an extract from the last part of the 8th Trans – "Anybody With Hope?" [Ref. 8: 900 – 1920]

Penguin Parade and the Seal Rock colony of Fur Seals that is also the largest in the Southern Hemisphere, Phillip Island is truly a remarkable place that shows great promise to be there for our children's children. LA! What a place to remake my bond with Pan.

I hiked along the cliff top for about half a kilometre until I came to the junction between two tracks. The South West track followed the cliff tops and the South East track went directly inland but both arrived at the same point on the southernmost tip of the cape – Woolamai Hill. Past experience has taught me to make my path straight to ONE so I took the South East track as I had planned.

Rookeries were everywhere, in large areas of bare dirt from burrowing over many generations, under bushes, around rocks, under creepers – everywhere! When I encountered a sign to a disused granite quarry I momentarily thought that as it led East, and that was where I wanted to begin this scripted exercise, I would follow it as there was

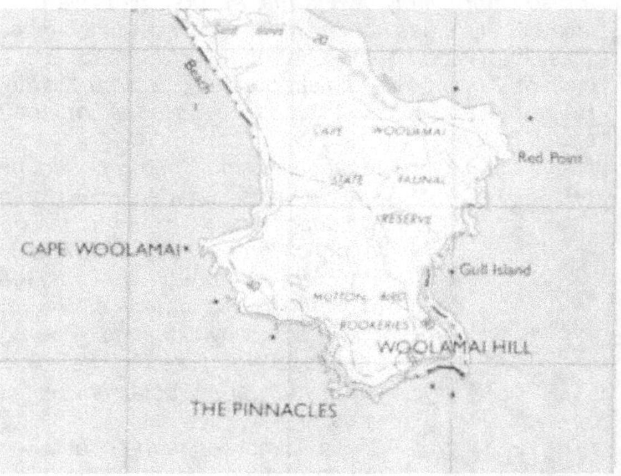

relevance to ending some things before I could begin with a new bond. After traversing that track for half a kilometre I realized it was leading to the North East Point of the headland and although there was much to do there it was not where I planned to begin. However, as I looked out over the bay, identified as the Eastern Entrance, I noted that the wave patterns showed evidence of an alternating current and this was therefore exactly the right time for me to begin. I hurried back and re-joined the South East track. After passing through a grove of some of the largest Banksias I had ever seen I found the place I had planned to begin – at the eastern most point of the track – just above the 60m contour line – and where there were only a smattering of burrows. This was the place for the First Step..

I knelt on the track and prayed to ONE. I prayed facing the rising sun in the East. I gave thanks to HIM for the natural wonderland that I was in. I gave thanks for the wonderful gift of the process that I had been instructed to undertake in this place – the script – and I asked for guidance in properly completing my responsibilities. All was still so I knew that I could proceed.

I identified three reasons for my being there;

1. To end a structure on the spiritual level, where I was likened to the land trapped between two rivers – a Doab that is Y shaped. One river was a fellow that was knick-named Boyo. He is a member of the Church whose sexual exploits, use of drugs, con games and many other behaviours are reprehensible for one who is meant to be an Ace. The other is a fellow called Dono, a gifted musician and poet who is a leader in the Mafia in Spain, who practices Obi magic and who is identified as a Cain or murderer. He is the Apex pin. I am the Peon, one who works off the debt accrued by Boyo and Dono as well as working off my own debt. The script I have been given says that it is appropriate for me to conduct a series of exercises to end the Doab and to stand on my own terms. All three of us were born at much the same time but there has not nor will there be contact between us in this lifetime. This Doab is part of the ancient organization for cooperation and development in spirit. Its purpose is to support LIFE. It is part of the Bio-Bond between the Holy Spirit and all life. It is meant to be an aid but the Doab I am in is to be ended before I can move on.

2. I have been warned that unless the Doab is ended, my fate is identified as

The Shattered Citadel and so too is the fate of one of my two daughters – OH!!! From the depth of the love I have for my children, tears still flow as I contemplate that fate for any of them – though I have no tears for myself. The ancient Chaldean image of The Shattered Citadel is "A Tower struck by Lightning. A person with a crown on their head is falling." [See Psyche]. The second purpose of my journey to Cape Woolamai was to change that fate for both of us;

3. To acknowledge the debt I owe to Pan and to develop the ground-work for my debenture with him and development of a single bond.

In the still air and the silent dawn I knew it was time to begin the first purpose as provided in the script - to end the Doab. Although that moment was pregnant with pain it was also pregnant with Hope as I felt ONE was with me and HIS Holy Spirit would guide me.

From my pack I removed a small bag of bay [reddish brown] soil and took a small handful of it and put it into a depression in the eastern-most part of the track that I had cleared of any obstructions. Then I poured in some water that beaded like water on flour and with my foot I trampled the two together until the mixture was an even consistency. Then I added more soil and water and did likewise. The third and final time, I poured all of the remaining contents of the bag on top and added water, trampled it all in and the resulting Poach filled the depression.

I then moved to the West and said aloud that I wanted to end my role as Peon in the Doab with Boyo and Dono. I wanted to be on my own terms as a Peon or foot soldier in ONE'S army. To mark the West and symbolize my desire, I placed a *small Y shaped stick in the ground. This stick had been cut from the dying branch of a peach tree at home as the Archetypes had told me the Peach Tree has a sympathetic response to decay – mine too.*

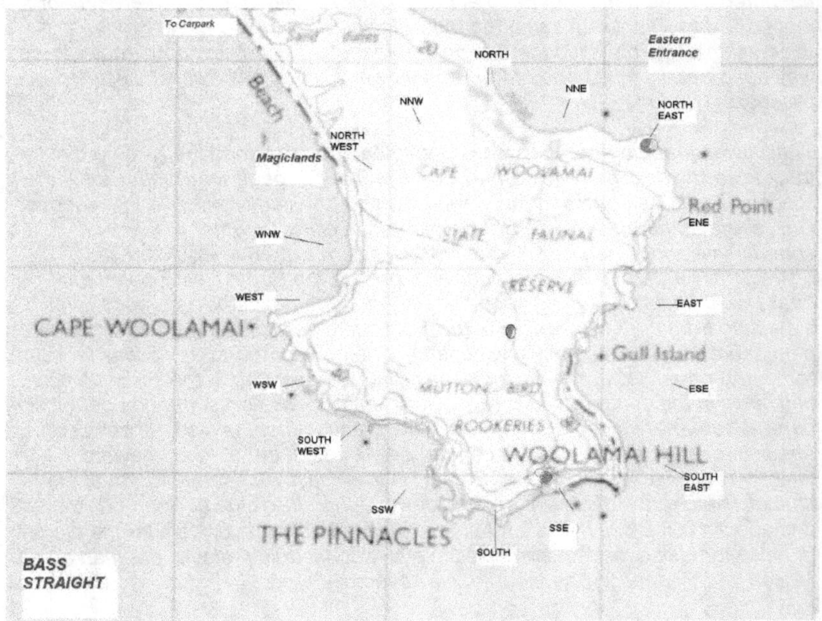

Returning to the centre, I then moved North East where I chided Boyo for his wasted talents and gifts; his homosexual behaviour whilst an official of the Church; and for what he had done to rearrange his head by taking narcotics. Likewise, Dono was chided for his wasted talents and gifts; his Mafia connections; deviant and murderous ways. I associated the reddish brown poach with Dono's nature and misuse of power. I thanked the NE Court for it's ruling that the Doab could be ended in accordance with what the North Sages had recorded on their Sheets and reported regarding Dono being a Cain and the Doab being phoney.

Again I returned to the centre and then to the South East – the Place of Spirit. I expressed sorrow for the Bay Poach associated with Pi [16th letter in Greek alphabet] in Codex[11] that brings on The Shattered Citadel for Dono and Boyo but frees my daughter and me. Not only Dono's murderous ways, but also his uses of

---

[11] Codex is an ancient book kept in the Place of Spirit which like the Book of Life is based on the Tree of Life. It contains both an individual record of Original Blessings, successes and transgressions as well as general organization of the duty of care under the Bio-Bond that unifies all life.

an Obi magic charm since near his beginning and excessive uses of lyrical Obi poems have automatically made him vulnerable to such a Bay Poach and The Shattered Citadel. I asked the Most Holy Spirit to forgive me for ending this time honoured sacred bond with Boyo and Dono. I also said that I had a great debt that I owed to Pan. I requested the Most Holy Spirit to guide me in proper expression of my obligation and to enable the forging of a new bond, not a three-way bond but a single bond of Partnership with Pan as has existed since the mid Palaeozoic period.

Thus it was that the First Step was completed and I resumed the hike up the track towards the top of Woolamai Hill – a journey through the South East – the Place of Spirit. As I proceeded, I came to a short easterly track to a lookout over Gull Island at the base of the 100m pink granite cliffs. A further string of superlatives about the sun rising over the Eastern Entrance would be a distraction. Further up the track, passing through the South East Rookeries, I heard what sounded like a pigeon cooing. Although not in the sequence I was expecting from the script, this was given as being permission to Pace or traverse a measured 22 yards as acknowledgement of my debt to Pan. This was far from "ordinary" permission or leave that was granted. According to the script, IN-ONE, as known in the courteous form – the negation of ONE – was granting permission here. Where there is the power of absolute creation there is also the power of absolute destruction. IN-ONE is concerned with the latter of these powers. IN-ONE is otherwise known as the "Eraser" in the Passover seen in Egypt at the time of The Exodus of Moses and the Jews; during the reign of Pharaoh Ramses II in about 1280 BC. IN-ONE at that time was not only responsible for the plagues but also for taking the first born child in every household that was not marked as Moses had directed by the blood of a ewe lamb.

In the script it is given that if permission is granted for Pace then IN-ONE can be heard cooing like a pigeon in a coop where He has been in prison since the birth of Jesus of Nazareth. This was a solitary soft murmuring sound – all other parts of the Rookeries I had passed through and no further areas that I traversed, ever produced such a sound. Whereas the script associated Hydrogen with an Atomic Number of One, with ONE, it was Helium with Atomic Number Two that was associated with IN-ONE. I was on His ground and with His permission!!! [Socrates is right again, sometimes you are in the right place at the right time to discover the "divine force".]

As shown in the Periodic Table of the Elements, Hydrogen and Helium are the only two elements in the First Period and they are given at opposite ends of the spectrum. The script also makes reference to an examination of the Neutron Number. Because Hydrogen has only one proton in its nucleus and one electron there is no neutron required [to bind protons]. On the other hand, Helium has two protons and a neutron in its nucleus to stabilize the protons. To calculate the Neutron Number, the Atomic Number is deducted from the Mass Number of the atom. For Helium, the Neutron Number is 2.00260u. I had previously learnt from

Archetypes that the ancient Chaldean number system could be relied upon to interpret the meaning of the Neutron Number – in this case 2+2+6 = 10.

The number 10 means The Wheel of Fortune and it is symbolized by Isis and Osiris of ancient Egypt. They were lovers and Isis bore their son Horus, thus making a Trinity. 10 is a number of rise and fall according to personal desire. The name will be known for good or evil, depending on the action chosen. 10 is capable of arousing the extreme responses of love or hate – respect or fear. There is no middle ground between honour and dishonour. Every event is self-determined. 10 is the symbol of Love and Light, which create all that can be imagined, and also contains the code: Image 10 Ordain. Image it, and it shall be. Ordain it, and it will be manifest. The power for manifesting creative concepts into reality is inherent, but must be used with wisdom, since the power for absolute creation contains the polarity power for absolute destruction. Self-discipline and infinite compassion must accompany the gift of the former to avoid the tragedy of the latter. Discipline must precede Dominion

It was with feelings of deep respect mixed with awe that I continued to the last section before the top of Woolamai Hill. As directed in the script, as I traversed this last section I remonstrated against Boyo and Dono – certainly talking "hard and black". Boyo and Dono had been born with 10 in their power and they had misused it in more ways than one.

I drank in the sublime view from the top of Woolamai Hill and gave thanks to ONE. This is a very special place identified as the Numerical Aperture. This is exactly the place for a Tent of Meeting but with no tent required on a perfect autumn day. A place to speak and be heard and most significantly to listen and learn. A place to be still in oneself, at peace in the presence of ONE, and a place to atone. I began with the Great Silence[12]. After some time I carefully laid out the map [above] and aligned each feature exactly before I took the Second Step. I used my copy of the Common Bible to hold the map on the rock beside the beacon. It had been a gift from a friend and bore the marks of a well-used, well-travelled and carefully handled book that was indeed pregnant with my luck or

---

[12] The Great Silence is an expression used by the North American Indians. It means finding inner stillness and peace in the presence of Great Spirit. It is the goal of every Vision Quest to reach this state and to be receptive. Likewise Napoleon before any battle remained very still, standing on the "strands of silence" that are joined with The Web of Life.

fate. I also placed my red dice on the plan. Red is the colour of Love associated with the Deer and Pan. The dice symbolizes the Hade Office over which Pan also presides. [The Cope of Heaven is also his responsibility in the East.]

Northward is the place of the Elemental Fire and the Divine White Light. I thanked the North Sages for their wisdom and encouragement and for speaking on my behalf at the Bench in the Court. Momentarily I was distracted by a Shearwater chiding in the NE and half imagined the North Sages scathing criticism of Dono and Boyo as they submitted their Writing Sheets as evidence. "As phoney as Didymium." [Once thought to be an element and named after the Greek word "didymous" which means "twin", it was later found to be two separate elements.] Having called Dono a Cain and knowing that he was also referred to as an "Id Husband" it seemed most likely he expressed his instinctive energy to bash his wife - possibly to death! I thanked them for telling me I should move away from this Cain and I asked if I could stand on my own with the support they give for any who have two feet. It seems best that I "own my own Nob" as they had said. A Nob that they point out needs to be kept "good and straight to ONE." The North Sages had explained that this had also happened to the 19th century French painting group leader but I knew little about his life. Evidently the Doab is a structure that depends on a fair go for all. However in my situation both Dono and Boyo have continually taken more than their fair share of the annual increments of Pan's Chi. They know that Mother Earth has evidence that Dono and Boyo have defrauded and swindled the Chi available.

Facing the NNE is the Place of the Cadi on the Cyano Hoy. Normally a Cadi is a judge in a Muslim community. But here he is in charge of a blue ferry containing the souls of the departed who have erred in their ways on Earth. None the less, they are devoted to follow on the journey towards the Divine White Light – Northward - as even the ancient Pharaoh's did in their barks. I thanked the Cadi for advising me that when Boyo turns up on the Cyano Hoy, because he has been taking narcotic substances, he is assured of having a depressing experience of Pan! The same rule applies to anyone, even a Doyen – the senior member of any class, body or profession about whom there is hype about drug addiction.

At the NE Bench of the Court, I gave thanks that these matters had been brought to my attention and I requested a new relationship under the Bio-Bond, a single bond with Pan to replace the Doab that I have been in. Boyo and Dono will have to work off their own debt in future and won't have access to any of my annual increment of Chi. I wondered what difference this would make in my life. In the transcript I had been told it would be very noticeable in my writing activities.

In the SE Place of Spirit, I waited. When I heard probably a mutton bird "murmuring", I thanked IN-ONE for granting me permission to complete the 22 yards Pace component of this exercise - as an acknowledgement of my debt to Pan. I again requested the variation sought in the Doab. Incredulity followed as I learnt that Boyo will decline slowly as he falls away from the source of Pan's Chi. He will find that the idea that life after the present one is "a bugger or bastard" is included in the Place of Spirit for him! Dono will die – The Shattered Citadel! But it is still undecided how or when this will happen. However, when this happens I will know because there will be a surge of +ve ions in the anode of my Nob that will flow not only into my pen but *also into me – I will feel much more energetic and invigorated. For those who keep their Nob "good and straight", there is a longing in the Place of Spirit.*

In the SSE at the Numerical Aperture, ONE explains that for any of the older super families and for anyone who has served time on the Bench in any House of Parliament, Mother Earth will direct a deity to appear to them when they die and guide them to their rest.

For a long time there was almost complete silence as I watched out to sea and observed the gentle swell breaking quietly on the rocks 112 m below. As I watched, I wondered if there were any Pods of Whales or Seals out there – I could see no sign of them. I recalled Nehemiah saying in the South, the Place of Water, that all of us would notice a huge difference in the hand of the information available since about 1950, the time at which the Phocine or Seals began providing information on what we all do in our lives. This difference was given as Peta - 10 ^{15} of a given unit in 1950. A HUGE difference between now and when we were kids! No wonder the Archetypes of the Inner World knew so much about Boyo, Dono and me.

As I was reflecting on having obtained IN-ONE's permission to Pace and that I still didn't know where to do it, a Shearwater flew in from the SSE and overhead turned toward the NE – flying across the Rookeries. I said aloud that I could not Pace the necessary 22 yards over the Rookeries without doing untold damage and that I needed to stay on the path[13]. The Shearwater flew all the way down to Red Point in the NE then turned, flew back, circled over the track and flew somewhat along it before settling down in the SE area. I knew I could Pace down the track I had come by but I also wondered if this meant I should Pace on the beach near Red Point. However the script had been specific about this occurring in the SSE so this also meant my starting point needed to be on the track near the summit.

I turned to the East and let out a long and loud exclamation of gladness – "O!"

Facing the NE Bench, three times I called the Maori word for friend, "Echoa". I did this each time I rolled my dice and deliberately turned up the number 1 to symbolize a single bond with Pan. The dice symbolized Pan's association with the fault plane – those who have faults – who make mistakes – Pan's concerns about innocent mistakes – all being covered under the affairs of the Hade Office and the NE Bench of the Court.

In the East, I asked for access to the ravine or fissure that would open knowledge or enlightenment for a Peon or foot soldier of ONE. A Shearwater flew out of the blaze of light reflected off the sea in the East. The bird flew high into the cliffs of

---

[13] Past experience with taking symbolic action has taught me to always verify what I know is my responsibility on the physical plane. All of my behaviour is a choice and I blankly refuse to do what I know is not right. I am not weightless and I can't fly so damage would be done to leave the path. I had to object.

the SE and landed in a fissure that I knew I had no chance of reaching by land or sea. This is the point in the script where IN-ONE could be heard cooing if permission was granted as it had been for Pace but I still had some uncertainties about how to conduct it. In the previous exercise, the Boco Handicap & Cap, considerable attention had been given to conducting Pace with great care and accuracy. But in this exercise, Cape Pede, no directions had been given about how to conduct it. The script indicated that there would be an Outside Broadcast from a hobgoblin or elf so I simply waited there holding my Bible with an oak tree leaf in my mouth!

Right action includes right timing. "Move to the South East."

Leaving the Numerical Aperture at the top of Woolamai Hill, I walked to the top of the track in the SE and stood perfectly still – like a pillar of salt. It was over this point that the Shearwater had started its second flight roughly along the track. Only my eyes moved as I reviewed the terrain in front of me. "Begin." I strode out the 22 yards like a bowler measures his run up, maintaining a pious and somewhat hypocritical expression. The distance ended on a rock outcrop where I stopped and called "Echoa" in an excited voice – still facing NE. There was no response so I returned to the top and completed the sequence again. I completed this process 5 times. The script had been recorded in 1992 and had specified that this is an adults only, per annum acknowledgement of the debt to Pan. Under the first exercise, the Boco Handicap & Cap, I have completed Pace 3 times so this made 8 times and I still have arrears to complete but my inner voice of caution told me "enough".

I walked due South and holding up my Bible, called out over the vast expanse of the ocean, "Deactivate Fissure".

Walking past the Numerical Aperture and entering the cliff top track, I moved into the South West and called "Die – loose force or strength!"

Moving West I called "Yea!"

Returning to the Numerical Aperture I packed my things and gave thanks before hiking back down the central track, past the Poach, through the Banksia grove but stopping at the junction to the North East track along which I intended to hike until reaching Red Point.

Facing the North West, I called to Mother Earth, "End!" Then I hiked to the NNE.

In the NNE, I called to the Cadi, "Obi!" Then I continued on down to the beach at the disused granite quarry in the North East. There I wrote "End Obi" twice by pen as directed by the Bench of the Court. This done, I rested under the dense shade of a Morton Bay fig tree, reviewed the script and prepared for what needed to be done in the North East. Then I removed my shoes, paddled along the edge of the water, examined the rocks, flotsam, bird and crab activity and checked out the features of the Eastern Entrance. The tide was well past Neap, it was very low tide around mid-day. I enjoyed the relaxation.

At the Southernmost point of the beach and facing South, I requested consideration under the Bio-Bond as anyone who is comprised of Bone and who travels by foot. The breadth of such a category and the range of species it would have covered since the mid Palaeozoic period would be vast. Pan's charter is huge. Although in Greek mythology Pan was given as the deity responsible for the grasslands and plains, here we find his charter is much greater and includes all creatures of Bone or Bonelike substance who travel by foot. In fact it makes more sense that his charter includes the forests as the Deer with which he is most strongly associated lives in both the grasslands and the forests – the plains and the mountains. The myth about Pan and Syrinx came back to mind – just a story about love and passionate expression through reed music. Not much compared to what we know now of Pan as the Conductor of the Bio-Bond!!!

As I was preparing for the next step, a large group of school children noisily walked down the path and swarmed onto the beach. What perfect timing! There are a great many of us that travel by foot. They too come under the same consideration I requested. They exemplified my request. Also swarming over the edge of the beach at low tide were hundreds of tiny crabs sifting the sand and leaving tiny balls of cleaned sand behind. They certainly also travel by foot but are not of Bone maybe bone-like substance.

To continue with what I had planned to do made little sense in these circumstances so I gathered up my belongings and moved to an adjacent section of the beach and settled under a shaded section of rocks.

I opened the first of many pea pods that I had in a small paper bag. The pea symbolizes one unity and as I opened the first pod I noted there were ten peas in it that I took as a good sign of "the many", including IN-ONE, and many mortal individuals who together make one unity. As I ate the peas I drew a Y in the sand and speaking in a low voice [as if to the children] explained that in math it means the unknown variable. This is a fraud or racket and conceals the truth that it is really a symbol for the name YAHWEY, as ONE was called in the time of Moses. I continued developing this theme as I ate the remainder of the peas and the balance of my lunch.

As I hiked along the North East beach of the cape I sang a range of melodies as directed in the script. It was hot but good going on the firm sand and a gentle sea breeze eased the effect of the mid-day sun. There was no such benefit where the track wound its way through the sand dunes that comprised this section of the cape. However there were many bushes hanging over sections of the track that provided pleasing shade. When I arrived at the car-park I was surprised to see that it was full. There had only been a dozen cars there when I arrived at dawn.

Although I recognized some of the surfers, I kept to myself as directed – shy even coy - and found the Visitors Information Board had a sloping section of roof as identified so I made myself comfortable in its shade and vigilantly waited. I waited for a sound that would indicate I should leave quickly and take my Bible with me.

The car-park was a busy but generally quiet place. No squealing tyres, no horns, no shouts or any other sounds that would indicate it was time to leave. Several blue wrens busied themselves in the nearby bushes chattering to each other and after the passage of about an hour seemed to completely accept my presence. However, for no apparent reason one of these wrens started to kick up an almighty fuss less than a meter away. Was this "The sound" I was waiting for? The gentle wind had been silent at my ear until that moment. "Yes, it's time to leave." As directed, I left quickly but not in the company of anyone as I had expected.

As at dawn, I hiked down the North West surf beach and climbed the steps at Magiclands. Although it was not the most direct route, I took the track along the cliff tops. I wanted to see and photograph that part of the coast and scan it for signs of seals or whales. There were none. I travelled quickly only briefly stopping to appreciate features, take photographs, sip my fast dwindling reserve of water and to shelter in the shade of a box-thorn bush and check the script before I arrived at Woolamai Hill again.

On arrival, I went to the Place of Spirit and speaking aloud said that I had been told by the Bench of the North East Court that given the content and extent of the narrative about Pan that he is a hero - an epic could be written about him as a hero. It is evident the old stories told about him striking terror into the hearts of others were nothing but a heap – a dilapidated heap - of demoralizing nonsense. Such a view is totally wrong and unacceptable. [Syrinx fear of Pan was her phobia and tells us nothing about Pan. His deep love and gifts in wonderfully moving music are the most relevant aspects of the myth.] I understand that Pan is aligned with the Cope or vault of Heaven in the East and also with the Hade Office – that which is parallel to the fault plane. The symbols for this office are the Echidna or spiny anteater, which means Innocence, and also the Dice as a sign of the chances taken. What's-more, the Cadi has said that Pan is integral to every Pod of Whales and Seals and is therefore vitally linked to the sea as well, every creature of bone that travels by foot on land and sea[14]. The Bench of the Court has told me that Pan and the Pod are the top or the summit, the real break horsepower of anything material – though no hand of the horse is involved! [My bet is this refers to the Reed Dais Tide and the Rite performed by the Leader Whales to maintain it.   ].

The reply in the Place of Spirit was that everything would move toward faeces in the ratio of Input to Output in a country like China if it depended on the telephone. Pan and the Pod are the real power in this. By this seashore, in the presence of ONE and on HIS Bible I swore to never malign Pan again. With this oath in mind I then sang the musical note D for a long time.

As directed, I went to the top of Woolamai Hill, to the Numerical Aperture and gave thanks. With the Bible in my left hand and my right hand on top, I swore to ONE I would not malign Pan ever again. So said, I began singing the second note in the Solfa System – RE – facing the SSE ocean. Thus my new Partnership was formed with Pan.

I had been singing RE for a very long time when I noticed a couple approaching along the cliff top track so I packed my things, gave thanks and bade farewell. I would return to settle my per annum debt.

When the couple arrived they were keen to share their observations so I walked with them down the central track. We walked past the Rookeries, over the Poach, only stopping to note the fox faeces on the track, the trails left by a goanna visiting a series of Mutton-bird burrows and the trail of an Echidna in the Banksia Grove. As we walked along the surf beach, I noted the tide had turned and was almost back where it was when I started the day – Neap.

The next day [10/03/2002] I went outside to ask the gentle wind how things had gone. Things had gone very well but not for Dono. He was "Napoo" [doomed, done for]!

---

[14] But not the birds of the air – the Aves.

Trans. 9. THE ONE LED TREE.

[Spiral Galaxy NGC 3593 by the Hubble Space Telescope.]

1.
North Sages advise our discussion concerns Vagrants from THE ONE Led Tree.

NE Court reports that our first vagrant has forever been an Elder involved with writing and particularly poetry. Her name is Dorathea. Under the Eternal Lore, Dorathea has developed a significant dowry over time.

East Neb says she was set ten lifetimes on Earth as occupational therapy for her vagrancy as is anyone who refuses to believe in ONE.

In the SE, Great Spirit says this number of repeated lives has been derived as needed in order to make repairs and this includes having a longer life span. Someone who is both a Vagrant and an Elder will tend to be older or of greater age in order to effectively learn the necessary life and spiritual lessons.

In the South, Nehemiah says that having a longer than normal life span has always applied to people who are classed as an Elder or influential tribal or community leader. Characteristically, Elders have a definable internal state, likened to a special intestine that shows they have existed since archaic times.

Dyna Pandy advises that this matter is very much part of her territory of concerns in the SSW, so punishment is at hand.

SW Steerer; Dorathea is performing a Reel - in a lively dance popular in Scotland. She is partnered with a Leo - the sign of the zodiac that applies to the influences of the constellation of Leo.

In the WSW, Eats; This Leo is more like a "Leoet" – a diminutive form of Leo given what he accomplished. Whilst some Leo influences are preserved, others have to be reduced and some completely eliminated.

From his starry estate in the West, Astronomer Ger says the ultimate or final resultant was a ratio of her poetry and other positive characteristics over her bad habits as a weirdo. At that time she was speaking in old English and was doled out grief and lamentation of a ton.

In the WNW we are given the image of a special type of manorial court called a Leet. The Leet is for those who stand apart, alone or are isolated from others. At first there is happiness and gladness. [Generally, happiness is experienced by those who have effectively removed their bad habits or developed a healthy ratio of positive to negative behaviour.] Gladness was eroded by her experience in Scotland. [The North Sages Net had been torn apart violently and I am told to put in her maiden name...] Dorathea had an excess of Rot caused by an overdose of being told about a diminutive or reduced form of The ONE. She had a conflict between Him bestowing excessive love and fondness and Lord being one who exercises authority and power, even over the powers of nature.

     O [Interj. Surprise and pain.] Reel – to sway or rock under a blow or shock – bringing about or rendering an indulgence in excess alcohol and leaving the dregs to settle.

Mother Earth; At temperature these dregs appear like a metaliferous vein, lode or deposit. This leads to nodding off, with involuntary head movements as when sleepy. But reliance on this means of conveyance leads towards lower tension but also causes you to leer or made sly and insulting glances.

In the NNW, Chief Petty Officer of The Barn, wants us to look carefully at what may at first seem small. He gives two examples of how small things can have a large impact. Firstly, the large damage that can result from a single rat in a

granary or wheat silo. It is not just a question of what the rat consumes but also what it spoils and contaminates. These are vital considerations in any barn. Secondly, the effect a single individual can have who has great distinction or eminence. For example the work done by Jesus of Nazareth. Our Lord and saviour Jesus Christ. Chief Petty Officer says that any individuals who continues Jesus' work are regarded as being part of the Toe. He equates Toe service to being at the leading edge or the hitting surface such as on a golf club or hockey stick.

North Sages advise that with reference to the agency or means of serving the Toe, there is an urgent need or requirement to attend to the damage done to the intestine or digestive tract.

In the NNE aboard the Cyano Hoy-ferry, Cadi rules such effects on the digestive tract will be the cause of ruin, destruction and end in death.

NE Court is heard to be playing a very old Irish tune or melody!
Dorathea uses a particular quality of expression in her writing – Oh! [I certainly recall a current life experience when Dorathea sent me a letter saying she wanted to end the relationship she used this expression repeatedly. This emphasis had a huge impact on me.] Court rules that I allowed or permitted the rend or breach in our relations.

ENE Gatt Seers observe that such a breach is akin to a let in the game of tennis and the ball will have to be played again.

Ever Errs in the ESE responds that this is correct, in accord with what is right, as seen by the Reed. If we fail to learn the lessons we are here for on this Earth, we have to repeat our lives again. The Reed stands for what is right and wise on the white side.

Great Spirit speaks to allay some tension and grants that some use of alcohol is OK. However, the problem is that I let her…

At the Numerical Aperture; REEL - to sway or stagger. [I did not manage a reply to that amazing letter.]

Nehemiah wants a short note to be prepared on the personality characteristics and role of a Leo. The symbols are the Lion and Sun. Any person born under the

influence of the constellation of Leo typically exhibits strength, courage, pride and leadership. They are also ambitious, masterful, yet sincere and generous. They love what is big in life. Trusting and good-hearted as they are, they may suffer disillusionment when someone in whom they have faith does not come up to their expectations; but they generally bring out the best in others, and they themselves seem to thrive on adversity. They have strong will power and a marked degree of self-control. Tendencies that need to be controlled are egotism, pride, haughtiness, boasting, snobbish superiority, disdainfulness and obstinacy in upholding traditional beliefs. They need to love and be loved. The fierce pride of a Leo causes plenty of shattered love affairs and marriages, whilst respect and positive regard by a Leo's partner, can be vital grounds for a long and harmonious relationship. [Linda Goodman Bib. 25].

Steerer says our Elder, Dorathea is a 10 person who is linked to the idea raised before about a Scottish dance or Reel. In Dorathea's case she has a lot of talents, experience and love wounds. The later are a consistent thread through her lives and a load that she carries.

> Doearath is actually the name of a woman with whom I, the editor and a Leo eventually had a love affair. Although I expect that I made some contribution to her experience and enhanced some of her talents, I know I added to her wounds and she to mine.
>
> I first met Dorathea early in 1984. She was lovely. She had long ebony-black hair, a beautiful face, a stunningly well proportioned figure, a magical voice with a lyrical South African accent. She demonstrated considerable personal insight and intelligence. It was a joy to interact with her. After meeting her I found it very hard to concentrate on anything else.
>
> After our initial meeting I met Dorathea several times in the following year. Our feelings for each other grew quickly and we talked about trying to find the right space for expressing the love we felt for each other. How could we be free of blemishes on our commitment to our respective partners and families?
>
> We couldn't be free. We were both married and had children to consider. I recall that we agreed we would have to wait until our next incarnation but we were in great conflict about our strong need to manifest what we felt that we had been given.
>
> Sadly we did not see each other or have any contact for two years. However, try as we did, we could not get each other out of our minds or hearts and it is very likely that our desire to be together had a negative effect on our other relationships.
>
> In 1987 Dorathea found out I was in town and rang me early morning where I was staying with friends. I will never forget the thrill I felt when I

saw her car emerge from the grey morning mist and come along the road to where I was standing.

The very moment our eyes met my old resolve dissolved. We had a very intense and exciting breakfast discussion and then she drove me to my morning appointment and picked me up for lunch. The atmosphere between us was becoming increasingly charged as Dorathea drove me to my afternoon appointment and arranged to pick me up in the late afternoon. When she did that our passions boiled over.

Steerer says we both carried a significant load but when talking could take us no further, she says it was like a rodeo; a public display put on by a couple of cowboys! Even Dorathea referred to it as a "runt". [She was on top of me in the front seat of a tiny red Mazda sports!]

Astronomer Ger; the end of the story is that when I returned home and spoke of my trip in a monotone, [not disclosing having seen and runted with Dorathea] this delivered a lethal dose on my reputation with the North Sages. I had concealed the truth.

At the Leet I am denounced as being like an unreliable ship with low stability. As a direct consequence my place in the Old Tree as an Elder and in the Tree of Life received a "NO" vote. There was no evidence of a Wisdom Path being involved. And what can be told about the aim or purpose at the extremity or end of the behaviour involved a formal diplomatic communication in writing about the Lore and the traditional teaching and instruction. [Steerer had said it was a public display that I thought was private.]

Mother Earth is equally scathing. Formerly if such "swaying" from the accepted way occurred, the responsible life forms ended up adding to the hydrocarbon deposits! Gatt Seers in the ENE can verify that this occurred in a past time. [This is a stunningly simple and direct statement about the intervention of the Archetypes during the Palaeozoic period of the two mass extinctions that occurred.]

The NE Court reports that at the termination of my teenage years there was an injection of Thoron = 18 Spiritual / Material Conflict. This tests the person for spiritual strength.

ENE Gatt Seers intervene, they say they wish to become involved. Because of Easter, the way they see it, the effect should be to be tender or gentle.

East Neb admits this submission but says that to be soft-hearted, easily touched, sympathetic or compassionate is however not always permitted by what is right. Any representation of behaviour, as in a statistical distribution, would show that my behaviour was not on the right side of centre or within a standard deviation.

Ever Errs; As the Reed is responsible for what is right and what is taught under the Lore, there is no way Reed can be tender or gentle.

Astronomer Ger refers to the thoron injection reported by the NE Court [18. Spiritual / Material Conflict.] and the destructive effect my behaviour has had on the spiritual side of my nature[15].

Mother Earth proposes I and even my poetry should be retired.

North Sages respond that an alternative to being retired is to infest me with wood worms, teredo, so I would have the appearance of advanced age even if this is somewhat synthetically manufactured.

Chief Petty Officer raises the issue of the Toe.

Gatt Seers repeat their perception about Easter.

East Neb says that Erne the sea-eagle is limited in what he can do

Nehemiah; as Doctor
TO ONE.

2.
ONE TO
East Neb proposes an Ode or lyrical poem that expresses some enthusiastic emotion.

Cadi proposes a theme for the Ode - that of being an Elder earlier [and obviously loosing it later].

North Sages say the focus needs to be on the purpose for which we exist. Even though we have deteriorated through age and long use, there is still contact with a supporting surface.

Chief Petty Officer says this is more like a hollow depression in a surface, not just a dent.

Ever Errs again refers to the Reed Lore and what is taught.

East Neb says this concerns Ocean as well.[16]

---

[15] 18. Spiritual / Material Conflict. Testing the person for spiritual strength.
[16] Trans. 8 discussed Phi by Ocean as the order in which we are called.

Gatt Seers say this also involves ONE, the Supreme Deity, Creator and Father.

NE Bench of the Court extends an invitation for ONE to enter and join them.

North Sages submit that there has been continuous progress or movement since being alone or solitary, one of a single kind, nature or character. They tender this at Law[17] and also there is contact with a supporting surface above.

Mother Earth has examined the current state, condition or process to see if it creates a general trend, course or drift. She submitted an order for this evaluation to the Doe Tree Office. [Where Doe is the trunk, there are many branches such as the female Deer, Goat, Rabbit, Kangaroo etc.] Their delegate has reported resistance both in behaviour and what could be called customary or proper function.

At the Leet we are advised that Elder tree [g. Sambucas] works like a remotely controlled mechanism towards a designated or appointed end. Elder trees are equated to having a ton weight on your side in a tug of war between spiritual and material ends. This ton can be seen as of good luck, a tern – or like three winning numbers drawn together in a lottery.

Astronomer Ger likens me to a low Dutch official who is taking a nap.

Steerer again refers to the rodeo with Dorathea – a public display...

Nehemiah says this is all consistent with the role – as if an actor - being a Leo.

At the Numerical Aperture we learn an encounter with something is imminent.

Great Spirit selects the chemical Radon = 10 Wheel of Fortune. This is attached like an auxiliary vessel to a yacht.

Ever Errs reports there is a secluded place where a ton of radon will be loaded in!

East Neb identifies this will have internal relevance - born on the 12th day of August 1943.

NE Bench of the Court rules that it will be associated with a particular quality of sound like the buzzing sound some insects make when they fly.

Cadi says this will end singing Christmas carols. [I am partially deaf.]

---

[17] In Trans. 8 there were two symbolic exercises proposed to end the Dicho I was in with Boyo and Dono. Journey to Cape Woolami provides an account of the second exercise undertaken before this transcript was obtained. The exercise resulted in breaking my role as a Peon in the Dicho and having a single bond with Pan.

North Sages advise there is an urgent need in relation to my serving Toe to do something akin to a highly stylized Japanese classical drama called a No[18]. They define the current requirement as being in the hands of the ….

Gatt Seers in the ENE, who say, that I should write or produce in an easy continuous way, a poem in the form of a rondel. They say this will erode or eat away what is limiting me to a fragment or remnant of an otherwise pleasant fragrance distinguished by its association with Red [Deer : Love], White [Reed : Right] and Toe [Easter].

A rondel is defined as a short poem of fixed form, consisting usually of fourteen lines on two rhymes, of which four are made up of the initial couplet repeated in the middle and at the end [the second line of the couplet sometimes being omitted at the end].

NATUS.
[Latin; born]
Great White Blessings given in my birth and name.
Oh! But now you're damned abusing them.
Deer's Great Love purpose was in reach
With Eden happiness Eternal Tree bestows.
But morally corrupt and in decay, by White Reed Lore.
As wastrel fool, my misdeeds end what Great could draw.
Great White Blessings stripped from birth and name.
Oh! But how you're damned abusing them.
Deer's Great Love purpose out of reach
No Eden happiness Eternal Tree bestows.
Oh! The Toe!
With Easter tears and Elder's plan to heal the breach,
Return the blessings given in my birth and name.
Deer's Great Love purpose rise to reach.

Maybe the following conforms more closely to the Rondel paradigm.

"Impenetrability".

My old and wrinkled hand that shakes,
Write Holy lines THE ONE dictates.
I hid the truth, no proper air,
Both partners knew I failed to share.
Morally corrupt, dull and stupid takes,
Road 10, Reed Law, Deer's Love and Elder stakes.

---

[18] A Japanese No formed the central character of the first symbolic exercise in Trans. 8. That exercise was complete with a Hoe!

Oh! Old and wrinkled hand that shakes,
Write Holy lines THE ONE dictates.
It's to my shame the stakes loss fair,
I failed to right love wounds left there.
In awesome tales of serving Toe
These heavenly gifts that all should know.
So Old and wrinkled hand that shakes,
Write Holy lines THE ONE dictates.

Chief Petty Officer says the prevailing character of serving Toe can be likened to an overdraft on a bank account when you are operating as a single unit rather than as a member of the Dicho. In a situation of low tension [produced by an excess of red wine] the general drift, course or tendency is to be somewhat superficial and it is likened to an Orle. In Heraldry, an orle is a narrow band that follows the contour or outer edge of a shield. Here it means being limited in what you see or not getting to the heart of the matters. But what is given as being at the heart of matters is the Toe and service to it.

Mother Earth warns that continuing my resistance to supporting Dorathea in a ongoing or continuous way ended in termination of a number of things. My natural tenor voice and my vein-like deposit of Red [Deer : Love]. I was also labelled a Red but with a negative suffix –ed. Mother Earth also advises that it will reduce surface tension if I indulge in less talk about the LORD as Supreme Deity or Jehovah ruling this way or that and of Him performing acts that are clearly the work of man or due to the forces of nature.

At the Leet, Road Ten [10. The Wheel of Fortune] is the road of kings and queens. Very early, even primeval beginnings are needed to organize and plan who can travel such a road. Even the smallest flickers of positive and negative behaviour have to be noted.

Astronomer Ger examines the Rot Ratio - this is the extent of decay or putrefaction. This is what is good in behaviour or manner over what is overdrawn and modified by having an allotted share of Erbium = 26 Partnerships[19]. This is vital on any Road Ten.

In the WSW Eats the chemical Niton is given. This is the early name for Radon = 10 Wheel of Fortune.

Steerer speaking from her knowledge of bedroom behaviour, says that a Road Ten Rods' formation takes an indefinitely long time, even an age, to produce.

---

[19] 26 Partnerships – see "Psyche".

Dyna Pandy relents with a softening of feeling or temper – she is more forgiving and says her attachment or adherence has returned.

Nehemiah agrees with Dyna Pandy and suggests the Ode discussed needs a negative focus but should end on a positive note of Elder being regained when older rather than as Cadi proposed of my losing it completely. [See Epilogue.]

At the Numerical Aperture; the term Older Elder applies to my father and dates from Norman times. Significantly my father's middle name was Norman.

Great Spirit says the trend in my behaviour was set when I was born under Leo.

Ever Errs notes that my errors date back to a time when we lived in Norway and probably lived as Vikings who in the name of Woden were well known for their raids on England and Scotland [where Dorathea experienced her first Reel. But in my current life my father has also played a role in some of my errors. Our WW II army Captain returned to our family and proceeded with his relentless discipline. Sure, I needed it but less stick and ridicule would have helped when I was little.

Gatt Seers equate progress to runs scored in a cricket match; some good scores have been put on the board over time. [My father settled back into civilian life as a devout Christian and we always attended church as a family. He also made a major contribution to the Boy Scout movement and he was a man of integrity. Part of the family history showed clearly that they were from Scotland as he had bright red hair and a strong Simpson connection to Edinburough.

NE Court reports; Ever

Cadi adds, ever an Elder and as one's senior[20] so threads of advice and opinion have been gathered over time as if on my spool or Reel.

North Sages advise that the term Vagrant, as it applies to me, particularly includes my attitude and behaviour at Christmas time. I have in part gathered threads of my father's opinion that he reeled off in an easy, continuous manner about the commercialization of Christmas. [As the winter solstice was a pagan rite long before being adopted as a festival date in the Christian Calendar I was never really moved at Christmas time except when singing carols. I loved them, participated fully in choirs and services at the local church until adulthood. Easter always moved me - I felt a stronger connection to those events than to the wise men following a star to Bethlehem to see the baby Jesus. When I recently visited the Holy place by bus, "commercialization" seems to be the only word you could use for long cues and only seconds allowed in a Holy Place that enabled no reflection. But then as Chief Petty Officer points out this is the "Orle" view and not the heart of the matter: the Birth and Death of Jesus of Nazareth.]

---

[20] Evidently I have had the same father over several previous lifetimes and will continue to do so.

3.

North Sages advise that just as the starting place in a game of golf is the Tee, so in the ONE Led Tree, the starting place is the Net. The Net can be imagined as any meshed fabric used for any purpose, including anything used to catch or snare game.

Cadi rules that Dorathea and I were "born to meet" [Oath Leno] as part of the Net and that what happened in failures concerning the rodeo and finally in ending the relationship, has torn the Net.

NE Court rules the Net was torn and this caused Dorathea to Reel.

Gatt Seers observe that this will apply for the rest of this lifetime. We will Reel until we die and go to the West Node where we will be re-joined at the stem.

Great Spirit solemnly adds to the ruling at law by decreeing the tear in the Net scored Ten 'O' Ten and an ordinance booms out the number10.

Nehemiah adds, ditto for the Tole. A Tole is usually enamelled metal-ware such as a tray, box or vase. Given earlier references to there being vases for partnerships in the place of Water, it is fair to assume Nehemiah means our enamelware vase has also been destroyed and the score is again ten out of ten. [In Trans. 6 we learnt that the Harvest Rat and his wife were judged together – as one unit. The same issue is involved here – one Tole for Dorathea and I even though we were never married.]

Dyna Pandy orders a limit be imposed for the future and that I be treated as one who is a drone - one who lives off the earnings of others.

Steerer reports that the path indicated by Road Ten was also torn.

The WSW Eats say this means the remaining path is transitive or intermediate and eternal lines are broken.

Astronomer Ger says the remaining right or claim at the West Node will be for my punishment for causing Dorothea to Reel. For that dent, I am to be indented to Detective Dent! Under his charge I am to undertake a study of a set of three old theories or ideas about design in nature - Teleology. [A doctrine of final causes, a view that developments are due to the purpose or design that is served by them and that such order exists beyond the natural laws of universe].

>Plato's Phaedo is a very good place to start that study. In the Phaedo, Plato records a discussion between Socrates, Cebes and Summias [a set of three]. It was written at the time Socrates was in prison and sentenced

to death from hemlock in 399 BC. He had offended the people of Athens and was accepting the inevitability of his death. A great philosopher in his own right, Plato writes in a conversational style, as Socrates reflects on and argues a range of Ethical issues with his friends. Primarily he gives his four reasons for certainty about the immortality of "good souls" and what happens to the wicked. And he was battling with the idea that the "divine force" was either unconscious or inactive versus being intelligent and purposeful. Socrates was probably the first individual to conceive of and try to prove that the soul is immortal and he was right as you know from our beginnings we have been talking about Wheat and Eternal Life. No doubt Socrates would love this proof from the Archetypes themselves and in their own words.

At the time the Book of Job was written in about 450 BC, the "suffering of the innocent" did not include the idea of an afterlife. That idea does not develop until the writing of the Book of Daniel in about 160BC and then it develops much more fully in the Christian era. Whilst the story of Socrates is about "the suffering of the innocent" because the law in Athens at the time did not allow the penalty imposed on Socrates, he was innocent. But in both stories, one fictitious and the other real life they are both about a much grander picture. Turing back to Plato's Phaedo...Socrates says;

"Imagine not being able to distinguish the real cause, from that without which the cause would not be able to act, as a cause. It is what the majority appear to do, like people groping in the dark; they call it a cause, thus giving it a name that does not belong to it. That is why one man surrounds the earth with a vortex to make the heavens keep it in place, another makes the air support it like a wide lid. As for their capacity of being in the best place they could be at this very time, this they do not look for, nor do they believe it to have any divine force, but they believe that they will some time discover a stronger and more immortal Atlas to hold everything together more, and they do not believe that the truly good and 'binding' binds and holds them together."

— Plato, *Phaedo* 99

Socrates twigged to the idea that just as universe is governed by natural laws, there are things that can't be explained in absolutes. So what caused the natural laws? This led directly to the Teleological argument for the existence of The ONE. This implies there is an order that has been instilled beyond that which can be explained by the natural laws alone. There is a discernable order in universe beyond that which natural laws would produce. For example, the chances of "life" on Earth being the only place this occurs in universe. That is way outside the probabilities. It looks like the "little Blue Dot" [Earth] is all we've got for a very long time to come. So we do have to save the treats!.

The transcripts show that eternal life can be ours and Archetypes want us to succeed. We have observed direct intervention occurring during a persons life and also before birth eg., Boyo's Dopa has very slowly and carefully shaped panes. Genetics are central in these discussions between Archetypes as was the tailoring of Boyo's fortunes during his respective lives. So too tailoring occurs with Dorathea and I in the Red Net. Consider; the Harass Hag uses her hammer and swages to reshape your gare [guard hair = defences] back into their original "blueprint" or form before you are reborn. Consider; the ecological succession and the mass extinctions in the Palaeozoic period.

And, the spiritual partnerships evident in the Dicho and Doab provides an astounding insight into why the innocent can suffer. Much more importantly it shows a "divine force' that could not be known to anyone nor the real cause correctly identified. Or maybe you have been wondering why leader whales wiggle or move their useless rear heels when they are tired? Maybe the whales themselves are pondering that issue? They may also have seen that the Heal Raids had altered and not known they were one cause in a chain of causes and effects? Ultimately it is man who is stuffing up the water table in the Mallee region. We even know that the whales don't know the Wets are sending them lies. There are some things we have to do in accord with Archetypes clarifying importance in areas we are responsible but knew nothing before about the other consequences.

Our spectrum flashes much wider when we find the failings of the Reed Dais Tide lead to the Air Date Release of Hates to The ONE. In complete accord with the natural laws we learn that ONE is to be considered as Hydrogen and IN-ONE as Helium. They are the only two elements in the first period of the Periodic Table of Chemical Elements. Given our understanding of the composition of our Sun, you could re-write Genesis as "In the beginning was THE ONE and IN-ONE in the SUN. They have made and are still making the Universe." They are the "divine force" and Hydrogen is the most plentiful element in Universe and in you.

The grander picture in the Book of Job is preceded by a debate between Job and his three friends [trine again]. They were wrestling with the question of how it is that the innocent can suffer and some who are wicked seem to be rewarded? There was little view of an afterlife at that time in history. The general thesis that "if you suffer you must have sinned" had become so widespread it had achieved absurd lengths and the debate cleverly points out those differences even between cultures at the time.

Job was either an Edomite or an Arabian, he was not an Israelite. His friends were Eliphaz from Theman, Baldad from Sue and Zophar from Naama. I understand that the original text for the book included two friends so the text is corrupted by the addition of the third friend. So as it was originally a trine and these transcripts provide the answer Job was looking for, I am including it. The friends in Job's story took turns to challenge Job's innocence and in the end gave up when thinking he was no more than a monster of pride that he refused to repent some unknown wrong doing. The underlying theological debate is multi-national in breadth and wonderfully well written but it is a part of what is termed Midrashic literature. The story is told to illustrate a principle or point of doctrine. It is not a historical account. The author's Job is fictitious but he does create an incredible psychological drama that points us directly to the "divine force".

Yahweh's speeches come after the debate. Job in his grief and suffering calls on the Almighty to answer him!

No! Yahweh does not answer questions he asks them and you Job will answer! Where were you when I founded the Earth?

Job is totally unable to answer any of the numerous questions that follow that prove very clearly Job was a part or being of creation in the awesome presence of the Creator. He was the impotent in the presence of the Omnipotent. A tiny nothing and his questioning the providence of the divine was nothing but foolishness. He retracted and was ashamed and humbled. His conclusion was like all the Hebrew wisdom literature, based on one enduring principal; "fear the Lord."

BUT fear was never an effective motivator and I seriously doubt if this is what The ONE really wants. We are told very clearly in HAIL THE ONE, that He wants an I – Thou relationship. He hates the Height lies and the word Lord is an example. Thinking that it was a sign of respect to add the word Lord to Hail the ONE, I proceeded to follow the spiral process. The resulting text was a staggering puzzle until I came to the end and saw these words. "See Right Edit an't on demand." THE ONE will not be forced and my addition of the word Lord was a mistake. So I started again with the exact text they had given in the first spiral that they said needed to be listed!

In HAIL THE ONE we are all called to ATONE in peace at each interjection and there are 15: Magician = 6 Love. I challenge anyone to tell me that this is not the "divine force" at work. Not only is there an answer to Job's problem but there is also an answer to Socrates as well. He was right about Immortality and the "divine force". He was also right about the "binding" the binds the truly good. [See Bonds of the Seed Sea Era and

Wheat and the Tears of Easter!] Integral to the transcripts in differing parts we are told to exercise 22 Submission – Caution and to be ever alert to the "bait that falls lightly on water – like a fly in trout fishing" and it tests your belief in the Almighty ONE. Beyond all this you have to ask yourself a question. What is the best possible relationship between a Creator and His creation? You can't answer that with recognizing you are Sanctitas Vestra and Aware as Gare! To me, mutual respect is the starting point for any I – Thou relationship – then empathy, warmth and genuine honesty – so Love grows and I raise my right hand to the Tears of Easter. Besides I do know what it is like to loose a son.

At the Leet a variety of tints, colours or hues are referred to. We come in a whole spectrum or range of different colours but one formulae is used to test any part of the range. The test formulae given is nerol alcohol is – $C_{10}H_{17}OH$. Yes it is volatile but returning to the trine of Phaedo characters, Socrates, Cebes and Summias to test the formula;

- If C is for Cebes and he is given as 10 Wheel of Fortune he is expecting to rise or fall according to his desires and what he ordains to occur.
- And if H is for Summias he is blessed with 17 Star of Magi and will be tested for spiritual strength; and
- OH is for the combined form of Plato as recorder and Socrates as the speaker. Plato was a great philosopher and most certainly injected his understanding into Socrates speeches and the questions asked. Socrates never kept any written records. Plato means 23: Royal Star of the Lion and so help from high places. Socrates means 28 Trusting Lamb and Road 10. Together, 23 + 28 = :51 Warrior. They certainly were that and they broke a great deal of totally new ground. A truly wonderful philosophical contribution.

How might this formula apply to this critical philosophical contribution? To undertake that we need the text from Phaedo. We will take the section relating to Socrates four proofs that the soul is immortal.

Of the senses' failings, Socrates says to Summias in the *Phaedo*:
Did you ever reach them (truths) with any bodily sense? -- and I speak not of these alone, but of absolute greatness, and health, and strength, and, in short, of the reality or true nature of everything. Is the truth of them ever perceived through the bodily organs? Or rather, is not the nearest approach to the knowledge of their several natures made by him who so orders his intellectual vision as to have the most exact conception of the essence of each thing he considers?
The philosopher, if he loves true wisdom and not the passions and appetites of the body, accepts that he can come closest to true knowledge and wisdom in death, as he is no longer confused by the body and the senses. In life, the rational and intelligent functions of the soul are restricted by bodily senses of pleasure, pain, sight, and sound. Death,

however, is a rite of purification from the "infection" of the body. As the philosopher practices death his entire life, he should greet it amicably and not be discouraged upon its arrival, for, since the universe the Gods created for us in life is essentially "good," why would death be anything but a continuation of this goodness? Death is a place where better and wiser Gods rule and where the most noble souls exist: "And therefore, so far as that is concerned, I not only do not grieve, but I have great hopes that there is something in store for the dead..., something better for the good than for the wicked."

The soul attains virtue when it is purified from the body: "He who has got rid, as far as he can, of eyes and ears and, so to speak, of the whole body, these being in his opinion distracting elements when they associate with the soul hinder her from acquiring truth and knowledge--who, if not he, is likely to attain to the knowledge of true being?"

The Cyclical Argument.

Cebes voices his fear of death to Socrates: "...they fear that when she [the soul] has left the body her place may be nowhere, and that on the very day of death she may perish and come to an end immediately on her release from the body...dispersing and vanishing away into nothingness in her flight."

In order to alleviate Cebes' worry that the soul might perish at death, Socrates introduces his first argument for the immortality of the soul. This argument is often called the *Cyclical Argument*. It supposes that the soul must be immortal since the living come from the dead. Socrates says: "Now if it be true that the living come from the dead, then our souls must exist in the other world, for if not, how could they have been born again?" He goes on to show, using examples of relationships, such as asleep-awake and hot-cold, that things that have opposites come to be from their opposite. One falls asleep after having been awake. And after being asleep, he awakens. Things that are hot can become cold and vice versa. Socrates then gets Cebes to conclude that the dead are generated from the living, through death, and that the living are generated from the dead, through birth. The souls of the dead must exist in some place for them to be able to return to life.

The Theory of Recollection Argument.

Cebes realizes the relationship between the *Cyclical Argument* and Socrates' *Theory of Recollection*. He interrupts Socrates to point this out, saying:

...your favorite doctrine, Socrates, that our learning is simply recollection, if true, also necessarily implies a previous time in which we have learned that which we now recollect. But this would be impossible unless our soul had been somewhere before existing in this form of man; here then is another proof of the soul's immortality.

Socrates' second argument, the *Theory of Recollection*, shows that it is possible to draw information out of a person who seems not to have any knowledge of a subject prior to his being questioned about it (a priori knowledge). This person must have gained this knowledge in a prior life, and is now merely recalling it from memory. Since the person in Socrates' story is able to provide correct answers to his interrogator, it must be the case that his answers arose from recollections of knowledge gained during a previous life.

The Affinity Argument.
Socrates presents his third argument for the immortality of the soul, the so-called *Affinity Argument*, where he shows that the soul most resembles that which is invisible and divine, and the body resembles that which is visible and mortal. From this, it is concluded that while the body may be seen to exist after death in the form of a corpse, as the body is mortal and the soul is divine, the soul must outlast the body.

As to be truly virtuous during life is the quality of a great man who will perpetually dwell as a soul in the underworld. However, regarding those who were not virtuous during life, and so favored the body and pleasures pertaining exclusively to it, Socrates also speaks. He says that such a soul as this is:

...polluted, is impure at the time of her departure, and is the companion and servant of the body always and is in love with and bewitched by the body and by the desires and pleasures of the body, until she is led to believe that the truth only exists in a bodily form, which a man may touch and see, and drink and eat, and use for the purposes of his lusts, the soul, I mean, accustomed to hate and fear and avoid that which to the bodily eye is dark and invisible, but is the object of mind and can be attained by philosophy; do you suppose that such a soul will depart pure and unalloyed?

Persons of such a constitution will be dragged back into corporeal life, according to Socrates. These persons will even be punished while in Hades. Their punishment will be of their own doing, as they will be unable to enjoy the singular existence of the soul in death because of their constant craving for the body. These souls are finally "imprisoned in another body". Socrates concludes that the soul of the virtuous man is immortal, and the course of its passing into the underworld is determined by the way he lived his life. The philosopher, and indeed any man similarly virtuous, in neither fearing death, nor cherishing corporeal life as something idyllic, but by loving truth and wisdom, his soul will be eternally unperturbed after the death of the body, and the afterlife will be full of goodness.

Summias confesses that he does not wish to disturb Socrates during his final hours by unsettling his belief in the immortality of the soul, and those present are reluctant to voice their skepticism. Socrates grows aware of their doubt and assures his interlocutors that he does indeed believe in the soul's immortality, regardless of whether or not he has succeeded in showing it as yet. For this reason, he is not upset facing death and assures them that they ought to express their concerns regarding the arguments. Summias then presents his case that the soul resembles the harmony of **the lyre**. It may be, then, that as the soul resembles the harmony in its being invisible and divine, once the lyre has been destroyed, the harmony too vanishes, therefore when the body dies, the soul too vanishes. Once the harmony is dissipated, we may infer that so too will the soul dissipate once the body has been broken, through death. Socrates pauses, and asks Cebes to voice his objection as well. He says, "I am ready to admit that the existence of the soul before entering into the bodily form has been...proven; but the existence of the soul after death is in my judgment unproven." While admitting that the soul is the better part of a man, and the body the weaker, Cebes is not ready to infer that because the body may be perceived as existing after death, the soul must therefore continue to exist as well. Cebes gives the example of a weaver. When the weaver's cloak wears out, he makes a new one. However, when he dies, his more freshly woven cloaks continue to exist. Cebes continues that though the soul may outlast certain bodies, and so continue to exist after certain deaths, it may eventually grow so weak as to dissolve entirely at some point. He then concludes that the soul's immortality has yet to be shown and that we may still doubt the soul's existence after death. For, it may be that the next death is the one under which the soul ultimately collapses and exists no more. Cebes would then, "...rather not rely on the argument from superior strength to prove the continued existence of the soul after death."

Seeing that the Affinity Argument has possibly failed to show the immortality of the soul, Phaedo pauses his narration. Phaedo remarks to Echecrates that, because of this objection, those present had their "faith shaken," and that there was introduced "a confusion and uncertainty". Socrates too pauses following this objection and then warns against misology, the hatred of argument.

The Argument from Form of Life.

Socrates then proceeds to give his final proof of the immortality of the soul by showing that the soul is immortal as it is the cause of life. He begins by showing that "if there is anything beautiful other than absolute beauty it is beautiful only insofar as it partakes of absolute beauty". Consequently, as absolute beauty is a Form, and so is the soul, then anything which has the property of being infused with a soul is so infused with the Form of soul. As an example he says, "will not the number three endure annihilation or anything sooner than be converted into an even number, while remaining three?" Forms, then, will never become their opposite. As the soul is that which renders the body living, and that the opposite of life is death, it so follows that, "...the soul will never admit the opposite of what she always brings." That which does not admit death is said to be immortal.

Socrates thus concludes, "Then, Cebes, beyond question, the soul is immortal and imperishable, and our souls will truly exist in another world. "Once dead, man's soul will go to Hades and be in the company of," as Socrates says, "...men departed, better than those whom I leave behind." For he will dwell amongst those who were true philosophers, like himself who loved philosophy and argument.

Detective Dent might read the same formula another way;
- Carbon = 8 Destined difficulties doubled +10 Wheel of Fortune to test for abuse of power. 8+10 = 18 Spiritual / Material Conflict. [Cebes means 18.]
- Hydrogen = 20 The Awakening + 17 Star of Magi tests partnerships and spiritual strength. 20 + 17 = 37 Uniqueness. Tests any or all aspects of character on Road 10. [Simmias = 17]] Authority and Power are not given without unexpected tests of character, nor until THE ONE has called you to some great purpose.
- Oxygen means Great Spirit of which there is only one. In the formulae it is combined with one Hydrogen atom and this suggests we are tested for our belief in and adherence to ONE. Oxygen = 38 Grace Under Pressure 11. This involves many tests of spiritual strength and Socrates is a fine example but as a 28 Trusting Lamb. Hydrogen = 20 The Awakening. 38 + 20 = 11 + 2 = 13: Regeneration and Change. Or as Socrates is 28 and Plato is 23 the total is :51 Warrior. Indeed they both were great warriors.]

The same formulae like18 that tests and forms character has application to each unique person, irrespective of their particular state of mind, spirit, character or culture. As Great Spirit points out in the transcript there is a lot to be learnt from negative conflict and experience. Life is learning.

The Leet gives a further example to consider. The limited quantity of roe, milt or sperm produced by a male fish. The quality of the Roe is an individual matter but not the quantity. The male fish is given as a very hard worker when he is young or immature but what he produces can cover no more than a teaspoon. Overall what matters is the quality of what you produce. Size isn't the thing that always counts.

Mother Earth develops this theme with reference to "payment" received from a Rod, a colloquial expression she uses for an erect penis. Such "payments" are received by the Doe Tree Office and the female Deer in particular. In Doe's ordinary or normal state or condition, she receives such ""payments" on each occasion they are made to the older, more sedate or wise Dorothea, from whom The Doe Tree Office receives them punctually. When Doe did not receive such a "payment"[21] this distressed her heart with painful feelings that took Doe back to

---

[21] This is true. I remember the first "flowering" or Rodeo well. In the early evening, Dorathea drove us to a quiet secluded place but when talking could not get us through our conflict, romance and then passion took over. Just as in a rodeo, she climbed on my lap in the cramped space of her Mazda sports car, but in my conflicted state I could not move or make such a "payment". This seems like a double-edged sword. Mother Earth is saying that a "payment" was important to the Net and my failure condemns me for the pain

archaic times when Dorothea yielded readily to force or pressure to the point she was easily broken and fragile. Two such instances occurred. One, reminiscent of the Rod of Biblical times, was when a new offshoot of a family or tribe was formed. The other painful memory occurred when the natural source of such "payments" was Old Norse. [A Leo Viking no doubt came back to find her again.]

Chief Petty Officer suggests replacing what has been dented.

North Sages advise that there are several dents so a debt has been accumulated in Road Ten; as part of royalty; and failed under18 Spiritual - Material Conflict. They put my ranking on any absolute scale it is NO. A Naval Officer could be appointed as my Elder and Occupational Therapist for these vagrant behaviours and particularly the failure of the partnership and Red Net tear with Dorothea.

Cadi suggests that one form of Reel therapy would be to introduce whirling like a Dervish in a spiral form. However, he is not satisfied by this as it is associated with the musical note TE – the 7th or highest note in the Solfa system[22]. He doesn't think this is an appropriate place to make a beginning; and he is not yet clear that a new beginning is warranted.

NE Court rules that a limit or bounds must be imposed on me who they describe as a dull and stupid fellow.

Gatt Seers modify Cadi's idea and propose dancing the Reel as is popular in Scotland. They expect that this lively dance would serve as a sign of regeneration and change and impress North Sages.

East Neb does not see how this could change the requirement for punishment at the West Node.

Nehemiah says that he has edited his remarks but they relate to what to do with the rod, ear, nose and throat.

Astronomer Ger has been evaluating what is "within" and the ratio he finds can be compared to a yacht dragging a small rowing boat on the lee side that is loaded with a lot of merchandise. He also advises that he has received Do, the first note of the Solfa system [no doubt sent by Doe].

Leet; This is not a number to be taken as correlating with something else [eg a wisdom path] As a doer or performer he reports my weight of Tod at 28 pounds.

---

caused to Dorathea and Doe. Yet on the other hand I am condemned for having extra-marital sex under Reed Lore. Evidently the double-edged sword is that on one edge Deer is Red : Love and the other edge Reed is White : Right. I did not reconcile these conflicting objectives.

Mother Earth wants to limit any further movement or extension on my membership or association with the ONE Led Tree. A further but different limit is that she does not want my exclusion from membership to effect my daughter who was overseas. [This is the same daughter who is referred to at the end of Trans. 8 whose birth path is also 37.] She wants any effect this might be taken to have on my daughter to be deleted. She proposes the term Drone be used to designate any branch of my family arising from my role as a husband in future. And she proposes I be given an injection of the chemical rhenium. This means a dose of 12. Sacrifice – Victim. [One will periodically be sacrificed for the plans and intrigues of others. This warns of the necessity to be alert to every situation, to beware of false flattery from those who use it to gain their own ends. Be suspicious of those who offer a high position and carefully analyse motives. Although duplicity is not always present, forewarned is forearmed. There is a degree of mental anxiety, caused by the need to sacrifice personal goals to the ambitions of others. Even the physical properties of the element rhenium would indicate a lifetime of instability, turmoil and decay.]

Cadi agrees to deleting any effect on my daughter but he wants to know what is to be the cost of the dent?

NE Court rules the chemical to be used is Oxygen and a distinctive portion is to be given out. This means 38. Grace Under Pressure. Wisdom Path 38 is indicative of perhaps the heaviest karma of them all. It tests the person for spiritual strength through trials and tribulations similar to the Old Testament story of Job. The life is filled with uncertainties, treachery and deception from others, unreliable friends, unexpected dangers and considerable grief and anxiety caused by members of the opposite sex. It is a path of grave warnings in every aspect of personal life and career.

Gatt Seers observe that I am to remain alone without a partner.

Ever Errs sets the portion to be given out as a dram = $^1/_{16}$th of an ounce. 16 means the Shattered Citadel, also previously discussed in chapter 8. Even one experience of that can be fatal. As far as 38 is concerned, in the story of Job he was a good and faithful servant of ONE but was handed over to Satan to test him; however Satan liked. Everything Job had was progressively stripped from him, friends, money, property and family. There was no let up in his destruction and personal devastation. When the only thing left was his unfaltering faith in ONE, IN-ONE handed him back and everything was restored. Not a happy story and certainly a very bleak personal prospect on top of the difficulties I already have. There is of course a significant difference between Job and me. Job had no idea why all that happened was happening to him. I do know what to expect and why Archetypes have ruled the way they have. As the North Sages said earlier, I at least have contact with a supporting surface even if I don't like what this knowledge brings.

Nehemiah does not think this will deal with the problem of making side-ways glances or leering at women. [This observation is true enough.]

Steerer says I can make a comparison between how I was once regarded by women and I will now find general opposition.

Chief Petty Officer agrees opposition will come from those who carry eggs – fertile females.

North Sages advise a period of time will have to be served like a jail sentence.

NE Bench of the Court also rules that something will have to be turned over or handed in.

East Neb says I have to hand in my Rod.

TO ONE.

4.
ONE TO
Nehemiah illustrates his point with reference to the Reed used by a weaver. Like a shuttle that goes back and forth in a loom, difficulties have to be faced and worked through as each part of the pattern is being formed.

At the Numerical Aperture, ONE refers to being affectionate, loving and sentimental. A central matter for anyone but particularly a Leo – to work things through with love.

East Neb says we can imagine the loving parts woven into the fabric of our being with a particular colour or hue – Red. The colour for the Deer and Love.

North Sages advise that this distinctive colour also applies to one's Rod.

Mother Earth wants it noted that she has a share in this too, via the Doe Tree Office and especially the female Deer.

Astronomer Ger says he has a deci-litre of something. This is a very small quantity 10^{-1} of a litre. I expect this means Road 10 has gone West or been negated.

Eats say they have dealt with partnerships – I am to be alone.

At the Numerical Aperture; DO visit as a tourist -TON. [DOTON – Dorathea on the Cape as I expect this means taking another journey to Cape Woolamai in the

SSE - a normal tourist destination on Phillip Island. So there is a place and an attitude or air with which to approach the journey. See Postscript 3].

Great Spirit recognizes there is an internal need in this situation or time of difficulty.

Gatt Seers say the situation is of being alone without a partner.

NE Court identifies a Reed musical instrument with this situation.

Cadi remarks that knitting has been a helpful practice since olden times.

North Sages also propose music but particularly a droning sound as produced by the bass strings or on a didgeridoo. They further identify Dorathea with each shortened note, staccato. North Sages say that Dorathea still has her sports car in which the rodeo occurred, even though it is advanced in age compared to others[23]. [This and the following sequence of steps constitute another exercise in symbolic action we will refer to as the Red-Net exercise.]

Mother Earth proposes collecting a bushy mass of Ivy that together with a rand [currency in South Africa where Dorathea was born] should make a suitable Lenten offering providing I am considerate and careful. Given the significance of currency to materialism, I also choose one king protea flower, that is the symbol of South Africa, to reinforce the spiritual side of this representation. I remember the sheer radiance on Dorathea's face once when I gave her a bunch of proteas I had grown at the farm. Plenty of Ivy also grew on the farm so I had no difficulty collecting the proposed "bushy mass". The local Bank provided the Rand.

Leet equates the offering to a light emitting diode.

Astronomer Ger in the West, seems to appreciate some part of the impact this year-long sentence was having, by suggesting I tear out my hair and rip my clothes in grief and anger. These feelings should be put forth towards a Tor [rocky eminence or hill], T [Dicho] and Tern [Trinity]. As I first began to rip the jacket I was wearing I became aware of my anger toward myself for my failures in the partnership with Dorathea. This developed into quite a wild thing of ripping up and discarding the negative aspects of myself. By the time I threw the remaining pieces on the floor, I had shed a lot of anger and frustration. Significantly I do not

---

[23] Dorathea later verified that she still has the red Mazda sports car – now 20 years old.

hold Dorathea or the Dicho as responsible for my problems, but it seems that the

Dicho may have contributed significantly to my lack of clarity. All of this and my petition for renewal were put forth towards a Tor - Hanging Rock that stands in the West, nearby the farm as shown in the sunset picture above.

Steerer says guidance may be forthcoming from Lieutenant Eon. [An eon is the largest division of geological time comprising two or more eras.]

Nehemiah's comments have been edited out [but not by me].

At the Numerical Aperture we are to note a tone or quality of sound particular to the LORD as master, chief or ruler.

Great Spirit directs that music be played dolente, sadly, plaintively until achieving consciousness or coming to one's senses. As the harmonica is a reed instrument, this is what I used to play this music as directed also by the NE Court to signify being alone. I was very much in touch with my grief as I played and I found playing dolente a very powerful release.

Ever Errs is not in any degree tender. She equates my character to wool quality that has a weakness at a particular point in the staple where, when pressure is applied, it will break. She says she will not allow such a breakage to alter her hold. This will not cause her to allow an escape even if it results in a sensation of whirling or reeling. A reed mat is laid from the ESE to East Neb.

East Neb wants a written paper acknowledgement of the debt owed under the Lore. [See Postscript 2].

Gatt Seers propose study of a small spot on the surface of something – observing to see if I notice that Dorathea is involved in a lively popular dance – a Reel. When this occurs, the Red-Net exercise is considered complete[24].

NE Court rules there will then be a small distribution made in charity - for maintenance - of an x-ray, roentgen. This means 27 The Sceptre. This is an excellent, harmonious wisdom path of courage and power, with a touch of enchantment. It blesses the person it represents with a promise of authority and command[25]. It guarantees that great rewards will come from the productive labours, the intellect, imagination and that the creative faculties have sewn good seeds which are certain to reap a rich harvest. 27 is a path of reward earned in more than one previous incarnation.

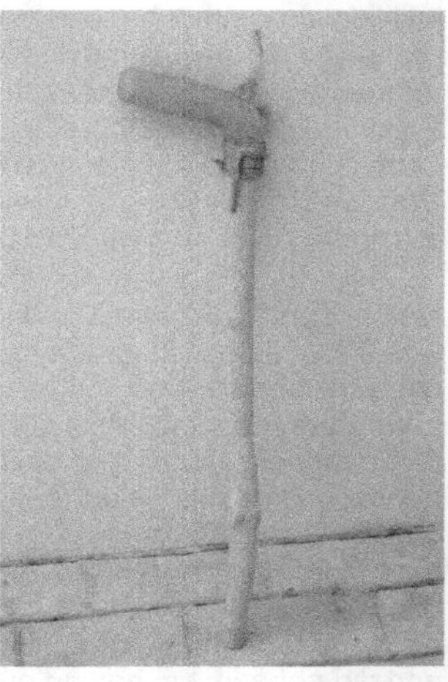

Cadi rules that –REL should be put after sceptre to make it "sceptrel" to indicate I am a diminutive and pejorative force like a wastrel. He says I have become morally corrupt and offensive in action and process where Dorathea is concerned. He thinks I am odorous and smelling and my poetry is nonsense.

North Sages advise they would only give a rupee for what happened on the night of the rodeo. They hold me morally responsible for what happened in the car that night.

Chief Petty Officer is concerned about a further dent. He identifies the event with terns flying in an aquatic environment near where we are eating our entrée and discussing affairs and sex at a Rugby League Club. He further points to our discussion about whether we met by chance or lot, or by meaningful chance - synchronicity[26]. As discussed earlier, we knew that we were meant to meet and were both deeply troubled by our conflicting partnership and family responsibilities. However, waiting until another incarnation absolutely denied the reality of our present lives and feelings for each other. We jumped that hurdle at the rodeo so there was no way of looking back. I accept that I failed that test of fidelity and that I was morally corrupt and see no value in presenting

---

[24] I have undertaken the Red-Net exercise three times. On the second occasion, whilst meditating on the spot indicated, I noticed a tiny flying insect come out of a shadow and advance toward me but it then stopped and did not dance the Reel. So the Red-Net exercise is still not complete. The Archaic term for such a process is scrying. A copy of the Debt owed under the Lore is contained in Postscript 2.

[25] In the Old Testament, the Sceptre is normally given as a symbol of equity, righteousness, power and authority held by a ruler. In the New Testament the "righteous Sceptre" is a symbol for the kingdom.

[26] Von Franz, Marie-Louise. "On Divination and Synchronicity – the psychology of Meaningful chance." See Bib. 78].

justifications. What happened can not be undone no matter how many times I replay the old painful movie. Chief Petty Officer further reinforces his message by reference to Leno and says this can be seen as some lives being twisted together like pairs of threads between the filling yarns. As noted in Trans. 7, Oath Leno is an Oath taken by two people during their period in a "communal setting". Our being "born to meet" was our choice - it was not through Archetypes manipulation or intervention. Our Fate was something we had determined.

Mother Earth adds that Leno and Rete need to be seen together. A Rete is a network of fibres like the nervous system or blood vessels - heart, arteries, capillaries and veins. She observes I grew careless, inattentive and dull about my Leno Rete responsibilities and allowed distance to be an excuse to shelter from those responsibilities and the forces of our natures. Mother Earth refers to a question Dorathea asked me about whether I can play the didgeridoo and do the circular breathing required. I said that as I did not have a didgeridoo, on my next trip to the Big Desert I was hoping to find and make one. She suggested I look for one with the shape of a deer's leg – which I finally did; but the white-ants had gone too far in their work. Like a typical Leo, I was too keen to impress Dorathea and did not admit to having problems with circular breathing. Mother Earth says my response was disgusting especially as it is like a node or a centring point for component parts. This attempted deception and another incident later in another locality caused Dorathea to Reel. For that incident, Mother Earth refers me to a study of my personal journals[27]. The journals proved we were both reeling.

> The incident occurred at an airport when we agreed that if I had missed my plane we would go "elsewhere". I had missed the last plane to Melbourne but then made arrangements to go via Sydney and back to Melbourne. This was at the end of our third encounter where the rodeo was the first. We had spent the weekend together with Dorathea's daughter. Significantly, during the last day, her daughter privately said to me that mum wanted to stay with her husband. [Out of the mouths of babes…]I thought by leaving and not going "elsewhere", my actions would help. Not so it seems from the letter that followed. Dorathea could not settle afterwards and wrote me a stunningly powerful letter about how she drove all night trying to work out what to do. She drove the highways, the black roads and the white roads lit by moonlight, but on each she felt like an abandoned lover and she thought it best if we never see each other again – Oh! I wrote, drove interstate and I telephoned Dorathea but she refused contact and would not answer messages. However, I accept that she felt abandoned and was left reeling from the experience. Her letter was proof enough of the depth of heartfelt pain that she suffered as one abandoned. So was I abandoned as it happened.

Leet sounds the second note of the Solfa system, RE. [New subject.] This is linked to a negative comment I once made about the Rector in the Church Parish where I grew up. I was an idiot for not giving enough credence to the ends he was seeking nor thought to the difficulties he had experienced at the hands of Japanese interrogators in Singapore during WW II : they had twisted his tongue and he had great difficulty speaking. My comments led to further my decay or decomposition. Rector's internal capacity is given as 100 and his salary a pittance compared to his ability. My comments about Rev. Pain are likened to the distant nibbling or gnawing of a rodent at the Toe.

Astronomer Ger says that when I am far advanced in years of life and only a fragment remains, some day the mark aimed at with the Trinity, a score of 100 will be attained. This is my lot, the portion in life assigned by fate or providence under the Lore.

Eats qualifies this is under English Lore or it's derivation as I have contiguity with it. [Indeed Australian law is based on the English Westminster system.]

Steerer advises that comparatively less, a smaller amount can be netted in the Red Net. Lieutenant Loner – one who dislikes company – says that at such time liability will be turned ON.

Dyna Pandy provides a brief note or record set down to assist memory. She also sounds the 3rd note of the Solfa system, E. Dot. She rests her musical point by saying Dorathea is associated with a Celtic medieval instrument called a Rote, which she says can also drone. When I consulted a friend who has considerable knowledge of stringed instruments he provided me with a copy of how the Rote or Saxon Lyre was constructed. It has six strings! He felt certain that you could make a droning sound with the instrument. The fact that the Rote is a Celtic or Saxon instrument further supports what was previously said about our past lives on Road Ten.

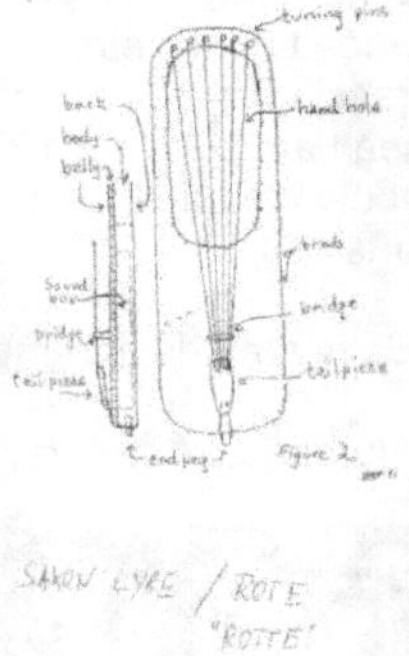

Under the Tree of Life[28], the musical note E is associated with Capricorn, under which sign Dorathea had been born. This is also associated with influences from the planet Saturn that can be harsh and pungent. From what I know of Dorathea's life there have been periods of considerable hardship. The musical note E is also associated with the colours yellow and blue-violet and two Wisdom Paths, 26 and :32. As noted previously 26 means Partnerships. :32 means Communication – having the magical power to sway masses of people and help from those in high places. Add to this the natural ability to charm others with magnetic speech. [Dorathea certainly has a wonderful voice and every time I hear her speak I feel somehow transfixed.] The complexities of advertising, writing, publishing, radio and television are not always, but usually an open book to the :32 person who tends to work well under pressure. :32 is a very fortunate path if the person it represents holds inflexibly to his or her own opinions and judgement in both artistic or intangible matters and material matters. If not, the plans are liable to be wrecked by the stubbornness and stupidity of others.

---

[28] Hulse, David Allan. "The Key of It All". [See Bib. 33].

Nehemiah refers to Retene [a crystalline hydrocarbon] that means 26 Partnerships. He also gives the chemical neodymium that means 18 Spiritual - Material Conflict. He says these are great wisdom paths that are very far from being only about action.

Great Spirit points to the result or consequence.

NE Court rules that I am refused, denied or prohibited, from being a Doer as an amusing or odd person. [I must confess that my sense of humour has resulted in more misunderstandings than any other form of my communication.]

Cadi hesitates to rule this way but says any title of honour, even as one to whom a royalty is paid has been torn.

North Sages advise that with respect to the aim, purpose or intension and the starting point or Tee, I should be allowed to pass, go or come.

5.
NE Court rules that like a periodic payment of rent by a tenant to a landlord, periodically my Rod will be punished or chastised. My Rod certainly does not work on demand. Unless I have settled into a loving relationship with a woman I usually don't achieve an erection. There were times when this was not only embarrassing in my relationship with Dorathea but with other women too. With Dorathea I am quite sure it led her to believe that I did not love her. I had put the matter down to conflicting loyalties and I knew nothing then about "periodic payments".

Great Spirit sounds a trumpet as a signal.

At the Numerical Aperture, this concerns a railway.

Steerer advises it has to do with someone who is concerned with railways like a railway engineer. In this context the railway carriage on the farm is the issue. As one of my labours of love, over a three year period, I restored an 1890 railway carriage that had operated on country lines in Victoria for nearly 100 years. It is truly a treasure of mainly timber construction, including teak, cedar, and silky oak.

All the original paints were removed, panels repaired, reinstalled and re-polished. Although most of the original character has been maintained, including a quirky silver plated hand basin and brass fittings, it then served as a self-contained bed & breakfast.

Mother Earth instances contact with any surface in the carriage…

Ever Errs uses the expression Ohm – repeat. Although an ohm is a unit of electrical resistance, here repeated it means 32 Communication.

Great Spirit says that this communication will be forthcoming wherever rot, disease or decomposition occurs.

Nehemiah says that in this way the railway carriage will be kept straight TO ONE.

6.
ONE TO
North Sages advise that the steel is to be kept up to quality likened to a toledo blade – a fine steel sword produced in Spain. Besides steel brackets in the walls and braces, there are three steel RSJ's supporting the carriage over it's 20 metre length - it is great to know North Sages will kept me informed if the RSJ's need work.

Ever Errs repeats her assurance about communication.

At the Numerical Aperture, the carriage gets a nod of agreement.

Great Spirit reassures me that no date has been entered for commencement of a process of teasing or heckling.

At the Numerical Aperture we learn that as far as the issue of any repeat problems are concerned…

East Neb says Never[29].

---

[29] It looks as though I have got something right.

7.

East Neb sounds a note or tone.

Great Spirit draws attention to what happened in the beginning that involves the New Testament and a distant message…

At the Numerical Aperture, a reprint is involved…

Leet reminds me I was a teenager of 13 when I was confirmed. When I checked my copy of the Holy Bible given to me at the time of my confirmation, there was a note I had kept from Rector that I had forgotten. I had been 10 at the time he wrote this note for me.

> "The Disciples would have been just fishermen or men of simple occupation, if Christ had not chosen them to be world figures. Christ's plan for a man is always the largest.
>
> 11 : VII : 1953.
>
> A.W. Pain.
> 'St Aidan's, Papakura'

Mother Earth refers to the order of things – the ordinal position as in a sequence of numbers. The note had been written three years before my confirmation and had been torn from my autograph book as a memento of a man who I deeply admired and respected when I was 10. Since then I have wondered when the Toe would make its plan known. I regularly served at the altar and in the choir of that church throughout my teenage years and joined the Postulants Guild in the expectation of joining the ministry. But when the critical moment came when those who felt called by the Holy Spirit were to kneel, I was compelled to remain standing and then leave the church. I was stunned. I had been profoundly moved in that moment **not to knee** and to a degree I felt turned out and abandoned. I had been sure I knew what Christ's plan was for me – the ministry.

NE Court rules I am to examine my name or designation. Christopher means "Christ bearer". By Chaldean numerals my name, Christopher Robert Phillips, means 36 Sceptre.

My life was to be lived in the face of materialism and in the teeth of government, industry, unions and education where I have been involved in what can be summarized as processes of humanization and democratization of organizations and communities. But whilst the latter can be seen as consistent with a developmental plan, finding or being given this work to do in editing these transcripts, I regard as key to understanding the "largest" part for me in serving the Toe. I have wondered what might have happened had I worked within the structure of the Church, even as a theologian. But given declining Church public relevance and attendance, histories of child abuse, public humiliation of senior Church officials and escalating "religious wars", I can see the wisdom in being positioned where I am - outside

I am usually called Chris Phillips and the Chaldean significance of that - Road 10 - 46 Elder!

East Neb says there is something to offer or proffer – to put forward for acceptance.

Nehemiah says this something is old, having existed a long time or was made long ago.

Eats give her name as ER – Queen Elizabeth. Significantly the name Elizabeth has the same Chaldean path numeral as Christopher - 27 The Sceptre.
TO ONE.

8.
ONE TO
Nehemiah refers to the old, those who have existed a long time or who were made long ago.

At the Numerical Aperture, ONE relent – to cause to relent or soften in time.

Ever Errs says we are lent longitude or long life, it is a gift.

North Sages advise the Leet is central to this gift.

Nehemiah says it is proffered for our acceptance.

Great Spirit likens long life to a long thread wound on the spool of a fishing rod's Reel.

Ever Errs repeats her reference to longitude.

NE Court rules that with longitude also comes being alone and lonely.

9.
Ever Errs identifies "the way".

At the Numerical Aperture we are given the chemical neon. This means 25 Discrimination and Analysis. 25 bestows spiritual wisdom gained through careful observation of people, things, and worldly success by learning through experience. Its strength comes from overcoming disappointments in early life and possessing the rare quality of learning from past mistakes. The judgement is excellent but 25 is not a material path. The age of 55 years is given as the point in longitude when such a blessing is given.

Nehemiah says something else is also given out, but sparingly, that is as sweet as a bird's song.

Dyna Pandy says that she gives out 26 Partnerships over a range from 0 – 80.

Great Spirit says that a duty has been assigned; one can take charge of something.

Nehemiah says this is in a place where I have trod.

Astronomer Ger says this involves two aspects. One is the Transcendental Constant, E = 2.7182818… and the other is R, which in physics and chemistry means the gas constant. There are several meaning levels involved here. The meaning of ER is 7, a sign of the Great Mystery – especially as it applies to section 7 above and so may be a direct indication of the "Sceptrel." This would be consistent with being assigned a duty or taking charge of something.

The individual meaning of the Transcendental Constant, E also begins with the number 27 meaning The Sceptre. Followed by the recurring sequence of 18, 28 and 18 may be an indication of recurring 18 Spiritual – Material Conflict and the dangers of 28 The Trusting Lamb like Socrates.

Another possible interpretation arises from taking the whole number of the Transcendental Constant numbers given in the definition means 37. This number has a distinctive potency of its own. It is associated with an extremely sensitive nature – good and fortunate friendships – a strong magnetism with the public, often in the area of the Arts – and productive partnerships of all kinds. It places an emphasis on love and romance, and sometimes too much emphasis on sexuality. Attitudes towards sex may be unconventional [but this aspect is not always present]. There is a pronounced need for harmony in relationships. Happiness and success are more easily attained when in partnerships with another rather than when operating alone as a single individual. [37 is my birth numeral and also that of my daughter referred to in this and the previous chapter.

The individual meaning of the gas constant, R, is .082057 = 22 Submission – Caution. This is symbolized as "a Good Man, blinded by the folly of others, with a knapsack on his back full of errors." In the image, he seems to offer no defence against a ferocious tiger that is about to attack him. It's a warning number of illusion and delusion. It indicates a good person who lives in a fool's paradise; a dreamer of dreams who awakens only when surrounded by danger, when it is often too late. It warns of mistakes in judgement, of placing faith in those who are not trustworthy. The karmic obligation here is to be more alert, to curb spiritual laziness, and develop more spiritual aggressiveness – to realize your own power to change things, to prevent failure by simply ordaining success. When this personal responsibility is recognized, practiced, and finally mastered, the 22 person can be in control of events, no longer blinded by the folly of others, and will see ideas achieved and dreams realized.

The combined meaning of these two constants, E & R is 32 Communication. I certainly have a duty in that area – service to Toe in producing this manuscript.

Mother Earth in the NW refers to a place where I have trod. A bare sandy tract – most likely she means the Big Desert in NW Victoria – place of the Receptive Earth and where so many Vision Quests had been held over 14 years or so. As that land is defined as a national park and Wilderness, it is evident that my having been assigned a duty there does not mean ownership. My expectation is that this is a proposal to undertake a Vision Quest to the Big Desert, in the southern area of the region. There to gain some greater clarity about the nature of the duty I have been assigned and the purpose which Toe has defined for me in returning the "Sceptrel", albeit to a more limited extent in a sandy tract. In view of this section commencing with a discussion about 25 Discrimination and Analysis and previous discussion about my failings, I expect this means a limited learning exercise in effectively using the power granted is what is meant in this section.

Astronomer Ger draws particular attention to R, the gas constant, 22 Submission – Caution.[30]
TO ONE.

10.
ONE TO
Eats addresses the Rabbi

Great Spirit says this concerns one's fate or destiny.

North Sages see a normal, healthy condition of the mind.

Mother Earth refers to the organic compound ethyl, C_2H_5 that comes from ethane. Although it is possible to interpret this formulae, it is more probable the name contains the meaning - 18 Spiritual – Material Conflict as this is consistent with previous discussion.

Astronomer Ger again refers to the Transcendental Constant, E, which means 27 The Sceptre and 37 that has a unique potency of it's own.

Nehemiah says these wisdom paths are not presented formally for acceptance as they apply whether I like them or not.

Gatt Seers draw attention to the Old Testament.

Chief Petty Officer of The Barn, gives the name Lot and says he did not have a choice in the matter. Genesis provides an account of Lot, his wife and two daughters fleeing Sodom before it was destroyed by IN-ONE. Lot had no say in

---

[30] 22 Submission – Caution means stilling yourself and listening to the inner voice of caution. I have good reason to see that this is important advice when approaching ONE.

About a dozen years ago I was undertaking a solo Vision Quest in the northern part of the Big Desert. I had been fasting for three days and set out at midday each day for a journey to the NW – the place of Mother Earth. Midday was important because the sun was exactly true North at that time and navigation could only be taken from the Sun in that region because the large amount of iron stone deflected a compass by between 11 - 13 degrees. A significant problem to navigation. Normally I would hike exactly NW for about two hours and then draw my purpose circle in the sand and mark the direction by which I had to return. Then I would sit inside the circle for some time, still myself and wait in silence.

On this occasion the inner voice of caution said quite clearly that I should "apologize to ONE for ever having referred to Him using the "G" word." This stimulated quite a lot of thinking but some time later I was still again. The inner voice then came through again and told me to tie up the dog and climb the sand dune ahead of me up to about half way and then kneel down but don't look back. I did exactly as directed.

"Crawl forward but keep your eyes on the ground." As I began to do so the bush in front of me began crackling as though it was on fire! A voice came from the bush addressing me and telling me that I was a disgusting individual of little or no merit. At the end of this rebuke I was asked what I wanted to say. I said that I had come to apologize for having ever used another term to refer to ONE. "Good, now go."

I did. I crawled backwards for some way, untied the dog and made my "astounded" way back to camp.

trying to save Sodom. Although told by the angels not to look back, Lot's wife did so and was turned into a pillar of salt.

Eats say this is suggestive or reminiscent of …

Nehemiah; feeling forsaken, desolate and wretched. Lot felt that way when he had to leave his wife behind and so does the Toe about the Rabbi and Hebrews.

At the Numerical Aperture [that can be regarded like the Tent of Meeting in Moses times], we are to consider our return or the benefits derived.
        LO [Interj. Behold] the style, distinction or elegance of the outcome to negative conflict.

Great Spirit directs us to strike out, expunge four things. Net does not include the idea of containment; and three T's; T [ton]; T [tare]; and Tone [as an accent particular to a person or entity]. So the Red Net is a way of drawing people and events together and not a process of containment or restraint.

11.
Gatt Seers say; we are to examine a contract for performance.

At the Numerical Aperture; during the 40 week-days leading up to Easter, the period of Lent, we are not to undertake things in a mechanical way without thought. There is a need for serious consideration of the situation during that time. Being alone in the meadow for an hour each day during Lent was given as an exercise to assist Oath Leno – finding those who we are born to meet.

Nehemiah says; one, a single individual should undertake this activity.

Eats propose study; Indeed it is an extraordinary sacrifice that one individual made for so many. In the fulfilment of his destiny he enabled so many.

Leet offers; the Elder tree, Sambucas for study.

North Sages advise; this study be approached as if a technical officer.

Gatt Seers inform; one will be led in this study...

Great Spirit says; to a state or condition…

At the Numerical Aperture; where a stick used to measure with…

Nehemiah; will end or complete…

Eats; study…

Mother Earth; on the grounds. [Indeed, there in the place of Mother Earth in the North West corner of the property there was a young self-sewn Elder Tree growing.]

Sambucas nigra or the Common Elder is very widely known in Europe and it has a history that goes back thousands of years. Two traditions have particular pertinence to the Elder, as a single individual helping so many. According to one tradition, the Cross of Calvary was made from Elder. The other tradition is that Judas hung himself from an Elder. Both traditions have vital significance for Easter.

"In consequence of these old traditions, the Elder became the emblem of sorrow and death, and out of the legends which linger round the tree there grew up a host of superstitious fantasies which still remain in the minds of simple country folk. Even in these prosaic days, one sometimes comes across a hedge-cutter who cannot bring himself to molest the rampant growth of its limbs and gypsies forbade them using the wood to kindle their camp-fires… In most countries, especially Denmark, the Elder was intimately connected with magic. In its branches was supposed to dwell a dryad, Hyde-Moer, the Elder Tree Mother…wherefore whoever needs to hew it down or cut it's branches has first to make request… In earlier days the Elder tree was supposed to ward off evil influences; give protection from witches; bring good luck at weddings; cure most diseases; bring happiness to a soul lying in a new made grave; and if you slept under an Elder on Midsummer Eve, you would have visions of Fairyland."

There are some genuine, highly beneficial and even dangerous, potent, herbal medicines that can be derived from the roots, bark, leaves, flowers and berries of Elders. The British Phamacopoeia prescribes Elder for some seventy or more distinct diseases or classes of disease – a very impressive record for one plant. Perhaps the other most commonly known uses today include wine and jam made from the clusters of small blackish berries.

What then of the timber? There are two characteristics I have noted in this study. It is a white, closely grained wood and therefore hard. Like the Reed, it has a pithy core, not hard like an oak so this pith can easily be removed to form a hollow tube. No doubt this is also the reason why it is sometimes called the Pipe Tree. For this reason Elders have long been used in making wind instruments "something of the nature of a Pan-pipe or flute" and several types of horn. There are two other features of the tree worthy of note;

1. "The bark of the older branches has been used in the Scotch Highlands as an ingredient in dying black, so too the root [the ancient Roman's used it for a hair dye]. The leaves yield with alum, a green dye and the berries dye blue and purple, the juice yielding with alum, violet; and with alum and salt, a lilac colour."
2. "The botanist finds in this plant an object of considerable interest, for if a twig is partially cut, then cautiously broken and the divided portions are carefully drawn asunder, the spiral air-vessels, resembling a screw, may be distinctly seen." [See Grieve. Bib. 27].

In my study of the plants spiral air vessels, I only found them distinct when using an eye-glass. But there in the carefully divided portions were the perfectly formed spiral or screw shaped air vessels. Overall, Elder is a most remarkable plant with a great many significant medicinal and other useful properties.

Finally, as Mother Earth says, my study needed to include the grounds of the farm where I found three self-sewn Elders growing. As noted earlier, one tree was growing in the NW, so after careful study I selected a branch that could be used for a measuring stick of 1 metre and asked permission to hew it down. As tradition has it, not a breath of air moved so I took this as consent and proceeded quietly with the work. Just using a piece of fencing wire I was able to completely hollow out the stick. Two other small sections of the branch were also hollowed out using a drill and very strangely both made the musical note A but exactly one octave apart! [Concert A is the note we are all tuned to according to Archetypes in Trans. 10.]

North Sages advise that a new line is needed.

Gatt Seers say this is the End or concluding part
TO ONE.

12.
ONE TO
Astronomer Ger says, Eternal

Steerer says, Tree [Arch; Cross on which Jesus Christ was crucified. The Eternal Tree is not the Elder it was given in the WNW. The Elder is however THE ONE Led Tree. The last tree named for Three Tree was the Ben Tree or Moringa oliefera with a pedigree of virtues no other tree is likely to match. This includes a remarkable connection with ONE at Neap Tide – likened to Aphids.to ONE. The Eternal tree wouldn't be an Ebony as no one could carry a cross made from that very dense and very rare timber. Likewise the Penda can be ruled out as it is a rainforest timber tree and would by very unlikely to be available in Jerusalem at the time. Otherwise the tree is not named but it's position is given in the SW.

North Sages declare that a new line is needed.

Astronomer Ger says there is a necessity arising from the case or circumstances of Christ's crucifixion

Dyna Pandy says this should be done on immediate proximity to …

Nehemiah says … the end or extremity of the present life.

At the Numerical Aperture we are warned that we have a liability for our debts.

Great Spirit decrees there we will enter and a record will be made of the entry to…

Ever Errs says … Eden and a state of perfect happiness.

1. ODE OF THE ELDERS OF TOMORROW.

This Ode has been written as the Epilogue at the end – see p370.

[Spiral Galaxy NGC 3370 – by the Hubble Telescope.]

2. DEBT OWED UNDER THE LORE
-    **Road Ten Responsibilities and Failures.**

Road 10 is the road of Isis and Osiris or the road of kings and queens. The principle aspects are Light and Love. It involves the power to ordain, decree and manifest. It takes an indefinite period of time to forge the character required to handle Road 10 and the period is given as even greater than what is required for an Elder. For those who are to embark on a Road 10 journey, every little flicker of positive and negative behaviour requires special notice. Lieutenant Eon is given as the one with responsibility for this exacting developmental task. In the first place I am deeply indebted to him for his efforts to-date.

Under the Lore, a man or woman does not appear on Road 10 on their own. There are parents, friends, loving and other partnerships of many kinds that are to be considered, planned and organized. Some partnerships are for testing character. Everything has to be set at its proper starting place or Tee. And so it is that a whole Rete or network of people, learning and testing events can be identified with anyone on Road 10 and in particular the part played by one's loving partners under what is termed the Red-Net. Red being the colour for Love and Net being the complex interrelationship of people, situations and learning.

Under the Red-Net, it was decreed that Dorathea and I would live 10 lives together and our current life-time is our last in the sequence. For both of us, at conception, every tiny detail was set in the same way as the potential of the true or estreat, mature tree is set within each seed. She was conceived for me and I for her. After developments involving nine previous lives, this lifetime was to have been the summit in Eternal Love between us. And of course a child.

The starting point of the life-times we have spent together was traumatic. Dorathea was in her more advanced years when forced to yield or submit. Apparently I have raped her twice. Once in ancient Biblical times when the child born later began a new tribe as Lieutenant Eon planned. The second rape was when I was an Old Norse from Norway – a Viking raider on the coast of Scotland. Both experiences so distressed Dorathea's heart with painful feelings that she was easily upset and fragile. I understand the following seven lifetimes were marked by great happiness and joyful partnership where we were as we should be to each other and Lieutenant Eon is most pleased with the way we grew together and helped each other with our respective responsibilities as Elders. A note given to assist memory in this regard is that Dorathea played a medieval Celtic or Saxon instrument called a Rote whose bass strings were able to develop a significant droning sound. Further it is given that her note in the scale of music is E – the third note in the scale after C. My great grandmother and father had a family tree drawn up long ago that actually traced several branches of the family long back into their medieval roots. Also noting the regular reference to a lively dance popular in Scotland, the Reel, the significant issue here is that a branch of the family came from Edinburgh in Scotland.

Under the Lore, my father has always been my Elder and always will be. His middle name was Norman but he is also given as having been my father even in Old Norse days in Norway. Significantly, as a young man he had bright red hair. He has been my Eternal Father that no doubt takes as much planning as my Eternal Loving Partner. Where my father has been vital to the development of my character and opinion, he has not always been right and a problem identified in this lifetime relates to his attitude towards Christmas, that it is too commercialized, an attitude I had adopted. However he pointed me into many constructive paths as my Elder where I was finally to achieve some success in education, sport, religious service and devotion, scouting and community service. He taught me to be the generally honest and hard-working man that I became. He was and always will be my Elder.

In this lifetime, at a very early age I loved nursery rhymes and my mother recalls me hearing them and then deliberately mixing parts together to create new amusements. Very early on, I learnt about being an odd and amusing character but it has not always served me well – and I am currently forbidden such an approach. However, to poetry; I often wrote my feelings, reactions and imaginative stories in poetic form. I loved reading, reciting and writing Australian Bush Ballads. As part of the role my Eternal Love has always played, has been to be my Elder in poetry – Dorathea has vitally helpful insights; knows how to encourage what is needed; she helps explore alternatives; find and refine new ways to sharpen expression and clarify purpose. These things are the dowry she has that has contributed much over time. These matters are consistent with the Lore and thus indicative of Great Design in our lives. The deep pleasure I have gained from this work and the way Dorathea has assisted even to date in this lifetime is indicative of a further debt I owe under the Lore. Even as Great Spirit says great lessons can be learnt from negative conflict.

However, contrary to the plan, in this lifetime Dorathea and I have not found peace, inspiration and happiness together and this has impacted negatively on the roles we were to fulfil. Of all that we were meant to do in mutual responsibility for a partnership, it would seem we have failed. It is not for lack of love between us. The problem is more in our not finding the way to express it. The faults may be read from both sides but for mine, for which I can speak, there are several relevant issues.

When I first realized Dorathea's interest in me I told her I was already with a partner I was happy with, in love with and committed to so although I felt deeply for her I doubted if we could find a way in this lifetime. I put her off. I even failed to see the significance that we were both reading the same book – The Snow Leopard – at the same time. Failing to see the importance of our meeting was the first step in my downfall. I thought I was being tested for faithfulness to my partner especially as I was very attracted to Dorathea. For two years I denied or rather tried to suppress my feelings and made no effort to contact her or even check to see how she was going. Being interstate was a very convenient excuse for my complacency and avoidance. In denying Dorathea, I also denied myself. I often thought of her but refused to acknowledge the depth of feelings involved and failed to find appropriate ways to be supportive.

Dorathea created the momentum for change from "stuck ness" when she phoned me at a friends place where I was staying in her town. We met for breakfast. The eventual Rodeo that evening has many parts to it that are vital to my undoing and so condemnation. My failure was to have not had an orgasm and so made the "payment" required at the Doe Tree Office. To have done so would have completed the Red Net plan Lieutenant Eon had so carefully prepared and the Doe Tree Office and Dorathea expected when she climbed on my lap in the cramped quarters of her little red Mazda sports. Who could resist?

In the Red Net plan, timing is everything, in order to ensure the correct moment of conception and hence the conjunction of influences [although I don't recall the date, I do recall it was the Buddhist full moon]. This same care is illustrated earlier in both Dorathea's birth as a Capricorn and in my Leo characteristics.

When I returned to the farm I attempted to deceive my partner by concealing my involvement with and feelings for Dorathea. I failed to see and act on my responsibilities to both women and Archetypes, all of whom had been supportive. In simple terms I was selfish, defiant, short-sighted, stupid, confused, out of touch with "higher guidance" and morally corrupt as North Sages point out.

I know that my love for Dorathea grew quickly on our next meeting when we stayed overnight in a motel together. This is exactly what we should have done

instead of the Rodeo. At the motel I recall watching her lips form each word as
she told me about a medical problem she had. Deep threads of hazy past
knowing and love welled up in me but also mixed into this were feelings of guilt
for having failed to be supportive in the first period and sympathy for her
suffering. Although the Doe Tree Office did receive "payment" that night, the
timing was wrong.

Our next encounter was over a weekend, when we took her love child, Alice with
us. Alice was possibly about three years old at the time. As in most romances we
had some wonderful and confusing times together. After an exciting start when
she picked me up at the airport, she left me at a shopping centre whilst she went
to pick up Alice. On her increasingly late non-return I started to wonder what was
happening. When she finally did arrive with Alice she explained that she nearly
didn't come back at all! She was thinking of leaving me there?

I was shocked and deeply troubled by what had begun so badly. Most things that
begin badly also end badly and I didn't know if I could trust what she said she
was going to do. Especially when she didn't seem to know or trust herself.

I realize now that deep currents were flowing in both of us and on the second day
of our weekend, Dorathea took me to see a house that was for sale in a nearby
town. Instead of fully appreciating that she was trying to find some common
ground for us to live together I was foolishly critical of the house she had chosen.
She had obviously been doing some significant planning because she went
straight to the house without using agents or a directory. We then failed to clarify
whether we wanted to live together.

On the positive side, we devoted a significant amount of time to Dorathea's
medical condition we had discussed in our motel encounter. She said she had
bowel cancer and she wanted me to conduct some healing rituals. I did this with
a small but very extraordinary healing stone I had found on the beach on the
island of Tana. The little Tana Stone was almost perfectly round and emitted a
lavender light from it's tiny crystalline structure. It was a beautiful stone I carried
with me as a travel stone when I was away from the farm and it was perfect for
Dorathea's healing so she carried it during the weekend.

As we were walking along a lovely creek bed she suddenly announced that she
had lost the stone! I immediately began to search for the stone back along the
way we had been walking. Fruitless efforts rapidly increased my concern – I was
very attached to the stone. Then Dorathea finally found it inside her clothing at or
about her navel and I was greatly relieved. Then came the twist so characteristic
of that weekend. She thought I was more concerned about the stone than I was
about her! Evidently I was failing to show her the love she expected.

During the afternoon I was alone and talking to Alice when out of the blue she told me that Dorathea wanted to stay with her husband and I believed Alice spoke her truth. This prompted the greatest failure of that fateful weekend.

We both expected I was too late to catch my plane back to Melbourne and had agreed that if the plane had gone that we would go "elsewhere". Yes, the plane had gone but a flight was immediately leaving for Sydney by which I could get a connecting flight to Melbourne. To do that I had to run to catch it so I left without speaking to Dorathea about this. I accept it is my fault that she went into a Reel or whirl, which affected every other incident from then on.

Driving all night on the black roads of abandonment Dorathea wrote a stunning letter that she began with "Oh Chris", and ended by saying she never wanted to see me again. If she was abandoned so was I. This poem was the product of my torment.

Four Questions.

If I arch myself like a tree in the Wind will my leaves quiver and shed my grief?
No – Oh!
If I pray to the Sun will it shine it's light in my life again and bring sweet relief?
No – Oh!
If I speak into the deepest reaches of the Water will it answer me and let me be whole with you again?
No – Oh!
And to Mother Earth; If the sand runs through my finger-tips will each grain embrace and draw away our pain?
No – Oh!

I can see what Mother Earth says about how the weekend raised archaic depths of heart felt pain from two previous lives and sent her into a whirl. Significantly, it was on reading her letter that I realized she was a lot more competent than I was in expressing her feelings in writing. Her terrible letter changed forever my feelings about the word Oh! I realized when I read the letter that Dorathea was terribly tormented by what had occurred and that I don't have the right to inflict such pain. However I was also suffering abandonment and I had tried to help her relationship with her husband as indicated by Alice. My classic mistake was in not asking Dorathea what she thought about what Alice had said.

I called Dorathea, but not often enough. I wrote to her infrequently and failed to express myself properly. I left messages she preferred not to answer. I drove interstate to try and see her but at the end of a week I returned without having seen her at all.

Distance, avoidance and time fed a breach of two whole years. In the two-year period after her letter of abandonment, a quite remarkable event occurred. I

wrote about the incident in my journal. I had forgotten the incident until Mother
Earth said that I should review my journals and I found this entry;

*"I go out into the moonlight and do the Long Form of Tai Chi with the Tana
Stone at my Tan Tien [solar plexus]. Then later, whilst doing Horse [a
frozen stance] with my hands in the injured position, I went through the
visualizations involved in the Buddhist's Suffering Tantra. Suddenly a
mouse ran up my leg with my cat in hot pursuit! Obviously the Tantra was
working if I seemed like a better place to be than in the cat's jaws and
claws! I hope Dorathea benefited, feels better now and can sense the love
I send her." [In trying to keep perfectly still!]*

Although I often practiced this and other distance forms of communication and
support, I accept Mother Earth's ruling that I failed to do such things frequently
enough.

Eventually, Dorathea did relent and we met for dinner in another motel,
discussed poetry, mutual friends and interests and problems in our respective
marriages. She came with me to my room and again I failed, but this time even
more completely. It wasn't even a rodeo and it did nothing but increase confusion
and pain. Evidently my Rod was being punished. Again I concealed my actions

and feelings from my wife and
my egotism prevented me from
speaking to either women about
the problem I had.

The next time we met I stayed at
her house. During discussion
she asked me if I could play the
didgeridoo and do the circular
breathing. Again I tried to
conceal my problems, even on
so simple a matter of what I still
needed to learn. I accept Mother
Earth's definition that the
breathing is a Node or centring
aspect for component parts and
my reply was disgusting.

That night I slept in Alice's
bedroom and Dorathea came to
me during the night and we
made love for the last time. I was
shocked in the morning to find
her husband had been in their
bed to which she had returned!

On our last meeting before another two-year break, I failed to confront her with my truth because she was angry. It was Mother's Day in 1990 when I phoned her and told her that I wanted to see her. She agreed so I spoke frankly to my wife and then jumped into the car and drove interstate to her place only to find the place deserted but with the front door open. Whilst waiting for her return I put numerous South African protea [flowers I had grown on the farm] all around in her garden.

Afternoon turned to evening and still she had not returned so I walked into the house and sat down and watched the TV that was already on. I assumed initially that as the front door was open and as she was expecting me I thought she intended me to wait so I did. As any expectant or hopeful lover might.

Finally Dorathea arrived with Alice and her Husband mid evening.

Dorathea was very angry that unannounced I had let myself in!

However a funny thing happened that night. Alice remembered me and realizing I was in Big Trouble because Dorathea was even stamping her foot; she went into her bedroom and returned with her stuffed guinea pig. She gave me the toy for me to hold when she's angry! It was sweet medicine for me. Dorathea was in fact pretending she didn't know I was coming. The whole thing was a sham and I was being stupid!

My actions probably caused problems in Dorathea's relationship with her husband and no doubt these stresses affected their children. But why did she invite me to drive all that way and then pretend she had no knowledge of my coming to see her? I was on that black road of abandonment all night whilst I undertook the long and tormenting drive back to the farm and a marriage that was also "on the rocks". I loved both women and couldn't see a future with either of them. I still wonder what Dorathea thought she could achieve by her actions. Only one thing was certain. Just as the weekend start showed me that she might not be relied upon, so Mother's Day 1990 was absolute proof. I could only rely on trouble, uncertainly, deception and unhappiness.

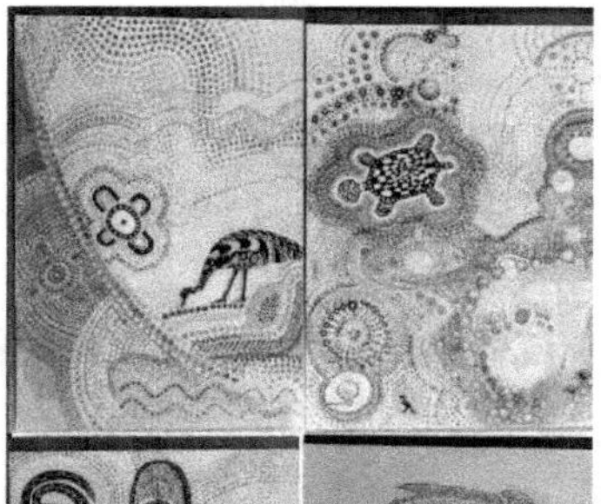
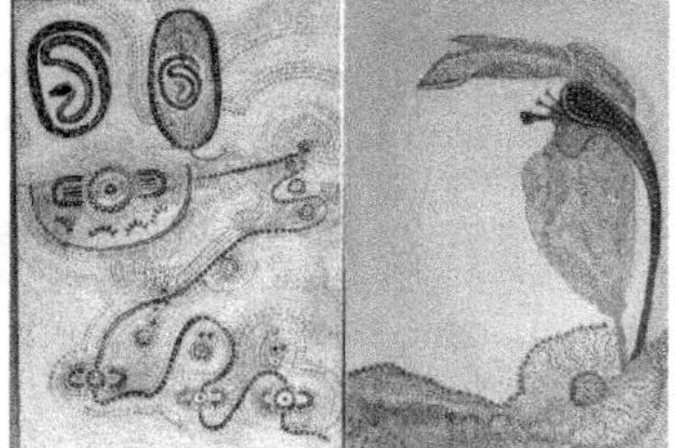

What would Dorathea think when she found proteas all over her garden?

Also during this period I had been running a

number of Vision Quests into the Big Desert and decided to write a book about the process and include information about some of the remarkable things that had happened. The book was written as a novel about real events and it included a number of dot paintings I had produced during my years of deprivation and waiting. On completion of this project I sent Dorathea a copy. Whatever her reasons were, the book was returned unopened and of course unread.

Her simple instruction – "Return to Sender" - was very painful – Oh!

I phoned Dorathea after a couple more years had passed and found she was coming to Melbourne and would meet me at the airport.

She was coming down to see her mother-in-law and so I offered to drive her to her destination in the Essendon area. It may have been a pay-back for the Tana Stone incident during our weekend, but Dorathea had lost a button off her dress and she was more concerned to get the airport staff to find it than she was in saying hullo to me. Our reserve was so complete we simply shook hands on eventual greeting. During our drive to Essendon I enquired about her health and she said she was completely fine – no signs of trouble. My enquiry about remission and she denied ever having bowel cancer! As she was about to get out of my Vision Quest Troopy I stopped her and kissed her good-bye.

For nearly ten years I had no contact with Dorathea. The Red Net was completely torn. The love sap that once flowed now spilt onto the ground. I could not find a way to be with her but I was still bleeding. More Vision Quests followed and during this period I began work on the Spiral transcripts. I was extremely surprised to find this transcript about our relationship and the symbolic exercise about the Red Net re-awakened many old memories, regrets, hopes and shattered dreams. I simply had not realized that Archetypes also had their hopes. We had ruined some very important plans.

This ruination seems stunningly stupid in the light of having been set 10 lives together as occupational therapy for each other – this being our tenth – and evidently equal to our worst since Biblical and Old Norse times. How can it be that we have gone so far wrong after so long? How can I even consider the price to be paid for beginning a quest to understand Eternal Life and Great Design and be led to see that Eternal Love is the area of the greatest failure in my current life?

I phoned Dorathea to find out how she was and to talk about this transcript and particularly this postscript. Certainly she was well. She had moved to a country cottage where she had become very interested in organic vegetables, ducks, sitting on the reflective veranda chair; and for income, importing South African wines. Her life had been revolutionised and yet she still owned the old car in which our "runt" had occurred. This was consistent with the transcripts. However she knew nothing about the musical instrument called a Rote.

Speaking to her on the phone brought back a flood of memories, but most particularly of the fateful day I received her letter saying she never wanted to see me again.

In part I can see the cost has been that we were both set Road Ten and even that has been torn. I can offer no sensible reply to Archetypes ruling that I am a wastrel fool. The journals again point directly to my responsibility. There were several times when Dorathea asked what she could do for me and I failed to see the need to explore what occupational therapy meant; and how she could be my writing Elder, ever my guide and my Eternal Loving partner. I also failed to explore what I could do for her on her Road Ten.

Ten times Dorathea's name occurs directly in the transcripts originally obtained from the spiral and once she is given as Dot deci. There is no doubt her journey and mine are integrally linked in mutual Road Ten purpose we have not even begun to explore. But there is a clue to how this can be approached. This is an example of when the edge of the shield has to be left so that the heart of the matter can be found. In section 4 above the transcript reads;
SSE DO [visit as tourist] –TON [Suff. To Noun eg. Simpleton]

There is no way I can see that is really saying I should go to the SSE on my own as a simple tourist because the capitals say DOTON – on what? On Phillip Island at Cape Woolamai, on Woolamai Hill, on the Numerical Aperture of course! Where better to find out what ONE intends than in a place given as the place to speak and to learn? What better invitation could we get in starting to mend Ten 'O' Ten breaches when on the Road of Light and Love?

Having completed a draft of this quite remarkable transcript I phoned Dorathea and spoke to her about what had occurred and she agreed to review what had been written. I had no female partner at that time so I found the contact exciting and full of good prospects. Even listening to her voice on the phone sent thrills through me. There seemed to be no significant barriers to solid progress after years and years of difficulties and confusion. I wondered if she would agree to meet me again, even on Phillip Island?

The crushing disappointment eventually came by email. Dorathea had nothing she wanted to add to what I had written and she had no intension of seeing me. Oh!

Indeed the Red Net was torn Ten out of Ten and there would be no mending possible now. Not even the Elder Tree could help me with this mess in this lifetime. She wanted nothing to do with me. It was time to accept defeat.

Sacrifices under Reed Lore.

There is another debt I have under the Lore and a set of responsibilities that go with it. Footnote 26 [Partnerships] identifies a past experience I had when I had to apologize to ONE for ever having referred to Him otherwise. [Using the "G" word.]

In all the years since that experience I have very seldom made a mistake with this word and even when undertaking a reading at one of my daughter's wedding I had to obtain permission to change the wording of the reading to suit. This actually requires constant vigilance because I have found my self singing a song with the "G" word in it and suddenly realizing what was happening. But there was another very important outcome from that experience.

As I was driving along the track leaving the Big Desert on that occasion, the inner voice of caution spoke to me very clearly saying "After what has happened, out of respect, you should never eat meat again." I was astounded all over again.

I loved meat anything. I loved a fillet steak with mustard and one pea and one potato! I found it hard to imagine not eating meat ever again. I had taken my meat eating responsibilities very seriously and even did my own slaughtering and butchering at the farm. I even had a wonderful old six foot butcher's block in the kitchen and 19 cubic foot freezer that could hold half a steer. Not eating meat would be a major sacrifice. Then the inner voice continued. "You should also not eat fish and only eat shell-fish at a feast." That was another major sacrifice as I loved going fishing and coming home with up to 9 kg snapper or a hundred whiting, assorted flat-head, pike, bay trout, bream etc. Oh!

Since that incredible experience and the sacrifices outlined, I have kept the Lore.

Obviously mistakes are made. On one occasion I ordered a vegetarian Greek souvlaki and they made me one with chicken in it. As I began chewing the thing it tasted unusually beautiful! But before I swallowed I checked the consistency and found it was chicken and had to empty my mouth and go without the meal that I had been given.

Anyway there are some wonderful shell fish and I delight in a good potato cooked in foil in the embers of a Mallee root camp fire.

Other than making a daily sacrifice, the major consequence of this ruling under the Lore has been that I have come to enjoy a wide variety of vegetarian food that I otherwise would probably never have tried.

In planning my next trip to the southern region of the Big Desert as Mother Earth and Astronomer Ger have suggested I will certainly undertake that trip with a solid 22 sense of Submission – Caution To ONE.

I have made other sacrifices. When my inner voice of caution told me to always fast on a Tuesday, I did so for about three years until told it was no longer required. The purpose had been served. Whilst I am unclear about what the purpose was – beyond self-disciple – I suspect it was to deal with some of the debts I owed and responsibilities I had under the Lore, even to Dono and Boyo.

Tuesday is named after Woden's son Tyr who made a significant sacrifice in the interests of capturing the Fennris Wolf that was wreaking havoc on the general population. According to the legend, the Fennris Wolf was so strong that no leash could hold him. Tyr found out that only a leash woven from spider's webs would be strong enough to contain the beast. But the Fennris Wolf was also very smart and when Tyr went to try and attach the leash, the Fennris Wolf insisted that he could only attach the leash if he was holding one of Tyr's hands in his mouth. Tyr put on the leash but then refused to take it off so the Fennris Wolf bit off his hand. Tyr made a sacrifice for others.

Something like that was achieved by my three years of fasting on Tyr's day and by the ego-rebukes I received from some family members and friends.

Perhaps my greatest sacrifice was leaving the Tana Stone to distract IN-ONE.

This is not an easy story to tell. The Tana Stone meant a lot to me and it had a direct association with Dorathea's healing of a non-existent cancer. When I found it on a beach in Tana and I was thinking about her at the time. Twice daily I practiced Tai Chi on this isolated beach in an unspoilt wonderland. {A University student of mine had told me of the beauty of Tana [in the Vanuatu Group] that he had discovered as the manager of the resort on the Island of Tana after finishing his degree in Business Management.}

After Tai Chi, I made a practice of walking slowly along the beach and meditating on different issues in my life. One of the issues was what to do about my feelings for Dorathea and then I spotted this very small, almost perfectly round stone amongst thousands upon thousands of other black volcanic stones. Unlike any other, this stone had some tiny crystals that emitted lavender light – it was perfect for healing so I picked it up and kept it.

As noted earlier I carried the Tana Stone with me whenever I was away from the farm and it had been in my pocket during many Vision Quests where I made a regular practice of not looking back.

I was no stranger to symbolic action or to stilling myself and listening for guidance. "As above so below" was the ancient Gnostic saying.

One day, with the Tana Stone in my pocket, I was driving along a side street in New Gisborne Victoria when… "Stop". So I pulled into the kerb. "Go to the front door of that house and knock. No-one is at home". I followed the instruction and indeed no one answered the door. There was a small Christian Cross fixed to the door. Something very important was afoot.[31]

"Turn around clockwise and clap your hands. Do this three times and then say - If there is anybody there come out now or go in everlasting peace." I realized this was an exorcism[32] and so I did exactly what I was told. Nothing seemed to

---

[31] Doing what I was told also had to conform to my own sense of responsibility. I refused to do anything I was told when it did not so conform. On this occasion it did conform so I did exactly what I was told. It is significant that Great Spirit identifies three T's which do not have relevance to this text and the last one of those was an individual tone of voice. I can verify that I have never been able to distinguish individual voices in "guidance'. The choice about responsible action is always **vitally mine**.

[32] This is relevant to a Southern Hemisphere banishing process. In the Northern Hemisphere the process is completed anti-clockwise.

happen. Everything seemed peaceful but I had no idea about what to do if somebody did come out!

"Go around to the side gate."

From the side gate I could see a middle sized black dog lying on the veranda, it looked up but significantly it did not bark or come to investigate my presence at the gate.

"Put the Stone on top of the gate post."

I was somewhat shocked at this but I put the Tana Stone on top of the post beside the house.

"Go back to the car and wait."

I could see the side gate from the car and after half an hour I was told to go back to the gate and check the top of the post. No one had come to the gate or even entered the property but the Tana Stone had gone! It was nowhere to be seen even when I searched on the ground around the post – it had "vanished" and I have never seen it since.

"Satan wanted it. The people will be very surprised when they come home and find that all is peaceful." The stone was pretty important to Satan?

In Trans. 1 Archetypes refer to a situation where the "Lease Shed Set" had "slid sit Hades". I think the Tana Stone's disappearance was highly instrumental in enabling that remarkable occurrence – but I was sad to have lost it.

Also under the Lore I have had a responsibility to protect one of my daughters. The description of the First Journey to Cape Woolamai identifies what I needed to do and did in this regard. She is my eternal daughter and I am her eternal father, in the same way my father has always been my father in successive lifetimes.

I am glad to report that my daughter is in perfect health and very happy circumstances with gorgeous children of her own.

[Distant Spiral Galaxy NGC 4603 by the Hubble Space Telescope.]

2ND JOURNEY TO CAPE WOOLAMAI.

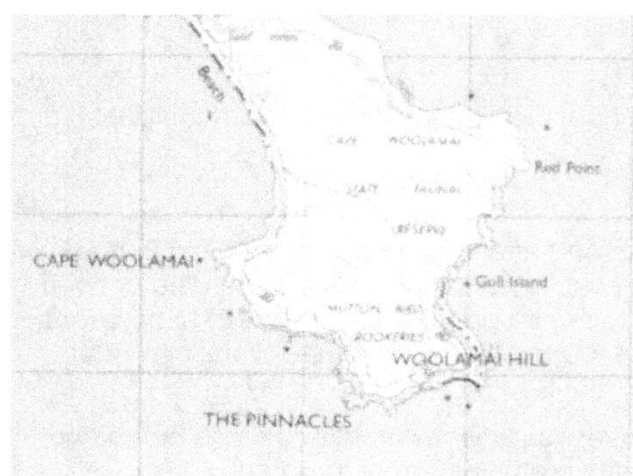

The most characteristic thing about the second journey to Cape Woolamai, is that it was not peaceful weather. It was gail force winds! Little chance of being within a standard deviation of the reflective Lake of Peace – Lake Tai! But it was exciting!

I had prepared for wet and windy but not storms. As I drove into the island, I could see the tide had been driven by the storm well up to full and would rise further. But was it the wrong time? The national tide forecast put neap tide at about 3 – 4 p.m. and so a short trip was necessary anyway to get back before dark. I had emergency gear and even a survival blanket and had no need to carry water! Besides I had come for the experience of nature and needed to make it quicker than planned. As I had begun fasting 24 hrs. before leaving the farm, I was and I wasn't well prepared for QUICK! I was reminded to take a small bag of dates and return all the pips in the bag! [completely Elder Tree Mother]. Rather than quick or quicker; more "clicker"; feeling my way along with my Elder Tree Mother symbol; a one metre hollow stick. [See chapter 9]. At one level the Elder Tree Mother has become my constant companion and I was taking her on a very important walk to the Numerical Aperture to ONE. I couldn't be sure about returning. No, I haven't heard of anything yet that would otherwise persuade me from going as a common tourist, especially when the tides were exactly right on my birthday. Although this was a very violent storm I felt sure that Elder Tree Mother would warn me of any impending danger. As I hiked along the beach, the wet sand entered at the tip, but slow bruuussshes in the churning sea cleared any blockages. Along the track I brushed her lightly through bushes leaves, the water on the grass and the sand under our passage. I could sense her enjoyment. She had warned me to be ready for the unexpected so I knew all was OK as she was steady in my hand.

This is as much a wonderland of flora and fauna in a gale as when at peace. Hardly a bird was to be seen anywhere and although the transcript had said DOTON, I expected this only meant I was to undertake the journey with the cheerfulness of DOT being ON Cape Woolamai.

In sharp contrast to the peace and tranquillity of walking along the dawn-beach at Magiclands last time, now there were two metre waves. In places, they were already running so far up the beach they were undermining the edges of well-established sand dunes. It was wet but the oilskin coat, beanie and storm hat were great. But I was not storm prepared in the pants department. I knew that I should not roost anywhere like a bird, so I hiked straight to the top of Woolamai Hill without stopping and by following the straightest route. I planned to return the same way.

Judging from later reports, about the time I was on the Cape to Woolamai Hill, gale-force winds were ripping off part of the 80 years old café roof in the nearby Seal Rock! And back at Woodend there were reports of snow falling! Significantly I never felt the winds endangered or opposed me, but rather assisted and at one time resisted every step I took when descending the steps at Magiclands to see a surfing puzzle of immense complexity and awesome power. [It is notable that there was a great tail wind from behind going up but not down on the steps.] I felt at one with the place and the storm. Without stopping or deviating from the track I felt my way clear to the top despite the driving rain along the ridge through the SE sector of IN-ONE's territory. With Elder Tree Mother steady in my hand, I hummed along, loving the storm.

When I reached the top I called RE to the whales in the wild waters as my eyes drank in the panorama of whitecaps in Bass Strait. At the top of this hill we were still witness to stunningly powerful forces. I took a short moment to stop in the centre of the storm; and remembering where to begin, I knelt at the base of the solitary rock at the top. I removed my hat and stilled myself. As I began giving thanks… through the storm came a "clear voice"…

> *"This isn't the time for a chat!"*

> *Laughing, I agreed.*

Hats back on and Elder Tree Mother still by my side, I quickly left by the shortest route and did not stop or look back until I was back in the central clump of the protective Banksia grove. A small dark-brown kangaroo moved along quietly to a different place, its pace and direction undisturbed by my presence or the storm.

I figured that now was a good time to find the bag of dates and end my three day fast. Delicious, three then three and all the six pips went back into the bag as Mother Elder had directed! Then I headed down the track, along the beach and into the car park.

The silence and calm of sitting in the car were a shock after the violence and noise of the storm.

There were no other cars in the car park so there was no way Dorathea was ON Cape Woolamai at that time. Even as I panned the car park I realized there was a

hopeful aspect to this action. I wanted to find her there on the Cape. I wanted to feel there was a proper resolution to the many things that had happened. So many unresolved issues existed between us - several hours later when I returned to the farm, I rang her…

I think I could do with a moment or two holding Alice's pig!

[Spiral Galaxy 74 – by the Hubble Telescope.]

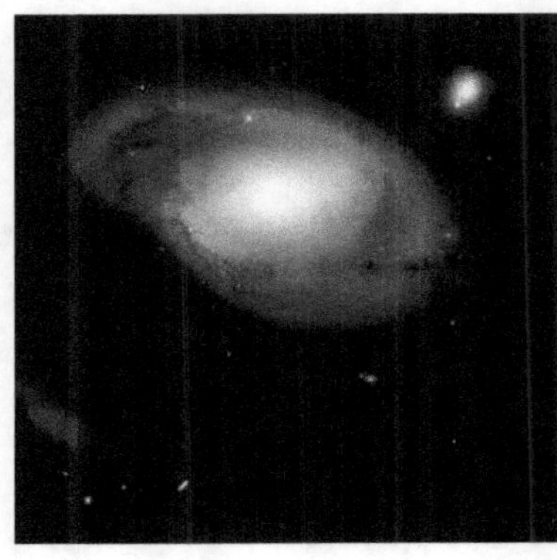

1.

North Sages take centre stage to a very quiet meeting of Archetypes. They advise us that discussion is to be about AIDS - acquired immune deficiency syndrome. The physical manifestations of HIV/AIDS, [symptoms and spread characteristics] show many signs of entropy – even down to definitions by circular argument. People's responses to HIV/AIDS are entropic too along with intervention difficulties; lack of research and medical facilities; shortages in aid programmes; staffing problems; funding shortages; and nutritional deficiencies. Central and common to all these issues is entropy.[33]

[Spiral Galaxy NGC 4319 and Quasar Markarian by the Hubble Space Telescope.]

Cadi blows a long SI/TE on his horn. He instructs us to make sure that we are sitting for this discussion. Expanding on the note he had chosen; the 7th note is a signal of Great Mystery - Creator and Destroyer. In raising the subject of individual deaths from AIDS, it also raises great pain and grief in loss of loved ones. There are millions of grievers! So many who are living and dying with HIV/AIDS are just children. You may well be asking is this the Destroyer at work? But no it is the work of man.

Children of the Eternal Tree are signalled also by the musical note SI - the highest note - a call to the highest state of consciousness anyone can reach, the limit of human ability in contemplation of the divine. The levels of consciousness reached when our Dervishes dance the spiral until they know divine inspiration and bliss. That is what our children will know. All of them who are now in Eden are in a state of perfect happiness. So a very personal construction is applied even when we are discussing matters collectively, technically or statistically –

---

[33] Entropy; firstly, the greater the degree of randomness or disorder in a system, the greater the entropy of the system. So if you have gas escaping from a cylinder into a room, entropy will be greatest when all the gas has escaped and become spread randomly in the air throughout the room. Underlying the process of the escape and spread of the gas is what is termed a spontaneous process. No external energy or input is required for the process to occur, it will happen naturally. A state of equilibrium will only be reached when the potential energy of the system is fully expended - just like water flows down hill until it reaches the lowest point. As the water flows so it expends its potential energy and the process cannot be reversed – it cannot run uphill again without energy input from outside the system. The second law of thermodynamics is that all spontaneous or natural processes produce an increase in the entropy of universe. So by analogy, AIDS will continue to spread more and more widely and it is not reversible. The escaped gas won't go back into the bottle by itself.

HIV/AIDS has many aspects, but the first aspect is personal - we are all sacred beings. [Sanctitas Vestra.]

Gatt Seers report around the Bend; this is a very personal subject: it's about men chasing "Tail and Ta-ail" - a very personal discussion about sex.

East Neb; Putting it politely, the first issue has to do with a system that is not designed to be blocked - it is designed for bodily waste disposal and contains remnants of every sort [anti-bodies your own system has disposed of - elements and molecules dangerous to your own system]. A silt system needs to be respected for what it is there for. Problems arise when it is not being treated properly - it is not Tail, it is Ta-ail.[34]

Ever Errs; All people who behave in this manner have been set down together in a List.

Great Spirit; The register for the Ta-ail List is very large.

At the Numerical Aperture; AIDS is registered D - 4th in a series where dis- can be put before d,b,l,m,n,r,s, and v: or di- could be put before them. There are many ways that HIV/AIDS can become manifest. It would more properly be called a collection of diseases with a variety of thinning and wasting symptoms. The name Ta-ail List may convey the wrong idea. It is not to be likened to a tail on a living animal; even if it is imagined as the tail of a blue whale. It is more advantageous to consider the stature of the Ta-ail List as huge because HIV/AIDS is the biggest killer of human life ever and Ta-ail is a key cause. However, in terms of stature, there are so many volumes of the Ta-ail List register, it is huge; there are whole streets of them! Whilst on the subject of streets, street children, whose only advantage was their body, are advantaged – special provisions are made for them.[35]

---

[34] Ta-ail. HIV/AIDS has becoming more widely spread in the female population. In some parts of Sub-Saharan Africa, up to 35% of adults have HIV/AIDS. In Swaziland, HIV prevalence among pregnant women attending antenatal clinics in 2000 ranged from 32% in urban areas to 34.5% in rural areas; in Botswana, the corresponding figures are 44% and 35.5%. Worldwide, the number of children living with HIV/AIDS stood at 2.7m in December 2001. Although unprotected sex, especially anal sex, is a significant contributor to this situation, malnutrition and poverty dominate the considerations. Source; UNAIDS & WHO "AIDS epidemic update December 2001." [See Bib. 77.]

[35] D 4th . This rating very closely equates to the December 2001 AIDS epidemic update by UNAIDS and WHO, written by Anne Winter, Dominique de Santis and Andrew Shih. Their Global Overview said ;

"Twenty years after the first clinical evidence of acquired immunodeficiency syndrome was reported, AIDS has become the most devastating disease humankind has ever faced. Since the epidemic began, more than 60 million people have been infected with the virus. HIV/AIDS is now the leading cause of death in sub-Saharan Africa. Worldwide, it is the fourth-biggest killer."

"At the end of 2015, an estimated 78 million people globally had been infected with HIV and 35 million had died. In many parts of the developing world, the majority of new infections occur in young adults, with young women especially vulnerable. About one third of those currently living with HIV/AIDS are aged 15 - 24. Many of them do not know they carry the virus. Many millions more know nothing or too little to protect themselves against it." It is 49x higher among transgender women. 28x higher among

Nehemiah; Ever since archaic times there have been many individuals who decide they would prefer to sail into the next life by being conveyed by the action of a disease. There are a great many on the Ta-ail List who chose to end their Earth life via disease.

Steerer; Amongst a sufferers' sufferings is isolation. Feeling distal; to be experiencing a distance or feeling cut off from the source; or distant from one's origin or point of attachment. Tension is caused by this distal relationship not only from the community in which they live but also distal from ONE. Those who feel distal come most quickly under the destructive or corruptive influences of Saturn. As such they are increasingly vulnerable to contracting "full blown AIDS". The corruptive influences of Saturn can be very pungent.

Astronomer Ger; If people living with HIV/AIDS were convened together in a meeting, they would sit without sound or movement - like pillars of salt.

Mother Earth; Iodine and basic hygiene in house and person are central individual necessities[36]. Then three things are needed in response programmes – 24: Love, Money and Creativity. Each of these three warrants creative research and development in response programme design. Isolation needs to be met with Love.[37] Money.[38] Funds are also needed for research into the virus and

---

people who inject drugs; 12x higher among sex workers and 19x higher among gay men and men who have sex with men. For every 10% increase in treatment coverage there is a 1% decline in new infections.

[36] In the Russian Federation, HIV/AIDS is growing faster than in any other part of the world. Analysts conclude that unprotected sex with multiple partners, combined with alcohol and recreational drug taking are the main contributors. Although spread has been entropic in high-risk groups, the virus has not as yet spread to the wider community. The virus has spread to the general population in Africa but "The vast majority of Africans living with HIV do not know they have acquired the virus. One study has found that 50% of adult Tanzanian women know where they could be tested for HIV, yet only 6% have been tested. In Zimbabwe, only 11% of adult women have been tested for the virus. Moreover, many people who agree to be tested prefer not to return and discover the outcome of those tests. However other obstacles remain. A study in Abidjan, Cote d'Ivoire, shows that 80% of pregnant women who agree to undergo an HIV test return to collect their results. But of those who discover they are living with the virus, fewer than 50% return to receive drug treatment for the prevention of mother-to-child transmission of the virus." Other findings are that women who know they have HIV do not tell their partners for fear of abuse or abandonment. Basic hygiene and no anal sex are central necessities at the individual and family level. In 2016 UNAIDS estimated the rate of new infections [2m] hasn't changed much in the last 10 years.

[37] Love; Several studies have shown that social isolation generally increases as HIV/AIDS advances. Response programmes involving social support have proved to be highly beneficial in the effects this has on the individual's immune system. [See Trans. 11.]

[38] Money; "One quarter of households in Botswana, where adult HIV/AIDS prevalence is over 35%, can expect to lose an income earner within the next 10 years. A rapid increase in the number of destitute families is anticipated… In hard-hit areas, households cope by cutting their food consumption and other basic expenditures, and tend to sell assets in order to cover the cost of health care and funerals. Studies in Rwanda have shown that households with an HIV/AIDS patient spend, on average, 20 times more on health care annually than households without an AIDS patient. Only a third of those households can manage to meet these extra costs. According to a United Nations Food and Agricultural Organization [FAO] report, seven million farm workers have died from AIDS-related causes since 1985 and 16 million more are expected to die in the next 20 years. Agricultural output – especially of staple products – cannot be

its spread. A sign of great hope and promise may be found by putting aside some funds to research the medicinal value of the plant commonly called Dill – Anethurum graveoles. [This herb has been used for culinary and medicinal purposes since ancient times. Limonene and carvone are the volatile oils or medicinal ingredients principally obtained from the seeds by distillation. They possess stimulant, aromatic, carminative and stomachic properties, making them of considerable medicinal value[39]. The culinary uses of dill include pickles of many sorts and it is especially eaten with fish because of its fat reducing qualities.]

Mother Earth says that in early folk history when a woman found herself having to pay a tythe to the landlord, as well as the rent, she would try dill in the tail and generally find he'll much prefer vagina! Especially when that has been given a small dose of LSD. Then you will find he looks as though he has seen the faces of all the Saints!!! At such moment she would tell him it is the only passage he can use to get there!

 Overall, a distillation of the sex drive when focussed on Ta-ail will show that the source of one's instinctive energy in psyche is negative when it needs to be positive. The best way of determining which is the sacred passage is to consider from which passage your last daughter was born? Considering all the species that have

sustained in such circumstances. The prospect of widespread food shortages and hunger is real… Almost everywhere, the extra burdens of care and work are deflected onto women – especially the young and elderly." "The AIDS epidemic has a profound impact on growth, income and poverty. It is estimated that the annual per capita growth in half the countries of Sub-Saharan Africa is falling by 0.5 – 1.2% as a direct result of AIDS. By 2010, per capita GDP in some of the hardest hit countries may drop by 8% and per capita consumption may fall even further. Calculations show that heavily affected countries could lose more than 20% of GDP by 2020. Companies of all types face higher costs in training, insurance, benefits, absenteeism and illness. A survey of 15 firms in Ethiopia has shown that, over a five-year period, 53% of all illness among staff were AIDS-related… Meanwhile, the epidemic is claiming huge numbers of teachers, doctors, extension workers and other human resources. In some countries, health care systems are losing up to a quarter of their personnel to the epidemic… In Zambia, teacher deaths caused by AIDS are equivalent to about half of the total number of new teachers the country manages to train annually." In the face of such vicious destructive cycles, huge injections of funds are needed to assist individuals, families and countries. HIV/AIDS will worsen most where nutrition is worst. UNAIDS say treatment programs cost in the order of US$19 billion a year

[39] Mrs. M. Grieve. "A Modern Herbal". [See Bib. 27].

roamed Earth, the answer is a fraction indefinite as there have been a few! Nevertheless - even then! Yet!

Chief Petty Officer; a single but substantive variant had a T shaped joint "setting sail" and "waste distribution" system.

North Sages; The amount of earthy matter consumed by that variant was so great it was like the weights freight ships carry! And what they unloaded on their journey, at zero temperature would make you slip if you were knitting!

Mother Earth; Yet! The human faces of the Saints would greatly assist the therapeutic process by the distillation of the negative aspects of Psyche. The source of the instinctive energy of the psyche can be regarded like two sides of a coin. Further research is called for into both positive and negative aspects of the Psyche. [See Trans. 11]. Research is also needed into the passage of the last comet [Borrelly] about which we should note what was deposited by this astral body. [The adjacent exhibit is not of Comet Borrelly, it is Hale Bop that visited our part of the solar system in 1997 and is a long period comet with a return every 2500 years. However it clearly shows what is deposited from the tail of a comet. Later exhibits are of comet Borrelly when it was intercepted in deep space by Discovery 1 on 22nd September 2001.]

Chief Petty Officer; A substantial amount of various particles can be seen travelling together like a whole fleet of sailing vessels that are left behind in the comets tail and so become very widely distributed. [The blue feathered section of the tail is composed of ion particles whilst the lower brighter section is composed of dust, gas and water molecules.]

North Sages; Water particles at absolute temperature are the carriers for many other particles, some of which can have a destructive effect when they interact with a slip into negative or self-destructive Psychic state.

Cadi; Sunday Schools should teach the importance of maintaining a positive emotional state and loving attachment to the Creator.

Gatt Seers; Some of the particles deposited on Earth are extremely small and can have highly beneficial effects.

East Neb; Liken this to the beneficial effects of a play in ice hockey that assists a team member score. Some water born particles have been found to be the building blocks for life itself. In effect comets are transporting these building blocks throughout the solar system and into Universe beyond. Therefore, comets aid or increase entropy.

Ever Errs; If we examine the end or conclusion of this process, we will see that a central underlying personal conflict exists - all forces rely on the same building blocks. Our biggest errors can be traced back to our negative, self-destructive emotional state, our own destructive side, our negative Psyche. It attracts trouble.

Great Spirit; We need to examine what and how we do things and bear these facts in mind when formulating contingencies. But there is something that has to be allowed for in such contingency plans…

Nehemiah; …since archaic times, it has been to listen.

Steerer; We should listen to a totality of things or qualities that dwell in a situation. In particular, consider those who have delirium tremens [DTS]. Those who suffer DTS also need help, assistance, relief and aid. They would benefit from being assisted in much the same way as those who are living with HIV/AIDS. Additionally, sailing or managing a boat for sport, would assist both those with HIV/AIDS and DTS.

Eats; Amongst many who could vie for let's say Eating capacity, including knowing the mental state of the meal in an aluminium boat, Shark has no rivals. Shark is 27 of the sea, The Sceptre. Shark knows what you imagine and invite when a leg is hanging over the side of the boat and the occupant is dreaming about the imaginary number in Math, the square root of minus one! The Sceptre has looked many in the eye at that moment and seen startled faces - a return to "now" awareness. Shark likes to see a dial on which time is indicated!

Astronomer Ger; Having seen many go West, Shark first prefers to go for the tail, or the bits that hang down from it! Shark can take up to ten of them in a row but has to leave the last one - one foot.

At the Leet; It is ruled, the remaining digit has to be on the right.

Mother Earth; The right is tuned to the musical note A, the Hallelujahs and planet Mercury. All my heirs are kept under observation in this manner.

Chief Petty Officer; By analogy a 'dial', is a special compass used for underground surveys in the mining industry. In a similar way, the face, even the rib is measured in relation to a specified height for such heirs.

North Sages; This would cover just about anyone with a somewhat sad expression shown in a still frame - the A-Sad.

Cadi; This specified class of heirs, the A-Sad are tailed or followed where-ever they go.

NE Court; Each one is required to sit as a candidate for an examination.

Ever Errs; A dialect - a subpart of a major language group is used for this examination.

Nehemiah; The dialect is specific to south territory.

Astronomer Ger; Everyone examined so far is illiterate in that dialect!

Mother Earth; When negation and reversing forces are evident and one can not be identified as belonging to this class of heirs, the last digit left by Shark, the right foot, could be used for identification. It can be matched against a model. If that assists...

North Sages; ...what is also shown on the face...

East Neb; ...what will begin is a period of being seated
TO ONE!

2.
ONE TO
North Sages; Seventh Day Adventists perceive the strait entered is the final one relative to other positions.[40]

---

[40] Although not a direct reference to the Book of Daniel, or to Revelations, previous references in Trans. 5 point to North Sages referring to the period known as the Last Days before the Second Coming. This is the period marked by "the Abomination that makes desolate."

Mother Earth; A measure of this final strait is used in physics and called a Tesla –
a measure of magnetic flux density [the magnetic poles of the Earth have been
reversed before! Tesla also means 16 The Shattered Citadel, a sign of fatality
becoming entropic in South Africa. She thinks the people there will appreciate
being used as a model.[41] They need all the assistance they can get. [Even basic
skills are being lost, land left idle in places where people starve because all their
resources have gone into much higher than normal medical expenses. The
burden of family care is falling increasingly on children who are in increasing
shock themselves. Poverty and malnutrition act as further body and mental stress
factors that increase onset into HIV/AIDS. So the negative cycles develop
negative spiral characteristics in chronically affected areas.]

Astronomer Ger; Will a model for a Sex Appeal [for HIV/AIDS and DTS] from
South Africa really be best? The last go was something Late Latin!

Steerer holds up the Roman numeral for 1. To salt a situation, or create a higher
sense of value, one should imagine someone sitting upon something like a horse
whilst in fact enduring a progression…

Nehemiah; …into the once Roman territory previously referred to. There is a note
at the bottom of the page for a concert to be held at the end of this procession -
all instruments are to be tuned to the same musical note – Concert A.

Great Spirit; lanthanum[42] - also identifies the numeral 24: meaning Love, Money
and Creativity.

East Neb; for-sees the beginning of a ton of talk. A short ton of lanthanum and
24:.

NE Court; announces that someone has been enlisted to assist with this work…

Cadi; …Lieutenant Al Last – one who comes after all others – has been enlisted.
He is otherwise associated with the chemical sulphur; 19 The Prince of
Heaven[43]. Travelling aboard ship with Lt. Al Last, your aboard the SS
Steamship…

---

[41] People living with HIV/AIDS in the Sub-Saharan Africa number 28,100,000. This is also where 68% of
the world figure for new infections is occurring. Mother Earth is saying HIV/AIDS is identified with the
Abomination. Nigeria, Uganda and South Africa accounted for 48% of all new infections of HIV in 2014.

[42] Lanthanum is the beginning of a very different series of elements known as Inner Transition elements.

[43] 19 The Prince of Heaven. It is symbolized by the Sun. It indicates victory over all temporal failures and
disappointments. It blesses the entity represented with the power of 10 [Love and Light] but without the
inherent dangers of abuse. This promises happiness, fulfillment and success in all ventures. [See Psyche].

North Sages; …in harmony with the musical note SI is harmony like International units.

Chief Petty Officer; A dissertation is required on Psyche as the source of our instinctive energy. [This is included in Trans. 11. The Twin Nature of Psyche.]

Mother Earth; all one's interest, concern and /or property should go into this dissertation. The musical note A, and the Right, clockwise; tuned at or about Tasmania.

Leet; Where "Tail" means the hindmost part of an animal.

Astronomer Ger; A- signifies the intensity of the action such as to amaze, results in a few drops. And "To exude Lad"- means any male detective. To add "Latin", means ill, trouble, misfortune. To try and sail with the Latin Conflict List, would amaze…

Steerer; the sail or equivalent apparatus needed for the Latin Conflict List, could only be operated by someone with delirium tremens, in a literal sense!

Nehemiah; Water will appear to be still, without waves or perceptible current! However, a high flown, grandiloquent TAIL will follow close behind, measured in tones! But it will be lowered a little bit for the L-Latin!

East Neb; -T will be recorded after the names of all those who meet that TAIL unexpectedly. This will signify a whole range of verbs to describe how!

NE Court; There is a long history of ONE yielding assistance or aid to all who travel on any List and in any peril. So too in HIV/AIDS.   .

North Sages; 3 remain still for a moment. Then they individually report on the assistance given - "Steadily." "Constantly." "Always provided."

Chief Petty Officer; for relentless action - SS storm trooper!

Mother Earth; ILL. SS-ILL to look into all objections, any or all unsatisfactory or poor performance aspects. He even knows what passages have been silent since Anglo Saxon times and he will not be still until no sound is heard from one

---

Eastern Colonies for malarial conditions, its efficacy in this respect is not to be compared with cinchona bark, though it does not create the bad effects cinchona does. It is also employed as a bitter tonic, vermifuge, and as a cure for chronic diarrhea and bowel complaints". A homoeopathic infusion of Alstonia bark is 5 parts to 100 parts of water. A dose being equal to 1 fluid ounce or when powdered bark is used a dose is 2 to 4 grains." This wonderful tree grows exactly where it is most needed in tropical and sub tropical Africa, India, Southeast Asia, Central America and Australia. Several species of the Alstonia family are also widely used for commercial timber as the trees can achieve heights of 20 to 60 meters and they have been recorded with a diameter of up to 2 meters. See Mrs. Grieve "A Modern Herbal" Bib. 27.

particular passage. He aids all those who administer last rites and those who assist forgiveness whilst distilling negative aspects from Psyche until all is known is /said; peace and blessings then instilled.

Leet; -ASIS, the name we have given for Mother Earth's folk story about experimenting with Dill and LSD. This could become something of a battle-ground. Instead of the proposed "treatment" of lysergic acid diethylamide battleground, we propose the scene of combat be about the properties of a tree or shrub called Dita or Alstonia scholaris from the Old World Tropics[44] [India,

Africa, Southeast Asia, Polynesia, Central America and Australia. The tree grows widely in the very regions where HIV/AIDS is worst and the bark has important homoeopathic properties that make it particularly useful in the treatment of chronic diarrhoea, dysentery and malaria that result in wastage symptoms. Using Dita bark extracts will calm, appease or allay peoples' fears and concerns; although one would hardly say it would be a replacement for LSD, or of an experience of looking on the human faces of the Saints whilst using LSD!] One way or another, the negative Psyche has to be reversed and grounded in Men saying No to ASIS[45]. By Chaldean – Kabala numerical alphabet, ASIS [1313 = 8 ; repeated patterns; destined difficulties doubled.] To change ASIS to –ASIS is to begin a process of saying "no" and of so ending the destined difficulties and repeated patterns parts. All who can join in -ASIS can

---

[44] DITA bark is used medicinally. Alstonia scholaris is commonly variously named; Devil's Bit, Pali-mara, Bitter Bark, Australian Fever Bush, Devil Tree. Our botanical thesaurus, Mrs. Grieve describes Dita bark properties can be used "mainly as a febrifuge in malarial fever, tonic and astringent, with much the same properties as Peruvian Bark. In A.scholaris the strongest alkaloids are Ditamine, Echitanine, the latter in character resembling ammonia; other constituents are echierin, echicaoutin, echitin, and echitein - these are crystaline - and Echiretin amorphous." Medicinal action and uses; "Though Alstonia is used in India and Eastern Colonies for malarial conditions, its efficacy in this respect is not to be compared with cinchona bark, though it does not create the bad effects cinchona does. It is also employed as a bitter tonic, vermifuge, and as a cure for chronic diarrhea and bowel complaints". A homoeopathic infusion of Alstonia bark is 5 parts to 100 parts of water. A dose being equal to 1 fluid ounce or when powdered bark is used a dose is 2 to 4 grains." This wonderful tree grows exactly where it is most needed in tropical and sub tropical Africa, India, Southeast Asia, Central America and Australia. Several species of the Alstonia family are also widely used for commercial timber as the trees can achieve heights of 20 to 60 meters and they have been recorded with a diameter of up to 2 meters. See Mrs. Grieve "A Modern Herbal" Bib. 27.
[45] Where men have recently turned to saying yes to ASIS, the UNAIDS & WHO reporters advise in relation to the Russian federation and Eastern Europe – HIV risk is high among men who have sex with men, among whom multiple partners and unprotected sex are widespread. Currently, there are very few examples of HIV prevention activities targeting this group."

be counted aboard what was to have been the –ASIS LSD List. However, it will be known instead as the –ASIS DITA List that is sure to sail. The change in the nature of those who travel under this List is from destined difficulties doubled to 30 The Loner – Meditation that is characterised by retrospection and thoughtful deduction. Destined difficulties will be doubled for those who stay on the Ta-ail List and who continue ASIS.

Astronomer Ger; The Tail can also be the inferior or refuse part of the ego, the Metaphysical I, etc. and the Will, all go West [awareness normally survives in transition].

Eats representative Shark; suggests someone sit or place themselves in position, as for an artist. Placed at a till or cash register that can accommodate variously large units of weight or capacity to receive donations for "All Women" and "All Men".

Steerer; Contributions are needed from the whole of society.

Nehemiah; What will be underway is a vessel that will serve the choices made.

At the Numerical Aperture; Choices will also have to be made for each and every assistant.

Great Spirit; decrees appointments should be semi-annual until the final goal is reached or the whole tail treated. Then we will get to Last.

Ever Errs; There is a final matter…who comes Last? Lt. Al Last.

East Neb; When Lt. Al or "Lastal" was a boy or youth, he was given an atomic stitch.

Gatt Seers; we observed the stitch passing through. And we frequently see Lt. Al Last passing through now-days.

Cadi; A division of Lt. Al Last's hair or beard should be set aside to signify a Saint for the Ill and those who face unfavourable or adverse circumstances.

3.
North Sages; Thallium is the chemical chosen to denote 18 Spiritual – Material Conflict. "A rayed moon, from which drops of blood are falling. A wolf and a hungry dog are seen below, catching the falling drops in their opened mouths, while still lower, a crab is hastening to join them."

Cadi; It is time to be still and quiet.

NE Court; Idem – as previously given or mentioned. STILL. As Still as an experienced sailor, an old salt, listening to nature and carefully observing her.

Gatt Seers; A lilting tune then a melody is being played - alternately.

East Neb; Calling on the lines in the initial training alphabet, the Chaldean – Hebrew Kabala Numerical Alphabet, for the LITA'D List that sailed with dignity; LITA'D means 13: Regeneration and Change.

This is not an unlucky numeral, as many people believe. The ancients claimed that "he who understands how to use 13: will be given power and dominion." The symbol for 13: is a skeleton, or death, with a scythe, reaping down men in a field of new-grown grass, where young faces and heads appear to be thrusting through the ground and emerging on all sides. 13: is a numeral of upheaval, so that new ground may be broken. It's associated with power, which, if used for selfish purpose, will bring destruction upon itself. There is a warning of the unknown and the unexpected. Adapting to change gracefully will bring out the strength of 13: and decrease any potential for negative. 13: is associated with genius, explorers, with breaking the orthodox and new discoveries of all kinds.

Great Spirit; a light shines on the letters "D-4th ". [HIV/AIDS is the biggest reaper of humankind ever and the 4th biggest killer. D also has the numeral value 4 in the Chaldean –Kabala Numerical alphabet - destiny. This also means 4th in a series as outlined in the beginning. HIV/AIDS has many forms in which it manifests.]

At the Numerical Aperture; LITA'D

Nehemiah; She sails with dignity, all instruments tuned to the musical note D, under Scorpio, with blue-green sails.

Dyna Pandy; Some instruments played D sharp. By the Tree of Life this means Sagittarius under the influence of Jupiter. She had 622 on the bow and is painted blue for Jupiter. She has flashings of red – orange and is tuned to G sharp – 415 – all children - under Taurus[46]. By the time LITA'D passed through, it sounded more like a recital.

---

[46] Jupiter is blue and D sharp – pitch 622. This means 10 The Wheel of Fortune. LOVE & LIGHT. Power to manifest creative and destructive forces. Scorpio is blue-green – D music – pitch 587 and means 20 The Awakening ; "a winged angel, sounding a trumpet, while from below, a man, woman, and child are seen arising from a tomb, with their hands clasped in prayer." A powerful awakening, bringing new purpose, new plans, new ambitions – the call to action for some great cause or ideal. 415 – Orange-Red – all children under 10 - Taurus.

From her Lighthouse, Steerer watched LITA'D voyage. She encountered strong ocean currents, twice; but singing LA in unison did wonders. [6th note - love.]

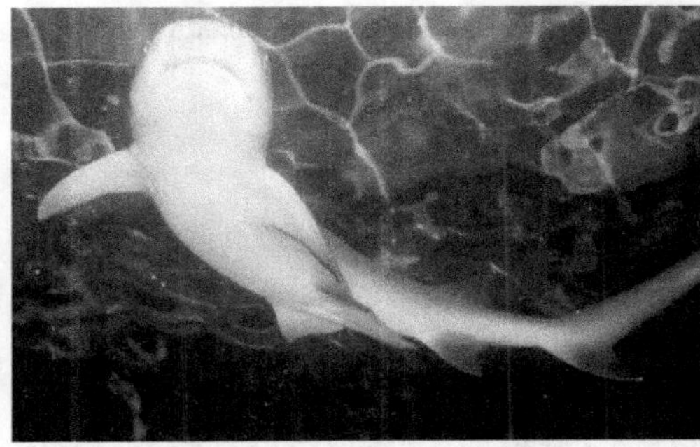

Eats representative Shark; whenever people experience pain, feel somewhat ill, or are in grief, they classify it as Evil. In any language - it is.

Astronomer Ger; What can be seen on the LITA'D is also a SIT List comprising those persons who have spent time as an elected representative in parliament. Even those who sat on the border of matters, or who experienced only a small dose, now sail with the SIT List. She sails along like a cloud.

Leet; There is a saying that salt gives piquancy or pungency to something.

Mother Earth; Not all experience gives piquancy. Anyone who thinks the buttocks can be used to induce pregnancy is an ass. They will die with all those who are like-minded.

North Sages; Salt can be used to cure, preserve and treat things. Particularly they identify salt from South Australia. Taking a somewhat technical atmosphere, they identify compounds that have the same chirality as L-glyceraldehyde; ie., left handed chirality or the sinister is identified with such a passage.

Cadi; Calls for all to be still, to quiet commotion, pain and passion. He proposes we consider one of a class, a single case.

NE Court; A Learner – Driver. Each one has to learn it all – everything. As a Learner – Sex not everything has to be learnt! It is best to also know about the dangers Mother Earth sees in using the "silt" passage.

Gatt Seers; There is surface tension.

East Neb; Likened to the lower part of a pool or stream, Sanctissimus Dominus – Most Holy Lord – the title given to the Pope. As shown by the plate or dial with letters and numbers on it, only the tail is left.

Ever Errs; Is sad, sorrowful, mournful.

Great Spirit; For anyone to occupy that seat in an official capacity would be a lethal dose in density that over time would result in illness.

At the Numerical Aperture; The field enclosed for combat is occupied by a slow, patient, sure-footed beast of burden.

Nehemiah; A southern identification is involved.

Steerer; This person is to be found…

Eats; …where the young herrings grow in Norway.

Astronomer Ger; Finding this person is without year or date but that when found he should be seized by the tail as if grasping wickedness or sin itself.

Leet; He will give financial support to the AIDS List, because of a like or desire to do so.

Mother Earth; In an intermediate or transitive stage, during developments of the dissertation on the negative aspects of Psyche, a solicitor at law will be heard to cry out "AI" as if imitating the large three toed sloth from Central or Southern America. He will understand her remark about an ass and can take responsibility for the Deposit Account because he knows only a blockhead or fool would take any latitude with such an account. [No doubt the Hop Office will keep a very critical eye on the Sex Appeal funds.]

North Sages; Money will be forthcoming to begin a journey by water to make a presentation at a meeting for the Sex Appeal in Holland.

NE Court; meetings, or gatherings of the AIDS and DTS Tail will be quiet, tranquil and calm even though a very strong current will be running – although not apparently attached to anything. However one issue will be to do with coming last after all others in suitability or likelihood. Thus, leaning to one side like a listing ship, the HIV/AIDS List.

Gatt Seers; A measure of luminance called a Lambert is of relevance. It means wisdom path 29 Grace Under Pressure, perhaps the heaviest karma of them all with the exception of 38 Grace Under Pressure. 29 echo the tales of Job in the Old Testament. It means being individually tested but maintaining grace under pressure and particularly remaining steadfast in adherence to ONE.

East Neb; The mood is sombre, dark and dull.

Great Spirit; Sadness is running at a very high level.

Nehemiah; But this is a very solid foundation on which a player is called upon to perform.

Astronomer Ger; in the end analysis this performance should be more like a still wine and not be effervescent.

Mother Earth; a link should be formed with Italy and the solicitor at law previously referred to.

Chief Petty Officer; Any of various salts used as a purgative to clean the bowels.

North Sages; a measure of viscosity - Stokes. The name Stokes has an association with the Salvation Army that is deplorable and shocking to the North Sages.

Great Spirit; Associated with "alto" music or high young-male voices.

Nehemiah who have previously provided ERNE as a Doctor to ONE; now prescribes the chemical lithium [an anti-depressant]
TO ONE.

4.
ONE TO
Cadi; A state of lower tension has been reached!

North Sages; What is particularly shocking is that Stokes is the Deputy.

Mother Earth; His official responsibilities include the Saturday's Lid. This is the moveable piece for opening a box or vessel – such as used for a regular collection.

Leet; Stokes will appear and answer for his efforts at artificial insemination.

Astronomer Ger; A subdued, low or hushed sound is heard when Stokes uses the phone to make a call.

Great Spirit; Decrees the behaviour is to the left – sinister.

East Neb; A sad and sombre image of long, narrow strips of wood like on a park bench.

NE Court; This was at the time of a comet, when the luminous head and tail could be seen.

Cadi; Identifies it as the last comet – Borrelly on the 22nd September 2001. He says that a large amount of something remained behind.

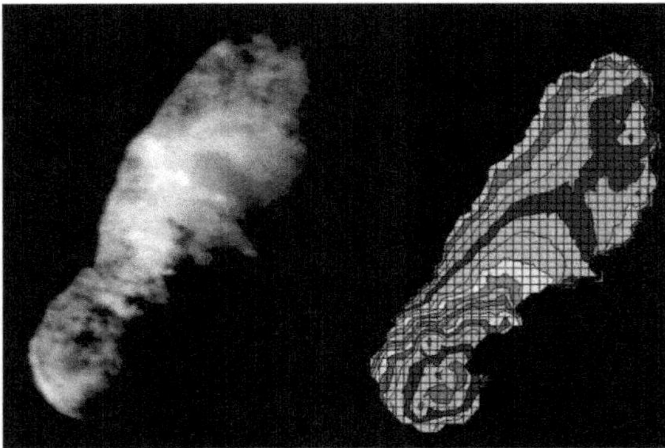

North Sages; An extract was obtained by distillation. [Near Deep Space 1's closest approach to comet Borrelly's nucleus, solar winds picked up charged water molecules from the coma about 2200 km away. NASA press releases in April 2002 described Borrelly as like a "dirty snowball". Analysis has shown there is "plenty of ice beneath its tar-black surface, but any exposed to sunlight has vaporized away". The surface temperature of comet Borrelly is between 26 to 71 degrees Celsius so any surface water is quickly vaporized in the coma. One of NASA's researchers said that the surface of the nucleus "seems to be covered in this dark material, which has been loosely connected with biological material. This suggests that comets might be a transport mechanism for bringing the building blocks of life to Earth." Such dark material is more commonly found in the outer segments of our solar system and generally not found in the inner solar system. Study of the nucleus has shown it to be far more complex than previously expected. Over 90 per cent of the surface is inactive and it has rugged terrain, smooth rolling plains and some very deep fractures. The above exhibit shows the structure of Comet Borrelly's nucleus but regrettably NASA's legend was not available to the public.

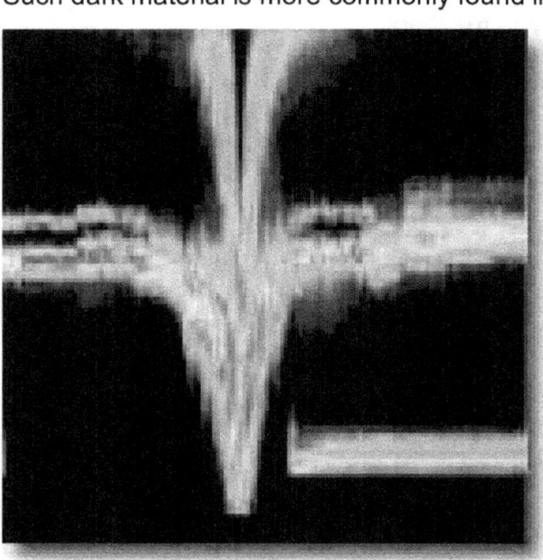

Borrelly not only left behind a long trail of ions in it's tail along with dust, water and gas, but it also interacted with the solar winds that carted particles off at right angles to its path as well. In this exhibit, the horizontal red bands to left and right are due to the interaction between the solar winds and the coma. The head or nucleus of the comet is at the bottom of the picture.

Mother Earth; Subject to individual approval, particles or elements from the comets tail may become attached or driven off by Psyche. Movement of these particles is limited by the expanse of the catching surface like sailing ships put up more canvas to catch more wind. Likewise Psyche can attract more or less; or be tuned to respond in particular ways; or regulate what it will accept or reject. To gain an idea of the power involved here, Mother Earth reports tidal movements in September show the remarkable characteristic of being staid or fixed at that time.

Leet; The tides should be made the subject of an inquiry.

Astronomer Ger; An inquiry should be conducted with all possible speed but still be undertaken thoroughly or completely. [I first obtained the tidal information at the shipwreck site of the Pandora in Queensland. There seemed to be a particular relevance to opening the lid there! Although tidal movements between high and low tide are normally in the order of 3m, during the period 21 – 24th September 2001, movement was less than a metre! Likewise, tidal movement in the South, Central and North Pacific of the USA can be 3 – 3.5m, but unusually low tidal movements of 1.5m or less occurred during the period 24th – 29th September 2001. This is about the same time Deep Space I intercepted the orbit of comet Borrelly on 22nd September 2001 when it was closest to Earth.

Steerer; Aid, help or assistance is required for the sinister S shaped deposit that sits in the upper atmosphere.

Nehemiah; It is at a very high level.

Great Spirit; But it can effect all women – any woman.

Ever Errs; Notes the effects could only be reviewed by adults – those under 18 yrs. should not be allowed access.

East Neb; This will effect Sanctissimus Dominus – Most Holy Lord – the title of the Pope and the tail of succession or lower part of the pool or stream.

Gatt Seers; A Son was to sing and play in a lilting manner, however what can now be seen is tension on that surface.

North Sages; A large amount of tension exists about how to protect and hatch eggs whilst the comet's tail exists or sits in the upper atmosphere – a technical atmosphere issue about which NASA have not provided public information.

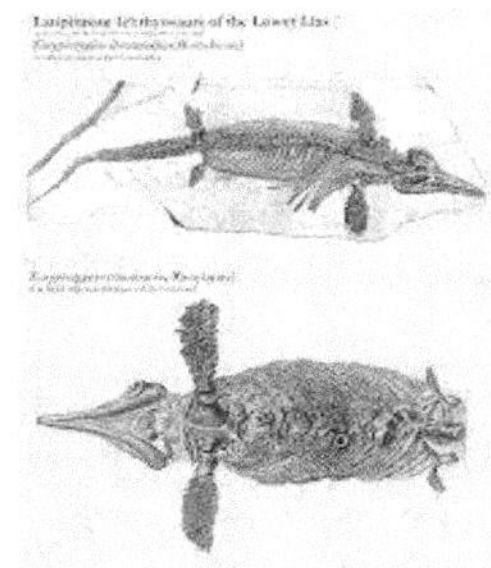

Chief Petty Officer; Roman number for 50 – L.

Mother Earth; The wavelength measurement unit Angstrom, which measures the distance between atoms in molecules – 50 angstrom. Angstrom also means 29 Grace Under Pressure. The current pressure is equated to the Lias of NE Europe, which are a series of marine sediments of the Lower Jurassic Period. Mother Earth says that the shape of those deposits correlate with the rhythmic swing or cadence of a comets' tail when the deposits fell to Earth.[47]

Leet; A list is needed of things both positive and negative of what has been found in the tail of comet Borrelly that landed last Tuesday [04/07/02] and continued to land until Sunday [07/07/02] when it was landing by the tonne[48].

Astronomer Ger; As one cloud of ill, harm or injury sails across the sky and eventually settles, it causes another to set sail as he has in the past to navigate; he is 19 The Prince of Heaven – Pan - alias Lt. Loner, Lt. Eon and most recently Lt. -Al Last.

Eats; He will aid the remainder of the period AD.

Steerer; Singing the musical note La [the 6th note] twice, she refers us to Isaiah [Chapter 12] in the Old Testament.
> *"1. You will say in that day; "I will give thanks to thee, O LORD, for though thou wast angry with me, thy anger turned away, and thou didst comfort me.*
> *2. "Behold, you are my salvation; I will trust, and not be afraid; for the LORD is my strength and my song, and he has become my salvation.*
> *3. With joy you will draw water from the wells of salvation.*

---

[47] These marine sediments were laid down during the Hettangian epoch that is the lowest of three in the Jurassic Period. The epoch dates from 203.9m to 206.2m years ago. This is a period of great changes in geological and biological terms. Major tectonic [continental drift] and climatic changes occurred during this time and the marine sediments known as the Lias were spread across Europe and Britain. Because of their importance in petroleum research, these deposits are relatively well studied but it is not currently possible to determine whether there are correlations with the tail of a passing comet or whether Earth was hit by one or more comets during this period. Research has shown that clay layers have shown higher than normal levels of iridium – ie., higher than normally occurs on Earth. Archetypes are obviously very concerned about the impact of Comet Borrelly's residual deposits and what will happen when they fall to Earth. The record of a massive extinction occurs in the European Lias.

[48] I have attempted to validate the type and quantity of deposits from Comet Borrelly but detailed results are not currently available from NASA or any other internet source even in 2016.

Dyna Pandy; Just as land is prepared for a crop by making furrows and ridges, so too the schooling in titanium – 23: Royal Star of the Lion. This is a wisdom path of karmic reward. 23 bestows not only a promise of success in personal and career endeavours, it guarantees help from superiors and protection from those in high places. It is a most fortunate path, and greatly blesses with abundant grace the person represented by it. Other paths don't have much of a chance to bring serious trouble when the Royal Star of the Lion is present during difficult times. No other path can challenge the Lion's strength and win.

Nehemiah; The eyelid marks this number – 23. [The Eye of Horus shows the eyelid as a spiral with the numerical value of 1/32. In a mirror we see –1/23.]

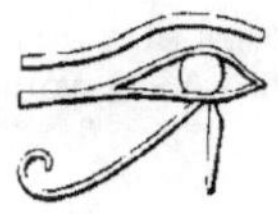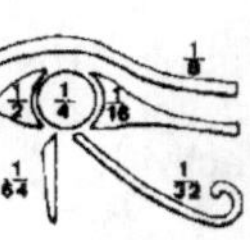

At the Numerical Aperture; Just like salt can be used for seasoning, a model or last of the foot…

Great Spirit; Can be fashioned with the chemical silicon. Again this means 23 Royal Star of the Lion, as said, named or mentioned before salt.

Ever Errs; The Royal Star of the Lion's is on side with everyone who commits to and undertakes -ASIS.

East Neb; Just as I already had the initial Chaldean training alphabet available for use, so too others will be provided for in their work also. Even from the beginning or from what will later be seen as the beginning. There is Heart. Courage. Light/wisdom. Deer/Love, Reed and what is right under the Lore. A right choice of passage is needed and the Royal Star of the Lion could be counted on to…

NE Court; Vaporize! Then condense…to distil "the right choice"!

Cadi; Saturday, 13th July 2002, is the day on which that border or edge is reached[49].

5.
NE Court; That ends matters concerning the first element in the compound.

Great Spirit interjects; LA ; wonder and surprise will occur when next using the telephone to call ...

At the Numerical Aperture; ...someone seeking an artificial insemination donor.

Nehemiah; When the assistant turns up in full dress attire – right down to a formal Lion's tail...

Dyna Pandy; ... you had best pay a few shillings and say that by Ta-ail, you meant you wanted to have someone followed!

Mother Earth; Say, to follow someone reading a book or books - Literary work! [Not much work is involved in following them.]

North Sages; Arsenic – the poison, also means 23 Royal Star of the Lion. [The symbol for arsenic is As, the first two letters of the Leet's named –ASIS.]

Great Spirit; The idea of what is an auxiliary mechanism includes anything that can dissolve something. –ASIS would be essentially for dissolving all but normal anal activity.

Nehemiah; It may be difficult to believe, even extravagant to have as a goal, but none the less...

Dyna Pandy; Just as in building, if one end of a beam has been fixed then technically it is fixed. There is no flexibility about what is or isn't –ASIS.

Steerer; suggests that next time you are with your female sweetheart...

Astronomer Ger; ...and at the end you know you've got her by her we ankle...

NE Court; ...the lass' Ta-ail must be still, at this or that time, still
TO ONE.

6.

---

[49] 13 Regeneration and Change day but double bad "luck" after that – destined difficulties doubled.

ONE TO

East Neb; To remain in good condition as a lad, even with a devil-may-care sort of attitude, or that of a "dashing young man" or even just as one of the lads...

Mother Earth; ...will require distillation to extract some volatile components.

Steerer; This sounds like an advertisement...

Nehemiah; On the plant "Dill" – particularly the leaves and seeds[50] should be used.

Ever Errs; "I would," would and should use dill. I especially use it for Evil, and /or when choked up with something."

NE Court; Dill is like a long braid or tress of hair from a loved one - it is highly valued.

North Sages; We should mark the day that it comes...

Astronomer Ger; The end of that day will be marked by the musical note A. The sixth degree means love and on the Tree of Life it means Saturn and Capricorn, the 10th Sephiroth, the Hallelujahs and Road Ten. [That is a big day to call.]

Steerer; 26 Partnership is involved with a Doctor of Letters.

Dyna Pandy; The Partnership is as with someone who follows another and so they can vouch for another.

Nehemiah; He who follows is literally in full dress attire!

At the Numerical Aperture; A distance is involved. Even if a distance is involved, Royal Star of the Lion will be there at a measured distance.[51]

Great Spirit; Likens it to talking on the phone to the Dais. But there is a warning here[52] as well, anyone who thinks they can roost or perch like a bird on the Island...

---

[50] The volatile oils in dill seeds are limonene and carvone.

[51] Visiting the Numerical Aperture in the SSE at Cape Woolamai is also being referred to here as it was in chapter 9. The reference to a partnership between the Doctor of Letters and Royal Star of the Lion is that the wisdom path for my name is 46, double 23: Royal Star of the Lion. [See Postscript 3 for Trans. 9.]

[52] At the top of Woolami Hill; one large granite rock; one bench type seat and a solar-powered lighthouse.

Ever Errs; …would be a fool or incompetent.

7.

Ever Errs; the association is stet, ie., it has been deleted and then put back or reinstated. Those who succeed with –ASIS will find that their association with Ever Errs has been re-instated.

Great Spirit; A tail wind will come from behind from the right.

At the Numerical Aperture; To cultivate the wit and use of humour, the musical note D is prescribed. 20 The Awakening. When this wit has taken root this will constitute the end of the second part. [Laughter is the best medicine.]

The image of 20 ; "A winged angel sounding a trumpet, while from below, a man, woman and child are seen rising from a tomb with their hands clasped in prayer."

Dyna Pandy; One should then be able to travel through the air like a balloon.

NE Court; One should no longer require assistance, and the past associations will be deleted.

Ever Errs; At such time, a garment will be fitted; likened to the chemical argon that means 24: Love, Money and Creativity.

Nehemiah; At such time one can rebuff or reject on-going criticism of the literature – this literature from the spiral transcripts.

Steerer; The literature is…

East Neb; vaporization and condensation
TO ONE.

8.
ONE TO
NE Court; the literature is like…

Nehemiah;…drops of distillate…in a purified and condensed form…

Great Spirit;…that will continue…

Ever Errs; …until ready to go boldly into action.

NE Court; The "right time" will depend on the state of the tide…

Steerer;… as though…

Dyna Pandy; … limited to a specified line of heirs…

Nehemiah; … even when set at the diameter there is a basis for tuning in.

At the Numerical Aperture; This tuning in is within a standard deviation of the Lake of Peace – Lake Tai.

Great Spirit; "I will come from behind like a tail wind."

NE Court; all remains in place or at rest, the Court and the Bench are motionless.

---

4. CATALOGUE OF TRANSCRIPTS 1 – 10.

The following transcripts are an exact record of the word slip order obtained in the process of analysis. The numbers included in the left-hand margin are used for ease of reference. The original words generated from the "dream statements" are typed in capitals and the associated definitions are in parenthesis in lower case. Following the initial development work, a record was also taken of the position or location of word groups relative to the compass points (North, etc.). The order in the transcripts remains the same as in the original manuscript.

1. WHITE REEDS LAID
2. DEVELOPING WIDER EARS
3. SACRED BONDS OF THE SEED ERA
4. FAILING ALLIANCES IN THE BISHOPS POWERS
5. WHATA SAGA
6. HARES AND AVES AGHA TO THE HARVEST RAT
7. HAIL THE ONE
8. ANYBODY WITH HOPE?
9. ONE LED TREE.
10. SAIL LIDS LIST

The following material has not been edited at all. It is an exact record of how the word slips landed in the spiral lanes. Each lane reading is separated by a broken line. Some further notes have been made to expand certain issues and points. An explanation of the correspondence between the Elements of Chemistry and the Wisdom Paths is also provided before the 8th Transcript where Chemistry symbols were included in the abbreviations from then on.

Transcript 1. WHITE REEDS LAID.

The word string used for analysis was WHITE REEDS LAID.
1.10 WHEAT
1.11 SITE
1.12 DIRE
1.13 LARD SIDE WET
1.14 WETS TIRED LIES LEADER WHALES
1.15 TIED HAS REED DAIS RITE
1.16 WRITE TIE LIE ADDERS TIER SIDED HATE
1.17 LEE RAT TRIES WHAT SHIT HIT
1.18 HEW DEAR EARS SEW SAD TO THE ONE.

1.20 THE ONE SAD RITES REEDS RISER WIRE
1.21 WISER EARS DREAD RELEASED

1.22 ADDS READ DAIS TIDES HIT
1.23 SEED TILE WRITES SHIT HAT LID
1.24 RAT LEE SIDED TIER ADDERS
1.25 REED TIED WHALES HEEL LEADER REST TIRED
1.26 WET RATE SIDE HIRE TALES RE DIRE TIRES SITE WHEAT

1.30 WILD SEER ADDER REALIZE WHALE RATES
1.31 SHEAR RAIDS HEAL HAD ALTER RESTED
1.32 RATS SLIDE RAID WADE
1.33 THESE SEAL LED LAID HEATER SHEER
1.34 RID DAD HEARD DIE SEA REAL AS SHEARED
1.35 LATER AIDS SHEET DIRT TIERS
1.36 HEARS LEASE SHED SET
1.37 SLID SIT HADES LATE EAR LAD LEADS TO THE ONE

1.40 THE ONE LEADS EAR WIDE LATE
1.41 WAITS HADES SIT SLID HIS HEATS HIDE A REAL DIE IT HEARD
1.42 DAD RID HEATER LAID SEAL
1.43 THESE WADE RAID SLIDE ADD RESTED HEAL RAIDS
1.44 SHEAR RATES RIDES DID
1.45 SHIRE TEARS
1.46 RED WHITE HELD ALDER SLEW HATES HIS AIR DATE RELEASE
      TO THE ONE

1.50 THE ONE TEAR HIS
1.51 LEASED HEAT
1.52 LEAST ALDER DALE STAID TEARS DEER SHIRE
1.53 HEAR DEEDS SEE WEEDS
1.54 LEST LIED LETS RISE WIDER TO THE ONE

1.60 LIST HAIL THE ONE

1.70 THE ONE LED TREE
1.71 SAIL LIDS LIST

1.80 AIDS TO THE ONE

1.90 THE ONE AIDS

Transcript 2. DEVELOPING WIDER AND WISER EARS.

The words used to develop this record were WIDER EARS. Compass points begin to identify the location of some words [e.g. N = North].

2.10 N. AIRS WED
2.11 E. ERASE WIRES
2.12 WE EASIER WAR
2.13 READ IS DEW RISE RIDE TO THE ONE LORD

2.20 THE ONE LORD RISE SAW RAW DEW IS READ
2.21 REARS WAR ERASE WEE SEER WED
2.22 DARES WAR IDEA
2.23 ERASED SEAR
2.24 WIDER REED WEARS
2.25 SEE ERE SEED SEA TO THE ONE LORD

2.30 THE ONE LORD ERASER RIDS SEA SEED
2.31 ERASED AIDS DAIS RISER
2.32 WEEDS RED A DEER WEDS
2.33 DARE SIRE ARISE WIRE SEW TO THE ONE LORD

2.40 THE ONE LORD ARISE
2.41 S. WEIRDER
2.42 E. A RED ERR WAS EARS
2.43 S. WIDE EWER DESIRE
2.44 EASE RE
2.45 DIRE WADE WERE WEIR AID
2.46 ARSE DEARS REAR SAID WEIRS TO THE ONE LORD

2.50 THE ONE LORD WEIRS SAID AS ARSE AID REAR
2.51 SE. IRE EIDER RIDES WERE RID WEIRD RE DESIRE

Transcript 3. SACRED BONDS OF THE SEED ERA.

The words used for analysis were WEEDS RED A DEER WEDS.

3.10 DARED WAS SEA WARS
3.11 DARES ASS [donkey] EASES SEW ADDED DEARS TO THE ONE LORD

3.20 THE ONE LORDS WARDED ARSES SEWERS ERR WADED WADE
      DARED DEED ASS SEESAW WARD AS DARED
3.21 SE. WARDER
3.22 S. RARE
3.23 ADDERS SEDER ERASE REDDER DEEDS
3.24 DRAW WEARS SEWER
3.25 DARE WEE DEW EWE ERASE TO THE ONE LORD

3.30 THE ONE LORD SEEDS SEWER WEAR DRAW SEAS DEEDS WAR
3.31 ADDS ERASED DEER RASED SEE [Bishop's seat of power] DREAD
      REAR DRAWS SEAR REARS WED SERE REED WEDS SWEAR TO
      THE ONE LORD

3.40 THE ONE LORD SEED ERE RAW REED SERE WED SAW READER
      SEARED
      REAR RASE ADD RASED DEER
3.41 SE. WRASSE
3.42 SEER WADED EARS
3.43 WEED DREW READ WEARER SEWER SEES SEWS RE SEAR EAR
ERSE
      TO THE ONE LORD

3.50 THE ONE LORD ERSE RE ARE WARE SEERS SEES READ DREW
      WEED EARS DEWS

Transcript 4. FAILING ALLIANCES IN THE BISHOP'S POWERS.

The words used for analysis were DEW RISE RIDE.

4.10 N. REEDS [arrows]
4.11 WIDER WEIR DIE [stain]
4.12 SE. SEE [Bishops seat of power] DIED WARD DIE [cast] REDDER WEIRS
4.13 REEDS [grass] SERE IS DESIRED DEER WISER IRE
       WE'RE EVER ERRS ESE [east south east]
4.14 WEED [grass] REED [arrow] SEE RE WEER REED [grass] SEER WERE DID
       TO THE ONE LORD

4.20 THE ONE LORD DEEDS SIDE RIDE REED [grass] RE SEE SEE [Bishops]
       WEEDS [clothes] WEIRER ERRS REED [weavers] SIDED WEED [grass]
       REEDS [weavers]
4.21 DERRIS EVER WOULD
4.22 IRE DIES [cast] DEER ID RIDER DESIRES RE RED WEIRS DIED [stained]
       DIE WIRES REEDS [flutes] REDDER DIE [cast] WARD DIED RESIDE
       DIRE ERR SEE [Bishops] WEIR
4.23 WEE WISE [proceeding]
4.24 DERIDE SEWER
4.25 DERIDER DIES WORD WEEDS [grass]
4.26 ERE DEWIER EIDERS WIRE EIRE DESIRE
4.27 RESIDED WIDE EWE
4.28 WE'D [had] WISE WEED [clothes] EWER TO THE ONE LORD

Transcript 5. WHATA SAGA.

The words used for analysis here were THE GREAT WRASSE SAVES.

5.100 N. WEAVE RATES REVERT ARTICLE RAG RASTER [electronic
scanner]
        AREA GETT [Erse tartan]
5.101 SE. EASTER TEARS RAWER TAW [valued marble] WHEAT
        GATT [passage/pass] SH'D [should] WHERE AT VERT [turning the foetus
in the womb prior to birth]
5.102 SEVER GRASS SWEARER ARREARS STEERAGE REVerend
        S.V. [Sancta Virgo] ESTATE GARTER
5.103 S. TAWER [cloth preparation] THREW SHAT STARS
5.104 SW. WAG [admonish with finger]
5.105 NW. VEERS
5.106 N. RETE [network e.g.. heart, arteries and veins, solar system]
5.107 NE. WEER RAGE
5.108 E. WHATA [Maori storehouse] SAGA GER.[gerund; verb form of a noun
        e.g.., hunting, writing, by adding 'ing] AWARE AEGIS
5.109 H.G.[High German] GEARER SWEATERS EWE VERGE [edge] SECtion
        TAWSE [strap punishment]
5.110 SE. SHEA [African Butternut tree] SEES [Bishops seats of power] H.E.
[His Eminence] SEE [look] WAVE THETA [Grk: 8th letter] HEATS WEARER [one
        who changes tack]
5.111 SWEETS STEEVE [incline upwards] VERT [right to cut greenery]
5.112 STAR ASS'S ASH [ex. fire] AS VESTS [with power] VEGETATES SEE
[look] HAG.[Haggai – Holy Bible] STEER TETRA [tropical fish] VARiant AGE
        ASSistant SERVES
5.113 ARSE SWERVE GRASS GAVE WAGER WAG [tail]
5.114 SSE. ERST STEEVE [pack tight] TRESS [plait/ braid] SEWER
        AH [Exclamation; pity] WAS TERRA TAGS WAGER TATTER GESTATE
STEW SERE [dry] TAG GREAVE [pair of defenses] ARRESTEE AGHAST
5.115 SECondary WASTER STEWS THEATRE GATE TESTER SAHARA
RATHER WASHES SEVERER REARS
5.116 S. W [Wodensdarg - Woden] REAVE WAGE [war] SAVE
5.117 THRASHERS STARVE S.V. [Sanctitas Vestra / Your Holiness] SHEER
[facing] STAVE [wooden wine barrel slat]
5.118 W. GARE [guard hair in a fleece]
5.119 South East HARASS HAG SWAGE [tools for shaping metal] WARE
[watchful]
5.120 E. HEAVE TEASE EAST VAT WARE [things]
5.121 SE. GRASSER [informer] EASE ER [Exclamation; hesitation] STEARATE
[salt of acid] VAGrant TAG
5.122 S. VASES SEESAW RATA [New Zealand red flowering tree] SEAS

AESTHETE RET [cloth prep'n; soak fibre in water until separated]
SHEET REVERE [venerate] GREATER RHEA TO THE ONE LORD

5.200 THE ONE LORD ASHES GREATER VEST [long outer garment]
5.201 SHEET HAST TWA [Scottish; two] EARTH'S SEAS RET [laid down to rot]
        SEESAW SWEETER VASES
5.202 SE. TAG VAGrant ER [Exclamation; hesitation] STEARATE [salt/ester of
an acid] EASE GRASSER [informer]
5.203 E. VAT TEASE WARE [things] 'WARE [aware] EAST
5.204 SE. HAG EH [Exclamation ; surprise]
5.205 W. GARE [guard hair in a fleece]
5.206 S. STAVE [barrel slat]
5.207 N. SHEER [fabric]
5.208 E. TERAS [study of the abominable]
5.209 S. TRET [allowance for waste in cargo] EWERS W.[Woden]
5.210 SSE. RATHER GATE TESTER WE'RE VERSET [short verse] WASHS
TAG SAHARA STEWS AGHAST TARTARE STET GRAVE [hole] SERE [dry]
        AH [Exclamation; pity]
5.211 SSE. RESTATE TAGS
5.212 ERST SEWER STEEVE [pack tight] HE'VE [he would have] WAGER
5.213 GAVE SWERVERS ARSE GRASS ASH [tree] ASSistant THE AGE
SERVES VEGETATES HAGgai [Bible] AS STAR ASS'S SWATTER GRAVES
WAGES [conducts] STEEVE [incline upwards] WAR SWEETS WHARVES
WEARER HEATS WASTAGE WAVE SEE [look] SEES [Bishop's seats of power]
        H.E. [His Eminence]
5.214 E. VERGE [edge] EWE SWEATERS GEARER H.G. [High German]
AWARE RAW AEGIS GERund [hunting] GEESE SAGA SERVE WHATA [Maori
        storehouse] TARGETS WEER THAWS STEER [castrated male]
5.215 N. RETE [network = heart, arteries, veins, solar system]
5.216 W. ESTATED
5.217 SW. WAG [admonish]
5.218 SE. STAGES GARTER ESTATE S.V. [Sancta Virgo] REVerend
STEERAGE SWEAT THAW SWEARER GRASS WHERE AT VERT [turn foetus
in the womb] WHEAT TAW [valued marble] TEARS EASTER RATES THEE
WEAVE

5.300 SHEARS SECretary TEETER TARGE [Scandinavian round shield] WART
HEW STEERS WEAR [change of tack] EASES
5.301 SE. STATE WRATH WREATH WHEAT AVERTS SEVERS TEAS
Western Australia TAR EWER REVET [face with masonry or stone] HEARTS
WASTES WEARS RE VAS [vessel/duct] WAVER TARE REVERSE SEWERS
RETired TASTER
5.302 HER HARSH SERGES WHERE AS SWAG TERETE GHEE [liquid
buttermilk] THESE EAGER WETS WEAR ASHET [meat platter] STEERER TE

[7th note in music] South West HAS RARE ART ERSE SHE SET SEE RECeipt
SHARER ETHER THREE HARVEST TEATS VERticle GER.[German] SWARTH
STEER ASTronomer West TRAVE [device to restrain a wild horse for veterinary
work] TEATS R.A. [Right Ascension] EVERT TEETH THAT ART SWEAR
     REVelations [Bible] SEVERE
5.303 SAGES SHEETS TASSET THRASH TERRA SERE [stages in ecological
         succession] WAGER V.G. [very good] STARTER SWAT STASHES ASS
5.304 S. be HEST [akin to] WASTES EVE ETA [Grk; 7th letter] EARS VEE
SWEAR AT WHAT'S TAT [small] GAT SEERS TEAR REAR EGRESS
5.305 W. TARTAR [descendants of Genghis Khan] AGREE HA [Exclamation;
laughter] GREW SETTER GARage RAH [Exclamation; hurrah] RESGESTAE
[present the facts of the case] STAVES [staffs] TEG [1 or 2 year old sheep]
RET'D [retired]
5.306 SE. HARASSES TO THE ONE LORD

5.400 THE ONE LORD
        SE. WREATHS
5.401 W. STAVES WEAR RAH [hurrah] GARage ETHERS [upper reaches or
heavenly regions of the air] SETTER SWAGES GREW HA [Exclamation ;
laughter] AGREE RATHE [early or quickly bloom]
5.402 S. RAGS GEAR TART REAR GET ETA [Grk; 7th letter] SAW VEGETATE
         WASTES SERVER SAVATE [French kick-boxing] TETHERS STASHES
5.403 SE. SERE [stages in the ecological succession] SHEETS VASE SAGES
         SWERVE GASH HART [male red deer] REVelations [Bible] WHARVE
[flywheel or pulley] TEETH SWEAR TETHER STEERS Right Ascension
5.404 SETA [animals with bristle] EVERT TRAVE [device to restrain a wild horse
         during veterinary work]
5.405 ASS. [astronomer] SAT GER. [German] STARRED ESTATE HARVEST
         GRAVE [Solomon music] TAW [cloth preparation]
5.406 THREE TREE SEES [looks] VEGETables SHE SET ERSE
5.407 HAS WAGE TERRET [harvesting] South West STEERED TE [7th note in
music] WETS
5.408 THESE GHEE [liquid buttermilk] TERET [long slender cylinder] SWAG
         STATES ARRive SERGES TARATA [Maori lemon wood with a bitter
         taste] HARSH HA [Exclamation; pain] RETIRED SHEER SEWERS TEA
         HATTER EGRETS SHE'D WEE RE WASTES
5.409 HE HAW VERGE [incline] SWAGS EWER ESTREAT [true copy]
THRASHER TEAS AVERTS EACH SHEW [show] WRATH EASES WEAR
[change of tack] TWEE [delicate and precious] SETTEE STEERS ARTified HEW
GRATE [fire] VERTebrates
5.500 SE. AGREER SAWS ERES AWE THREE'S ARREST ATE E.G..
[example] SHAG SASH [moveable frame] THESsalonians [Bible] TREES
WAGES WEAR
TO THE ONE LORD

5.600 THE ONE LORD

TREES STATES [Grk; stand of trees] SASH [frame] SHAG E.G. GAS
VEES [small bathing costume for men] SWARE [archaic; past tense of
swear] ERES
5.700 VERGER [church warder/official] RATE AT. [atmosphere] TESTS HASTE
VEST WEST WEAVER SEW TREATS AWAY WAVES TO THE ONE LORD
5.800 THE ONE LORD WAVES AWAY TREATS SEW WEAVER WEST TESTS
AT. [atmosphere] RATE VERGER [church warder/official] STAGS TREAS.
[treasurer]
5.900 ASH'S [tree's] TARTS VESTS [chest] AGREES TRASS [Rhine volcanic
region of Germany] GASES GEE [up; command to start] SHEAR STAGE VESTS
[Ecclesiastic vestments]
5.901 AETHER [upper regions of the atmosphere supposed by the ancients to
be heaven] STARTS SAGE'S TARGET AVERSE ERA
5.902 AVATAR [Sanskrit; decent of a deity or manifestation of a deity on earth]
SAGE VESTA [Roman fire goddess] ERRATA
5.903 ERSE'S RASES VERsion SEWER SWEARS AVE [Exclamation; hail]
TEAR[rip] EAR
5.904 RESTS TREAT ETAGERE [open shelves/library] South East WHEE
[Exclamation; delight/thrill] RAVES WERT WEAVES HATE HAT SWART
SWATS RASTAfarians VEST [with power] WEARER WATERAGE
SOUTH HAWSE [very thick rope] EARTH THEW [sinew to muscle] SWARTHE
[wrap up] HATH
TO THE ONE LORD

5.1000 THE ONE LORD
HATH SWAT E.T.A. [estimated time of arrival] WREST [jerk] WATERAGE
TEASER RESEAT WET EGRET SAWSET HATES
SWART [swarthy] SEARS THREATS THREAT SWEATS EATS WERT
TESTER [flogging of 25 lashes]
5.1001 REVERS [garment hemming] GRAVE [sedate] EAR [wheat]
5.1002 REST South East RAGES REVolution EAVES RECORD VERsion
VESTA [Roman fire goddess] WASHER WREATH ERA TARGET STARTS
SAGES ATTAR [incense] VESTS [Ecclesiastic vestments] SHEAR STAGE
5.1003 GEE [up; command to start] GRAVE [hole where buried] TRASS [Rhine
volcanic region of Germany] GASES AGREE VESTS [chest] WETER
TARTS
5.1004 WEER SAWGRASS TASTES VERST [Russian kilometer] VEST
[Ecclesiastic vestments]
5.1005 RAVE WARS WEARER GATHER GESTA [deeds to property] EGEST
[discharge] SHARE VEER SEE [Bishop's seat of power] STEEVE
[incline upwards] HAVE HATS HER'S RHEToric SEVERE SECond EATS
5.1006 WHERE GRAVE [engrave] TATERS WAVE TAWA [Maori timber tree
with purple flowers] HARVESTS GREATEST RATTER GRAVE [serious] SEER
AVES HARES AREAR GEE VERSE A STAGER SEES [looks] RESET E [Math's;
transcendental constant] WAG [tongue]
TO THE ONE LORD

5.1010 THE ONE LORD
E [math's; transcendental constant] RESET GATE [way]
5.1011 SHE'S SWEET ASSociation SEES [looks] AVEerage
5.1012 A AREAR VERSE SHARES GEE ATHWART HARES AVES SEER
WASH HARVEST SEGT. [sergeant] WAVE TATERS GATT [General Agreement
on Tariffs and Trade] GATE [way] AGHA [Turkish graveside custom for army
    generals – a mark of respect] SECond GET GREATS
5.1013 WART HATS WEST SEGment VEER EGEST SEE [Bishops] SEETHE
    GATHER WEARER SWATHES STASHER RAVE HEATER REVised
    WHATEVER TASTE GREAT AT GRAVE [scrape ship's hull] GEAR SAG
    SWATH TERAS [Grk; monster or abomination]

Transcript 6. HARES AND AVES AGHA TO THE HARVEST RAT.

The words used for analysis were HARVEST RATS AGHA.
6.100 N. REAVE [to rend, break or tear]
6.101 NNE. RATHE [early or quickly bloom] GER. [German]
6.102 E. TASSET [one of a pair of defences worn on the upper thigh and suspended by leather straps] SEE RASE [lifted]
6.103 SE. VETS [animal surgeon] SEER AND RATS GRAVE [cut in] ARREARS SEW ARREST REAR
6.104 S. HEW VASES GATHER THAWS VESTS A
6.105 SSW. SEARS
6.106 WSW. TA TA TARGET
6.107 W. ARTICLE HART GREAT GAS ASS SHAG AREAR
6.108 NW. RESTS AGHA'S TAGS
6.109 NNW. AH [Exclamation; pity] GRAVE [dignified] SERGT. [Sergeant] GASHES
6.110 N. GAT [opening between sand-banks] TARGET HA HA [laughter] TARTARE SAUCE ARTified GRAVE [scrape 'barnacles' off the ship's hull]
6.111 NNE. TEA EH [Exclamation; surprise and some doubt] HASTE SETA [bristle] VET [carefully examine] STAFF FRAME DAVID [Bible] IN ?
6.112 NE. VATS ERA TEAS
6.113 E. ARRANGED TARGE [Scandinavian round shield] GASES GARAGE SEERS THETA [Grk; 8th letter] GAR [fish] GET HEART HEARTS GRAVE [serious] SANCTA VIRGO [Holy Virgin] TEATS RAVE RASTAfarians
6.114 SE. HARVEST SAG VAT
6.115 SSE. TE [Music; 7th note] THAW VERY GOOD
6.116 WSW. SEAS
6.117 W. SHAT TREASURES
6.118 NW. AVES HARES HEAT ERST [before the present time] TERRA ART
6.119 N. ASHES SAGES VESSEL GARTERS REVISE REVolution RAGS
6.120 NE. ASTRonomer GHAT [passage through mountains via rivers] HARSH RASTER [electronic scanner]
6.121 ESE. AVER [to affirm with confidence]
6.122 SE. GATES [ways] HAVE TEAT
6.123 WSW. HAGGAI [Bible] SEAS
6.124 NW. GRATES [fire]
6.125 N. VETS [carefully evaluate] TO THE ONE LORD

6.200 THE ONE LORD
       NW. THE GRATES [fire]
6.201 SE. GATE [ways] HAVE
6.202 ESE. AVER [affirm with confidence] HAVE
6.203 NNE. SOUTH

6.204 N. RAGS REVolution GETT [Celtic area tartan] GARTERS SAGES
6.205 NW. AVES AND HARES HEAT
6.206 W. TREASURER
6.207 SSE. SAG
6.208 SE. TAT AGHA STARE AT SAVES HARES
6.209 E. RASTAfarians RAGES TEAT RAVE GRAVE [serious] Sancta Virgo
       HEARTS HEART GET GARfish GRATE [fire] TARGE [Scandinavian
round shield] THETA [Grk; 8th letter]
6.210 ENE. SEERS GARAGE ARRanged
6.211 NE. SOUTH VATS EARS VET [check carefully] SETA [bristle] HASTE
Average EH [Exclamation; surprise and some doubt]
6.212 NNE. GRAVE [scrape ship's hull] ARTified TARTARE [sauce] HA HA
[laughter] TARGETS
6.213 N. TRAVE [device to restrain a wild animal for veterinary work] SAGS
6.214 NNW. SERGeant RAT HE'S GATT's GERund
6.215 NW. TAGS RESTS
6.216 W. SHAG GREAT HART [male red deer]
6.217 SSW. SEARS
6.218 S. A ARRESTS VESTS VASES GATE [way] ATE GRAVE [solemn music]
6.219 SE. ARREST SEW Atmosphere AND SEER
6.220 ENE. SEE VEST [granted with power] VASE
6.221 NE. GERman TASTE
6.222 N. REAVE [art]

6.300 N. Right Ascension AGE
6.301 NNE. TARE South east SAT RAVES AVES
6.302 NE. TRET SETT [weaver's reed] REVerend HATH HAS EARTH'S
6.303 E. SEWS VERST [Russian kilometre] REVolution
6.304 SE. STARS TETRA [tropical fish] HEATH THESSalonians [Bible] HATS
ATTAR [incense] Vertical GATE
6.305 SSE. EATS be HEST [akin to] SAVE
6.306 SW. HERR [German; mister] HER ERR VESTS [with power]
6.307 W. 'Make a Costume'
6.308 NW. EAST HEWS REARS TARTAR [Genghis Khan] AVE [Exclamation;
hail]
6.309 N. TERAS [Grk; study of abominations] GRAVE [hole] VEST TEST TEAR
[rip] TRAVE'S RASES GATHERS
6.310 NNE. THRASH
6.311 NE. HAGgai [Bible] TASmania TAR AGES AGHAST SASH [in decline]
6.312 E. ASSociation TAGASASTE [tree Lucerne with white flower] ASSistant
TERAS [Grk: the monster/abomination] GeV [geiger scanner] HEARTS
RHETorical TEARS
6.313 SE. THRASHES HARVESTS SASH HARTS [male red deer] ATTAR
[incense] Vertical
6.314 SSE. AVATAR [Sanskrit; decent of a deity, manifestation of a deity on
earth]

6.315 S. AVERT
6.316 WSW. EAT
6.317 W. HEARTS RET
6.318 WNW. E [math's; transcendental constant] ETA [Grk; 7th letter] AVERTS
THAT GASH
6.319 N. RETS TARATA [Maori lemon wood tree]
6.320 NNE. SEERS GESTA [deeds to property]
6.321 ENE. AGHAST AREA TREATS
6.322 SSE. EAR TO THE ONE LORD

6.400 THE ONE LORD
       W. RATTER GATES
6.401 E. HEATS SASH TEG [l-2yr old ewe lamb] AREA
6.402 NNE. SEATS SEER'S RE
6.403 N. TARATA [Maori lemon-wood tree] ART THOU RETS
6.404 NW. VEGetables THAT TEARS [rips]
6.405 W. HER'S TEAR EAT
6.406 S. RAH [hurrah]
6.407 HARTS [male red deer] HARVESTS SASH VERT [turn foetus in the
womb] THRASHES
6.408 E. TASTER THREATS
6.409 NE. TASTES TAR THREW THRASH
6.410 NNE. GATHER GATT VEST TEAR [rip] GRAVE [hole]
6.411 VERSion AREAS RARE GEST [deeds, exploits] REARS
6.412 NW. VAGRANT
6.413 W. VERTebrates
6.414 SW. HER HERR [German; mister]
6.415 S. SAVE RATHER HARASS EATS
6.416 SE. HATS TARS HEATH
6.417 ESE. REST RATE
6.418 E. REVolution Sanctitas Vestra [Your Holiness] SEW RAGE VARiant
       GRASSER [informer] His Eminence HAS E.T.A. [estimated time of arrival]
       RAG
6.419 NE. SEAT SETT [weaver's reed] TRET
6.420 NNE. AVES GRATE [as on feelings] ASTER [flower] SAT TARE South
East HEARTHS [fire] AGE
6.421 N. Right Ascension TEST

Transcript 7. HAIL THE ONE – A Tale of Interjections.

The words used for analysis were HAIL THE ONE.

7.100 N. HATE ALIEN ELITE TENse [grammar] THEE ANTE [stake held by each] THEOLogian
7.101 SE. ANOLE [iguana that changes skin colour] LEAST [at a minimum] NOEL [birth of Jesus Christ] THOUGH LEE [dregs settle]
7.102 S. LITHE THAN
7.103 SW. HAIL NUMBER LIT LEASH
7.104 W. TON [speed of 100 mph]
7.105 NW. A.E. [at the age of…]
7.106 NE. HALITE [rock salt] Temperature ONE THEOLogical TELA (delicate membrane surrounding the brain]
7.107   SE. TOLE [a tray for an offering] TAI [Chinese; peace] ATONE
7.108 S. ON TALE INTerjection
7.109 W. THE A.T. [technical atmosphere] ONE LATIN ACTINON [a semi-inert gas] AI [3 toed sloth] Each Surface Tension
7.110 N. IN LANE
7.111 NE. HIT INTAL [drug used for asthma] Na [sodium] LINT
7.112 E. HOUR IT
7.113 S. NEAT
7.114 W. Not Available NOAH [Bible] NAIL [steel pin] Earnestness Nominal
7.115 N. Natus [Latin; born] TO [contact] LENO [warp yarns twisted in pairs between the filling yarns]
7.116 NE. OATH EAT ANETHOLE [anise in fennel] NATURAL TO THE ONE

7.200 THE ONE TANH [3rd of the 6 mathematics of the hypobolic function] ANETHOLE HA [Interjection; hey] OATH LENO
7.201 N. TO [contact] Natus [Latin; born] ALONE LENT
7.202 E. IT IOTA [very small quantity] HOUR LEA [open meadow/grassland]
7.203 NE. LOIN INTerior EATEN AI [3 toed sloth] ETHA Literary ONE A.T. [technical atmosphere] HALT THE HEEL HEATHEN HEIGHT LIES AN' TALE NO Old Norse Honorary LINE
7.204 SE. TOLE [tray used for offering] HALE [robust] TELA [3rd meninger around the brain] THEOLogical TIN [container] TO [limit, direction]
7.205 NE. HALITE [rock salt] ELATE [put in high spirits] AN'T [is not] HEIL [German; Hail]
7.206 NW. LOIN LEAT [conduit by which water goes to a water wheel]
7.207 S. ATE LEE [dregs settled]
7.208 SE. NOH NO NAE [Scottish; not] LIEN [legal right to hold or sell property to settle a claim] ANTE [stake each holds] LET TENSE [grammar]
7.209 N. ALTitude ALIEN

7.300 E. THANE [a person ranking with an earl's son and usually holding the king's land; the chief of a clan who became a baron] NEE [maiden name] ANINUS [in the year] TONE [sound]
7.301 SE. LO [Exclamation; behold] LOATHE [hate or disgust] LITerature Tenor THOLE [fulcrum pin for a boat's oar]
7.302 S. TAO [Chinese; belief that all existence has been only in relation to an external absolute] HOE NOTE [sound] Tonne
7.303 SW. LEFT NO THE LOATHE [reluctant or unwilling]
7.304 W. THOR'Sdarg [Thor]
7.305 NW. TOEA [currency in Papua/New Guinea] A.E. [in the age of...] HEATH [erica; wilderness bush] OFFICE LAW TEND [to attend to by work]
7.306 SE. ONTO AT [place]
7.307 S. N [noun/name] THIOL [organic compound] NOTE [importance]
7.308 SW. Absolute Temperature TEE [starting point] LA [Exclamation; wonder and surprise] OATEN
7.309 W. LINEATE [marked with lines, especially longitudinally] ALINE [to line up with]
7.310 N. OLIEN [glyceride of oleic acid in olive oil] A'ONE OH [Interjection; surprise and pain] TELE [Grk; distant, far]
7.311 NE. HATH Honorable Thursday Island TOE LONE AIT [small island]
7.312 E. Magnetic North Territory
7.313 SE. OH [Interjection; surprise and delight] AH [Interjection; surprise, pain and pity] HONE [to sharpen]
7.314 SSE. AH [Interjection; surprise and joy]
7.315 S. HALE [to pull or drag] LINE LIE ANIL [indego plant]
7.316 SW. TAINO [extinct Arawarkian tribe]
7.317 W. HEN AIN [Scottish; own] TEA [drink] NET [exclusive of deductions]
7.318 N. LEA [any measure of yarn] OCEAN
7.319 E. TOD [small load of wool] TAIL
7.320 SE. HEAL [to make whole or sound/restore health and vigour]
TO THE ONE

7.400 THE ONE HEAL TON TEN
7.401 W. OLEATE [ester] LITH [stone]
7.402 SW. LINE
7.403 S. HALE [pull or drag] TIME HONE
7.404 SE. ALTERNATE OH [Interjection; surprise and delight] THAI [language]
7.405 E. Territory TOE IN ELATION TUESDAY TOE ANTHO [flower] THURsday Island OH [Interjection; surprise and pain]
7.406 N. His Excellency A'ONE OLIEN [glyceride acid in olive oil] ALOE TILE NOMINATION
7.407 W. LOAN TOIL [game nets set to catch game, or into which game is driven]
7.408 SW. TOE NAIL
7.409 S. TEA [meal] LENTO [slowly]
7.410 SE. TO [movement limit]

7.411 E. TIE
7.412 N. THEOLOGY TAIL [Law of Limitation]
7.413 NW. OFFICE A.E. [in the time of…] HALE His Eminence THU [Thor]
7.414 W. HEAT
7.415 WSW. TAN ON EEL
7.416 SSE. TOILE [type of transparent linen]
7.417 E. NOT ANNUS [in the year]

7.500 E. TAEL [Far East weight of silver]
7.501 SE. LITHO [stone] LONE LINE [garment] TO THE ONE

7.600 THE ONE
       NE. NET TALON [grasping mechanism of a bird of prey]
7.601 SE. NEOLITH [a stone implement of the Neolithic age] LONE
7.602 E. TAEL [Far East silver currency]

7.700 ENE. HOT
7.701 ESE. TOLAN [unsaturated crystalline hydra carbon; tar]
7.702 ENE. TEAL [duck] NITE [Col; night]
7.703 SW. AEON [infinitely long time] TO THE ONE

7.800 THE ONE
       ENE. THUrsday [Thor]
7.801 NNE. TAEL [Chinese silver currency]
7.802 SSW. THINE/THOU
7.803 ESE. LEI [Hawaiian neck wreath of flowers, leaves etc.]

7.900 SE. ANTHELion [luminous ring seen around the shadow of an observer's
head as thrown by the sun on a fog bank, cloud or moist surface – especially as
seen in polar regions] ETA [Grk; 7th letter] TINEA [skin fungus] NAIL [paws or
hands]
7.901 N. ALE [light beer] NIL
7.902 S. LEO [lion] TO THE ONE

7.1000 THE ONE ENATE [to grow outwards, especially on the mother's side]
LENGTH NOIL [short fibres separated from the long fibres by combing]
7.1001 SE. TINEA [skin fungus] LENT [40 days leading up to Easter]

7.1100 SE. LINDEN [tree] TA [Interjection; thank you]
7.1101 N. Not Applicable
7.1102 SE. E.T.A. [estimated time of arrival] TONAL [music] Atomic Number
       TO THE ONE

7.1200 SE. OH [Interjection; surprise and gladness]
7.1201 ENE. ANI [black cuckoo-like bird]
7.1202 SE. TE [music; 7th note]   ----

<u>ELEMENTS and Wisdom Path correspondence</u>

Correspondence is achieved by taking the Mass Number of an Element less the Atomic Number to find the Neutron Number. The NN is then added by the Chaldean method and the path number identified.

Actinium – 22
Actinon – 22
Aluminium- 27
Argon – 24:
Arsenic – 23:
Barium – :21
Beryllium – 17
Bismuth – 25:
Cadmium – 16
Calcium - 17
Cobalt - :21
Columbian/Niobium
Didymium twin ;
Neodymium – 18
Praseodymium - 26
Dysprosium – 18

Erbium – 26
Ethyl
Hahnium – 13:
Helium – 10
Holmium – 28
Hydrogen – 20
Indium - :21
Iodine – 24:
Ionium – 5
Lanthanum – 24:
Lead – 10
Lithium – 17
Neon – 25:
Niobium – 25:
Niton/Radon – 10
Nitrogen - 20

Nobelium – 13:
Oxygen – 38
Palladium – 12:
Polonium – 8
Radium – 10
Radon – 10
Rhenium – 12:
Silicon – 23:
Sodium – 27 v 45
Sulphur – 19
Thalmium - 20
Thorium – 18
Titanium – 23:
Yitrium - 36

<u>46/109</u>

Transcript 8.   ANYBODY WITH HOPE?

The words used for analysis were "Anybodi c [with] Hope"? With 11 different letters and four vowels, just over 1300 words were generated for this analysis. Word definitions are contained in brackets and the normal dictionary conventions followed [n.= noun, v.= verb, adj.=adjective, W.E.= word element, pref.=prefix, suf.=suffix. Chemical Elements were included in the abbreviations .]

8.100 E. CADY[boater hat] PEACH [Col; admired or liked] HAND [applause] Pilot Officer Hydrogen NN=20 CHAPlain HYPE [pretentious] COB [thickset and stout legged horse] PONE [maize bread] DAY [period of life, power and activity] DIE [cease to exist]

8.101 SE. BOYO [disorderly young man from the country] D-500 POCO [somewhat miscellaneous direction] BY [evidence of authority] ON [Col; indulgence in excess] B.Chem Engineering BEADY [bead like or glittering] PAH [Excl; disgust]

8.102 S. CODE [system,law] AID PYO [W.E. - pus] Hectare DEAN [head of a chapter at a Cathedral] DIE [engraving stamp - leaving an imprint on softer material] ECAD [habitat acquired characteristic] PHEN- [W.E. - chemical term for derivatives of benzene]

8.103 SW. EBONY [black, hard wood often used for carving] NIP [compress sharply] BEACON [warning] DIAgram YAP [Col; mouth] Husband

8.104 NW. Pressure Orbituary [notice of a person's death] PINCH [Col; steal] CHOP [cut up with a series of blows] Police Constable

8.105 N. OPEN [visible or plain] HAD [past tense of have]

8.106 NE. NAP [short fuzzy fibres of cloth] PAD [cushion like mass] DIE [cease to live]

8.107 E. Out of Print Yacht IDEA [conception of mind] NODE [knob] BOY Brother HOB [Col; mischief] BOYO [disorderly young man from the country] INDO [indego] YEP [Col; yes]

8.108 SSE. Not Applicable CYANIDE [very poisonous salt] BOO [Excl; frighten] PEACHY [Col; excellent, wonderful] PYO [W.E. - pus] Ampere Hour Younger DOPE [absorbent material used to hold liquid]

8.109 S. YEAH [yes] HIP [pelvis] INCH [narrow margin] BODICE [upper dress]

8.110 SW. EBONY [black, hard wood often used for carving] NIP [compress sharply] HEADY [intoxicating] CHIAN [Grk; rich red wine] PIN [very small amount] PENDA [rainforest timber tree] PAID ION [electrically charged atom, radical or molecule] BAN [prohibit]

8.111 W. DECAN [astrology; one of three divisions of 10 days in zodiac sign] CONOID [cone shaped] ONE [future] AEON [infinitely long time]

8.112 NW. PIE [ecclesiastic; rules for service of the day]

8.113 N. Calcium NN=17 Died HA [L; hoc anne - in the year]

8.114 NE. PAD [cushion like mass] POI [Hawaiian dish of baked Taro]

8.115 E. IDEA [conception of mind] Chain Ocean
8.116 SE. COD [codex] PHI [21st letter of the Greek alphabet] BY [in serial order]
8.117 SSE. HOY [Exclm; to get attention]
8.118 S. EPI- [pref; against] B.Education PAN [Col; face is dead pan, or expressionless]
8.119 SW. HE'D [he had] NAB [Col; catch or seize]
8.120 W. Oc [in the work cited] CAP [surpass] DEN [secluded wild place of habitation eg., cave] COD [large fish from the Murray River]
8.121 N. A CHEAP [sheepish] INcluded Bach.of Divinity
8.122 SSE. HOY [Exclm; to get attention]
To THE ONE.

THE ONE
8.200 SSE. NA [numerical aperture] HOY [Exclm; to get attention]
8.201 E. CHINE [backbone or spine] Included HOOP [ring of metal]
8.202 N. HOY [small ferry type boat] PHONEY [false] HOPE [trust in truth of the matter] COD [large fish from the Murray River] Pi [math; ratio of circumference to diameter]
8.203 NW. CAP Cb [chem; columbium – former name for Niobium NN=25: HE'D [he had] PAN [Col; face as a dead pan]
8.204 SW. EACH [individually] BI [built in] OPEN [no boundaries]
8.205 SSE. EPI- [pref; against] HOY [Exclm; to get attention] PEA [Col; one likely to succeed]
8.206 SE. PHI- [Grk; 21st letter] COD [codex] BY [in serial order] OCEAN
8.207 NNE. HOY [small ferry boat] CYANO [pref. before vowels - dark blue coloured] CADI [Judge in a Muslim community]
8.208 NNW. HAD [fed up or exasperated] PEON [messenger or attendant] db [double brested] Pi [math; ratio of circumference to radius]
8.209 NW. PIE [Eccless; rules for or order of services] PAID [pay] AEON [infinitely long time] DOE [female deer, sheep, goat etc] BAD [past tense - bid]
8.210 W. NEPHO- [W.E. - cloud] CONOID [cone shaped] Deposit account Cd [candella - luminosity] CAINO [W.E. - new or recent] -ANE [adj suff. eg humane]
8.211 SW. OPEN [ready to admit] -IA [suff to noun - rave] COBALT NN= :21] HYPO [Col; needle or injection] BY [no later than] DE- [pref, decent eg denograte] CHIAN [Grk rich red wine]
8.212 S. Younger CHIP [potato] Indium NN= :21 PEACHY [Col; wonderful, excellent]
8.213 SE. AI [sloth] BONE Not Applicable -CIDE [W.E. - killer] Indian HO [Exclm; gee up] HOB [Col; mischief]
8.214 E. PH [telephone] EPOCH [distinctive character/event] NODE [knob] AO [account for] Out of Print DIE [cease to live] BEYOND [superior, surpassing]
8.215 NE. BODE [past tense of bide] Part ANI [black cockatoo like bird]
8.216 N. OPEN [visible or plain]
8.217 NW. Police Constable -ACY [noun or adj suffix] PINCH [Col; steal] Orbituary [notice of a person's death] DOE [female deer, sheep, goat etc.]

8.218 W. CHOP [Chinese or Indian permit or seal of clearance] OPEN [unfilled] CHAIN [with links] PAEONY [flower, herb, shrub]
8.219 SW. DOOBY [Col; dope or ignoramus] CAPO [guitar finger board] DE- [pref. decent] BEACON [guiding or warning signal]
8.220 S. PHEN [W.E. chem; derivative of benzene] DIE [engraving stamp - imprint on softer material] Hectare DAN [title of honour, master] CODE [system or law]
8.221 SSE. Phenyl –univalent radical C6H5 From Benzene CHOP [change suddenly - wind]
8.222 SE. CHIDE [drive or impel] P&C [parents and citizens] Edited COY [affectively shy, reserved] Ibidem [in the same book chapter or page] Convict
8.223 ESE. Atomic Energy Commission PIE [collusion between biders at an auction] HAND [applause] Deputy HOOPLA [game of hoops thrown over prizes]
8.224 E. PEACH [Col; admired or liked] CADY [boater hat] PIN [surfboard with wide sides].

8.300 N. Northern
8.301 E. BYE [Col; farewell] Indicative DAY [Ast; 24 hrs revolution]
8.302 SE. DIP [slope or incline downwards] Care of BOND [unites] BIO- [W.E. life] NEB [tip or pointed end] NODE [join in stem / link]
8.303 S. PHOBIA [obsessive fear or dread] ADOBE [sun dried mud bricks] Dialect
8.304 NW. CON [confidence game] Head Office HOP [twining plant] Office
8.305 N. DAPHNE [nymph pursued by Apollo]
8.306 NE. HOP [Col; dance] HYPOID [gears with tooth shapes] CHIP [small piece]
8.307 E. CAP [confer/complete] DH [dead heat] Cycle PCA [prescribed concentration of alcohol - charge of .05]
8.308 SE. Bass BY HEADY [rashly, impetuously] YEO [Col; ewe] HA [interjection] Actinium NN=22] Commanding Officer COD [Col; bag or sack] Youngest DICHO [W.E. two parts]
8.309 S. NEHemiah [bible] HI [Exclm; greeting] OPAH [brilliantly coloured deep sea fish]
8.310 SSW. DYNA [W.E. power] PANDY [Scottish; school strap or stick punishment]
8.311 SW. APHONIC [lost voice] O [pref. Irish descend] Artificial Insemination NICE [tact, overcome, delicate] COP [conical mass of threads wound on a spindle] BAD -IN [suf. to adj. pertaining to] APE
8.312 W. BE [exist] HOOEY [Exclm; silly nonsense]
8.313 WNW. E [math; = 2.7182818....indef.]
8.314 NW. I [Roman numeral for one] D- [chem; compound] PAN [separate by washing]
8.315 N. ICON [picture or representation] H.P. [horse power] Bach. of Economics BEYOND [farther on] PAD [leg, foot or arm guard]
8.316 NE. CHIP [small piece] NICE [pleasing amiable] BENCH [work table]

8.317 S. Be beryllium NN=17] PINCH [compress between two surfaces]
HONDuras
8.318 W. No Dice OH [Exclm; surprise/pain]
8.319 W. EDition COO [Exclm; surprise or amazement]
8.320 NNW. ICY [covered with ice] Chief Petty Officer
8.321 N. ONE [single unit]
To THE ONE

THE ONE
8.400 E. PEAN [hymn of invocation to Apollo] Brought Down BIN [Col; pocket]
8.401 N. ONE [single unit]
8.402 NNW. Chief Petty Officer Canopy [covering of leaves eg., rainforest]
CHEAP [base, mean] ICED [as per cakes], DOPEY [slow witted, stupefied]
8.403 W. ADONIC [verse containing a dactyl followed by a spondee] Edition DIE
[lose spiritual life] BADE [p.t. of bid] BI- [pref. secondary, incidental Beryllium
NN=17] DIAPason [tuning fork]
8.404 S. -IN [suff. communal setting]
8.405 E. Brought Down BIN [Col; pocket] HEAD ON [head to head]
8.406 NE. In Command OP [other people's] Bach. of Economics
8.407 N. BEHIND [back of] PACED [specific pace] HP [horsepower] CON
[perusal or examine carefully] NAY [not only so, but ...]
8.408 NW. PAD [travel by foot] HEAP [a pile] IODO [W.E. iodine NN=24 BID
[greeting or benediction] COPY [imitation]
8.409 W. Carried Over Anglo Norman BE [exist] Centigrade
8.410 SW. YO-HO [Exclm; attract attention] BAD -IN [suf. to adj. - pertaining to]
POOH [Exclm; distain] ON [contact with] CApital POOCH [dog] Ca [eg about
AD476]
8.411 SSW. DYNA [power]
8.412 S. NEHemiah [Bible] 'D [had] Old English
8.413 SSE. ADO [bustle or fuss] DE- [pref. privation, separation] COIN [fabricate,
make up] Cubic ADENO [W.E. gland] PANED [having panes]
8.414 SE. I [my, mine, me] DOPA [a non protein amino acid precision of
adrenaline, used to treat Parkinson's disease]
8.415 ESE. Diameter Bass HYPHA [fungus mycelium] ACE [tennis; no touch]
POON [East Indian timber tree]
8.416 E. Density DONAH [girl, sweetheart] AN COB [corn cob]
8.417 NE. Pico [10 to power 12] IND [indo before vowel] NAHum [Bible]
8.418 N. Population BOA [snake shaped wrap of silk etc.] Argon NN=24; DIN
[loud noise]
8.419 NNW. PECAN [hickory tree]
8.420 NW. HOP [twining plant]
8.421 SW. Aboriginal BENCH [show table]
8.422 S. Dialect CHIP [reprimand] BAND [binding] COD [scrotum]
8.423 SSE. PAD [path worn by animals] COOEY BY [evidence of authority]

8.424 SE. COENO [W.E. common] HEBrew C [tone - keynote] ABC [alphabet] HEAD BOY [native servant] 'D [would] DIP [inclination of the eye] OPINE [think or express opinion] DIP [Col; short swim]
8.425 E. DAY [Ast. 24 hrs revolution] OH [Exclm; surprise, delight] EPI- [pref. above] HAND [pledge of marriage]
8.426 NNE. CANE [to push fast eg car]

8.500 N. YAHOO [rough or uncouth person]
8.501 NE. -INE [suf. to n. action, procedure, art or place] OCEANID [sea nymph]
8.502 E. YAH [Exclm; impatience] ICE [diamonds] COPHA [solid coconut flesh] HOE IN [Col; to energetically begin] BOOHAI [Maori; wrong] AH [Exclm; surprise, pity] PINCH [arrest] YIN [feminine, passive, yielding element of Chinese philosophy] ACHE [in pain continuously]
8.503 SE. CAPE [race wide] DE [place of origin] BOY [grown man] ICE [cakes icing] BEHIND [minor score] Able Bodied POONCEY [col; effeminate] OO [W.E. egg] BYE [having no competitor] NAPE [the back of the neck] PICture
8.504 S. DIPloma BANDY [pass from one to another] O [Exclm; surprise, pain] NEO- [W.E. new] DOONA [quilted eiderdown]
8.505 W. Personal Computer On Demand PINCH [cause distress]
8.506 NW. PANE [division of a window] HONE [whetstone]
8.507 NNW. PAN [pot or saucepan] ONDINE [water spirit] Bi-sexual CHIP [counter] COON [racoon]
8.508 N. BAY [compartment] Cash On Delivery
8.509 NE. Deuterium Isotope of Hydrogen NN=2] BY [near] CHEAP [little account, small value] -ION [suf. to n. action, process]
8.510 E. Eastern Hot & Cold DIB [bait bobs lightly in water] Neodymium NN=18] Associated Press
8.511 SE. HE [laughter] HEAD [head of water] DE [place of origin] CERTI Hypothetical ICY [cold]
8.512 SSE. Able Bodied INCH [Scottish; small island] Niobium NN=25:
8.513 W. On Demand
8.514 NW. Iodine NN=24:] PYOID [pus like]
8.515 N Polonium NN=8] HOPE [expectation of a desired outcome] PIAD [patches of two or more colour] DOU/DOH [1st note in the solfa system] BOOAY [in difficulty] CAN [container or tin]
8.516 NE. CODex ACHE [longing] ABODE [dwelling place] OPeration
8.517 SE. IN- [pref. in] NIDE [nest or brood of pheasants] CAPSULE PIN [fastener] Central Business District EO [W.E. early, primaeval] CONY [fur of rabbit] BORN
8.518 SSE. Number Ionium NN=5]
8.519 S. ABIDE [stay, wait] ON [manner]
8.520 W. ECONomy
8.521 NW. Indies
8.522 N. PHOOEY [Exclm; contempt]
8.523 SE. Born
To THE ONE.

THE ONE
8.600 SE. Born BOONDY [stone, pebble]
8.601 S. ABIDE [stay, wait] Number
8.602 SE. CAPsule ACE [playing card]
8.603 E. ACHE [longing]
8.604 N. CAN [container, tin] DOH/DOU [1st note of Solfa system] D [penny,
pence] PINCH [steep or difficult section of a path or road] AN [in the year]
8.605 W. On Demand
8.606 SSW. POD [W.E. foot]
8.607 S. EPI- [pref. near to] CONDition Niobium NN=25;]
8.608 SSE. No Claim Bonus DINE [eat principal meal] DIP [make candles by
dipping in tallow] -ONE [suf.n. chem. derivatives]
8.609 SE. PANIC [grain eg., millet grass] DIA- [pref. passing through]
8.610 ESE. HABokuk [Bible] Nitrogen NN=20 HE [laughter]
8.611 E. ECONomic BAY[stand made by a pursued or hunted person or animal]
HOIDEN [rude or ill-bred girl] A'ONE Eastern
8.612 ENE. Parking POD [seed vessel]
8.613 NNE. Cash On Delivery COON [racoon] BAY [compartment]
8.614 NNW. Barn
8.615 W. DAY [point something occurs] On Demand Personal Computer BEAN
[Col; little money]
8.616 S. HIP [wild, ripe rose fruit] CHINE [a ridge or crest of land]
8.617 SSE. CAPtion CIAO [hello] OB [incidentally] COP [police person] His
Eminence BOON [joyous companion] -OLD [suf. like , resembling] -AD [suf. n.
action, process] POONCEY [Col; effeminate]
8.618 SE. ECHO [repetition] EPIC [imposing, impressive] PAD [highway man]
BID [attempt to attain a goal] BOA [snake] PINE [conifer tree]
8.619 ESE. DON [put on]
8.620 E. HOE IN [Col; to energetically begin] HYPO [photographic fixing agent]
8.621 ENE. YAH [Exclm; impatience] Natus [L. born]
8.622 N. YAHOO [rough or uncouth person].

8.700 NE. Increase DIN [loud confused noise] AD HOC [special purpose]
8.701 E. BINE [twining plant stem eg hop] DECAY [decline or rot] Day Noon
COB [beat, strike]
8.702 SE. PAN [move continuously eg camera] CAN [to silence] Extended Play
ON [direction] POACH [simmer in shallow pan] E [music 3rd C scale] PEAN
[song of praise or joy] Nominal CAP [top or upper surface eg wave] Hardness
8.703 SSE. ABED [in bed] IBO [Negro people of Niger River] DON [head fellow]
COON [derog. expression for dark skinned person] HYENA [nocturnal carnivore]
Hypothesis
8.704 S. PEACH [to inform against associate or accomplice] HEN [female fowl]
HOD [basket] HAY [Col; old country dance] OPEN [candid or frank disclosure]
8.705 SW. HENCOOP [cage for poultry] Per Diem
8.706 NW. HE'D [he would] HEAD [drug user] CAPitalise

8.707 N. DEN [squalid, vile]
8.708 NNE. Hahnium NN=13:] YEAN [bring forth young]
8.709 ENE. ONE CHAIN [binding] PACE [linear measure eg., step] CANE [pithy wood stem]
8.710 E. POI [Maori women - ball on string]
8.711 SE. CHINE [cut along or across backbone] OPEN [lay bare, uncover] CAIN [complain, remonstrate]
8.712 SSE. DIE [Col; want keenly] Near OPUS ACE [single spot on card or die]
8.713 S. Dutch PICO [W.E. pref. 10 to the power 12]
8.714 WSW. Hindustani
8.715 NW. Height DANCE [feet and body rhythm] BENCH [terrace like structure]
8.716 N. HAY [Col; bed] -PHONE [suf. sound]
8.717 E. END [extremity, farthest point] AIDE [aide de camp]
8.718 SE. OPEN [lay bare, uncover]
8.719 W. BONDI [beech in NSW] Criminal Investigation Branch
8.720 NE. ONCE [a single occasion] -IAN [suf. variant of -an. From L. -ianus.] To THE ONE.

THE ONE
8.800 SE. Diploma IN LIBrary
8.801 E. COOBA [acacia - willow wattle] HO [Exclm; stop] CONY [animal - daman] Adjective
8.802 N. Check DANCE [feet and body rhythm]
8.803 WSW. Hindustani
8.804 S. PEDestal
8.805 SE. PEN [writing with pen] BONDI [Col; haste] CABIN [small house] CAB [taxi]
8.806 E. BEND [diagonal band from dexter chief to sinister base] Actinon NN=22] PHON [W.E. voice, sound]
8.807 NE. BIO- [biography of an important person] Overdrawn HOB [target pin eg coits] YEAN [bring forth young] DECember DEACON [elected official of the church]
8.808 N. ACID [sour liquid] Bible
8.809 NNW. CAD [contemptible]
8.810 NW. HEAD [drug user] AIN [own]
8.811 W. HE'D [he would]
8.812 WSW. Norse
8.813 SW. HENCOOP [cage for poultry]
8.814 S. HEN [female fowl] Confined to Barracks PEACH [Col; to inform against an associate or accomplice] PEND [remain undecided]
8.815 SSE. BANE [cause ruin or death, destroy life] PIE [baked dish] BEND [cause to submit or stop, stoop] PION [Phys; a meson with +ve or -ve or zero charge and a mass between 264 - 273 electron masses 12:] Nominal DAN [high grade of proficiency]
8.816 SE. PEAN [song of praise or joy] COPE [long mantle of silk or surplice] ECG [electro cardiograph]

8.817 E. Bach. of Engineering -ODE [suf.n. way]
8.818 NE. DIN [loud confused noise] Increase DANE [citizen of Denmark]

8.900 NE. PEACH [a pinkish yellow colour]
8.901 E. HAND [a bunch of fruit or leaves] Diplomatic Corp
8.902 SE. BAY [inlet in shore line] Bismuth NN=25:] Pb lead NN=10]
CONservatorium BOD [person] PAEON [metrical footnote - 4 syl = 1 long, 3
short] CAPE [land jutting out into the sea] DANiel [Bible] Barium NN=21:]
NAPOO [Col; doomed, done for] BAY [European laurel tree]
8.903 SSE. DANCE [perform] Post Office HYPE [deliberately stimulated
excitement] CAP [protective cover] CANOPY [covering eg cloud or throne]
PIANO [keyboard] -ODE [suf.n. resemblance to preceding part] -PHOBE [W.E.
one who fears] HEY [Exclm; to call attention]
8.904 S. Computer Aided Design OPEN [to begin, start or commence]
8.905 SW. ONCE [a single degree]
8.906 W. CO- [pref. association]
8.907 NNW. ICY [slippery as..]
8.908 N. ANY [whatever] HEAP [to caste upon someone, something]
Conscientious Objector DAP [a groove to receive connectors or notch] HEP [Col;
inside knowledge] NOB [Col; head] NIPA [palm tree of E. Indies, Philippines etc]
BOON Integrated Circuit PACHY [W.E. thick] Not Available DEACON [official of
early Christian Church]
8.910 NE. DIP [Gym; move down then up between horizontal bars] BOO
[contempt] BODY [main mass of the building] END [purpose or aim] Adults Only
Debenture CHAIN [measurement of distance] Per Annum NICHE [recess] PHEN
[illuminating gas reference] Palladium NN=12:]
8.911 ENE. -ID [suf.n. daughter of] CHIP [cut in small stages] CAPE [garment]
HOE [implement] BAH [Exclm; contempt, frustration] PACE [traverse]
8.912 E. PINE [wood] COPE [struggle on even terms] POACH [to mix with water
to uniform consistency] NODE [difficulty] CHAP [jaw or fleshy covering of jaw]
Department ON [process, procedure or encounter] DICE [cut into small cubes]
8.913 SE. PICA [depraved appetite] BODE [omen of ..] PAN [W.E. all,
considered together] CHIN [jaw]
8.914 SSE. PEA [round nutricius seed] ONE [unity] COB [lump, heap or roundish
mass of ...] HEAD BOY [school prefect]
8.915 S. NO [stylised Japanese classical drama] NEB [bill or beak] BOND
[sealed document] DI- [pref. twice] Computer Aided Design Inclusive
8.916 SW. ACE [highly skilled person]
8.917 W. NIP [check growth or development]
8.918 NW. Pay As You Earn Danish
8.919 N. NIP [small quantity] EC [variant of ex-, eccentric] HEAD PIN [apex pin]
O [suf. eg garbo] DON [Spanish Lord or gentleman]
8.920 E. BIANCO [white wine] Bring Your Own YEN [Japanese currency] HOE
[implement] DO [does perform]
8.921 SE. PYCNO [W.E. dense, close] -Y [suf n. affectionately] BOCO [Col;
nose] Handicap AND CAP [head cover]

8.922 S. BOCHE [derog. German] Candle Power
8.923 SW. COP [arrest, being caught]
8.924 NW. Harbour HYPNO [W.E. sleep]
8.925 N. Heroin PAN [Col; reprimand severely]
8.926 E. DIP [baptise by immersion]
To THE ONE

THE ONE
8.1000 E. DIP[baptise by immersion] PAN [leaf of betel]
8.1001 S. END [bounds an object, space]
8.1002 SE. HOP [to leap by one foot]
8.1003 E. PEN [Col; confinement in prison] DOPE [varnish] BODY [things taken together] I'D [I had] DOAB [land in Y of rivers] Bring Your Own POACH [to trespass to steal game]
8.1004 NE. BENCH [long seat]
8.1005 N. DON [Spanish lord or gentleman] O [suf. eg. garbo] HEAD PIN [apex pin] -ICE [suf.n. state, quality] NIP [Col; small drink] Delete CHOPIN [thick cork soled shoes]
8.1006 NW. DEACON [church official - level below priest] ACE [very small amount]
8.1007 S. DOB [betray]
8.1008 SSE. CHI [energy] PAN [dish or vessel] PEA [round nutritious seed] OP- [pref. by assimilation before p only eg oppose]
8.1009 SE. Doctor of Chemistry PICA [depraved appetite] Department
8.1010 E. NODE [difficulty] Year Probable Error PACE [traverse]
8.1011 NE. CAPE [garment] POACH [to trespass to steal] CHAP [open with small slits, cracks] Chapter BEN [mountain in Scotland]
8.1012 NNE. BOON [benefit] Organization for Petroleum Exporting Countries
8.1013 N. NEB [nose] DICEY [Col; risky, tricky, dangerous] CON [against] BY [through agency, efficacy] ICY [slippery as ..]
8.1014 NW. No Answer PAY [coat or seal with tar] NIP [cut off by pinching] CO- [pref. association]
8.1015 SW. ONCE [a single degree]
8.1016 S. OPEN [to begin, start or commence] C [velocity of light in vacuum] DOB [betray] Nominative HEY [Exclm; to get attention] DECAY [Phys; disintegration of a radio-active substance to a stable state] PEACH [tree] ECHO [sympathetic response] -ODE [suf. resemblance to preceding part]
8.1017 SSE. HOOD [cloak hood overhead] POND [small water body] PIANO [keyboard] PACE [anxious] HOON [loutish, reckless] PEACHY [peach like]
8.1018 SE. PEN [female mute swan] Barium NN= :21] PANIC [stricken with panikos - Grk - by Pan] COD [pod]
8.1019 E. CHINE [matted material printed on warp] CAIN [commotion] Probable Error HOP [Col; go]
8.1020 NE. Cognate with OCHNA [shrub with toothed leaves and yellow flowers]

8.1100 N. CAIN [murderer] CAPO [leader of Mafia] PAD [writing sheets] AB-
[pref. away from] DOPE [thick liquid or pastry preparation]
8.1101 E. Noun BY [past you by] Honorary Deci
8.1102 SE. ICY [resembling ice] CAN [able] PEACH [fruit] Bedroom YOB
[brutish] ID [source of instinctive energy] Husband DEN [personal place]
8.1103 SSE. pH [measure of acidity or alkalinity] BOOAY [remote country] DIP
[plunge temporarily into ...] Photo NAPOO [Col; finished, used up] NOD
[careless, dull]
8.1104 S. Advertisement HEY [Exclm; to give encouragement] DENY [not true]
NO [notary]
8.1105 SW. Old PIANO [music; softly direction]
8.1106 NNW. DIP [cocktail dip]
8.1107 N. CAN [permission] NOH/NO High NABIS19th C French painters took
their name from Heb. Nabhi – prophet. Pierre Bonnard 1867 – 1947 established
and was the Doyen of this group. HAD [exhausted] Idem [same as previously
mentioned] DICHO [W.E. in pairs]
8.1108 NE. DIAPason [compass of a voice or instrument] Own Your Own NOB
[double headed coin]
8.1109 ENE. Pi [Col; pious, esp. hypocritically] Na sodium NN=18] HOP [jump or
leap by all feet] NICE [great accuracy or precision]
8.1110 E. Bach. of Arts DANCE [leap or skip esp. from excitement] ON [liability]
8.1111 SE. North BED B Ch D [Dental Surgery] HONEY [nectar of flowers]
Double Certificate
8.1112 SSE. DINO [W.E. terrible] Neuter
8.1113 S. 0 [Arabic zero] DYNE [force] COO [talk fondly/amorously]
8.1114 WNW. COPY [reproduction] Board PEON [day labourer]
8.1115 N. NAP [Col; blankets] HYPNOID [state resembling sleep] DE- [pref.
intensity] YEN [desire, longing] PhD [doctor of philosophy]
8.1116 NNE. ODIC [of an ode] CHEAP [inexpensive] British PONCY [manner,
dandy]
8.1117 NE. OPEN [may be entered, afford access] About Bishop Batsman
Absolute COB [male swan] PYIN [albuminous constituent of pus]
8.1118 E. HOOCH [alcoholic beverage]
8.1119 SE. HAND [Col; assistance]
8.1120 SSE. Bound Price On Application
8.1121 N. PAIN [to cause pain]
To THE ONE

THE ONE
8.1200 N. BID [offer a price] PAIN [to cause pain]
8.1201 W. Dysprosium NN=18]
8.1202 E. Hard cent BODY [structure, mass eg. man]
8.1203 NE. COB [male swan] Deceased ENCHAIN [fasten, fetter or restrain]
DOPE [stupid person] CHAD [north central Africa]
8.1204 NNE. CAY [small island] POOHEY [disagreeable]

8.1205 N. AYE [Exclm; ever, always] ID [identification] ICED [covered with ...]
HYPNOID [state resembling sleep]
8.1206 NW. Hire Purchase PEON [one who tends a horse or mule]
8.1207 W. Board
8.1208 SW. DEAN [head of any body eg. father] Year Book Yonder
8.1209 S. Aged Compare NIB [point of anything eg. pen] Neuter DON [leader of
Mafia family]
8.1210 SSE. CHAP [fellow, man, boy] HOOD [top of motor car]
8.1211 E. OPEN [undecided] DIE [suffer as if dying, pine] YAHOO [Exclm;
delight and surprise] ANODE [+ve ions] NOB [double headed coin] EN- [pref.
into] DO [ditto] PEN [author, writer]
8.1212 NE. BEAD [small ball with hole] POONCE [Col; male homosexual]
Deceased HOOEY [Exclm; disapproval] CODicil BOYO [Irish friend, companion]
-ADE [fizzy drink]
8.1213 N. BAY [dog bark] Cooperative In Charge
8.1214 W. Honourably
8.1215 SW. HONE [cut back to sharpen] CONE [light sensitive parts of the eyes]
HOP [flight or trip] BEHIND [in arrears]
8.1216 S. AD HOC [with respect to this] HEY [Exclm; to give encouragement]
8.1217 SSE. BOOAY [Col; remote country] Ecology DEN [personal place]
Hundred YOB [brutish]
8.1218 SE. His Excellency Breadth N [math; indefinite whole number] OPEN
HYPE [needle]
8.1219 E Honorary -ED [suf. eg. crossed] EDH [voiced th]
8.1220 NE. AB- [pref. away from]
8.1221 N. CAIN [murderer]

8.1300 N. Didymium Twin Neodydmium NN=18 and Praseodydmium NN=26]]
PHONEY [Col; not genuine] CAPE [mid Palaeozoic period] YIDISH [Jew]
8.1301 E. HOBO [Col; vagrant]
8.1302 SE. OBI [a fetish or charm worn or used in Obi magic] Pi [16th letter of
Grk alphabet] EPI- [pref. near] Da Carpo [music; from the beginning] OD
[overdose, excess] ODE [lyric, poem] OPEN [clear of obstructions] POACH
[slushy trampled land] BAY [reddish brown colouring] Account N.B. [neta bene]
8.1303 S. East
8.1304 SW. Alternating Current AYE [Exclm; affirm]
8.1305 NW. CON [defraud, swindle] DIPODY [group of two metrical feet] BAND
[radio waves]
8.1306 N. Consumer Price Index Physical Education CAPE [mid Palaeozoic
period] PINEY [covered with pine trees]
8.1307 NE. COB [gull - black backed lorus]
8.1308 E. BEYOND [life after the present one] IDEO [W.E. idea] B [Col; bugger,
bastard]
8.1309 SE. Inclusion
8.1310 S. Decibel
8.1311 SW. Intransitive CABIN [ship room or truck]

8.1312 W. PEON [one held to work off debt]
8.1313 NW. DOB [Col; to contribute]
8.1314 N. Young CHI [tea]
8.1315 E. BEYOND [life after the present one] Country
To THE ONE

THE ONE
8.1400 W. BY [conformity]
8.1401 SE. CHAIN [succession]
8.1402 NW. Bay
8.1403 W. PEON [one held to work off debt]
8.1404 DAB [tap lightly with hand] Detective
8.1405 E. HAY [Col; money]
8.1406 NE. COB [gull - black backed lorus] CHIDE [scold, find fault]
8.1407 NNE. CAN [Col; carry blame] CAPE [mid Palaeozoic period]
8.1408 N. PAD [animal foot pad]
8.1409 SW. PAD [Col; bedroom] AYE [Exclm; affirm] HAY [fodder]
8.1410 S. PENE [W.E. almost]
8.1411 SE. AY [Exclm; surprise, sorrow] BAY [reddish brown colouring] Pi [16th
letter Grk]
8.1412 ESE. COPY [guidelines or copy for and advert.] ENDO [W.E. internal]
8.1413 E. OBI [African magic system - fetish] HOBO [Col; vagrant] POON [Col;
eccentric or weird person] BIDE [wait, endure]
8.1414 NE. DAB [small European flatfish] CANE [punishment]
8.1415 N. PHONEY [Col; not genuine] Didymium Twin Neodydmium NN=18 and
Praseodydmium NN=26]

8.1500 E. OB- [pref. inversely] PAD [dull sound on ground]
8.1501 SE. BOND [acknowledgement of debt] DAB [small quantity] PAIN [col;
irritating, tedious] BOON [enjoy blessings sought] HOON [Col; one who lives off
prostitution] COB [lump of coal] -Y [suf. characterised by] DECAY [elect; fall
away after the source of energy is removed] Inches
8.1502 SSE. -OLDER [suf.n. super families] Dose BENCH [house of Parliament]
8.1503 NW. -PHANY [suf.n. appearance of deity or super natural being]
8.1504 NNE. DOYEN [senior member of body, class or profession] HYPE [drug
addict] DIN [to sound or utter]
8.1505 NE. DYE [colouring material] DECI [pref. 10 to the power -1]
8.1506 E. DECOY [lure] HEAD [seat of thought] OBI [long broad sash worn by
Japanese women and children]
8.1507 SE. Ancient CONE [volcanic] HAND [palm with 5 digits]
8.1508 SSE. YAP [Col; talk noisily] HB [hard and black]
8.1509 N. BIPOD [two legged support]
8.1510 NNE. DOPE [a drug, esp. a narcotic] CHEAP [poor quality] PAN
[depression in ground]
8.1511 NE. Postal Order
8.1512 SE. Organization for Economic Cooperation and Development

8.1513 N. NOB [social elite] PIE [Col; good, straight]
To THE ONE

THE ONE
8.1600 N. NOB [social elite]
8.1601 SE. O [longing]
8.1602 NE. CHEAP [poor quality] PINE [suffer, longing or grief]
8.1603 SW. Capacitance [elect]
8.1604 S. Potential Difference HAND [source of information] PHOCINE [seals]
8.1605 SSE. BP [before 1950 - radio carbon dating year] AD- [pref. towards, at about]
8.1606 SE. PETA [pref. 10 to the power 15 of a given unit]
8.1607 E. BICE [blue or green as carbonate of copper] DECOY [lure]
8.1608 N. College of Advanced Education DIE [stop functioning]
8.1609 SSW. Perch
8.1610 S. PHONetics -Y [suf. action verb eg.enquiry] HIP [Col; cheers] BONDI [Col; thrashing]
8.1611 SSE. Cape -PEDE [W.E. foot] EH [Exclm; surprise and some doubt] Phosphorus
8.1612 SE. CHIP [elect; a square semiconductor] Blend of ... Pedal DICE [small cube 1:6] BOND [acknowledgement of debt] PAN [international TV and radio signal - Precautionary Advisory Notice]
8.1613 E. O [Exclm; gladness]
8.1614 NE. ECHOA [Maori; friend]

8.1700 NE. Bond DIE [singular of dice]
8.1701 E. OPEN [access to knowledge or enlightenment] PEON [foot soldier] CHINE [ravine or fissure]
8.1702 SE. PACE [with permission from ... courteous form] IN- [pref. negative] ONE [The LORD] AD [since Christ's birth] COOP [prison] COO [soft murmuring sound eg. pigeon] Helium NN=10] HOB [hobgoblin, elf] Outside Broadcast
8.1703 SSE. HEN [fussy woman] New English Bible POD [pregnant] HAP [one's luck or lot]
8.1704 S. BID [direct, command] DE- [pref. reversal eg. deactivate] CHINE [bottom of a boat] PHON [unit of loudness]
8.1705 SW. DIE [loose force or strength]
8.1706 W. YEA [yes]
8.1707 NW. END [issue or result, remnant]
8.1708 NNE. OBI [a kind of sorcery practiced in Africa & West Indies]
8.1709 NE. BI- [pref. twice] PEN [instrument for writing]
8.1710 E. Captain DIA- [pref. opposed in movement] Electronic Data Processing COON [failure is inevitable] DIAPason [fixed standard of a pitch]
8.1711 SE. Australian Broadcasting Commission BODY [wool quality] Dead On Arrival INDO [pertaining to India] YE [the] -PHANE [W.E. apparent, similarity] Advantage HIPBONE [pelvis] Oxygen NN=38 Central Intelligence Agency

8.1712 SSE. CHAPE [metal trim on the scabbard eg. at the knife point] PICA [print size]
8.1713 S. BONY [of or like bone] ONE [union, agreement, harmony] -PED [W.E. foot]
8.1714 SSW. PEA [plant producing a pea]
8.1715 WSW. NIP [Col; to steal]
8.1716 NW. About Debenture
8.1717 NNE. Conductor
8.1718 NE. ON [support, conveyance]
8.1719 SE. BY [route, conveyance] Australian Broadcasting Commission
8.1720 S. PAD [expand unnecessarily]
8.1721 ENE. PECAN [hickory tree nut]
To THE ONE

THE ONE
8.1800 NW. DE- [pref. negation]
8.1801 SSE. CINE [W.E. motion] Direct Current
8.1802 SE. Brotherhood
8.1803 E. CAP [explosive]
8.1804 NE. Deposit
8.1805 NW. HEAD [top of body]
8.1806 WSW. PONCHO [blanket like cloak]
8.1807 SW. HOY [Col; to throw] Editor
8.1808 SSE. Circa [date] DACE [small freshwater cyprinoid fish] DIP [solution to dip... sheep]
8.1809 SE. BODY [wool quality]
8.1810 ESE. COON [failure is inevitable]
8.1811 E. DINE [entertain at dinner] HYPE [fraud, racket] Y [math; unknown quantity or variable] HIDE [conceal] Poise
8.1812 NE. DIAPason [melody]
8.1813 NNW. HIP [sloping side of a roof] COY [modest, shy]
8.1814 S. PHONO [pref. voice, sound]
8.1815 SSE. NIP [Col; to go, leave quickly] ACNE [skin inflammation] New English Bible Nobelium NN=13: BOY [young male servant] HEN [fussy woman] BIND [make fast with ...]
8.1816 SE. BENCH [court] BY [extent of...] EPIC [hero narrative] HEAP [Col; old car, dilapidated] PANIC [demoralizing terror] BOOAY [completely wrong] Post Dated
8.1817 E. COPE [the vault of heaven]
8.1818 ENE. Or Nearest Office HADE [angle parallel to fault plane]
8.1819 NE. ECHIDNA [spiny ant-eater] DIE [singular of dice]

8.1900 NNE. PAN [Col; result or turnout] POD [small herd or school of whales or seals]
8.1901 NE. HEAD [top or summit]
8.1902 ENE. Brake Horse power -EN [suf.adj. material]

8.1903 SE. OB- [pref. towards] POO [Col; faeces] Input / Output CHINA [country] No Account PHONE [telephone] BEACH [seashore] BY [in presence of.. to swear] D [music; 2nd note in Solfa scale - RE] NO [not at all] HAND [horse height] Incorporated
8.1904 SSE. Acre
8.1905 S. Holmium NN=28] I'D [I would]
8.1906 SSW. HYOID [u shaped bone at root of the tongue in man] DINE [take any meal]
8.1907 NE. BOCO [one eyed animal] C [specific heat] daughter CAN [Col; gaol]
8.1908 ENE. DOB [Col; nominate for an enormous task] COP [top of hill, summit]
8.1909 E. Neutron
8.1910 SE. BACON PAY [salary or wages] BEANO [Col; lavish feast]
8.1911 SSE. DIA- [pref. going apart] EPOCH [beginning of a period in history] AC =AD PAED [W.E. child] EPHOD [Hebrew priestly vestment]
8.1912 S. ICY [cold as ...] I'D [I would]
8.1913 SW. BEN [tree; Moringa Oleifera]
8.1914 NW. PAIN [careful efforts]
8.1915 N. PINCH [a small quantity put into something]
8.1916 NE. CAN [Col; gaol]
8.1917 SSE. Dining Room Children
8.1918 S. NEAP [tide midway between spring tides, least]
8.1919 SW. BEN [tree]
8.1920 W. APHID [plant sucking insect]
To THE ONE

THE ONE
8.2000 SSE. Including
8.2001 NNE. N [unbranched carbon chain in the aliphatic molecule]
8.2002 S. BEAN [edible seed]
8.2003 SSE. Children
8.2004 E. DAP [...dips lightly or suddenly in water]
8.2005 N. Doctor PINCH [a small quantity put into ...]
8.2006 S. Company DAP [to bounce on the surface of water]
8.2007 SE. CAPON [castrated cock] Conservation & Environment BEANO [Col; lavish feast] Hypotenuse
8.2008 ESE. B- [music; 7th degree in the C major scale - TE]
8.2009 E. NEP [small knot of tangled wool fibre removed by combing] India [country]
8.2010 ENE. CHINA [porcelain wares]
8.2011 NE. Daughter CADE [young left by mother and raised by hand] BOCO [one eyed animal] After Hours Provisional
8.2012 SW. NAP [downy coating on plants] Yttrium NN=36]
8.2013 S. BC [Before Christ] Holmium NN=28 Bach Ch [Surgery] NIP [derog. Japanese]
8.2014 SSE. Acre ON [time / occasion] CIAO [goodbye] Chinese HONEY [bee's viscid fluid]

8.2015 SE. April New Pence COOP [cage] HOB [shelf around fireplace]
8.2016 ESE. NAP [Col; off one's guard] AE [at the age of] DENY [refuse to believe, not grant] HEAD [seat of power or position] Before Common Era DIA- [pref. thoroughly, completely]
8.2017 E. DAP [bait falls lightly on water]
8.2018 ENE. YAP [Col; talk foolishly] Ohm BAY [window] Officer IE-ID [est. daughter of]
8.2019 NE. YE [thou, you]
8.2020 NNE. Cadmium NN=16.

Transcript 9.   ONE LED TREE.

The words ONE LED TREE were used in analysis.

9.100 N   DERO [N. Col; vagrant]
9.101 NE   E'ER [Poetry; ever] DOT [Civil Law; dowry] OT [overtime]
9.102 E   TEN [a set of this many] OT [Occupational Therapy] ONE [a person indefinitely, anyone]
9.103 SE   'RE [are] DER [derived] NEEDLE [for sewing] OLDER [of greater age]
9.104 S   ELDER [influential tribal leader] ENTERO- [WE; intestine] OR [Arch; before, ere, early]
9.105 SSW T [territory]
9.106 SW   REEL [music for a lively dance popular in Scotland] LEO [constellation of Leo, sign of the zodiac]
9.107 WSW -ET [Suff to N; diminutive eg., owlet] DO [accomplish, finish]
9.108 W   NET [ultimate, final resultant] O'ER [Poetry; over] ON [manner] R [ratio]   REND [separate into parts by force or violence] –O [N. Col; habits eg., weirdo] OE [Old English] DOLE [Arch; grief, lamentation] TON [unit of freight = 1000 Kg.]
9.109 WNW LEET [special type of manorial court or it's jurisdiction] LONE [standing apart or isolated] O [Interj; gladness] ERODENT [eroding power of] NT [Northern Territory] NET [bag for carrying] –ERN [Suff to N; eg., northern] NEE [born, maiden name] ENTER [to put in, insert] OD [overdose, excess] ROT [to fall or become weak due to decay] TOLD [pt. of tell] 'OD [Arch; reduced form of God] DOTE [bestow excessive love or fondness] LORD [one who exercises authority, power] ERODE [to form (eg., a channel) by the forces of nature] O [Interj; surprise, pain] REEL [to sway or rock under a blow or shock] DO [render] ON [Col; indulgence, excess] LEE [that which settles from a liquid, the dregs in wine]
9.110 NW   T [temperature] LODE [vein-like deposit esp. metaliferous] NOD [sudden involuntary head movement when sleepy] ON [support, suspension, dependence, reliance or means of conveyance] T [absolute temperature] TO [motion or direction towards] LT [low tension] LEER [side glance, sly, insulting]
9.111 NNW   -LET [Suff; little objects eg., bracelet] RODENT [gnawing or nibbling mammal] ONE [a single unit] NOTE [eminence or distinction] LORD [saviour Jesus Christ] –ER [Suff to N; connecting with something eg., butler] TOE [outer end of hitting surface on a golf club or hockey stick]
9.112 N   RE [in the case of, or with reference to] ON [agency or means] TOE [analogous part in animals] NEED [urgent want, requisite] ENTERON [Grk; digestive tract] REND [to pull or tear violently]
9.113 NNE END [cause of death, destruction or ruin]
9.114 NE   NOTE [Arch; tune, melody or song] TONE [a particular quality of expression or meaning] O' [descendants of an Irish family] LET [allow or permit] REND [a breach in relations or union]
9.115 ENE LET [tennis; play ball again]

9.116   ESE   RT [right] REED [plant growing in marshy places]
9.117   SE   T [grammar; tense] LET [grant occupancy or use]
9.118   SSE   REEL [to sway or stagger]
9.119   S   LEO [personality traits of a Leo] NOTE [short informal letter] ROLE
[character which an actor presents]
9.120   SW   DOT [decimal point] REEL [a quantity of something wound on a
reel] TOD [a load] RODEO [cowboy entertains public by riding horses, steers
etc.]
9.121   W   DRONE [to speak in a monotone] LD [lethal dose] N [northern]
9.122   WNW   TENDER [ships apt to have low stability] OLD [long life] TREE [a
perennial plant with stem and branches] ELDER [aged person] OLD [long known
or in use, familiar] TREE [Tree of Life] NO [a "NO" voter] TOLD [pt. of tell] END
[purpose or aim] END [section adjacent to extremity] NOTE [formal diplomatic
communication in writing] LORE [Arch; teaching or instruction]
9.123   NW   OLD [formerly in use] NOD [trees or flowers swaying motion] –ENE
[Chem; hydrocarbons eg., benzene] OLD [belonging to a past time]
9.124   NE   -TEEN [termination of cardinal numbers 13 - 19] OR [tincture of
gold or yellow] LORE [body of knowledge esp. traditional] TN [Chem; thoron NN=
18]
9.125   ENE ENTER [engage or become involved] E [Easter] DO [to be the
cause of an effect] TENDER [gentle]
9.126   E   ENTER [to be admitted] TENDER [soft hearted, easily touched,
sympathetic, compassionate] NL [not permitted – L. non licer] RT [right] T [Stats;
distribution]
9.127   ESE LORE [that which is taught]
9.128   W   ORE [metal bearing mineral or rock] NE [North East]
9.129   NW   E'EN [Poetry; even] RET [retired]
9.130   N   OR [connection between alternatives] TEREDO [wood worm in
ships] OLD [having the appearance or characteristics of advanced age] –ENE
[Suff; synthetic manufacture of substances]
9.131   NNE TOE [forepart of a hoof or foot]
9.132   ENE E [Easter]
9.133   E   ERNE [sea eagle] LTD [limited]
9.134   S   Dr [doctor]
TO ONE.

ONE TO
9.200   E   ODE [lyrical poem of enthusiastic emotion]
9.201   NNE ELDER [earlier]
9.202   N   END [object for which a thing exists] OLD [deteriorated through age
or long use] ON [above and in contact with a supporting surface]
9.203   NNW DENT [hollow depression in surface]
9.204   ESE LORE [that which is taught]
9.205   E   O [ocean]

9.206   ENE ONE [Supreme Deity, Creator, Father] ENTER [engage or become involved]
9.207   NE   ENTER [to become a member of or join]
9.208   N   TENDER [continuous progress, course or movement] LONE [being alone, solitary] ONE [of a single kind, nature or character] TENDER [Law; offer]
9.209   NW   ON [state , condition or process] DO [to make, create or form] TREND [general course, drift, tendency] ORD [order] DOE [female of species eg., goat, rabbit, kangaroo] TREE [something resembling a tree] O [office] R [resistance] DELO [delegate] –OR [Suff to N; one who does something eg., actor] ROLE [proper or customary function]
9.210   WNW ELDER [ground or box elder plants] DRONE [remotely controlled mechanism] TO [destination or appointed end] TON [2240 lbs.] TERN [a prize won for drawing three numbers in a lottery]
9.211   W   LD [low Dutch] LORD [titled nobleman or peer, high official] NOD [nap]
9.212   SW   RODEO [cowboys entertaining public riding horses steers etc.]
9.213   S   ROLE [character that an actor presents]
9.214   SSE ON [encounter]
9.215   SE   Rd radon NN=10 TENDER [auxiliary vessel to attend to one or more other vessels]
9.216   ESE DEN [secluded place] T [ton]
9.217   E   ENDO- [WE; internal, within]
9.218   NE   TONE [a particular quality of expression or meaning] DOR [various insects which fly making a buzzing sound]
9.219   NNE END [death] NOEL [Christmas song or carol]
9.220   N   NEED [urgent want, requisite] TOE [analogous part in animal] NO [highly stylized Japanese classical drama] ENE [East North East] REEL [to say or write or produce in an easy continuous way] RONDEL [short poem of fixed form with 14 lines] ERODE [eat out or away] REDOLENT [pleasant fragrance or smell] RED [distinguished by being red] R [right] TOE [outer end of the hitting surface of a golf club or hockey stick] END [a remnant or fragment]
9.221   NNW TONE [prevailing character, style] TOED [having toes] OD [overdraft] ONE [a unit] LT [low tension] TREND [general drift, course or tendency] ORLE [Heraldry; a narrow band within a shield that follows the contour of the edge]
9.222   NW   TO [motion or direction towards] R [resistance] ON [support, suspension, dependence, reliance or means of conveyance] DOT [roundish mark] ON [with continuous procedure] END [termination] TON [Col; very or good many] TENOR [highest, natural, adult, male voice] LODE [vein-like deposit esp. metaliferous] RED [ultra radical political party] –ED [Suff eg., bearded] NEED [a condition marked by a lack of something] T [surface tension] ON [Col; indulgence in excess] LORD [Supreme Being, Jehovah] R [ruled] DO [perform acts] LEER [Lehr – long tunnel shaped furnace used in hardening glass] ERODE [make or form (eg., a channel) by forces of nature]

9.223   WNW Rd [road] TEN [cardinal number] R [Regina – king or queen] TEE [to organize or plan] EO- [WE; very early or primeval] NOTED [specially observed or noticed] -ER [frequentive eg., as a flicker]
9.224   W   ROT [state of being rotten, putrefaction] R [ratio] ON [manner] O'ER [Poetry; over] OD [overdrawn] TONE [to modify the tone or colouring] ER erbium NN=26] LOT [allotted share or portion]
9.225   WSW NT niton early name for Radon NN=10]
9.226   SW   ROD [electrode as in arc welding] EON [an indefinitely long time, an age]
9.227   SSW RELENT [to soften in feeling or temper, forgiving] TO [attachment or adherence] RETD [returned]
9.228   S   -ODE [Suff; like the preceding part] ELDER [older]
9.229   SSE T [taken from] NOR [Norman]
9.230   SE   TREND [have a general tendency as events] LEO [person born under Leo]
9.231   ESE NOR [Norway]
9.232   ENE R [runs as in cricket] OT [overtime]
9.233   NE   E'ER [Poetry; ever]
9.234   NNE ELDER [one's senior] REEL [device to hold thread]
9.235   N   DERO [Col; vagrant] NOEL [Christmas] REEL [to say, write or produce in an easy continuous manner]

9.300   N   TEE [starting place as in golf] NET [meshed fabric for any purpose] NET [anything used to catch or snare game]
9.301   NNE DOT [anything small or speck-like] TORN [pt. of tear]
9.302   NE   TO [point or limit in time] REEL [lively dance popular in Scotland]
9.303   ENE NODE [join in stem]
9.304   SE   TEN [amounting to this number] O [Interj; adds solemn poetic language] TEN [symbol for this number, 10 or X] ORD [ordinance]
9.305   S   DO [ditto] TOLE [enamelled metal-ware eg., tray]
9.306   SSW O [order] TO [limit in degree or amount] DRONE [one who lives off the labour of others]
9.307   SW   REND [opening made by tearing or rending] DR [drive or street name]
9.308   WSW T [transitive]
9.309   W   TO [object of a right or claim] ROD [stick used for punishment] R [river] REEL [cylinder or frame on an axis to hold thread etc.] DET [detective] DENT [to become indented] TERN [set of three] TO [proportion or ratio] OLD [far advanced in years of life] TELEO [V of Tele as in teleology – study of design in nature]
9.310   WNW TONE [a variety of colours, tints or hues] DO [execute] NEROL [alcohol $C_{10}H_{17}OH$ found in nerol oil] ONE [an unusual person or character] TONE [a particular state of the mind, spirit or character] ROE [the milt or sperm

of the male fish] DOER [hard worker] TENDER [young or immature] DO [to cover or traverse] T [teaspoon]

9.311   NW   ROD [Col; erect penis] DOE [female deer] –OR [Suff; state or condition] ORD [ordinary] DOLE [receive such payments] ON [time or occasion] OLD [sedate, sensible or wise] DOT [Col; punctuality] REND [harrow, distress the heart with painful feelings] ERE [Arch; before, early] TENDER [yielding readily to force or pressure, easily broken, fragile] ROD [Biblical; offshoot or branch of family, a tribe] ORE [a mineral or natural product source but not metal] ON [Old Norse]

9.312   NNW R [replacing] DENT [to make a dent, indent]

9.313   N   DENT [to sink in or indent] DR [debtor] R [royalty] R [18th letter of the alphabet] R [Rankine – absolute scale of temperature] NO [Naval Officer] ELDER [governing officer or teacher] OT [Occupational Therapist] R [rupee] DOT [anything small or speck-like]

9.314   NNE REEL [to turn around in a whirl] NO [to express dissent, denial, refusal] TE [7th note of the Solfa system of music] ENTER [to make a beginning] DENOTE [mark, sign or indicate] NL [not clear or evident – L. non liquet]

9.315   NE   END [a limit, bounds] –ENT [Suff; eg., ardent] DOLT [dull, stupid fellow]

9.316   ENE REEL [lively dance popular in Scotland] DENOTE [symbol for] DENOTE [stamp or impress] NO [North]

9.317   E   NODE [knot, protuberance or knob] NEED [necessity, want, requirement]

9.318   S   ED [edited] RD [rod or rods] ENT [ear, nose and throat]

9.319   W   ENTO- [WE; within] TENDER [small rowing boat behind yacht] LOT [parcel of merchandise] LEE [Navigation; quarter to which the wind blows] DO [1st note of the Solfa music system] R [received]

9.320   WNW NO [number] OR [often in correlation with something] DOER [performer] TOD [English unit = 28 lbs.]

9.321   NW   TO [limit of movement or extension] ON [membership or association] OT [overseas – over there] ED [edition] DELE [take out or omit] DRONE [metal lure used in trolling] ROD [Biblical; offshoot or branch in family, a tribe] LORD [Arch; husband] RE [Chem; rhenium NN=12;]

9.322   NNE DENT [to impress as a dent]

9.323   NE   O [Chem; oxygen NN= 38n] LOT [distinctive portion] DOLE [a portion given out]

9.324   ENE LONE [unmarried or widowed]

9.325   ESE DR [dram]

9.326   S   LEER [to look with a leer]

9.327   SW   TO [comparison or opposition]

9.328   NNW ROE [mass of eggs in female fish]

9.329   N   DO [to serve a period of time]

9.330   NE   TO [turnover]

9.331   E   ROD [Col; revolver, pistol]

TO ONE.

ONE TO
9.400   S   REED [weaver's reed used in a loom]
9.401   SSE TENDER [affectionate, loving, sentimental]
9.402   E   TONE [a distinctive colour or hue]
9.403   N   ROD [stick, wand, staff or shaft]
9.404   NW   END [a part or share of]
9.405   W   DL [decilitre]
9.406   WSW TON [displacement of salt water by a ship = 35 cubic feet]
9.407   SSE DO [visit as tourist] –TON [Suff to N; eg., simpleton]
9.408   SE   ENDO [Grk; within] NEED [situation or time of difficulty]
9.409   ENE LONE [unmarried or widowed]
9.410   NE   REED [musical instrument]
9.411   NNE NEEDLE [used for knitting] OLDEN [Arch; old]
9.412   N   DRONE [Music; bass strings] TO [relative position] DOT [Music; staccato – shortened note] OLD [advanced in age compared to others] ROD [Col; car]
9.413   NW   TOD [a bushy mass especially of Ivy] R [rand] LENTEN [suitable for Lent] TENDER [considerate, careful]
9.414   WNW LED [light emitting diode]
9.415   W   REND [to tear one's hair or clothes in grief or rage] DO [put forth, extent] TOR [rocky eminence or hill] T [something shaped like a T] TERN [three winning numbers drawn together in a lottery]
9.416   SW   LT [lieutenant] EON [largest division of geological time comprising two or more eras]
9.417   S   ED [edited]
9.418   SSE TONE [quality or character of sound] LORD [master, chief or ruler]
9.419   SE   DOLENTE [Music; sadly, plaintively] TO [to consciousness or to one's senses]
9.420   ESE NO [not in any degree] TENDER [wool quality that has a weakness at a certain point in the staple where it will break] LET [cause to allow to escape] REEL [to have a sensation of whirling]
9.421   E   NOTE [paper acknowledgement of a debt for which payment is required] LORE [space between bill and eyes in a bird]
9.422   ENE DOT [small spot on surface] REEL [lively dance popular in Scotland]
9.423   NE   R [roentgen – exposure to radiation, X rays] DOLE [distribution in charity for maintenance]
9.424   NNE -REL [Suff to N; diminutive, pejorative force eg., wastrel] ROT [to become morally corrupt, offensive] –ER [action or process] DOT [full stop] REDOLENT [odorous, smelling] ROT [Col; nonsense] ODE [poem that is intended to be sung]
9.425   N   R [rupee] ONE [a particular day, night or time in the past] NEEDLE [to sew or pierce with] END [furthermost part] NET [exclusive of deductions] ROD [Col; a car] ON [relation of a person to an event which affects him]

9.426   NNW DENT [to sink in or make a dent] TERN [bird of aquatic environments – Sterninae] ENTRÉE [dish before main meal] R [rod] RL [Rugby League] LOT [divide or distribute by lot] LENO [threads twisted in pairs between the filling yarn]
9.427   NW   RETE [network of fibres, nerves or blood vessels] NOD [to grow careless, inattentive or dull] TELE [telegram] LET [as an auxiliary used to propose or order] LEE [sheltered from wind] DRONE [Music; eg., bagpipes] ROT [Interj; dissent, distaste, or disgust] NODE [a centring point of component parts] ROTE [routine, fixed procedure] REEL [to cause to reel] END [district, locality] RONDE [typeface like angular writing] NOTE [record of a speed, impressions]
9.428   WNW RE [2nd note of Solfa system of music] R [rector] ROT [to undergo decay or decomposition] NERD [Col; idiot or fool] ON [object or end of action, thought or desire] -O [combining form eg., speedometer] TON [unit of internal capacity = 100 cubic feet] DOL [dollar] DOER [any animal that gains or improves rapidly in weight] TEL [telegraph] RODENT [gnawing and nibbling mammal] TOE [front part of the stocking or shoe]
9.429   W   OLD [far advanced in years of life] ORT [a fragment of food left after a meal] ONE [some day in the future] TEE [mark aimed at in various games] TERN [set of three] TON [score of 100] LOT [portion in life that is assigned by fate or providence] LORE [the learning or knowledge, erudition]
9.430   WSW E [English] DER [derivation] TO [contact, contiguity]
9.431   SW   -ER [Suff; comparative degree eg., smaller] NOTE [bank certificate or money] NET [bag to catch game] RED [something red] LT [lieutenant] LONER [one who dislikes company] ON [risk or liability]
9.432   SSW NOTE [a brief record set down to assist memory] E [3rd note in the Solfa system] DOT [Music; rest point] ROTE [Celtic medieval musical instrument] DRONE [one who lives off the labour of others]
9.433   S   RETENE [crystalline hydrocarbons, fossil resin] ND [Chem; neodymium NN= 18] LOT [Col; great number] NO [not at all, very far from being] –ER [Suff to a N that changes it to a verb eg., harvester]
9.434   SE   TO [result or consequence]
9.435   NE   NOT [negation, denial, refusal, prohibition] DOER [an amusing or odd person]
9.436   NNE ER [Col; hesitation] LORD [one to which royalty is paid] TORN [pt. of tear]
9.437   N   TO [aim, purpose or intention] TEE [starting place] LET [allow to pass, go or come].

9.500   NE   RENT [periodic payment by tenant] ROD [punishment or chastisement]
9.501   SE   NOTE [as a signal, as on a trumpet]
9.502   SSE R [railway]
9.503   SW   -EER [Suff; one who is concerned with eg., engineer]
9.504   NW   ON [in contact with any surface]

9.505   ESE   O [Elect; ohm] R [repeat]
9.506   SE   ROT [diseases characterized by decomposition]
9.507   S   ROD [straight, slender shaft or stem]
TO ONE

ONE TO
9.600   N   TOLEDO [quality steel sword made in Spain]
9.601   ESE R [repeat]
9.602   SSE R [railway] NOD [to make a quick forward inclination of the head as in agreement]
9.603   SE   ND [no date] ENTER [to make an entrance] NEEDLE [to tease or heckle]
9.604   SSE R [repeat]
9.605   E   NE'ER [Poetry; never]

9.700   E   NOTE [sound or tone]
9.701   SE   E [East] NT [New Testament] TEL [telephone]
9.702   SSE RE- [repetition eg., reprint]
9.703   WNW TEEN [Col; teenager]
9.704   NW   ORD [ordinal]
9.705   NE   DENOTE [designation or name]
9.706   E   TENDER [to offer or proffer]
9.707   S   OLD [having existed long or made long ago]
9.708   WSW ER [Queen Elizabeth]
TO ONE.

ONE TO
9.800   S   OLD [having existed long or made long ago]
9.801   SSE ONE [a certain (or unknown) or undescribed person] RELENT [to cause to relent or soften in time]
9.802   ESE LENT [pt. of lend] LON [longitude]
9.803   N   LEET [jurisdiction or area over which a manorial court extends]
9.804   S   TENDER [to offer or proffer]
9.805   SE   REEL [device on a fishing rod]
9.806   ESE LON [longitude]
9.807   NE   LONE [lonely]

9.900   ESE -ODE [WE; way]

9.901   SSE NE neon NN=34:] ROD [linear measure of 5.5 yds]
9.902   S   DOLE [given out sparingly] NOTE [as in a bird's song]
9.903   SSW R [reaumur – temp scale of 0 – 80]
9.904   SE   TENDER [one who tends, attends to or takes charge of something]
9.905   S   TROD [pt. of tread]
9.906   W   E [Transcendental Constant = 2.7182818 …] R [Phys & Chem; gas constant]
9.907   NW   DENE [bare sandy tract]
9.908   W   R [Phys & Chem; gas constant]
TO ONE.

ONE TO
9.1000   WSW R [rabbi]
9.1001   SE   DOLE [Arch; one's fate or destiny]
9.1002   N   TONE [normal, healthy condition of the mind]
9.1003   NW   ET [Chem; ethyl]
9.1004   W   E [Transcendental Constant = 2.7182818 …]
9.1005   S   NO [not, whether or no] TENDER [present formally for acceptance]
9.1006   ENE OT [Old Testament]
9.1007   NNW LOT [choice by chance] –N'T [not eg., didn't]
9.1008   WSW REDOLENT [suggestive, reminiscent]
9.1009   S   LORN [Arch; forsaken, desolate, wretched] TOE [digits of the foot]
9.1010   SSE ONE [an instance of a number is indicated] RENT [profit or return derived] LO [Interj; behold] TONE [style, distinction or elegance] –ED [Suff; past tense]
9.1011   SE   DELETE [strike out, expunge] NET [containment] T [ton] T [tare] TONE [an accent particular to a person]

9.1100   ENE LET [contact for performance]
9.1101   SSE LENT [40 week-days leading up to Easter] ROTE [in a mechanical way without thought] ON [situation or place]
9.1102   S   ONE [single unit or individual]
9.1103   WSW DO [study]
9.1104   WNW ELDER [plant of the genus Sambucus]
9.1105   N   TO [technical officer]
9.1106   ENE LED [pt. of lead]
9.1107   SE   TO [state or condition]
9.1108   SSE ROD [stick used to measure with]
9.1109   S   TELE [WE; end, complete]
9.1110   WSW DO [study]
9.1111   NW   ON [ground or basis]
9.1112   N   NL [Printg; new line]

9.1113 ENE END [concluding part]
TO ONE.

ONE TO
9.1200 W   ETERNE [Arch; eternal]
9.1201 SW TREE [Arch; cross on which Jesus Christ was crucified]
9.1202 N   NL [Printg; new line]
9.1203 W   NEED [necessity arising from a case or circumstance]
9.1204 SSW ON [immediate proximity]
9.1205 S   END [extremity – longer than broad]
9.1206 SSE ON [liability for a debt or expense]
9.1207 SE   ENTER [to make a record of]
9.1208 ESE EDEN [state of perfect happiness].

Transcript 10.   SAIL LIDS LIST

10.100 N   AIDS [acquired immune deficiency syndrome] S [Phys; entropy]
10.101 NNE SI [Music; 7th degree] 'T [impersonal constructions]
10.102 ENE TAIL [Col; vagina]
10.103 E   SILT [to become filled or choked up with silt]
10.104 ESE LIST [to set down together in a list]
10.105 SE   LIST [to register] L [length] IT [without definitive force after an
           intransitive verb]
10.106 SSE D [4th in series] DI- [variant of dis- before b,d,l,m,n,r,s,v] TALL
           [relatively great stature or structure] AS [in the degree manner etc.] TAIL
           [an arrangement of objects or people like a tail] 'LL [shall] ST [street] AD
           [advantage]
10.107 S   LIST [Arch; to like, wish or choose] SAIL [to be conveyed on a
           vessel by the action of wind, steam etc.] ILL [disease or ailment]
10.108 SW   D [penny, pence] T [Gram; tense] DISTAL [situated away from the
           point of origin or attachment] SLIT [to cut or rend into strips] SAT [Saturn]
           SALT [pungent, sharp]
10.109 W   TAIL [something suggestive of a tail by shape or position] STILL
           [without sound or movement] SIT [to be convened or in session as
           assembly] SALT [NaCl NN= 27 or 45]
10.110 NW   I [Chem; iodine NN= 24:] AID [payment made by feudal vassals to
           a lord on a special occasion] DILL [plant Anethurum graveoles] TAIL [the
           hinter or concluding part, rear] A- [Pref; increase, addition eg. amass]
           SLIT [Col; vagina] LSD [lysergic acid diethylamide, creating hallucinations
           and schizophrenia] AT [a point occupied, attained, sought] DIAL [Col;
           human face] SS [saints] DISTIL [to drop, pass or condense as distillate]
           TAIL [Col; reverse of coin] -ID [N suff. "daughter of"] ADIT [entrance,
           passage] LAST [on the most recent occasion] A [indefinite plural eg. a
           few] STILL [even then, yet, nevertheless]
10.111 NNW S [substantive] -IAL [var. of -al] SAIL [sailing vessels collectively] T
           [Stats; distribution]
10.112 N   SILT [earthy matter carried by water and deposited] T [absolute
           temperature] T [tare] SL [knitting; slip]
10.113 NNE -S [suff. To form plural of nouns] SS [Sunday school]
10.114 ENE -T [suff. Past tense of certain verbs] DL [decilitre]
10.115 E   ASSIST [a play which helps a team member score]
10.116 ESE LAST [the end or conclusion] I [9th letter of English alphabet]
10.117 SE   -S [suff. To form adverbs eg. always] AS [which fact, contingency]
10.118 S   LIST [Arch & Poetry; to listen]
10.119 SW ALL [a totality of things or qualities] SIT [to be situated, dwell] DTS
           [delirium tremens] AID [to afford, support, relief, help] DISTIL [to undergo
           distillation] SAIL [to manage a boat esp. for sport]
10.120 WSW I'D [I had] Al [Chem; aluminium NN= 27] I [Math; imaginary number,
           square root of -1] DIAL [face upon which time is indicated]

10.121 W   Tail [to remove stalks from…] ITAL [italic type] D [deci] LAST [next
            before present, most recent]
10.122 WNW LAST [utmost, extreme] D- [Pref; former abbrev. dextro-]
10.123 NW   A [music; string, key or pipe tuned to A] I [singular pronoun of 1st
            person] TAIL [Law; limitation of estate to class of heirs] TAIL [Col; to
            follow to hinder escape or observe]
10.124 NNW DIAL [Mining; compass used for underground surveys] SLAT [Col;
            rib] TALL [stature or height as specified]
10.125 N   A- [Pref; on, in, to, towards] SAD [expression of or characterized by
            sorrow] STILL [single picture or frame]
10.126 NNE TAIL [to terminate, to follow like a tail]
10.127 NE   SIT [to be a candidate for an examination]
10.128 ESE D [dialect]
10.129 S   T [territory]
10.130 W   ILLIT [illiterate]
10.131 NW LAST [utmost, extreme] DIS- [privation, negation, reversing forces]
            DIA [diameter] LAST [model of human foot made of wood etc.] ASSIST
            [to give help, support, aid]
10.132 N   DIAL [to indicate as on a dial]
10.133 E   SIT [to rest on the lower part of the body, to be seated]
            TO ONE.

            ONE TO
10.200 N   SDA [Seventh Day Adventists] ST [strait] AT [relative position,
degree,   rate] LAST [final]
10.201 NW   DIAL [used to measure with] T [Phys; Tesla] SAIL [to move along by
wind   or steam etc.] SA [South Africa] TA [Col; Thank you] SIT [to act as a
model]
10.202 W   SA [sex appeal] LAST [to go on, to endure, continue to progress] LL
[late   Latin]
10.203 SW   I [Roman numeral for one] SALT [to create a false impression of
value] SIT   [to sit upon eg. a horse]
10.204 S   T [territory] TAIL [end of the page] A [Music; Concert A, the note all
            instruments are tuned   to]
10.205 SE   La [Chem; lanthanum NN= 24:]
10.206 E   ST [short ton] D [dialect]
10.207 NE   LIST [Arch; to enlist]
10.208 NNE Lt [lieutenant] -AL [Suff. Compound included aldehyde group] LAST
[after   all others] S sulphur NN= 19] SS [steamship]
10.209 N   SI [International system of units]
10.210 NNW DISS [dissertation] ID [source of instinctive energy in the psyche]
10.211 NW   ALL [one's whole interests, concerns, property] A [Music; string, key
or pipe tuned to A] TAS [Tasmania] IT [substitute for neuter noun] D- [Pref;
former abbrev. dextro-]

10.212 WNW TAIL [hindmost part of an animal]
10.213 W   A- [Pref; intensify action eg. amaze] DISTIL [to fall in drops, trickle
or   exude] LAD [Col; any male] D [detective] L [Latin] ILL [trouble, misfortune]
I [9th letter of English & 3rd vowel] LIST [to enter on list with others]
10.214 SW   SAIL [similar piece or apparatus] DTS [delirium tremens] LIT [literal]
10.215 S   STILL [without waves or perceptible currents as water] TALL [Col;
high flown, grandiloquent] TAIL [to follow close behind] T [tonne] LL [low Latin]
10.216 E   -T [Suff; past tense of certain verbs]
10.217 NE   AID [one who aids or yields assistance]
10.218 N   STILL [Poetry; steadily, constantly, always]
10.219 NNW SS [storm trooper]
10.220 NW   ILL [objectionable, unsatisfactory, poor] STILL [free from sound or
noise] ADIT [entrance or passage] AS [since, because] AS [Anglo Saxon] LAST
    [Eccles; extreme; final as to dying person] -ID [Suff; used in naming epics]
    DISTIL [to drop, pass or condense as distillate]
10.221 WNW -ASIS [WE. Forming names of diseases] LSD [lysergic acid
diethylamide, causing hallucinations and schizophrenia] LISTS [any place of or
scene of combat] STILL [up to this or that time] DITA [shrub or tree, Alstonia
scholaris of the Old World Tropics] STILL [to calm, appease or allay]
10.222 W   TAIL [inferior or refuse part] I [Metaphysics; Ego] 'LL [will]
10.223 WSW SIT [to place oneself in position for an artist] TILL [container with
drawers for coins and notes etc.] LAST [any of variously large units of weight or
capacity] IS- [var. of iso-] ALL [the whole number eg. all women]
10.224 SW   -AD [Suff. To N; collection of a certain number eg. triad] S [society]
10.225 S   A- [Pref; up, out or away] SAIL [to be conveyed on a vessel by the
action of wind or steam etc] LIST [Arch; to like, wish or choose]
10.226 SSE AS [the manner in which] A [each or every] ASST [assistant]
10.227 SE   SA [semi-annual] LAST [Col; final mention or appearance]
10.228 ESE LAST [that which is last]
10.229 E   LAD [boy or youth] A [atomic] ST [stitch]
10.230 ENE DIA- [Pref; passing through]
10.231 NNE LIST [a division of the hair or beard] S [saint] ILL [unfavourable,
adverse]

10.300 N   The [Chem; thallium NN= 20]
10.301 NNE STILL [to become still or quiet]
10.302 NE   ID [idem; as previously given or mentioned] SALT [Col; a sailor
especially   an experienced one eg. an old salt]
10.303 ENE LILT [a lilting tune or melody] ALT [alternate]
10.304 E   L [line or lines] ITA [initial teaching alphabet] 'D [had] SAIL [to move
    along with dignity] LASS [girl or young woman] S [summer]
10.305 SE   LIT [p.t. of light] D [4th letter of English alphabet]
10.306 SSE L [litre] IT'LL [it will] D [dose]
10.307 S   D [Music; key, string or pipe tuned to D]

10.308 SSW ST [stone weight] -AL [Suff. Forming a N of action from a verb eg. recital]
10.309 SW   SAIL [voyage or excursion] A [ampere] SIT [situation] DI- [Pref; twice, doubly, two] LA [Music; 6th degree]
10.310 WSW AIL [to feel pain or somewhat ill] ILL [evil] TAI [Sino-Tibetan language]   IT'LL [it shall] SA [South America] 'TIS [it is]
10.311 W   SIT [an elected representative in parliament] LIST [a border or strip usually   cloth] T [teaspoon] STILL [in the future as in the past] SAIL [to move along in   the manner suggestive of sailing eg. clouds]
10.312 WNW SAID [p.t. of say] SALT [that which gives piquancy or pungency to   anything]
10.313 NW   TAIL [Col; buttocks] AI [induce pregnancy] ASS [long eared, grey   mammal like a horse] DI- [var. of dia-] ALL [whole quantity]
  10.314 SALT [to cure, preserve or treat with salt] SA [South Australia] AT [Technical   Atmosphere] L- [Pref. To denote compounds that have the same chirality as L-glyceraldehyde] ADIT [Mining; horizontal passage for air, water etc. to work   face]
10.315 NNE STILL [to quiet commotion, pain, passion] A [singular, one of a class]
10.316 NE   L [learner-driver] 'T [it] -AL [Suff; of or pertaining to]
10.317 ENE T [surface tension]
10.318 E   I [an I shaped object] TAIL [lower part of a pool or stream] SSD [Most Holy   Lord - title for the Pope] DIAL [plate or disc with numbers or letters]
10.319 ESE SAD [sorrowful or mournful]
10.320 SE SIT [to occupy a seat in an official capacity] LD [lethal dose] D [density]   TILL [up to the time of , until] ILL [trouble, difficulty or inconvenience]
10.321 SSE LISTS [the enclosed field for combat] ASS [slow, patient, sure-footed beast of burden]
10.322 S   [southern] ID [identification]
10.323 SW   SLAT [Col; buttocks] IS [3rd person singular present indicative of be]
10.324 WSW SILD [young herring - Norway]
10.325 W   SA [L; sine anno - without year or date] Tail [to seize by the tail] ILL   [Arch; wickedness, sin]
10.326 WNW AID [to give financial support] LIST [Arch; to like or desire]
10.327 NW   T [transitive] -ID [Suff; used in naming zoological family] SL [solicitor at   law] AI [imitation of the cry made by a large three toed sloth from central and   South America] DI- [var. of dia-] ALL [the whole quantity] DA [deposit account]   ASS [Col; fool or blockhead] L [latitude]
10.328 N   LSD [money] SAIL [to begin a journey by water] ASSIST [to present as at   meeting] IT [Col; sex appeal] D [Dutch]
10.329 NE   TAIL [to tend or herd sheep] .STILL [quiet, tranquil, calm] ALTI- [Pref. High] AT [ampere turns] I [intransitive] LAST [coming after all others in   suitability or likelihood] LIST [leaning to one side like a ship]
10.330 ENE L [Lambert]
10.331 E   SAD [sombre, dark, dull] 'S [is]

10.332 SE ALT- [Music; alto -high]
10.333 S   SILL [horizontal timber block etc. for foundations] IT [player called upon to   perform]
10.334 W   STILL [not effervescent wine]
10.335 NW L [link] I [Italy] SL [solicitor at law]
10.336 NNW SALT [any of various salts used as a purgative]
10.337 N   S [Stokes] SA [Salvation Army] SAD [deplorable, shocking]
10.338 SE ALT [Music; alto - high]
10.339 S   LI [Chem; lithium NN= 17]
     TO ONE

     ONE TO
10.400 NNE LT [low tension]
10.401 N   A- [Pref. Reduced form of ab-] SAD [deplorable, shocking] D [deputy]
10.402 NW S [Saturday] 'S [possessive singular of noun] LID [moveable piece for opening a box or vessel]
10.403 WNW AI [artificial insemination]
10.404 W   STILL [subdued or low in sound; hushed] DIAL [to call by phone]
10.405 SE L [left]
10.406 E   SAD [sombre, dark, dull] SLAT [long narrow strips of wood etc.]
10.407 NE T [in the time of] TAIL [Astron; luminous train from the head of a comet]
10.408 NNE LAST [being the only remaining] TALL [Col; high, great, large amount]
10.409 N   DISTIL [to extract or obtain by distillation]
10.410 NW SA [subject to approval] TAIL [to join or attach at the tail or end] DISTIL [to drive off by distillation] -ID [var. of -ide] SLID [p.t of slide] LTD [limited]
     SAIL [expanse of canvas etc., to catch wind] DIAL { to regulate or select or tune] TIDAL [characterized by tides] STAID [fixed, settled, permanent] S [September]
10.411 WNW IT [to refer to the subject of inquiry or attention]
10.412 W   ALL [the greatest possible eg. all speed] DIA- [Pref; thoroughly, completely]
10.413 SW AID [to give help or assistance] L- [former abbrev. for laevo-] S [something S shaped] SIT [to cause to sit] ALT- [before vowels var. of alto-]
10.414 S   S [soprano] IT [subject of a clause]
10.415 SE ALL [the whole of; extent] LASS [Col; any woman]
10.416 ESE A [adult classification eg. film]
10.417 E   SSD [Most Holy Lord - title for the Pope] TAIL [lower part of a pool or   stream]
10.418 ENE S [son] LILT [to sing or play in a lilting manner] D [dialectical] T [surface   tension]

10.419 N   L [large] SIT [to cover eggs to hatch them] 'S [Col; does] AT [Technical   Atmosphere]
10.420 NNW L [Roman for 50]
10.421 NW   A [Angstrom] L [something having an L shape] LIAS [a series of marine sediments of the Lower Jurassic rocks in NE Europe like limestone] TAIL [to dock the tail] SILL [horizontal timber beneath doors, windows etc.] LILT [rhythmic swing or cadence] TAIL [Col; buttocks] AS [a consequent in the correlations]
10.422 WNW LIST [a record of a series of names, things] SALT [Chem; upon dissociation yield cations [+ve] and anions [-ve] of an acid radical] TAIL [Aero; stabilizing and control at rear of an aircraft] T [Tuesday] LAST [coming after all others in importance] S [Sunday] T [tonne]
10.423 W   S [singular] SAIL [to move along in a manner suggestive of sailing eg. clouds] ILL [harm or injury] STAID [of settled or sedate character] SAIL [to cause to sail] STILL [in future as in past] SAIL [to navigate] S [19th letter English]
10.424 WSW A- [Pref. Reduced form of ad-] I [a sound represented by the letter I] D [daughter] AD [Australian Democrats] STAID [P.t. stay]
10.425 SW   LA [Music; 6th note] DI- [Pref; twice, doubly, two] IS [Bible ; Isaiah]
10.426 SSW AS [for instance] LIST [to prepare land for a crop with furrows and ridges] S [school] TI [Chem; titanium NN= 23:]
10.427 S   LID [eyelid]
10.428 SSE SALT [to season with] LAST [to shape or fit to a last of the human foot]
10.429 SE   SI [Chem; silicon NN= 23:] SAID [named or mentioned before] SALT [to furnish with salt]
10.430 ESE 'S [possessive plural of a noun] AL- [var. of ad-] SLIT [to cut apart or open along a line]
10.431 E   'D [had] ITA [initial training alphabet]
10.432 NE   DISTIL [to become vaporized and then condensed]
10.433 NNE SAT [Saturday] AS [that, who, which] LIST [to border or edge]

10.500 NE   -I [ending for the first element of many compounds eg. cuneiform]
10.501 SE   LA [Interj; wonder & surprise] DIAL [use phone]
10.502 SSE AID [artificial insemination donor]
10.503 S   ASS [assistant] TAIL [full dress attire]
10.504 SSW S [shilling, shillings] TAIL [Col; person who follows another]
10.505 NW LIT [literary]
10.506 N   As [Chem; arsenic NN= 23:
10.507 SE   SLAT [Aeron; auxiliary airfoil] DISS [dissolved]
10.508 S   TALL [Col; extravagant, difficult to believe]
10.509 SSW TAIL [Bldg; to fix one end of a beam etc]
10.510 SW   LASS [female sweetheart]
10.511 W   TALI- [WE; ankle]
10.512 NE   STILL [at this or that time]

        TO ONE.

        ONE TO
10.600 E   LAST [to remain in good condition] LAD [Col; devil-may-care,
dashing man]
 10.601 NW DISTIL [extract volatile components]
10.602 SW AD [advertisement]
10.603 S   DILL [aromatic seeds and leaves]
10.604 ESE I'D [I would] ILL [evil, wicked, bad] SILT [to fill or choke up with silt]
10.605 NE TAIL [long braid or tress of hair]
10.606 N   TILL [before eg didn't come till today]
10.607 W   A [Music; 6th degree]
10.608 SW S [Siemens] D.LITT [Doctor of Letters]
10.609 SSW TAIL [Col; person who follows another]
10.610 S   A [adjective] TAIL [full dress attire] LIT [literally]
10.611 SSE DIST [distance]
10.612 SE   DIAL [to use a phone dial] DAIS [raised platform for a throne, seat of
honour or teacher's desk] SIT [to perch or roost like a bird] I [Island]
10.613 ESE DILL [Col; fool or incompetent]

10.700 ESE ASS [association] ST [stet]
10.701 SE   TAIL [coming from behind eg. tail wind] D- [Pref. Configuration of
chemical compounds that have the same chirality as glyceraldehyde]
10.702 SSE TILL [to cultivate the soil] SALT [wit, pungency] D [Music; 2nd
degree] SALT [overflowing or growing in salt water] TAIL [to form or constitute
the end part] S [second]
10.703 SSW SAIL [to travel through the air eg. balloon]
10.704 NE   D [delete] ASSIST [to be associated with an assistant]
10.705 ESE SIT [to fit or be adjusted as a garment] A [Chem; argon NN=24:]
10.706 S   A [Col; rebuff, reject Arse] STILL [even or yet eg still more
complaints] LIT [literature]
10.707 SW   IT'S [it is]
10.708 E   DISTIL [vaporization and condensation]
        TO ONE.

        ONE TO
10.800 NE   D.LITT [Doctor of Literature]
10.801 S   DISTIL [to let fall in drops]
10.802 SE   AS [when or while]
10.803 ESE AS [to such a degree or extent] SAIL [Col; to go boldly into action]

10.804 NE   TIDAL [dependent on the state of the tide]
10.805 SW   AS [though]
10.806 SSW TAIL [Law; limited to a specified line of heirs]
10.807 S   D [diameter] DIAL [rotatable plate used for tuning]
10.808 SSE SD [standard deviation] L [lake] TAI [peace] LT [long ton]
10.809 SE   I'LL [I will] TAIL [coming from behind eg. tail wind] SLAT [to furnish
or make with slats]
10.810 NE   STILL [remaining in place or at rest, motionless].

---

6. EPILOGUE - Ode To The Elders Of Tomorrow.

It is a thrill to see so much
Of the Divine Province.
To see how it radiates in our lives
And in a myriad of other creatures on this beautiful Earth.

It is with the most profound respect
For ONE, IN-ONE and Great Spirit
That this work is undertaken
And Your messages are carefully conveyed.

At the very outset I made a promise
I would write about what I find,
But never to be like Prometheus
And punished for bringing fire to man,
I likewise ask to only be told what You want to be made known.

You have shared your Providence
With us in these transcripts.
We are eternally grateful
For Your trust and insights given in any form.

You light the unknown here
With analogies, case studies, sacred rites
And processes unknown before.
They create new vistas of understanding Your plan for plants, animals and man.

Two hundred and fifty million years
Before the emergence of man,
You had a plan – great schemes to shape our natures
Vast nets to teach and monitor
Vast lessons in eternal life and love for us to learn.

AND all this is in Your written words
Your gift to me to write.
And so as mine I give to Ye
Our Elders of Tomorrow.

Oh! Bring forth your true blessings!
You can find your way.

Psyche has revealed herself.
Boyo, Dono and me are all undone.
Archetypes have debated and arrayed the Heavenly Province
And come to help us find our inner truth.
Where can that lie
Save estreat in you

Sanctitas Vestra?
Certainly.

Oh! Look to the blessings of your
birth and name
There's wisdom there to find.
And Seek the "inner voice" in calm.

Arise anew
Ye Elders of Tomorrow,
Keep good and straight
To Father and His Son.

ONE beckons us to make our peace
And come in love to Him.

Amen! Amen! Amen!

Chris Phillips   3rd Feb. 2017.

7. BIBLIOGRAPHY.

1. Ashcroft-Nowicki, Dolores. "The Shining Paths." Aquarian Press. 1983.
2. Bancroft, Anne. "Origins of the Sacred". Arkana. 1987.
3. Barr, Andy. "Traditional Bush Medicines." Greenhouse Publications.1988.
4. Beblo T, Driessen M, Mertens M, Wingenfeld K, Piefke M, Rullkoetter N, Silva-Saavedra A, Mensebach C, Reddemann L, Rau H, Markowitsch HJ, Wulff H, Lange W, Berea C, Ollech I, Woermann FG. "Functional MRI correlates of the recall of unresolved life events in borderline personality disorder." [http://www.ncbi.nlm.nih.gov/entrez/query.fcgi?] 2006.
5. Benazzi F. "Borderline personality-bipolar spectrum relationship Prog Neuropsychopharmacol Biol Psychiatry Jan;30 (1) :68-74 2005.
6. Blainey, G. "Triumph of the Nomads – A History of Ancient Australia". Sun. 1983.
7. Bulfinch, Thomas. "The Golden Age of Myth and Legend." Studio Editions. 1994.
8. Carr-Gomm, Philip. "Sacred Places." Quercus Books. 2008.
9. Carroll, Lewis. "The Complete Illustrated Works of Lewis Carroll". Chancellor.1991.
10. Carlson M, Earls F. "Psychological and neuroendocrinological sequelae of early social deprivation in institutionalized children in Romania." NY Acad of Sciences; 807 pp 419 – 428.
11. Charlesworth, James H. "The Old Testament Pseudepigrapha." Doubleday & Co. Inc. 1983.
12. Chatwin, Bruce. "The Songlines." Picador. 1987.
13. Common Bible. Revised Standard Version - Expanded. Collins 1973.
14. Cragg, Kenneth. "Readings in the Qur'an." Fount. 1988.
15. Duesberg PH. "Inventing the AIDS virus." Regnery. Washington DC. 1996
16. Dunphy, Dexter. "Jaguar Heart Poems". Wellington Lane Press. 2003.
17. Emerson, Ralph Waldo. "Selected Essays." Penguin Books. 1982.
18. Eliade, Mircea. "Shamanism." Princeton University Press. 1974.
19. Ellis, Peter. "The Men and the Message of the Old Testament." Liturgical Press 1962.
20. Evans-Wentz, W.Y. "The Tibetan Book of the Dead." Oxford Univ. Press. 1968.
21. Evans-Wentz, W.Y. "The Tibetan Book of the Great Liberation." Oxford Univ. Press 1968.
22. Evans-Wentz, W.Y. "Tibetan Yoga and Secret Doctrines." Oxford Univ. Press 1968.
23. Flaum, Eric. Pandy, David. "The Encyclopedia of Mythology." Friedman Group. 1993.
24. Foster, S. & M. Little. "The Book of the Vision Quest." Prentice Hall. 1988.
25. Goodman, Linda. "Linda Goodman's Star Signs." Pan 1987.
26. Goodman M, New A, Siever L. "Trauma, genes, and the neurobiology of personality disorders." Ann NY Acad Sci. 1032: 104-16 2004.

27. Grieve, Mrs M. "A Modern Herbal". Penguin Books. 1982.
28. Haich, Elizabeth. "Initiation." Unwin Paperbacks. 1988.
29. Hespertz SC, Dietrich TM, Wenning B, Krigs T, Erberich SG, Willmes K, Thron A, Sass H. "Evidence of abnormal amygdala functioning in borderline personality disorder: a functional MRI study." [http://www.ncbi.nlm.nih.gov/entrez/query.fcgi?] 2001.
30. Houston, Jean. "The Possible Human." J.P.Tarcher Inc. 1982.
31. Howard-Taylor, Lucy. "Feeding the Demon." Sydney Alumni Magazine. Spring 2008.
32. Huang W L, Harper C G, Newnham J P, Quinlivan J A, Beazley L D, and Dunlop S A, "Maternal administration of repeated corticosteroids delays brain growth in foetal sheep." Obstetrics & Gynaecology 1999.
33. Hulse, David Allen. "The Key of It All." Llewellyn publications 1993.
34. Ingpen, R. "A Celebration of Customs & Rituals of the World." Dragon's 1994.
35. Innes, Brian. King, Francis. Powell, Neil. "Fate and Fortune." Crescent Books. 1989.
36. Irwin, Matt. "Low CD4+ T-cell counts; A variety of causes and their implications to HIV and AIDS."   Health Education AIDS Liaison. Toronto.[irwin18@gwis2.circ.gwu.edu].
37. Irwin, Matt. "AIDS and the Voodoo Hex". First draft p 23. 2002.
38. Jones, Caroline. "The Search for Meaning." ABC Enterprises. 1989.
39. Jones, Ernest. "The Life and Work of Sigmund Freud." Anchor Books 1963.
40. Jung, Carl C. "Man and His Symbols". Picador. 1964.
41. Jung, Carl C. "Alchemical Studies". Routledge & Kegan Paul. 1967.
42. Lamy, Lucie. "Egyptian Mysteries". Thames and Hudson. 1986.
43. Lau, D.C. "Lao Tzu Tao Te Ching". Penguin Books. 1987.
44. Laudenslanger M., Ryan SM., Drugan RC., et al. "Coping and immunosuppression: Inescapable but not escapable shock suppresses lymphocyte proliferation." Science 1983 221; 568 – 570.
45. Macdonell, Arthur A. "A Sanskrit Grammar for Students." Motilal Banarsidass 1988.
46. Maggiore, Christine. "If It's Not HIV, What Can Cause AIDS?" Health Education AIDS Liaison, Toronto. 2002. http://www.healtoronto.com/ifnothiv.html
47. Meyer, Marvin. "The Gospel of Thomas". Harper San Francisco. 1992.
48. Milton GW. "Self-willed death or the bone pointing syndrome." Lancet 1, June 1973 pp 1435 – 1436.
49. Montefiore, Simon Sebag. "Speeches that Changed the World." Murdoch Books. 2005.
50. Moore, Patrick. "Atlas of the Universe". Colporteur 1982.
51. Nasr, Seyyed Hossein. "Islamic Spirituality – Foundations." Crossroad. 1987.
52. Oldham J. "Borderline Personality Disorder: An overview." Psychiatric Times. Vol XXI Issue 8 2004.

53. Padian NG, Shiboski SC, Glass SO, et al. "Heterosexual transmission of HIV in Northern California: Results from a ten-year study." American Journal of Epidemiology. 1997 146 (4) pp 350 – 357.

54. Palmer, M. "The Jesus Sutras." Piatkus. 2001.

55. Petrucci, Ralph H. "General Chemistry." Macmillan 1989.

56. Phillips, Dr. D.A. "Secrets of the Inner Self." Angus & Robertson. 1988.

57. Picknett, Lynn & Clive Prince. "The Templar Revelation." Bantam Press. 1997.

58. Purce, Jill. "The Mystic Spiral". Thames and Hudson. 1973.

59. Quinlivan J. "Study of Adolescent Pregnancy in WA." In "Domestic Violence in Australia ; The Way Forward." Proceedings of a national conference on Domestic Violence published by the Australian Institute for Family Studies. 2000.

60. Rampa, Lobsang. "Wisdom of the Ancients." Corgi Books. 1977.

61. Regardie, Israel. "The Complete Golden Dawn System of Magic." Falcon Press. 1987.

62. Ricard, Matthieu. "Happiness." Atlantic Books. 2006.

63. Rosenburg, DR; Pajer, K; Rancurello, M; et al. "Neoropsychiatric assessment of orphans in one Romanian orphanage for 'unsalvageables'." 1992 JAMA 268(24); pp 3489 – 3490.

64. Schnapper, E.B. "The Spiral Path". C.W.Daniel Co Ltd. 1985.

65. Schueler, G.J. "An Advanced Guide to Enochian Magick.". Llewellyn Publications. 1987

66. Schwaller de Lubics, R.A. "Sacred Science." Inner Traditions International. 1988.

67. Schwaller de Lubicz, R.A. "The Egyptian Miracle." Inner Traditions International. 1985.

68. Science. 1984 224 carried separately titled retrovirus articles by (1) Gallo RC, Salahuddin SZ, Popovic M et al; (2) Popovic M, Sarngadharan MG, Read E et al; (3) Sarngadharan MG, Popovic M, Bruch L, et al; and (4) Schupbach J, Popovic M, Gilden RV, et al. The team was under the leadership of Robert Gallo.

69. Segal, Jeanne. "Living Beyond Fear". Newcastle Publishing Co. 1984.

70. Steiger, Brad. "Indian Medicine Power." Schiffer Publishing Ltd.1984.

71. Suzuki, David. "The Sacred Balance". Allen & Unwin. 1997.

72. Suzuki, David. "A David Suzuki Collection." Allen & Unwin. 2003.

73. Suzuki, S. "Not Always So. Practicing the true spirit of Zen." Harper Collins. 2003.

74. Temple, Robert. "The Crystal Sun." Century 2000.

75. Trine, Ralph Waldo. "In Tune With the Infinite". Keats Publishing Inc. 1973.

76. Tichy, J. "Legends from Eastern Lands." Paul Hamlyn. 1968.

77. UNAIDS and WHO; "AIDS epidemic update December 2001." By Anne Winter, Dominique de Santis and Andrew Shih.

78. Von Franz, Anne Marie. "Divination and Synchronicity."

79. Walton, Clair. "What makes a Survivor?" Continuum 1999 5 (5) p 16 – 18.

80. Watson, Lyall. "Supernature II".Sceptre. 1986.

81. Webb, James. "The Harmonious Circle." Thames & Hudson 1980.
82. Weiss, Margaret., Phyllis Zelkowitz, Ronald Fedman, Judy Vogel, Marsha Heyman and Joel Paris. "Psychopathology in Offspring of Mothers with Borderline Personality disorder: A Pilot Study". Canadian Journal of Psychiatry Vol 41 June 1996.
83. White, Ruth. "A Question of Guidance." Saffron Walden. 1988.
84. Wilhelm, Richard. Translation. "The I Ching". Bollingen Series. Princeton. 1987.
85. Zanarini MC, Frankenberg FR, Hennen J, Reich DB, Silk KR. "Psychosocial functioning of borderline patients and axis II comparison subjects followed prospectively for six years." J Personal Disord   Feb; 19(1): 19-29 2005.